From a Vantage Point: A Novel

By

John V. Tieso

With a Foreword by
Captain Michael Hayes, JAGC (USN, Retired)

From a Vantage Point

Copyright © 2012-2017 John V. Tieso
All Rights Reserved
Reproduction of this book in any form, in whole or in part, without the written permission of the copyright holder is expressly prohibited.

ISBN-13: 978-1537635057
ISBN-10: 1537635050
BISAC: Fiction / Espionage
Published by CreateSpace, an Imprint of Amazon, Inc.
Library of Congress Control Number: 2017911941
CreateSpace Independent Publishing Platform, North Charleston, SC

The main characters and events described in this book are fictitious, and any similarity to actual people is purely coincidental. This volume is a work of fiction, based loosely on a historical timeline, but is not a recounting of historical activity.

Original and Modified cover art by D. Sharon Pratt and CoverDesignStudio.com

From a Vantage Point

A Special Note from the Author....

The Fisher House Foundation
"Fisher House - because a family's love is good medicine"!

    The Fisher House Foundation is best known for a network of comfort homes where U.S. Armed Services military service members and veterans' families can stay at no cost while a loved one is receiving medical treatment. These homes are located at major military and Veterans Administration (VA) Medical Centers nationwide, close to the medical center or hospital they serve. Families share a common kitchen, laundry facilities, a warm dining room, and an inviting living room area. There is never a hotel or lodging fee. Since its inception, the Fisher House program has saved military service member and veterans' families an estimated $360.0 million dollars in out of pocket costs for lodging and transportation.

    The Fisher House Foundation also operates the "Hero Miles" program, using donated airline(s) frequent flyer miles or FFM's to bring family members to the bedside of injured U.S. Armed Forces military service members as well as the "Hotels for Heroes" program using donated hotel points to allow family members to stay at hotels near medical centers without charge. The Fisher House Foundation also manages a grant program that supports other military charities and scholarship funds for military children, spouses and the children of fallen and disabled American veterans.

- ✓ Families served: More than 28,000 in 2016
- ✓ Daily capacity: 970 families
- ✓ Families served: More than 305,000 since inception
- ✓ Number of lodging days offered: Over 7.0 million
- ✓ Student Scholarships: Over 11,000 students have received $18,000,000.00 in Scholarship Awards since inception
- ✓ Airline 'Hero' Miles: Over 65,000 Airline Tickets provided by 'Hero' Miles to service members and their families, worth nearly $100.0 million dollars

In grateful appreciation for all The Fisher House Foundation accomplishes each and every day, all royalties from this book will be sent to Fisher House

From a Vantage Point

Foreword

Please sit down in your favorite easy chair, re-arrange and 'comfort yourself', square your buttocks in the seat bottom, and prepare yourself for an enjoyable learning experience, a present-day novel adventure in fictitious literature. This adventure in literature is based upon a sociological paradigm that debunk and dispels several myths associated with the development of terrorism in modern day America specifically, the several myths associated with radicalization of today's homegrown "domestic terrorist"; as well as how and why they answer their 'mental clarion call', and to whom or what Cause Celebes', they claim to swear their allegiance.

In exhilarating chapters which follow, John Tieso takes us on an unparalleled journey into the world of terror and terrorism. He weaves the two separate but similar definitions of terrorism into this volume. "Terrorism" is defined in the United States Code (U.S.C.), in two ways: "international terrorism" and "domestic terrorism".

"International terrorism" means activities having three primary characteristics: acts involving violence or acts dangerous to human life that violate federal or state law; and which appear to be intended (i) to intimidate or coerce a civilian population; (ii) to influence the policy of a government by intimidation or coercion; or (iii) to affect the conduct of a government by mass destruction, assassination, or kidnapping; and, occur primarily outside the territorial jurisdiction of the U.S., or transcend national boundaries in terms of the means by which they are accomplished, the persons they appear intended to intimidate or coerce, or the locale in which their perpetrators operate or seek asylum.

"Domestic terrorism" means activities with these three characteristics: acts Involving activities dangerous to human life that violate federal or state law, and appear intended (i) to intimidate or coerce a civilian population; (ii) to influence the policy of a government by intimidation or coercion; or (iii) to affect the conduct of a government by mass destruction, assassination, or kidnapping; and, occur primarily within the territorial jurisdiction of the U.S.

In examining these definitions of terrorism, and particularly the definition of "domestic terrorism", John Tieso takes us on a journey into the 'creation of the terrorist's mind', rather than concentrating solely on the terror actions of an international or domestic terrorist and their intended consequences and desired aftermath.

He asks the seminal question, "Why do individuals become terrorists; or alternatively, why do groups bond, and become terrorists?" Then, he tries to answer this query with a wonderfully written fictitious adventure, based on concrete examples of diverse facts and circumstances, occurring both abroad in the Middle East/North Africa and here at home in the U.S.

The self-made "domestic terrorist" you will discover, is motivated by a personal sense of self-worth, a personal ideology, a desire for money, personal religious beliefs, or any number of other things. One thing is for certain; all motivations are utilized to make the 'terrorist' appear "larger than life", "bigger than they truly are", "more important than all else in their own minds eye". All "terrorists", be they an "international terrorist" or a "domestic terrorist" have a singular motto they live by: "To thine own self be true, to rest of the world lie!"

Terrorists live for, or abide by, a drug called danger. They suffer from 'delusions of grandeur' and an 'abundant arrogance of self-worth'. In point of fact, the fictitious characters or individuals in John Tieso's novel, like Will Johnson (i.e., Willard Johnson; a.k.a. Suleiman Ashkar), Josh Giddons (alias: James Atherton), Hakim al-Azahir, Ibrahim Maloof and Fatima Ahmad (i.e., the female feme-fatale, the double-agent provocateur who helps orchestrate "domestic terrorism" and plays both sides (i.e., the U.S. CIA and the Terrorist(s)) against each other, or so it appears or seems) are all simply liars, bullies and mercenary-criminals; it is just that simple.

They are common or uncommon criminals, depending upon your personal point of view; but, they are criminals nonetheless. It is this body of truth, exposed by the author, that shows them for no more than what they truly are – a violent, extremist criminal element – dwelling today within our nation-state society, here in the U.S. or somewhere else abroad. An extremist, criminal element comprised of individuals, or groups of individuals who on the one hand believe their own ideas and views are the only ideas and views to be tolerated, and followed without question; and, on the other hand, individuals or groups of individuals who believe that they are waging a Holy War [i.e., a Jihad] against all infidels. The "infidel" in their mind is anyone who does not agree with their ideas and views of the historic past, or the present-day world.

Their actions take many forms; but all forms fit the U.S. Code definitions articulated above nicely. Their objective is the terrorist's view or version of perfection in the present-day world; and anyone who opposes that view should perish from the face of the Earth. This is a terrorist, born from a form of 'education'; the 'self-education' of the subconscious mind with extremist views, leading ultimately to the adoption of a radical perspective as one's own.

This occurs, even though it is the antithesis of how one has been raised, how one has conducted oneself and one's life for a whole or entire lifetime, even up to that historic day/date or data point in time, where an act of terror is initiated. Hence, it is an 'educated terrorist' view, a social vision, which results in a passion play relying on terror and terrorist acts. It results in a self-assured, subconsciously educated terrorist; one spawned from a radicalized knowledge base, and a terror-infused rationalized view of the world today.

Moreover, this 'education' causes a person to adopt a view of the world that causes them to take abhorrent, extremist, terror-based criminal actions they would normally reject. Tieso exposes this process; and in so doing, he sheds the brightest of LED light(s) on this "world of the 'self-educated', 'self-made' terrorist" world. He answers the inquiry: "Why do individuals become terrorists; or alternatively, why do groups of individuals bond and become terrorists"? It is because, simply stated, they want to actively support their self-made, self-educated social vision of the world and for their personal, short-lived time, in the LED spotlight of 'terrorist' fame and notoriety, be it on the domestic or international level. Conversely, be proud that not all who are enticed end up as a radicalized terrorist.

Finally, John Tieso reminds us all that international or domestic terrorists cannot take away the fundamental message of mankind: that no one can take away the freedom, our freedom, to conduct oneself [or ourselves] with honor, courage, commitment, dignity, integrity and love. It is, after all, the fundamental tenet or ability of mankind to be able to conduct ourselves with reasoned, rationale based decision-making and love, which sets us apart from all other species on Earth.

It is our destiny to live on, to survive terror. It is our destiny to live on, survive and thrive in the wake of acts of international or domestic terrorism. Why? ...you may ask... because it is what civilized societies do.

The ending of this terrific novel of fiction will surprise the reader; you will not have seen it coming.

Kindly enjoy this latest novel from my good, dear friend and fellow Bostonian, John Tieso. It is an entertaining and wholly worthwhile fictitious read – a "fiction" that is much closer to a present-day reality than you might ever imagine. I wish you, the reader, a joyful, joy-filled, peaceful read.

Michael W. S. Hayes, Esquire
Attorney and Counselor-at-Law
{CAPT/O6, JAGC, U.S. Navy (Retired)}
Senior Attorney-Advisor/Ethics Counselor
Department of the Navy, Office of the General Counsel

From a Vantage Point

From a Vantage Point

Table of Contents

A SPECIAL NOTE FROM THE AUTHOR 3

FOREWORD 4

TABLE OF CONTENTS 9

DEDICATION 13

ACKNOWLEDGEMENTS 14

PREFACE 15

PROLOGUE 23

PART ONE: LOOMING CLOUDS 25

CHAPTER 1 TRAVELING EAST 25
CHAPTER 2 WILLARD JOHNSON, TERRORIST 27
CHAPTER 3 ENROUTE TO QATAR 41

PART 2: THE BEGINNING 53

CHAPTER 4 SIGHTS OF DOHA 53
CHAPTER 5 ON TO KHARTOUM 71
CHAPTER 6 TOURISTS 79
CHAPTER 7 BEGINNING OF THE CONUNDRUM 87
CHAPTER 8 AMERICAN EMBASSY, DOHA 89
CHAPTER 9 BACK TO KHARTOUM 99
CHAPTER 10 CHANGING PLANS 107
CHAPTER 11 FATIMA 119
CHAPTER 12 THE FLIGHT HOME 125

PART 3: EVOLUTION 133

CHAPTER 13 RETURN TO REALITY 133
CHAPTER 14 INTERROGATION 137
CHAPTER 15 HOME AT LAST 141
CHAPTER 16 FOLLOW-UP 147
CHAPTER 17 SAMMI 151
CHAPTER 18 INTEREST AT LANGLEY 157
CHAPTER 19 WIDENING THE NET 163
CHAPTER 20 NEW AWAKENINGS 173
CHAPTER 21 THE ESCAPE 181

PART 4 THREE MONTHS LATER 193

CHAPTER 22 THE COOPERATIVE 193
CHAPTER 23 CONTEMPLATION 197
CHAPTER 24 LONG DISTANCE TO ATLANTA 203
CHAPTER 25 A CHANGE IN PLANS 223
CHAPTER 26 THE START OF RETRAINING 231
CHAPTER 27 SLEEPING GIANTS AWAKEN 247
CHAPTER 28 THE PLAN 259
CHAPTER 29 CONDOLENCES 287
CHAPTER 30 DREAMS 321
CHAPTER 31 NIGHTMARES AGAIN 339

PART 5 WORKING THE PLAN 353

CHAPTER 32 APPROACHING THE EDGE 353
CHAPTER 33 THE NET WIDENS 375
CHAPTER 34 CONNECTING THE DOTS 403
CHAPTER 35 BREAKING THE CONUNDRUM 415
CHAPTER 36 DISRUPTING THE PLANS 431
CHAPTER 37 CLOSING THE LOOP 467
CHAPTER 38 CREATING AN IMAGE 475

- Chapter 39 Into the Jaws of the Lion 487
- Chapter 40 Boxes Everywhere 511
- Chapter 41 Chasing Ghosts 537
- Chapter 42 Encountering the Devil 551
- Chapter 43 A Fateful Trip 571
- Chapter 44 One Final Chase 599

EPILOGUE 611

- The End of A Dream 611
- A Day in Paradise 615

PERSONAE 617

From a Vantage Point

Dedication

THE UNITED STATES DEPARTMENT OF HOMELAND SECURITY

Research for this book led me in a very different direction than its predecessors. In one of those forays into what makes some people accept radical views as their own, assuming they will be better off than in the past, turned out to be a direct route to the many, varied activities of the Department of Homeland Security (DHS).

That agency, created shortly after the September 11, 2001 attacks on New York, Washington DC and Pennsylvania, is, on the surface, at least, a hodge-podge of agencies, ranging from the Secret Service to the Sky marshal's Service, with Customs, Border Control and the coast Guard somewhere in-between.

DHS is a critical player in the intelligence world, at many levels, none more critical than keeping those who wish to do damage to us out of the country, and identifying those who do enter, and then decide to adopt a radical, twisted view, which eventually contributes to terrorist fears and actions, in the US or elsewhere.

So, this volume speaks to the often-times extraordinary efforts of the dedicated personal, agents and investigators of the Department of Homeland Security—without whom, as a member of America's intelligence team, our citizens would be experiencing many of the actions, frustrations, and fears as other parts of the world.

Acknowledgements

Every book, regardless of genre, relies on many people who help to shape it, smooth out the plot, try to ensure accuracy, and often keep the author occupied, while others make the changes needed to turn something mediocre into something more readable. This is particularly so when you meld the world of pure fiction, with some historical happenstance.

As is the case with some of these type volumes, mentioning names gets people in trouble, so I will simply say that I had a number of friends, and professional associates in the Intelligence Community (IC), the Federal bureau of Investigation (FBI), The Department of Homeland Security (DHS), and others in several countries who contributed their thoughts and suggestions for improving my prose. Thanks to you all.

My proof reader, Rose Demma, has been with me since the first volume, *Bernie Minihan's Dilemma*, and I do appreciate the hard work she puts in to make things sound grammatical and readable. She makes the work of the staff at the publisher so much easier.

CreateSpace is an amazing publishing house. They are patient, willing to put up with late deadlines, will contribute as much as they can to making the effort a success, and their mix of assistance to and for the author is immensely appreciated.

MY wife, Therese had to put up with many hours of my hiding in the office at home, trying to research and figure out what I wanted to write. Her patience at my not doing other things, other than writing, is a testament to her willingness to let me do what I like to do – write.

To the readers, reviewers, and family, especially CAPT Jerry Norris (USN Ret.), CWO Ray LaPlante (USA RET.) and so many others, all I can say is thanks, and I owe you all a couple of beers.

Last, but not least, Captain Mike Hayes, who wrote the Foreword in his own inimitable style, giving the work a sense of class it did not have before, and his in-depth understanding of what happens at all levels of potential radicalization, tempered with his extensive service overseas during these past years, lent the air of authenticity an author always treasures.

From a Vantage Point

Preface

There is an old saying, 'suckers are born, not made.' In my view, that expression applies to virtually every possible action or profession involving humanity. More recently, it seems to apply to a new group—individuals and groups of 'homegrown' terrorists. With high ideals, they go off to change the world—usually to something more to their point-of-view—or even more often, to the point-of-view of those that entice them into that kind of life. They become *radicalized*, a favorite term with the media, and often adopt a way of life considerably different from their prior social and political views. They learn to hate, hurt, kill, and demean anyone, or any group, they perceive is opposed to them, and those they adopt as their life models.

This book aims, in part, to dispel several myths surrounding the development of a terrorist, particularly the homegrown domestic terrorist we are increasingly seeing in the news each day.

It is true that some people, later identified as terrorists were born into circumstances of conflict, depravation, and often-outright denigration, some for their beliefs, and some into long-term religious, social, or political upheavals. These people are a very small microcosm of the overall population, yet their actions produce immense after-affects. In several of my prior novels, I zeroed in on the effects of their actions, rather than the cause. This book departs from that trend, and looks toward the creation of a 'terrorist mind', rather than concentrating solely on the actions of the terrorist. Terrorists try to encourage, even coerce others to their point-of-view. Sometimes it works, sometimes, it does not.

Before we progress further, I want to point out one very important fact. Those who commit terrorist acts seldom do so for the reasons they espouse. Terrorism is not a religion (Although there are Islamic terrorists, just as there are terrorists who could be tenuously tied to a myriad of religious sects), but terrorism is not the practice of many, if not most of the population. It is the actions of a few, who want to be something bigger, and more important than they really are, and these types are willing to go to any extreme to be recognized for their actions.

As I started to write this book, the actions against the magazine *Charlie Hebdo* were occurring in France. Several radicals, calling themselves Islamists, broke into the magazine's offices, shot, and killed numbers of people, wounding others, and killing an unarmed police officer outside whose hands were in the air in an act of surrender. Several hours later, two other terrorists took over a Jewish kosher market, killing several people as they arrived, and stood off the French

From a Vantage Point

police for several hours before the hostages were released, and the ringleader killed.

By the time I finished, there had been many more major incidents, some overseas, and some here in the United States, many perpetuated by our own citizens. Some were particularly horrific, such as the latest (Late May 2017) bombing of a concert in London, where the deaths were primarily among young girls and women, killed using Improvised Explosive Devices (IEDs) filled with nails, bolts, and other shrapnel, designed to inflict major damage. Others have e involved trucks or other vehicles crashing into crowds of innocent people. There is no limit to what some of these terrorists will devise to get their place in the evening news, and too many started out as a 'hometown' person who was convinced to make radical changes in their lives. Several other incidents followed, including that at Nice, France, where the driver of the truck believed he was doing the will of Al'lah in driving through the crowd, killing as many as possible. They think they are right—most of us thing, rightly so that they are wrong.

These incidents gained an immense amount of publicity for the terrorists—something they wanted. Several al-Qaeda-based groups later claimed 'credit' for the actions, as did the Islamic State in Syria (ISIS). Everybody wants credit for this kind of thing. The 'credit' they got was death—suicide by police officer—because they wanted to die as martyrs to their cause.

In the *Charlies Hebdo* case, the French police had been watching these people for some time, but without overt actions that is all they did—watch. One of the men had been to prison several times for terrorism-related crimes. Another was a local fishmonger in a small market. Both appear to belong to the same local cell. They were known, but so many others are not—until they commit a crime.

In London, it was not just the cruelty and depravity of the crime, it was the exposure by the media so quickly, even before the police could begin to investigate, that boosted the morale and tenacity of the terrorists. After all, that is what they want, *fear in the public, uncertainty*, and *publicity*. Those are three essential ingredients of terroristic activity.

Even in the vilest circumstances, if the crime cannot be related directly to terrorism, it might well be overlooked, or downplayed, as happened in France. Without better understanding of what causes someone to accept radicalization, these kinds of events will continue to occur, and more people will be injured and die, as the public fails to recognize it for what it is, evil in its worst form.

Some people, especially those born into conflict, may have no way to remove themselves from the fighting, and simply take up with whatever side their family supports, or whatever war leader demands their service. In these instances, a very few people could be said to be 'born to be terrorists.'

From a Vantage Point

But what about the others? What about those people who have no obvious reason to be a terrorist, such as Will Johnson, the man whose travels, experiences, and actions, we discuss in this book? Why do they become terrorists? Why do other terrorists try to turn them into one?

There are no 'good' answers to those questions. There are answers, to be sure, in each individual situation, for the path they took toward terrorism. There is no 'good' general answer, no universal reasoning that says, 'Today I will become a terrorist because I suddenly feel this way." Some will argue that an important part of the process involves environment and community. As those of you who watched events unfold in France, could see the sense of *multiculturalism* the French Government adopted as national policy, later evolving into an environment, fostered and supported by insulated, ethnic communities in and around Paris. In these areas, French law gave way to Sharia law, and the police allowed the communities to protect themselves. There was little apparent effort to integrate these communities into the larger French population. Taken together with the numbers of young people who travelled to the Middle East, the Persian Gulf, and Northern Africa to learn and aid in radical Islamic causes, it is logical some will return to recruit others.

Will Johnson, as you will see, lived in very different surroundings. He was simply a farmer, worked with the larger community on social and business projects, and seen as an ordinary American. As you will see, there is usually more to the story. Take Mary Mulligan, a character in my first book, *Bernie Minihan's Dilemma*, and a homemaker in Charlestown Massachusetts. Both could be called terrorists, but they responded to the urging, which took them over the edge, in quite different ways. One was a mole—someone waiting to hear about action; the other was friend, and his so-called friends tried to cajole him into action. However, they both ended up reacting quite differently. They both accepted the call, for different reasons, were assigned a mission, and attempted to complete it—one at least partially successfully, and the other less so. Both worked to achieve success in their mission. In the end, both failed.

Therefore, we go back to our question, 'Why do people become terrorists?'

Terrorists, in some form have existed since antiquity.

Looking at a few examples, both across history, and in the more recent time, and see if there are similarities among these people that might give us some clues. Let's start by going to the early 20th century, and the anarchists for a little historical perspective, then to a couple of the 'newer' terrorists and see what the difference between the two groups has become over time.

First, let's understand what anarchism is, so that we can then see what it ultimately became over time.

According to **Merriam-Webster**, an "Anarchist" is (1) A person who rebels against any authority, established order, or ruling power; or, (2) A person who believes in, advocates, or promotes anarchism or anarchy; especially one who uses violent means to overthrow the established order. What we have then is a person who opposes the normal order of things for some, perhaps unspecified reason. Anarchists did not like the prevailing order of governments, mostly autocratic, in the days surrounding the onset of the 20th century.

The first, and perhaps most well-known example of an anarchist in the early 20th Century was **Gavrilo Princip**, the assassin who killed Archduke Franz Ferdinand, starting World War I. Born in 1894 in Bosnia, Princip was one of many children, born to poverty, but eventually able to attend school. He became a member of the Young Bosnians, an illegal group, and was eventually expelled from school for his political activities. A person of small stature, he was repeatedly rejected by several of the local opposition groups of the time as 'too weak and frail' to be of value to the groups.

So here we have a person who wants to participate in the overthrow of the established order, but has significant difficulty in doing so. He was finally accepted, sent for training in small arms, and prepared for a future event. No one knew at the time that his 'event' would be as calamitous or earth-shaking, but his fight to be included in the movement made him even more dedicated to whatever the groups has in store for him.

That day came on June 28, 1914, when Princip and others lined up along the route announced for the visit of the Archduke and wife the Archduchess Sophia in Sarajevo, Bosnia. Although not the principal leader of the group, it is Princip who is remembered for the act that eventually precipitated World War I. he was, of course, as history relates, later captured, tried and executed for his crimes. To this day, there is a major memorial to him and his fellow anarchist and he is remembered as a National hero.

Looking back at the Webster definition, Princip is easily seen as a person who came from poverty, never really rose above that level, but wanted more; an education and a country ruled for the people rather than the aristocracy. He was convinced that only the overthrow of the Hapsburg Monarchy, together with its aristocratic traditions was the only way to achieve those ends, and he was, with his cohorts, willing to kill to achieve those goals.

In this sense, the early days of anarchy were dedicated to change in the established order, and those who called themselves anarchists were dedicated to that effort. Their aims were political and social rather than religious or personal. They knew, as did Princip that the possible end was death, yet they considered their cause important enough to risk that potential fate.

By the end of World War I, several things happened to change the perspective on opposition to established states. First, the anarchist philosophy grew exponentially, aided in part by the rise in Italy and southern Europe of the "Black Hand', the Mafia, as we would call it in current day parlance, and the rise

From a Vantage Point

of Socialism and communism, notably in Russia and Germany following the upheavals in those countries after the war. With the ever-increasing immigration of people from throughout Europe in the later 19th and early 20th century, anarchism grew, particularly along the Eastern coast of the US where many immigrants arrived and settled. However, the US Government, having entered the war to defeat the Alliance of Germany, Austria, and others, and who watched the rise of Socialism in Europe and Russia, there was increasing tension over the possibility that these anarchists could attempt to overthrow the US Government as well.

Perhaps nothing thrilled the public and convinced the Government of this growing threat of anarchism than the celebrated **Sacco-Vanzetti Cases** in Massachusetts in 1920-1921. Once again, the circumstances were similar.

At the outset, it was clear that Nicola Sacco, a shoemaker, and Bartolomeo Vanzetti, a fishmonger, both from Italy, were anarchists. They were believed to be followers of Luigi Galleani, an ardent advocate of revolution, bombings, and assassinations. His followers were at the top of the FBI wanted lists, and Galleani himself was deported along with several of his more radical followers. These were the days of so-called "Palmer Witch Hunts", named after then Attorney General Palmer, and anyone suspected of any form of anarchism or communism was arrested and quickly deported.

Having laid the background bare, we turn to the robbery of the Slater-Morrill Shoe Company in Braintree, Massachusetts on April 15, 1920. Two men, paymasters, were shot and killed, and the murderers escaped. Sacco and Vanzetti were rounded up several days later by local police and found to own weapons identical to those which had been used in the robbery and murders at Slater Shoe. Most of the evidence was circumstantial.

The crux of the case turned on anarchism. The judge, Webster Thayer had recently given a major speech on his opposition to Bolshevism and anarchism, and he actively supported their suppression through any means at the disposal of authorities. In addition, he was known to dislike foreigners.

The trial proceeded, but neither man testified in their own defense. Much of the testimony on their behalf was by locals who themselves spoke broken English and interpreters disagreed on their statements. Much of the circumstantial evidence centered on the anarchist beliefs of the men, the weapons found on them when arrested weeks after the robbery, and the fact they were immigrants of some kind—still a point of contention for many people. The circumstantial evidence they committed the crime was lacking, but the circumstantial evidence and the bias prevalent at the time convicted them, they were executed by the State, and their case has continued to generate controversy to this day.

From a Vantage Point

Modern-day society has its equivalents to these earlier extremists and terrorists. Two of these, among so many, are an interesting introduction to modern terror tactics.

First, there is the story of **Richard Colvin Reid**, also known as the "Shoe Bomber", Reid, a British citizen, born in 1973, was arrested on December 22, 2001, just over two months after the Twin Towers Bombings in New York, for attempting to detonate explosives packed into the shoes he was wearing, on an American Airlines Flight 63 from Paris to Miami, Florida, during the height of extensive security increases following September 11th.

Reid had an interesting, almost compelling, story. His father was a career criminal, and Reid followed him in multiple petty thefts, eventually being arrested, convicted, and sent to prison, during which time he converted to Islam. When released from prison, he began attending Mosque in Brixton, then Finsbury Park Mosque in North London, headed at that time by the anti-American cleric Abu Hamza al-Masri, a cleric often referred to as ' "the heart of the extremist Islamic culture" in Britain. Succumbing to radicalization efforts, he was sent to Pakistan and Afghanistan, receiving extensive training, and declaring allegiance to al-Qaeda. During his later trips, he was introduced to the bomb-maker crafting specially-made shoes, containing plastic explosive, and designed to be detonated by a willing martyr.

Unfortunately for Reid, he was uncovered attempting to board an America Airlines flight on December 21st, but detained by security, mostly for being unable to answer their security questions, and his disheveled condition. French security arranged for him to board another American Airlines flight the following day, and he continued to act suspiciously, eventually tried to detonate his shoe bomb, but was overcome by passengers, and held for the police. The plane was diverted to Boston, where Reid was arrested, eventually tried for espionage, and sentenced to three life terms in a super-maximum-security prison.

One more case of interest is **Umar Farouk Abdulmutallab**, popularly referred to as the "Underwear Bomber". Abdulmutallab, was a 23-year old Nigerian man who attempted to detonate plastic explosives, hidden in his underwear, while a passenger on Northwest Airlines Flight 253, from Amsterdam to Detroit, Michigan, on Christmas Day, 2009. The youngest of 16 children, his father was a wealthy Nigerian banker and businessman, and described by *The International Times* in 2009 as "one of the richest men in Africa." He is a former Chairman of First Bank of Nigeria and former Nigerian Federal Commissioner for Economic Development.

Abdulmutallab, an adherent of Anwar al-Awlaki, and al-Qaeda in the Arab peninsula (Now ISIS), failed to detonate his bomb enroute to the US, was detained and convicted in a U.S. Federal court of multiple criminal counts, including attempted detonation of a weapon of mass destruction, and multiple counts of attempted murder.

On February 16, 2012, he was sentenced to 4 life terms plus 50 years without parole, and incarcerated at ADX Florence, the supermax federal prison in Colorado.

What did these men have in common? One born to poverty and crime, the other born to wealth and financial independence. Both were enticed into opposition, then terrorism through emulation of someone they considered important in their religious life. Both accepted the views of those leaders, and trained for their fate. Unfortunately, both also failed, and, instead of going to their 'paradise' as martyrs, they will spend the rest of their life in confinement. Few even remember these two, except perhaps for the terrorism-oriented magazines, and an occasional mention in the media.

Was it worth it? To them, perhaps, or perhaps not. We will never know, since they have said little. What we do know is that there are many others out there, with similar 'dreams' and aspirations of glory, ready to be the successful terrorist. When they choose to act is unknown. That they will choose to act is almost a certainty. We need to be prepared.

John V. Tieso
Arlington, Virginia
June 2017

From a Vantage Point

Prologue

"This is Jim Smead, Eyewitness News, reporting to you from a vantage point along the Mall near 14th Street. Just a short time ago, several small explosions were heard and felt along the mall from 12th to 15th Streets, with one of the explosions know to have damaged a building at the Smithsonian. That building is presently on fire, and ladder companies from throughout the District have responded. Traffic is totally snarled, and plans for the Inaugural Parade have been cancelled."

"So far, the White house has had no comment; the only response to inquiries has been from the Emergency Operations Center trailer, set up at 14th Street and Constitution, and their spokesperson has asked that people stay away from the Mall and downtown until the 'all clear' has been sounded." We have no word when that might occur."

"Joe Snyder, with us now, was a witness to the explosions. Mister Snyder, what did you see?"

"Well, I was walking along the Mall, just about here at 14th Street, when I heard an explosion behind me, and turned to see what it was. Then, I saw a streak in the air, coming toward where I was, and ran across toward the building, and fell flat on my face. I felt the second explosion, while I was down on the ground. I waited a couple of minutes, and then got up, turned around, and saw the museum in flames."

"What do you think it was, Mister Snyder?" asked the reporter.

"Hey, I was in the Army a long time, and I know a mortar coming in when I hear it. I do not know about the first blast, but the other two were mortar's coming and dropping on the Mall. Must have been from somewhere close."

"Let me interrupt. Thanks Mister Snyder, our own Rose Cello is over at the Emergency Operations Center, and has the Mayor of Washington with her. Rose."

"Thanks Jim. I have with me the Mayor, who just arrived with several senior officers of the Metropolitan Police, and was just briefed inside by his emergency response team. Mister Mayor, what happened here?"

"Rose, there is very little I can tell you right now. We did have two explosive devices come in and hit the Mall, and an adjacent building, a Smithsonian museum. There is considerable damage to the building, which is still on fire, and another large crater on the Mall. Further upon the street, the Alexander Hotel appears to have sustained damage on one of its upper floors. Several windows are blasted out, and at least one room seems to have smoke billowing from it."

"This is clearly a disaster for the Nation, and our city, especially when we are all here today to celebrate the inauguration of our president. As should be obvious along the route, many of today's events are cancelled. There will be further word from the White house, but we know the president has already taken his oath, and been moved to safety outside the city."

"The FBI and other agencies have already arrived, in force, and secured the area. No one is allowed into the explosion zone. We understand they are evacuating the Alexander Hotel guests to a safe area, and closed the streets around the hotel. The Director of the FBI, I understand, will have a press conference shortly, and more information will be made available at that time. In the meanwhile, I have declared the city in grave danger, and asked the President to call out the National Guard to assist in patrolling the streets. He granted that request about an hour ago."

"I can't tell you much more at this point. I hope you and your listeners will understand that this is a very grave situation; stay in your homes, and do not try to come downtown. Thanks." As he finished speaking, the Mayor was surrounded by police officers and escorted away toward his limousine nearby.

"Well, that's what we got from the Mayor. There have been a series of explosions downtown, along what was to have been the parade route for the Inauguration. All events have been cancelled. The President has taken the oath in private, and been taken from DC to a safe location. Now, I guess, we wait to hear from the FBI. This is Jim Snyder, Eyewitness News, speaking to you from the scene of possibly the most horrific crime ever committed in the nation's Capital."

Part One: Looming Clouds

Chapter 1 Traveling East

As was his custom, Johnson often stopped in Strasburg, VA for breakfast on his way to the city. He liked a small restaurant just off the Interstate, and the menu they provided their customers. Generally, he would have an omelet with toast and coffee, and some fruit, paying his bill with a credit card. When he finished his meal, he would get gasoline at the service station next door to the restaurant, and then start the trip toward his destination. Johnson took his time, leaving home about 8:00 AM, stopping for his meal and gas, and then travelling along the Interstate just below the speed limit, puffing on his pipe, and enjoying the scenery as he drove along.

When he was close to the Beltway surrounding the DC area, Johnson would stay on the Interstate until he reached the Rosslyn section of Arlington, just over the border from DC. There he would leave the major roads, go over the Key Bridge into Georgetown, and then down toward the center of the city, arriving at his hotel just in time for a late lunch, or early dinner, depending on the traffic.

This day was no different, except that the traffic was worse, due to the impending Inauguration only three days away. As he pulled into the drive at the hotel, the doorkeeper welcomed him as usual, and reminded him that parking might be tight in the garage, but that the hotel had other parking spaces in a nearby lot. Johnson gave the doorkeeper his keys, and started into the hotel, followed closely behind by a bellhop with a luggage cart containing the few pieces of luggage he normally carried.

"Good afternoon, Mister Johnson," said Emily, the front desk clerk, "We have your reservation, as usual, and we're glad to have you back with us." She handed him his room key, and, just as Johnson started to turn, another of the clerks stopped him.

"Mister Johnson, we also have several packages for you. Let me get them."

"It's not necessary right now," he responded to the desk clerk. "I am going to the bar, and then upstairs later, after dinner."

"No problem, Mister Johnson," said Emily, "Shall I have everything sent up for you?"

"Sure, but no hurry. I intend to have a very casual dinner, then probably turn in early."

The clerk went into the back, to the mail slot area, and retrieved several small packages stored underneath. "I have them here for you, sir," said the clerk, as she had one of the bellhops place the packages, packing cartons, on the luggage cart with his other things.

From a Vantage Point

"You can take them all to my room, please," asked Johnson, handing the bellhop a tip. He then started toward the stairs opposite the front desk, which would take him up to the bar area. The bellhop tipped his hand against his hat, thanked Johnson for his tip, and started toward the elevators, where he would deliver both the luggage and packages to Johnson's room.

Willard Johnson was well known to the hotel staff; he had a standing reservation over several years, and he was considered a 'regular' customer. Ten days before the inauguration, he called to confirm his normal reservation, and the room he usually reserved, which the hotel confirmed even though they were pressed by inquiries on available rooms for the inauguration. Johnson was too good a customer to turn down, even in the press of a new administration.

Four days before his arrival, several small Federal Express packages arrived for Mister Johnson, sent from his home address in West Virginia. The clerk who received the packages saw they were for Mister Johnson, and stored them under the mail slot area, to ensure he received them promptly on his arrival. The packages were very light, but bulky. The clerk could not ascertain what they contained nor did he care. Mister Johnson, after all, was a good customer, who gave extra-large tips to the staff for their services to him.

The room Mister Johnson usually occupied was on the front side of the hotel, facing the Washington Mall. On the ninth floor, the room afforded a panoramic view, and the wide glass windows increased the appreciation for the historic area of the Nation's capital. Johnson had stayed in this room, on each of his visits to Washington, for over three years. He was well-known to all the staff, particularly the bar and restaurants, where he often hosted meals and parties, and treating the staff very well.

Johnson lived in West Virginia, travelling to Washington to conduct his business. He would normally arrive late Monday afternoon during the weeks he was in town, and leave early in the afternoon on Friday to return to the country. Since he travelled along interstate Route 66, it was much easier to avoid the traffic that bottled up in the DC area, especially inside the beltway surrounding the city and its suburbs, and he often had comments for the desk staff on the traffic coming east.

Chapter 2 Willard Johnson, Terrorist

Johnson was not the man he seemed to be in public. In fact, his name was not Willard Johnson, but Sulieman Ashkar, and he was only an American by adoption; in truth, he was Lebanese, whose family had come to the US when he was young. He grew up in the country, went to local schools, enjoyed the friendship of classmates and friends, and eventually enlisted in the Army, serving for four years, with six more in the Reserve.

Despite his seeming acceptance of the American way of life, Ashkar eventually became a mole. That did not happen immediately. He worked hard on his farm, and actively participated in community development. He was a 'good citizen', looked up to by his neighbors, and even received an award as "Man-of-the-Year" from the local Farm Bureau. He nurtured his American ways and customs well, eventually aided further by a school, originally created in Sudan by the Government of Libya, to train future terrorists for operations in the United States. Ashkar, or Will Johnson as he was known locally, was a terrorist waiting to happen.

The terrorism school had as its model a similar operation, conducted by the Germans during World War II, where they trained men and women, born in the United States, or with a strong background that included American families. The Germans produced a cadre of well-trained, undercover insurgents, who could infiltrate the Allied lines in Europe, and disrupt operations, sending many men to their deaths. Al-Qaeda developed a similar school, first in Sudan, then Pakistan, and eventually Afghanistan, taking over a field training site used by the Russians during their occupation of the country.

Al-Qaeda, funded by Osama Bin-Laden, learned well from the Germans. There was no shortage of young men, mostly American or Canadian, who, like Johnson, were disenchanted about various US policy positions, particularly those relating, first to the Vietnam conflict, and later to the ongoing conflict between Israel and the Palestinians. Many volunteered to go to Sudan, where they entered the schools, preparing terrorists and infiltrators, for the war against first the Russians, and now the Americans. These men believed sincerely in their mission to create both a free Palestine, removing the yolk the Israeli's placed on freedom and commerce, in both the West Bank and Gaza, and in a greater, Islamic-based world.

Of course, as in all wars, there were also those who were involved for their own profit and excitement. They bore no real allegiance to any cause, but served out of a feeling of involvement, or, just as often, out of a sense of greed, for what they would be paid. Many of the early trainees in this school had long since been placed in the United States, mostly in rural or suburban settings, some even joining the military, and otherwise establishing themselves in their community.

From a Vantage Point

Johnson was one of these. Born a Maronite Christian in the Southern Lebanon, his family brought him to the US, escaping the civil wars in that country, and Johnson grew up in rural West Virginia. Johnson had been drafted into the US Army, receiving training in weapons and mortars. He received orders to report for service in Vietnam, but left the country to avoid the war, settling in Sweden, eventually becoming a 'protestor-for-hire' for several European peace causes. After President Jimmie Carter granted amnesty to those who left the country to avoid the draft, or who deserted during the war, Johnson returned to the US, and settled again in West Virginia, attending the University there to study business management.

Over the years, he became a successful businessman, traveling between his home, in a small West Virginia town, near where his parents had first settled, to the Washington area, selling various dairy and other farm-created products from the farmers in the region. He bought a small farm, with an old house and barn, which he quickly refurbished, as his base of operations.

Johnson had worked with several of the farmers to create a cooperative, where they would not only share their produce, but combine to sell it to the hotels and restaurants in the DC area. Over thirty farms, large and small, contributed to the cooperative; they purchased several trucks, and maintained two central receiving warehouses, where the produce would be collected, processed, packaged, and readied for shipping. That provided work for many of the locals, particularly their children, and the income was sorely needed. The whole community considered Johnson one of its valued citizens.

In August 2014, just before Johnson started his plan to develop the cooperative, he was visited by an old acquaintance; one with whom he had worked in Europe during the protest years, named Josh Giddons. That visit began a chain of events, which would eventually change his life remarkably.

Asked by his friend to meet him at the local train station, Johnson waited for the 10:35 local train to arrive from Charleston. While waiting, he spoke with several neighbors, and seemed to have a very positive outlook. He had already begun to formulate his cooperative plans, but felt the time was not yet ready. He snapped out of his haze just as the train arrived. Johnson looked at each of those who departed from the train, looking for his old friend.

"Will, is that you?" came a voice from behind him. Johnson turned, and a tall man, with a goatee, wearing jeans and a plaid shirt, stood in front of him.

"Sure is, Josh. Glad to see you." The men shook hands warmly, and Johnson showed his friend the way to his car in the parking lot.

"This is beautiful country," said Josh, "I can understand why you want to live here. Sure beats the big city." The two friends drove out the short road into the farmland surrounding the train station.

From a Vantage Point

"It sure does. The land is beautiful, and the people friendly. Where are you living these days, Josh," responded Johnson, "I've lost track. I do remember getting cards from several places over time, but the last one came nearly four or five years ago. What have you been doing since?"

"I travel a lot Will, all over the place. Really don't have a place I call home, just a place I stay for some period, I guess. Last place was Boston. I lived there for nearly three years. Do you remember Hakim al-Azahir? The guy from Yemen we roomed with in Sweden years ago?"

"Sure, I often wondered what happened to him. The last time we were together was in Gaza. We were running guns under the Egyptian-Gaza border for the PLO. That was an interesting time."

"Well, he and I have created an import-export company in Sudan this past year. We support several organizations in the Middle East, and other formerly Muslim areas. We get some support from the Egyptian Muslim Brotherhood, and other groups for our efforts."

"Really. I had not heard about any uprisings over in that part of the world lately."

"We're not into uprisings anymore, Will," responded Josh, "I work with a training group on organizing local relief and reconstruction efforts. We train Muslim locals on how to organize, and get ready to form a Muslim government, as time makes that possibility a reality."

"We have several high-profile groups, mostly from Egypt, Saudi Arabia, and Libya, who support and fund us, along with providing instructors. Currently, we are working in Sudan, but will be moving to Pakistan shortly. You might want to come and see what we are doing, if you have the time."

"I have the time, Josh; I'm just not sure I want to get back into the protest movement, even if it is for a more peaceful cause. I was born in Lebanon, you know, and of Maronite parents, growing up part of my early life in between the warring lines. Out here in West Virginia, we had little contact with our faith, but my mother and father continued to try to teach me as much as they knew. Unfortunately, after they died and I left for Europe, the sense of religion died with them, and I just never got back to it myself."

"Well," responded Josh, "Maybe this isn't the time to discuss old history. Let's just enjoy ourselves, for what little time we have, before I have to get going again."

"One more question," Asked Will, "Where is 'going next' going to be?"

"It will probably be Sudan, and then on to Pakistan. I'm waiting for a call on the move in the next few days."

"How do you pay for all this travel? I certainly could not do it, at least on what I am making right now?" asked Will.

"Generally, the groups I work with pay the freight. If they want me to go somewhere, they will tell me, and a ticket will be waiting for me, in this case it will probably be through Dulles Airport. OK, now let's figure out what we want to do for the next couple of days, friend."

In about twenty minutes, they arrived at a farm road and entered the drive. Ahead, about 200 yards was a small, while farmhouse, with a barn on the right side. Around the property, there was a farm fence about four feet high. Will pulled up in front of the house, hit the button for the trunk, and left the car to get luggage for his friend. Walking up the two short steps to the front door, bags in hand, Will led Josh into the house. He dropped the luggage near the stairs to the second floor, ushering Josh into the living room, and then toward the kitchen.

The two men got some beer from the refrigerator, and sat to watch a football game on the TV. Over the next hour, they discussed a bunch of issues, mostly the fun times they had travelling around the world, before Will decided to return to the US.

That evening, in his bedroom, Will thought a bit about the discussion he and Josh had earlier, before rolling over and falling asleep. Josh did much the same, except that he congratulated himself on putting a small seed in the mind of his friend; one he hoped would bear fruit sometime soon.

Over the next two days, the two men travelled many miles throughout the state, visiting small towns, the university where Will received his degree, and other nearby attractions, including the land where his parents once had their farm. The previous discussions were forgotten, until it was time for Josh to board the train, taking him back to Washington, and the trip to Dulles Airport.

The previous evening, Josh had received the call he expected, and he told Will the next stop was Sudan, although he really knew that beforehand. He made a deal of the call, and the plans to pick up his tickets at the international area at Dulles, where he would travel Emirates Air to the Gulf, and then over to Khartoum by a local carrier.

Will Johnson was impressed by the planning and the availability of funding for Josh's trips. He was also impressed that his friend would be travelling first class; something Johnson had never done in all his years on the road. He was impressed with the salary and expenses Josh had available to him while he worked for the import-export firm.

On his last day in the US, Josh and Will stood once again on the porch at the railroad station, waiting for the 10:56 AM to Washington. Saying their goodbyes, and each expressing hope the other would stay in touch, Josh again invited Will to visit he and Hakim. Josh promised to keep his cards, with a current address, coming, and Will indicated he probably would not be moving for a long time, so Josh could count on finding him here in rural West Virginia.

From a Vantage Point

With a handshake, Josh was on the train and headed toward Washington, and Will went back to his farm. Their separation would not last very long, however; barely a few weeks would go by before Johnson made contact, accepted the invitation to visit Josh and Hakim, and was on his way to Sudan to see the training camps.

Will could not be aware that his friends, Josh and Hakim, were well-known international terrorists. The 'import-export' firm they worked for was an arm of the al-Qaeda terrorist group in Yemen. The 'training' involved the training camps throughout Yemen, Sudan, and now Pakistan. The 'import-expert' business was involved with funneling arms, money, and other resources needed by the major terror groups, and their mole organizations. Both men had been looking for additional people they could count on for a new US operation, and their sights eventually settled on their old friend Will Johnson.

Josh had kept Will's address in his contact list over the years, occasionally sending cards and brief letters—none of which ever explained what he and Hamid were doing. Instead, they kept the contact alive, just in case they ever needed him. Both Josh and Hamid were professionals—even more so than Will had been. They were completely committed to their causes—and especially to the money their causes brought in for themselves. They also knew that Will was more of an idealist. Will would not work on a cause just for the money—it had to mean something to him.

In a few cases, they had worked causes involving the rights of Palestinians, and opposition to Israel. Will had strong feelings on that matter; partially because of his family background during the battles with Israel in Lebanon, and partially because he was an idealist at heart—one who felt that both Palestinians and Jews could live in harmony on the same lands—as they had done for centuries, before the current strife erupted. That was the very kind of person Josh and Hakim needed for their latest idea.

They had been working with a group planning a major event in the Washington DC area for nearly two years, this would be their opportunity to make it happen. To do it, the group needed someone like Will, and now their plan would start with Josh's visit to the farm.

Will Johnson thoroughly enjoyed Josh's visit. On many nights, long after Josh had returned to the Middle East, Will relived in his mind several of their escapades as protestors-for-hire, and slowly came to realize he still respected, even loved that way of life. The real question in his mind was what to do about it.

Those thoughts put him into a quandary; here he was in West Virginia, comfortable, secure, and no real responsibilities. Yet, he wanted more, and it seemed that the visit of his friend caused him to feel that the 'more' he sought might be in the adventure and travel he once enjoyed. While he might not return to his old life of wandering, at least he could go and see how his old friends lived. After all, he had nothing to keep him here anymore; his family was gone, and, while the community had taken him back with open arms after his return, he was still virtually a stranger to many of them. The community where he lived was predominantly Quaker, and they abided anyone who refused to raise weapons against another.

Three weeks later, Will e-mailed his friend Josh. He knew Josh was in Sudan, and Josh responded immediately, inviting Will to visit his two former partners and see what they were currently doing. It was agreed they would meet in Qatar, in the Emirates, and spend a few days together, before they went on to Sudan. Will quickly made plane reservations for a visit three weeks later.

Will had no idea this was always part of the plan, hatched between Josh and Hakim, to get him involved. They knew, once he arrived in Sudan, and saw their training programs, both men knew they would quickly have him hooked.

Making plans for at least a four-week absence, Will arranged with a local Amish farmer, who normally utilized Johnson's fields for crops, to have his son take care of his property, trading the fields for the farmer's efforts. He also deposited funds with the local bank, ensuring his house and utility payments were made during his absence.

Now, standing on the platform he had said goodbye to Josh some weeks earlier, and waiting for the same 10:56 AM train, Will Johnson looked around, knew he would miss the comfort and enjoyment he loved in the mountains, but looked forward to seeing his friends during the trip to the Sudan. As Josh had promised in his last message, a first-class ticket would be waiting for him at Dulles Airport for his trip to Africa.

The train lumbered into Union Station in DC, and Will went out to the curb to find an airport limo, which would take him on the hour-long trip to Dulles. A van, painted blue with huge yellow lettering was there on the curb. Johnson paid the fare, stepped aboard, and the van shortly left Union Station, making one stop over in Crystal City, across the Potomac River at a large Marriott hotel, and then drove to Interstate 66 in Rosslyn for the trip to Dulles.

During the journey, Johnson sat in the seat well toward the back of the van with an older gentleman who promptly fell asleep, quickly starting to snore. Johnson read a bit of a book he carried with him for the trip, but gave that up since the snoring interrupted his train of thought on the book's plot. Instead, he started to think about his two friends, and the last time he, Josh, and Hakim were together on one of their adventures.

It was 1977, and the struggles over rights and nationality in several nations were just beginning to make the front pages of American papers. The Shah was

From a Vantage Point

overthrown in Iran, in favor of an Islamist revolutionary government headed by an aged Imam. In other historically Muslim countries, similar events occurred, as one country after another changed its historic governmental structure; many adopting the more fundamentalist, and strident approach used to seize power.

For Will, Josh, and Hakim, their lives were a constant swirl in adventure; some foolhardy, some dangerous, and all enjoyable, for three young men experiencing life on their own. They met in Sweden, where Will had gone in 1969 to avoid serving in the US Military. He was nineteen years old then, and saw the world as a place for amazing experiences. There, in Malmo, he met another professional protester, Josh Giddons, from Detroit, Michigan, who saw the world much the same way Will experienced it. Together, they protested the US war in Vietnam throughout Europe, and gradually became a part of a core group, protestors-on-demand, for any organization willing to pay their expenses.

Josh had also left the country to avoid the draft, but not before he participated in several anti-draft demonstrations at local Detroit draft board offices. During the third protest, a police officer tried to push Josh with his night stick to get him away from a blocked doorway. Josh grabbed the stick away from the officer, beat him senseless, and then quickly left the city.

It was nearly five years before enough testimony was gathered by detectives hired by his family that the tapes of the demonstration surfaced, showing Josh protesting, but not actively resisting the officer. What the tape also showed was the officer repeatedly going after Josh, calling him a draft evader, and pushing his night stick into Josh's chest, and the side of his head.

Josh's family attorney proved conclusively that Josh was only protecting himself from the officer, and the district attorney decided to reduce the charges, then eliminating them after the officer refused to testify in a trial. By then, Josh was in Sweden, and would not return to face the other charges on draft evasion.

John and Will traveled throughout Europe, staying mostly in student pensions, small hotels, and slept in railway stations when they had no funds for better accommodations. They had just completed a demonstration in Germany when they were approached by another protest leader, who asked if they might be interested in going to South Africa to protest apartheid.

While neither man knew much about the apartheid movement, they were impressed with the group travel expense money, and daily personal expense allowance their acquaintance discussed. They agreed to meet with one of the organizers of a group going to South Africa shortly to work in one of the 'independent' black republics the South African government established as part of the apartheid program. Within weeks, they were in Cape Town, and took several trips to small villages where they worked with organizers of coming demonstrations in Pretoria.

From a Vantage Point

It was on one of these trips in South Africa, that the two young men met Hakim al-Azahir, a Yemeni citizen, wanted by the police in his own country for attempting to assassinate a political figure. Hakim explained that the politician had molested his sister, but because he was a member of an elite family, the police refused to investigate. Instead, Hakim simply walked up to the politician one morning as the man entered a government office, and shot him with an old pistol belonging to Hakim's father.

Unfortunately, the shot did not kill the man; Hakim was arrested, and placed in a cell to await trial. One evening, just before the trial, after he had been in jail nearly six months, his family paid a guard to enable his escape into Saudi Arabia, and then on to Egypt, where he enrolled in al-Azhar University in Cairo, home of the Muslim Brotherhood. Later, he became a member of the Al Gamaat al Islamiya wing of the Muslim Brotherhood, and attended classes on Fundamentalist Islam, taught by some of the more strident faculty at the University. Within the year, Hakim was organizing cells, and working with other Brotherhood groups in and around Cairo.

Hakim became a fervent and dedicated member of the Brotherhood, and the organization rewarded his fervor with increasing responsibility. He soon started travelling, first to other nearby countries such as Sudan and Libya, and eventually to further locations, such as South Africa, where the rising clamor against apartheid was a perfect cover for organizing the Muslim communities in that country. Hakim did very well as an organizer, and gained his own following for the principles he had learned early on in Cairo.

Hakim had another asset, one of value to the Brotherhood; his ability to mimic foreign accents and other effects. He would often regale his fellow protestors, playing an Englishman, an Indian, an oriental, or a member of another ethnic group, with all the mannerisms, gestures, and dialects that would make an unknowing person think he was real.

During the past two years, Hakim, changing organizational affiliation to a new group, called al-Qaeda, brought together others with similar skills and, these men created a special school outside Khartoum where others could be trained in the same skills. The school was funded by a Saudi national, Osama Bin-Laden, son of a prominent and politically connected family. Instructors were brought from all parts of the world, speaking myriad languages, and dialects. Each possessed a wide range of experiences, all of which were brought into the curriculum to train new cells for the emerging movement across the world.

The primary job of the school was to train those whose experiences would be needed sometime in the future. They would be trained in tasks ranging from demolition to computer hacking, and then sent to their respective countries, where they would wait for further instructions. If needed, they would also be trained in dialect and mannerisms of the countries where they lived after

From a Vantage Point

assignment. Until needed, they would act simply as local citizens; participate in their community, and be as patriotic as the person living near them.

Remembering his friend from protest days, the disillusioned Will Johnson, Hakim worked out a plan with Josh Giddons to re-contact their old roommate, first to see if he still might have a desire for adventure, and then as a possible instructor or perhaps student in the school. Giddons, who had kept contact periodically with Johnson, agreed to work with Hakim toward that end. He contacted Johnson, made a visit to West Virginia, and now Johnson was on the way toward their part of the world. It was agreed they would meet in Qatar for a holiday together. By that time, Hakim would fill Josh in further on his new assignment.

Will's thoughts of past days were interrupted as the van came to a screeching halt, and the driver yelled out they were at the arrivals section of the Dulles Airport complex. The driver stepped from the coach and directed the passengers toward the entrance that would take them up to the check-in area at the Dulles main building. Johnson entered the building, went up the escalator, and began to look for Zone Two, where the Qatar Airlines reservations area was located, eventually finding the check-in space where he could pick up the ticket waiting for him for his trip.

The stay in the line took about thirty-five minutes, since it was early in afternoon, about three hours before his flight would depart. He presented his identification, and his current passport to the counter clerk. Inside the passport was the letter from the Qatar Embassy with his visa information. He answered the usual questions, and waited for his ticket to be issued by the ticket agent.

Confirming his reservation, and printing his ticket, along with checking his baggage took only a few minutes, once he arrived at the front of the line. The agent took the ticket, baggage claims, and his passport, and brought it down the counter, to a person who appeared to be a supervisor. That person perused the documents, including the passport, looked at a document he pulled from his jacket pocket, and returned the documents to the agent, saying a few words to the agent Will could not hear. A few seconds later, the agent gave Will his ticket and returned his passport, pointing out where he had to go through security, and then how to get to Concourse 'A', where the flight would depart from Gate A-15.

Washington-Dulles International Airport was originally named after John Foster Dulles, Secretary of State under President Dwight D. Eisenhower. Appointment as the Secretary of State was the capstone of a long career, extending from his service as Legal Counsel to the Delegation that ended World War I, to his service on Several Federal boards and Commissions, and a short stint in 1949 as a US Senator from New York.

The airport was built in what was then the country in Chantilly, Virginia, as an alternative to the Washington DC Airport, near the Pentagon, in Arlington, Virginia, with the hope that moving the airport outside the city, would make air travel safer, especially during the Cold War.

Unfortunately, while it might have been good for the traveling public, it was not good for the public officials, the members of the Congress, and other senior Governmental officials, who liked the convenience of Washington-National at the Potomac River. The Congress approved the airport, but exempted itself from using it. For many years, it brought in international flights, but few domestic flights, whose companies continued to fight for lots at Washington-National.

The airport, opened in 1962, has a magnificent mail terminal designed by Eero Saarinen, an internationally acclaimed architect finally completed in the later 1990's, as the airport regained its stature as a premier site for international travel from the Washington DC area.

Over the last several years, the airport has been a testing ground for the Department of Homeland Security; introducing several innovations in passenger reviews and searches. It was the first airport in the country to have the so-called TSA 'Express lane' for trusted travelers, and it was toward that set of lines that Will was headed today.

Will had a strange feeling overcoming him since he arrived at the Airport. It seemed as if someone was constantly watching his every move for whatever reason. There had been the review of his ticket at the ticket counter, and then he remembered what happened as the ticket agent tagged his bags for loading on the conveyer belts at the Transportation Security Agency (TSA) checkpoint. When the agent placed the bag tag, it had a large 'X' in red marker on the tag.

Going over to TSA, Will started to place his bags on the conveyer belt, and a TSA officer, seeing the mark on the bags, asked Will to bring them over to the inspection area, and asked for his ticket.

"Sir, we need to inspect your luggage today. Please unlock and unsecure the bags for inspection."

"Why me?" asked Will. The officer gave Will what he considered to be a rude stare.

"Just routine, Sir," responded the officer, "We do random checks here, so may I please open your bags."

"Sure, I guess that's OK."

The officer opened the first bag, and started searching carefully throughout the bag, and then did the same with the second one, leaving Will to re-shift the contents, and re-zip and lock the bags. The officer them marked the tag himself, and placed them on the conveyer belt.

From a Vantage Point

"Have a great trip," said the officer, waving the next person in line over to have their bags inspected. Will noticed their bags had no red 'X' on them.

Walking around the TSA area, Will soon came to the start of the long lines that waited to go through the personal inspection area, which checked on the ticket, the person, and the carry-on luggage. Once at the lanes to wait for inspection, Will could see that people were going through quickly, with an occasional stop in the line, as a person was asked to go through a large body scanner.

Waiting about 15 minutes in the line, which wound around in several snake-like lanes before you reached the end at the inspection area, Will finally arrived at one of the inspection stations, put his carry-on luggage on the machine's moving belt, along with an extra basket for his shoes and coat, and started to move through the line. As he did, and handed his ticket again to a TSA officer, he was told to go over to the body scanner, and did so, placing his hands over his head, and following the officer's instructions while the scanner did its work.

As he exited from the scanner, two other officers were waiting for him.

"Sir, could you please show us which luggage is yours?" one asked.

"Sure, right over here," responded Will, as he pointed to luggage already scanned and waiting. The officers took the luggage over to a side are and began to search the carry-ons.

"Was there something in the scanning that showed I had something I wasn't supposed to?" asked Will.

"No Sir, just routine," responded the officer, just as the other officer at the entrance had done.

The officers rummaged for a couple of minutes, and then told Will he was free to go. The luggage was disheveled, and had to be re-arranged, but Will did it quickly, and moved on, putting on his shoes and coat, so he could leave the area as quickly as possible.

Once through the inspection area, Will went looking for Concourse "A" where his flight would depart. As he moved along the terminal, and down the escalators toward the aero train stop, he still had the nagging feeling he was being observed, although, in the crowd at Dulles that morning, close observation was surely hard to do. Nonetheless, this nagging feeling kept with him as he boarded the aero train for Concourse A, and his flight.

Looking along Aero train car, Will found a small group of flight crew members riding the train. With them were two TSA officers, having what appeared to be a lively conversation. Several times Will saw one or the other TSA officers looking down the car, where Will was seated at one of the doors.

Concourse A is a large, bustling terminal, connected to Concourse B, where most of the international flights depart for locations around the world. Alighting from the aero train at the Concourse "A" station, Will headed up the escalator toward the departure gates. He looked at the signs at the top of the escalator, and realized he needed to go to the left, and quickly found gate A-15, his departure gate. He also saw a camera, looking down on the escalator, moving periodically as the escalator rose toward the concourse level.

Looking at his watch, Will realized he still had nearly two hours before his departure, and decided to go to one of the restaurants near the gate for some food, and a beer. Luckily, it was still early in the terminal, so finding a seat at the bar was no problem. The bartender quickly gave him a menu, and took his drink order, promising to come back shortly to take his food order.

Will looked around, still feeling the sense of observation, but decided that it was simply the camera surveillance systems, and, after all, he was no criminal, and resolved to simply enjoy his upcoming trip. When the bartender returned, Will ordered a hamburger, with a bunch of additions, fries, and another beer. The bartender, took the order down, said thanks, and went over to put his order in the system.

On the television in front of him, above the bar, one of the national news channels was showing some recent carnage, this time in Sudan, outside Khartoum, said to be the work of a terrorist group Will did not recognize. As he shook his head at the death and injury, the man next to him, on his right, leaned over.

"These people sure make a mess, don't they?" asked the gentlemen.

"I guess they do," Will responded. "It sure seems to me to be something horrific, though. Why can't people settle their differences in ways other than blowing each other up? This is all that seems to be on the news these days."

"You're right, it is unfortunate, but that's the price people are willing to pay to get their views on the news. I'm Jim, Jim Davis, by the way. I'm heading for Qatar."

"Mine's Will, Will Johnson. I'm going to Qatar as well, and, unfortunately, as it seems, I'm going from there to meet some friends in Sudan. Doesn't look good right now does it?"

"Not really, but if you stay in Khartoum, you should be relatively safe. My job takes me over there periodically, and the center of the city is well protected. It's the outlying areas that have become infested with al-Qaeda, and the other splinter groups fighting with each other."

"That's good to know. I'm going over there on vacation, to see two friends I worked with some years ago. Kind of a return visit, since one of them came to see me a few weeks back, and we wanted to get together again."

"Good deal. What do you do?" asked Davis.

"I own a farm in West Virginia. Right now, I do a bit of farming, even though I am not much of a real one. I am also working on a deal, to help the locals in the area combine into a cooperative, to sell their goods and produce to the restaurants and wholesalers in the DC area. It's slow, but we have made some initial deals, and are working on several more."

The two men continued to talk over lunch, and a couple more beers, until they heard the first announcement of their flight to Qatar, departing at Gate A-15. Will started to ask for his bill, but Jim dissuaded him.

"We have plenty of time," said Jim, placing his hand on Will's arm. "The plane is not full, and there is still 45 minutes until departure. Let's enjoy the space while we can before we are cramped up on the plane for hours."

"Sounds good to me," Will responded, as they went back to talking and finishing their beers.

"So, what do you do Jim?"

"Oh, I work in security, mostly. I spend a lot of time flying to and from job locations. My firm provides security overseas, mostly. Been doing that for about five years now."

"Must be hard on the family life?"

"Not really. You have to have a family life first. I have been out on my own since I was a kid; spent some time in the military, and have been working in some form of security or another ever since. I have no one close, so travelling is easier than for some."

"Don't you ever get tired of the same travel grind?"

"Oh, sure, on occasion. I get thirty days off most years, and simply go off to do something else not related. Last year, I went on a safari in Kenya. A couple of years ago, I went to see Mount Everest. Lots of places still to visit in this big world."

Just then, another announcement on the concourse address system told them the flight was boarding, and the gate was looking for passengers who had not yet boarded.

"Guess we better get over to the gate," said Will, as he reached for his bill, putting down a credit card.

"I agree, we don't want to miss the flight or get kicked off, "responded Davis, as the two men started the short walk over to their gate for their flight to Qatar.

From a Vantage Point

From a Vantage Point

Chapter 3 Enroute to Qatar

The flight from Dulles International Airport to Qatar is a very long 14+ hours. Generally, the route is a northeast arc, extending over Europe, then down toward Saudi Arabia and Qatar. The expected arrival time in Doha is about Noon, the following day.

Will and his new acquaintance Jim Davis settled into their seats for the flight. Since the plane was far from full, Davis asked one of the flight attendants if he could have the seat next to Will, and she accommodated him just before takeoff. Once they were seated, the flight attendants took orders for drinks and small snacks.

"So, tell me Will, how is it again that you are going to Qatar?" asked Jim Davis, just after the attendant brought their drinks.

"Well Jim," responded Will, "I'm actually going to Sudan, where my friends are currently working. They have been overseas for years, and we lost track for some time after my military service time. We spoke occasionally, but I wanted to get back and remake my life; perhaps make up a bit for my wild years before my military service time."

"That seems reasonable," responded Davis, "Sounds like a good plan, but now, suddenly, you want to renew old relationships. I guess that is a part of growing wiser, but any particular reason why NOW is the time, rather than some other time."

"An interesting question, Jim. I thought about that myself. When Josh, my friend, came to visit, and we discussed the possibilities of going over to see him, and others, it seemed to me that I had a lot on my plate here in the US. Hopefully, I will have the agreements in place soon on our cooperative, and then it will be busy most of the time. It just seemed, if I was going to do it at all, now was the time, or I would miss the opportunity entirely."

"Again, that sounds reasonable, but the Sudan is not exactly a peaceful place these days, with many terrorist groups working out of there, and possibly capturing an American is good business for them. Aren't you afraid of some problems?"

"Sure, just like anyone else would be, Jim, but I wanted to go, had the time, and made the decision, come-what-may. It was now or never for me on this."

"Well, I applaud your spunk on this Will. Not sure I would have made the same decision. Enough for serious talk. The film will be on in just a moment, and then they will bring food. Need another drink? First Class does have its amenities, you know, especially on this airline."

Will looked at his mostly unfinished drink, and responded, "No, I'm just fine for now. When does she come by with the headphones?" Both men laughed,

From a Vantage Point

and grew silent for a few minutes, until the attendants started through the cabin with headphones, and snacks before the film started.

Sometime later, Will looked out the windows, after the film had ended, and saw that it was evening; the sun was setting brilliantly on the horizon, and he realized somehow that the sun was also setting on him, at least as he was at present. There was an uneasy feeling building in his psyche that told him he would not be the same person when he returned; something Will initially thought ridiculous.

In a short time, the attendants returned, this time to get orders for dinner, along with more drinks and coffee or tea for those that desired alternatives. Both he and Jim Davis ordered the chicken on the menu, along with salads, and wine. The dinner was delicious, as was the wine, and eventually the after-dinner aperitifs. They continued their light conversation, started before the film, until the cabin lights again darkened slightly as people started to wind down their day.

Will Johnson was no exception. Slowly, he fell asleep, ending a powerful day, with the thought still in the back of his mind that someone was observing his every move.

Jim Davis was, indeed, observing virtually every breath that Will took, assessing the possibilities of his honesty, and his loyalty. Jim Davis had two purposes on this trip; first, and foremost, he was a member of the Sky Marshal Service of the Transportation Security Administration, an agency of the US Department of Homeland Security. His job on this flight was to observe Will Johnson, a person flagged for review as a potential terrorist. Unlike other sky marshals, Jim Davis could eat and drink, and associate with flyers as he observed their behavior, and solicited information on their tendencies to commit acts of terror. He was well trained in this regard, as graduate of both the DHS training program and that of the FBI.

Prior to joining the Sky Marshal Service, Davis was a special agent with the Naval Criminal Investigative Service, NCIS, where he learned well the powers of observation, especially for those whose tendencies were to commit crimes against the Government.

There was a second, and even more personal reason why Davis was on this flight. Years earlier, his brother Joe was a draftee for the US Army, served in Vietnam, and died in a small battle that most historians have forgotten. He went to basic training at Fort Jackson, South Carolina, in the same company as Will Johnson, but then went on to serve at the expense of his life. No one cared in those days, and he was buried in the local veteran's cemetery with little fanfare.

Later, after President Carter granted his amnesties, a lot of men, mostly cowards who used 'opposition to the war' as their cover, returned home, and expected their communities to greet them open arms. A few did, and others simply, and quietly, allowed them to live within their surroundings. Some families

From a Vantage Point

never forgot the insult to their sons, who, after all, had served their country well, even if some disagreed with the government's policies.

Davis had become part of a select group of sky marshals whose job was to be on the watch for specific possible terrorists. When someone is identified through the database searches at DHS, and is shown to be planning a trip, especially outside the US, a member of the team may accompany that individual, to observe and report. The assessment of the marshal carries great weight on future actions of the agency.

Right now, Davis sat quietly in the darkened cabin, next to an identified suspect, and watched the film, wondering what this flight might bring. Was Will Johnson a terrorist; was he being recruited by others, or was he simply a young man, wide-eyed and adventurous, looking to see his friends.

Davis did know one thing; Will's 'friend' Josh Giddons was a known sympathizer of al-Qaeda, worked in Yemen, and other countries, providing training for future terrorists, and was shortly heading for Sudan, where he would meet Will Johnson. That information, combined with a review of Johnson's file, which brought out Johnson's connection to Davis' brother, made Davis want to take this particular case, and work it to whatever ending might occur.

The film on the flight was one of those 'shoot-em-up' terrorist thrillers that fill the movie theaters; something Davis had no real interest in watching. Instead, he put on his earphones and listened to the classical music station, which was playing parts of several Mozart and Bach symphonies. Davis learned to love classical music early in life, and still enjoyed hearing music he had heard so many times before.

One of the benefits of working in his profession is the opportunity to go to distant countries, where, if he had a long enough stopover, he would find the nearest place to hear his classics. It also gave him the opportunity to hear music from other cultures, many of whom used the larger symphony orchestras as well as their European counterparts to provide the most amazing musical compositions.

This evening, the movie, and the associated ads and trailers for other films, lasted nearly three hours, and Davis enjoyed every minute of the music channel, until the attendants came to inquire about his dinner preferences. Only then did he realize the film was over, and, coming back to reality, he heard Will ordering drinks before dinner.

'Wow, Jim, you were way out there with your music."

"Sure was, Will. Forgot the time and place. I really enjoy good classical music, and the selections, at least on this flight, really are first rate."

"Sir," asked the flight attendant, "Would you like something before dinner?"

"Sure," responded Davis, "How about some black coffee?"

"Cream and sugar?"

From a Vantage Point

"No, just black will be fine."

"Coming right up then," responded the attendant, marking down his coffee on her seating chart.

"Here is the dinner menu," she added, "I'll take your order when I bring the drinks back, if that is OK?"

"Sure. That's fine with me. Will, how about you?"

"Ok with me as well. Thank you for asking."

"Back shortly, then," said the attendant, as she started to the next row for their order.

"Will, how was the film? Asked Davis.

" It's just another of those 'shoot first' films, Jim. I probably should have done as you did, and listened to the music or something else on air. I can easily forget this one."

A few minutes later, the attendant brought the drinks, and took the dinner order, which she brought to them in about thirty minutes. They had a bit of light conversation through dinner, and afterward, until, about an hour later, Will fell asleep. Davis turned out the overhead lights and eventually drifted off himself.

"Ladies and gentlemen, this is the first officer. We still have about three hours to our destination at Doha, Qatar. Good morning. I hope you enjoy your breakfast. While most of you slept, we took a long northeast to south arc across part of Europe, and are now moving more southeast toward the Arabian Peninsula."

"This morning will be a bit busy," continued the first officer, "our flight attendants will serve breakfast, and the various lavatories are available to you throughout the plane to freshen up. It is now approximately eight o'clock AM, Greenwich Time. Our flight will be a bit early into Doha, with the help of good tail winds as we moved across the Alps and downward toward our present location in the Mediterranean near Italy."

"Once breakfast has been served, and the cabins cleared, the flight attendants will help you fill out the incoming customs declaration for Qatar. The Government here is quite strict, and some items, such as alcohol, are prohibited. Please be sure to list cameras, expensive watches, or other computers and electronic gear on the declarations. Otherwise, you may have problems with them going out of the country. This will be particularly true if you have a layover, and expect to see anything of the country."

"When we land, you will be shown to the Customs area. Please have your passports and visas ready. You may enter the airport without a visa, and stay in the airport area, but cannot leave the secured areas for the city without a visa inspection. Military personnel, and other official personnel will be met at the jet way by US Government and Qatari officials for processing."

From a Vantage Point

"For now, enjoy your breakfast. We have about three hours to complete everything we need to do before reaching our destination. Weather in Doha is very warm, sunny, and dry. The attendants will provide you with extra water bottles before arrival so you can stay hydrated until you get to your hotel or next flight. The airport is well air-conditioned. Thank you for flying with us, and have a great day."

Will woke slowly, as the message on the intercom system went on, and opened his eyes, just as it ended, to find Jim Davis putting on his earphones to listen to the morning news, showing on the screen in the back of the seat in front of him. The report was of a bus bombing in Syria, near one of the presidential buildings in Damascus.

"It's about time you woke up," said Davis, as he took off his earphones and looked over toward Will. "We have about three hours to landing, if you did not hear all the message from the cockpit."

"Heard some of it," responded Johnson, "Was just starting to wake up as it came on. Have they asked about breakfast yet?"

"Not quite, but there is stirring in the kitchen area, so I assume they are getting ready. Sure enough, here comes one of the attendants now, down the aisle."

The attendant had a tray in her hand, and was passing out warm towels, giving one to both Davis and Johnson, before she moved on to other passengers in the section. A few moments later, she returned with a plastic sac to retrieve the moist towels, and took orders for coffee and tea, or soft drinks.

"So, what's next for you, Will?" asked Davis.

"When we get to Doha, there should be two friends waiting for me. We intend to spend a few days in Doha, looking at the sights, and then on for a few days to Khartoum. I can only stay a week, or less, because I have to get back to work the cooperative deals."

"Sounds interesting. You said, two guys; you had only been mentioning one in our previous conversations."

"Yeah, there are two friends there. One, Josh Giddons, I mentioned already, and another, Hakim Al-Azahir. Josh and I were in the military together some years ago, and used to travel quite a bit when we were younger and adventurous. I met Hakim on one of our trips. Eventually, I came back to the States and settled down. They still like adventure, and do whatever they want, I guess. It's been a long while, and I have no idea what they are currently doing."

"That's a lot of trust to come half way around the world to see them, isn't it?"

"I guess so," Responded Will, "But we are friends, and friends do odd things sometime. I'm looking forward to seeing them both, and having some fun. That's about it."

From a Vantage Point

"Good luck on that. Just remember what I was saying about the dangers in Sudan. It is not peaceful there, and you really need to be careful."

"I appreciate the advice, Jim. This is supposed to be a fun trip, and, since they live there, you would think they know where to go and where to avoid."

"You're right, of course. I just like to think on the safe side."

"Are you going to be tied up much in Doha, Jim? Otherwise, why not join us for a look around?"

"Love to, and happy to accept the invitation. How about I call your hotel, and let's work out some time to get together?"

"Great. That will work out well. Might as well enjoy some of your time in Qatar."

"Agreed. Security can get boring sometimes. Luckily, there are times when it gets interesting as well. I'll call you soonest."

"Great, now let's have breakfast. I see the truck coming down the aisle. This is one of those times it is good to be in the first-row seats." The two men laughed, and the attendant soon arrived with their breakfast and coffee.

As they enjoyed their breakfast, time seemed to fly by, and it seemed like just a few minutes before the first officer was back on the speaker system announcing their initial descent into Doha.

"Ladies and gentlemen, this is the first officer. We will shortly be entering the airspace of Saudi Arabia, on our way to Qatar, and Doha International Airport. Many of you near the windows will be seeing military aircraft as we cross the Arabian Peninsula. Please don't be concerned; the Saudis are very protective of their airspace, and we do have permission to be crossing it today."

"Shortly, we will be passing over Amman, Jordan, and then quickly into Saudi Arabia. Most of what you see in Saudi Arabia will be desert, punctuated by some small villages and oases. The largest of these villages will be Sakaka, which you should be able to see from the windows on the right side of the aircraft. We will follow a line south east from Sakaka toward Riyadh, and then east toward Doha."

"I'll try to point out some of the interesting sights for you as we progress. You can see Amman, Jordan, ahead from either side of the aircraft, coming up in about two minutes." Periodically, Davis pointed to other sights, and Will clearly enjoyed the guided tour, at least until Davis indicated that soon they would be seeing Qatar and Doha Airport in the distance.

"Well Jim, looks like the last legs of travel for us."

"We still have about two hours, Will, but the scenery is interesting, if you have not seen this area before, take a look at Amman. It's an old and interesting city, with an interesting mix of the old and the new." Just as Davis made his statement, the first officer was again on the speaker system.

"As we approach Amman, two things will come into view of interest to most who travel to this part of the Middle East. First, on your left is a large building,

From a Vantage Point

with an ornate checkered roof; squares in black and white atop a large mosque. This is the Abu Darweesh Mosque, located on the highest point of Amman's hills. The other large mosque, seen off a bit to the right is the King Abdullah Mosque, a monument to the grandfather of the current king. This mosque has over 3000 people pray in it each day."

"Once we have moved through the city, going south, you will see the Queen Alia International Airport, a sprawling facility of three main concourses, and the main airport in this region, through which passes most of the major airlines of the world. Look out the windows for yourself. We will also turn on the external cameras on the plane, and project our pass over Amman on the screens on the back of each seat so all of you can see the sights of the city."

"Once we leave the Amman airspace, we have about two hours before landing. We'll leave the cameras on for a while to give you all a good view as we pass over, and then down toward Doha. Our general route will take us south over Burayadah and Riyadh, the capital of Saudi Arabia, then east into Qatar airspace, and the Airport at Doha. The views are spectacular, so enjoy the scenery."

Watching the screen, and alternately looking out the window, Will was fascinated by the scenery, and how villages, and oases seemed to pop up out of the desert. The plane seemed to be following a large, paved road that moved south and east through otherwise desolate desert dunes, pausing occasionally to stop at patches of green. Will was also amazed at the number of cars and trucks travelling along the route. Soon, in the horizon, he could see another, larger city looming. From the map is was Riyadh, the Saudi capital.

Riyadh was indeed a large city, at least for this part of the world surrounded by desert, and the military planes in the area seemed even more frequent than over Amman. Rising to a plateau, the gleaming city of skyscrapers and buildings, many of which rival those in the major western cities.

"Ladies and Gentlemen, this is the first officer. We are now approaching Riyadh, the capital of Saudi Arabia. Those of you watching the screens can see what a beautiful city it is, in the middle of the otherwise desolate desert. The capital city has several very interesting architectural structures, and I will point out three you should be able to see clearly as we pass by the city. As you can see, the city is built on a plateau, and rising high from that plateau is the highest, and largest, of the building, the Kingdom Center, a unique building, which changes color each evening to constantly give people a new view of this landmark."

"Nearby, Al Faisaliyah Center is the second largest building, shaped like a ball point pen, some would say. The other, more historical landmark is the Al Masmak Castle, built in mid-1800, as the current ruling family took over the country, and established what we now know as Saudi Arabia. Off to your right is the International Airport. Enjoy the sights. From here, we will be turning east to

From a Vantage Point

head toward Doha. We will fly south of Iraq, gradually turning east. I'll let you know when we are approaching the airport."

"We currently have about 40 minutes before we reach Qatari airspace, and about fifteen minutes after we enter the airspace until we are on the ground. The flight attendants will be coming through the cabin again, with customs declarations, for those of you who have not already filled one out. Please be very careful to declare everything of value you are bringing in. Otherwise, enjoy the view for what is left of our flight. That's it for now."

Finally, just beyond Riyadh, Will could feel the plane turning east in a banking movement, and heading in a new direction over the desert. It took about twenty minutes to reach another city, much smaller than Riyadh, and, off in the far distance, it was now possible to see the Persian Gulf.

"Looks like we're close now, Jim," said Will to Davis, just as Davis took off his earphones. He had apparently been listening to music, and experienced the turn himself.

"Must be, I felt the turn," responded Davis. "Do you have your declaration forms completed?"

"Right here," said Will, pointing to the forms in the pocket ahead of him on the wall. "You too?"

"I have nothing really to declare, Will. I take this type of trip so often; I leave most everything at home. If I need anything the client provides it. By the way, you haven't told me where you will be staying in Doha."

"A place called the Concorde, just outside the Airport. They have a shuttle, so Josh said in his message. My reservation is all made. What about you?"

"Interesting. I am staying at the same place. Looks like we are rapidly becoming soul mates here."

"Great, then I won't have to try and find you for us to get together. I'll just leave a message for your room."

"Good enough for me. As I said, I will be busy for a day or so, but then should be free for a couple of days. By the way, I like that hotel, and have stayed there several times in the past. It is clean, the staff is efficient, and they will get you anywhere in the city in one of their courtesy vans."

Josh and Hakim had arrived a day earlier, and were settled in at the Concorde, having had a late breakfast, and spent some leisure time talking in the coffee shop, before Josh was to depart for the airport to pick up Will.

"Do we have a plan, then, Hakim?" asked Josh of his friend, looking across the table.

"Of course, we do, Josh. The only question is if Will can be convinced to accept it, and work with us. Only time will tell that, and we must be cautious. He has been gone for a long time, and, as you saw in West Virginia, become again

From a Vantage Point

part of the America we hate. I still think we can bring him over, but we must be cautious, and patient in our efforts."

"Agreed," responded Josh, "We only have a week or ten days before Will has to return. At least we can plant a seed, perhaps."

"You better be going to the airport," said Hakim, looking at his watch, "Perhaps the hotel shuttle can take you over there when they go to meet the flight. At least you can ask."

"I will. That was my thought as well." Josh rose to leave the coffee shop, and walk the few steps to the concierge desk, where the driver was waiting to leave.

"See you in about an hour, then."

"OK, I will be right here waiting."

Josh walked over to the concierge, had a short conversation with the driver, and the person at the desk, and waved to Hakim to signal that he would ride out to the airport in the van. In a couple of minutes, he and the driver left for the short ride to the terminals at Doha International Airport, to meet his friend, and any others coming in on flights this sunny morning.

"Ladies and Gentlemen, this is the Captain speaking. We are approaching Doha on our final leg of this flight. We expect to be on the ground in approximately five minutes, and it will take another five to ten minutes to taxi to the arrival concourse. I want to thank you all for flying with us today, and hope you have enjoyed the flight. I will be turning the screens off shortly for our arrival, and, if you are not currently seated, please do so quickly so that the flight attendants can prepare for arrival."

Will looked out the window, and saw Doha looming on the horizon. It seemed to be a huge city, with large towers, and green space; something he did not really expect to see.

Jim Davis was busy putting away his earphones, and placing some magazines he had removed from his carry baggage earlier, then took his seat to prepare for arrival.

The flight attendants were coming through, taking trash and no-longer needed cups and other galley items. They started to ask those in First class about outer clothing, although it would not be needed here in Qatar. Some, who had arrived from the west coast of the US, had outer coats where the weather had been chilly on departure. Finishing their tasks, the flight attendants took their seats, just in time, as the plane wheels touched the runway, and the plane started to slow down to taxi to the concourses at the airport.

"Welcome to Doha, the time here is approximately ten fifty-five AM, and the weather, as you can see, is sunny and hot. Please be prepared to take all personal possessions with you when you leave the flight, since, when you depart the plane, you cannot return to it. The flight attendants will have water available

From a Vantage Point

for any who wish to take some with them, as they acclimate to the climate here, and for the wait at Customs. The airport authority advises us that the average wait time at Customs is approximately twenty minutes."

"Once again, thank you for flying Qatar Airlines for your flight today. We appreciate your patronage, and hope you enjoyed the flight. Have a great day."

Within a few minutes, the plane taxied up to the arrival gate, and the jet ways came forward to connect with the plane, in both first class, and coach sections. As they did, the flight attendants at the doors moved the security latches to allow the doors to open. Both Will and Jim felt the blast of the artificial cold air enter the cabin as the door opened wide. They both started to rise from their seats, to retrieve their under-seat carry-ons, and Davis moved to the aisle to open the overhead storage as well. He pulled down Will's bag first, then his own.

"Well, this is it, my friend. Here's your bag, let's get ready to get off this bus, shall we?"

"You are right, Jim. It has been one long flight. My back needs to walk a while to straighten out." Both men laughed, and started into the aisle toward the doors. Airline personnel were in the jet way with directions on how to proceed to Customs.

The customs review was very short, as the Captain had suggested. Both men went through quickly, and were out in the concourse in less than twenty minutes, since they did only cursory reviews of Will and Jim's bags. As they exited Customs, Will saw his friend Josh ahead, and yelled out to him, and waved in his direction. Josh saw him, and started down the concourse to meet him.

"Josh, it's great to see you again."

"You too, Will. I'm glad you came."

"Josh, this is Jim Davis. I met him at Dulles. We flew together from DC." Josh looked to Will's right and saw a tall, thin man, with his hand extended.

"Jim Davis. I'm glad to meet you."

"And I as well," responded Josh, obviously surprised that Will met someone on the plane. "Are you here for a visit as well?"

"No, I work for a company here, outside Doha. I generally travel around the area quite a bit. Just coming back from a short vacation in the US."

"Great. Hope we have the opportunity to get together with you while Will is here."

"Actually, I already asked Jim if he would like to do that over the next couple of days," responded Will.

"Great, then it's settled. The hotel shuttle is outside, so let's head toward the exit. The shuttle should be at the exit by the domestic baggage claim area. You guys start down the concourse. I need to get a paper, and will catch up."

"OK Josh, sounds like a plan to me," responded Will. The two men started to walk down the concourse, and Josh went over to a newsstand nearby, to buy a

From a Vantage Point

paper. He looked over the selection, picked up an *International Herald Tribune*, and went over to pay. As he did another man came up, and bumped slightly into him. They had a word or two, Josh paid for his paper, and quickly caught up with the other two men, who were just about to walk through the baggage claim area.

From a Vantage Point

PART 2: THE BEGINNING

Chapter 4 Sights of Doha

Outside the terminal, the Concorde Hotel shuttle driver waited patiently for his passengers. He knew there would be at least two on this trip; both coming from the flight that just landed from the United States. He also has his passenger from the hotel, who came with him to the airport to meet his friend. The driver assumed that person was one of the two arriving from the US on the same flight.

Sure enough, in his rear-view mirror, the shuttle driver could see the man he brought from the hotel with two other people, and he assumed, correctly as it turned out, they were the same two he expected. The side door of the shuttle van opened, just as the driver left the vehicle to help load luggage into the rear of the van. The two new passengers gave the driver their larger bags, each keeping one of their carry-ons for the trip to the hotel.

The two new passengers entered through the side door to the middle seat, and his original passenger again took the passenger seat in the front. The driver mentioned they would wait a few more minutes, to see if others also required a ride to the hotel. He also called the hotel on the radio, and was told no others had called. In about five minutes, he closed the side door, re-entered the driver seat in the front, and started to engine to depart for the hotel.

"Welcome to Doha, one of the pearls of the Arab world," said the driver, as he started the engine, "This is a beautiful city, both historical and modern, and I hope you enjoy your stay. We will be at the hotel in just a few minutes." The driver's English was flawless, although, had he sensed he had Arab passengers, his Arabic would have been equally so.

"The major arteries of the city are arranged in rings around the historic harbor, as is common in many Arab cities. The original city was close to the harbor, and grew outward over time, necessitating more roads. We now have a fine taxi service, and excellent bus service throughout the city, and, these you will not need, since the hotel vans will take you anywhere you want to go. The fee is very small," the driver continued, with a smile.

"Sit back and relax, as we go to the Hotel."

The Concorde Hotel is only a short distance from the Airport. Pulling out of the terminal drive, the shuttle van turned left on C Ring Road, the main road outside the Airport, went around the broad arc the road made as it went along the airport grounds, before coming to the intersection of and eventually turned right onto al-Matar Street, a road that would take it up to the hotel. The whole trip took perhaps six to seven minutes.

The Concorde Hotel, on the corner of al-Matar Street and B-Ring Road, is a large, pleasant, and modern hotel, with a lot of amenities, in addition to its

From a Vantage Point

convenience to the airport. The hotel has over 200 rooms, on 10 floors, with world-class services, and a worldwide clientele. In the midst of the historic district of Doha, the hotel is close by to several major tourist attractions, some within walking distance (If you can bear the heat of the day), and most open to the public, such as the Doha Fort, the National Museum, and the Museum of Islamic Art.

The hotel entrance is a semi-circular drive with a broad façade to the buff brick structure. The doors open into a magnificent lobby area, which boasts concierge services, and some front desk open 24 hours a day, and every day of the week. Most who have stayed in the hotel are quick to laud its services, and the availability of the quality staff.

The driver stopped at the front doors, and quickly left the vehicle, traveling to the right side of the shuttle, and concurrently opening the front passenger door, and the sliding side door for the two new passengers in the middle seat. Having done that, he moved to the back of the vehicle, to open the rear door with its access to the luggage.

"Please be careful stepping down," said the driver, in his traditional Arab dress, a flowing robe and Kaffiyeh, over more modern shirt and trousers, along with western style shoes.

"Welcome to the Concorde. I hope your stay will be pleasant. The weather has been as it is now, and will remain so, Praise All'ah. I will bring your luggage to the Bellman for you. Please enter inside, and out of the heat, to register. The Bellman will have your luggage to take to your rooms." Having said that, the driver went over and secured a luggage cart. He [pushed it toward the rear of the van, and was placing the luggage on the cart, as the Bellman came out of the hotel, and assisted in moving the cart inside.

"Let's all go inside," said Josh, "It's hot out here, even if you are used to it. Will, Hakim is in the restaurant waiting for us. Jim, would you like to join us?"

"No," responded Davis, "I think I'll go up to my room and get squared away. Thanks, though. Meet you all later?"

"Good deal," answered Will.

The guys walked into the lobby, went over to the registration desk, and completed Will and Jim's sign-in. Then, Will and Josh headed for the restaurant, as Davis headed upstairs to his room.

Will had just entered the restaurant, when he saw Hakim who, at the same time, saw him and Josh, and started over to meet them. Will and Hakim hugged, and exchanged handshakes, then the three went to the table that Josh and Hakim had been occupying before Josh went to the airport. The waiter came over and asked Will if he would like anything to drink.

"Sure, iced tea, unsweetened if you have it that way," responded Will, remembering that sweetened tea was common in the Middle East.

From a Vantage Point

"Coming right up sir, unsweetened iced tea. Anything else?"

"No, I think that will be OK. We just ate before landing." The waiter left with his order, after refilling the teas for both other men.

"I am so glad to see you," exclaimed Hakim, obviously excited, "We have been waiting for you since you said you would come over. We are going to have a great time, here and in Khartoum in a few days. We have a lot planned for you."

Josh looked over at Hakim, as he finished speaking, with a frown on his face, as if to say, 'don't say too much right now', without coming out and curtailing the conversation. Hakim noted the look, which he knew well, but Will seemed to be totally oblivious to it, with the excitement of being there in Doha.

Finally, the waiter returned with Will's tea, and they clinked their glasses, just as they always had, with even more potent beverages than tea, something they would not find in public places in Qatar.

"I hope you are ready for some exciting days, Will," said Hakim, bringing the conversation up again. "I have a whole agenda of places to see, starting with the museums; I know you always liked museums, and two of the best are here within a short distance."

"Great. I want to see as much as I can in the short time I have with you guys. When do we leave for Sudan?"

"In about three days, I think. I'm waiting for confirmation of our visas," responded Josh. "Meanwhile, we can enjoy the time here. When we finish our tea, let's get you upstairs, and settled in, then we can plan out our days together."

"Sounds good to me," answered Will, as he went back to his iced tea. "This is very good tea. Seems to have a bit of mint in it."

"It does. They like mint here, and the tea itself is Darjeeling; a remnant of the old days of the British occupation here."

They sat and talked, almost non-stop, for nearly an hour, before Josh asked for the bill, pulled out a wad of foreign-looking money, and paid the bill. The three friends rose, and started toward the lobby elevators, which would take them to the 8th floor, Will's room area, was part of a suite, with a common area, a kitchen, and rooms for the other two men. It was much larger than the rooms he would find in the Washington area, well-decorated, and boasting large television screens in each room, and the common areas. There was even a smaller TV in the bathrooms.

Josh took Will's bags into his room, and Will quickly excused himself to go get settled there.

"Back in a few minutes, guys," said Will, "I want to get a shower and change after that flight. Will only take a few minutes and then we can decide what to do with the rest of the day."

"Good idea, Will," responded Josh, "We'll be here waiting for you.

From a Vantage Point

Will closed the door, and a few seconds later, the others could hear the water running in the bathroom.

"Hakim, Will arrived on the plane with a guy named Davis. Says he is a contractor over here, but something raised the hairs on the back of my neck. Wasn't sure why, until I bumped into a guy in the airport lobby, you might remember him, his name is Jackson or something close. Anyway, this guy bumps into me and says, 'watch out for the guy with your friend. Not a nice person' then walks away. What do you make of that?"

"Interesting. Is the guy you are thinking of Chuck Jackson? The guy from Physicians without Walls, or someone else?"

"No, that's the guy, Chuck Jackson. Why would he say that to me though?"

"Not sure, but he is back and forth from the US all the time. He must have a reason. I'll go see him today, and ask."

"Good. I would be a lot more comfortable knowing more about him, before we start travelling around with him here in Doha. It could really put a crimp in our plans. Will asked him to join us."

"Agreed. We need to be careful what we say or do around him. Nothing about our plan until we are on our way to Khartoum."

"OK with me. Better that way anyway, in my view."

Twenty minutes went by before Will emerged from his bedroom, to the sitting area, where Josh and Hakim waited. Hakim spoke first. "How was the trip, Will? It really is great to see you after all this time."

"Trip was great. I don't travel that much anymore, and at least had someone on the flight I could talk to. It's great to see you guys as well. I can't tell you how much I think about the good times we had, and often wonder what I would do if I decided to go back to those adventures."

"We've missed you, Will," responded Josh, "We don't travel as much anymore ourselves. Right now, we have a steady set of work opportunities, mostly taking us between here and Khartoum. We work with several of the NGO's – the Non-governmental organizations -- that are all over Africa these days. Sometimes we help with security, and sometimes, we do training for the locals. It's interesting, and you get to meet a lot of people."

"That's true. We just did some work with Physicians without Walls, the group that provides medical care out into the desert village areas around here, and over in Sudan. That keeps us coming back and forth to Doha, and here we are." Hakim smiled, got up, and walked over to Will, who continued to stand, and patted him on the back.

"We have a lot to show you over the next week or so, Will," continued Hakim, "Sudan is a very beautiful country, even more so that Qatar, if you are careful not to get in too close to the marauding nomads and terrorists. Here, they have police on every corner, and watch out for the tourists, and foreigners in general.

From a Vantage Point

Over in Sudan, you are on your own, and should be careful. They'll take everything you have, and leave you for dead. We try to avoid those situations."

"Boy, do we ever, and sometimes it is not easy," added Josh.

"OK, so what do we have planned for today?"

"I thought," responded Josh quickly, "We might get our car out of the garage, and take you on a tour of the city. There are some really cool things to see here; this is one of the richer emirates, so their museums, especially those with Islamic art and other artifacts, are among the best in the Middle East."

"That's true," echoed Hakim. "Qatar is a bit more modern and western than many of the emirates, and Saudi Arabia. The Emir allows more freedom here, especially in dress, and associated with the people, especially women. While you will see some women wrapped totally in a burka, most wear a head scarf, or a modified veil, and want to converse with westerners. Others are more reluctant, and try to stay in the background. A lot depends on whether they are born and raised in the area, of have come here from other Arab countries."

"Let's go get the car, and be on our way. You never know when traffic is going to get messed up here, so luckily we have a lot of time, "said Josh, as he headed toward the door of the suite. Hakim and Will followed him into the corridor, then down the elevator, to the garage level where the valet service parked cars.

Showing his room card to the valet employee, it took only a minute, or two for the employee to bring the car to the waiting men. Josh and Will entered the front seat doors, and Hakim entered the right rear door. As soon as everybody was settled, with their seat belts engaged, Josh began to exit the garage, up one ramp, to al-Matar Street. There, he turned right, and they started their tour of downtown Doha.

"Doha is an interesting mix of a town, Will," said Josh, as they started to drive up what seemed to be Main Street. "Its history goes back to the 17th century, when the first sections of the old city, around the harbor, were created to house the ship owners, and those who supported the shipping trade. Today, the area is called the *Corniche*, and we will show you that section later this afternoon. Now, it houses several museums and other places to visit, and several world-class restaurants, one of which we will visit to have dinner. A friend of mine is the *maître d*. I'm sure you will enjoy the food."

"Josh, let's go to the harbor, and see the Museum up at the port first. That might give Will a sense of the culture here better than trying to explain it."

"Good idea, Hakim," responded josh, "The Museum has centuries-old artifacts from Islamic culture. It's one of the finest in the Middle East, and they have wide open hours so people can see it. We'll do that first."

From a Vantage Point

"Great," responded Will, "I love good museums. You remember, we used to frequent them in Europe. I have one question, though. How is it that you guys, working out of Sudan, can be here, and know a lot about Qatar?"

"Easy, my friend," said Hakim quickly, "We work for several organizations, and most of them have offices here, in addition to the on-site work in Sudan. We come over here for meetings, and to pick up supplies, or deliver reports, and try to stay a few days, such as we did here, knowing you were coming over. When you work for multiple firms, you have a lot of flexibility."

"I guess so," retorted Will, "Sure wish I had a job like that. It makes my operation in West Virginia seem tame in comparison. But then, I wanted to slow down a bit, and what I am doing there is really going to help people over the longer term. So, I make no apologies for my decision to become a farmer."

"What you are doing is important, Will," said Josh. "So often people forget the need to help the small guy, as opposed to the large companies. It's the big guys that have gotten us in trouble throughout the world, not the little guys, who want to earn a decent living."

As Josh finished speaking, they arrived at the end of al-Matar Street, at the *Corniche*, the long promenade that borders Doha harbor, with its spectacular views of the old port and the new age skyscrapers that seem to grow larger each year.

"We're almost to the Harbor, Will. You can see the Museum of Islamic Art off in the distance to the left," said Josh, as they drove along the Corniche, toward the peninsula that bordered Doha harbor.

"The gleaming white building in the distance houses one of the best collections of art and other artifacts from all over the Middle East, and covers virtually every aspect, and denomination within the Islamic culture and religion. The building was designed by I. M. Pei, who also did many buildings in the US, but this is one of his best works," continued Will.

"It sure is. Pei showed the rest of the world that Islam is important, and its art tells a story unique in religion and culture. I love coming here," added Hakim, "because it teaches me something new about my religion each time I can get here. You don't have that in western churches like we do."

"No selling Islam today, Hakim. Will is here to visit, not be converted."

"Ok, so I do go overboard sometimes, but the beauty of Islam is in its simplicity, and the beauty of its history. The artifacts and art tell that story."

"Well then, let's go see it," said Will, as the car started to enter the drive to take them to the Museum. "I appreciate you guys taking the time to show me around."

"We would not have it any other way, Will," answered Hakim. "You are our friend, for many years, and we want you to see some of the things we have come to love in this culture."

From a Vantage Point

" Thanks Hakim. You don't know how much this trip means to me."

"For us as well," responded Josh, driving around the grand fountain at the entrance to the access drive, which would take them to the small, artificially-built island, with its white granite main Museum building in the center. Driving down the access road, through the tall palms, and across the short bridge, gives the view of the museum ahead, even more magnificent than envisioned by Pei, when he designed the structure.

I. M. Pei, then over 90 years old, literally took a tour of the Islamic World, looking at building in every major city from Spain to the Middle East, with significant Islamic influence, to gain a perspective of the type of architecture that would be exactly what he, and his sponsor, the Emir, desired in a world-class museum. Pei eventually decided on the style of the 13th-century sabil (ablutions fountain), found at Ahmad ibn Tulun Mosque in Cairo, Egypt, which dated from the 9th century.

"The guy Pei, the architect, traveled throughout the Muslim world to see the great buildings before he attempted to build here," announced Hakim, as they drove down the access road.

"But they say this place is unique, and that Pei did not see in the other places what he wanted to express here. So, a man over 90 years old, used his experiences, and his mind to express his view of Islam, and created this wonderful place. Wait until you see inside, Will," added Josh, obviously excited at the visit.

"We have come here many times, Will," continued Hakim, "and each time, we see something different, something interesting, and something new about the Muslim people. This place gives you a totally different view from what you hear and see in the Western countries."

Josh pulled the car into the parking entrance to the museum, and quickly found a space on the first level of the garage, not too far from one of the elevators, which would take them to the main floor. Once they parked the car, the three men went to the nearest elevator, and started up to the museum. They emerged seconds later to the main level, at the courtyard, near the walkway to the entrance, and started toward the main entrance. Going through the security checkpoint at the doorway, the men found themselves in front of the massive spiral staircase to the other levels.

"Wow!" said Will, as he came closer to the center of the first floor, dominated by the staircase, with a large sitting area just beyond.

"This is magnificent, isn't it?" asked Josh, who had stopped briefly to get floor maps, and a brochure in English on the Museum from the security personnel, and the guide at the entrance.

"It certainly is," responded Will. "Where do we start?"

From a Vantage Point

"How about we go through the stairway area to the lounge; get come coffee, and figure out a plan here," said Hakim, who started off quickly toward the serving area to the right of the lounge. There, they could get coffee or tea, soft drinks, and small food items, which, the sign on the wall clearly said, had to be kept in the lounge area.

"Great, let's do it," responded Will, who quickly followed Hakim, along with Josh.

The men went over and ordered coffee from the vendor, and then sat down at a table in the lounge. Will picked up one of the brochures Josh had placed on the table. It showed the floor plan of the museum, and highlighted some of the exhibits, along with a special exhibit in the first-floor exhibits area. He quickly became amazed at what the museum offered.

"What would you like to see first, Will?" asked Hakim. "There are some really good exhibits here. Just coming here makes you proud of your heritage. Maybe a bit like your own American History Museum in Washington, DC."

"Don't know," responded Will, "Let's just start to walk and see what is here. It's hard to decide from the brochure, and everything here looks so fine."

"OK' said Josh, "Let's start by going up the staircase to the first floor. They have some good stuff up there, including a piece showing Saladin on a horse."

"Great place to start, Josh," answered both Will and Hakim, almost in unison. Getting up from the small table in the foyer, they walked over to the grand, double staircase that framed the center of the building, and began to walk up the semi-circular stairway to the floor above.

The three friends spent most of the afternoon looking over the exhibits, enjoying the pottery, ancient books and manuscripts, and all the other items in the vast collection held by the Museum. It was nearly six PM before they walked back down the stairs to the foyer, and decided to have another cup of Turkish coffee, before they went off for dinner.

"This place is completely amazing," exclaimed Will, as they took their coffee, and went over to sit at a small table, as they had earlier in the afternoon.

"As I said earlier, Will, we are very proud of our heritage, and our faith. We only wish the rest of the world understood us better. Perhaps then, we could finally live in peace here in the Middle East, and elsewhere as well."

"It's interesting, Will," responded Josh, "As we have travelled over the years, through countries with constantly changing governments, and upheavals, very little of that is seen in the countries where their laws are based on the principles first written by Muhammad. It's really interesting, to me at least, to see people live under a government with firm, consistent leadership, which cares about its people."

From a Vantage Point

"Well, in the US," answered Will quickly, "We have laws, and the people generally feel comfortable and safe on the streets, although I will admit the constantly changing laws sometimes make things a bit harder to grasp."

As the friends continued their discussion, eventually getting up to leave the museum, Hakim and Josh were careful in their conversation. They wanted only to plant a seed with Will and, hopefully, create a positive image of Islam with him; one which might make him more amenable toward it, as they travelled to Sudan in the next few days.

Josh drove away from the museum, and turned back toward the Corniche, to a place where they would have dinner. It was only a short trip, and they soon arrived near the Pyramid-shaped Sheraton Doha, and drive into the local parking area next to the hotel.

"This is the place to start looking for someplace to have dinner," said Josh, as they all left the car, and started toward the street. "This is the Corniche, Will, the center of night life here in Doha, and the location of some of the best, and sometimes the most expensive, restaurants in the city. Let's see what we can find."

"Good enough for me," responded Will, "You guys must be making some bucks with whatever you do to be able to afford this." Will looked around, and up at the hotels and other towers, and was frankly amazed at what he saw.

"We do a lot of freelance work, Will," said Hakim, with a shrug. "We have developed a set of clients over the years. Some want us for specific tasks, like security over in Sudan. We do some training, and we also do a bit of what you might call 'delivery service' work. A company will ask us to escort deliveries from Yemen, or Saudi Arabia, or even from Europe, to Sudan, to make sure everything gets there in one piece, and on time. They are willing to pay well for the services, and we pride ourselves in giving good service."

"That's true," added Josh, "We have three or four clients we work with a lot, keeping up busy, but not so busy that we can't take time to come here in Qatar and enjoy ourselves occasionally. That's why I suggested meeting you here; it's a beautiful place, with a lot of history."

"I guess so," responded Will, "I am certainly impressed by what I have seen. Let's find some place to eat, shall we?"

The friends strolled along one side of Corniche Street, looking at restaurants and bistros, with Hakim occasionally pointing out a place on the other side of the street as well, often commenting that the places close to the ocean were also the most expensive.

Finally, they decided on Balhambar Restaurant, one of the few on the Corniche which provides true Qatari food, rather that the cuisine of other Middle Eastern or Mediterranean countries. They went across the street, and into the restaurant, after passing by a huge statue of 'Orry' the mascot of the 2006 Asian

From a Vantage Point

Games, now in a place of honor on the large patio outside the restaurant. They looked at the menu in the window quickly, as they entered the restaurant, and were greeted warmly by the host, who led them to a table, looking out over the water.

"OK, so what do I order?" asked Will.

"The seafood here is great, as is almost anything else on the menu. This place has an international reputation. They also serve alcohol, by the way in case you want something to drink. Qatar is a bit more lenient than most Arabic countries, in that regard, so enjoy," said Josh, as he handed Will the drink and wine menu.

"Thanks Josh, so now what do I order? I have no idea what the food is here."

"Let me make this easy for you," responded Hakim, as he waved over the waiter. "What are the specials today? We have a friend from the United States, and we want him to have a good meal this evening."

"Well then," responded the waiter, "May I suggest you start with some *Hummus*, and perhaps some of our fresh-made *Taboulleh*, along with our flat bread for dipping. For the main course, I suggest *Ghuzi*, our lamb dish with rice. We can give you a smaller portion for three, if that is acceptable to you?"

"That will be fine. You suggest some fine choices," answered Hakim. "Also, please bring us a bottle of your house white wine, if you would."

"That will be right out, sir," said the waiter. "I will put in your order immediately, and bring the appetizers and wine as well. Thank you."

Qatar, unlike a few other Arab states, does allow the consumption of alcohol in its restaurants. Residents and visitors can buy their alcohol through state-run liquor stores.

The waiter walked toward the kitchen as Hakim turned to Will and said, "Will, you will love the lamb here. It is prepared with light oils and herbs, and is something you have never enjoyed as much before. This is going to be a great dinner."

"By the way, in case you have not had them before, *Hummus* is a dip made of chick peas, and herbs. You in America call them garbanzo beans, I think. The *Taboulleh* is made from Bulgur wheat, mixed with parsley and mint. The restaurant chef here also adds in a bit of tomato for taste. Everything is eaten by dipping with a toasted flat bread, like Greek Pita bread, cut in slivers. I hope you will enjoy it as well."

"I look forward to it, Hakim. I'm always looking for new foods, and new places to eat. This is a great choice. The restaurant is great, and the view of the water is phenomenal. Thanks for bringing me here, both of you."

In a few minutes, the waiter brought a bottle of white wine to the table, in an iced chiller, along with three glasses. Right behind him was another waiter with the appetizers.

From a Vantage Point

"Please try the wine, sir, and see if it meets your requirements." The waiter took the bottle from the chiller, and poured a bit into a glass he had placed in front of Hakim.

"Excellent, light and dry," responded Hakim, as he swirled the glass, and then tasted a small bit of the wine. "This will go very well."

"Thank you, sir," answered the waiter, "as he poured wine for the other two men, and refreshed Hakim's glass.

"As you can see," the waiter continued, "We have *Hummus* and *Taboulleh*, as you requested, and some bread for dipping. I also took the liberty of bringing some almonds, as is our custom. I hope you enjoy them as well."

The waiter bowed slightly, and walked away from the table, returning to the kitchen through the swinging doors that separated it from the main part of the restaurant.

The three friends sat back, tasted the appetizers, and enjoyed the wine over the next hour, as their main course was prepared. When it arrived, all three marveled at the amount of food they were served. Hakim ordered another bottle of wine to go with the main course, as the waiter separated the food into three plates, one for each man, and placed them on the table. Then, he again bowed slightly, suggested that he hoped they would enjoy their meal, and left with the cart, which had delivered the lamb.

"So, Will," asked Hakim, "What would you like to do for the next day and a half, until we leave for Sudan?"

"Not completely sure, except that, at some point, I hope that Jim Davis will join us for part of the time. It was great having someone to speak with on the long flight, and he seems to know a bit about this part of the world."

"Oh yes, Mister Davis," responded Josh, "I had nearly forgotten about him." When do you expect him to contact you?"

"Perhaps tomorrow," responded Will, "Otherwise, I guess we are on our own."

Josh and Hakim glanced quickly at each other, and then back to Will, trying to appear unconcerned, but they both had concerns over Mister Davis. They would let that wait, until they saw if he was really going to join them.

"How about a trip around the city, and out into the nearby villages tomorrow, Will?" asked Josh. "I'll give the hotel my cellphone number, so they can give it to Mister Davis, and he can get back to you if he calls. We can get back to the city quickly to pick him up, if he wants to join us. If we leave the hotel by ten AM, we still have time to see a lot, and it gives him some time to contact you. How about that plan?"

"Sounds good to me, Josh. I want to see as much as I can while we are here."

From a Vantage Point

"That will work out for me as well, Will," responded Hakim, "I have to see one of our clients first thing in the morning. We do some small things for Physicians without Walls, and I need to go over there about eight AM. I will be back in plenty of time for us to leave at ten."

Jim Davis, who had arrived with Will Johnson in Qatar, stepped outside the airport, and flagged down a cab to take him to his hotel in the City. He was staying at the same hotel, the Concorde, as Will, but wanted to let Will meet his friends, and go off on the city with them. Instead, he would go to the hotel, relax for a while, and have dinner there in the Concorde.

Stepping into the cab, and closing the door, he told the driver what hotel to take him to, and sat back to enjoy the ride.

"OK, Mister Davis, what have you learned on your trip?" asked the cab driver.

Davis looked up front, and saw the face of his counterpart Anwar Fazeel, an INTERPOL agent, and local resident of the emirate in the rear-view mirror.

"Anwar, how are you?"

"Pretty well, for a poor cab driver. Things are so slow here right now, and working as a cabbie is actually more exciting than being a cop. Yourself?"

"OK as well. Good trip. I met Johnson, and seemed to hit it off with him. So far, I'm undecided on whether he is a terrorist, one in the making, or simply wants to see his old friends. Time will tell, I guess."

"Sure will. We know they are all staying in a suite at the Concorde, and we have a guy at the desk to keep track of them. What are your plans?"

"I agreed with to see the sights with Johnson tomorrow with his friends. That will give me a better chance to evaluate how dangerous they are, and how Johnson fits in."

"Good, then I will be available at the taxi stand at the hotel for the day tomorrow, so, if you need someone, you only have to ask the concierge for a cab. Understand though, I do not know Giddons well, but I do know that al-Azahir is a very dangerous man. Do not lower your guard for a moment with him, my friend."

"Thanks Anwar. Let's hope this is a simple observation, and not a more complicated scene."

"I agree, my friend," answered Fazeel, "I prefer peace and quiet to running around like a cop myself."

A few minutes later, Fazeel turned into the drive of the Concorde, and Davis got out of the cab to go in and register. Being a good cab driver, Fazeel made sure the bags got to the bellhop, before he drove off to have dinner with his family, out in one of the villages. He would return in the morning, to be at the cabstand when needed.

From a Vantage Point

About two hours later, after enjoying their meal, and having desert, Will and his friends arrived back at the hotel, after a leisurely drive along the Corniche to see the lights, just as the sun began to drop on the horizon. Doha is particularly beautiful, as the buildings blaze with light in the early evening sky. It was no different today, with a clear sky, and a bright red sun just above the horizon to the west.

Josh pulled into the garage, showed his parking ticket, and left the car for the attendant; taking his two friends to the bar for a nightcap before heading to their suite. As they approached the bar, Will saw Jim Davis in the small shop off the lobby, and went over for a brief conversation. The other two men went to the bar, and saw Will and Davis enter, and go over to a side table a short time later, waving to them as he sat. Josh and Hakim had their drinks, and then went up to their hotel suite.

"Josh, I think I will go over to the Docs office tomorrow morning early and find out what this guy Davis is all about."

"Good idea, Hakim. We need to know what we might be facing. I thought that was what you had in mind, since we don't have any contract with them. Good for Will's consumption, though."

"Exactly, Josh. I want to be sure he sees us simply as small-time businessmen, couriers and helpers for various organizations, without going into too many details until we see what Will's intentions might be over the next week or so."

"When do we have to be back in Sudan, Josh?"

"I told our people we would be back by the beginning of next week, at the latest, figuring that would be enough time to plant some seeds with Will, before we took him over there. Today went well, I think, and he does seem to have an appreciation for Islamic heritage, even if he knew little about it. As I remembered, his family brought him to the US very early, and he had little time to start learning about Islam, even more so with his Maronite family."

"True Josh, but Will is a very interesting person. He is smart, but not in the street sense. He is very logical, and a planner, as well as a dreamer, from the sounds of his venture with the farmer's cooperative. Perhaps that is the key to success here. We need to keep his 'education' to a low level—emphasizing the approach of Jihad as a means of improving people's lives, and steer clear, as much as possible, from the sense of struggle. We can capitalize carefully on the struggles of his own religion in Lebanon, while showing that their struggles are no different from those of others. If we make a simple approach, perhaps we will catch the fish."

"You may have something there, Hakim. I agree Will is very down-to-earth, and practical. His interest in the exhibits on the local people, brought the highest reactions, but he also seemed to be fascinated by the religious artifacts as well."

"Agreed, so we have a sense of an approach. Right now, we need to get past his association with Davis, without making too much of our interests, just in case Davis is a plant. We will, hopefully, find that out tomorrow, and can react accordingly."

The men heard Will coming to the door, and punching the buttons on the door, to open and enter, so they curtailed their discussion any further, so that Will would not know their real purpose in getting him to Qatar.

"Hey guys," said Will, as he entered, "Saw Jim Davis in the lobby, and we sat in the bar for a drink. He would love to join us tomorrow. I told him we were going out about 10 AM. Is that OK?"

"Sure Will," responded Josh, "Ten is fine. Just the timeframe we were thinking. Let's look at some of the literature you got at the Museum, and figure out what you would like to see tomorrow." The three grasped at pamphlets, and started looking at various sites in Doha, occasionally speaking about one or the other, until they had a plan mapped out for the following two days. After that, they would get ready for their trip to Sudan.

The following morning, Hakim rose early, at least for him, and left the suite around 7:30AM, traveling across town to the location of Physicians without Walls, an international Non-Governmental Organization, or NGO as they were called, that specialized in providing physicians and other healthcare professionals in areas where medical care was sparse, but critical. The NGO maintained offices in Doha, using it as their central location for assignments, shipping of supplies, and coordination with other international organizations, many of which were also in Qatar.

Going inside, he stopped at the reception desk and asked for Chuck Jackson. The receptionist asked him to wait, buzzed for Jackson, and asked if Hakim wanted some coffee or tea. Hakim declined both, but took a seat in the reception area, waiting for Jackson to come out.

"Hakim, how are you?" asked Jackson, as he emerged from a door to the right of the receptionist. Jackson was dressed in camouflage pants, a polo shirt, and combat boots; like many of the staff at the doctor's group.

"Just fine Chuck," responded Hakim. "Wanted to come by to discuss something with you, if you have a moment."

"Sure, come this way." Jackson asked the receptionist to give Hakim a visitor badge, and sign the visitor's register. When she issued his badge, Hakim accompanied Jackson through the door, and into the inner area of the building, where he found several offices and cubicles, each with someone related to health care.

"This office is mine," said Jackson, as he opened the door, and let Hakim precede him into the office. When Jackson entered, he closed the door behind

From a Vantage Point

him, and went over to sit at a small table on the side of the room. Hakim joined him.

"What can I do for you?" asked Jackson.

"Well, Josh mentioned he saw you at the airport yesterday, and you might be concerned with a passenger who arrived with a friend of ours from the USA."

"Oh, sure, that's probably Jim Davis," responded Jackson, "He comes and goes from here a lot, and often goes over to Sudan and Somalia as well. Supposed to be working for one of the security firms here under government contract."

"Is there a problem with him?"

"Not sure, Hakim. I do know that several people who come and go from Qatar to Sudan and Yemen have disappeared over the past few months, and are no longer our contracts over here. I would bet money that each made acquaintance with Davis, because each time, shortly after I saw him, they no longer came to meetings, or were around town. I guess, I would simply watch out, and tell your friend to do that as well, at least until more evidence is in."

"What kind of evidence?"

"Several of our people here at the Docs think he is a US Government agent of some kind; others think he works here for the Emir, who really does the bidding of the US when asked. Either way, he could be a disaster in the making for someone who lives, shall we say, at the edge of the law."

"Understand completely, Chuck. I don't want my friend getting in trouble, so we will watch him. Will Johnson, that's my friend, is over here for just a few days, and I don't want him to get in trouble for any reason, even if unfounded. How is everything else these days?"

"Too much work, too little time, too few volunteers, and no supplies. Other than that, everything is peachy. What about you two? Still working for the Sudanese companies?"

"Sure am. They keep us bust ferrying back and forth. We're going back to Sudan in two days, and then on to Pakistan for a week or so, before we return to Doha. Everybody wants everything yesterday."

"I know that feeling only too well. Say, can you take some stuff to our people in Sudan? I can get it to the airport, and checked in at cargo. All you have to do is let our people know what is coming, and make sure they get to the cargo office in Khartoum."

"Sure, happy to. Just get me the Bill of Lading, and I will deliver it myself." Hakim was happy Jackson asked, because it would give credibility for his visit, and a cover story, which might impress Will Johnson.

"Thanks for your time Chuck. I have to get back to the hotel, and pick up the others for today's tour. We are taking this guy Davis with us, so I will have a chance to look him over myself. Will let you know my thought before we leave."

"Thanks Hakim. Hope everything goes well, and I am wrong on my gut assessment, but it pays to be careful." The men shook hands, and Jackson walked Hakim to the door by the receptionist, where he turned in his visitor badge before leaving for the parking lot and his car.

Returning to the hotel Concorde, Hakim hoped that Josh was up, and that the two would have a few minutes to speak between themselves, before Will joined them. As luck would have it, Will was still sleeping when he arrived in their suite, and Josh was making coffee.

"How did it go, Hakim? Any information from Chuck on this guy Davis?"

"Yes, the discussion with Chuck was interesting. The people over there are concerned that they had several friends and associates who seemed to disappear from the scene after they met Davis. What he relayed might be nothing more than a coincidence, but worth worrying about, especially since he will be with us tomorrow. We need to be very careful, I believe."

"Agreed. How about some coffee? I thought I heard Will stirring a few minutes ago. It's still early, so he might have fallen back asleep." Josh poured them both a mug of coffee, and they moved from the kitchenette to the living room, and were sitting reading the morning papers, as Will emerged from his room, heading directly from the doorway to the dinette to get some coffee himself.

"How goes it, guys? Ready for a big day today?"

"Sure enough," responded Hakim, "We have a lot of ground to cover, if we are going to get to everything you want to see. How about finishing your coffee and we will go to the lobby to wait for your friend Jim?"

"Sounds like a plan," answered Will, grabbing one of the English-language papers, to look at the headlines.

"Looks like they are getting ready in a big way for the Obama inauguration," said Will to the other two, "This will be a big change from George Bush, I guess. Perhaps things will slow down a bit, and be a little less tense under a new man in the White house."

"Possibly so," answered Josh, "You never know what will happen in Washington these days. Let's get ready to leave, shall we?"

"I'll be right back," said Will, as he went back to his room, to get the small backpack he liked to take with him on tourist trips.

"Still carrying a backpack, Will?" asked Hakim.

"Makes things a bit easier, and keeps the hands free," was Will's response.

"If everybody is ready, let's head out to the lobby and meet your Mr. Davis, then," sounded Josh.

The three left the suite, took the elevator to the lobby, and found Jim Davis waiting for them near the front desk. All four then headed for the parking garage elevator, found the car Josh had rented, and took off for a day on the town in

From a Vantage Point

Doha. Over the next few hours, they saw several museums, the Emir's Palace, other Government buildings, and then headed toward the outskirts of town to see a couple of the villages that surround the city. They returned to their hotel at dusk, tired, and looking for a drink at the bar.

"Jim, we're glad you could join us today," said Hakim, "Will tells us you come to Doha often."

"Yes, I do come here quite a bit, but I also travel all over the Peninsula, often, to Saudi Arabia or Aden, though."

"Really," responded Josh, "I love the port of Aden, with the US Fleet stretching out in the harbor sometimes. The sight is amazing; just like a smaller Norfolk, Virginia."

"Sure, except that the ships come into Aden as a stopping and refuel point, rather than a permanent port. My company does some security work for the Port Authority over there."

'I worked over there for a while myself, a few years back. Lived near the Sheba Palace, in a small inn. Most of the time the only other occupants were visiting physicians coming to the University Medical School a short distance away. Never got over there myself."

"That's quite some ways from the airport," said Josh, "Interesting you would want to go all the way over to the shore, when there are so many places to stay closer to the Airport."

"True," answered Davis, "A friend used to stay in the same place and introduced me to it, so I guess I just never looked closer to the airport. I was happy there, and it was away from the job over on Ummul Island, where we had a setup."

The men sat, and had another drink, discussing mostly minor topics, until Davis rose, and indicated he was going off to bed. The others agreed, since they had a flight the following afternoon over to Sudan themselves.

Davis took the elevator toward his room, getting off instead on the floor below his, and walked over to a nearby room, knocking on the door. A man answered, and Davis walked inside as the door closed behind him.

Will Johnson also left the bar, to return to their suite, while Josh and Hakim continued their discussion.

"What do you think, Hakim?"

"Still not sure, Josh, but he is either the smartest, or the dumbest guy I have ever met. His story on Aden fits, and there are a few small installations over on the Island. They do have private security, most of which comes in from Europe or the States. He could be legitimate, I guess. In any case, nothing we said today will give anything away for us."

"I agree. The faster we get Will out of here, and over to Sudan, the more comfortable I will be. Let's go upstairs, before Will starts to ask questions."

Upstairs, Davis and the man in the room he entered were engaged in a lively conversation.

"What did you get on these two, Saul?" asked Davis.

"Well, a lot and very little, Jim," the man Saul answered. "We know they work for several firms between here and Sudan, and do a lot of transfers of goods and papers for those organizations. One of our contacts in Sudan thinks they do *hawala* banking transfers as well. "

"That's interesting, but any indication they do their work for the Bin-Laden network?"

"Not so far, Jim. They seem to be merely small fish in a large pond, as you Americans would say."

"OK, but let's have the boys over in Sudan watch them while they are there."

"Sure Jim, we can do that. I go back tomorrow on the same plane your friend will be on."

"Thanks Saul. Let me know what you find." Davis went to the door, opened it, and looked out into the corridor. Just before he headed out, Saul shouted after him, "What do you want me to tell Washington?" Davis closed the door, and turned toward Saul.

"Better tell them I have found nothing to indicate that Johnson is a terrorist, or intending to become a terrorist, at least up to this point. Tell them I will continue to monitor. That should do it."

Then Davis turned again, and exited through the door toward the elevator, closing the door behind him. In just a minute or two, he was in his own room, where he sat down and began to read a book.

From a Vantage Point

Chapter 5 On to Khartoum

The following morning, Will Johnson and his two friends rose, and prepared to go to the lobby to have breakfast. While Will and Hakim entered the restaurant, Josh went over to the front desk, and paid the bill, letting the clerk know they would be leaving around noon. Then he joined his friends for breakfast. Three hours later, they would be on the way to Doha International, and on to Sudan.

When they finished, they returned to their room to complete packing, and get everything together for the bellhop.

Will packed up his luggage and brought it out into the sitting area of the suite. There the bellman could pick it up with the rest of the luggage slowly building in the middle of the room.

"Hey guys, what are all these boxes?" asked Will, as Josh and Hakim walked into the sitting area.

"Oh, that's paperwork, and supplies we bring back to Khartoum each time we make this trip," answered Hakim quickly. "We bring reports and files back, and they give us more stuff to take with us when we return here. Happens all the time."

"OK, so I guess we have to stop at Cargo when we get to the airport?"

"No, we just check it with everything else. It gets delivered quicker that way," responded Josh, looking unconcerned. "If we must haul a lot with us, cargo is always available as a backup," he added quickly.

Will looked quickly at the top package, and saw it was addressed to a company in Khartoum. Unconcerned, he piled his clothing bag over the top of it, and walked back toward the kitchen for some coffee.

Within the hour, the men had checked out of the hotel, packed their luggage into the hotel van, and were on their way to the airport and their trip to Sudan. The van left them off at the departure entrance for their flight on Sudan Airlines.

At the curb, Josh worked with a skycap to check in the boxes they carried from the hotel, along with their suitcases. That left each of the men with two carry-ons that were small enough to bring onboard. The skycap told them the flight today would be on an Airbus A320, so luggage would not be a problem.

Walking into the terminal, they went over to the departure board to check the flight to Khartoum, and get their gate number. Then, they went over to Sudan Airlines to check in for the flight. Forty-five minutes later, boarding started, and they were on their way to Sudan.

The three travelers could not know the extra effort on the part of a myriad of security personnel who explored the luggage, manned the x-ray machines at the baggage area, and the two US FBI agents, behind closed doors, looking closely at the monitors in the airport security area reviewing room. Finding only papers, and having no further comments by the local security personnel, the flight could depart on time, and the agents filed their reports through the Embassy.

During the short flight, Will sat at the window seat, with Josh in the middle, next to him, and Hakim taking the aisle seat, in the same row. Will and Josh exchanged mostly small talk, while Will read the magazines in the pocket on the seat in front of him. In that pocket, he found a recent copy of *The Economist*, as two other European publications on current events he did not recognize. Inside the *Economist* was an article on the changing face of Africa, and the rise of the militant Islamists in places such as Yemen and Sudan. Will made a mental note to ask Josh later if he had seen those types of changes in the two countries he knew both frequented in their travels.

The articles were interesting to him, in that they presented a view quite different from that he usually read in the Washington DC area papers. In the US, al-Qaeda was usually viewed from a militant, overly aggressive perspective, which highlighted mostly bombings and the extreme application of Sharia Law.

In the article though, the impression left was quite different. Will looked at the cover, and saw that the *Economist* was the European Edition, and was much larger than those he saw in the supermarkets in his area. He wondered about the reason for the difference in coverage. He read on, but decided he would discuss his issues with Josh after they arrived in Khartoum.

One interesting thing he found was a discussion of the investments made by Bin-Laden and his followers in the infrastructure of Sudan. To date, he had built and managed a chemical factory, developed several major roads, and contributed, according to the article, several public works projects to help the more unfortunate among the population in that country. He realized, as he read through the article, that one of the companies mentioned was the same name as the labels on the packages the three brought with them to Khartoum. His biggest surprise was the lack of any mention of pervasive terrorism or armed camps in the articles, as he had been led to believe by the US press. That confused Will even more.

Eventually finishing his reading of the *Economist*, and looking quickly over the other two publications as well, Will placed them back in the pocket in front of him, and sat back to enjoy the trip. The flight attendants were coming down the aisles asking about food, drinks, and snacks. Just before they got to Will's aisle, Josh reminded him that if he wanted a drink, he had better get it now, since there was no drinking in Khartoum. Will nodded his understanding, and waited for the flight attendant to come by their seats.

As the plane slowed dipped through the few clouds into the airspace of Khartoum, Will looked out the window, and saw a more desolate area on the

From a Vantage Point

horizon than that he had seen in Qatar. The desert quickly gave way to a beautiful city, sectioned in what appeared to be three parts by two large rivers.

"Josh, this place is huge, and right out of the desert."

"Yes, it is, Will. The city is formed at the crossing of the two parts of the Nile River—you know, the one that ends up in Egypt. There is the Blue Nile, and the White Nile, and they merge here in Khartoum. The various villages that bordered the rivers eventually grew large enough to merge into one large city. Last I heard, there were over four million people here."

"Wow, that's impressive. You would never think there were cities like this, outside of the large ones along the Mediterranean."

"That's the way people think, but it isn't true, like a lot of things about Africa, and the Islamic countries," echoed Hakim, as he looked over toward the other two.

"Khartoum has a long and proud history, since the late middle Ages, and has been a center for commerce, of some kind, along the trade routes to Egypt, since the days of the Pharaohs," Hakim added.

"I'm looking forward to see it, then," responded Will, sitting back and watching, as the city came into view in the distance, and eventually became larger, as the plane reduced speed and altitude, preparing for its final approach to land.

" Ladies and gentlemen please prepare for landing. Place all tables back in their position behind the seat in front of you, and turn off your computers, and other devices. We will be touching down in just a couple of minutes, and will be in Khartoum, capital of The Sudan. Thank you for flying with us today. Our flight attendants will be coming through to pick up papers, and any trash you may have. Please do not leave anything in the pockets of the seats."

Will started to pull out the magazines and papers he had placed in the pocket to give to the flight attendant, as she arrived their row, then changed his mind.

"I think I will keep these to read later," he said, as she held out the trash bag for him to drop his papers.

"No problem," the attendant answered, "Have a nice day in Khartoum," she continued, smiling as she went to the next row.

A minute or so later, Will felt the thump as the plane reached the runway, and set down, rolling toward the terminals far ahead.

"Ladies and Gentlemen, this is the first officer. We have arrived in Khartoum. I would ask that you not yet use phones or other computing devices, until we reach the off-ramp going toward the tarmac. There are many small planes that enter and leave Khartoum, and some of these computing devices may affect their navigation, especially with wireless communication capabilities. We will let

From a Vantage Point

you know when it is safe to use your phones. Thank you for your patience, and welcome again to Khartoum."

The plane continued its way along the main runway, until it reached a tarmac to the left, where it turned, and started toward the terminal buildings. Once the turn occurred, the First officer allowed the passengers to use their phones, and many did so almost immediately, including Hakim.

"We are here," Hakim said into his headset, "We will be in the terminal in about five minutes, so the truck can come to get the packages. Go to cargo, as usual, and they will be there. We will take our own luggage, and be at the front of the terminal in about thirty minutes." Will turned, as Hakim hung up his phone. "Will there be someone to meet us Hakim?"

"Yes, from our company here in Khartoum," came the response. "Our car is at our apartment. It is easier to come and go from the airport this way." Hakim almost seemed distant and detached, and Will wondered why.

Our company, thought Will; *do these guys work for Bin-Laden? Is there something more here I need to know?*

"Ladies and Gentlemen," said a flight attendant, into the passenger space intercom, "We will be arriving momentarily at the gate, and you will need your passport, visa, and your customs documents for inspection at that time. Please have them ready for the customs inspectors. Airplane personnel will be at the doorway to the terminal to assist you in going immediately to customs."

Since the three men had filled out the brief forms when they boarded the plane in Doha, it was simple to get it out, along with the other documents they each carried. Hakim had a manifest for the boxes as well, and he put that inside his passport for the customs people at the terminal.

The plane arrived slowly at the gate, pulled the last few yards by a tractor, called a mule, and stopped about fifty yards short of the terminal building. Trucks quickly brought wide stairways to the two departure doors of the plane.

"Ladies and gentlemen," the flight attendant intoned, in a clearly foreign accent, first in English, and then in Arabic, "The plane arrived today at a gate other than the one scheduled, because another plane had mechanical problems, and could not be pulled out in time for our arrival. We have two sets of departure stairs for you today, which are currently being put in place. We will open the doors in a minute or so, and you will be able to depart for Customs inspection. Follow the directions of our ground crew, please, to expedite your processing through the airport customs area. Please have all documents ready."

Will looked out the window, to see the stairways being put in place, and noticed that several soldiers had entered the tarmac, and placed themselves around the plane. He tried to remember if that had happened in Doha, but do not recall. Then, he remembered there had been troubles in this country over the past year, and attributed their presence to some form of maintaining security.

From a Vantage Point

Shrugging his shoulder, Will stood, and took his carry bags from the overhead, and started to leave the plane, following Josh and Hakim out the door and down the stairs to the terminal.

The three men entered a nearby doorway marked 'Arrivals', which took them directly to the Customs examination station. There, they were asked to form lines, and bring their carryon luggage with them. As Will entered a line, he saw the luggage racks coming in with the checked baggage, and he was sure he saw that one of the racks contained several the boxes like those Hakim had checked. Hopefully, he thought to himself, this will be a quick process, so they could get out of the airport, and off into the city.

"Your passport and papers, please," said the uniformed officer at the head of the line, as Will approached his station. Will passed the officer his passport, with his custom declaration inside.

"I see you are American," said the officer, "We do not see many Americans these days. Why are you here?" he continued, as he looked through the passport, and read the Sudanese visa.

"Visiting friends, and looking forward to seeing your country," replied Will.

"Very well," answered the officer, "You may not find the people friendly to Americans, but you are welcome. Do you have anything to declare?"

"Nothing at all. You will note I have my watch and camera on the form." The officer looked at his watch, and asked Will to bring out his camera from his carryon bag."

"Where is your other luggage?"

"Over there," said Will, pointing to the pile of luggage which had been brought into the room.

"Please go get it, and bring it back here." Will did as he was asked, found his two bags, and brought them to place beside his carry-ons.

"The officer stamped the tags on the bags, and told him he could go through, pointing to the exit door. "Have a good stay, Mr. Johnson," the officer said, as he looked over, and passed Will his passport, after stamping it, and the customs declaration as well.

Will stepped away from the officer's station, and joined Hakim, who had already been through another of the lines. They waited for Josh together. It took only a couple of minutes for him to join them so they could leave and enter the main terminal.

Will, Josh, and Hakim passed through two wide glass doors to enter the main terminal, after leaving the customs area, and found themselves in a bustling hodge-podge or varied costumes, carts, and headdresses, so common in a well-traveled country in Africa. Passing out of customs took them into another world, and Will soaked in as much of the atmosphere as he could.

From a Vantage Point

One thing he noticed was the large number of police, and military, walking through the terminal area with some standing in front of gates, and other closed doors along the main terminal walkway. He had seen this outside, as they arrived, and he remembered he would discuss it with the others as they reached their hotel.

The military and police were both very different from what Will was used to seeing in airports. First, they were mostly dressed in camouflage uniforms, although with soft, baseball-type caps, and they all carried an automatic weapon in addition to their side arms. Some wore a white turban, with the ends of the long, wrapped scarf dropping down from their shoulders.

The Sudan is an interesting country, with influences from many of the surrounding countries, particularly Egypt and Ethiopia, and religiously is two countries; the North predominantly Islamic, and following Sharia Law; the South mostly, Christian. As a result, the dress of the people differs markedly. Those in the north, are often seen in turbans, loose fitting clothing, and for the women, a combination of long dresses and veils, which completely cover the body. In the South, it is more common to see Western dress.

In just a few seconds after the three men had reached the sidewalk outside the terminal, a truck drove up and stopped in front of them. The truck was gleaming white, had no markings on the side, and appeared to be simply a late-model Mercedes-Benz panel truck. A man exited from the right front door, and walked over to where Will and his two friends stood on the sidewalk, extending his hand to Hakim.

"Peace to you, my friend. Your journey was a success, and we are pleased to have you back with us," said the man, quickly moving to Josh as well with a firm handshake.

"It has been long, Saleem. I want you to meet our friend Will Johnson of the United States." Hakim pointed to Will, and Saleem turned, and extended his hand to Will as well.

"I am glad to meet you, Will Johnson. I hope you enjoy your stay with us, and have the opportunity to see our city."

"Thank you, and it is good to meet you, as well, Saleem," responded Will, returning Saleem's handshake with his own.

"The truck is here, and the boxes were loaded at the cargo dock," said Saleem, as he pointed toward the truck. "All we have to do now is get them down to the office. I will take care of that, and drop you at your apartment, so you can get settled. Sabah would like to meet with you later in the day. Please call him,"

"No problem," answered Josh, nodding toward Hakim. "I want nothing more right now than to get out of these clothes, and into something more comfortable." Josh started to walk toward the side of the truck, and the others followed. Saleem opened the side door, and inside there were two wide seats,

From a Vantage Point

one a bench seat, and the other really two bucket seats, with space between the buckets seats for their carry bags. Josh entered first, taking the rear seat, closest to the back, where the boxes were stacked, placing his bag on the empty portion of the bench, and Hakim and Will took the middle seats, behind the driver's seat, and placed their bags in the open space waiting for them.

Driving from the airport to the downtown area, where their apartment was located, is itself an interesting experience. People drive as if their final days on earth are approaching, and they care little who they cut off, how they approach intersections, or especially it seemed, those who might be on bicycles or scooters. Saleem weaved in and out of the lanes, taking advantage of sometimes very small spaces, and roared down the highway from the airport toward downtown.

From a Vantage Point

Chapter 6 Tourists

The din of the city by mid-morning is deafening, as the workers in their cars and motorbikes move through the city, competing with farmers, truckers, and a host of others whose business takes them to Khartoum. This day was no different from others, and Will heard it loud and clear through the windows of the apartment, as it woke him from a sound and much needed sleep.

Climbing out of bed, Will realized he was the last to rise and greet the day. Josh was in the living room, reading the International Herald Tribune, while Hakim was busy in the kitchen cooking something for breakfast.

"Welcome to the world," shouted Hakim, as Will entered the living area. As he did so, the telephone rang, and Hakim quickly picked it up; engaged in what sounded to be a heated conversation in Aramaic, then slammed the phone back into its cradle.

"We must head out toward the desert quickly this morning," Hakim announced to Will and Josh. "It will be a long trip, and we should leave soonest to avoid the biggest part of the sun and the heat."

"I agree with that," responded Josh, "But what's the hurry here? I haven't even had breakfast."

"I second that," chimed in Will, "Breakfast first, then the trip to the desert."

"All right," said Hakim, somewhat glumly. "A quick breakfast. I want to be on the road within the hour." He turned, and left the room to his bedroom. Josh followed, and an argument in Aramaic ensued behind closed doors.

Will devoured his breakfast of eggs, sausage and toast, and waited for the other two to return so they could leave for the desert. He picked up a copy of a magazine on the coffee table, and started to leaf through it. It took only seconds to realize that it was a propaganda piece from some part of the al-Qaeda terrorist group. *What dribble*, thought Will as he looked quickly through the pages. *But then, you can't complain about someone unless you know them,* he continued to himself.

After about five minutes, the two emerged, and Will asked if he could have the copy of the magazine to read on the way home. Both nodded in approval, and sat down to eat their breakfast, after which the three headed out to the car. Before they left, Will stashed the copy of the magazine, called *Inspire*, into his backpack.

Hakim seemed anxious as they left the building, looking in all directions, as if he expected someone to be waiting for him. They moved quickly toward the car, entered, and darted out into traffic as they headed toward the edge of the city.

They had only gone about three blocks when a large explosion sounded behind them, and a cloud of black smoke rose quickly toward the bright sky.

From a Vantage Point

Several additional explosions followed, and it was clear that something important had blown up in the area where they were staying, just as they left the area.

"What happened?" asked Josh, as the car continued its route out of the city.

"Probably the Americans again," responded Hakim. "They have been sending their drones over the city lately, looking for terrorists, they say, but all they kill are civilians, women and children mostly."

Really," said Will, "We see nothing of that in the US papers or media. Are you sure?"

"It's true," offered Josh, seeming depressed at the thought. "They bring their drones over and kill one or two terrorists, or more usually a possible terrorist and a lot of civilian bystanders. It really is disgraceful, but they claim the right to do it if they feel like it. The UN and the other international puppets do nothing to stop it. These people die, and no one cares. Disgraceful."

"How often is this happening," asked Will.

"Too often," answered Hakim, continuing to drive along what was now a desert road that seemed to lead to nowhere. "Too often," he repeated. "They do this here in Sudan, and anywhere else they feel like killing people in the name of terrorism, but they are the real terrorists. They care nothing about humanity, or people—only their own political agenda to win votes."

"OK guys, let's enjoy our vacation together, and stop this talk," interjected Josh. "It is painful Hakim, and Will can't do anything about it, so let's just enjoy our time together as best we can."

"I know," responded Hakim, "Sorry Will, I just get so frustrated sometimes at my adopted country, and what it is doing to people who have done nothing against America." They drove in silence, until, about two hours later, they reached a small village, where Hakim said he knew a family, and they would stop for lunch. He beeped the car horn as they approached, and pulled into the small garage—really a car port, where their car would be out of the direct sun.

Ahmad Shipping, Khartoum, Sudan Jim Davis walked slowly down Gamhouria Street at the Dinder Bazaar, looking left and right for an address. Clad in a combination of European style clothes, and wearing a Kuwaiti Kaffiyeh with his deep tan, he easily passed quick muster from the locals as he strode toward the address he sought.

Finally, about half way down the narrow, bustling street, filled with merchants selling from their storefronts, and a myriad of carts and stalls that clogged and prevented an easy walk, he saw a sign to the left that read "Ahmad Shipping", and he walked quickly toward the entrance to the shop.

Davis knocked at the closed door, which opened slowly almost as quickly as he finished knocking.

From a Vantage Point

"May I help you sir?" asked a smallish man in a bright red short, and tan pants, wearing an equally red fez on his head, and a large, red scar on his right cheek. Looking carefully, Davis saw the large bush of black hair that protruded from under his hat, and the large, furry eyebrows which accentuated his large, dark eyes.

"Yes," answered Davis, "I need to see Fatima, if she is in this morning."

"She is, sir. Please come in. May I say who is calling for her?"

"Tell her it is Davis," Jim Davis responded.

"Davis, sir?" asked the small man, as if expecting more for a name.

"Yes, Davis. I will wait if she is busy."

"I will ask sir, and return to you immediately." The man quickly went back into the shop after signaling that Davis should enter, and rushed quickly behind the counter, and through a door on the side of the shop.

Davis looked around to see what was in the small room. All he saw were several pictures of mostly Middle Eastern cities, ranging from Riyadh to Tripoli and Tunis, and all of which showed large mosques, or other prayer sites in the region. As he looked around the man returned and stood before him, with his hands on his hips.

"Fatima will see you shortly, sir," said the man, probably a clerk. "She says to welcome you to Khartoum, and asks if you wish some tea of coffee?"

"Coffee would be fine," returned Davis. "Do you have Turkish?"

"Of course, sir. Would you prefer our demitasse, or your own larger coffee cup?"

"Demitasse is fine, and thank you. No sugar is necessary."

"Of course, sir. Right away," answered the small man, who again went through the door, toward the back of the shop. Davis continued to look over the pictures, admiring several of them for their panorama sights, especially those in Cairo, which he particularly enjoyed visiting.

"Well, Mr. Davis, what brings you to Khartoum?" asked a voice who had come up behind him as he viewed the various pictures on an opposite wall. He turned to see a young woman, about his height, her head wrapped in a scarf, and wearing a long, flowing gown of bright colors. "This is an honor for our house. We do not get visitors such as you very often."

"That's unfortunately true Fatima," responded Davis, "Right now, I am here tracking the visit of a young American, who arrived with two friends of yours only two days ago."

"Oh, yes, the man who arrived with Giddons and al-Al-Azahir from Qatar. We heard about him. Why is he important to you?"

"Not sure, just yet. We know, of course, about the affiliations of Giddons and his buddy, and we want to know if they might have another recruit that we need to watch. My current understanding is that the three were in the Army together,

From a Vantage Point

and Giddons invited the American, Will Johnson, to visit them here. We also know that Giddons visited Johnson earlier in the year in his home in West Virginia. You can expect, as a result, that we are concerned and interested."

"That seems reasonable, but how can I help in your effort?" asked Fatima in return.

"I flew over here seated with Johnson, by design, and can't be seen too often by him, or perhaps his friends, whom I have also met, or they will begin to suspect some ulterior motive on my part."

"Well said, Mr. Davis. So, you want my people to follow and report, as you Americans say, and get as much information as we can, and probably as quickly as we can. Is that right?"

"Exactly. Can you do it?"

"Of course, we can do it. Will we be receiving some formal tasking from the Agency, or is your word good enough for us?"

"Please start right away. I will confirm with Doha that you are taking the task."

"Good enough. We will take him under our wing then. Be assured we will keep you informed. The three are out sightseeing right now. We already have them under our eyes, anticipating someone would be coming to ask about them."

"Good. I expected that from you. Please call me on my secure phone when you have information for me."

"Of course, Mr. Davis," responded Fatima. "We are always happy to see you. Will you be going back to Doha today?"

"Actually, I have never left there." Davis turned, and left the shop, moving quickly toward the right side of Gamhouria Street, until he reached an intersection at where he met a Land Rover occupied by two men dressed in local garb. Taking the right rear seat, he closed the door sharply, and the car drove swiftly into the mid-day traffic.

Early the next morning, Davis was at the airport, waiting for a flight to Doha, when his phone rang.

"Mr. Davis, this is Fatima," said the voice in the phone. "We need to talk." Then, the phone clicked off to stony silence. Davis reached into the backpack he carried, and retrieved another phone, walked toward the concourse, and stopped where few people passed, and pressed a series of number.

"Ahmad Shipping," said the voice on the other end of the connection. "How many I help you?"

"Fatima, please. This is Mr. Davis."

"Mr. Davis, I am glad you called me back. Something has happened. The bird flew into Khartoum just a few moments ago, and there was considerable damage just a short time later in the area where the person of interest was staying. He

From a Vantage Point

was not in the building, but had driven off just moments before with his friends. What do you wish to do?"

"Damn," responded Davis, "Nothing right now, except to continue to monitor our person of interest, and report back on his whereabouts. I will contact Doha on what they are doing here. Thank you." Davis ended the phone call, and dialed some more numbers, waiting for dial tone, and then the call to be connected through his secure phone."

"Coggins," said the person Davis had called. Can I help you?"

"Tom, Bill Davis. What the hell is going on here in Khartoum? The guy I am supposed to be monitoring was nearly executed by a bird. Are we monitoring, or doing something else here?"

"Bill, let me get back to you. I ordered nothing. Back shortly."

"OK Tom, I'm waiting in the airport for a flight to Doha. I need to know what comes next." He clicked off the phone, and placed it in a pocket in his shorts, then walked back toward the departure lounge. He was forty minutes before departure.

Hakim, Josh, and Will came to the door of the home, just as a man emerged wearing local dress, and obviously carrying a handgun in his right hand.

"Hello Hakim," the man said, as they walked toward him. "I thought it might be you and your friends. Looks like you got out of the city just in time. They blew up your apartment building, along with two others. Many people killed, and many more wounded; the damned Americans." As he finished, he looked menacingly at Will, who was behind the other two.

Hakim, sensing the animosity, quickly said, "This is our friend Will, Ibrahim. He is to be trusted."

Ibrahim looked again, and responded, "Trust comes with time and experience. One stays alive that way. In the meanwhile, welcome to my home, all three of you." Ibrahim turned, and started back for the front door of the house, standing to the side to let the men enter.

"Welcome to my humble home, Mr. Will," said Ibrahim, as they came through the door to the main room. "Please have seats, and my wife will bring refreshments." He waved to a woman standing in the doorway of what was probably the kitchen. She seemed younger than Ibrahim, and looked to be western, with a light complexion, and light blond hair.

Josh spoke first. "What is the news of the explosion, Ibrahim?"

"The report from the city is that the buildings on either side of your apartment, together with your building were totally demolished by what appeared to be a small plane or drone. The first reports were that 17 people were killed outright, and about 50 were wounded. Several people remain unaccounted for in the rubble. The Red Crescent is there to help with the search.

"Anything else on the news so far, Ibrahim," chimed in Hakim.

"The US State Department and the American Ambassador both have issued statements that the attack was to kill some terrorists who were in one of the buildings. They did not identify who yet. I will expect they will come up with something to justify themselves, though. There are too many dead this time to sweep it under the rug as they usually do. The Government has demanded answers, but they are so weak the US pays no attention to them."

"There have been previous incidents like this?" asked Will.

"Of course, this is the third in less than a year, all in the city, and all supposedly to kill terrorists, none of whom has even been identified," responded Ibrahim. "They do this in several countries here in Africa, as if the Americans own these places too."

"But aren't there terrorists here in Sudan?" asked Will.

"Of course, young man," responded Ibrahim. "There are terrorists everywhere, depending on how you define the terrorist. The US uses definitions to suit itself. They never want the world to forget September 11th, just like the Jews never want the world to forget the Holocaust. At least the Jews have a better reason than the Americans for their feelings."

"Agreed," answered Will. "My family came from Lebanon to the US to avoid the civil war there. I remember as a small boy how the US Marines attacked and invaded our country when I was a small boy, and the hatred of the people for the invaders. We had no choice then. The Government invited in the Marines, and they roamed through the city and countryside arrested and disarming anyone they chose. A lot of people were injured and many died during those days before my family came to the United States."

"Things have not really changed in Lebanon, or anywhere else for that matter since," responded Ibrahim almost sadly. "Here is my wife Sarah with refreshments. Let us have better conversations over what she brings."

Sarah brought in a large tray, full of bread, dates, and hummus, along with small aperitif cups for coffee. She went back to the kitchen for a moment, returning with a large urn apparently full of very aromatic coffee, along with cream and sugar.

"Enjoy the meager amenities of our house," she said, returning to the kitchen to leave the men to speak freely.

Bill Davis sat for nearly the entire hour before the flight was scheduled to depart, and, at the last minute, the phone rang. It was Coggins.

"Bill, we have a real mess here. Are you somewhere that you can speak without being overheard?"

"Sure, but it has to be quick, Tom, my flight leaves in less than five minutes.

"OK. Here is the short version. One of the men involved in your assignment is staying with a very dangerous man. Name is Hakim al-Azahir, and he is a leader of one of the cells that supply the Taliban training leadership in Khartoum."

"Sure, I met him at the airport."

"All right then, we were targeting him, and did not realize he was with your detailee. We sent a bird to wipe out al-Azahir's residence. Lots of damage, And some deaths. Your guy is not among them. They left the city just before the attack. The Ambassador is on the line to Washington to come up with a reasonable excuse for the bombing. One thing we have been told, no more birds until we sort this out. Go to Doha. I will join you there tomorrow."

"Great. See you tomorrow then. Out here."

Davis headed back to the gate and arrived just as the gate attendant was about to close the doorway to the overhead walk to the plane.

"Mr. Davis, you just made it," she said and opened the door to let him pass through.

"Thanks. Appreciate it," he responded, and headed down the jet way, and the plane to Doha.

From a Vantage Point

Chapter 7 Beginning of the Conundrum

The four men sat speaking quietly as they ate their cakes and drank the rich Turkish coffee so common in this part of the world. Most of the discussion centered on current events, other than the bombings and just an occasional mention or aside on the many bombings, killings, and other attacks going on around the world. Will was enjoying the companionship of the group, and mentioned several times his awe and appreciation over the people he had met thus far, and the beauty of the places they had so far visited.

What Will did not know was that Ibrahim, friend of Hakim and Josh, was Ibrahim Maloof, a key member of the committee that coordinated training for future Taliban and other terror groups in Sudan. Several very remote sites remained in the country, even though al-Qaeda and some major terror organizations had been banned and expelled. However, the country is very large, and some groups still managed to retain their ties to central and southern villages where they continued to train for future terrorist acts.

Hakim and Josh were 'runners.' They brought in goods and money, which were funneled to the villages through contacts in Khartoum. Goods would come in from Europe and other eastern countries, be stored in dispersed warehouses, and go out in small amounts in a small truck fleet owned by the coordinating group. Never more than one or two trucks at a time, and in random order and schedules, the trips were nearly impossible to plan or track.

Will sat comfortably, mostly listening to the conversation, and occasionally contributing some small comments. He was fascinated by the history and geography issues, as well as the religious issues that seemed to be discussed around him. In a short time, he had received a vast amount of information, even though he probably did not realize it at the time.

Three hours elapsed before Hakim looked at his watch and said, "We need to be going shortly, Ibrahim. Anything we can send you from the city?"

"Let me think and call you later," Ibrahim answered, with a shrug of his shoulders. "I am glad you came out to see me today. Even more so, since danger came so close to you in the city. Take care my friends, and be safe. These are terrible times." Ibrahim rose, as did his visitors, and started to move toward the door.

"You especially Will. Take care. This is a dangerous place, especially for an America; even one of Lebanese descent. People don't always ask your real nationality before they make decisions on how they will act."

"I will Ibrahim," responded Will. "Thank you for kind hospitality, and a really great discussion. Peace to you also." He extended his hand to Ibrahim, who shook it forcefully, and then patted him on the shoulder as they moved toward the front door.

From a Vantage Point

Will asked several questions during the return trip to Khartoum, answered mostly by Josh, while Hakim paid attention to driving along the dusty roads they had to traverse before they reached the outskirts of the city. As they entered, it seemed the police were out in greater force than Will had seen previously.

The three drove past their apartment building to see the extent of damage, continuing down several streets before stopping in front of a small building with a driveway along the right side, into which Hakim drove the car, and parked under an overhead cover.

"We sleep here tonight, and go over to the building tomorrow to see what is left," he announced as he stopped the car and killed the engine.

Inside was a small, sparsely furnished, but clean home, with comfortably furnished three bedrooms. The three spoke into the evening before they went to their respective rooms to sleep. Will stayed awake a long while, thinking about the trip, and going over in his head many of the things he had heard from Ibrahim earlier in the day.

Chapter 8 American Embassy, Doha

The ride from the airport was pleasant and fast, for once, and Davis appreciated that as he needed to be at the US Embassy soonest. Luckily an embassy car awaited him on his arrival, and he moved through the arrival and customs quickly—showing his sky marshal identification and was out to the curb in just a few minutes.

The ride was smooth and quiet, interrupted only by a phone call on the embassy car phone, which he answered to hear the voice of the CIA station chief Jeff Namers.

"Jim, glad you're back," started Namers, "Come to my digs as soon as you arrive and check in. We have to talk."

"Will do, Jeff. That feeling is mutual. There is a lot to discuss here."

"Sure is. How far out are you?"

"On Doha Boulevard, about to take the curve," responded Davis.

"Five minutes, then. See you in about 15-20."

"OK, out here."

Davis put the phone back on its cradle, and sat back in the rear seat, folding his hands on his chest and began to plan what he would say to Namers when they met.

The Marine guard saluted as the embassy limo drove slowly past the entrance guard post at the side of the Embassy grounds. Davis looked out to see a large, glass-enclosed building with what seemed to be a number of people coming and going through the entrance. He assumed that to be the normal business of the consular office on the first floor of the building; something he noticed as he looked at the Embassy website in preparation for his visit.

As the limo moved past the people toward another entrance, the numbers dwindled, eventually consisting only of guards and Marines walking the perimeter, and casually observing the area. The limo stopped by a large doorway, and a man emerged from it to greet the limo.

"Mr. Davis, I presume," said the man as he opened the rear door, and held it open for Davis to emerge.

"Sure is. Jim Davis," he said as he extended his hand to shake the outstretched hand of his greeter.

"The station chief is waiting to see you, but first you've got to meet the second-in-command, and make your formal entrance into the Embassy. Did your flight go well?"

"Exceptional," responded Davis. "The airlines in this part of the world have not discovered the lousy service we put up with in the states. It's a pleasure to be flying in this part of the world. Even coach is treated well."

From a Vantage Point

"I agree, sir. This is a great part of the world; except, of course, for the wars, pillaging by terrorists, and sometimes virtually being a prisoner in the Embassy, everything is great."

Davis looked quizzically at him.

"Only kidding. Things are good here. Let's go inside, shall we?"

"Lead the way," responded Davis. The two men entered the doorway, which led down a short walk to the main area of the Embassy—but behind the security perimeter that separated those coming to the consular offices from the rest of the facility.

The two men entered an elevator, after his escort had punched in a number on a keypad by the elevator button, and they were on their way to the third floor.

"Right this way, Mr. Davis," his escort indicated, pointing to the left in a corridor. The corridor looked much like a hotel with many rooms, only the signage in a hotel that indicated room numbers was absent.

They arrived at a room, about the sixth room on the left side of the corridor, and the escort punched in a numerical code. The door opened.

"Your code is 2234, Mr. Davis. Remember it. It gets you in and out of your room here. We maintain a high level of security on our guests."

"Thanks," responded Davis, as he entered the room, and quickly walked around. "Looks good to me. Thanks for the hospitality."

"No problem sir. That's what we are here for. Please remember you have an appointment with the station chief. Use the '2234' code to get around in the building."

"Will do," said Davis. He found his small amount of luggage already in the room, and he started to place his clothes in the cabinets along the left wall.

Hakim and Josh let Will sleep in the following morning, leaving a note on the table that they had gone for a short time for business. Instead, they were going over to see the damage to their apartment building. Driving along the side roads, just in case they were being followed, it took longer to get to their neighborhood than by the major roads in the area.

They were still blocks away when they started to see damage to buildings, and, soon enough piles of rubble where damage was evident. About six buildings, including their own, were now piles of stone, brick, and steel; it was clear that everything within had been destroyed, or at least damaged beyond recovery.

While the two had nothing incriminating in their apartment that, if discovered, could be incriminating, the same was not true of the 'business office', and they left the area quickly to drive to that location as well. As they suspected, there was considerable damage to nearby building. They were shocked, as they got closer, that what was left was literally nothing more than a hole in the ground. The blast had blown everything into the air, and around the

From a Vantage Point

area. Money, jewels, and parts were strewn everywhere, and a large group of people were searching the site for everything they could take away.

"What do we do now, Hakim?" asked Josh.

"We walk quickly back to the car, then to our living space, before Will wakes and realizes we are gone. He may start to ask questions. We will bring him to the apartment area later in the day, and he will want to get more clothes, so we will take him to a men's shop to buy clothes. We will treat this as simply another American attack. Nothing more."

"Good plan," said Josh, "What do you think he would ask?"

"Not sure, but I want to steer away from direct discussion. Let him form his own opinions about this."

"OK, but what about our offices?"

"That's another thing. We need to notify our contacts, and get replaced what we can soonest. We had one shipment ready to go that is critical to our contacts in the US. I had hoped to have it there even before Will returned to America. I will deal with that this afternoon, while you take Will to see the apartment."

"Sounds like a plan. Let's get back. Nothing else to see here, right now." Josh started toward their car, and Hakim followed, stopping to pick up a white jewel in the dirt. He rubbed it with his fingers, and placed it in his shirt pocket. In a minute or two, they were again navigating the small side streets that would lead them back to their temporary living space.

Jim Davis sat for a few minutes in one of the high-back arms chairs in his bedroom, thinking about what he would say and ask of Jeff Namers, the CIA station chief, when they met. His brief conversation with Tom Coggins had not yielded much information on which to rely in a conversation, which could become heated, with a man he had not previously met.

Davis did know the reputation of Jeff Namers, and it was a varied one. Namers started with the CIA nearly twenty years ago, spent time in both Europe and Asia, eventually ending up in the Operations Directorate, now the Clandestine Services Directorate, headed by his classmate Bernie Minihan.

As Davis understood it, Namers hated office work, and wanted back in the field. He got Doha, a critical listening post in the Middle East, much like Lisbon Portugal had been during World War II and into the Cold War. Namers had been in Doha over five years, and developed an exceptional network throughout the region.

Now he and Davis were going to discuss the collision between his needs in Doha, and his instructions from Langley, aimed at monitoring gain Intel on Will Johnson. One of the men would come out of the meeting a winner, and Namers had a strong reputation for being that person as often as possible.

The phone in Davis's room rang, and Jim picked it up to answer.

From a Vantage Point

"Jim Davis."

"Jim, this is Jeff Namers. If you have a few minutes, how about coming to the second floor. My office is the glass-enclosed space as you exit to the right of the elevator. Come on in. Mollie, our secretary, will show you to the conference room where we are meeting."

"Sure Jeff. Be right down," responded Davis. *OK, so I am going to a meeting in Namers' conference room—already in progress. Be sharp Davis, something is not quite right here,* he said to himself, as he left the room headed for the elevator. *Time will tell, but be sharp. Let him do the talking.*

Davis entered the elevator, pushed the button for the second floor, entered his code on a keypad next to the floor buttons, and the door closed to take him down to his destination.

Josh and Hakim returned before Will awoke. That was good. They threw away the note they had left, turned on the local TV, and waited for Will to begin to stir. Josh eventually made some coffee. About thirty minutes went by, and eventually the two men heard activity in Will's room. Just as Will emerged from the room, the two began a conversation, based on the television program they were watching.

"Look at the devastation, Josh. Why does no one other than the local stations show the extent of damage from these damn drones? You would think that the world would be interested that real people are being killed by real bombs", offered Hakim.

Josh was initially taken aback by the onset of the conversation, but quickly responded, "That's the way the media works these days. Anything that supports the West is blared over the news. The real killing and horror, the deal damage to families is not considered, except perhaps by the Arab press. Even then, the West disregards it in favor of whatever Israel and the other nations considers their personal perspective. People are dying while the West defends the killers."

Josh looked over, and saw Will entering the room. "How did you sleep-, Will?" he asked.

"Not well, actually," Will responded. "I dreamt a lot of what we had seen over the last day or two, and tossed and turned. It reminded me of my early days as a kid in Lebanon."

"Sorry about that Will," answered Hakim, "We wanted you to enjoy your time with us. Unfortunately, controlling events is not among our capabilities. Nonetheless, let's try to enjoy what limited time we have left, and go do some real sightseeing."

"Good for me, Hakim. What about my clothes and stuff in the apartment? Can we go there and see what we can get out?"

From a Vantage Point

"Sure Will," responded Josh, "We can go after breakfast if you like. Let's go to a local restaurant, have something to eat, and then go by to get your stuff. Not sure what is there, but let's go anyway and see what we find. We may luck out. Whatever fell might have hit on another building in the area."

"Great. Thanks guys. I sure appreciate it." He went over to where the coffee brewed, poured himself a cup of black, and sat down on a small chair in the room, sipping, and trying to make sense of everything.

"Gentlemen, our other guest is here, so we can start," said a man with graying and receding hair, dressed in a comfortable blue short-sleeve shirt. "You must be Jim Davis, our 'Air Marshal' associate," he added, as he stood to greet Davis. "I am Jeff Namers, and this is the ground zero of the Middle East. Guys, introduce yourselves so we can get acquainted and then let's begin." The other five men around the table introduced themselves; the only one Davis knew was Tom Coggins, who sat near the end of the table farthest away from the door.

"Jim, grab a seat, and let's go. OK, so as usual, Langley screwed up in its efforts to meddle in our affairs here. The attempt to get al-Azahir and his American buddy failed. The bird blew up three buildings but didn't get him. And, at the same time, apparently screwed up the op you were conducting, Jim, to monitor another American, a guy named Will Johnson. Langley neglected to read us in on his arrival under escort to visit our two pigeons. Who starts?"

"We aimed the strike for a period when most of the people would not be in those buildings," said the man sitting next to Davis at the end of the table. "Al-Azahir has tried to surround himself with people to prevent an attack, so we acted to create minimal collateral damage. Unfortunately, our people on the ground say he and his friends left in a hurry just before the attack. They barely got out."

"How did we not see them leave, and redirect?" asked Namers.

"Well Jeff, it's like this," responded the briefer, "Our eyes on the ground either did not see them leave or did not tell us. There were several cars leaving the area at the same time, and our aerial recon did not pick up one of the cars as theirs."

"OK. Shake down the people on the ground. I want to know if all of them are 110%. If not, get them out of there. We can't afford another blunder. The ambassador is already after my ass for screwing this up. Aerial must do a better job. Don't we have his car tagged?"

"We do," answered another at the table. "No tagging active to identify and effect a redirect. Either he has two identical cars, or someone got to the bugging device. Either way, we lost them."

" OK. Let's rotate a bit here, and get to our new arrival. As I said, this is Jim Davis. We have him posted from the Air Marshal Service for 'special actions',

From a Vantage Point

those that involve people we want to watch as they travel. Jim, give us an update on what you are doing here."

"Sure, thanks Jeff. About three months ago, one of the men you are following, Josh Giddons, arrived in the US to visit an 'old military buddy' in West Virginia. He and Will Johnson served together in the Army, along with Hakim al-Azahir, by the way, and they traveled extensively during their service in Europe, after they first deserted from the Army and fled from the US, landing initially in Sweden."

"Giddons spent nearly a week with Johnson at a farm in West Virginia, then returned to the Middle East. Johnson followed him to Doha a few weeks later, Meeting there, and traveling to Khartoum with al-Azahir. I was on the plane with Johnson, arranged to sit next to him on the flight, and struck up a good conversation. I also met the other two here in Doha while they were sightseeing."

"OK Jim," interrupted Namers, "What's your impression thus far?"

"Not completely sure, but my initial impression, at least is that Johnson has no idea what he might be involved with here. At this point, I would put a good bet on him thinking he is just at a reunion with his buddies. Johnson gives nothing really to indicate any direct current involvement with the other two, although I can't really rule it out 100%."

"Thanks Jim," responded Namers, "Action number one for you remains the surveillance of Johnson. Keep Coggins in the loop for anything we might need to know. Now that he is in the mix, we need to rethink how to deal with the other two."

"Tom, I want these guys under 100% coverage. Use only people you can trust absolutely. The failure of the bird is giving me a feeling that we have an internal problem, possibly someone feeding information to al-Azahir. I want that determined, and any problem if there is one, to go away. Soonest."

"Meanwhile," continued Namers, "No more attempts on the group. Find out where their other caches of supplies and equipment are, and get those if you wish, but I want nothing happening to the men, at least until we can determine what part Johnson might play here. Understood?"

"Sure Jeff," responded Coggins. "My guys will make that happen."

"Good. Anything else to discuss? Nothing? OK, get back to work, and Jim, Tom and I will go have some coffee to discuss baseball."

The men slowly rose from the table and started out of the room. A couple went over to shake Davis' hand before they left. Only Namers, Coggins and Davis remained in the room.

"So, what are your plans, Jim?" asked Namers.

"Right now, I need to reestablish some contact with Johnson in Khartoum, but that may be difficult, without knowing where he might be."

"We can help you with that," responded Coggins. "We know they went out into the desert, visited a contact of al-Azahir, and have returned to a safe house. What bothers me is that the person they visited is Ibrahim Maloof, a member of the training coordinating council for al-Qaeda in the Arabian Peninsula, presently living in the Sudan. That man is particularly dangerous, even more so than al-Azahir."

"So, do you think that Johnson has begun an assimilation into their organization?" asked Davis.

"Not necessarily," interjected Namers. "Maloof meets many of the people brought to Sudan by al-Azahir. Not all have panned out as future terrorists. Sometimes, we think he just makes a point of sending us in disparate directions—wild goose chases-for the fun of it."

"You need to continue to monitor Johnson as best you can, and look for subtle signs. Use the assets we have in Fatima's organization in Sudan as well. See where he goes, and what he does with the others. It may be just a social visit. Johnson has one thing on his side; his family came from that part of Lebanon which was very anti-Hezbollah, so there is no natural affinity for these terror movements lurking under the skin. It can be developed, of course, but it would take some major event for that to happen, at least in our experience. Let's just see how everything pans out with him."

"Fair enough, Jeff. I'm going back to Sudan tomorrow on a routine flight, and will try to link up with Johnson to update myself. Frankly, I would love to say he not a threat, and get on with other issues."

"Understand, Jim," responded Namers, "Just don't underestimate the man, that's all. Good luck. Let us know how we can help. Coggins will be back in Sudan tomorrow as well. Let him help you, if you need assistance. Good luck. Wish we had more time together. Those things just don't happen these days," Namers ended the conversation, as he rose to leave.

"Thanks for everything Jeff," inserted Davis, "I'm sure we will see each other again."

Ditto." Namers walked out of the room, leaving Coggins and Davis at the table.

"Well Jeff, I guess that's it. I'm back to Khartoum for a day or so, then on to a couple of flights to maintain my marshal presence. I'll work with Fatima to keep an eye on Johnson while I'm gone."

"That's about all you can do, Jim," responded Coggins. "This was not the best thought out Langley plan, but we'll make it work. From what I have seen thus far, though, I think you have a visitor, and not a terrorist. It's still the best approach to continue to monitor, though. People have a way of turning for odd reasons these days."

"Agreed," said Davis, as he rose to leave as well. Coggins followed, and they started to walk to the door. "When will you go back, Jim?"

"Have a flight tomorrow Doha to Khartoum early in the morning. Can I get a lift to the airport?"

"Of course. Just tell the first-floor security desk what time you need to be ready to go, and a car will take you to the airport, discreetly, of course. No fancy limos now." He extended his hand to Davis, who responded, shaking it firmly.

"Thanks for your help Jeff. Appreciate everything. See you soon."

"Good trip, Jim," responded Coggins as he turned and walked down the corridor, leaving Davis at the elevator.

Hakim drove through the winding streets with a speed that only a long-time resident could offer without attempting to lose their life to people, animals, and other cars in the narrow passageways. Finally, he pulled over into a small outcrop from a side street and stopped the car in front of a small building without markings, and a bright red door.

"Here we are," announced Hakim. "The best food in this part of town." The three got out of the car, and walked toward the red door, entering one at a time to see a brightly lit and painted interior room with tables and chairs. Along the walls were posters of various sites in Sudan, mecca, and other religious sites throughout the Middle East. A man came through an interior door, and waved them to a table. He was dressed in baggy pants, a loosely fitting white shirt, with the sleeves rolled partially up his forearm, and wearing a New York Yankees baseball cap.

"Good morning. How are you all today? Can I get you some tea or café?" he said as he handed out menus written in both English and a Sudan dialect. Will looked at the menu and wondered at the broad selection.

"I will have coffee," responded Hakim. Josh nodded that he wanted the same, as did Will. The man disappeared through the door from which he had come, and the sounds of cups and preparation filled the air. In just a few minutes, he returned with a large tray, carrying both coffee urns and a teapot.

"I brought tea as well in case you decide later. Please enjoy," he added, as he filled the coffee cups and placed them before each of the men. "I will come back shortly to take your order. Enjoy."

As the man entered the kitchen area, a shadow emerged from the side of the large freezer, and a woman stepped out into the light.

"Fatima, what are you doing?" asked the man.

"I understand you have visitors," she responded.

"There are three men out in the restaurant. One is the man Hakim you have been seeking. He is with two others. You should not be here. The walls are paper."

From a Vantage Point

"I am leaving immediately," she responded to his entreaty. "But I want you to remember everything that is said in your hearing. You will come to me later, after they have departed. Do you understand?"

"I do," said the man, dejectedly. "I will come as soon as possible."

"Today," she said, as she went out a rear entrance, and closed the door. The Man could hear the roar of an engine as a car left the side of his restaurant, and spend down an alley toward a street.

The man sat at a small table, buried his face in his hands, and thought to himself, *"What have I done? That woman will get me and my family killed. This man Hakim has strong friends, and people do not want to be their enemies. What can I do?"*

The man rose from the table, took a small pad of paper and a pen from the table, and walked out into the restaurant toward the table where the three other men sat.

"Can I take an order for food, sirs?"

"Sure," answered Josh, "This is what I will have." The other two followed with their breakfast orders, which he quickly went to the kitchen to prepare.

From a Vantage Point

Chapter 9 Back to Khartoum

A 5AM knock at his door told Jim Davis it was time to depart for the airport, and return to Khartoum. Unlike many cities, where early travel means light traffic, it was just the opposite in Doha. People travel early, before the heat becomes unbearable. They work early, travel early, and then stay inside where, even with air conditioning in many places, the heat of the desert is still felt until; well after dusk.

The unmarked car, with local plates, pulled up in front of the main terminal, Davis took the small bag he carried, and entered the wide front entrance. He walked along the terminal until he came to a door, marked simply, *Official Use Only – No Admittance,* punched in a code and went inside.

This was the operations office, and it was here that he would confirm his flight, sign on as a sky marshal, and retrieve his weapon for the flight. Davis also kept the rest of his bags here, preferring to take with him only a small overnight bag, along with the bare necessities for a stay of a day or two at the most.

The flight from Doha to Khartoum was uneventful. About the only commotion was a young child crying unceasingly several rows behind Davis, who spent most of the flight working a crossword puzzle book he brought with him on the flight. Entering the final approach to the airport, Davis thought through what he knew to date about Will Johnson, and how he would approach the next few days—his final opportunity to evaluate and then recommend next steps to the Agency.

Will, Josh, and Hakim worked their way through the truly magnificent breakfast at the restaurant. Each had on his mind what they might see at their former residence, now a pile of rubble from the drone attack.

Hakim also had other things on his mind. He only had about two more days to put some thoughts into Will's head, if the plan to make him a member of their team—albeit an absent one in the US, waiting for further instructions.

That was the real purpose of getting Will out to see Maloof, especially after he had received a call from one of his contacts that their building would be the subject of the drone attack. Hakim had contacts all over Khartoum, both government and private, even contacts with the US Embassy who provided occasional information.

The most recent occasion had been two days ago. Hakim received a short message from his contact in the US Embassy detailing an overheard conversation about an attack the following day on an unknown target in the city. While there was no more definitive information from the informant, other than a follow-up call to say that the bird was flying, both men thought it prudent to get out of the city and into the countryside, just in case the bird was meant for them.

Josh and Hakim had worked out an arrangement to protect themselves some time earlier. Each man knew some of the informants and contacts, but

From a Vantage Point

neither knew them all. That way, if one was captured and interrogated, only limited information could be obtained by whatever means the interrogators chose.

It was one of Hakim's contacts who overhead the conversation at the Embassy. What pleased him most was that he managed to get it from right under Jeff Namers nose, without Namers even thinking twice about it. These two men had a love-hate relationship; they respected each other, but both wanted the other silenced. Hakim had no inhibitions about telling his contacts to kill Namers, if they had a chance. Namers had more rules to follow, and the drone strike was apparently his opportunity—or so Hakim thought.

"We need to leave soon, if we are going by the apartment guys. The sun will be up in full force shortly."

"OK Hakim," said Josh. "Let's go Will."

"Sure guys," Will responded, "Let me go to the head first, though. There is one here, I assume?"

"Right through the door over there on the left, Will," pointed Josh to a door with no markings. "It's the first one on the left." Will rose to go toward the door, just as Hakim took out his cell phone to make a call.

Dialing a number, Hakim said into the phone, "What's it like over there Amoud?"

"Really trashed, huh," he continued. "Anything salvageable?"

"Nothing of real value here."

"OK, we are on the way over. Should be there in about ten minutes. We have our American friend with us. I want to show him what they have done, so let's put on a bit of a show. You know, lots of people walking around, ladies crying, everything in a shamble. Just like it would be for some nosy reporter. Can you do it?"

"Good, One more thing. Is the old lady still around who says she was from Lebanon? If she is, then she just might do as a relative of the guy we have with us from the US. He is from some small village in Lebanon, before his family came to America. Make it happen if you can. We will see you shortly." Hakim hung up the phone just as Will entered the room.

"Ready to go now," asked Josh.

"Sure am. Let's go see what is left of the neighborhood—our former neighborhood, that is," said Will, continuing to stand and obviously anxious to leave.

Josh pulled out some money, left it on the table, and walked toward the other two as they went through the front door. The restaurant man never came out from the kitchen, but was listening through the kitchen door, still scared.

As soon as they left, he made the phone call to Fatima, and recounted what they said, and where he expected them to go next.

From a Vantage Point

"Fatima," said the server, "The men you called me about just left. They are going to some place where something blew up, to see if their American guest has anything to recover. Does this make sense?"

"it is all right," responded Fatima, "I know what they are doing. Thank you for calling." After her response, she hung up the phone.

The drive across town was yet another puzzle—a maze it seemed—as they wove through small streets, staying off the main roads, and darting through intersections, until they reached the area of the most damage—right near what had been their apartment building.

All they saw was rubble, and many people milling around, some trying to pull personal possessions out of the rubble. Hakim pulled the car over to the left side of a small road and stopped the car. The three men left the car, and started walking toward the other side of the street, where a large pile of rubble represented all that was left of their previous abode.

"It's the American bastards again, with their drones," yelled Hakim for all to hear. "They don't care what they do, or who they kill," he added, as he could see a small group bringing a body out of the rubble. Walking behind them were several women, their heads covered, loudly wailing for the loss of someone. Will watched, and swore he heard a dialect he knew from his childhood.

"Hakim, who are these people? Do you know them?" asked Will.

"Not all," Hakim answered, "But some I recognize from the area. One of the women lived in my building with some of her relatives. They are from Lebanon, originally, I think. One of the men works here. He left his country during the battles between the Jews and Hezbollah. I don't see him, though"

Do you know where in Lebanon?"

"Not really. Why?"

"My family came from Lebanon, and brought me to the United States as a child. I thought I heard a Lebanese dialect. I am probably wrong, though. I have not heard the language for many years."

Perhaps it is true, then," responded Hakim. "When you hear something once, you always remember. Hakim waved to one of the men, who walked over to where they stood.

"What happened here?" asked Hakim.

"As you said, it was the Americans, we think. I was outside, going to the local shops, when I heard a whistling sound, then I was knocked to the ground. The building blew up in front of me. It was another of those bombs the Americans fly in to kill us all. We have done nothing to them, why do they do this to us?"

Another man, who had also walked over to where they stood added, "Now we have nothing. What do we do?" The man pointed at Will, and said, "You are American. Why do you do this to us? We have done nothing to you. My friend is dead, with many others. He came here from his own country to work and avoid wars. It came to him and his family anyway. Now we will bury him, his wife and family, and there is no justice? Why is that American?"

Will did not know what to say, so he remained silent. Then a woman walked up to him as well. "You," she yelled as she pointed her finger at him, "Why did you kill my Habeeb? What am I to do? Do you have no shame, to come here to gloat on our misery? Go home to America and leave us in peace." Then, she reverted to her own language, and Will's ears perked up as he again recognized the accent.

"Are you from Lebanon?" asked Will.

"My Habeeb and I came here from Lebanon to seek work during the last fighting. He got a good job in a local hotel, and I worked there as well. We lived here in a small room we could afford. Now that is gone."

"Where did you live in Lebanon?"

"In a small village in the south. When the fighting started, my people escaped mostly went to America, but we stayed longer until it became impossible to live. Then we came here, because we heard there were jobs, and companies would pay to bring us here. Now I do not know what I will do. I am alone without my Habeeb." She started to wail again as the body was brought out to a waiting ambulance.

"That was my Habeeb, at least what we could find from your bombs." She spat at Will and walked away, with a defiant wave of her hand while looking away toward the ambulance.

Will asked if any of the men knew what village the woman and her husband came from in Lebanon. One said he was not sure, but it was in the south, and volunteered that her name was Maryiah Ashkar. Will's face went pale as he heard the name, and started to walk toward the ambulance, following the woman.

"The men told me your name is Ashkar. Is that true?"

The woman turned, and said, "Yes, it is true. I am Maryiah Ashkar, and this was my husband Habeeb."

"What village did you come from in Lebanon?"

The woman responded with two names, and a short tale of their travels during the fighting.

"My father was from one of those villages. His name was Suleiman Ashkar, and I had his name, until we came to the United States. We were proud of our heritage, and glad that we could escape the fighting."

"I remember," the woman said, "Habeeb had a cousin named Suleiman, who left to go to the United States during the earlier fighting, when the Americans invaded our country. We never knew what happened to him. If you are my kinsman, then avenge this crime," she said, as she entered the ambulance and

From a Vantage Point

the doors closed. The ambulance sped off, siren wailing, and lights blinking, trying to make its way through the rubble.

Will stood on the street, dumbfounded, watching the ambulance move off into the distance. How could this be, he asked himself. Why is this happening? Why would his own government kill innocent civilians? There were too many questions, and too few answers.

Standing off a bit in the distance, partially hidden from sight was Jim Davis, who had received the messages from Fatima on the conversations in the restaurant between Will and Hakim, and the alert they would be going to the apartment area. He could not hear all the conversations, but he heard enough to realize that Johnson had apparently found a relative. That did not bode well. He slipped away to get to the American Embassy to call Jeff Namers.

Will, Hakim, and Josh stood quietly for a few moments after the woman left in the ambulance. It was truly an emotional moment for Will, and Hakim used that moment for all it was worth.

"Sorry about the outbursts, Will. These people have lost everything, and they are very emotional about it. Especially around here. A few weeks back another strike killed two small children playing in a side street. A wall came down and crushed them to death. This is just the latest of a string of these attacks. We see the US claiming credit on the international news all the time. Sometimes, it makes me sick that I served my country, and now they seem to be coming after even Josh and me."

Will continued to stare ahead at the rubble and watch the people digging out what few possessions they had.

"We never know when they are coming," added Josh, just as Will seemed to be coming out of the trance he had entered earlier. "Are you OK Will?" he added.

"OH, sure," answered Will. "There is so much damage here, and people dying. What did they do?"

"Nothing quite frankly," responded Hakim. "They were simply here when the Americans dropped their bombs. Probably a drone of some kind. We won't know until they parade it in the news today or tomorrow, if they even do. No one has a chance to get away from these things. Lucky for us we had planned to go out into the country, or we would be right in the middle here."

Josh picked up the tempo of the conversation as well. "Will, they do this somewhere around Khartoum all the time. You probably see it on the evening news at home, but it is very real to the people here, as you can see. Most of these people have come from war only to get attacked here. The US will say it was killing terrorists, but that man Habeeb was no terrorist. He was nothing more than a hotel worker. Why kill people such as him?"

"The US Government has declared these people terrorists, but they are not. They are simply innocent people caught up in a political war, one where there are

From a Vantage Point

no winners—only losers, such as Habeeb. At least he no longer has to worry about it." Josh turned, and walked over to where two men were moving bricks. Underneath they found a doll, tattered and muddy. A small girl ran up and snatched it from Josh's hands, and hugged it as she walked away.

Turning again toward his two friends, both could see tears in Josh's eyes as he returned to where they stood. "This is so unfair, and what makes it even worse is the fact that it is my own country doing this to these people. It really sucks. Let's get out of here. There is nothing to save here that belongs to us."

Josh turned again and started to walk back to where their car sat on the side of the now-destroyed street. The others quickly followed.

Jim Davis moved quietly among the buildings and alleys and finally reached his car, safely placed away from the site of the bombing. He drove quickly out of the area and headed for the US Embassy. Showing his credentials to the Marine guard, he drove through the gates and found a parking spot near the entrance. Jeff Namers met him at the entrance.

"Well," said Namers," how is your investigation going Jim?" He turned and walked into the building with Davis, as they moved toward the stairs and his office.

"All right, I guess. Johnson is going all over the place with his two friends, but there is nothing clear that links him to anything other than a holiday with old war buddies. Unless I see something in the next day or so, it's about time to go home, I think."

"Perhaps you're right Jim," responded Namers. "What about their meeting today at the building we trashed with the drone?"

"They were there all right, and Hakim put on a show, but it didn't seem to overly impress Johnson. The crowd even dragged a body in front of him, with the women wailing and yelling at him. I think it scared him more than anything else."

"Are you sure? Is there a possible alternative here?"

"Jeff, let's talk. I have mixed emotions here. What we know from our information on Johnson is that he has Mid-Eastern Christian heritage, and he came to the US following the American Invasion. He has lived a perfectly normal life, except for his short military service, later becoming a respected citizen in his community. There is no real reason to believe he is a mole or secret terrorist of any type."

He contacted two of his former military buddies—both of whom are on our terrorist watch list, only after one of them contacted him. One eventually visited him, and then Johnson decided to visit them. The three have been travelling and seeing the worst of what we do to stop terrorism in this part of the world. I really don't know what influence they have had on him. So far, from my observations, there is no change from the person I met on the plane to Doha."

From a Vantage Point

"Can I guarantee that? No, I can't. I have no particular view presently, but I have no potential opportunity to change my mind. He seems to be simply visiting his friends, however vile they may be, and is oblivious to their current position in the Jihadist community."

Davis raised his hands, seemingly in a level of frustration. "I want to believe he will return to the US and simply go back to being a farmer. That seems to be the situation."

"Well, let me know what you want to do from here. Does seem like a dead end, but better to follow it to the real endpoint. We don't want a homegrown terrorist on our hands in West Virginia. Take what time you need, and have Fatima follow up on him after you leave. Get me a report before you go home."

"Ok Jeff. Will do. I'm going by to see Fatima today to tie up some loose ends. I also have one of her men following the boys to keep that contact."

"Good, anything else you need from me?"

"Nothing right now. Will call you tomorrow or the following day to close the loop. Right now, I really need to go to see Fatima."

Good, let's get together before you go back to New York." Namers extended his hand, and Davis shook it, turned, and started back down the stairs to make the trip over to see Fatima.

From a Vantage Point

Chapter 10 Changing Plans

"Let me have the keys," yelled Josh to Hakim, who was quickly catching up to him, along with Will.

"Sure, here they are. You drive. I want to make a phone call."

"Where would you like to go?" asked Josh.

"Let's go to the Ferzzan Café, first. I need a drink, and we can get rooms at the hotel next door. I forgot its name." Hakim and Will climbed into the back seat, as Josh got behind the wheel, and turned over the engine of their small car. They were out in traffic and driving through the narrow streets, around several corners, and finally reached a main road. There, they encountered the maze of traffic so common in Khartoum.

In the back seat, Hakim pulled out his phone to make a call. After dialing, he put the phone to his ear. "Meet me at the hotel near the Fezzan, the one with the Red overhang. We will be there in about 10 minutes." He closed his phone, and put it back into his pocket.

Josh looked back through the rear-view mirror and smiled. Then he looked over at Will, and saw him gazing out, looking at the city, obviously in deep thought.

So much had happened in the last two hours that Will rapidly became even more confused. He saw all the damage to the apartments; the woman wailing over the loss of her family members, and the sheer devastation caused by whatever bombing had occurred. His mind raced between the vision of the woman, and a similar view of a drone or bomb coming down, much like the bombs had rained down on his family in Lebanon when he was young.

In fact, as he recounted, the woman was from Lebanon, and from the area where my family had lived. Now she had nothing to live for, and she had nowhere else to go. So many of his relatives and friends had the same future. As the thoughts bounced through his head, especially the vision of the old woman, Will gradually became more upset over the indiscriminate killings and damage that solved nothing.

What Will could not have known is that much of what he saw was staged for his benefit. There were bombings, of course, and just that day. The neighborhood where they lived had been hit by a US military drone, hoping to bomb the center Hakim ran for the local branch of the Muslim Brotherhood. They missed the apartment building where Josh and Hakim lived—it was still in good condition, a block away from the site bombed by the drone, and distant from where the three visited in the same neighborhood. Will had not idea they were not in the same location as the original apartment. Everything looked alike to him in this foreign city.

From a Vantage Point

Hakim took no chances that the bombing might hit them, so, when he heard of the impending attack from his contact at the American embassy, he arranged to have the three go to the countryside for a visit. When they returned, an elaborate subterfuge was played out for Will's benefit. It was designed to cause a reaction, something it did well.

Just ahead, on the right, Josh could see the red overhang on the hotel to the side of the Ferzzan Café, and he pulled into a parking space on the side of the restaurant. As they left the car, Hakim separated himself from Josh and Will.

"I'll be in shortly. Want to go get us rooms in the hotel. You two go to the Ferzzan, and order me a Turkish coffee with milk."

"Sure, Hakim," responded Josh, "See you in a few minutes, then." Josh walked with Will toward the door of the Ferzzan, and Hakim headed toward the hotel entrance. Going through the left front door, he entered the lobby and saw the person he needed to see sitting on a chair over to the right side of the lobby, nearly out of view from the main part of the lobby.

"My people saw you three at the site of the drone attack," said the woman, looking up from her newspaper.

"Really, and what did they see?" asked Hakim.

"Not much. They could not make out most of what you said. It seems, though, you put on a good act for the American. Did he buy it?" Hakim sat down next to Fatima, who was his contact with the CIA and the US Embassy, although not for their benefit, but for his.

"It seems he did. When we brought out the old lady from Lebanon, we set the hook. Now we need to reel him in."

"You know," answered Fatima, "He is being watched by another American, Jim Davis, who has been following him on his trip. He is here in Khartoum. I am supposed to meet him shortly."

"What are your instructions from him?" asked Hakim.

"Have my men watch him, and report. Nothing more. No contact directly."

"Good. Then your report is that you and your men have heard and seen nothing out of the ordinary, but will keep watching him until he leaves. Report back to me what Davis responds, and his next steps."

"As you wish Hakim. Where shall I reach you?"

"I will call you in two days. By then, I will have a new phone. My old one, the one I used to call you is no longer in operation. We must be very careful."

"But I thought one of al-Asiri's men gave you a phone which could not be traced. Is that not true?"

"It is true. He did give it to me, but I trust no one, not even you my cousin, not even my mother if that were possible."

From a Vantage Point

"May Al'lah give her rest, Hakim? She was a good woman. She believed in you, even to her death from the American bombs. Was the phone blown up in the latest bombings?"

"No, my home is still intact. We were away from the building, blocks away from what I showed to the American. He thinks everything is gone. He could know no better. I will leave it that way."

"All right, I will do as you ask. Call me at your will. I must get back, because Davis is coming to see me today. I want to be there when he arrives."

"Go then, and keep the man away from us." Hakim walked away toward the Ferzzan Café bar, and saw Fatima leave by a side exit to his right. He gave a short smile, knowing she would do what was required of her with the American Davis.

Davis sped through the traffic between the Embassy and the Gamhouria Street, where the Dinder Bazaar sold the wares of the world, weaving in and out, and doing the same jerking to a stop, then speeding up that every driver experienced in the chaotic world of driving in Khartoum. He wanted to reach Fatima, hear if she had any further news, and then head to his hotel to pack before leaving the city. He approached the street from the south, just as Fatima, one block over, entered an alley where she parked her car, and rushed inside Ahmad Shipping; to be there waiting for Davis.

The small brass bell tinkled as he entered the shop. A salesman looked up, saw the American, and quickly came over to try to make a sale. Americans' always wanted something, and were usually willing to pay without regard for price.

"May I help you?" he asked, as he approached Davis, dressed in a subdued colored flowing gown, with a bright red fez on his head. "Is there something I show you, perhaps? Something to bring home to your wife? Or perhaps even your lady friend?" The salesman's right hand swooped out over the panorama of goods in the shop.

"I am looking for Fatima, actually," responded Davis. "Is she here?"

"I will have to see sir," said the salesman, "Let me look in the back and see if she is here. I have not seen her this day yet." The salesman left Davis' side and started toward the rear of the shop, then turned and said, "I will return immediately. Please be patient, and look around to see if you might wish something." Then, he turned again, and left through a door, partially covered by a large rug on the wall.

Davis thought for a moment, and became a bit concerned. *Why*, he asked himself, *would the salesman not have seen Fatima? Surely no one else would open the shop without her. That could compromise her situation here in Khartoum.*

Just then, the door opened, and Fatima came into the room. "James, so good to see you. How have you been since we last met?" Fatima seemed cheery and friendly as always.

"Just fine, and you as well?"

"I am myself. I never seem to change."

"When I came in, and the salesman greeted me, I asked for you. He said he had not seen you, and did not know if you were in."

"The old fool. Of course, I am here. Who else would open this shop? I did leave for a few moments to go to the grocery down the street. Mostly, I stay in the back working on the books or ordering so the salesmen do not always see me. They should know I am here, since they could not enter themselves without my opening the shop. None of them have keys, or access to the office if I am gone. The doors to the back are locked. Have no fear, I keep the shop secure from all—even those working for me here."

"All right, then. I will be returning to the States in a day or so. What have you found on Will Johnson and his friends?"

"Pretty much nothing, I am afraid, Jim. They have been sightseeing, visited a couple of small villages, and then came back to Khartoum the day after the missile attack the part of town where Hakim al-Azahir and Parsons were living. Too bad, by the way, the missile missed its target by a couple of streets. The only damage was to an old building housing mostly refugees from Lebanon. The three are staying at a small hotel nearer the airport. I have a man there watching to see if anything happens."

"So, no indication of any activity involving Johnson, then?"

"Nothing we have seen. I tend to think you have a young man visiting two men he thinks are his friends, and who are showing him a good time. Perhaps there is more, but we have not seen it. I have someone close to them at all times."

"Just keep looking, and let me know. Thanks Fatima. As always, you are a friend I can count on."

"Absolutely, Jim. What time is your flight?"

"Tomorrow evening at 7:50PM."

"I will call you well before then with another report. Enjoy your brief time left with us. Go have a good dinner and relax."

"Thanks, I think I will. Any recommendations?"

"Perhaps the Club Mediterranee. It is just down the street a block or two. The owner, Faisal is a friend. Tell him you know me. He will take good care of you. The food is excellent, and they have the best private wine cellar in Khartoum. Go early, or you might wait a while, even if you are a friend."

From a Vantage Point

"Thanks again for the tip. I'll try it. Hear from you tomorrow." Davis waved as he turned and left the shop, headed for his hotel to change, and then dinner at the Club Mediterranee.

Will and Josh were laughing loudly as Hakim entered the bar area. It was easy to find them, and he sat down just as Will was telling a story.

"Josh, do you remember the day in Malmo, when we were protesting the Vietnam War, and a guy came up to me to object?"

"I sure do," said Josh, "He thought you were a classmate in whatever college he went to back in the States, and decided he did not like protesters, so he tried to hit you in the face."

"That's right. He did. Unfortunately for him, I put the heavy sign between us and his fist hit the sign pole—broke his wrist in several places, and the cops hauled him away for creating a disturbance."

"They sure did," Josh continued, "And he went screaming, resisting all the way despite the injury and the pain. I heard later they put him on a ferry back to Denmark, where he had apparently come from earlier."

"Yeah, he wanted to make a statement, but the only real statement was the publicity we got for the incident. We could not have paid for a better opportunity. I even heard from my family back home that it was on the evening news." It was clear that Will enjoyed reliving the old times.

"Those were the good days," added Hakim, as he sat down with the other two. "We still have some good times here, even though the things we do have more depth than the old protests. The situation around the Middle East is very poor. The US and its cohorts are trying every trick they can to prop up Israel, destroy the Palestinians, substitute their western ways for our own heritage. You two are different, and do not understand the needs we have to keep that heritage alive, along with our religion."

"I think we do try to understand your point-of-view Hakim, at least I do, travelling with you for years now, and I think Will does as well. He saw today what happens to us frequently—the Americans simply won't leave the people alone to determine their own fate. Instead, they think bombs will bring them to submission. They are very wrong."

"Hakim, I think Josh is onto something here. I have been away from my own heritage for many years, but that does not mean I do not care. I do, and I felt a lot of pain today seeing one of my countrymen in such unnecessary distress. I care, but there is little I can do from my home in the US. I live in a community among people who believe in peace and harmony. They would hurt no one. They don't even have television or radios to hear or see the violence going on outside their small world. To them, the world is family, children, their churches, the cattle they farm, and the crafts they produce for their subsistence. That's their world."

From a Vantage Point

"If only the rest of the world could live as they do Will," responded Hakim. "Unfortunately, the outside world is much different, as you have been seeing. Times do not get better here, or in Afghanistan, or in Africa, only worse. People are persecuted for their faith in Islam, and when they react to persecution, they are the ones branded as inhumane and barbaric. A missile is launched from Gaza, and hits a fountain in a small Israeli town—injuring or killing no one."

"The next day, sections of Gaza City are bombed by the Israeli Air Force, killing, wounding and driving people from their homes. They attack schools, churches, even mosques, without regard for what they cause is suffering and death. They are applauded by the press, and we, the innocent, are condemned. It is not right."

"Before we get too deep in philosophy, let's eat. I'm starving for some good food," opined Josh.

"Agreed," responded by Hakim and Will, almost in unison. Just as they finished, the waiter arrived with menus for their order.

Fatima had operatives all over Khartoum. The waiter at the Ferzzan Café was one of her men, as was the maître d' at the Mediterranee, who greeted Davis as he entered the restaurant. Each would dutifully report back to her on the visits. What she did with the information, however, was decidedly different.

"Good evening, sir," intoned a man standing at the inner door of the Café Mediterranee as Jim Davis entered. "May I help you?"

"Yes, a friend of mine, Fatima Ahmad told me you have excellent food. I wanted to try it myself."

"Then you must be Mister Davis," responded the man, "I am Suleiman, the maître d'. Fatima called to say you might be coming. I have a very nice table for you. Our food is excellent, and I know you will enjoy it. Please follow me"

Davis followed into the restaurant, and was taken to a table on the left side, in a small alcove where he could see throughout, including the small stage at center front, where a small group of musical instruments sat waiting for their owners.

"You will find our menu to be very varied. We offer both local custom and some more western dishes, if you prefer, sir. This is Abdala, who will be your waiter. He will take good care of you." Suleiman pointed to a short, rather overweight man, with a goatee on his chin, and an oversized red fez on his head. "Have an enjoyable visit, Mister Davis. If you need anything at all, simply have Abdala bring me to you. Salaam." Suleiman gave a graceful sweep of his hand in the traditional greeting, and turned to walk back to the door.

Davis looked quickly at the menu, turned the page over, and then looked up, just as Abdala asked, "Would you like something cold to drink, Mister Davis?"

"What do you have available, Abdala?" was the response.

From a Vantage Point

"We have everything here, sir. We are licensed to serve foreigners, and can offer drinks, which must not be taken outside, even to our sidewalk tables."

"Thank you. I will have some wine. Do you have a recommendation?"

"Sir, our house wine is a Sauvignon Blanc from France. Most find it excellent."

"Good, then bring me a bottle. I will order later."

"As you wish, sir," responded Abdala, as he turned to enter the order and retrieve the wine.

Davis sat thinking about the trip, and revisiting his views on Will Johnson. Over the past two years, as he was detailed from the Sky Marshal Service to Homeland Security, and then to work overseas with the CIA, he remembered being told not to take everything at face value; that people are all too often not what they seem.

Thinking about Will Johnson, and what he knew to date, Davis was in a quandary. On the one side is a farmer from West Virginia, who happens to have two friends who are active mercenaries and now terrorism supporters, but with whom Johnson seems to have no frequent long-term relationship. He worked with them in his younger days, after his desertion from the Army, but that had been years earlier.

Then, suddenly it seems, Josh Giddons contacts him, visits him in West Virginia, and invites Johnson to visit he and his other protest buddy Hakim overseas. Johnson agrees, they meet in Qatar, and eventually end up here in Khartoum, where they seem to be sightseeing. So far, Fatima's people have found nothing to show they are recruiting him for something in the future. Yet, there was this nagging in his mind that something more was happening.

Davis came out of his deep thought as Abdala arrived with the wine, placed a glass on the table, opened the bottle he brought with him, and poured a small amount into the glass for his taste. He also positioned the wine cooler close to the table, so that, after pouring the glass, he could place it in the ice that partially filled the cooler. Near the top of the ice was a semi-transparent listening device, shaped like an ordinary ice cube.

"Will you be dining alone, sir?" asked Abdala.

"Yes, I will," Davis replied, "Although I am expecting a call later in the afternoon. It should come to my cell phone, but it may come to the restaurant as well."

"Certainly, sir, we have a wireless phone and can bring it to your table as soon as it arrives."

"Thank you, Abdala. The wine is excellent," added Davis, and Abdala poured half a glass, and placed the wine bottle in the cooler.

From a Vantage Point

"Please let me know when you wish to order sir," responded Abdala, as he started to walk toward another table of guests, who had just arrived. "I will be happy to serve you."

Davis sipped his wine; it was an excellent Blanc from a better year, and he enjoyed simply sitting, watching the customers as they arrived and sat to dine, and blew away most of his fears and concerns.

Twenty minutes later, his cell phone rang. He looked at the face of the phone and saw only a number. It was not Fatima; he had her listed in his contacts.

"Davis," he answered as he picked up his phone. "Jim, Jeff here. Anything new. You are booked for this evening. Be at the airport an hour ahead. Use your usual airport pass to get through security."

"Thanks Jeff. Nothing new here. Hoped to hear from Fatima, though. We spoke at length earlier at the bazaar. She had nothing from her people, other than a man visiting risky friends, and on vacation. Will call you if that changes, otherwise, I expect to be on the flight you all arranged."

"OK Jim. Send the report in the normal way. Thanks for the effort, my friend."

"Enjoyed the visit," responded Davis, "Love to come back soon. This part of the world really intrigues me."

"It is interesting, isn't it," said Jeff Namers, as he hung up the phone.

Abdala heard the conversation from a small earpiece in his left ear. As soon as Namers hung up, Abdala was on the phone to Fatima.

Will enjoyed the dinner with Josh and Hakim. They continued to tell and retell stories of their travels throughout the world, and what the future might bring. As for Will, he spoke of creating a farming cooperative for the neighbors in his small town; one which could sell their produce and crafts in the Washington area, bringing needed income to their otherwise meager lives. Will related his desire to establish a working relationship with the Amish, indicating the immense respect he had for their views on peace and living in harmony with all others.

Josh and Hakim both listened intently as Will spoke of his renewed interest in his family and heritage, an attitude which they could possibly exploit in their desire to create cells in the US, helping advance their cause. The only remaining question was how they could involve Will without his realizing their subversive intentions. They only had a limited time, since Will had already announced his intention to return to the US in the next few days to get back to his farm.

Josh, sitting next to Will, extended his hand toward him and grasping his left arm, spoke first. "Will, believing in family is a great asset. I know you have been mostly separated from them for years, especially those still in Lebanon, much like Maryiah Ashkar who lived in our building. I hope someday you will restore what you can of those relationships, wherever they might be. All a man really has is his family. Hakim and I travel a lot, but we have no family to speak of ourselves. You do, and you should search out where they are, and how to reconnect with them."

"If I have the chance," added Josh, "Would it be OK with you if I give Maryiah your address in the US? If she is related, you might find this a good first step in rejoining your extended family."

"Sure, that is fine with me Josh. At least I will eventually find a relative, if I do have one over here. What about you Hakim, didn't you have a sister in one of these countries over here?"

Hakim had been sitting quietly, listening to the conversation, seeming to be thinking about other things. The question from Will jarred him, and he turned to face him, saying, "Yes, I did have a sister, over in Yemen. She worked for the International Red Cross, going from place to place trying to help those caught up in the conflicts here."

"Three years ago," Hakim continued, "She was killed by a rocket attack, one similar to what you saw today. She was in a compound in Gaza, clearly marked with Red Crosses, when the Israelis attacked with fighter jets. They destroyed the compound, and later tried to explain that it contained terrorists. There was no investigation. The United States and other countries simply accepted the Israeli version, and the case was closed."

"The Red Cross tried to demand more answers, but was told to leave the area when the Jews invaded Gaza City. We have never had the opportunity to even get what might be left of her body. The Jews bulldozed the site and covered it over with dirt. Now, I have no family left." Hakim went back to whatever he was thinking about, and Josh quickly intervened.

"Anyway, you will be leaving soon, and you need clothes, and other things to take back with you to the States. Let's finish eating, relax a bit, and find a store close by to get you re-outfitted."

"Agreed," Responded Will, "Looks like a floor show is about to begin." The lights had dimmed somewhat, and the café staff was arranging a space in the center for entertainment. They waited to see what kind of entertainment it would be, and both men continued their small talk for nearly an hour.

Across the city, Jim Davis had finished his meal, enjoyed the last of the wine, and was about to leave as his cell phone rang for a second time. It was Fatima.

"Jim, this is Fatima. My two men following the three have returned. They are having some food over at a café near to where two of the men lived, as you know. We arranged to have a listening device near them, but their conversations were about long ago, when they were in the military, and in the protest movements across Europe. Nothing major. Johnson has decided to return to the United States, probably tomorrow or the next day."

"Nothing more interesting? No plans or discussions for future meetings?"

"There is nothing like that on the recordings, Jim. What speaking they did was mostly personal, and telling of tales. A small discussion of families, but nothing serious at all."

"All right Fatima. Thanks for the effort. I'll let Namers know, and will probably go home tomorrow myself, perhaps even this evening if I can get a flight. Thanks for your help. Talk to you again, I'm sure."

"Goodbye Jim. It has been a pleasure working with you. Please do come visit us again, and soon." Fatima ended the conversation, and Davis clicked off his cell phone, placing it on the table, although he knew he would pick it up again quickly to call Namers.

Now Davis had a decision to make. What report would he give Namers? He thought through the options again, mulled over the information from Fatima, and picked up the phone, dialing a number.

"Namers here. Can I help you?"

"Jeff, this is Jim. I just heard from Fatima. She gives the boys a clean slate, at least as it relates to Johnson. I have thought the thing through as well, and, despite a couple of misgivings, this is probably a dead end. Johnson is going home in the next day or so; back to West Virginia. Maybe it's hard to make a farmer into a terrorist, who knows."

"OK Jim. That's it then. You get on your plane. I will file my report, and let's move on. No sense trying to make something out of nothing, at least for now. I will recommend a cursory follow-up on Johnson in the states. The Terrorism Task Force people can follow-up on that. Thanks for everything. Get on your plane and go home."

"Will do, Jeff. Hope I helped."

"You have Jim, now enjoy a few hours of peace and quiet and go home. Talk to you again soon, I'm sure." Namers ended the conversation, and Davis put the phone back where he had picked it up to make the call.

Abdala, in the kitchen, listening through his ear piece, quickly called Fatima.

"The man is going home, Fatima. He told someone there was nothing further to do. I believe he will leave this evening."

"Thank you, my friend. You have done a good service. It will be remembered." Fatima hung up her phone, and immediately dialed another number, which rang at a table at the Café Ferzzan, next to Hakim.

"Everything is done, Hakim. Davis is leaving for the United States, and has reported as you desired that nothing was occurring among you three. You are safe for now."

"You did well. Thank you. I will speak more with you later." Hakim pressed the end button his phone and put it back on the table, looking over to Josh, who seemed to understand its meaning. The three watched the dancers for nearly an hour before they left to find clothes for Will's return to the US.

Khartoum International Airport is an imposing place. As with many of the Middle Eastern airports, it shares its facilities with the military, and is securely guarded by each nation's military. This is equally true in Yemen, and even more so. It is a secure place, and the military security forces freely shoot, even if questions seem to be more appropriate.

Sudan Airlines is the main carrier connecting Yemen to the rest of the world, although there are also a few regional carriers within the Middle East also serving the airport. The government-owned airline is a main link to Europe and normally the way that passengers visiting Sudan return to their countries of origin, especially Europe and the United States.

Jim Davis rushed to return his rental car, get on the shuttle to the main terminal, and be on time for his flight. He heard the first call just as he entered the terminal. Today's fight itinerary was a Sudan Airbus A320, recently introduced in the airline's fleet, to Cairo, change planes there for Frankfurt, and then Delta Air to Atlanta, GA. At least the plane changes would keep him awake for part of the flight.

Entering the terminal, Davis looked for his flight on the departure board and headed for the security area. He looked for the special access entrance, approached the security guard standing by the swiping machine, inserted his card, and entered the departure terminal for his gate.

"Sir, Mister Davis," yelled someone behind him at the entrance. Jim turned around to see who it was, and found a man in suit and tie coming toward him.

"Can I help you sir?" asked Davis.

"Mister Davis, I am Basur, security officer in this terminal. Your name flashed up on the screen as you entered. Can I ask if you are traveling on official business today?"

"Returning to my duty station in the United States, Mister Basur. Is there a problem?"

"None at all, my friend," responded the security officer, who had produced his identification for Jim Davis to see. "I like to keep up on who boards our planes, especially when they are, shall we say, security personnel themselves."

"I appreciate that sir, but I am simply returning to the US. Have been in the area mostly for vacation over the past ten days, and now I need to get back to work. I have thoroughly enjoyed your country though, and hope to return in the near future."

"Of course, we hope you will as well, Mister Davis. Have a nice flight," answered Basur, as he turned and moved back toward the side of the security area, where he spoke briefly to a uniformed officer, and then went through a

From a Vantage Point

door, presumably to his office. Davis did the same, turning back to face the corridor to his gate, walking slowly along, looking at people and shops as he moved toward his gate. He stopped once to buy a book and several papers for his trip, and again to get some snacks, assuming there would be none on his flight.

Will, Josh, and Hakim left the Café Ferzzan to find a clothing store for Will. They asked the Maître d', who suggested they go down the street, about two blocks to the right, where they would find a European-style tailor shop for their American friend. That man, the maître d' said, would have everything they need. Josh paid the bill, and the three left the restaurant to find the nearby clothing shop he recommended.

Deciding to walk the short distance to the shop, they engaged in a conversation on Will's upcoming trip home. Neither Josh nor Hakim thought they had enough time to persuade Will to join their cause, but at least they could plant some seeds, perhaps for future growth. In any event, they would try as best they could.

Chapter 11 Fatima

Fatima, as is already obvious, is a complex person, in the pay of both the Americans and the Jihadis. The American CIA had originally set her up in the shipping business as a means of moving small items more easily through the often-complex regulations of the Sudanese Government. Over time, they expanded her business into surveillance activities, and she hired several operatives who could be her eyes and ears around the city. As she had done with both Davis and Hakim, she steered people toward those places and activities where she had the ability to listen, record, and report on activity and behavior.

Her principal contact at the Embassy was Jeff Namers, the station chief. Two years earlier, she had a brief affair with him, and remained on good terms. Fatima was also a very careful person. While she and Namers discussed Agency business, she provided little in the way of substantive information on the growing network she cultivated in the city. For him, it was better not to know; for her, it provided an opportunity to sell some information to the other side.

One item Namers did not know was that Fatima Ahmad was a cousin to Hakim al-Azahir. Fatima's mother and Hakim's mother were cousins, living in widely separate villages after they married. When Namers did a background check on Fatima, the information on the relationship never came up, since the two mothers seldom saw each other, their last visit occurring nearly twenty years earlier. Fatima and Hakim only met about a year ago, purely by accident.

Another aspect of Fatima's background that went unnoticed was her relationship, through marriage, with several village chiefs, all of whom were covertly supporting Osama Bin-Laden's opposition to the Saudi Royal family, and his desire to reinstate the Caliphate and Shariah Law throughout the Middle East. Those lapses provided her opportunities to create relationships on both sides—the Americans and the Jihadis—as it suited her, without fear of discovery.

Fatima was equally careful in developing relationships. She worked with Jeff Namers, and with Jim Davis—among others—giving them support and information, while ensuring that she controlled the relationships.

Hakim found he needed a shipping company who could do some of his work with exceptional discretion, and he was told that Ahmad Shipping might fit what he needed. He decided to visit the shipping company and see what potential there might be for doing business. The name Ahmad was not lost on him; realizing he had relatives with that name, but also knowing that Ahmad was a relatively common name in the Muslim world. He gave the possibilities no further thought, until he entered the shipping company one morning to seek out its owner.

From a Vantage Point

Hakim drove purposely through the back streets of Khartoum, to assure he was not being followed, then headed for Gamhouria Street in the Dinder Bazaar. He parked his car to the side of Ahmad Shipping, and entered through a service door, coming into a small main display room. There he met an older man who appeared to be a salesman of some sort. Hakim looked him over, seeing the rumpled trousers under a short robe coming down to his knees, and a braided skullcap on his head. "I hope this guy is not the owner," Hakim thought to himself. "This might not be the right fit for what I need."

"May I help you sir?" asked the old man.

"Perhaps," Hakim responded. "Are you the owner?"

The man looked intently at Hakim, finally saying, after a few seconds, "You look so much like someone I knew many years ago. Is your name perhaps al-Azahir?"

Hakim stood back shocked. "Why should you want to know?" he stammered, somewhat in a daze.

"If your name is al-Azahir then we are kinsmen. My name is Ibrahim Ahmad, and I work here with my kinsman Fatima, the owner."

Hakim thought quickly, trying to remember the stories his mother had told him when he was young about kinsmen in other villages. He tried to remember what she had said, and remembered in his childhood meeting and playing with a cousin named Fatima.

"I am Hakim al-Azahir, and if you are Ahmad, then we may be related. I have not seen my relatives in years, so I cannot tell you very much more. I remember playing as a boy with a girl named Fatima, who was my cousin.

"Let me find her," responded Ibrahim, as he turned and rushed out through a door to the back of the shop. 'I will return shortly. I know she is here somewhere."

The old man disappeared through a side door, and Hakim could hear loud talk behind the door between the old man and someone else, a woman. After several minutes, a youngish woman emerged through the door and faced Hakim." I understand you wish to see me," she said in a subdued voice. "How can I help you?"

"Two friends suggested we could do some shipping business, if you wish to do that work. They claimed you had done some work for them, and I need similar work now. Are you interested?"

"Perhaps. The old man told me he might be related to you. Is that true?"

"It may indeed be," responded Hakim, "Only time will tell. I am Hakim al-Azahir. The old man believes I am a kinsman. Perhaps we are, and perhaps we are not. My father came from a village not far from Khartoum, Wad Hassoun, but moved to work for oil companies in Yemen when I was ten. So, perhaps it is true, perhaps it is not. Is that important to anyone?"

From a Vantage Point

"It may be to me," responded Fatima, "I want to know more. What village? who was your father?"

"My father's name was Massoud."

"If that is true, then we may be kinsmen. Our family lived about ten miles from Wad Hassoun, and some still do. My name is Fatima. I remember a young boy, with a scar on his left arm where I cut him one day when we were playing."

Hakim pulled back his shirt on his left arm, and a long, thin scar was clearly visible diagonally across the forearm.

"It is you, then Hakim. I cut that with an old knife when you hit me."

"It took a long time to heal," responded Hakim, "The cut got infected and had to heal slowly."

The two embraced, and then Fatima showed Hakim to the office. As they went through the door, Fatima's uncle rose from his chair.

"Well, is it true?" he asked, looking toward Fatima.

"It is true, uncle. This is Hakim, son of Massoud, your kinsman. He has come to visit us. Come and embrace him."

The old man placed his hands to Hakim's face, and smiled. "I am glad to see you, son of my old friend and kinsman Massoud. I have missed him for many years. Is he well?"

"No, my father died in an American bombing in Yemen several years ago. My mother died with him as they blew up his house in an air raid. I was living in Sudan when it happened. I never got to bury them, as there was nothing left."

"They are in the hands of Al'lah, my friend. May they be in peace in his arms. That is for the best. You father was my friend, and now you are my friend. What can we do for you?" The old man looked at Fatima, who had moved to the back of her desk and sat down. She nodded, and the two went to chairs on the sides of the desk.

"You said you needed some shipping, Hakim. What is it you need from us?"

"That will come Fatima. I do have need of a shipping agent, since I ship many things to Yemen, to Pakistan, and other places on a frequent basis. We will speak of it later. For now, it is good to meet you both, and to find family again. We will speak again soon."

The conversation turned to families, and older times, perhaps happier times for both, as Hakim and Fatima renewed their acquaintance, and retold the stories of their youth. Both clearly enjoyed their reunion, and Hakim found some peace, as they discussed his parents with his kinsmen. He stayed nearly two hours before he rose to leave, saying simply that he needed to go. He promised to return.

Fatima walked to the outer door with Hakim, looked in his eyes, and saw a man with many problems, and dark secrets. She knew the relationship with her cousin would not be easy, but she was clearly happy to meet him again. Hakim

From a Vantage Point

left, disappearing into the crowd in the bazaar, and Fatima returned to her shop, going through the public area to her office, then closing the door.

The meeting with Hakim quickly turned from elation in renewing a youthful friendship, to concern for herself, her uncle, and her relationship with Namers and the intelligence community in Sudan. She knew immediately from her brief discussion that Hakim was somehow involved with one terrorist group or another; they teemed in Sudan and Yemen, and Hakim worked in both places.

She knew she should report the contact to Namers, but then Hakim was her kinsman. By declaring Hakim his friend, as had been his father, her own uncle had taken Hakim into their family. Therein lay the dilemma. She would have to think about what to do. For now, he was simply a relative, and she would not make her uncle unhappy by causing difficulties for Hakim. Little did she know what the future might bring for her. For now, she would find out more about this 'new' cousin from her youth.

Hakim also had concerns. He told Fatima about his father's work in Yemen for an oil company, but left out his father's later work for an organization controlled by Osama bin Laden, which originated in Sudan and later transferred its operations to Afghanistan. It was that work which caused the deaths of both his father and mother.

Hakim's father had been an early member of bin Laden's entourage, attending the 1998 al-Qaeda Congress, and helping to plan several of the bombings against US property that year, while still working for oil company—an effective cover. Eventually, he gave up his position with the oil company to work directly for one of bin Laden's companies—a 'shipping' company, providing mostly courier services for money, diamonds, and other commodities, such as small arms, needed by the al-Qaeda network in trouble spots around the world.

The killing of Hakim's father was basically an extra opportunity. The bombing that day was meant to kill someone else; another member of the bin Laden network responsible for a US Embassy bombing earlier that year. Hakim's father happened to be in a building near the site of the bombing, and was killed by explosive shrapnel caused by the blast, along with his wife. With their deaths, only Hakim and his sister, a nurse with the International Red Cross, survived.

The US never admitted they conducted the bombing, nor did they admit that his father had been one of the casualties. It took three weeks for the couple to be identified, and another month for the authorities to locate Hakim to inform him of the deaths. The only real evidence was some fragments attributed to both a man and a woman, and an identity card for his mother.

Hakim returned to Yemen, saw the place where his parents were 'interred', although it was mostly a sign with their names. He immediately sought to associate himself with the same group as his father. Hakim the protester and mercenary quickly became Hakim the terrorist. He was sent to Pakistan to learn the finer points of terrorism. In the small village where he trained, pictures of his father and mother were prominently displayed on the wall of his small room, placed there by the training team to remind him of his purpose and resolve.

From a Vantage Point

Chapter 12 The Flight Home

The departure area of Khartoum International Airport is a maze of glass and steel, with sky-high ceilings and bright, effusive lighting; a comfortable welcome for those flying to destinations around the world. On any given day, it is possible to see people from as many as fifty different countries, each with their own dress and customs, all vying for position in the security lines to reach their departure gates, and eventually fly off to their preferred destination.

Throughout the concourses are international shops, myriad food offerings, small shops providing almost anything a passenger might need or want, and many military and security guards, making sure people depart safely, and those whom the government wants to stay in the country do so.

Josh drove their car to the center portion of the departure entrance walkway to drop Will Johnson off for his flight. Knowing that Will would be flying Lufthansa to Frankfurt, Germany, and then on to the United States, stopping near the center of the long drive at the departure building made Will's trip to security much faster.

Will was excited about returning home. He had been gone for over three weeks, and needed to return to his farm, and take up where he had left off. The trip exhilarated him, seeing his old friends, and visiting new places, all were exciting, but he had to return to reality. His fledgling effort to create a cooperative needed his personal time; it could not be left to others. He needed to work out arrangements for selling the produce and other goods the farmers had committed to the effort, and he needed to do it before the fall and winter seasons cut off his visits to outside West Virginia. It was time to go home.

The three friends stood at the entrance to the departure building and looked at each other for possibly the last time in a long while. Josh and Hakim would be heading to Pakistan shortly, and could (or would) not say when they might return. Will hoped they would remain safe, but he knew there were no guarantees.

"Well gents, looks like this is it. The entrance to the outside world is ahead," said Will, as he started to pick up his luggage. As he did, a porter came and took the bags, along with his tickets, to check them in. The two bags, both new, were filled with the clothes and other items purchased in Khartoum after everything was lost in the bombing.

"This has been some trip," he continued. "I am so glad I came to see you, even if we were nearly blown up in the process." They all laughed.

"I can tell you Will," retorted Josh, "We did not plan to have a bombing, although we might have considered fireworks for the occasion. Remember the time in Sweden when we blew up some cherry bombs and the Swedish police chased us out of St. Charles Square?"

From a Vantage Point

'That is not all we did in Malmo, as I recall," added Hakim, "There was the curious case of Will punching out the Army deserter, and the police putting us on the hovercraft back to Denmark as well. Those were exciting days."

"Sure were," responded Will. "But now we are older and more mature, right?"

"Right," both Josh and Hakim responded in unison.

"First call," the loudspeaker blared, "First call for Lufthansa Flight 3301 to Frankfurt, Germany is now ready to board. Flight departure is in 25 minutes. Please proceed through security to the gate for boarding."

"Guess that is me, guys. I better get inside and through the security lines. Thanks for a great time." Will went over and hugged both Josh and Hakim, and turned to start through the wide doors to the security area. He turned briefly to wave to his friends, and they returned the wave. Hakim also performed the customary *salaam* gesture with his right arm, so common in the Middle East. Will returned the salute in his own clumsy way.

Entering the terminal, going first to a small news stand near the entrance to purchase several magazines to take on the flight. Will stuffed them in his carry sack with the other magazines he took from Hakim days earlier. Going toward the security area, he was surprised to see a small line, and his porter already starting to put the baggage on an inspection platform as Will walked up to the location. A customs inspector, flanked by a soldier was waiting for him. The customs inspector asked in English for his passport and custom papers.

"Where are you travelling today sir?" The customs officers continued to look at the luggage, and not make eye contact with Will.

"Through Frankfurt, Germany to Washington DC."

"Oh, the United States. I see you are an American citizen. What brought you to Sudan this time?"

"Visiting friends, and enjoying the scenery," responded Will.

"And now, you are returning to your own country?" the customs agent asked, and then continued without waiting for a reply, "Are you taking more than $100 American in our currency with you?"

"No, I am not," Will answered.

"Anything to declare? Have you taken any old artifacts or anything which might be prohibited? Do you have any weapons to declare? "Added the agent in quick succession.

"No, none," was Will's answer.

The customs agent marked a cross with chalk on each of WIll's bags, and said, "Thank you sir. Have a good flight. Please return to our country again in the future." The customs agent returned Will's passport, along with his tickets for the flight, and allowed him to take his carry-on bag.

From a Vantage Point

"I would love to," Will responded, "Perhaps in the future," He added, as he walked past the customs agent, who placed his bags on a moving ramp going out to the cargo area to be loaded on his plane. He walked casually down the corridor filled with shops toward his gate, thinking about buying a book, but decided he had enough to read on the plane.

Will arrived at the departure area, and found a seat where he could put his carry-on pack next to him, and was near an English-speaking television station. He started to watch the local news, although that proved boring, except for the brief mention of the bombing of the neighborhood where he and his friends had stayed. The news announcer was discussing the attack in English—he called it a drone attack—and described the devastation it had caused to the people in the neighborhood. Surprised the news was in English, Will turned to a traveler next to him and asked about the English translations, finding out that many monitors in the airport provided English-speaking news, due to the large number of visitors and tourists.

In scenes that followed, the news station showed demonstrations in front of the American Embassy, and people throwing stones and debris over the high fences, along with other screaming about the deaths which had occurred. One of the people interviewed, a woman, Will seemed to recognize as the lady he met when they were looking at the damage. He still wondered if this might be a relative from Lebanon.

Will's attention to the news was interrupted by an announcement blaring through the departure area. "Flight 3301, a Lufthansa jet to Frankfurt, Germany is departing in five minutes. This is the final call for all passengers to board the flight. Please have your ticket and boarding pass ready for the agent at the gate. Lufthansa flight 3301 to Frankfurt, Germany is boarding now."

Grabbing his carry-on pack, Will started toward the departure door, gave the agent his ticket and boarding pass, which he quickly received back, and walked down the short jetway to the plane. He was on his way back home, tired, but enjoying every minute he spent with his friends.

Once on board, Will put on his earphones attached to an I-Pod, filled with all kinds of music, including some he had downloaded featuring middle-eastern songs, but fell asleep almost as soon as he sat in his seat, dozing off to the sights and sounds of an area of the world he now appreciated so much more.

Jim Davis left Khartoum the previous day, still troubled somewhat, but feeling better about his concerns after hearing one final time from Fatima on his person of interest, Will Johnson. Fatima reinforced her previous comments, and tried to make Davis more at ease that Johnson was no terrorist, although his friends could hardly be considered model citizens, even in their own countries. She told Davis that Will Johnson would be leaving for the US on the following

From a Vantage Point

day, and that any follow-up could be accomplished in the States. That information seemed to be well-received, and exactly what Hakim had told his cousin to say.

Davis flew out of Khartoum on the same flight that Chuck Jackson, the physician from Doctors without Walls was taking to meet with several of his counterparts in Frankfurt. Jackson saw Jim Davis enter the departure security area, swipe a card through a security ID reader, and simply walk through to his gate. That confirmed his earlier views that Davis was a government agent of some kind, not knowing for certain whether he was a sky marshal, or an agent of some other agency. Now, with Davis leaving Khartoum, if really didn't matter.

Fatima sat in her office at the shipping company thinking about how deeply she was involved in whatever Hakim, her cousin, was doing. Even though he was a kinsman, she disliked the secrecy and stealth that these people brought to whatever they did, and most of all, she disliked the danger that having these people in Khartoum brought with them. Nonetheless, as her kinsman, Fatima respected the cultural values of her family, and her people in general. She would decide later how far that loyalty would go. For now, she could live with herself.

Picking up the phone, she dialed Hakim on a number he had given her just a day ago.

"Yes," she heard.

"This is Fatima," she responded. "Both men are now leaving Khartoum. Davis left yesterday, just after I gave him the last of the information you asked me to convey. He went to the airport, and entered through security with an ID card in one of those readers for special flyers. The security people seemed to know him, I am trying to find out what he actually was, but my guess is that he worked for the CIA, or another American agency."

"Johnson left this morning, as you know," she continued. My men saw you all at the airport departure area. They said it was an intimate scene."

"Do not be sarcastic, Fatima."

"I am not, but simply reporting what my men said, as you requested."

"Thank you for the information," responded Hakim, as he hung up the phone. Fatima did the same, and returned to her thinking, and eventually her work, posting a pile of bills that covered her desk.

Frankfurt, Germany *Davis reached Frankfurt and was met by two men. They introduced themselves as National Security Agency officers, and asked him to accompany them to a side room in the arrival area of Frankfurt International. There, they asked that he wait a few moments while his luggage was searched. Davis protested. He was informed of his rights, stripped of his badge, and asked*

From a Vantage Point

to accompany the agents to the local American Consulate for further questions. Davis complied, but not without concern.

Davis was caught in a web. His identity, once known, caused a chain reaction in the intelligence field. Jim Namers in Khartoum had received an anonymous message that Davis was involved in an affair with a double agent—Fatima—operating out of the city with the al-Qaeda operations managed by Hakim. When Namers heard of the problem, he immediately notified the Embassy security officer, who called in the Homeland Security liaison. That started a chain reaction of events, including notification of the potential breach with the National Security Agency, leading to the detention of Davis in Frankfurt. At Namers request, no further inquiry was initially made of Fatima.

Davis was shuttled quickly onto a flight to the US, where he would be met by DHS officials concerned about the potential breech. Any information he had, or any possibility of a problem with Will Johnson died silently and quickly.

"Fatima, I need to see you. Meet me at 5PM in our usual place," said the message on her voicemail. She knew at once it was Jeff Namers. She also knew how and why he called so infrequently; usually sending messages instead. She also knew, just by his tone, it was not an invitation.

Later that afternoon, approaching 5PM, Fatima arrived at the Assyrian Café, a meeting place for all sorts of people, especially those who wanted to remain anonymous. The Assyrian was a small café, off the usually-travelled routes, and located on a one-way street, going south. It had barely fifty seats, mostly at tables, and a small bar, seating perhaps six or seven people. The atmosphere was Middle Eastern, lighting was dark, and easily concealed meetings where people did not want the world to know they were meeting for any reason.

Fatima entered, and saw Namers sitting at a side table, away from the bar, and in a corner where privacy was probably better than the rest of the restaurant.

"Well, Jeff Namers, what can I do for you? We do not meet frequently. What is happening?"

"Davis was nabbed as he left a flight to Frankfurt. He was taken for working with a double agent—you, in fact."

"That is ridiculous," responded Fatima. I have worked for you nearly ten years. In all that time, I provided information, following, and anything else you requested. I thought of Davis as one of your agents. Is that not so? Why am I now being called a traitor?"

"Calm down Fatima. The allegations have been made. We need to work through them. I need you to look me in the eye and tell me there is nothing here."

"There is nothing, my friend," Fatima answered, "I am your informant, and you have treated me well. Why would I turn?"

Fatima felt a pang in her heart that her dear friend Jim Davis was now under suspicion, but that was part of the trade, part of the business. She had to protect herself if possible.

"What would you have me do?" she added.

"For now, nothing, Fatima. We will cool off our relationship for a short while as this blows over. I expect nothing else will come of it, but we need to be upfront and careful. Return to your company and conduct business as usual. I will contact you again when it is safe to resume our work. Trust me though, as I trust you. If I find that what you say is not true, you want to be as far away from me as possible.

"I understand Namers. When all is over, we will still be friends."

"Good. Have a drink. We are still friends, after all."

Fatima returned later to her shipping office, going immediately to a small space in the back where she kept imported goods. Reaching into a box on a high shelf, she took out a box containing a cell phone. Quickly putting it together, she turned it on after connecting to a charging cable, and dialed a set of numbers, listening in to be sure the activation worked. Then she dialed a phone number.

"Hakim," she said into the phone. "They have taken the man Davis in Frankfurt."

"I know all that. It was me that turned him in. We need him out of the way for our plans."

"Hakim, you are a fool. Do you realize what you have done? I just left Namers, who was told I was a double agent. My contacts with the CIA are now useless to us. They will be watching, and we have lost our ears to the intelligence people."

"It will be worth the risk, Fatima. Just do your shipping business and wait. I will call you when I need you. Do not call this number again." She heard the phone go dead. A chill came over her, as she slowly realized her kinsman Hakim was leaving her to fend for herself. She feared for her and her uncle.

Returning to the front of the shop, Fatima recognized several customers, some of whom were being helped by her uncle. She stepped up to one to assist him in shipping a package, making everything look as normal as she could in this new uncertainty.

Namers likewise returned to his office, and went immediately to the signals area of the embassy.

"Joe, what do we have?" Namers asked Joe Reardon, the signals chief.

"Not much, Jeff. No routine phone calls from the shipping company. There was one burner phone call. Too short to monitor. There were a few people in the shop at the time, so sorting out who used the phone is impossible. It was a call to a local number, though because of the number of digits dialed. That's about all we know."

From a Vantage Point

"OK, keep at it, will you? We want to know what comes out of the shop, and who they talk to. We may have a critical breach here."

"Will do, Jeff. Happy to be of service."

Namers walked from the signals area to the Embassy security office across the hall. Walking through the door, he stopped at the desk of the admin assistant, Scott Blankenship.

"Scott, is your boss in?"

"He is sir."

"Anybody with him?"

"No sir."

"Thanks, Scott," Namers responded as he walked through the inner door to the Embassy security officer, Charles Irving.

"Charlie. I need to give you a quick update on the Davis matter."

"OK Jeff. Sit down. Let's talk," responded Irving. "What do I need to know?"

"Well Charlie," said Namers, "Since the NSA took Davis into custody in Frankfurt, we started doing some security oversight of our contact here, Fatima Ahmad. The signal boys are watching the telephone and internet traffic for anything. I also met with her to see a reaction to the Davis situation. Hard to say what her reaction really was, but she seemed somewhat ruffled by it, and maintains she is not a turnover."

"So, you ruffled some feathers in the hopes of her making some kind of mistake?"

"That was the plan, and still is. If she is a turnover, then she should fear uncertainty, since I cut off her access here. That was her value if she was working for the other side."

"Are you sure she has no continuing contacts among the locals working here Jeff?"

"Pretty sure Charlie. We checked everybody out for any potential relationship, even a small possibility of local living or contact, and nothing has come up. We'll watch carefully for any activity in our sections. Need your help though on anyone who might have secure access in other parts of the Embassy. Until this is over, we will use our own security to transmit traffic, especially anything related to Davis. That keeps you in the loop, but it will go out on our encrypted lines, and back in on yours. It gives us a bit of a firewall, since none of the locals I know of here in the building have that kind of access."

"Agreed, Jeff. I'll put a track on our lines at enhanced level as well, and let the Ambassador know what is happening. He can decide who else has a need to know."

"Thanks Charlie. Have a great day."

"I always do Jeff, at least on those days when the world is not blowing up in my face. See you later." Namers rose from his chair, and walked out of the room, waving to Scott as he left for his own office down the corridor.

From a Vantage Point

PART 3: EVOLUTION

Chapter 13 Return to Reality

Will awoke from his brief nap to the sounds of a service cart being pushed down the aisle by a flight attendant headed for the business class cabin. Just behind him was another attendant, and she walked up to where Will sat, asked if he had enjoyed his nap, and did he want something to drink or eat.

"Love something," responded Will." I feel like I haven't eaten in a week."

"What would you like, then? We have all kinds of juices and drinks. We are now outside the Sudan airspace, so we can serve alcohol if you wish. We also have a wide range of food and snacks. There is a card in the pocket on the seat in front of you."

Will looked toward the card, and then said, "I think I will have coffee for now. Do you have some Irish Whiskey as well?"

"We do sir," the attended answered.

"Good, then please bring me the coffee and some whiskey then."

"Of course, sir. We have Jameson's and several others."

"Jameson's is fine. Thanks again." Will turned his eyes to look at the card he took from the seat pocket as they were speaking. He saw the menu was in English, Arabic, and German. Reading the English portion of the menu, Will marveled that a plane could provide this much food. They were certainly superior to what he was used to in an American flight.

The attendant returned in less than five minutes, carrying a small tray with his coffee and whiskey. Just as she was setting them down on his tray, a cabin announcement started.

"Ladies and gentlemen, this is the First Officer. We have approximately ninety minutes before we enter Mediterranean airspace on our way to Frankfurt Germany. If you have items required to be declared under German Customs Law, please be prepared to do so. All passengers debarking from this flight are required to go through customs in Frankfurt, even if connecting to another flight. The flight attendants will provide you with forms for the customs inspection. Look at them carefully, and complete them, if required. The flight attendants are well-versed in customs requirements; ask if you have any questions. Trust me on this; getting it right on board will save a lot of time in Frankfurt. Thanks for your cooperation. Out here."

Will looked around and saw that he was not nearly alone in the First-class cabin. To his right, on the window seat was a gentleman reading the *International Tribune*, one of the papers Will could have picked up as he entered

From a Vantage Point

the jet way to the plane. He noticed that several sections of the paper were in the seat pocket in front of the passenger.

"Excuse me, sir," said Will, "Might I look at some of the paper sections you have already read?"

"Certainly sir," was the response, as the passenger took the paper sections, and handed them to Will. "Enjoy."

"Thanks again," will responded, as he started to look at the news. The first article was on the bombing in Khartoum—and he began to read avidly. They might have been the same bombings that he and his friends had avoided just barely a few days before. He followed the story to Page 3, where additional paragraphs and some pictures showed the destruction of the area. The news reporter noted that this area had a large population of people from Lebanon and Syria. These were émigrés from their respective countries during the upheavals, and most were Christians.

Scanning another article, also on page 3, Will noted a demonstration in Chicago against a mosque being built in the city, with demonstrators coming from both sides of the issue. During one part of the demonstration, a Molotov cocktail had been thrown into the construction site, and demonstrators refused to move for the firemen until the resulting fire spread throughout the construction.

Will closed the pages of the newspaper and handed it back to the man in the next seat, thanking him for allowing Will to read it. Then he put on the headset provided by the airline, hoping to find a music channel to enjoy the rest of the flight toward Frankfurt.

Hakim and Josh drove out of the airport, heading back to their neighborhood, and their apartment, feeling they had a new convert to their cause—eventually.

"What do you think he left with?" asked Josh.

"Not sure, my friend, but I do believe we have a possibility there. We will wait about a week and send him his backpack and some of his things. Use the excuse that they were found mostly untouched in the rubble. Then send him the latest issue of the magazine. Perhaps he has already read the one he took with him. We must tell our friends in Washington about him as well. Perhaps they can make quiet contact."

"What about the other guy, you know, Davis?" asked Josh.

"Now that we know he is an American agent; we can have our people on the watch for him. We will know if he has any further contact with Johnson. Our people will see him arrive at the Washington airport, and discreetly make sure of what he does. They have ways to do that. Tiny steps only. That is what we must do. Tiny steps only."

As the two pulled up to the front of their untouched apartment, Hakim saw two people standing out in front, as if they were waiting for the men. "Drive along without stopping," Hakim told Josh. "Go around a large block, and we will return. I don't like the looks of the men in front of our house."

Josh drove around for a few minutes as Hakim requested. Josh looked out the rear-view mirror to seed if anyone seemed to be following them. Hakim did the same with the right outside mirror. When they were satisfied, they returned to their street. The two men were gone from the front, so they parked.

"Be careful, my friend," said Hakim, as he reached into the rear of the car for his carry pack, which contained a small Beretta pistol. "We may still have visitors."

Both men walked slowly toward the apartment building, looking to the sides to be sure of their safety. Once inside, they went directly toward their apartment, taking the stairs up the three flights rather than the elevator.

Josh looked out into the corridor on their floor, and stepped out carefully. Hakim moved around him and they both stepped toward their apartment, arriving at the door, which still appeared closed and locked. Hakim pressed the doorknob softly, and felt resistance.

"Still locked," he said to Josh standing behind him.

"OK, then," replied Josh, "Next steps?"

"Use the key, and get out of the way quickly," was the reply.

Hakim put his key into the lock and turned slowly, pushing the door open, while he quickly stepped back into the corridor, using the wall as a safe barrier. As the door opened, they heard sounds in the apartment sounding like the opening of a window. They rushed in and saw someone going out the rear window and down a rickety stairway to the street. When they reached the window, the intruder was gone.

"Quick," said Hakim, "Look around for anything obvious." Both looked through their four rooms and nothing seemed to be out of order, except that is for the room Will had occupied. The carry sack Will left on his bed was gone.

"Hakim," yelled Josh, "Will's pack is gone. I looked around the room. It isn't there."

"Let them take it," responded Hakim. "Nothing in it anyway. We were careful enough. He is simply our old war friend, and they have nothing else. Hope they enjoyed the visit."

"So, what do we do about our plan?" asked josh.

"We send a message to Will in a few days saying nothing was left. He won't know any different, and we don't have to worry about what they found in his sack. It's the new sack he bought with the magazines that is important, and they don't have that. Let's go have some dinner at the Casa."

From a Vantage Point

Will opened his eyes, suddenly realizing he had fallen asleep listening to the music on the headset. He was apparently startled as the music stopped and an announcement from the cockpit, began through the cabin.

"Ladies and Gentlemen. This is the co-pilot speaking. We will be shortly entering the airspace of the Federal Republic of Germany. We expect to reach Frankfurt in about forty minutes, and should be on the ground just a few minutes later. The weather in Frankfurt is a bit chilly today, at 38-42 degrees, with a short wind to the east."

"In preparation for landing and debarking, please look over your customs forms and make sure that everything you need to declare is listed. There is a place on the form for expensive items, such as cameras or jewelry, which you may have purchased. These items need to be documented, so you will not have a problem leaving Germany for the next destination."

"The German customs officials and security officers are very thorough in their customs checks. Please understand this is for your safety, and those of us who fly around the world. We appreciate your being with us today, and hope that your future travel plans will again include Lufthansa. Flight attendants, please prepare the cabins for arrival."

The music began playing again in Will's earphones, as he took his customs declaration from the pocket on the seat back in front of him, and reviewed it quickly. He had really nothing to declare, so he put the form back in the pocket and sat back to listen to more music.

From a Vantage Point

Chapter 14 Interrogation

The flight from Frankfurt to Washington DC was less-than comfortable for Jim Davis. He sat between two men, both security officers for the National Security Agency, who had picked him up in Frankfurt. There was little conversation, and only a couple of magazines to read. Davis rose once to go the lavatory, accompanied by one of the security men who stood outside the door.

'At least they let me ride without handcuffs,' thought Davis to himself.

During the flight, he ate a meal, although he really had no appetite. Mostly, he thought back to how this chain of events could have happened, and what might happen next. He was still mostly in the dark on any real charges, although he did hear them speak of Fatima as a suspect of his 'crimes'. He wondered if she had turned on him or what was really happening. Nothing made much sense at this point.

Arriving at Washington Dulles Airport, Davis was whisked through Customs into a waiting van taking him to the Department of Homeland Security in the District of Columbia. There, he was again read his rights and turned over to the DHS agents. Brought inside, Davis went up an elevator with three DHS agents, and down a corridor to a room where another agent waited at a closed door.

"Davis, you will wait here, until we are ready for you," said one of the agents who entered the door, closing it behind him. Inside, Davis could hear several conversations going on at once until the door completely closed. Then there was silence. For the next 30 minutes, Davis stood against a wall to the left of the doorway with an agent by his side, waiting for the next step in this seemingly endless saga. Finally, the door opened, and a man in a dark suit came out and faced Davis.

"Jim, I'm Fred Pullery, Special Agent, Washington FBI Office. Come on in." He pointed toward the door and let Davis enter first. Inside, Davis faced a table with several men and women sitting around the table with piles of paper in front of them.

"Have a seat here," said Pullery. "Sorry for the rather rough way you were treated in Frankfurt, but we needed to get you out of there quickly, and make it look like you were in deep trouble."

"What is happening here?" asked Davis.

"What's happening, Jim, is that you were set up, we think. Let me start first with the people at the table. I'm Fred Pullery, as you know. I chair the Interagency Review Board that oversees the Joint Terrorism Task Forces operating overseas. Each of the people in the room are from agencies with representatives on those panels, including Alice Sawyer from DHS, whom I believe you know."

From a Vantage Point

Davis looked over at Alice and smiled as he waved hello. She smiled back as his eyes reached hers, and raised her thumb in recognition.

"About two days ago now," Pullery continued, "An anonymous call came in from a source in Khartoum, a burner phone, that one of the contacts working with the CIA station chief there was a double. In fact, it also stated the contact, a woman, was having an affair with you. Luckily, that call was taken by Jeff Namers, who passed it outside his normal chain to us, with the highest priority."

"We have two issues here we need to discuss. First, about the status of the contact. Second, your involvement with her, if any. Then we need to figure out what to do next. There is no question you have been outed, and we can't use you again in Khartoum. It also means that, for now at least, we should make it seem that you are in some sort of trouble. We solve that by putting you on administrative leave. Officially, you are under suspicion."

"Ok sir," responded Davis, "I understand all that, and have no problem where we are going here. Let me respond by speaking of the contact in Khartoum, at least from my perspective."

"Floor is yours Jim," answered Pullery, sitting down at the chair next Davis.

"Jeff Namers and I have been in contact with a young woman, Fatima Ahmad for over two years. She runs a small shipping company that does a marginal business, mostly because the Company funded her, took care of her father and uncle, and occasionally has her do some shipping to and from Kabul for us. She is very discreet, has been checked out completely and I still believe she is not a turn."

"We now know," Davis continued, "she is a cousin of Hakim Al-Azahir, whom we have been trying to nail for several years. We occasionally feed her information she passes to Hakim. Mostly, it is either incorrect, or at least imperfect information, but it keeps her in his good graces, and gives us an eye on him."

"Let me interrupt a second Davis," asked one of the men at the table. "Why not just go in and get him?"

"Simple answer, sir," responded Davis, "We want to know who his bosses are, and what their plans are for the future. Hakim, and his friend, an American named Josh Giddons are former protesters, mercenaries, or whatever you want to call them. Mostly, they are middlemen. They move money, supplies, and anything else one or another of the al-Qaeda tentacles wants moved, and we can usually trace what they do. That has led us to several of the bigger boys, some of whom have, shall I say, met a drone in their living room."

The people around the table gave out a muffled laugh at the obvious mention of drone attacks.

"Hakim also uses his cousin for shipping, and some of her employees for his eyes and ears when he wants someone observed for whatever reason. Fatima

From a Vantage Point

always has different people doing work for Hakim than she does for us. We get two sets of eyes and ears that way, and each group does not know the other. We get the reports of what Hakim is doing, and, to be sure, Hakim gets some reports of what we are doing; either through Fatima or another source in the city."

"Now, about any relationship with Fatima. It is true that Fatima and I are friends—professional friends for the most part. I have not, and would not compromise my situation with a deeper relationship. Nothing of what seems to be alleged here occurred, if I read your comments correctly, except in the mind of the person making the anonymous call. Happy to take a poly to confirm that if you wish. I have nothing to hide here."

"All right then, Jim, who do you think made the call?" asked Pullery.

"For my money, it was probably Hakim. I met him twice recently. He had a friend of his, Will Johnson, in tow when I first met him in Qatar, and then again in Khartoum. I came over this last time on the same flight as Johnson. He was informally flagged because he was apparently a friend of both Giddons and Hakim. They worked together after Johnson deserted from the Army, and more recently Giddons visited him at his farm in West Virginia. We heard later from Fatima he had been invited to visit his friends in Sudan, so we thought it prudent to keep tabs on him. I arranged my flights to coincide with his on the way over."

"Jim," asked Alice Sawyer, "What's the latest on Johnson?"

"Alice, I watched him, and had Fatima watching him, and my thoughts are still unclear. He seems to be an OK guy. I don't think he selects the right friends, but there is nothing overtly showing that he might be turning toward organizations such as those Hakim espouses. The guy lives on a secluded farm in West Virginia, bordering an Amish community, works his tail off to make a go of it, and is starting to work on plans for a farmer's cooperative. Not exactly terrorist work. I would still keep him under observation when he comes home, but he just doesn't fit any of the usual profiles."

"Agreed Jim," responded Alice, "I read in the file he was Lebanese, and the family left to come to the US during the upheavals over there nearly thirty years ago. Shouldn't that ring some bells?"

"Could be, but Johnson's family was Maronite Christian, not Islamic, and they were part of the communities driven into Syria and Jordan that never went back. Their relatives eventually ended up in many places, among them, Khartoum, in the Lebanese district there. As I said, we should continue to monitor, but I don't think at this point that he is a future sleeper."

"OK, any other questions for Davis?" asked Pullery. He looked around the room, and saw no indication of further interest.

"These are the next steps, then," continued Pullery. "Jim, you will leave this room with one of the agents, go down to main office, and turn in your badge and weapon. You will receive a receipt and notice of your administrative leave. You are to leave the building, and go directly to your apartment. You can stop for food, or anything else you need, but then go directly home. When you get to your apartment, you will find a package in the bottom left drawer of your desk. Open that package. Any questions?"

"None sir," responded Davis. "Thanks for filling me in." Davis rose, as did one of the agents who brought him to the meeting, and they walked out the door, taking the elevator down to the main administrative office. There, he turned in his weapon and badge, and received his paperwork. Within minutes, he was on the street, hoping to hail a taxi for the ride to his apartment, but then decided the DC Metro was the better choice. He decided to walk the distance toward Judiciary Square, where he could get a train toward his apartment in Crystal City, over the river in Virginia.

Chapter 15 Home at Last

Coming into the Washington, DC airspace is a marvel for many people. Looking out the window to the left of his seat, Will Johnson saw clear skies, lots of farmland, interspersed with massive areas built up with buildings, wide roads, and lots of cars. Off in the distance, you could make out the District of Columbia, and he thought he could see the dome of the Capitol. The plane seemed to move slowly over the terrain, until it suddenly speeded up approaching the runway, the pilot putting on its brakes, and gliding down to a smooth landing at Dulles International Airport in suburban Virginia.

"Ladies and Gentlemen," blared the loudspeaker system. "Welcome of Washington-Dulles International Airport, the termination of this Lufthansa flight. It is clear in Washington today, temperature about 56 degrees, and a slight breeze of less than five miles per hour. We want to thank you for flying with us today. We hope you will do so again in the near-future."

"Please have your customs declarations ready as you depart the plane. Please also take all your carry-ons and anything else you brought on board with you, as you leave the plane. Our airport staff will direct you to the US Customs arrival point, where your luggage is being routed. If you have newspapers or other small items you wish to dispose of, a flight attendant will have a disposal bag at the doors for you to drop your discards. The local time is approximately nine twenty-five AM, and thanks again for flying Lufthansa. The doors will be opening momentarily."

It felt good to be home on US soil again. After all, Will had seen overseas, he valued being back in his own country, and looked forward to getting back to the farm. He could hear the doors both in front of him and behind his seat opening, and felt a gust of cool air breeze through the cabin as the doors opening completed the depressurization process. Will stood in the aisle, and reached overhead to get his carry-ons, and then reached into his left jacket pocket to be sure he had his customs declaration, then walked forward to leave the plane.

Two Lufthansa employees waited at the end of the jet way to show the departing passengers the route to Customs, although that was probably not necessary, since the only exit from the plane was through Customs. He looked for his luggage, and then approached a line waiting for the customs agents. Finally, after about ten minutes, it was his turn to see the agent.

"Good morning sir," said the agent, "Your customs declaration and passport please."

"Sure," responded Will, handing the agent the form he had taken from his pocket while he waited.

"Anything special to declare?" asked the agent, quickly scanning the form. "Anything not on the list?"

From a Vantage Point

"Nothing else, sir," responded Will."

"I see you have been to Qatar and Sudan over the past few weeks' sir," stated the agent. "Have you brought in any prohibited goods or material from either of these countries?"

"No sir," was the response.

"What was the purpose of your visit to these countries, then?"

"Pleasure trip to visit friends that live over there. We were in the military together."

"I see," retorted the agent. "Just a moment please," he continued as he went over to a laptop near his stand. He took Will's passport, and typed in information. Will could see the screen change, and a photo of him, from his passport, show up on the screen. The agent scanned the information, and closed the cover, returning to Will.

"Are these your bags, sir?"

"Yes, they are," Will said as he pointed to the two small bags. The agent looked them over, and then handed Will back his passport and said, "All right sir. Have a great day."

Will walked to the site of the customs station, picked up his bags, and started to walk toward the exit. Going through the doors to the terminal, he really felt he was now home, and he started to move toward the front of the arrival area, to take the bus to the area where he had left his car in the long-term lot.

Khartoum, Sudan Sitting comfortably in their living room, Hakim and Josh were reviewing their situation. Josh turned to Hakim and said, "Well now that Will has gone, we need to review next steps here, I think. He went home thinking we were in danger, I'm sure, and that is good, but we have also lost our best connection at the embassy through Fatima. What do you propose we do now?"

"I propose we do two things right away, Josh," responded Hakim. "First, we need to move out of here without creating a lot of suspicion. We need to get out of here before they come after us again, even if they do miss with their drones."

"OK, so we move, what's next?"

"Then we start to put our plan in place, the one involving Will."

"You never have said what you really have in mind for Will, Hakim. We need to discuss that."

"Better we do not for a while, my friend," Hakim responded. "The less you know, the better off we are, just in case one or both of us gets grabbed by some intelligence people. I will fill you in on that gradually, but I still want the world to think you are a legitimate shipping and training guy if possible. With Davis out of the way, we have a better chance of extending that."

"I'll go along with that Hakim, but what do you want me to do?"

From a Vantage Point

"Find us another place to live, while I go make some plans, and meet a contact who will be leaving shortly for America. See you later this afternoon." Hakim rose from his seat and went to his bedroom, leaving Josh on the couch pondering what to do next.

Closing the door, Hakim quickly pulled out a cell phone and dialed a number.

"Meet me in ten minutes at the Place of the Dove', he said into the phone and quickly hung up. Hakim was especially sensitive about phone calls, even with a burner phone he might change often, for fear American intelligence would pinpoint him and launch another strike against him.

He followed up with a call to Fatima.

"Are you somewhere not to be overheard?" Hakim asked.

"I am," she replied. "What do you want? You have caused much damage already."

"Be patient," Hakim responded, "You will know all shortly. I need to go to the Dove in a few minutes. Do you still have a man there?"

"Yes, Ahmad is there. Ask for him at the front desk, and they will get him for you. Say you wish to buy some American wine. They will call him to come to see you at your table."

"Good. Thank you. You have been of help to me. I will remember."

"Of course, Hakim. Remember as you always do," she responded, as the phone went dead.

Washington D. C. Jim Davis walked out into the afternoon air from the Metro at Crystal City, and decided to do something he seldom did—go get a bunch of drinks. He knew his own situation, and he also knew the pretense would be to have someone following him, just in case he was being otherwise pursued. That made sense to him, but he still wanted a drink.

Coming up two sets of escalators, he looked out onto 18th Street and started to walk under the overpass to the right toward Eads Street. Then he walked across the 18th Street intersection to the local Westin Hotel, just across from his own apartment building complex. Going in a side entrance on 18th Street to the small bar in the lobby, he sat at a stool at the left end of the bar, pondering what he would order, as the bartender approached his location.

"Can I help you sir," asked the bartender. "My name is Luis. I would be happy to take your order." As he spoke, Luis dropped a small beverage napkin in front on hi, waiting for his order.

"Sure, let me have a Grey Goose martini, straight up with a twist and a menu."

"Sure, coming right up sir." The bartender walked toward the middle of the bar to make the drink, as Davis viewed the large mirror behind the bar. In it, he saw a man enter and take a seat at one of the small tables. He looked curiously

From a Vantage Point

out of place, with an ill-fitting suit, a garish tie, and a large, bushy moustache. At the same time, another man entered, taking a seat next to Davis at the bar.

"Jim," the man said, "How are you? Haven't seen you in a dog's age. What's new?" He leaned over to Davis and said in a subdued voice, "I'm Joe Lawson from DHS. The agency sent me to make sure everything was OK. I picked up this guy outside the building as you left, and followed him, and you, through the Metro to the hotel."

"Joe," Davis responded, "Glad to see you. Really didn't expect to see anyone during the day here. This place is usually very quiet. That's why I decided to come over after I got back this morning. How's the wife and kids?

"Everything's great Jim. We haven't had you over for a while. Must have been a long set of trips?"

"Yeah. I have been gone a lot. Me and the agency are a bit on the outs right now from my overseas travel. Things will get better hopefully. What have you been doing?"

"Not much actually. They put me on administrative duty a couple of months ago when I hassled an Arab at Dulles. You know how sensitive this administration is. They took me off the internationals and gave me a desk for a while writing policies. I guess that's OK, but it sure puts a crimp in the goodies coming home from overseas though."

Both men watched the mirror in their peripheral vision to see the reaction, and they got what they expected. The man was clearly listening to their conversation, took out his cell phone, and made a call. Then he stood up and left without making an order. The bartender, who had started over to where he sat was returning to the bar clearly miffed.

"Jim, it looks like he got what he wanted, so let's have a drink." announced Lawson as the man at the table left the hotel. The bartender came over and asked about a drink. Lawson replied, "Give me what Mr. Davis having, and put both drinks on my tab."

"Yes sir," responded the bartender, walking away to make the drinks.

Davis and Lawson had an animated conversation that lasted over an hour. It turned out that Lawson was the equivalent of an internal affairs officer of a local police department, sent by Alice Sawyer after the meeting to keep track of Davis, protecting him where he could.

On the road to West Virginia Driving out of Dulles Airport onto the toll road connecting the airport with the major routes, Will Johnson followed the signs over to Interstate 66, then headed west toward his home in West Virginia. Traffic was light going west, and he had the opportunity to think about his trip, and his excitement at seeing his friends. He also relived the confrontation with the woman in Khartoum, but did not know quite how to deal with or respond to it.

From a Vantage Point

As the afternoon progressed, he reached Interstate 81, the North-South route, turned south passing Strasburg, and the long trip down I-81 toward I-64, then local roads taking him across into West Virginia and home. Once he began to see large green fields and farm houses, he really felt he had returned. Now, hit was time to work on his cooperative project.

From a Vantage Point

Chapter 16 Follow-up

Hakim made a second call that morning from his room at their apartment in Khartoum. This time, the call was to the United States. He dialed a number on his burner phone to Atlanta Georgia. The phone rang for several seconds before someone picked up the receiver and answered.

"Salaam Hakim. What can I do for you?" came the voice on the phone in Atlanta. "May the wisdom of the Prophet be with you."

"May the Prophet be with you as well," answered Hakim. "The person we spoke of two days ago has begun his return to America. You will have your people watch and report on what he does, and I will give you further instructions on what we wish done with him. Make no effort to have him see or know any of you. Do you understand?"

"I do my friend," came the response, "I have someone, whom you know well, who works in a small town near this person's farm. He is nearby, and is ready to do as you wish."

"Good. I will tell you what to have him do. For now, all I want is for him to be watched."

"Understood."

"Good. We will speak later." Hakim finished the sentence and hung up the phone, not giving the person in Atlanta the time to respond. He turned off the cell phone, threw it in the trash and went over to a small desk in the room, opening the left upper drawer, taking out another phone, which he placed in his pocket. Completing what he had to do, Hakim walked back into the living room where Josh waited.

"Josh, I thought you were going out?" asked Hakim as he entered the living area.

"Decided to wait for you. That way we can go look together," Josh replied.

"Ok, let's do that. Anything else on your mind?" Hakim asked as they rose to leave.

"Nothing major. I am a bit concerned about our involving Will in all this. Our dedication to the cause involves us over here, and I'm not completely sure extending that to Will is a good idea."

They walked out into the morning air, and over to where they had parked their car, still talking quietly as they walked.

"So," asked Hakim, "What are your major objections?"

"Not sure I have major objections, my friend," responded Josh, "Just one of my uneasy feelings about all this. On the one side," he said as he entered the car, "This is a perfect scenario. We recruit someone completely away from our world, and include him in a major undertaking. That takes brass."

From a Vantage Point

"On the other hand," he continued as Hakim got in to drive, "We have the interest from Davis, and we're not sure how far that information may have gone. We might be walking eventually into a trap."

They drove down the narrow street, then onto a main road, having decided to look for a new apartment in another section of the city. After a few seconds, Hakim responded.

"Josh, we take chances all the time. Everything we do is dangerous. As far as the guy Davis is concerned, he is back in the United States, answering for having an affair with Fatima. He will be very busy for a long time. He won't have the time or chance to second guess us anymore."

"Wow Hakim. You outed your own cousin."

"One has to do what one has to do on occasion, Josh. She will be fine. They have nothing on her, and she will be back in their good graces soon. They need people such as her, since so few trust the Americans. We will shift to another shipper for a time, making an apparent clean break, and give her time to work her way back into their graces."

"What about Namers at the Embassy?" Josh asked.

"He has lost his eyes and ears, so he is the loser. We will slow some activities, and go black for a while. Let him wonder what we are doing. If we move quietly and slowly, we can stay under his radar. After all, his only connection to us is through Fatima, and he can't use her to get to us if she is under suspicion."

Hakim turned the car into an apartment complex just ahead, much newer than those where they had been living, and very close to a World Health Organization community health center. He pulled up outside the nearest building off the main street and stopped.

"Here is where we will soon live, at least until we leave for Pakistan," said Hakim as he opened the front door to leave.

"Pakistan?" responded Josh, "When are we going to Pakistan?"

"Right after we go to the United States for a short time. Let me correct that. Shortly after you go to the United States for a time, and return. Then we go to Pakistan."

"There are too many things I don't know Hakim? Is there a reason?"

"Again, my friend, the less you know about some things the better off we are. We will speak more of them later. Now let's go look for a place to live, shall we?"

Josh was leaving the front of the car as well, with a very puzzled, almost hurt look on his face, shaking his head, and seemingly deep in thought. Together, they walked toward the entrance of the first building to the right, just ahead of where they parked.

The building was tall, about 10 stories, with a driveway to what seemed to be a garage. They entered the wide doors at the entrance and came up to a desk

From a Vantage Point

where a young woman sat reading. She wore a grey *hijab* around her face and head, and was dressed in a colorful, but subdued dress, unusual, but not unknown in Yemen. It sufficed for the level of modesty expected among those who did not go out frequently in public. When she heard the two men coming toward her, she looked up and faced them.

"May I help you sirs?" she asked.

"Yes," answered Hakim, "I need to speak with Amal. Is he in? Please tell him Hakim al-Azahir would see him."

"I will see and give the message, sir. If you would please take a seat here," she responded, pointing to an area to her left with several chairs and a couch. Hakim and Josh walked over to the area she pointed out, and took seats.

The woman picked up a phone, and dialed a number. "Suleiman, is Amal back there. He has two guests," she said into the phone. "I see," she added, and hung up.

"Sirs," she said looking toward Hakim and Josh, "Amal will be with you in about five minutes. He is with someone, but he will be disturbed, and told you are here."

"Thank you," said Haim in response. "We will wait patiently."

"May I offer you some coffee? We have some excellent Turkish and I would gladly make it for you."

Both men answered together and declined, as they looked at the stack of magazines on a small coffee table in front of where they sat. Hakim picked up the *International Times* and Josh the *Economist*; both editions from the previous day, and started to read to pass the time.

From a Vantage Point

Chapter 17 Sammi

Will put his key to the door of his farmhouse, reached in and hit the light button on the wall to the right, turning on the living room lights. He entered the living room to find the house well-kept in his absence, and found a box of mail and magazines on the couch, to the left of the door.

A great pile of mail had accumulated during his absence, and he knew instinctively that his first two tasks for the morning were to go downtown to the store for groceries, and then sort the mail. Hopefully, he would find that his major bills had been paid, as he arranged before he left on his vacation. For now, he dropped his bags in the living room and went to the kitchen to make some coffee.

Elias, West Virginia is a small town nestled in the hills, and available through a county road that connects to the Interstate on the way to Wheeling. It has a few small shops, a restaurant, a gas station, and a church a short distance from town. The minister is also the owner of the gas station. Some families in town have lived there for generations; other are more recent arrivals, but they all enjoy the benefits and solitude of a small town.

Sammi Khan came from Pakistan, hoping to work for the railroad. He worked for several years for Norfolk-Southern, the largest of the railroads in the area, but then hurt his back, and could no longer do much heavy lifting. The railroad gave him a small disability pension, and Sammi moved to Elias, purchasing the local restaurant, which had been empty for over two years. It seemed that reopening the restaurant breathed new life into the town; people again had a place to congregate and talk over breakfast or coffee, and the ladies came in the afternoon, waiting for their kids to arrive on the school bus from a neighboring community. The bus stop was right in front of Sammi's restaurant.

Coming from a very poor section of Lahore, Sammi managed to get several years of schooling in the local Madrassa, eventually going to the local university, where he took courses in religion and philosophy. His aim once was to become an Imam, and help his people. Unfortunately for Sammi, his companions during his university years had different views of their future. They included Sammi in their ideas, and eventually a group of five went to Afghanistan to fight against the Russians, who had invaded some years earlier.

Sammi was not an overly religious man, even in the face of his earlier desire to become an Imam, but he did learn early to hate the Russians. Sitting outside a café one morning in Kabul, a group of Russians came into the café, and simply threw those sitting at the tables out, injuring several in the fracas during the expulsion of the locals. One of his friends went back to his living quarters, and brought back an AK-47 rifle, using it to kill the five Russian soldiers who had pushed the group out of the restaurant.

From a Vantage Point

When the Russians discovered who had done the killings, they found out who his friends were, arresting them all, including Sammi. Several days of beatings followed—torture really--until one of the men told the Russians where their friend fled. Rounding him up the next day, the Russians hauled his friends out into a courtyard near their makeshift prison in Kabul, and made them watch while he was brutally killed, then thrown into a pit and buried.

Two weeks later, a missionary family from England, who had worked in Afghanistan for many years, arranged for Sammi's exit visa from the country, sending him first to southeast England, the home of their missionary society, and then on the United States. One of their friends in Kabul, Hakim al-Azahir, made the introduction to Sammi, and they liked the young man from the first. A branch of their society arranged for Sammi to travel to Roanoke, Virginia, where he worked for the railroads for several years, until his injuries forced him to leave the railroad.

During that time, he had kept contact with the missionary society, who arranged to lease the former restaurant on the Main Street. Sammi paid back their investment within six months, as people in the local community flocked to the restaurant for his food and a place to meet with their neighbors.

One of these neighbors was Will Johnson, a young farmer with a checkered past, deserting from the military, but later returning to the community to farm, living quietly outside town. Gradually, he made Sammi's restaurant his place to stop while in town doing business, and the two men quickly became friends.

Will Johnson intended to walk his farm early the next morning, to be sure all was well. On his arrival home, he sat in an easy chair in the living room, quickly falling asleep, waking only the next morning from the sound rest he needed after the constant activity in the Middle East with his friends.

Looking at the clock on the mantle over the fireplace, he realized it was now 6 AM, and he still needed to walk the farm; something he did over the next hour, and was pleased at the work his friend Sammi at the restaurant had done while he was away. The local minister had suggested Sammi as the person to care for his farm, since, while Sammi was successful with the restaurant, and already had a reputation as a hard worker, someone to be counted on in the community, he needed the additional income as he paid back the missionary society.

Will and Sammi had met before Will's departure, agreed on terms and what needed to be done while Will was away. It was obvious to Will that the minister's references, and his own first impressions of confidence in Sammi had not been misplaced.

Shortly after his return from his walk, there was a knocking at his front door. Will, hearing the rapping from the kitchen where he was beginning to make breakfast with what was left in the refrigerator, walked over to the door, opened it, and saw Sammi in the doorway.

From a Vantage Point

"Welcome back, my friend," said Sammi as soon as the door opened. "I hope that everything is to your liking. I came every day, and saw to the herd as well," Sammi continued as he entered the living room.

"Everything is fine. The animals seem to have thrived. Thank you for the care you took while I was gone."

"No problem. That is what friends are for. I'm glad to be able to help. Was your trip successful?"

"It was," responded Will, "I had not seen my friends in some time. They were both doing well, and even with the uncertainty over there, they looked good, and in good spirits."

"Will you begin working on your cooperative idea now, then?" asked Sammi.

"I thought about that on the way home, Sammi," responded Will. "This is as good a time as any to begin to work on that plan. The farmers need it, and working out arrangements in the bigger cities is the way to go. I am sure of it. I will get a group together next week, and start to work with them to organize the cooperative."

"I am glad, my friend," countered Sammi, "These farms certainly need something, and you are the person to do it. When will you go to Washington to get the effort approved?"

"I think we will start more local first; perhaps Wheeling or Charleston, depending on what deals can be made. Then we will expand to the Washington area. That might take months, though. I want to be on firm ground as we expand, especially if we want to approach the Agriculture Department for their help."

"That is a good idea. Please let me know how I can help."

"I sure will Sammi," responded Will, "I'll see you in the morning. I need to go to town to buy groceries, and stop at the bank. Let's get together at your place for early lunch."

"Great Idea. It's on me. Welcome back," Sammi offered, he walked back through the doorway to the drive and his car.

Johnson started unpacking his carry bags and what little clothing he had left from his trip. It was unfortunate that the place he and his friends had stayed was destroyed but, as it seemed to him that was the way it was in that part of the world. Will unpacked his carry sack, finding the magazines he picked up in the airports. Among them was the magazine *Inspire* he found on the tabletop at the hotel room where he had stayed with Josh and Hakim, but had not yet had the chance to read.

With some time to spare before he went to town, Will picked up *Inspire* and started to read it. He quickly realized it was not what he expected, but still he continued to read it. The edition he picked up spoke of *dar-al-harb* (The land of War), and why Muslims around the world should join in the war against the non-Muslims—the infidels. Will knew very little about much of what was contained in the articles, since he was not Muslim, having been brought up a Christian, but it peaked his interest. He put the magazine away to read it later, and reminded himself to ask Sammi some questions about his readings as well.

Turning on the TV to catch some of the morning news, Will tuned to one of the DC stations, hoping to find out a bit of what was happening during his absence. He flipped the channels, until he arrived at CNN, then showing the mid-morning news.

"Good morning. This is Jack Ewing for CNN, reporting on an announcement coming from Sudan this morning about a drone strike in Khartoum several days ago, which apparently struck the wrong building, killing several families, mostly refugees from Lebanon. We are also reporting this morning on a new Obama initiative to reduce illegal immigration through education and compassion in Central American nations. Stay with us for the news happening now."

The pictures showing on the screen were virtual images of those Will had seen days earlier in Khartoum, in the block where his friends lived. He seemed to recognize several faces, including the woman who spoke with him at the site.

"CNN's sources in Khartoum indicate the use of an American drone aimed at a housing complex in downtown Khartoum three days ago. An entire city bloc, as you can see from the footage available, was leveled in the attack," said Ewing, as he returned to the screen after a commercial announcement.

"From what we know," Ewing continued. "There were several deaths, including two families with small children, a local religious leader, and a small shop selling groceries. Eleven people in the store at the time perished in the attack. Local medical personnel also confirmed at least forty people injured, although that number may rise as the building walls are removed in the coming days."

"Let's go to Samantha Carlson, on the scene from the Guardian-Mail newspaper in the UK, who was present at the time of the attack. Samantha, what happened here?"

"Well," responded Carlson, "It was mid-morning, and the people were out on the street doing errands, and buying groceries when a low whistle seemed to fill the air, and suddenly a huge explosion blew rock and dust through the streets, accompanied by the screaming of the injured, and those close to the injured. I was a corner of two small streets, which both collapsed, bringing people and rubble outward. I ducked into a passageway to avoid the shrapnel. Just as I entered a space, I saw a small boy, and grabbed him, pulling him in close to me. It probably saved his life."

From a Vantage Point

"Why here?" asked Ewing.

"Not really sure, Jack," responded Samantha. "The area is no hotbed of terrorism, or anything else for that matter. It is primarily a section where refugees from the Lebanese civil wars, and the latest Hezbollah-Israeli conflicts have come to live. People came here to work and be safe. Apparently, they are not though. We asked the government spokesman about their views, and all we get is a 'no comment'. It will take some time to sort this out."

"I do know one thing, though. In the minds of the people, at least as I hear it, the locals think this is yet another stupid act by the Americans without any real provocation, and designed only to hurt people who have no way to defend themselves. We are still waiting for the official government explanation, though."

"One final thought here. Many of these people, as I have said, come from Lebanon, and other points in the Middle East, usually as refugees from the fighting. Why they would come here, with its known al-Qaeda presence is a mystery. I asked several about this and they said they felt safer under the protection of the terrorists than either government in Lebanon or Sudan. What a commentary for the state of the society."

"Thanks Samantha. Now, on to other news. The President announced new initiatives today on immigration. There were also two important votes on the house floor today regarding the ongoing arguments of trade authority. Back in a moment with updates."

Will switched the channel again to see if other stations were carrying the same story on the situation in Sudan. Most seemed to be using the same footage. Turning the channel again, he found the local news, listening to it as he finished dressing, then had a cup of coffee before he left for town, and a visit to Sammi's for a late breakfast.

What Will did not know was Sammi's connection with Hakim and Josh. Hakim had been the real ringleader of the group who killed the Russians, not the man he turned in to them to escape more torture. Sammi regretted his act, but grew closer to Hakim, and to Josh, who had taught him how to use explosives, and fire a variety of weapons then in use in Afghanistan by the insurgent Mujahidin. Hakim used the knowledge of his act to draw him in further into their future plans.

When Hakim introduced Sammi to the missionaries, and heard that Sammi would be leaving for England, Hakim used him as a messenger to several small cells already organized in the south of England. Sammi brought diamonds sewn into the lining of his clothes, each near a button or snap to fool the customs people. When he was safely in the country, Sammi withdrew the diamonds, and arranged to meet those on a small list provided by Hakim, which he had carefully memorized.

Sammi heard nothing further from Hakim after his trip to England, until he was ready to move to Virginia under the sponsorship of the society. One of the missionaries, travelling to Kabul, had seen Hakim and mentioned Sammi's good fortune, giving him an address Hakim could use to contact his 'old friend'. Making good use of that information, Hakim arranged to have Josh travel to England and meet with Sammi, bringing instructions on who he was to contact when he reached Virginia. That contact, a person from Atlanta Georgia, was also a 'friend' of Hakim. Over time, as Sammi moved once again to Elias, his contact continued to provide information and instructions, including the assignment to monitor Will Johnson, his friend.

"Is all well?" asked the voice on the other end of the phone in the back office at Sammi's restaurant on Main Street. Sammi was in the office, listening to evening news, and the recent strikes in Sudan on CNN, when the phone rang. Sammi rose and closed the office door before answering.

"Yes, all is well," responded the restaurant owner, "Johnson returned today, and I saw him this afternoon. He will come to the restaurant tomorrow morning, and we will begin a conversation. Is that satisfactory?"

"What is satisfactory is the results, if they favor what we want to do. You know that. Report after he visits. I must contact our leaders with a response. It should be positive."

"I understand," Sammi answered quickly, though not fast enough to beat the sound of a disconnected call.

Still not completely sure of what he was supposed to do, Sammi sat back and thought about an earlier call, also from Atlanta, and about his friend Will Johnson.

Chapter 18 Interest at Langley

Jeff Namers remained unconvinced that his friend Jim Davis could have compromised their efforts. He was determined to use what resources he had to exonerate him, even if it meant problems with the Agency. He put the small technology staff he had to work trying to get a lead on Hakim, asking them to isolate cell phone traffic from burner phones, and see what they could find for locations and information.

In at least one way, his staff succeeded in locating several calls from burner phones, each with sequential telephone numbers, and all purchased from the same firm—Ahmad Shipping in Khartoum.

"Damn," said Namers as he heard the news," How could these guys be so stupid?" Then, it came to him. Fatima gave Hakim the phones, who used them once, or perhaps twice, and then discarded them to prevent tracing of his calls. The sequential numbers, though, stood out like a sore thumb, with only one or two calls not keeping to the sequence. These phones must have been used by Fatima, Namers thought. He made a mental note to ask her when he brought her in for questioning the following day.

In the meanwhile, Namers had his people work with their counterparts at the National Security Agency to trace the usage of the phones, and began to get a feel for the patterns they represented. The first several phone calls, originating in Khartoum, were used in the area where he knew Hakim and his friend Josh lived, before the drone attack, and then followed a pattern of their probable movements around the city and into the countryside. The last call they could trace was made just a few hours before, and came from the Place of the Dove Restaurant on the edge of the old part of the city. Namers had been there many times himself.

A prior call had also been made with another phone at an apartment complex not far from the Place of the Dove. Namers noted the location, and decided to send one of his locals to check it out. Looking at the tracing pattern on the screen, Namers also noted several calls from an apartment building about a mile away from the area of the restaurant. At this location, several calls had been made, each with a different phone, and one to the United States.

"Gotcha," yelled Namers. "Get the info on the phone call; the one to Atlanta, Georgia. Ask NSA to give us what they know. I want to know who received the call," barked Namers to the IT staff member.

"Sure Jeff, but what do I tell them?"

"Tell them we've got an active terrorist. Give them Hakim's name, and ask them for the linked calls to whoever he called in Atlanta. Tell them we need it post-haste. We finally have a chance to get this guy for real."

"OK, understand all that, but I have to go through Langley."

"No problem. Just tell them what I told you, and if they have concerns, have them call me here."

Namers turned and walked from the room, feeling elation he had not had in a long time. In the back of his mind, he felt that getting Hakim would aid considerably in proving that his friend Jim Davis was not involved in any plot. They had worked together too long for him to believe the charges against his friend.

It took less than two minutes to compose and send a secure message to Langley asking for the information Namers wanted. The IT staff member composed it carefully, as Namers had requested, hoping to get the widest possible information search and return with cooperation from NSA for the data search. That should be no problem, since the drone strike put Hakim and his friends at the top of the interest lists at most of the intelligence agencies and working groups.

>
> FR NAMERS KHARTOUM
> OPS (SPEC ACT) LANGLEY
> SUBJ: Hakim al-AZAHIR
>
> Need info on telcom traffic, phone number xxx-xx-xxxx-x this AM. Bundle:61-5AH, PKG:514-555-B. Origination, Khartoum. Destination, Atlanta GA, recipient unknown.
>
> Request trace of message, and call tree (Domestic/International) for period following call, and similar trace for any previous calls from Khartoum.
>
> Azahir know to use burner phones in sequence. Other calls expected from closely aligned numbers.
>
> ADVISE
> NAMERS, CHIEF

With the message out, they could only wait to see what the trace would provide.

The drive into town was short, and Will enjoyed looking at the scenery as he moved along in his small Dodge Pickup truck. He took the truck this morning so he could get groceries, along with some equipment he needed for work on the farm. Sammi had left him a list of what repairs were needed, and they all meant small parts, nails, boards, and other items he could get a Harry's Hardware on Main Street.

From a Vantage Point

    Ahead, as he reached the crest of a small hill, he could see Elias in the distance. It was truly a small town—the entire population could not be more than 500 people, plus those on the outlying farms. He knew many of these people, worked with them on community activities, and felt they were his extended family. Shortly, as he began work on his farm cooperative project, he would get to know even more of them, particularly those on the farms furthest from town.

    The country road began to widen a bit as he came closer to town, and turned into Main Street (Actually the only major street in the town). Both sides of Main Street shad small, antiquated brick buildings, some with dates going back to the late 1800's. There were also several newer buildings, but none newer than probably 1960, and all not more than two stories. The single exception was the Beaumont Hotel, named after its founder Charles Beaumont, who came to the state to find coal, and instead became a hotel owner after he was injured in the mines.

    Will drove along Main Street, eventually pulling over to the right side of the street, into one of the diagonally marked parking spaces in front of Sammi's Restaurant, and stopping in front of a parking meter. The metering system was somewhat new; parking cost a quarter for four hours. If you stayed longer, you were expected to put another quarter in a box, placed periodically along the sides of the street. There were no tickets, and no police officers walking along writing them.

    Every Friday morning, a clerk from the town hall would go out and collect the extra money in the boxes. Sometimes, he would come back with as much as five dollars in quarters, but usually it was less. People parked and then drove on; if they stayed longer they would pay the box. The whole situation was interesting, since people could put more money in the meter, but most chose to pay the box when late, if they were, and even, on occasion, added additional money.

    Will put his quarter in the meter, and walked directly into Sammi's Restaurant, taking a seat at a small table near the front window, where he could look out and see people walking through town. Mack Burnett and his wife, both farmers just outside of town, sat at the table next to him, and similar small groups of people were at other tables, all waiting for the great food Sammi provided.

    Sammi was in the kitchen working with the cook when Will arrived, but looked out through the open space behind the counter connecting the dining room to the kitchen, and saw Will come in.

    "Hello, Will," yelled Sammi through the open space. "Be right out as soon as we get these meals for the folks done." Sammi sounded just like a native West Virginian, something he felt good about. Will could see Sammi periodically place plates of food on the shelf above the counter, and looked around the restaurant, realizing the fairly large number of patrons this morning. One of them, toward the back, waved at Will and shouted welcome back, before returning to his breakfast.

Sammi came through the kitchen door with a rush. He had on a spattered white bib apron on, mostly from cracking eggs. He had told Will once that his worst effort in the kitchen was cracking eggs, getting everything in the mixing bowl, and not have the shells go with the rest of the egg.

"Will, I am glad you came. Is this your first stop?" asked Sammi in a rush.

"Sort of my friend. Next stop is Harry's for the supplies I need. Thanks for the list. I added a couple of things as well for the house. Not in a real hurry though. Thought I would have a breakfast-lunch and then go do my errands."

"Great, let me get you some coffee? Black, or with sugar?"

"Black will be fine," responded Will, and Sammi left to grab a cup next to a large coffee urn, then pour out some regular coffee. He also grabbed a spoon and a napkin from the stacks next to the urn and returned to Will's table, placing the items before him.

Sitting down across from Will, Sammi spoke, "Happy to be back? You still look tired, you know."

"I am happy to be back among my friends. It was an interesting trip into literally another world. Seeing Qatar, and then Sudan, was eye opening, at the least. I had no idea of that part of the world. All we ever hear is 'the third world' or the 'middle east'. Qatar is desert, but its cities are large and modern, with skyscrapers larger than our own. Sudan is more picturesque, but much more dangerous. The building where I was staying was bombed while I was there. Lost all my clothing and other stuff."

Will rattled on about ten minutes about the cities, the people, the villages, and anti-American feelings, especially in Sudan. Finally, he stopped, as if to take a real breath, and picked up his coffee.

"You were actually in a bombing area, Will?" asked Sammi, astonished. "What did you think of it?"

"It's hard to describe Sammi. I can still see the pictures vividly in my mind of the destruction, and the people milling around who had lost everything. I guess what bothered me the most was that buildings had large numbers of Lebanese refugees living there. My family came from Lebanon. I met an old woman who said she came from the same village as my father. Imagine that?"

"There are many with no homes due to bombings and other things in wars Will. It is a fact of life. In my own country, and Afghanistan especially, we have some who fought to free the country, first from the Russians and then the Americans. They don't get to see the good things in the world as do you and I, only the misery of war." Sammi sat back in his chair, appearing to be thinking about other places and times.

From a Vantage Point

"You are right Sammi. The people I saw, especially the woman and her family, are Maronite Christians, as was my family. I always thought this war was a fight for Islam among the fanatics."

"There are many kinds of fanatics, Will. We must talk about that more some time. In the meanwhile, what would you like for breakfast?"

"Wow, I almost forgot about that. How about one of your cheese omelets with home fries and toast. Make it wheat toast."

"Coming right up," responded Sammi, as he rose to go back to the kitchen. Will noticed a local newspaper on the table next to him, probably left by a prior customer, and he picked it up to read the latest news of Elias.

US Embassy, Khartoum, Sudan Two days later in Khartoum, the cyber room at the Embassy came alive as an 'Eyes only" message came in over the secure network from Langley. Three of the IT staff stood around as the message printed out. When it was complete, one of the staff took it immediately to Jim Namers. Hopefully, it was what he wanted.

        EYESONLY—EYESONLY—EYES-ONLY
FRM OPS (LANGLEY)
TO; STACHIEF KHARTOUM
SUBJ: HAKIM AL-AZAHIR

....

From a Vantage Point

TAKE ACTION AND NOTIFY THIS OFC.

CHIEF,

Namers looked at the message, shook his head, and threw it in the shredder. "What a bunch of fools," he mumbled to himself. "How can anyone take action on something unreadable." He made a mental note to call Langley directly, something he did, loudly, within the hour. By early afternoon, another message arrived, this time un-redacted.

Chapter 19 Widening the Net

Khartoum, Sudan Josh and Hakim entered the Place of the Dove and looked to find a table out of the main part of the restaurant. They found one over to the side of the bar, and took it, looking around for a waiter. A young man in traditional Sudanese clothes, with a red fez on his head came from the shadows and stopped at their table.

"May I help you sirs?" asked the boy.

"Are you our waiter," asked Josh, incredulous that such a young boy was waiting tables.

"I am sir. This is my family's restaurant, and I help out here. What can I get for you?"

Hakim responded first. "I will have a *Guhwah* with sugar, no milk. Do you know if Ahmad is here as well?"

Guhwah is pan-toasted, ground coffee prepared with spices (usually cloves) and served from a 'Jebena', a special coffeepot.

"Ahmad is here, sir."

"Good," Hakim interrupted, "Please tell him I wish to buy some American wine."

"I will, sir," the boy responded, as he turned to Josh. "And you sir?"

"I will have the same, with no sugar, if you please."

"I will be happy to get those for you. This is our menu, if you wish food later in your visit."

Having taken the order, the boy disappeared again into the shadows to get their drinks. Just as he did, a cell phone in Hakim's packet rang.

"Yes," responded Hakim, then added, "I see," and hung up.

Shortly after the call, a man came up to their table and stopped. "I understand you wish some American wine, sir? I am Ahmad at your service."

Hakim looked up and seemed to recognize the man. "Do I know you?"

"Sir, I am Khalil Ahmad, owner of this place. My sister, Fatima introduced you to me many years ago. We are kinsman, although we have not had the opportunity to know each other. I hope that will change, now that you have come to see me."

"I should have known," responded Hakim, as he rose, and embraced his kinsman. "You are the image of your father. It is sad we have not had the opportunity to know each other. Please sit with us for a moment. I have something I would like you to do for me, after we get to know ourselves more."

Namers read through the un-redacted message, realizing quickly that he had a gold mine of information. Not only that, the message from Langley gave

From a Vantage Point

him a virtual grid of calls from a series of numbers on either side of the last cell phone number used by Hakim, the dates the calls were made, the destination of the calls, the length of the calls, and other meta-data useful in tracing his whereabouts and who he conferred with over time. His instructions were clear.

Pulling out both a map of the Sudan region, and one for the city, Taping them up on his white board, Namers started to mark the location and date of the calls, and the phone number Hakim used. Within the hour, he had a roadmap of where he had been in the country.

Then, something struck him like a thunderbolt. One of the phones had been used at an apartment complex just a week ago, before the drone strike, and another phone used two days later close by the area of the strike. However, yet another phone, with two others, had been used two blocks over, and for more than one call. That could only mean the drone strike hit the wrong location. Despite the Agency's best efforts, they used faulty information for a strike that killed numbers of people, but not Hakim.

Looking further at the list, Namers saw that another phone had been used out in a village about 30 miles from the city at about the exact time the strike was occurring. Could it have been that Hakim knew about the strike in advance? But how? He would have to find out. One thing was sure; Davis knew nothing in advance about the strike, so he could not have leaked the information.

Elias, West Virginia The *Elias Courier* came out three days a week, and generally was about 6 pages, partly ads, and the rest local news. The big story in this edition was the local hog auction on the upcoming Saturday, and the participation of the local 4-H Club in that event. There was also a birth on page 4, a son to a local farmer, and on page 2 a short story about Will coming home from a vacation overseas. There was not much to the story, and it did not mention where he had been; only that he had been gone three weeks, and the community welcomed him back. A bit embarrassed, but also pleased, Will put down the paper as he heard a commotion on the other side of the kitchen door, and expected Sammi to be flying through with his breakfast.

Not to be disappointing, Sammi came bursting through the door, both hands full of food, and a big smile on his face.

"Will, I made this breakfast myself. You will love it. See, I made you a three-cheese omelet, fresh cooked home fries with onion, and wheat toast. I also have some butter, jam for the toast, ketchup for the home fries, and everything else you need is on the table." Sammi took great pride in his cooking, and the beam in his face, showed it well.

"Sammi, this all looks great. I can't tell you how I have missed this kind of a meal. What you get overseas is just not the same. I'm glad to be home."

"Well then, enjoy, my friend," responded Sammi. "I will be back in a few minutes and we can talk some more. Let me go see the new customers first."

Five or six tables had filled with customers since Will arrived, and Sammi liked to walk around and greet each person as they came in. Today, working in the kitchen, he had to settle for walking to the tables to greet them. Some were simply locals whom he greeted by name, asked if all was well, and then passed on to those he did not know.

One customer, over in a corner toward the back wall, was sitting reading the *Charleston Gazette*, which he probably got from the rack outside the restaurant. Sammi had both the Charleston and Wheeling papers, along with the *New York Times* and *USA Today* in the newspaper dispensers each morning. Some were delivered very early, before he opened, and the *Times* and *USA Today* came around 9 AM. Those papers, along with the local news, which he had for free on the counter inside, gave everyone who wanted news their own brand of journalism. Most took the local paper.

The man, who looked to be in his early forties, was reading and occasionally sipping from a cup of coffee at his table. As Sammi arrived near him, he looked up.

"How is everything, sir," asked Sammi.

"Just fine," responded the diner. "Your coffee is great and I look forward to my meal."

"Has it been long, I will check for you?"

"No need. I just put the order in. Your server is excellent. She left me to read the paper with my coffee, and came back just moments ago to take my order. Is your restaurant like this every day?"

"Most days, in the early morning until noon it is, then things get a bit quiet until the late afternoon and evening, after people finish their work on the farms. Then we get busy again."

"Well I hope you enjoy your meal. If there is anything I can do for you, please do not hesitate to ask me or the server. We are here for you. We want you to come back again."

"Thank you," responded the diner. "I'm sure everything will be just fine."

Sammi walked toward the next table, but had a sudden feeling that he either knew the person he just met, or something. He could not put his finger on why he had the feeling. He shrugged it off and walked around the restaurant, greeting the rest of the customers, and eventually went back to the kitchen to help with meals.

Khartoum, Sudan Assembling his small group in a conference room, Namers outlined the information he had received, and what he felt it meant. Still, he needed more information.

From a Vantage Point

"Gentlemen, look at the maps I taped to the wall here. On the left, a larger map of Sudan, and to the right, a close-in map of Khartoum and the surrounding villages. The marks on the maps are locations where specific cell phones have been used over the past several weeks. I believe these cell phones belong to Hakim al-Azahir and his associate Josh Giddons. The numbers represent burner phones used on specific dates. I also believe these phones came from a purchase made through Ahmad Shipping here in the city."

"There are some we need to confirm, and others where we need to know with whom he spoke, and why. This is our first real opportunity to get something concrete on this guy and I don't want to lose it. We will need to bring in a few of the trusted locals on this, but I want them to know only the bare minimum. They go out to get information and bring it back. That is all they do."

"Use only those you completely trust," Namers continued, "and then apply the 50% rule. Assume that one or more is a double. We cannot take chances that Hakim is alerted to our interest. He certainly knows we are after him, but I don't want him to assume we are actively pursuing beyond our usual efforts."

"Stay away from Fatima Ahmad and her company. I will deal with her myself. Now, let's look at the maps." Namers walked over close to the larger map on the left, and pointed to a notation over a small village about two hours out of Khartoum.

"Billy, this village," continued Namers, "is where they went the morning of the drone strike. I want to know who and why they went there."

"OK Jeff, will do," responded his team member.

"Jack, the morning of the drone strike, Hakim received a call about two hours before the attack at their apartment. We know the number of the caller, but no any other information. Can you use your contact at the phone exchange to get something for us?"

"Sure Jim, assuming it was not another burner phone."

"Fair enough," responded Namers. "Watts, I want you to concentrate on the Khartoum map, and particularly the area of the strike. We see calls from the strike zone before the attack, and then new calls, with different phones after the strike. Get me what you can on where they went, where they might be living, and who they talked to."

"That's a tall order Jeff. Especially with burn phones."

"Do what you can. Right now, we have nothing but numbers. We need to put names and faces where we can. Use locals where possible, and stay out of the sunlight yourselves. Let's meet again tomorrow afternoon with an update on what we have."

Namers scratched a note on his pad to call Fatima on the burner phones. Then he changed his mind, scratched it out, and decided they would meet instead. A discrete message through one of his locals was just the thing, he decided. It could wait though, until he heard from the others.

The other items he saved for himself were the two calls made to Atlanta, Georgia; one from Hakim's apartment and the other through a burner phone. For that information, he needed to call Langley. He knew the exact person to call to get the information—Sarah Minihan.

Jeff Namers always liked talking to Sarah. She had a straight way of working with the desk officers, and always responded quickly to his requests. Importantly, she was married to Bernie Minihan, his old friend and classmate at the Basic School. He looked forward to their conversation.

Elias, West Virginia Will Johnson finished his meal and rose to leave, dropping some money for his food on the table, and yelled into the kitchen to Sammi that he would see him after his trip to the hardware store. Sammi waved from the kitchen, and Will went on his way to Harry's. The gentleman at the table in the back looked up from his paper, saw Will leave, and went back to reading the sports section.

A few minutes later, Sammi again emerged from the kitchen with plates of food, this time headed for the gentleman reading the paper, stopping in front of the table, in preparation for placing the plates and condiments where it would be convenient for the customer.

"Your breakfast sir," said Sammi. The man looked over from the paper.

"Oh, yes. Place it anywhere. Thank you. Might I also have more coffee as well?"

"Of course, sir," responded Sammi, waving to the server who already had a coffee pot in her hand to come to the table. She walked over and refilled the cup, then left.

"Is there anything else you require?"

"No," responded the customer. "Not right now. This will be fine." Sammi walked toward the front of the restaurant to greet some other customers. Suddenly, as he walked, it came to him. *The voice, it was the voice I have heard before.*

A sense of fear came over Sammi as the recognition of who this customer was sank into his brain. *This is the guy from Atlanta that has called me before. What does he want? He told me to look for Will and I am doing that. Why is he here?*

"Hello Harry. Long time no see," announced Will as he entered the hardware store.

From a Vantage Point

"Long time Will. How was your vacation? See some interesting parts of the world? I was thinking about you earlier. Some guy came in I had never seen before and asked about you. Told him you were out of town. Missed you."

"I was until; yesterday Harry. Just got back last evening from Africa. Great trip. How's the family?"

"Just fine. Everybody healthy and the kids are in school. What could be better? Say, now that you are back are we going to get back on track on the cooperative? Lot of people asking."

"Sure am. Aside from some supplies, that's what I wanted to come talk about. I thought about it a lot on the trip. We need to have a meeting early next week, get an idea of what we want to offer, and how much we think we can bring to the table. Then I will go to Charleston to speak with the extension people on setting up the organization. Last time I was there they were telling me about some people at the Department of Agriculture in Washington that could help. Do you think we are ready?"

"I sure do Will. We already have several of the farmers going out of town into Virginia to farmer's markets and such. We could do much more if we were organized."

"My thought as well, Harry. Could you arrange with the Elks Hall for a meeting next week?"

"Sure will. My best guess is Tuesday evening. That's the day nothing much is happening. I'm sure they will give us the hall. They wanted to be involved as a sort of community project for them."

"OK. Let me know and the guy over at the paper as well. He can get the notice out. Thanks for all your help on this."

"What helps the community helps me Will. They spend more when they have more, and they grow more when they can afford the seeds. Once in a while I even get paid on time. Before you forget, where's your list?"

"Right here, Harry. I can pick it up later. I need to spend some time with Sammi on this as well." Will gave Harry the list, who looked it over and put it on the counter.

"Got everything you need. Should have it all packed up in about two hours. That OK?"

"Sure Harry. Take your time. I'm enjoying being in town."

"All right then. See you in a couple hours. Bring me a coffee when you come back if you would?"

"You've got it Harry. By the way, who was asking about me?"

"Some guy, never saw him before. Looked like a foreigner. Suit and tie, and a big moustache. Seemed to just be passing through."

"Don't know anybody who looks like that so I guess we will meet if we meet. Thanks again Harry."

From a Vantage Point

"See you later Will." Harry waved as Will left to walk along the street, talk to a few people, and then cross the street to walk back to Sammi's restaurant.

Finally, as the early breakfast crowd left, Sammi looked out from the kitchen and saw only one table still occupied; the one with the guy whose voice he remembered. Sammi left the kitchen and walked up to the table.

"Sir, have we met before?"

"Sit down, Sammi. We have not met, but we have spoken before."

"Why are you here? I am doing as you asked."

"I wanted to see for myself," said the man in the suit with the large moustache—the same man who had gone over to Harry's Hardware first asking about Will. "This is a very nice town. I have enjoyed coming here. What do you have to tell me?"

"Will Johnson will be back shortly. We will talk about his experiences. That is all I am supposed to do is it not?"

"Yes, you are to report on him, and then I will tell you what else I need. Do you have any other questions?"

"No sir," responded Sammi.

"Good, then I will leave and return to my home. You have a nice restaurant and good food. Do a good job for me as well." The man rose to leave, and waited a moment or two, as he saw Will emerging from the hardware store, and turn left to walk down the street. The man then went through the front door to his car, and quickly drove away down Main Street.

Sammi sat down at the table the man had left and put his head in his hands—shaking from fear, knowing that Will would return shortly.

CIA-Langley. McLean Virginia Sarah Minihan was at her desk in Langley, eating some peach yogurt, which she seemed to love when she was pregnant—as she was now by seven months—when the phone rang.

"Special Ops, this is Sarah Minihan. Can I help you?"

"Sarah, Jeff Namers in Khartoum. Costs a lot of money to have you answering the phone."

"Hi Jeff. Well, Bernie is out, as is our secretary, and the other desk officers are in a meeting on something. I'm not really sure what, and Sheila is meeting with the Ops Director. So, you have me. What can I do for you?"

"Social time first. How are you?"

"Feeling great. Very large. This kid kicks like a bull, and I'm eating gallons of yogurt. How's that for an update? By the way, don't you owe me a shawl?"

"Guilty. I will get it out today. I did promise that a short while ago, didn't I?"

"Sure did. Almost a year ago to be exact. I'm sure that is not why you called. Always happy to hear from you, by the way."

"No, it's not why I called, but I'm glad you reminded me. Did you see the message traffic a couple of days ago on a call from Hakim al-Azahir to someone in Atlanta from a burner phone?"

"Sure did. We had a real time trying to trace that phone call. It was burner to burner, but we picked up the call from a transatlantic node that bounced through Brazil, then Mexico, and into the US grid. That allowed us to trace the IP address to a location in Atlanta. I have that info right here. Sorry, I thought we sent it to you. Let me see. Here it is."

"The phone was purchased in a small convenience store in Atlanta and activated, along with another phone bought at the same time by the same person. He purchased the phones with a debit card drawn on an Atlanta bank, with the name Jamil Ashran. The card and account are real. We are looking into who really owns the accounts now," Sarah continued.

"We have a driver's license on the guy from Georgia Motor Vehicles, with a picture and ran it through the system. The real name is Jamil Ahmad. He is a Sudanese who lawfully immigrated three years ago, and has lived at the same address since. He works for Georgia Power as a grid technician. We have no record of any arrests or contact with local police. Sending all of this to you now."

"Got it. Thanks, "responded Namers, "An interesting character by the look of the picture. That's some moustache. Anything else on the phones?"

"Only that the first phone was used just one time after the call came in from Sudan, and then probably disposed of later. A call was made to a person in West Virginia about a week ago. Nothing on the first phone after that. The second phone was used in West Virginia—a little town out there—Elias—yesterday, and then went off the grid about an hour later."

"Do we know to who?"

"We know the call on the first phone was made to a restaurant—Sammi's Restaurant—in Elias, West Virginia. It's a small town outside Charleston. The single call on the second phone went to a burner. We can give you the number, but our FBI trace is getting nowhere. Will keep you informed if they get anything."

"OK Sarah. Got it all. Will let you know what else I might need from this end. We might have to get Bernie's Task Force involved here. Not sure yet. How is Bernie, by the way?"

"Bernie is fine. He misses Rex still, and they brought Sheila Williamson in to be Director, Ops, as you know, after Bridgett retired. He spends a lot of time in meetings, and misses the field. He loves the kids, and at least has time to play with them, on occasion. All's right with the world."

"You sound down. Everything OK?"

"Sure. It's just the weather and the baby kicking, and the office, and even the yogurt tastes terrible today. Woman stuff. Anything else I can do for you?"

From a Vantage Point

"No, just take it easy. I should be over there in about three weeks for Rex's memorial. It's about time for my trip to the company. "

"It is. Bernie and I were just talking about that the other day. We wanted to have a memorial for Rex, but have been holding it up until your class gets here, since he was closest to you all. Don't even think of not coming."

"I'll be there, don't worry. Besides, I want to see the kids. Got to go. I have a meeting waiting myself. Take care Sarah."

"You too Jeff," Sarah answered as she hung up the phone.

As he hung up the phone, a flash went through Jeff Namers' brain—AHMAD—Jamil Ahmad. He thought about Fatima Ahmad, Kahlil Ahmad. "Of course," he said to himself, "Must be the same family," making a mental note to speak with Fatima soonest.

From a Vantage Point

Chapter 20 New Awakenings

Will Johnson walked along Main Street, enjoying being back in his home town and looking forward to his next adventure to create a cooperative for the farmers. He had thought a great deal about the cooperative effort during his trip, and wanted to get moving on it before the planting season went too far this year. His goal was to have produce for the market this year, if possible.

To do that, he needed members, and Sammi and Harry were working hard to make that happen. Sammi had already had two meetings in the evening at his restaurant, and Harry, active in many community organizations, talked it up to the farmers frequently at the extension service meetings occurring throughout the area.

Now it is time to put it all together, thought Will, as he crossed the street, barely missing a dark blue car moving quickly past him. Will looked inside and saw a man with a bushy moustache, but had little time to really get a good look. The car sped down Main Street and out of town.

Wonder where he is from, thought Will, looking at the out-of-state plate, but not getting a clear look. It had to be out-of-state, since it was not the distinctive blue and yellow of the West Virginia plate. Looking up the sidewalk, he saw Sammi sanding outside, waiting for him.

"Have to be careful crossing the street these days, I guess Will. That guy was speeding though," Said Sammi.

"Sure was. Where are the cops when you need one?" responded Will, using an old cliché. Both men laughed.

"Come on in, and have some more coffee," responded Sammi. Will caught up to where Sammi was standing and they both went inside. Will took his usual seat, and Sammi brought coffee and two cups, then sat down.

"Quiet today?" asked Will.

"Sure is. We have these days occasionally, especially during planting. People stay home to work, and I get bored. It will pick up at lunch. Gives us some time to talk though."

"That's great," responded Will. "We need to move on the cooperative. I asked Harry to arrange with the Elks Club for a meeting next week, possibly Tuesday evening. Harry seemed to think that might be the best day."

"I agree Will. That is a quiet day, and more likely we will have people coming out, assuming the meeting is early. What do you plan to offer them?"

"Well Sammi, I thought about this a lot during my visit overseas. Right now, we have a bunch of individuals taking produce to local farmer markets outside the area on their own. From what some have said, they get mixed results, and they have no way of knowing what people might buy. My thought is to bring as many together as possible, especially those with differing produce, with a unified

From a Vantage Point

approach to the farmer markets, and to the towns in the outside area—say under 100 miles to start. We could offer the small towns a good deal on produce for their schools, and shelters. We could also offer competitive rates, for the stores outside the farming areas, for fresh delivered produce. We split up the deliveries among the members so everyone has a place on the schedule for delivery of their goods."

"We would need a central place to collect, process, and ship produce," Will continued, "With parking for pickups, and perhaps a small store for the locals, although I would be open to simply supplying the local market, and have our price go down a bit in the area. Just a lot of thoughts, I think, that need refining and discussion, as well as commitment."

"It sounds like a good plan Will," offered Sammi. "It will be important to get the local stores to support this, and not feel we are putting them out of business, possibly. I think we can work that issue easily, though."

"Good, I'm glad you like what I have thus far. I will work out a written plan for next week, and get it back to you to read beforehand. Is there anything else you think I should consider?"

"Only the next steps after that. Where do you plan to try to take this? How far might we go before we strain our resources too far?"

"Not sure on that. I need to go to DC sometime soon to speak with the Agriculture people. The guy I talked to early on said there were programs where Agriculture would pick up some goods themselves, if we gave them a reasonable price. I want to pursue that. I agree, though, that we can only go so far with our small undertaking, without outside assistance. I will speak to the future, but had not wanted to put it in a plan yet."

"I think you are right there," said Sammi. "Don't raise people's expectations before we have something more solid to give them. Good plan, drink your coffee."

Will took several short sips of the coffee, and then turned to Sammi and said, "I need to discuss two things before I take the trip back to the farm, if you have time."

"Sure, ask away," responded his friend. "What do you need to know?"

"The note you left me on the fence over near the grove. Does it need fixing right now; or can it wait?"

"Well, on that, I suggest you fix it as soon as possible. Your cows don't really go over there, but that is one of your log and wire fences for keeping the outside critters from getting in. My suggestion is to fix it before the weather turns."

"OK, I can buy that," responded Will. "My other question is about this mess I saw while in Khartoum. One thing I really don't understand is how so many of these groups are fighting each other, AND those they perceive as their enemy—

From a Vantage Point

usually at the same time. You were in Pakistan and Afghanistan; why do they do that?"

"That's not an easy question Will," said Sammi, sitting back on his chair and alternating from looking at Will and toward the front of the restaurant. "The main groups fighting right now, al-Qaeda if you want a name, believes it is fighting for Islam. They call it Jihad, and believe in it strongly."

"I understand some of the sense of Jihad," Will broke in, "I started to read a magazine I found in Khartoum. But why fight their own people?"

"Will, as I said the answer is not an easy one," Sammi continued, "First there are extremists in any society—those who believe that only their views are the correct ones and they follow those ideas, often in conflict. In this case, they think their conflict is with the United States and its allies, but they also are fighting what they see as a holy war beside. That part of the conflict is often against anyone who does not agree with their religious principles. In Islam, there are many beliefs, both religious and cultural; some arise from the days after the Great Prophet Muhammed died, and conflicts arose over his successors. Today, we have Sunni and Shia for that very reason, and they disagree, often violently, with each other."

"That's OK, I guess," responded Will. "Let me give you a specific example. You may have seen on the news a drone attack, supposedly by the US against an apartment complex in Khartoum a few days ago. I saw the damage, and spoke to some of the people, none of whom were Islamic; most, in fact were Lebanese Christians. A number were killed, many injured, and all had no place to live. The news says the government was going after known terrorists."

"They probably thought they were, Will," offered Sammi, "Sometimes from the news it seems that the US has bundled everyone that looks Arab together, and considers them all terrorists and fair game. I really don't know. All I do know is what I see on the news. Killing is cheap these days on both sides."

"Probably so," answered Will, "but it bothers me that these people in Khartoum may have been some of my relatives—those who were driven from their country by the civil wars and the terrorism like my family. There is a large number of Lebanese refugees in Sudan, where they thought they could work and not be bothered. As an old woman said to me, they know the dangers of war, but being in Sudan was less dangerous to them than Lebanon, their own country."

"As I said, Will, it is a long, complex situation in that part of the world. There are no ready answers or solutions, and people so mistrust each other, or are religiously in opposition, the slightest pretext can cause fighting. The US doesn't care about the Arabs fighting among themselves, and they spend precious little time trying to figure out the good people from the bad people. That's the way war works."

"I guess so my friend, but the whole thought of it stinks."

"Drink your coffee Will. We will speak some more about this if you wish. We will not solve it today, or even tomorrow. Right now, the cooperative is more important."

"Agreed. Thanks for the coffee. And the conversation."

Will was still clearly puzzled, and decided rather than prolong the conversation, he would simply enjoy being back home, leaving serious thought for later. He looked up and out toward the street, watching people as they moved along the sidewalks, some going into Harry's or one of the other small shops, and could not help but think of the small shop area destroyed near his friends' apartment. In his mind were vivid memories of the destruction, and the faces of the people whose livelihoods had been shattered in moments by a bomb.

What did they do to deserve that treatment, Will asked himself, *Why them and not those who are the warmakers?* Returning to his coffee and current reality, Will shrugged off his thoughts and simply tried to enjoy the company of his friends and surroundings.

The man with the moustache drove several miles out of town, eventually pulling over to a small gas station, with a diner attached, and just a few cars outside. It looked to be a quiet place to stop. He pulled up to the pump, had the attendant fill the tank, and paid cash. Then he pulled over to the parking area, and left his car to go into the diner, which turned out to have only one customer, an older man in farmer's overalls, with a beat-up baseball cap. He entered and took a seat at a table near a window so he could look outside.

"How are you doing, stranger?" asked a waitress arriving at his table. "Can I give you a menu?" she asked, laying one on the table.

"Coffee please, strong and black," Came the response from the stranger.

"Sure, coming up," responded the waitress, who then walked back to the counter, fetched a coffee mug and saucer, poured the coffee from an urn, and brought it back to the customer's table, along with a napkin and spoon.

"Do you need cream? Sugar is on the table," said the waitress, suddenly remembering that the customer had asked for black coffee. "Will you be eating with us today?"

"I have to make a phone call, and will look at the menu afterward. Thank you for the coffee." The customer pulled a phone from his pocket, giving the waitress a cue to leave him to make his call.

"Take your time sir. I'll be back after you make your call."

"Thank you," responded the customer as the waitress left.

The man with the moustache dialed a number and spoke without waiting,

"I have been to Washington and seen Davis. He was at a bar in Virginia, and has been placed on suspension pending some kind of action. It was not clear what that will be. I have also been to West Virginia and seen our friend. He knows what he is to do. Johnson is there and was in the restaurant. He was returning to it from another store as I left the town. I will follow up with our friend tonight." Completing his short statement, the man hung up the phone and placed it back in his pocket, then picked up a menu, expecting the waitress to return and take his order.

Khartoum, Sudan *Jeff Namers added a map of the US to his whiteboard, and put two pins into the map, one with information on a call from a burner in Khartoum to Atlanta, Georgia, and a pin on Elias, West Virginia, noting two calls with two separate phones.*

Right now, they seemed to be the least of his problems. The FBI's terrorism task force would eventually have to track the domestic calls, and what he had to deal with in and around Khartoum was going to keep his small team busy on Hakim and Giddons for a while yet.

At the Place of the Dove, Khalil Ahmad was becoming uneasy as he sat with Hakim and Josh Giddons in his restaurant. Fatima had warned him of the activities of Hakim, and he also knew of the recent drone strike in the area. He assumed the Americans were looking for Hakim, or someone like him, and really did not want to be involved in their activities. Unlike his sister Fatima, Khalil had remained outside the world of terrorism and subterfuge, preferring to run his restaurant, provide good food, and stay well below any type of radar the local police might have in Khartoum. So far, he had been successful in that effort.

Now however, his cousin arrived with a friend and wanted his help. In the tradition of their culture, he should provide the help requested because it was asked by a kinsman. But what if the help requested got both himself and his restaurant in trouble with the police? What would he do then?

"What would you have me do, Hakim?" asked Khalil, looking over at Hakim.

"I need something very simple, my cousin, responded Hakim. "I Need you to report to me on a person who may come to your restaurant named Namers, or someone who works for him at the US CIA. They will probably come simply as US Embassy employees, or even as local people, but they will be from the CIA. I need you to tell me what they want and what they say. That is all."

"Why do you need me to do this?" asked Khalil.

"Because they do not know you, and they will think of you simply as someone with information. If someone comes in and asks about me or Fatima, it will be the CIA people, and you should tell them you know nothing. You should say you have nothing to do with your sister or me. If you do that I will be grateful. Is that acceptable to you?" asked Hakim.

"I can do it if you wish," Khalil responded, still clearly puzzled at the request.

"Good. Now we will eat. First, tell me what you have been doing my cousin. Is this restaurant doing well?"

From a Vantage Point

"It is. We have many people each day, and most return because they like our food. I will get you two menus." Then Khalil saw the two menus to the side of the table, near Josh's arm. "Oh, I see you have them already. Order anything you wish. I am pleased to have you here this day."

Just as Khalil finished speaking, one of the waiters came over to him, and whispered in his right ear. "I am sorry Hakim. I must go. There is a problem in the kitchen. I will return later." Khalil rose to leave, and he patted Hakim on the shoulder as he left.

"Hakim, you are confusing me more all the time," offered Josh. "What was that all about? We came all the way over here to get him to say and do nothing for people who may not even come here. That's a bit bizarre. Then a cryptic phone call. What are you doing?""

"No Josh, just part of my plan. I threw one of my old burner phones in the trash as we came in. We must assume that the CIA's Namers is watching us, and following my phones. He must have figured out already that the numbers on the phones go in sequence. We will not use them anymore."

"I have arranged for new phones, and here is one for you. The numbers are completely different from those we used previously, with scattered numbers and different national codes. These will keep us safe. Use one only when absolutely necessary." Hakim handed Josh a phone, which he put quickly in his pocket.

In the kitchen, Khalil called Fatima at the shipping company.

"Fatima, it is Khalil. Hakim and his friend are here."

"What does he want?" asked Fatima.

"He says the American CIA people will be coming and I am to say nothing. What am I to say nothing about?"

"I do not know, Khalil, but if Namers comes, tell him what you know. He is our friend. Be safe."

"I will try sister, but I am very much afraid of Hakim. I will let you know if Namers comes to see me."

Khalil looked out into the restaurant and saw that Hakim and his friend were ordering from a waiter. He turned and went into his small office and shut the door.

On the Highway Outside Elias, West Virginia The man with the moustache finished his coffee, and a croissant he ordered, paid his bill and rose to leave, asking the waitress the name of the place.

"Glad you came in sir," the waitress responded. "We call this the Roadside Diner, and I am Sally, the owner. We don't get many out-of-town people here, and I'm sure glad you came. Perhaps you will come back soon? We hope so." Sally smiled then turned to another customer who had just arrived, sitting at the small

From a Vantage Point

counter. "Have a great day now," she added, waving back to the stranger as he started for the door.

Heading toward Charleston, the man listened to the radio, which consisted mostly of country music and religious programs in that part of the state, and began to drive up an incline, passing a long-haul truck and several cars. He reached the top, and almost immediately began a downward drive as the angle steepened, entering a sharp curve, and moving over to the right lane.

Just then, a shot rang out, mostly unnoticeable. It went through the right front tire, causing the car to jerk right toward the shoulder barrier, careening over it and flipping the car upside down as it started down the steep slope. The driver side window smashed in as it overturned, and glass struck the man with the moustache on his face, also ripping through the thin shirt he wore, spraying blood across the disintegrating windshield.

The man was dying as the car careened over the side of the steep drop-off. Hitting the bottom, what was left of the car burst into flames as it broke apart on the side of the hills, creating a large fire, fed by the full tank of gasoline. Several cars stopped, but there was nothing anyone could do, except for calling the State Police. Most of the traffic simply continued their journey along the road.

From a Vantage Point

From a Vantage Point

Chapter 21 The Escape

Khartoum, Sudan Hakim and Josh ordered their meal and mostly sat quietly while they waited for its delivery. Finally, Josh turned to Hakim.

"Well, my friend," offered Josh, looking over at Hakim. "I guess we could call this an eventful time, especially the last week or so. Let's see. We have been nearly killed by a drone strike, lost our apartment with most of what little belongings we had, sent our friend back to the US wondering if we were international criminals, arranged to out your cousin Fatima, and now, I believe we are being hunted by the CIA. Yes, sir that is what I would call eventful."

"You are right there, Josh, and more to come shortly," responded Hakim.

"What is it I don't know? We don't usually keep things from each other. I'm a bit confused."

"Relax Josh. Everything is going according to my plan. Let's wait until we get back to the new apartment and talk then. I don't like talking in public about things better left in private."

"Good enough for me," responded Josh, just as their meal arrived.

Jeff Namers walked in the side door of the conference room as the last of the several staff members arrived and were seating themselves. Looking toward the front of the long table, where Jeff traditionally sat, those attending could see a white board, filled with maps and notes; the same board Jeff prepared in his office.

"All right folks, let's get going. We all have a lot to say and do today," said Jeff as he took his seat.

"Look at two of the maps on the whiteboard," Jeff continued, "You see the map of the city and the larger one of a broader area. We know that Hakim and his friends have been moving around since the drone took out their living spaces. What do you all know that I need to know?"

Charlie Irving, the security officer spoke first. "Jeff, there is a lot of chatter right now about an impending move. There are plans to move some folks from here in Khartoum to Peshawar, and the chatter seems to be one-way chatter. It doesn't sound like simply a meeting to attend; more like a transfer of people. Nothing firm, just a lot of short bursts between some cells in Peshawar, one cell outside Kabul, and another along the Russian side. Most of it garbled, and we are not sure we got it all, but what we do have seems to indicate people will be in transition here in Khartoum."

"Thanks, Charlie," Any possible links to our friends?"

"Nothing specific, Jeff," continued Irving, "But the traffic is sometimes clear and sometimes seems coded. There are instructions moving, but who it applies

From a Vantage Point

to is unclear. I think we must assume, though, that Hakim is part of that traffic. He is clearly in the lead here, and these other locations would not be talking around him."

"Implications?" asked Namers.

"Simple," responded Irving. "We need to get a link to his comms, and quickly assess the extent of his involvement. He has gone to new burners, and changed locations numerous times. I need to be able to zero in on him to develop patterns where the phone traffic ties to him."

"Thanks Charlie, anyone else?"

"Jeff," responded Alex Hales, one of his analysts, "You asked me to put locals on the street to see if we could locate Hakim. I put everybody I could out on the streets, both his known locations, and other areas where he might go. One of my contacts said he saw Hakim and Josh Giddons at the Place of the Dove yesterday having lunch. Just the two of them, but before their meal, they sat talking, and Hakim received a phone call. It was very short, and Hakim barely spoke, but he did receive a call. Will that help Charlie?"

"Absolutely Alex," responded. "We'll look at the numbers after the meeting ends. I bet we get some info from the repeater pole just south of the restaurant. We used that before to trace some people living in the area. If we assume he might have kept the phone in his pocket before and after his meal, we just might be able to trace something here."

"Great, anyone else got something?"

"Jeff, if I remember my families correctly," said another of the analysts, "One of the waiters at the Dove is a relative of Fatima Ahmad. You want me to check it out?"

"No, I'll do that myself. The relationship we have with Fatima and her family is very touchy," responded Namers, "We need to tread carefully here. I do not want to involve her any more than we need to at this point." The staff around the room looked at each other quizzically, but stayed silent.

Then Jeff Namers continued, "If no one else has anything to add, this is what we need to do. Charlie, work what you can on both angles brought up. Try to refine the chatter and scope in as well on calls from the Dove. See if we can get somewhere there. Alex, I want you to get your people over in that area of town to see if the possibility exists that Hakim has found a new living space in that quarter. Don't move in on him, but let's see if we can at least locate and observe. Use only the most trusted. I don't want al-Azahir to know we are looking. I will contact Fatima and see what she can provide us. Anything else?"

"How do we treat this with Langley?" asked another of the analysts.

"We treat this with discretion right now," responded Namers. "We let them know about the chatter we have heard, provide them a dump, and above all, do

From a Vantage Point

not implicate Hakim as yet. We want to have better intel before we open that avenue of concern there. Understood?"

Everyone nodded, and they rose as Namers left, lingering to speak among themselves.

Charlie Irving walked out with Namers into the corridor. "Jeff, how long do you think you can keep this thing in house?"

"Charlie, I want to deal with Langley carefully. Bernie knows my feelings on dealing with al-Azahir. We have tried to eliminate him as a threat for a long time with no success. I have had the hairs on the back of my neck up for a considerable period, as if we have someone among our people who is feeding him information. I don't think it is any of our own, but it might well be one of the 'trusted' locals," Namers said, as he raised his hands to make the quotation marks gesture. "We need to be very careful, that's all. "

"OK Jeff. I understand," responded Irving, as he dropped off to his own office as they walked down the corridor.

Josh and Hakim finished their meal and waited for the waiter Khalil to bring the check. When he did, they rose to leave the restaurant. As they did so, two local policemen came in and sat down near the door, and both Hakim and Josh saw then.

"Be calm," said Hakim, as he touched Josh's arm. "We walk out quietly and calmly; all will be well." Both men walked normally toward the door, and left the restaurant, turning right down the street away from their new living spaces.

Just as they left, one of the policemen rose and looked out the window, watching the two men going down the sidewalk, then pulled out his phone and called in a message that he had seen them. As he returned to his seat, Khalil, who by then had returned from the kitchen, saw what transpired and walked quickly back again to his office, shaking his head with a look of fear on his face. He knew what Hakim wanted him to do, but no one asked him anything. It was certainly not the CIA, but two local police officers who came to the restaurant. In his mind, he had nothing to do, so that is exactly what he did--nothing.

Charlie Irving walked into his office, sat down at a screen and brought up the wireless telephone grid for Khartoum. It only took a moment to find the repeater closest to the Dove Restaurant, and, in a minute or so, he was looking at a scrolling set of calls made through that repeater.

Typing a few strokes, the list came on the screen again, this time with far fewer lines of calls. Irving took out the list of phone number Namers had given him that belonged to Hakim. Typing in a request, he saw one of the numbers active at the site of the restaurant. No calls had been made for some time, so Irving assumed the phone had been dumped on the premises. He typed a few

From a Vantage Point

more commands and brought up another screen with still far fewer calls, and then reached over for the office phone and called Alex Hales.

"Alex, this is Charlie. That sighting you discussed at the meeting, what time were they in the restaurant?"

"Gee, Charlie, I want to say it was about 12:30, if my memory serves. I can ask my guys and get back to you if you wish."

"No, that will not be necessary," responded Irving, "I see a call from a phone about 12:45. Thanks." The call he saw was not from the burner phone, but from yet another phone at the same location. He printed the page and noted the number on a small pad. Looking again at the list, there were only two other calls from the restaurant during that period, one from a house phone, and the other from a phone registered to the local police.

Irving took a chance on the information he had and pinged both phone numbers—the burner phone he knew Hakim had used, and the other number, which had come up in his search. He found the original burner phone still active, and at the restaurant. The second phone had moved from the restaurant down toward an apartment area.

"Bingo. Got you now," yelled Irving in his office, though speaking only to himself. *This could be good. Better tell Namers,* he thought.

Irving took the list and headed back down the corridor toward Jeff Namers office with his news. Unfortunately, he was only half right in his assessment. While he was checking his information, one of Khalil's staff was emptying the trash, and the original cellphone was now in a trash barrel behind the restaurant, where it would be thrown away to a local dump. The other phone, the one in Hakim's pocket, would similarly find itself in a trash pile down the street from the restaurant. It would provide no apparent help, since Hakim and Josh, seeing the police officers, headed in the opposite direction from their new apartment, and took a circuitous route back to avoid further detection.

Khalil was truly scared. Not only had he seen his cousin the terrorist, but he saw two policemen, who apparently recognized them, and called in their location. All of this was conjecture, of course, but that scenario was now fixed in Khalil's head. He did not know what to do next. Pacing his office, he decided to call his sister.

"Fatima, they were here," Khalil literally yelled into the phone.

"Who was there, Khalil?" she responded

"Hakim and his friend, and the police, they were all here. What do I do?"

"Stop Khalil. Tell me what happened," she said, reassuringly.

Khalil explained that Hakim and Josh had arrived, had a brief conversation, then ate a meal. As the two were ready to leave, two local policemen entered the restaurant and sat down near the door. Hakim and Josh walked calmly by them

From a Vantage Point

and down the street. One of the policemen called in on his phone, although Khalil could not hear the message.

"Calm down, Khalil," answered Fatima. "I understand it is stressful, but you did well. You are not in trouble with anyone. Listen to me. Go about your business. If the police ask you questions, tell them you do not know who the customers were. They will probably believe you, since they do not know you. Above all, be calm. Looking agitated only implicates you in whatever the police might think is going on. Calm down before you go back out into the restaurant."

"Thank you, my sister. You always know what to do. I am sorry for bothering you with this trivial thing."

"It is no bother. You are my brother. Again, calm down, and then go back to the restaurant. Everything will be fine." Fatima hung up her phone, and Khalil sat down at his desk.

A few minutes later, he looked through the window from the kitchen and the police officers were gone. He breathed a sigh of relief, and went back out to clear tables.

Josh and Hakim took a long walk around the area before going back to their car, driving the short distance back to their apartment building, along al-Siteen Street, then parking in a rear area behind the building, out of sight of the street. They entered the building through a rear door, and went up the stairs to their third-floor rooms. Once inside, Hakim dropped down onto the sofa, and Josh sat in an arm chair across the room. Between them was a long cocktail table containing several local magazines. They said nothing for several minutes, just looking toward the ceiling as if meditating.

It was Josh who spoke first.

"We need to make some plans, Hakim."

"I have a plan, Josh, but it appears that it may need to become reality sooner than I thought."

"OK, so what's the plan, then?"

"Josh, it has two parts. First, I need to go to Pakistan shortly, as you already knew. Only, that part of the plan must change. I need to stay in Pakistan for a while—perhaps a long while—until some of this goes away. I need to find alternative ways and people to do the work we have been doing, and get the blessing of the Imam for that work."

"What about me?"

"I have been thinking on that as well. You need to go back quietly to the United States for a while, and work with our cells there to expand our recruiting and activities on the East Coast. My thought is to send you in through Canada, and then down into the US through Vancouver, where we have many people, under a new set of papers making you a British citizen. You can then travel to the east coast, contacting our people in Atlanta. They will protect you and provide a

From a Vantage Point

safe place to live and work. They also have the means to maintain contact between us as needed."

"So, we break up after all this time together. Is that wise?"

"Brother, it is both necessary and wise. Together we are a very large target right now, and we need to disappear below anyone's radar if we are to continue our mission. It is the only way I see."

"I'll accept that, I guess," responded josh. "When does all this happen?"

"Within three days, if I can make arrangements in that time. Four days at the longest."

"Seems that we have a lot of work to do. I assume I will use my old British passport?"

"No, a new identity is being prepared. You are a businessman from just outside London. Your parents are British, but you have an aunt and uncle who are American, and with whom you lived for some time before they died. That will cover your accent. You are in Vancouver as a consultant on international shipping issues, something of which you know a lot. That will cover your presence in the country."

"We will get you into Canada on the west coast, at Vancouver, as I said. From there, you will take the train south to the US, and into Seattle. From Seattle, you can take a plane to Atlanta. By the time you get to Seattle, you will have several customs stamps that will legitimize your presence," Hakim continued. "It will also show that you were checked out by the US people—even if they did nothing but stamp the book. Pick a time when there are a lot of people in line, and be patient. You will get through."

"OK, so I do that, and get to Atlanta. What happens then?"

"When you get to Atlanta, you will be met by one of my people in that city, and he will have further instructions for you. It is important that you work through the network, and not contact me directly. That way the US intelligence people will not connect us. You will also receive new phones in Atlanta to contact others, but not me. Do you understand?"

"I do, but I am confused. Why not simply tell me what I need to do? We have been friends too long for this kind of secrecy?"

"My dear friend," Hakim responded, "Our friendship is exactly why you need to know as little as possible right now. You need to go to America, and then you will understand. The less you know now, the less you will worry, and the information you have for the authorities if you are caught up in their nets. Appreciate what I say—this is for the best for both of us, and the Movement."

"Hakim, I trust you with my life, as I have so many times. What will you do?"

"As I said, I am going to Peshawar for a meeting. I expect to stay there, or in the general area, about six weeks, with possibly a visit to Afghanistan, perhaps Kabul, to meet with some of our people, and form new links to those here in

From a Vantage Point

Sudan, and over in Yemen. How that will develop depends on the meetings, but I know one thing. We need to leave this country quickly, before the US CIA or someone else gets us. I do not worry about the local people; I worry about the foreigners who really control this country right now. We have overstayed our welcome and need to move on"

"I wish I could give you better answers, Josh," added Hakim, "But we need to make new plans and forge new contacts to keep doing our work for the Imam. Let's focus on that task, and worry about other things later. Right now, the first thing is getting out of Sudan and we must do that quickly. I want you to prepare to leave tomorrow evening for Canada. Is that OK with you?"

"Of course, if that is what we have to do. I'll pack and be ready."

"Good. Then I will get tickets for you under your new name, James Atherton. Now, let's think about dinner and discuss your new identity."

" Charlie, one of my men saw al-Azahir and his buddy walking along al-Siteen Street, near the apartment complexes. He wasn't completely sure, but the descriptions of both fit al-Azahir and Giddons."

"Great," responded Irving, "I'm sure that Jeff would want your guys to look further into the sighting, and be careful. We don't want them to get on to us. I'll be meeting with Jeff again in just a few minutes. I'll add your sighting to my information. Might want to look at the Dove as well. It's in that area, and you might get a sighting there as well."

"OK Charlie. Will do," answered Hales, as he left the office to get his people in motion.

Hales put his people out on the streets in the area where the sighting occurred. Two visited the Dove Restaurant, interviewed the employees, showed photos of Hakim and Giddons, and tried to create links between the men and the neighborhood. None of the employees, nor anyone on the local streets claimed to have seen either man, certainly not the two together. Khalil was not in the restaurant when they arrived, but neither of the agents asked if anyone else was employed there.

Irving checked out the police call from the restaurant, and found that one of the officers was responding to another call he had received-something which had nothing to do with Hakim or Giddons. Neither officer remembered either of the men, although one of the officers thought he had seen an American in the restaurant.

The locals working for Hales also travelled along al-Sittan Street looking to see if Hakim and his friend had rented rooms in the apartments nearby. That also came up blank. The possible sighting turned up dry, and the men returned to the office.

From a Vantage Point

Outside Elias, West Virginia Two West Virginia State Police officers looked down, over the steep precipice, viewing the remains of a car at the bottom of the steep cliff, which had been burning for some time. Two citizens driving by called on their cell phones to report the accident, and one remembered hearing what might have been a loud pop, but was not completely sure.

A rescue team was called, and three emergency rescue personnel went down the cliff on ropes to survey the scene. They reported a man in the front driver's side of the car, slumped over the steering wheel, obviously dead from the effects of the fire. A basket was dropped, and the driver was removed from the car, laid on the litter basket, and hauled up the cliff to the waiting ambulance, in which it would be transported to a local hospital to be seen by the local coroner.

An autopsy was performed. Fingerprints were taken, which turned up negative on the FBI Fingerprint System, and the man had no other identification. DNA samples were taken, and the body x-rayed for dental and other potential identification marks or scars. Everything turned up negative. This was a man who was completely unknown in police circles, with an obvious wound to his chest, a wound which the coroner attributed to a large piece of glass penetrating the body near the head, causing a bleed out.

Following the autopsy, the body was removed to a local funeral home, waiting for identification. While the automobile was a rental, the license used was fraudulent, and the address on the license was to an empty lot in Virginia, owned by another person. The police returned to other duties as the trail on this accident quickly grew less important.

Khartoum, Sudan As Hakim and Josh ate dinner, they discussed the new persona Giddons would assume, and who he was to work with in Atlanta. Josh found out that there were considerable assets in the Atlanta area, extending up the East Coast to Washington and New York. He would meet many of these during his time in the US. For now, he was to travel, as they had discussed, and see the country. When he arrived in Atlanta, he would be met and carefully protected by the local cell members. During his stay, he would learn more about the more militant side of the organization, and their plans for Jihad activities in the US and Canada.

Hakim emphasized that Josh was there to learn, and help organize new cells, leading up to the use of those cells in various actions over the next few months. He would hear indirectly from Hakim, and would have an avenue to send him messages as well.

The person he was to be become—James Atherton—was a consultant currently residing in Minneapolis, MN. He was born in the northern area of England, and came to the US to live with an aunt and uncle on their farm for

From a Vantage Point

several years. He attended the University of Minnesota, majoring in marketing, and worked in various industries as a salesman, or a manufacturer's representative, travelling widely along the East Coast until about ten years ago, when his aunt and uncle died. He returned to England, secured employment with a major manufacturing firm as their American representative, returning to the US periodically to meet with his customers.

Now Josh would assume his name and use it as a means of covering his entry into the US. Since Atherton worked only on the west coast, or closely inland states, Josh would have no problem using his identity on the East Coast. Should someone recognize the name, Josh was to say that he was distant cousin whom he had never met.

The following morning Hakim placed a call to Atlanta to put the movement of Josh in motion. He dialed a number from his cell phone, listened carefully while the call rang, trying to hear the tinny noise which often accompanied calls being monitored out of Sudan. Had he heard that sound, he would have ended the call.

"Hassan, listen carefully," said Hakim, as the phone was answered. "Our plan will happen in two days, so be prepared. The subject will take the route we discussed. Meet him there in five days. He will call to tell you the arrival time."

"I understand," came the response. "I will meet him as you wish."

"Good. Has everything else been cared for?"

"It has," responded Hassan.

"That is also good," replied Hakim, as he pushed a button to end the call; putting the phone back in his pocket carefully after turning it off completely. Even though the phone had no GPS, he was taking no chances. Then he sat back on the couch and began to sip his coffee. His friend Hassan Yasin came from a very prominent family in Sudan. Although he had lived in the US for many years, Hassan was still very much a Jihadist, and hated the US Government for what the military strikes did to his country. Both his mother and a sister had been killed in one attack, and he was unable to go to their funeral, on the possibility he would not be allowed back in the US.

Hassan met Josh and Hakim when they all ran guns for the Mujahidin during the years of the Russian occupation of Afghanistan. Hassan had come with one group from Yemen and had stayed to fight the Russians. He was eventually sent by the mullahs to school in the US, before the September 11th bombings, and had kept a very low profile as a simple Sudanese student, supported by a scholarship from his government. Using that money, he had managed to graduate from Georgia Tech, and then the graduate school in economics, and was employed by a marketing analysis firm in Atlanta.

He purposely associated mostly with his American friends, living and dressing as a modern American, giving no indication of religion, other than to show respect for the beliefs of his friends and associates. A year had passed

From a Vantage Point

since he took the oath as a US citizen, and the certificate he received from the Federal Court had a prominent place on the wall of his living room.

There was a dark side to Hassan, however. Periodically he would go to a local Madrassa to continue his religious education; not often, but frequently enough that he gained a perspective on what the Qu'ran taught on holy war—Jihad. He still retained communication with his friend Hakim, but now through intermediaries and messages he would receive occasionally from the Imam at the madrassa. He and the Imam spoke several times of their mutual friend, and Hassan kept the confidence. Little-by-little, Hassan was drawn deeply into the confidence of both the Imam and Hakim, and created a small cell of similar-thinking dissidents for some undefined future action.

Most of those he recruited had families in Sudan, Yemen, Pakistan, or Afghanistan, and they felt the daily pain of fear and anxiety for their well-being. Many of these were easy to turn into fellow Jihadists; others took more time, and needed more encouragement to bring them in the small circle.

Sammi Khan was one of those that needed a lot of time. Hassan acted as an informal mentor for the new recruits, counselling them on American customs and habits, and finding them places to work or live. In Sammi's case, a minister of one of the international religious groups providing humanitarian assistance in Afghanistan, found Sammi shortly after his release from Russian detention, and found a way to get him an exit visa, allowing his to travel to the United States.

Sammi worked for a while in Roanoke Virginia for the Norfolk-Southern Railroad, but became disabled, and turned again to the humanitarian group for assistance. This time, they arranged to place him in a remote town in West Virginia where members of their flock lived and worked. Knowing Hassan, the minister asked Hassan to come to West Virginia and help where he could with Sammi. Responding to the request, Hassan travelled several times from Atlanta to provide encouragement for Sammi in establishing his restaurant and getting to know the community. He also made sure that Sammi knew of his relationship with Hakim, his erstwhile friend from the earlier days in Afghanistan.

Hassan considered his nurturing of Sammi one his prouder achievements. Now, he would use Sammi as Hakim demanded, and he sent another of his early recruits to West Virginia to speak with him on the current matter of Will Johnson.

The man who went to visit Sammi had to do so with great care to prevent any possible knowledge of the reason for his visit. There could be no slipups; after all, this man, Will Johnson, was a friend of Hakim and Josh who was to be brought into the cell. This kind of inclusion had to be done carefully, and over time.

Regrettably, it was also Hakim's way that nothing would be left to link his activities to others. That meant Hassan had to arrange for an 'accident' after the visit; one that would preclude anyone from knowing the truth. The person he

From a Vantage Point

sent had no known record. His family was all dead overseas, and he had no one here in the US who would care if he simply did not show up later. Arranging the accident was the easy part; it was cleaning up the rest of the situation that was important.

As soon as the cell member who did the shooting reported back, Hassan arranged to have the apartment of the person who was killed cleaned, with all personal items removed. He had a friend with a cleaning service who would do that, for a fee, and since the apartment belonged to yet another friend, he was assured of privacy in the matter. The man with no identification simply disappeared.

For Hakim, making Josh disappear was not as easy a task. First, he had to get him out of Sudan, and out of the Middle East. That would be easy—he was not prohibited from travel, so Hakim simply put him on a flight to Turkey. On his arrival, he would be picked up at the airport in Ankara, and quickly hustled off to a local safe house, where he would stay for two days. In the safe house, he would undergo his metamorphosis into his new persona, and then be booked on another flight, through Lisbon, and over the Atlantic to Canada, and eventually Atlanta Georgia.

Hakim's task was eased somewhat by the physical attributes of Josh Giddons. Josh was a tall, slender man, with small hands and a fair set of features. There was really nothing outstanding about him; he looked very much like a local American boy, with a bit of a tan from being overseas. When Josh reached Ankara, all of that would change.

In Ankara, there was a woman named Assiri Benaziri, and this woman was a genius in disguises and cosmetic body changes. For Josh, Assiri would create a set of very realistic hand covers, complete with fingerprints of a person unknown to the police. These covers fit like real skin, and were made of a polymer that looked and felt like real skin as well. With these covers on his hands, which reached up about half-way on his arms, Josh could cover them with a shirt cuff, and it would seem real to the average customs or immigration inspector. She could also do other minor alterations in his physical view which would redefine him from Josh Giddons to James Atherton, his new persona. Josh Giddons would technically no longer exist.

The next day, Hakim and Josh travelled to the airport, and made no effort to conceal that Josh was leaving the country. The customs inspectors asked what his business was outside the country, and he replied that he was going on vacation to Turkey for two weeks. The inspectors bought the story, and he left soon after on a commercial flight to Ankara.

Three days later, Hakim also left Sudan; his destination was Pakistan.

From a Vantage Point

From a Vantage Point

PART 4 THREE MONTHS LATER

Chapter 22 The Cooperative

Elias, West Virginia "Ladies and gentlemen, let's call this meeting to order. We have a lot of work to do tonight, so we need to begin," announced Mayor Jim Flood. "We have a couple of small things to consider for the schools, and then we need to get to the main part of the meeting, the newly formed Elias Produce Cooperative. Will Johnson is here to give us an update and plan for getting it on the road." Mayor Flood nodded over to where Will sat, near the edge of the stage.

This would be the tenth time Will updated the community on the progress of creating a cooperative through which the local farmers could sell their milk, produce, and other craft items in the regional markets. A lot of work had been done since the first meeting in the Elk's Hall, just after Will's return from overseas, and he had done monumental work in moving the project along, with the help of Sammi, his friend.

Will knew there was great interest in the project; as soon as it was announced, the first meeting had over forty local farmers attend and voice their support. With that kind of support, it would be easier for Will to convince the State of West Virginia and the US Department of Agriculture (USDA) that they deserved a chance to make it work. Will traveled to the state capital several times, and made a number of trips to Washington, securing information the local USDA office could not provide. After these several months, he was now ready to complete his plans, and get the cooperative moving.

That morning, the Elias Courier, the local paper, had an article in the center

---

Elias Courier, the Community Newspaper

This evening at the Elk's Hall, the town council will hear the latest report on the progress of our soon-to-be Elias Produce Cooperative, a project led by our own Will Johnson. He, and several other members of the community have been working to find outlets for the produce, milk, and other products produced in the community. Their plans include regional farmer's markets, and eventually expanding to the Washington DC area markets.

The project is a possible breath of fresh air for Elias, which has not had any real industry, other than a small coal company, for many years. As Will said, in another recent meeting, "This is the time for Elias to get back on the map doing what we know how to do well. We need to take the initiative to pull ourselves up because no one else is going to come in and do it for us."

From a Vantage Point

of the front page, announcing the meeting that evening, and carrying a picture below it of Will and Jim Flood shaking hands at City Hall.

During the effort to get to this point, Will relied on Sammi and his friend Harry over at the store for support and encouragement. Harry arranged the meetings, with the community and local as well as state-level Department of Agriculture people. As the time went on, Harry accompanied Will on two trips to Washington DC to meet with the Agriculture national office people as well. Will trusted Harry, who was well-liked by the community, and had known Will since he came to town years earlier.

Sammi helped mostly with the farm, making sure that everything stayed in working order, fixing fences, milking cows, and keeping the house in order while Will travelled. He also spent considerable time working informally to get Will to understand and appreciate his heritage. These 'discussions' started out quietly and infrequently. Will asked about the magazine *Inspire* he brought back with him from Sudan, and Sammi showed him several others, all displaying degrees of what initially seemed to Will to be inflammatory language, and early on he really did not appreciate the approaches and suggestions of many of the magazines. He would try to look attentive at a magazine as he and Sammi discussed some of its articles, and then, after Sammi left, put it discreetly on a pile near his easy chair.

"And so, fellow members of the community, I want to bring up here our friend, and the sparkplug for this new effort, Will Johnson," said the Mayor, bringing Will out of the reminiscent haze he was in during the speech. He looked over at the Mayor, stood up and started to walk to the podium, smiling. They shook hands, and Will stood before the crowd.

"This has been a long journey," Will started, as his hands grasped the podium on either side.

"So many of you have come forward, agreeing to provide what you grow and make, and we have now been to four farmer's markets in the immediate area, plus one in Charleston, and we all made some money. That's progress," Will continued. "As we continue through the season, I have arranged for several more dates, and Otto over at the truck garage has agreed to let us use his trucks some more times to get our stuff to market." The crowd applauded as Otto stood and waved his baseball cap to the crowd.

"On Monday, I go to Washington to have more discussions with the Department of Agriculture. Their question is whether we can provide enough produce, milk, and cheese to support part of their food support program in the DC area. They have several plans which will produce the powdered milk and cheese; we need to provide the milk. What we need to consider this evening is whether, with everything else we are doing, could we produce the numbers of gallons of milk they want to contract for with us."

"Will," asked a farmer near the front, "How are we going to get large amounts of fresh milk to the Agriculture people? We don't have anything that big to do the job?"

"I'm glad you asked that question, Nate," Will responded, "My understanding is that the Agriculture people will provide the transport; large haulers will come here to get the milk from the farms, just as the smaller dealers do now, and they will transport it to processing plants. What we need to figure out is if we can provide enough milk, without disturbing your current customers in the local and regional areas."

"Well," said another man, "We still got a number of farms in the outlying area. Maybe we get them involved too, and then we might have enough and perhaps some to spare. Sure sounds like a good idea to me to work with these Agriculture people. I know most of those outlying folks. How about I invite them to my place, and you come and speak to them to try and get their support?"

"Happy to," responded Will, "In fact, any of you who know someone who could contribute to the co-op, and is not currently involved, ask them, and if I need to speak with them or encourage them further, I would be happy to do so. We need to get the whole area involved if this is going to work over the longer term."

"Any other questions?" asked the Mayor. He looked around the room, and saw no one raising their hand. "Well then, I guess this meeting is adjourned. Will, you have our support for your trip and come back successful."

"Thanks Jim. I believe this will work, and thank you all for being a part of what I hope, we all hope, will be a great enterprise."

From a Vantage Point

Chapter 23 Contemplation

The evolution of a person into a terrorist, at least from those whose stories we know, does not occur overnight. Their experiences, pain, suffering, and privation generally set them on the path toward what they eventually become. In fairness, this does not always mean violence, or anything close to violence, for there are many types of terrorists. There is one common denominator for their actions, or their attempts at action—they are opposed to something, and want to respond to what they perceive is required to exhibit their opposition, in a striking and meaningful way.

Their actions take them beyond the usual opposition figure we see commonly in politics in many nations, including the US, and other advanced countries. Often, we hear instead terms, such as 'fanatic', 'zealot', or some similar term defining a person opposed to the majority view. What separates them from the 'terrorist' is more than simply giving a person the title; it is the depth and breadth of the actions they take against a government which earns them the stronger epithet.

Moreover, while both opposition forces and terrorists have as their aim a change in a nation-state, their methods and actions are often quite different. The guerrilla, or an organized opposition force creates chaos and strife to force change through military-type actions. The terrorist, conversely, more often intends to cause fear in the people—a heightened sense of fear causing the people to rise against the government, forcing change. In addition, the guerrilla and opposition forces are politically-inspired for the most part, while a large part of the terrorist networks throughout the world are religiously inspired—even if those 'religious' beliefs are radially misplaced.

Additionally, while some are literally 'born' to the title, such as those where civil strife and upheaval are constant in their country, others eventually realize their opposition over time, and realize their desire to respond in a much subtler way; often coming under the influence of another person, a group with whom they empathize and perhaps consider friends, and then begin to absorb some of the tenets of opposition under these influencers. The change which occurs does so over a longer period, and may not result in a violent outburst or action, but it does change the individual—in both mind and soul.

Will Johnson saw at first hand the deprivation and poverty of those in harm's way in the Middle East; including the perception that this was happening to some of his kinsmen. He was constantly, but subtly influenced by his friends, who had already determined they wanted to add him to their terror network.

While Johnson had carefully repressed his familial influences over the years, gradually becoming an "American", rather than a 'Lebanese-American', as his

From a Vantage Point

father had always considered himself, Any remaining memories of his past were occasionally rekindled by events reminding him of his heritage, mostly from news reports of hostilities in the area of Lebanon and Syria, where he assumed he still had relatives. Otherwise, Will had his farm, with its many memories, some of which reminded him of who he actually was—not Will Johnson, but Suleiman Ashkar, formerly of Lebanon. other 'friends', like Sammi, and others, would also refer to his heritage, and its importance in the months elapsing after his return.

Elias, West Virginia "Will, my friend, if we are going to get you to your plane, we must be leaving," said Sammi, banging on the bedroom door in Will's house. "We only have two hours to get you to Charleston for the Washington plane. You must hurry."

"I know, Sammi. I'll be right out."

"Is there anything I can do for you while I wait?"

"Nothing. I am just about ready," responded Will, as he opened the door. On his bed was an overnight case, and in his hand, a computer case.

"This is it. Let's go," added Will, picking up the overnight case, and walking into the living room.

"Your flight leaves in a bit over four hours. We just have time," said Sammi, taking the overnight bag from Will and walking toward the door, where he had the car waiting, with its trunk upraised and ready.

Will followed him to the car, turning to lock the front door as he passed through, and then opened the right front door stepping in and placing his computer case at his feet. Sammi saw two magazines sticking out the edge of the side flap of the computer case.

"I see you brought reading material for the plane. That is good; you will not have to stop at the airport store."

"You worry about everything, Sammi. Yes, I brought some reading material with me. I thought I might read some of this stuff I got from Hakim."

"Better not to do that on the plane, Will," answered Sammi. "It might be misunderstood."

"You're right, Sammi. I'll stuff them into the bag and read them later when I have time in the hotel room. Now I'm back to getting something at the airport store."

"Buy quickly, after you have gone through security, then"

"Of course. Now, let's get moving or I miss the plane."

Sammi grumbled a bit as the car passed down the driveway and started out onto the country road, which would eventually lead them to the interstate and the airport.

"What caused you to bring those magazines, Will. I thought you were not interested in them?" Sammi asked about twenty minutes out into their drive.

"Oh, I really am not," responded Will. "It is more out of curiosity than anything else. Somehow, I figured I might like to understand what Hakim and Josh are somehow involved in. I must admit, I still do not completely understand a lot of what I saw in Sudan. Over the past few days, I have thought about what I saw of the destruction, and the injuries to innocent people. It just sticks in my mind, and I really need to sort those things out. In my heart, I truly hope that Hakim and Josh aren't in the middle of all this. We have been friends for so long, but I really lost touch with what their current thinking processes might be. More than anything, I guess it is just curiosity; nothing else."

"It is always good to try to understand something new or different, Will, especially when it involves good friends."

"That's right, they are good friends."

"Well then, after you return, I look forward to continuing our conversations. I will be happy to have any discussion you wish."

"Thanks, Sammi, you too are a very good friend. I appreciate everything you do for me, especially getting me to and from the airport like this."

"No problem Will. That is what friends are for," Sammi responded with a smile and a pat on Will's left leg. "That's what friends are for," he repeated as they drove along, an hour away from the airport.

The two men did not further discuss the pamphlets Will brought with him. Sammi felt he had accomplished his purpose, and he steered the conversation back toward the community, especially the cooperative, in the time they had left.

Finally, they arrived at Charleston Airport, and Sammi pulled up at the arrivals entrance.

"Do well, my friend," said Sammi, as Will opened the door to leave, took his bags from the back seat, and took one last look through the window at Sammi.

"I will. Take care of things, and I will see you in three days."

Will turned again, took his two bags, and walked toward the entrance to the airport. As he did, Sammi waved and drove off toward the Airport drive exit and the interstate.

US Embassy, Khartoum, Sudan. The calls and messages between Khalil and Fatima were reported immediately to Namers and his staff. As each new message came in, Jeff Namers was even more convinced that Fatima was loyal to him rather than her cousin Hakim, although he obviously could not prove it. Over the years, Namers had developed a gut reaction, as did many of his counterparts, and his gut was generally not wrong.

Now, he knew Fatima had been sacrificed for Hakim's safety, drawing the interest away from him, and onto Fatima and Jim Davis. The real question was how to prove it. That proof was not long in coming. As he sat thinking about the issue, the phone rang at his desk.

From a Vantage Point

"Namers. Can I help you?"

"Jeff, this is Fatima. I need to speak with you urgently. I have information for you."

"Fatima, I appreciate the call, but as I said before, we need to put space between ourselves for a time. This situation with Davis has put a black cloud on our relationship."

"Jeff, there is nothing to the Davis rumor. There is something to what Hakim is doing, and we need to discuss it. He visited my cousin Khalil, with his friend Giddons."

"Really, what did he want of Khalil? I always thought he was not involved in all this mess."

"Hakim was concerned that you, or your people would arrive at the Restaurant and ask questions."

"What kind of questions?"

"He did not say, just that you would ask questions. He said nothing more."

'What do you make of it?"

"I think he is creating a trail for you to follow. There is an old Arabic saying that says if you want to catch a small animal, then lead it to you. Create a trail of things it likes to eat, and set a trap. When the animal enters the trap, you have him. Hakim thinks carefully about everything. He is setting a trap for you. I know it was him who called your office to give the information on me. He told me that himself. Now, he is setting out other bait. Be careful."

"I will, and thank you Fatima. My faith in you has never faded. We will work through things here, but it will take time. Have patience and worry about your business. My people will be watching to be sure you and your uncle are safe. Now, we will watch for Khalil as well. Just in case."

"Thank you, my friend. I appreciate your friendship more than you know."

"Take care Fatima. I will get back to you." Namers hung up the phone only to realize his intel analyst Alex Hales was in his doorway.

"What's up Alex?"

"Not much Jeff," hales responded, "I was working on the intercepts trying to pinpoint Hakim and his buddy, but it appears they switched phones."

"I thought that might happen. It was too easy to see they were using sequence numbered phones. Any chance we pick up the new numbers?"

"Actually yes. It appears the two went back to their old apartment, just as one of our guys was going through the place. He got out onto the outside ledge and dropped down to the street as they entered. We got a backpack that was there. It seems to be Johnsons."

"Anything in it?"

"Nothing spectacular. Looks like he might have brought it with him from the US. Just personal stuff."

"OK, so now we know that the drone did not take out their apartment when it hit the building."

"That is the only interesting thing, Jim. Their apartment was reinforced somehow. It still looks the same, but the walls are very solid—not even a crack from the blast. The apartments of either side have extensive damage but not theirs. We went to the next apartment, and it looks like the walls between were reinforced with some bars and plate. That was a real fortress. I'll bet all four walls, floor and ceiling were all redone the same way."

"Interesting. So, they came in as one of our guys was leaving."

"Quickly, I might add. He just got out as they entered."

"All right, as long as our guy is safe. Were they able to put any listeners in?"

"We got in four, and heard some conversation after al-Azahir and Giddons entered the apartment. Mostly small stuff, some about Johnson. The impression they give is that he is completely out of their orbit."

"Why would you say that?"

"Well, Hakim noticed that Johnson's backpack was gone, and he assured Giddons they would simply say nothing survived the attack, if asked. That and other small talk rings loudly that he isn't involved in what they do."

"Ok, I need you to do two things; first, write everything up, and second, try to find out where they are living now."

"Will do Jeff. I have a man on their tail as we speak."

"Somehow, I knew you would Alex. Appreciate it. I have to go to see the ambassador."

"Understand. Will get back to you on the address."

"Thanks."

From a Vantage Point

Chapter 24 Long Distance to Atlanta

The Peshawar Valley in Pakistan. In the heat of the summer, the Peshawar Valley often reaches nearly 120 degrees, although the average is closer to 108-110 degrees. Starting in late March and early April, the temperature quickly moves above 100 degrees, and stays there until the late Fall, when it drops to about 70 degrees for the winter.

The Valley is a delta of the Kabul River, consisting of silt, rock, lime and other geological ingredients collected over time. It is here in the Plain that the Kabul River separates into channels. Here also is the City of Peshawar, fifth largest in Pakistan, and the capital of the Khyber Region. There are also some smaller cities and towns within the larger district, but these are all under the administrative governance of the district. Outlying the towns are some small villages and enclaves of people, some nomadic, and others there to support and fight for one or another of roving bands that compose the Taliban and, in turn, Al Qaeda.

The al Qaeda movement was originally formed in Peshawar in 1988, following a meeting between Osama bin Laden and others, resulting in the establishment of a complex training camp system across both Pakistan and Afghanistan, funded through contributions of wealthy Arabs. The camps were set up originally to train locals to fight the Russians, then occupying Afghanistan. After their expulsion in 1988, the attention of the opposition fighters turned toward the United States and other power, for a myriad of reason.

Financial support flowed through a 'Service Bureau' set up to provide men and equipment for the movement, and it was to this part of the organization that Hakim al Azahir had gravitated with his friend Josh Giddons, first to Yemen and Sudan and then to the Peshawar. Living in one of the small villages outside the city, Hakim worked for one of the early supporters of bin-Laden, Amoud Tabriz, known to most people as 'Fatool', an Egyptian businessman, with large shipping contacts throughout the world.

Hakim developed a network for securing supplies, providing training, and publishing the many tracts on terrorism and terroristic activities needed for their cells throughout the world. Both Hakim and Josh traveled extensively, coming under the radar of several nations, none of whom could tie them directly to al Qaeda. Nonetheless, they appeared on several watch and no-fly lists around North Africa and the Middle East.

Both men developed multiple personas under which they could travel with some impunity, and they could also rely on numerous networks of favorable allies, including the Pakistani Secret Service to ease their way around the region. On one occasion, Hakim had been given a diplomatic passport, ostensibly from

From a Vantage Point

the Pakistani Government, to travel back and forth between Khartoum and Peshawar.

This time, he returned to Peshawar on a Pakistani intelligence services jet, which left Khartoum, traveling through Egypt, and then on to Peshawar, delivering him to the Bacha Khan International Airport, where he was met by several officials of al Qaeda, returning to the local village in which he first became associated with al-Qaeda, and greeted as a hero.

The Swedish Saab 2000 Turboprop touched down casually at Bacha Khan as it had done so many times since being put in service in 2008. This time the plane, being used by the Pakistani Intelligence Service, had several special customers arriving. Some had come aboard in Khartoum, including two men who had slipped across the borders from Yemen, and five others who enplaned in Cairo, Egypt after a meeting with Egyptian Intelligence. There were several other passengers as well on the plane, unmarked except for a tail number, and a small Pakistani flag emblazoned on the cabin door.

Rolling toward an area of the tarmac with little activity, the plane stopped just short of a cargo area, and a portable stairway was quickly whisked out to the plane, while a ground crew member rushed up the stairs to bang on the cabin door, which was quickly opened from the inside.

The ground crew person quickly started speaking in Urdu and gesturing to the cabin attendant who appeared at the door.

"Did you have a good flight?" the crew member asked.

"We did," was the response from the cabin attendant.

"Anything to report that we need to do?"

"Nothing major. Let me get the passengers off, and I need to show you two things in the galley," responded the cabin attendant.

"OK, then tell them to come out quickly," said the crew member, starting to rush down the stairs, nearly tripping and falling as he reached the bottom step—his feet not as fast as the rest of his body.

The first person out the cabin door was a tall, heavyset man in a western-style suit, with no tie. He came to the top of the stairs and looked around to his left and right, and then did the same a second time. Apparently satisfied, he turned back toward the cabin door.

"All right," said the tall man, turning back toward the inside of the plane, "you can come out and start down the stairs to the terminal. Go to door number three. There you will be met." He began to walk down the stairs, stopping at the bottom for the others to depart the plane.

It was only seconds before a total of twenty-eight people had departed, including the flight crew. They all walked quickly toward a door about forty feet away with a large number "3" across the door window. As they did, other ground

From a Vantage Point

crew members came with a tractor and two luggage carriers to take their baggage to the terminal.

Nearly the last to deplane, Hakim looked around as the security guard had done, and walked briskly down the stairs, carrying with him two small bags, one over his shoulder, and one in his right hand.

At the bottom, the guard leaned over to him and whispered, "Sir, you should go through door number four. There are no customs people there, and you will be met."

"Thank you," responded Hakim, as he looked over to the terminal where he saw the door with the large "4" on the window. He walked quickly to the door, opened it, and found himself inside a short corridor. Standing at the end were two men in military uniforms.

"Mister al Azahir, please come with us," said one of the men, pointing toward the exit to the terminal. Hakim could see a car waiting outside.

"Thank you."

"Enjoy your stay," said the soldier as they approached the outside doors. "This man will take you wherever you need to go." He saluted and walked away.

Outside was a Mercedes sedan. Standing next to it in native dress was a tall man wearing a sidearm. Hakim could not see what it was.

"Good morning sir," said the man. "I am Saide, and I am your driver. Where do you wish to go?"

"I am going to the Ekhwan Hotel. Do you know it?" asked Hakim.

"Of course, sir, I know it. I will be happy to take you there. Please step into the car," the man said, as he opened the rear door. "There is water in the cold box on the seat, if you wish some. Please take it if you wish."

Hakim entered the car, and the driver closed the door, moving to the left front and opened the door. He sat in the driver seat, started the car, and quickly drove off in the afternoon traffic, going right on Khyber Road to exit the airport, and then weaving in and out of traffic, as he turned onto other larger roads within the city, dodging one military convoy and two military busses, as the driver pointed out interesting places and living areas, even though Hakim probably knew the city better. The final drive up Saddar Road to the hotel was much like driving in any major city; completely built up with modern and semi-modern building interspersed with older buildings and homes.

The Ekhwan Hotel was a middle-class hotel, probably rating about three stars, if that, but Hakim really did not care about the rating. He was there to stay only for a day or two until arrangements were made to bring him out of the city, and over the mountains of the Kush to Afghanistan. Staying at the Ekhwan gave him some cover as well, so he would not be seen or recognized by any foreign operatives in the city.

From a Vantage Point

    Hakim made the necessary plans for his travel before he left Khartoum. From Peshawar, he would travel north out of the city by car. Then he would take a small boat along the Kabul River west to the major bend of the river, crossing the border into Afghanistan, and meet some of his people on horseback, which would take him through the mountainous area few traveled, keeping him relatively safe. His goal was Gerdi in the northwest, where the major route into Jalalabad skirted the southern edge of the mountains. With care, he would be in Kabul in several weeks.

    The trip was not without danger, and it took much longer than the more usual routes between the two countries. While he traveled on a passport from Saudi Arabia with the name Kassim Said, there was always the possibility he could be seen or stopped along the trip. By taking his time, and avoiding public places, Hakim felt safer. He looked forward to seeing his comrades, renewing relationships, and working out the details for his next effort, in the United States.

    Enroute to Atlanta, Georgia. Josh was due to check in at the Omni Hotel in downtown Atlanta after the final leg of his flight from Seattle, Washington. Leaving Khartoum, Josh had flown to Lisbon, Portugal using his new alias, Jim Atherton, enjoying the sights in the city for three days. On the fourth day, Atherton boarded a British Airways flight bound for Montreal, Canada. With his passport identifying him as a consultant, he traveled light, carrying only a small bag with a personal computer, and checked the rest of his luggage. Nothing in his luggage, or on his computer would give him away as Josh Giddons.

    In Montreal, he again spent another several days seeing the local sights and enjoying the meals in local pubs. From Montreal, he took a flight to Calgary, and then drove a rental car through the hills from Calgary to Vancouver, British Columbia. So far, everything was going according to plans. His passport was unchallenged, as were his credit cards, and he used public phones for innocuous local calls. Nothing in his behavior would point to terrorism in any way.

    Atherton stayed a week in Vancouver, then drove down the coast to Seattle, where he turned in his rental car, and registered at the Hilton Hotel downtown. As before, he took in the local sights, ate several times at the fish pier, and enjoyed a baseball game. Josh enjoyed being back in his own country for a while, and took in every sight he could, although carefully not contacting his family or friends.

    The plan he and Hakim worked out called for him to be completely on his own until he arrived in Atlanta, and then he would be contacted by a member of a cell in that area. Since he was not in any way lacking funds, Atherton simply enjoyed himself until it was time to leave for Atlanta, taking care to keep in the background, and under anyone's radar while traveling.

When his week was up, Atherton went to Seattle-Tacoma Airport, and came into the terminal, trying to find the departure boards so he could determine where he had to go to get his Delta Air flight to Atlanta. He stopped at a news store, bought the New York Times, and headed for the concourse where he would depart. With only his small carryon bag, he passed easily through the TSA screening area.

What Atherton did not know was how close he came to discovery at SEA-TAC Airport. As he went through the TSA screening, and heading down the concourse, he passed a small restaurant. Sitting at the bar, sipping on a tall coffee, was Jim Davis, the sky marshal. Davis looked at the mirror behind the bar and saw a man walking casually down the concourse, looking into the various shops. He passed quickly by the bar, and for a moment, Davis thought he recognized him. Davis thought quickly who he might be, then turned back to get his drink. When he turned again, drink in hand, the man was gone. Davis stood and looked down the concourse filled with people, and could not see him. Unable to make any connection, other than a vague glint of recognition, Davis returned to the bar stool and continued to drink his coffee.

Atherton, in turn, saw Davis sitting on the bar stool and recognized him immediately. With a cool head, he continued to walk and look around, not seeming out of place, and passed by the bar. As soon as he was clear, Atherton joined a group moving down the concourse, and was soon in the middle of the pack. He continued to walk with them far down toward the end of the concourse where his flight would depart. Only when he reached the gate did Atherton turn to make sure he had not been followed. He had nearly an hour before his flight departed, and he kept himself among the crowd waiting for the flight for additional protection.

Much later, the realization dawned on Davis that he was looking at Josh Giddons, and by then it was too late. He pulled out his cell phone and dialed a number.

"Alice," yelled Jim Davis into his phone as a person answered, "Alice, its Jim. The guys we have been looking out for may be in the country."

"Slow down, Jim," responded Alice Sawyer, "What are you talking about?"

"Remember our last conversation, after I was brought back from Sudan? I briefed the group on Hakim al-Azahir and Josh Giddons, the two we have been trying to get in Sudan, and who also know this guy Will Johnson, a farmer in West Virginia?"

"I do remember that briefing, Jim. So, what do you think you have?"

"Alice, I am sitting in the Tiki at SEA-TAC, waiting for my flight to Japan. A guy walked by me in the concourse about an hour ago, never looked my way, but I could swear it was Giddons. He had the look, the mannerisms, and everything that spoke 'this is Giddons'."

From a Vantage Point

"OK, Jim, so what did you do?"

"That's the problem Alice. I looked and had a vague recollection, but could not place the man with a name. I walked over to the concourse and he was gone in the crowd. It was only a few minutes ago that the light dawned, and I'm sure it was Giddons. At least one of the two is in the US."

"All right, so we assume he is here for a moment. We need to confirm that. How much time before your flight?"

"About two hours. What do you want me to do?"

"Go over to operations, and ask for Jeff Crenshaw. Identify yourself, and tell him you want footage from the concourse cameras for that period sent to me here in DC. He will know where to send the film streams. Do we have a good picture of Giddons?"

"Sure do. I snapped one in Khartoum, and sent it to the file."

"Good. You go see Crenshaw, and we will look at the films; hopefully we will see something, and have an idea where he might be going. Call me after you get to Japan."

"Will do Alice, and thanks."

"Jim, if this pans out, you might be back with us. I hope so. We need you badly. Your replacement is not exactly a live wire."

"I accept the compliment Alice, and hope this is what I think it is. Talk to you tomorrow." Jim hung up the phone and put it back in his pocket. He asked the bartender for his bill, paid it, and walked out into the concourse on his way to see Crenshaw in support operations.

Jalalabad, Afghanistan. It was after midnight before Hakim and his two companions on their trip finally reached the city, after nearly two weeks of travel. As his friend Josh Giddons had done, Hakim took his time. The automobile ride out of Peshawar was uneventful; his Saudi passport gave him quick movement through the occasional temporary roadblocks set up by the Pakistani Army, and in less than a day, he was in a small village along the Kabul River where he would go by boat on his next leg of the journey.

Meanwhile, Hakim made several calls with a secure satellite phone given him by his contact with Pakistani Intelligence. He knew the Pakistanis would be listening in, but that was less important to him than getting in contact with his leader in Kabul. When making these calls, he often used a code to tell the person on the other end who might be listening; giving that person the opportunity to couch the conversation in terms that would not give away any important information.

"This is Kassim Said," said Hakim (using his alias) after dialing a number and waiting for a response. "I expect to see you in three weeks. Be ready."

From a Vantage Point

Disconnecting the phone call, Hakim looked to one of the men who accompanied him, and related, "They will be waiting for us at the bend of the river in three days. I want to be there first, so we will move with all speed to get there quickly."

"As you wish, sir," responded the man, who pointed to the boats at a small dock on the side of the hut where they were staying. "These boats will get us up the river quickly, but they are humble enough no one will suspect us as anything but fishermen or tourists going to the see the river."

"Good, when do we leave?" asked Hakim.

"The men are packing the boats now, sir, and will be ready within the hour."

" Fine; let me know when we are ready," responded Hakim, "I will be at the hut." Hakim walked over to the front of the one floor hut and pulled out the satellite phone, dialing a number.

"We leave within the hour, going up river to the great bend," Hakim spoke into his phone, "Make sure your men do not make mistakes and think we are Taliban. Be sure they give us space to move." Finishing his statement, he hung up the phone, placed it in his pocket, and then sat watching as the men finished packing the two boats.

Hakim, like many of his cohorts, had developed contacts within the Pakistani Intelligence service, and the Army. These contacts were important in situations such as this, since the Pakistani Army actively watched the river and the mountain areas, often from aircraft, to publicly show they were preventing terrorists from moving between Pakistan and Afghanistan. Most of that, however, was for show to its ally, the United States. Many of those they did attack were Taliban renegades, rather than members of the main al-Qaeda groups.

Washington, DC. As Alice Sawyer hung up the phone from her call with Jim Davis, several thoughts passed through her mind. On the one hand, Jim could be right; Giddons could be in the US, and she needed to vet that possibility. On the other hand, she was concerned that Jim, having gone through his ordeal of being removed from Sudan might proverbially be seeing terrorists 'under every rock'. In her mind, she did not think that Jim was doing that, but she had to consider all options, assuming his information was accurate.

Just as she was ready to leave, following the call, another call came in, this time from her counterpart at the FBI on another matter, and they spoke for about 15 minutes on a pressing issue involving increasing cross-overs at border check points from Canada.

Rising from her desk, Alice walked the short distance to the communications group to see what they had received from Seattle.

From a Vantage Point

"All right, guys," said Alice, as she entered the room, "What do we have from Seattle? Does anything match the pic Davis sent earlier?"

"Actually, we are not sure, Alice," responded on of the technicians. The pic Davis sent was not that great. We needed more pixels to do a really good job, but the good news is that we did get several matches, or at least possible matches."

"Show me," she answered quickly.

"Right here on the big monitor in the center. First, I put up the Davis photo. Then, we start running the tapes closest to the Tiki Bar where Davis says he first saw Giddons. Running the analysis of the two, we get four people who come close to the identity points on the Davis photo. Since all of their faces are somewhat obscured, we can't give you a definitive match."

"We followed the people down the concourse to see what gate they were departing from, and to see if we could get a better shot, "the technician continued, "At two of the gates, we eliminated three of the men through better images; that left one to follow further. Unfortunately, moving down the concourse, the scanning application also picked up several more men who might be Giddons. We are chasing them now. Will probably have a better answer for you in about 20 minutes."

"That means if Giddons is at Sea-Tac, we can't stop him from boarding a plane about to leave?"

"Yes Ma'am, that it does. We don't have enough information right now to get a stop order."

"Damn. Keep at it guys. If Giddons is there, or was there, let's try to nail him at his arrival point if we need to. Thanks." Alice waved her left hand in the air as she left to return to her own office.

Seattle Sea-Tac Airport, Seattle WA. Atherton (Giddons) sat waiting for the call for his flight to Atlanta, and worried about seeing Jim Davis at the bar up the concourse. He thought he had covered himself well, moving among the crowds, and staying near a small group at the gate area, but he also knew that numbers of cameras could be capturing his movements, and worried about that possibility.

Twice he moved with others heading for the restrooms, or over to the small shop to purchase a paper—always with others surrounding him. He stayed particularly close to two other men, roughly his size and height, hoping that might make any identification, if one was contemplated, harder to accomplish. Finally, he sat in a seat away from the loading area, where the cameras were most likely and buried himself in the Seattle paper until boarding stated.

"Ladies and Gentlemen," blared the loudspeaker in the departure area, "We are about to start boarding Delta Flight 2210 to Atlanta-Hartsfield International

From a Vantage Point

Airport. We will board by sections. Please have your boarding pass ready to show the attendant. Thank you."

Atherton looked at his boarding pass, realized he was in boarding group one, and stood awaiting another announcement, which came quickly.

"Those in boarding group one may now board, along with our Platinum frequent fliers, and all first-class customers. Please move toward the attendant at the door and present your boarding card for validation. Thank you."

Atherton walked over to the attendant, careful not to make himself conspicuous, showed his boarding pass, and moved down the entranceway to the aircraft. Looking again at his boarding pass, which he had placed in his pocket, Atherton started to look for his seat, 4-A, as he entered the plane. Stowing his one carry-on under the seat in front of him, and then taking his own seat, Atherton waited patiently, if not anxiously for the flight to depart.

People milled aboard, looking for overhead storage and seat assignments, but eventually the plane settled down for its departure. Flight attendants walked up and down the aisles assisting people as well. In first class, the flight attendant asked everyone if they wanted drinks or small snacks before takeoff, and Atherton ordered a Bloody Mary, stirred and hot. The attendant nodded and went on to complete her list, then to the galley to make the drinks.

Atherton made every effort not to seem anxious, but did look periodically toward the doors, subconsciously thinking he would be discovered after his brief brush with Jim Davis. That never happened, and fifteen minutes later, the doors closed, as the flight continued preparations to depart for Atlanta.

Washington, DC. Alice Sawyer made every effort to try to keep busy while waiting for the results from her technical staff. She went through her inbox, sorting documents she had not had the opportunity to read or act upon; initially some, and placing them in the out box. Others she put into several piles depending on the action needed, all the while expecting one of her team to come through the door to tell her they had found Giddons. Finally, about 30 minutes later, one of the technicians came in and walked up to her desk.

"Well Alice, we have been through all the footage we can get; called SEA-TAC twice for more views, and what we have is still inconclusive."

"How inconclusive?" Alice responded.

"Enough that we cannot positively identify anyone as Giddons. We do have two leads; one, a person going to LA, and the other going to Atlanta. Neither exactly matches, but we have sent Davis' photo to both stations and asked that they be sure the video is rolling in the arrival gates at both locations."

"OK. Get me the flight numbers and arrival gates, and I will have people at both places to see if we can get this guy, if he is in the States. Thanks for the effort."

From a Vantage Point

"No problem, that's what we are here for," responded the technician, as he turned and left. Just a minute later, the information Alice needed was on her e-mail screen. It listed two flights, one an American Eagle flight 1651 to LA, and the other a Delta flight 2210 to Atlanta. Alice forwarded the information to the two stations, asked that it be disseminated and that agents or sky marshals be at the gates for possible identification. Then she went back to her paperwork, confident she had the situation under control.

The routine of the airlines was basically the same; send a copy of the picture to the crew, with instructions to discreetly determine if the person was on board, make no effort to confront the person, but report back and action would be taken on arrival. At this point, Giddons was not considered dangerous, and was probably unarmed. The American Eagle report came in within minutes, since the attendants on this relatively short flight were already serving beverages and snacks; a good cover for observing passengers. They reported no person matching the photo.

Forty-five minutes later, the report from the Delta flight also came in, and they reported the same; no person matching the description in the photo. The information from both flights was forwarded to Alice Sawyer.

On the Kabul River, Afghanistan. The boat was a bit larger than Hakim expected, but it also contained two more men than he thought would make the trip. The man who arranged the trip, and was traveling with him was named Abadi, and he, along with his brother had met Hakim at the airport, bringing him to the village. Hakim thought only the three of them would travel up river, along with a pilot for the boat. In that he turned out to be wrong.

Abadi and his brother were members of Haqqani, a terrorist group supported by the Pakistani Inter-Services Intelligence Service (ISI), which had sponsored numerous domestic terrorist groups during its long war with India over Kashmir. Hakim had worked with these two men many times as he traveled to and from Afghanistan, generally through routes such as they were taking on this trip. While he trusted them, and appreciated his contacts and support within ISI, he still was cautious in what he said and did in front of them.

Now, at least in his mind, his trip was further compromised by two others who arrived at the last minute, expecting to take the trip up the river. He had never met the men before, but Abadi assured Hakim they were loyal members of the Haqqani, and their trip had been blessed by the same local ISI leader that approved his trip. Nonetheless, this made Hakim very uneasy, and he watched both especially carefully as they progressed up the river, keeping his American-made Glock 9mm pistol close to him.

"Abadi," asked Hakim, "Will we be at the place we need to be within three days?"

From a Vantage Point

"We will sir," responded Abadi, "Assuming we do not face bad weather or some calamity. I expect us to be right on time, as you wished. Would you like some food, perhaps? We have good food on board for the trip."

"A bit later perhaps. Right now, I would simply like to look at the river and scenery. Perhaps also I will rest a bit."

"As you wish sir," came the response. My brother will be here with you when I go forward to pilot the boat for a while."

"What are the other two men here for?"

"Our leader has need of them up river. We will leave them when we leave the boat. I am sorry this happened at the last minute, but I only received a message a short while before we left, and they have no other way to get up river themselves. A thousand pardons for the inconvenience."

"Watch them carefully," responded Hakim, as he pulled his hat over his eyes to rest.

Atlanta-Hartsfield International Airport, Atlanta, GA. Josh had slept part of the way from Seattle to Atlanta, awaking to the periodic announcements of the flight attendants, and the last one alerted the passengers that the plane was approaching Atlanta in about 20 minutes.

"Is there anything else I can get you before we land," asked the flight attendant, as she came up the aisle to where Josh sat.

"No thanks. I'm fine," he replied.

Josh thought about his next steps. He knew he was to meet two men at the airport, go to a local hotel, and then be briefed on the plans Hakim made for an event in the US. Other than that, Hakim had kept him in the dark, probably for fear he might be apprehended somewhere along the way, and it was better not to have him know too much.

He looked out the left window from his seat, and saw Atlanta as the pilot turned the plane toward Hartsfield Airport, and felt the descent as the plane entered the path for the runways looming far ahead.

Suddenly, he began to perspire, then felt dizzy and faint, a pain coming up in his chest he had not felt before. Raising his hand to push the call button, he had just reached it as his hand came back down and he lost consciousness. The last he heard was what seeming like loud voice—yelling in his ear to stay with someone—then nothing.

"Hartsfield, this is Delta 2210 with a medical emergency. We need immediate clearance to land. Repeat, this is a medical emergency. We need immediate clearance to land." The pilot, hearing the rushed call from the flight attendant who responded to the call button, then seeing Josh slumped over, and rapidly turning red in the face, pushed the emergency button, and rushed to a

From a Vantage Point

phone to talk to the cockpit. The result was the emergency call to the Hartsfield tower.

"Delta 2210, what is your emergency." asked the tower controller.

"Man, about 40 years old, with what appears to be a cardiac arrest. We need to get this bird down now."

"Roger, Delta 2210, a medical emergency is in progress, and you are cleared to approach and land on runway 12-North. Make a turn at zero seven zero degrees west, and descend to 1200 feet."

"Roger, tower, turning to seven-zero degrees and descending to one thousand."

"Delta 2210, you are one thousand. Turn to one two zero degrees, and descend to five hundred. Departing plane on your three o'clock. Continue on flight path and descend to designated altitude."

"Roger, tower. One-two-zero degrees and five hundred feet."

"Delta 2210, you are on path. Descend to two hundred fifty feet, and proceed to landing marker. On landing, turn right at marker 11-e, and gate C-26. Medical personnel are on hand at the gate for your emergency. All flights in path have been cleared. You are confirmed to proceed."

"Confirmed tower. On path at 200 feet, and descending. Thank you."

"Good luck, Delta 2210. There are better ways to welcome you to Atlanta."

"Roger that. Out here," echoed the captain, as his tires hit the runway.

"Ladies and gentlemen, we have a medical emergency on board, so the landing was a bit rough. We are taxiing to Gate C-26, where medical personnel will meet us. Please stay in your seats until told to move. We will open doors in the coach cabin to offload as many as possible, and as quickly as possible. Thank you for your patience, and welcome to Atlanta Hartsfield International Airport."

"When departing," the pilot continued, "Our ramp personnel will be available to assist you in getting to your next flight or destination. Thank you again for flying Delta, and have a good day. Flight attendants, please prepare the cabin for landing and the arrival of medical personnel."

An ambulance and a fire vehicle were racing along near the plane, intending to reach the arrival gate before the large jet. As the plane started to taxi into the gate, the firemen and EMTs were already on the ramp with a gurney and equipment, and entering the gate area. Two EMTs had lugged the folded gurney up the stairs to the jet way, entered the door, and quickly unfolded the gurney in preparation for arrival.

Meanwhile, gate personnel and other Delta supervisors were moving people from the gate to provide sufficient room for the emergency personnel to work, and eventually remove the patient through a short section of the terminal to the waiting ambulance. Emergency situations such as this were almost never private

From a Vantage Point

situations; virtually anyone in the terminal could see the assistance team provide emergency care.

"All right, the flight is in," shouted a ramp supervisor, as the jet arrived and the jet way was extended to cover the front door of the plane. At the same time, another set of stairs was brought to the middle door of the jet to allow passengers to depart.

"Let's move," shouted the ramp supervisor again, as she opened the gate departure door, and started down the ramp, followed quickly be two ticketing agents and two other ramp workers. They were moving slowly as the jet way finished its moves to cover the door. This was not standard procedure; used only when there was an emergency.

The ramp supervisor pushed the codes to unlock the door, and pulled out the opening latch of the door, and inside, the flight attendant looking through the port in the door started to do the same, breaking the air seal, and pushing the door out toward the jet way. The EMTs rushed in to the seat where Josh Giddons lay unconscious.

"Get rid of the shirt, and get him hooked up to the box," the lead EMT told another member of the team. Another EMT brought Josh forward to aid in removing the shirt, while the lead EMT tried to find a pulse in his neck.

"No pulse, no breath. Let's put the paddles to him and see what response we get," the lead EMT said as he grabbed a defibrillator box, opened it, and set up the equipment. He placed two small paddles on either side of Josh's chest, after attaching some electrodes to various places on the chest.

"Everybody off." Came the call as the EMT hit the shock button on the defibrillator, sending a jolt through Josh, and his body flexed in response.

"No beat," announced the EMT. "One more time," he said, as he twisted a dial slightly on the machine to increase the voltage, then hit the shock button.

"Still nothing," he announced. How long has this person been out?" he asked and a flight attendant responded, "About 12 minutes."

"OK then, one more jolt and we move him. The EMT hit the button and Josh jolted again, this time trying to push forward in the seat, and he gave a slight gasp, as if trying to breathe, then gave several more breaths hoarsely.

"We have a beat. Not much but we have a beat. Get a line in, and push air with the bag, and let's get him onto a board and on the gurney. Then we are out of here. Notify the hospital we are on our way with a live one." One of the EMTs went to the front near the cockpit and spoke into her radio, pinned to her shoulder loop, and gave the emergency room a report on the patient, and a status on arrival time.

Meanwhile, other passengers were departing the plane through the center door, and moving off toward a doorway below the arrival gate, where they were met by airline personnel. A few watched from their seats before departing as the

EMTs placed Giddons on a wooden board atop the gurney, and then placed him on it, covering him with a blanket. The vital signs monitor attached to him by cables was placed on the end of the gurney, and the bag of IV solution, which had been started was placed on a pole above his head.

Collecting their equipment, the EMTs started down the short aisle to the door of the first-class cabin, and out into the jet way toward the terminal. An airline supervisor went ahead to make sure the way was cleared for them to depart the gate and the terminal.

Outside the TSA secured area were two men in grey suits, standing near the opposite wall from the security entrance, one of them carrying a sign labeled "Mr. Atherton". Both wore dark glasses, and appeared to be two of the innumerable limo drivers so frequently seen at Hartsfield Airport. They stood there motionless, and silent until the gurney with Giddons emerged from the jet way, and they saw who it was on the gurney.

"Frank, it looks like our pigeon will not be riding with h us today."

"I think not," replied the other. "I better call and let them know what is happening."

"Right. This is not good at all."

One of the men, the one with the sign, left to go toward a small area in a vacant gate area to make a call, taking the sign and throwing it in a wastebasket as he went past.

"Problem here," said the man into his cell phone. "Looks like Atherton had some kind of medical problem. The EMTs hauled him out on a stretcher, and they were moving fast."

"OK," the man continued, in response to something he heard on his phone, "We will stay for a few minutes to see what falls out. I will try to get a location where they are taking him. Call you back later." That man stuck his cellphone back in his left jacket pocket, and walked back to where the other man stood.

"See if you can get one of those airline people to tell you something," he directed.

"Sure, I'll go," the other man responded. He walked slowly over to the counter and asked, "What happened to the guy? That was unusual, wasn't it?"

"It happens once in a great while sir. The man had a medical emergency. The EMTs are taking him a local hospital—Mercy, I think, but I am not really sure. Are you a relative?"

"No," responded the man, "Only interested. As you say, this doesn't happen very often I guess. Thanks." The man turned, and walked back to where his associate stood, and spoke briefly to him. Shortly after they turned and walked out to the parking lot to their car, driving away from the airport toward downtown.

From a Vantage Point

On the Kabul River, Afghanistan. Hakim woke with a start, hearing a weapon firing nearby. He sat up quickly, looked around for the two men who boarded with them, and found both sleeping further along the deck.

"It is all right, sir," assured Abadi as Hakim looked over to where he stood at the rail of the boat. "There are men firing on shore. We are quite close, as you can see, but they are not firing at us. It is quite common here. They are probably firing at poachers on their land. Everything is all right. Sorry it woke you up so quickly."

Hakim looked around some more, and then started to rise slowly, grasping for the deck rail and pulling himself to his feet.

"Where did the firing come from?"

"Over there, on the shore," responded Abadi, pointing to the shore off the port side of the boat. They were probably hunters. No one else comes out here.'" added Abadi excitedly.

"How much time do we have before we get to the bend of the river?" asked Hakim.

"About four hours more, we will see the bend ahead, and the one hour more to get there where you want to go," was the response.

"Good. Then let us prepare for the end of the trip. Is there breakfast?" asked Hakim, as he could smell something cooking.

"Yes, sir, I have made some small thing for you," said Abadi in a rush, as he moved past Hakim, and down the hold stairs to the small galley on board. Hakim could hear pots and pans clanging and then Abadi, food in hand, rush up the stairs.

"Thank you, my friend," offered Hakim, as he took the plate, which had some vegetables on it, and a fork.

"Eat, and then we can prepare for our arrival at the bend," said Abadi, smiling, and hoping Hakim would approve of the breakfast. Abadi had secured some small vegetables in Peshawar for the trip. It was just about all he really could cook, so he was proud of his creation.

The food actually tasted terrible; it was cooked in some kind of oil, and heavily seasoned, but Hakim was hungry and food was food on a remote river in Pakistan. He forced a smile as he ate to give Abadi the feeling he appreciated the effort, and continued to scan the shorelines, not completely comfortable that Abadi was right about the shots being from simple hunters. He would stay on guard all the way to his rendezvous at the bend with others he trusted more completely.

Mercy Hospital, Atlanta, GA. A nursing assistant stood at the doorway to the emergency department entrance as the ambulance drove onto the hospital property and up into the circular drive at the entrance. There was no siren

From a Vantage Point

blaring, nor flashing lights, and the nursing assistant knew that meant the patient. Had not survived.

"Hi guys, what do have," the assistant asked the driver, as he stopped the vehicle and left the truck cab to come to the rear and open the double doors.

"A DOA from the airport. We had the guy for a while, but his last breath was about two miles ago. He never had a chance. We only got a small pulse on the plane, and he barely breathed; needed bagging most of the way."

"OK, so you don't need me then," she responded, as she started to push the gurney back toward the emergency room doorway."

"Nothing for you to do. I never have figured out why they send you out with a gurney. We always take the patients in on ours. Seems like a total waste to me," said the EMT who climbed down from the back of the vehicle.

"You and me both," she replied, "But its protocol." She shrugged her shoulders as she pushed the gurney back inside, and left it along the wall.

The two EMTs brought their own gurney with the late Josh Giddons out of the ambulance, raised the heights and sides, and moved it into the entranceway, stopping to give the clerk their clipboard forms.

"DOA," the clerk responded as she reviewed the form, "You are taking the body to the morgue?"

"We will," answered the driver. "Nothing else to do right now. Can't exactly leave the stiff in front of your desk, can we?"

"You are so kind," the clerk responded, as she turned to enter the name "Atherton DOA" into her log. As she did, the EMTs took the gurney and turned right into a side corridor where an elevator would take them to the morgue.

Downtown Atlanta, GA. The two men in the car drove down a side street near the arena, and turned into a parking garage entrance. The driver took out a card, pressed it against an electronic pad, which brought up the barrier, and they drove into the garage; going down two levels to a waiting parking space near an elevator. Taking the elevator, they soon arrived at the 14th floor, waited until the door opened, and then walked directly across to an office. The glass walls had large letters saying, "Diamond Imports – Gems from South Africa – Wholesale Only."

One of the men took a plastic card from his jacket pocket and scanned it across an electronic reader, the door lock clicked to allow their entrance. As they went through the door, another man, standing in front of a cubicle, saw them and waved to them.

"You two go to my office. I will be right there," he shouted across the room. The men walked to the left and down a corridor, entering an office with the name 'James Withers' on the door panel.

"Did he see you?" asked the woman at the desk.

From a Vantage Point

"He told us to come in here. Sounded angry. Is there something going on?"

"Don't know. No one tells me anything. Better that way, I think. What is happening with Ike and Mike?"

One of the men scowled at the names, but answered, "Nothing, we just watched a still go to Mercy Hospital; the guy we were supposed to pick up." She shrugged his shoulders, and the two men sat down waiting for Withers to return.

"That news is really going to make him happy. You two are just a bunch of good news today. I think it is time for me to go to lunch," she said, as she grabbed her purse, and started for the door. She was barely there, and about to turn the doorknob when Withers walked in. As he came in, she left.

"OK you two, where is Atherton?"

"Dead," answered one of the men. "Apparently had a heart attack on the plane. They did an emergency land, and the EMTs took him to Mercy. When they got there, he was dead, so they put him in the morgue. Anything else you need us for?"

"Don't be a smart mouth. Any impression they might know who he really was?"

"Don't think so Jim," responded the other. "I asked the gate people about him, and they just thought he had a heart attack, nothing more."

"All right. Get our people over there to get his ID and effects. They will know soon enough who is he anyway, but let's make it harder."

"Sure boss. I can take care of that. Anything else?"

"Did anyone see you guys at the airport?"

"I don't think so. We stayed close to the walls to reduce the camera possibilities, and I had my sunglasses and hat on when I went to get the car from the airport garage. Joe here met me outside and he was wearing shades as well."

"Change the plates and registration on the car, and put it out in our garage for a while, until things cool down. Get another car for you to drive."

"Sure boss. Who is this guy anyway?"

"You really don't want to know. Just get me the effects and I will take care of everything else. Get moving now."

Withers walked past the men into his own office and closed the door. Sitting down at his desk, he sat for a few moments before opening his desk and taking out a small notebook. He flipped through several pages before putting his finger on a number inside, and then dialed the number on his phone. The phone rang several times before someone answered.

"This is Withers. Tell Harold that the person he expected to arrive here today will not be with us. He died of a heart attack on the plane before it arrived. He needs to let me know about an alternate plan." Waiting a few seconds to hear the person on the other side hang up, Withers did likewise, and sat looking at the door to his office.

From a Vantage Point

Morgue at Mercy Hospital, Atlanta GA. The clanging of a gurney coming down the tiled corridor could be heard at the other end, just like an echo. The two EMTs brought their 'passenger' in through the wide doors, and waited for one of the technicians to come into the room. One of the technicians had seen them come through a set of wide glass windows, and walked through from the laboratory to where they stood waiting.

"What you have guys? Don't see you two down here often."

"A stiff from the airport. Heart attack on the plane."

"Probably the food," responded the technician. They all laughed.

"OK, let's put him on this table. You guys get one end and I will grab the head end, and lift and pull. That's all there is to it. No pain involved." They laughed again, as they lifted in unison and dropped Atherton on the table.

"Where are his other effects?"

"Up at the admissions desk. They wanted to log him in, I guess."

"OK, I'll get them to send them down. Thanks for the delivery. Sorry, but I don't have anyone you can take back with you."

"Comedian," one of the EMTs yelled back at him, as they took their gurney, removed the rest of the covering sheets, tossed them into a laundry hamper and started to leave. "We'll tell the clerk to send his stuff down."

"Thanks," answered the technician, as he started to remove some clothes from the body, and get him ready for autopsy.

Ten minutes later, an older gentleman arrived at the admissions desk of the emergency room, asking about the Atherton personal effects, with the story they were requested by the morgue for identification. The clerk found the bag with what had been in his pockets, and gave them to the messenger, who started down the corridor toward the morgue.

As soon as he was out of the line of sight from admissions, the man went off toward an outside door, dropped his messenger jacket near a waste can, and walked out into the sunlight, going over to a car where a man waited for the bag the messenger was carrying. Once it had been handed over, the messenger went back inside, retrieved the jacket, and took it back to a locker room, where he hung it back up on its hook behind the door.

In just a minute or two, the man was back outside, entering the passenger side of the car and the two men drive off into the afternoon sunlight. They had Atherton's belongings, and could go back to the office and complete their mission. It had been a long day.

Along the Kabul River, Afghanistan. The last leg of the boat trip up river turned out to be uneventful. When Hakim had finished his breakfast on the boat, he and Abadi discussed the plans for moving further into the country when they

220

From a Vantage Point

reached the bend of the river. Hakim knew there would be two men waiting with horses and equipment to take them on the next stage of the journey, and Hakim looked forward to that, since he was a much better horseman than a sailor. Abadi was just the opposite; he disliked horses, and they disliked him for some unknown reason, but he would survive as he always had on these journeys. For now, he would simply enjoy the short remainder of this part of the trip.

"Sir, you can see the bend ahead," Abadi announced to Hakim, who had been looking in another direction, but quickly turned to see for himself.

"I see Abadi, how much longer?"

"About an hour Sir," was the response, followed by "The men with the horses should be there waiting."

"What happens to these other two when we arrive?"

"They will be met by others, and go on their own way sir," Abadi replied. "They have orders for what they will do. We will not see them again."

The boat moved smoothly along, it seemed like much less than an hour, when Hakim saw two men waving along the bank ahead, one of them with both arms to signal them.

"We are here, Sir," announced Abadi, "These are my men, and they are very trustworthy, as you know. We will do well from here. They are ready for us."

Hakim looked intently at the shore, and saw a third man, a face he thought he recognized, and wondered why another should be waiting.

As they came close to the shore, the person Hakim saw was indeed an old friend. "What are you doing here meeting us Saleem?"

"I came myself to give you news, Hakim. Come ashore and we will talk," he added waving them toward the shore. Abadi threw a rope to help pull them toward the shoreline.

"What is this news you have for me Saleem," asked Hakim, as they embraced, not having seen each other for over a year.

"I am afraid, my friend," responded Saleem, "Your friend Josh Giddons has died."

"How?" asked Hakim, obviously shocked at the news.

"A heart attack as his plane was approaching the airport in Atlanta, Georgia in the United States. We do not know much more; only what information we received from our friends in Atlanta who were to pick him up when he arrived."

"Do the Americans know who it is yet?"

"We think not. Our people took his belongings and identifications, but they will in a short time. We must make plans to replace him if we are to succeed with your plan."

"I know what we must do Saleem. First, I must get to a telephone. How can we do that out here?"

From a Vantage Point

"I have a satellite telephone for you to use Hakim. It is new, and safe, and secure as it might be. Please use it if you wish while we prepare for departure. Abadi, you come help us." Saleem waved to Abadi, and the two men walked off toward others holding horses.

From a Vantage Point

Chapter 25 A Change in Plans

Morgue, Mercy Hospital, Atlanta, GA. The shift had changed before the autopsy on the man named Atherton would begin. The technician who covered the body with a sheet, after removing his clothes was gone for the day, and two new technicians had arrived, along with Dr. William Scully, a pathologist. One of the technicians, Jim Shadd, was a medical student in his third year at Emory, and was always anxious to assist in any case which might come in. Today was no different.

"Hey doc, what about this new body? Are we working tonight?" asked Shadd, as he looked under the sheet at Atherton.

"We certainly are, young man," responded Dr. Scully. "Just as soon as I can find the information on this guy. Did anyone ask for his effects and papers?"

"The day guy said they did," answered Shadd, looking around on the desk to the side of the autopsy room. "They don't look like they are here, though. I'll walk over to admitting and see where they are."

"Good, I would really like to get this done this evening," said Scully, waving Shadd off to go on his errand.

Barely five minutes passed before Shadd was back, this time with a set of papers in his hand, but nothing else.

"Doc, emergency admitting claims they sent everything down here earlier, personal stuff as well. They gave me a copy of what they had, though."

"Good, let me see what it says then," said Scully as he extended his hand to receive the papers. "Not much here. Arrived from the airport via ambulance. Apparently had a heart attack on an incoming plane over at Hartsfield. Died in the ambulance according to this."

Dr. Scully pulled off the covering sheet and looked over the body.

"First look agrees with the cardiac arrest scenario. There does not seem to be any other obvious indicators. Let's reserve judgment until we do the work though. Jim, get his prints and run them through Atlanta PD, and let's be sure who we have here."

"Sure doc, no problem," said Shadd, as he went over to the shelf above the desk and took down the fingerprint device they received from Atlanta PD. The device records the prints, and then checks with FBI and others to confirm the identity. Shadd carefully took the print of each finger, recording which finger, and what hand, and then pushed the 'check' button, putting the device down on the side of the autopsy table waiting for a reply.

"That took no time at all, Jim," exclaimed the doctor. Let's see what we have here. Well, well, please meet Mr. Joshua Giddons, formerly of the Sudan. He is

From a Vantage Point

wanted by the FBI on several terrorism charges. Better expect a visit from those boys shortly."

Dr. Scully took a blank sheet from the desktop and started to fill in the blanks on the autopsy cover sheet, putting Giddons name as the name, and Atherton as an alias.

"OK Jim, let's do this," the doctor said, as he looked over toward his technician, who walked quickly over to the table. "Get everything ready, and let's start in about five minutes."

"Can do Doc," was the response. Shadd took a small cart near the table, and started walking with it over to the storage cabinets in the room, taking out instruments and other equipment needed for the autopsy. In five minutes, he would be opening a body with his mentor.

At the Bend of the Kabul River, Afghanistan. Hakim dialed a number, and then waited. He could hear through the phone some type of connection being made, and then a voice came on.

"Hakim, I thought you would call quickly."

"I am here. What has happened?"

"Your friend had a heart attack on the plane into Atlanta. He died before he reached the hospital. I sent men to the hospital to get his effects. We have friends there. There is only limited time before his real identity is known. What would you have us do?"

"Do nothing until I call you from Kabul. Is there any possibility that your men will be discovered?"

"None. They are all unknown to the police or the Federals."

"Good. On second thought, there is one thing I want you to do. You must get a message to Sammi that our plans are changing, and he will need to do something for us. I will speak to you further on that from Kabul."

"All right, Hakim. I will wait for your call." Both men hung up in tandem, and Hakim passed the phone back to Saleem, and went over to where Abadi stood and said, "Abadi, my friend, our plans are changing, but we go on to Kabul. We need to hurry though."

"As you wish Sir, we can leave immediately."

"Good. We will do that then."

Within minutes, the men were on horses, headed for Kabul with Saleem and the other guide. It would be a perilous journey, and Hakim was now worried as much about himself, as he was for his friend Josh.

Washington, DC. Alerts went off at nearly the same time, at both the FBI and the Department of Homeland Security, with the news that Josh Giddons was dead in Atlanta. For Alice Sawyer, it meant that Jim Davis was right; Giddons had

From a Vantage Point

been in the United States, and she had to figure out how and why he was here. She considered notifying Davis about the information she received from the FBI as she walked the short distance to the office of her technical staff.

"OK boys, we have Giddons," she announced to the small staff, who looked over at her, and waited for more information.

"How do we know?" asked one of the technicians.

"The FBI called, and he is on a slab in Mercy Hospital in Atlanta; died of a heart attack on a plane to Atlanta. One of you get Mercy on the phone, and get the information. We want to know the flight number, so we can back-check where he has been. We need that now."

Two of the technicians immediately jumped to computers, and one other picked up a phone after looking at a list, and started to make a call.

"I have the EMT report. Giddons was on Delta flight 2210 from Seattle. That was one of the flight numbers we had where we could not get a clear shot of faces."

"All right, then get Mercy Hospital to send you a face shot, and let's do some checking."

"Will do Ma'am," responded one of the technicians, again picking up a phone and calling the hospital. Within a minute or two a photo came up on his computer screen.

"Got it," yelled the technician. "I'll pass this against the partials we had from the stream at Seattle, and we'll see what we get." On the screen, almost a blur was visible as the head shot was scanned against all the footage from the airport in Seattle, and then the movement stopped, and a group of three shots were on the screen—one at the terminal entrance, one at the gate where 2210 had departed, and one in the main terminal area, where the man had gone to purchase a newspaper.

"Here he is, and you can barely see across the terminal where Davis was sitting in the bar waiting for his flight."

"All right then, we can validate what Jim Davis saw, and we need to let him know soonest in Japan. Have him hop a flight back. We will need him on this."

Alice returned to her office and made a phone call to an old friend at the CIA. She had served with Bernie Minihan on the Overseas Joint Terrorism Task Force in its early days during the Bush Administration as Homeland Security formed from several agencies.

Alice had been with the Coast Guard Interdiction office in those days, chasing down drug smugglers; her first introduction to Josh Giddons and Hakim al-Azahir. She was moving to Homeland Security as they went dark during the buildup days in Afghanistan. Now, she was concerned about what they, at least Hakim, was up to, and why they were in the US. "Mr. Minihan's line, may I help you, Ms. Sawyer?" said the voice from the other end of the line.

225

"Hello Agnes, how are you," Alice responded. "Is Bernie available?"

"For you he is. He just finished a meeting, and walked into his office just a moment ago. Hold for just a sec."

"Alice, what can I do for you this fine day? Are you catching some of my spies?"

"Bernie, you never change. I am chasing someone you used to be interested in, though," responded Alice.

"I know," said Bernie in return, "Sarah told me there were rumbles about Hakim al-Azahir and his buddy, but I thought they were running around the Sudan somewhere. What's happening?"

"Josh Giddons came up dead of an apparent heart attack on a plane coming into Atlanta early this morning. We don't have all the details yet, but he was coming in from Seattle, and who knows where before that."

"That is definitely not good. Any thoughts here?"

"One of my guys, from the Sky Marshal's Service, was on a plane recently with a guy going to Doha; a farmer from West Virginia. He turned out to link up with both of these characters there, and then went onto Sudan. We know the three of them were in the military together, and then did some time running guns and goods for various causes in Europe and the Middle East."

"Eventually, the farmer, Willard Johnson, returned to the US to work on a farm his parents owned in rural West Virginia. As far as we know, he has stayed there until now, over ten years, and hasn't seen either of those men to our knowledge."

"OK," responded Bernie, "Then two questions; one what do you think you have here, and two, how can I help?"

"I hoped you would ask that Bernie. One of your own guys in Khartoum was following those boys. I need to know what he knows."

"You mean Jeff Namers?"

"Yes, Jeff was working an issue on one of my sky marshals, Jim Davis, and a relationship with one of Hakim's relatives which blew up a few weeks ago. I brought Davis home under arrest as a subterfuge, but I imagine Namers might still be following up. We need to know where Hakim is presently, and what has been happening over there. Can you help?"

"Of course. I will get one of Sarah's people involved, and she will get back to you soonest. Will that work?"

"Absolutely. Any help I can get would really be appreciated. Come downtown sometime soon and have lunch. You and Sarah are always welcome."

"Love to, but I get lost down there. Better out here in the country. About the only time I go downtown is to the Kennedy Center. I can get there from the Parkway and don't get lost. This afternoon, I have another meeting. Sarah will call you within the hour."

From a Vantage Point

"That works. Thanks, my friend."

"Any time for a woman who saved my life once or twice. Take care." Bernie hung up, took a sheaf of papers, and walked out of his office. He had just started down the corridor to the conference room when he saw Sarah coming out of hers. She waved hello when she saw him.

"Don't I know you from somewhere?" asked Bernie.

"I think you are the father of my children, or maybe a clone. Either way, I don't see you very often."

"Meetings my dear. Did you get a babysitter so we can go out to dinner this evening?"

"I did," she responded. "The girl across the street, but we have to be back early."

"Works for me. By the way, I got a call from Alice Sawyer on the case you discussed weeks ago with Jeff Namers. Could you get an update, and call Alice? Apparently Giddons was in the US; died in Atlanta of a heart attack yesterday. It is really blowing minds over at DHS."

"Sure, I can do that. Will call her within the hour. Jeff should be in the office."

"Thanks. Got to go." Bernie kissed Sarah on the cheek as he walked by, and entered the conference room for hopefully his last meeting of the day. Sarah continued down the corridor, finally entering another office.

Within the hour, Sarah had returned Alice Sawyer's call to Bernie, and both she and Jeff Namers patched into a conference call on a secure line so they could discuss the information Alice needed.

"Alice, I have Jeff Namers, our desk officer in Khartoum on the line with me. Jeff has been following the al-Azahir-Giddons enterprises for some time."

"Hello, Jeff. Appreciate your return call. I know you both are busy. Let me fill you in on what I know first, then, hopefully, you can fill in some blanks for me."

"Works for me," responded Namers.

"All right then, one of our sky marshals identified Josh Giddons a couple of days ago in the Seattle Airport, headed down toward a gate. Unfortunately, he only got a fleeting look, and by the time he went out into the terminal, Giddons was gone. We checked footage at all the gates and could not complete a good enough ID to stop a flight to pull him off."

"Later," Alice continued, "We were notified that a body in the morgue at Mercy Hospital in Atlanta had a body with the fingerprints matching Giddons from his Army service. He apparently died of a heart attack. So, we traced backward from his flight and saw that he arrived at Sea-Tac on foot. Further checks showed that he returned a rental car he had secured in Vancouver. We are still tracing further back."

"Our concern is why he is here, and why not with his cohort al-Azahir. Any thoughts?"

"Sure, I do," responded Namers. "We did some checking here and found out that al-Azahir and Giddons both left the country at the same time; one bound for Montreal, and the other, al-Azahir, simply disappeared. As I said, we are still checking on his whereabouts."

"Any idea why the sudden moves?" asked Alice.

"Only one. It may be that Khartoum was simply getting too hot for them. Hakim knew we were on his trail, and watching him closely. Normally, that would not have mattered to him, but the present government also sees him as a problem—a pest really—but they would be happy to see him gone as well."

"I will say though," Namers continued, "Hakim does nothing by chance. He has an organized plan for everything he does. The trouble is that he is normally one step ahead of us. We tried to off him with a drone, and he simply vacated his apartment a day before the strike. He has people everywhere who both protect him, and provide him intelligence as good as ours."

"For a while, we thought he had a mole in our shop, which might have involved one of your marshals. We checked all that out and the guy was set up. We think because he may have known too much from whatever Hakim may think he learned from their friend Will Johnson. Nothing for sure, just a hunch there, but it does fit the patterns."

"Tell me a bit more about this Will Johnson please?"

"Alice, I can help there," answered Sarah. "Johnson owns a farm in West Virginia. He had a somewhat troubled history; came to the US with his parents who fled the Lebanese Civil War. They were Maronite Christians right in the middle of that mess. His father got the family out, and they eventually settled in West Virginia. He bought a farm and worked it for years."

"When Will turned 18, he enlisted in the Army, eventually went AWOL to avoid Vietnam, and ended up in Europe, where he met two of his former military buddies—Hakim and Giddons. They basically became mercenaries of a type, and supported a number of terrorist groups—mostly moving money and supplies around Europe, the Middle East, and eventually to Yemen and Sudan supporting Bin-Laden."

"Johnson did this for about two years, and then turned himself in and returned to the US. The Army gave him a general discharge under the Carter amnesty program, and he went back to the farm. After his father died, he took over and has been very successful, as far as we know. You might check his domestic record, but we see nothing other than a farmer right now."

"Thanks Sarah, we will check out Johnson, just to be sure. Can you send us your files on Hakim and Giddons Jeff?"

"Already on the way, Ma'am. Your comms people should have them. I sent them to the address Sarah had for you."

"That will do it. My guys will bring them in. Thanks. I will keep you informed of what we find. Right now, I need to close the timeline between Montreal and Vancouver, and then get an answer to the basic question; why is he here?"

"Get the answer to that and the whole thing unfolds," responded Jeff. "Well, out here unless you have anything else you need from me."

"No Jeff, I think we are done here," said Sarah.

"Yes, we are done. Thanks for the info," added Alice. "Talk to you both again soon, I will bet."

The conference line went dead. Alice sat thinking for a moment or two, and started down the hall to the commo room to get her documents.

In the Afghanistan mountains. Hakim loved Afghanistan. Riding along as the group rode higher into the mountains, along the narrow paths that only locals knew, he could feel the cool, clean air, and quickly lapsed into Pashto, as they rode along. This was the native language of most of the group, and one which Hakim knew well from his years in the country.

Some of their discussion centered on families and local happenings; things which happened since his last visit. One of the men had a new daughter, and would show Hakim her picture proudly when they camped for the night. Others discussed holidays, and new members of the various groups he supported. None, however, asked, or was expected to ask why Hakim was in Afghanistan. There was a firm rule among these people; keep what you know to yourself, and ask little, since you might be forced to give it up later to others.

By late afternoon on the first day, all the men were tired, and since they reached a place where they could stop, they decided to do so. They arrived at a short outcrop in the higher hills, with a small cave where they bring in their horses, and make camp, having a small fire which would not be seen from the outside. Two of the men went ahead to make sure no others were in the area, and one entered the cave to inspect it, making sure they were safe. When all returned, the men entered the cave, tied up their horses, and unpacked what they needed for the night.

Over the small campfire, they cooked what they had brought, both from the boat, and what the two men on horseback had brought with them, and continued to talk about their villages and of other things of interest. This routine continued, as they gradually made their way up and then west along the mountain range until they neared Gerdi, where their two guides would leave Hakim and Abadi. The other two men on the boat left them after the second day, riding north as they reached the crest of the hilly area, and onto a path in the direction of a nearby camp only about twenty miles away.

All the while, Hakim thought about the changes needed in their plans for what they would do in the US. Without Josh to guide events, Hakim had to rely

From a Vantage Point

on his cells in the Washington and Atlanta areas, and he remembered vividly the prior experience with a cell in that same area which had destroyed a drug shipment, but failed in its overall mission to extend their drug-related trade to US servicemen in the Norfolk, Virginia area. He did not want a repeat here.

The men he had chosen had no links to any prior efforts. They were businessmen, most of them not even Muslim, or in any way related to their causes. In several cases, they were refugees and immigrants passing legally into the United States through the government's immigration program. All had been investigated, cleared, and granted visas allowing them to live and work in the US. None had committed any crimes, and even the one who contacted Sammi and was eliminated, was shown to have had an auto accident, with the car burning up enough to prevent a clear identification of the small caliber bullet which had entered his neck and severed his artery before passing out of the body.

Now, Hakim would use Will Johnson, his farmer friend, as the lead for his next adventure. He would likewise be untraceable, but if caught, they could prove nothing. It was time to wait a while and let the education process take itself to Johnson's heart and mind. In that effort, his 'friend' Sammi would take the lead. All the while, Johnson would continue to be the gentleman farmer with a mission to help his neighbors.

Chapter 26 The Start of Retraining

Jalalabad, Afghanistan The sun was high in the sky, and the heat was nearly unbearable for the two men on horseback as they arrived on the edge of the city. Their trip had been an arduous one; ranging over often narrow and ill-defined trials through the hills as they drew nearer to Jalalabad, and a brief respite before riding the last leg to Kabul. This evening Hakim and Abadi would be in a real room, with running water and a bed to sleep in.

Hakim still had a major decision to make; how to deal with their plans in the United States now that Josh Giddons was dead. He needed to do something, and, as they rode down leisurely toward Jalalabad, he formed a new plan in his mind. To put it in place, he needed a secure phone to make a call to Khartoum. He decided not to wait until he had arrived later in Kabul to start working out the details.

In Jalalabad, Hakim owned a small house in a concentrated section near the Afghan Army Warehouse complex. It was small, off a side street, and very safe. Hakim had spent his career working both sides of the political climate; he had friends in the Government and among the Taliban, with whom he frequently did business. While his primary sponsor was officially al-Qaeda's supply organization, he was very comfortable moving goods, money, and providing other services to anyone who would pay.

He and Abadi came into the city along the western edge, near the airport, where they brought their horses to a small stable—a friend who often provided this service for his people. In turn, he got the keys to a small four-wheel drive vehicle, which he and Abadi used to carry their equipment to his house. When they pulled up along the street, there were no vehicles, and no people around, something they preferred, as they parked, looked well in every direction, and then exited the car for the relative safety of the house. Once inside, they dropped their equipment and both went looking for water from the tap, one of the few amenities they had due to their proximity to the military base.

About an hour later, Hakim went looking for his satellite phone, finding it in his pack, and started to make a call. Abadi was in the kitchen making something for them both, since one of Hakim's people who lived nearby brought over some food when he realized Hakim was there. Lunch consisted of vegetables, fruit, dates, and local bread, but it was enough for them, having become used to trail food for the last several weeks.

"Akram, it is Hakim. Assalam Alaikum."

'Alaikum Assalam, Hakim. How are you? I did not expect to hear from you yet."

"I know," responded Hakim. "I need to put a new plan in motion, and it could not wait until we reached the city."

"I understand. The loss of Yusha was very close to your heart. May All'ah hold him in his hand? What do you wish me to do?"

"Who do you have in our brethren in the United States that is a female, and can pass for someone of the faith from Lebanon?"

"Just a short time ago, perhaps a year, a woman went to a place called Delaware in the United States, to be married to one of our brethren. We arranged it to get her into the country. She is working in a house as a servant."

"Good. Can we arrange to send her to our friend Sammi Khan? We will tell him that she will work in his restaurant."

"That is easy to do, and she is from Lebanon, although she was born in Syria. She is very bright and also a good cook."

"Fine. Get information to her on the background of Will Johnson. We introduced him to one woman he thinks is his cousin from his father's village. I want this woman to begin his training. She will do for us what Josh was to have done."

"It will be done as you say Hakim. I will send the messages today, and she will go to Sammi. Can I also send the one she is to marry, since she received papers based on getting married?"

"Yes, have Sammi find something for him to do as well. I need this done quickly, and we need to be sure it is done well. We do not want another error like what happened in South Carolina."

"What is your will is also mine, my friend. It will be done. I will tend to it myself."

"Good, then I will see you in Kabul, and we will renew ourselves in each other."

"I await your arrival Hakim. Everything will be prepared. Be careful, the government police are everywhere, as like the old days, even worse."

"I will, my friend. Have peace."

And may All'ah protect you my friend." Both men hung up at the same time, and Hakim returned the satellite phone to his pack.

"Are you ready for lunch, Hakim?" asked Abadi, as Hakim ended his conversation.

"I am. Thank you Abadi, you are a true friend." Abadi brought in food for both and set it on the small table in the living room, where they ate the first real food in weeks.

Washington, DC Alice sat looking at the documents the CIA had sent, looking over Hakim and Giddons first, and then spent more time reviewing those of Johnson. She saw his history; born in Lebanon, an Eastern-rite Catholic, both

From a Vantage Point

parents dead, and their emigration to the US, where they settled on a farm in West Virginia. What interested her most was his decision to desert from the Army and head for Europe, the eventual home of hundreds of former soldiers, at least until the Carter Amnesty Program brought many home.

Somehow, Johnson seemed different in her mind. The only thing really bothering her was his association with the other two fugitives; spending nearly two years roaming over Europe and the Middle East working for whatever insurgency or group of malcontents that would hire them. She saw nothing in the records to indicate he had returned at any time to his native Lebanon, nor did she see much in the way of a listing of relatives who might still be in that country.

I'm not going to spend much more time on this right now, Alice said to herself, throwing the files into her inbox, and reminding herself to get someone to review it in the next day or so. She knew she could not use Jim Davis, since he already knew Johnson, and that might tip his identity, so she would have to find someone else for the job.

Just as she did so, Tom O'Neal, one of her analysts from the FBI loaned to the Task force, came into the office with a piece of paper in his hand.

"Alice, "said O'Neal, "This guy Johnson you have an interest in; his name just came up on the NCIC on a records check. Thought you might like to know." He handed her the printout of the request.

"Interesting. From the Agriculture Department. It seems he is working a plan to create a cooperative among the famers in his town, and wants USDA assistance. Hmmm. Tom, how would you like to be a farm cooperative agent for a while?"

"Alice, I can smell the wood burning. What do you have in mind?"

"Agriculture will appoint a contact for Johnson, and I want that contact to be you. That gives you an excuse to visit the farm, meet the people, and do an assessment of Johnson Interested?"

"Sounds like something different. It gets me out of the office, and out of DC. Of course. When do I start?"

"Let me talk to the people over at Agriculture and I will get back to you. In the meanwhile, here is a file on Johnson for you to review. He is an interesting man, by the way. Has two friends on our really, really wanted list."

"OK Alice, let me know when you are ready," answered O'Neal, as he waved and walked out of the office and down the corridor toward his own, file in hand.

Alice sat back in her chair, and formed a plan. She had no idea where it would lead, but she was going to bring down Hakim Al-Azahir.

Tokyo, Japan "US Passenger Davis, James Davis, please pick up a courtesy phone along the side walls in the terminal for a message. Passenger James Davis, please pick up a courtesy phone for a message," the public-address announcement continued to blare for nearly twenty minutes, before Jim Davis heard it and headed for a courtesy phone.

"This is Jim Davis; how can I help you?" Davis spoke into one of the myriad red wall phones connected to customer service.

"Mr. Davis, you have a call from Washington DC. Could you come to operations to take the call? We have them waiting for you."

Davis looked around and realized he was nearly at Operations. "Sure, I'm in the main corridor now, and will be there in about two minutes. Are they still holding?"

"Yes sir, they are. It sounds important. The code is 2Y16."

When he heard the code, Davis knew it was from Alice. He picked up some speed and headed for the operations office. Reaching the door, he punched in the code on the keypad at the door and entered.

"Marshal Davis, you can take your call over at the phone by the side chair, if you wish," said the guard inside.

"Thanks, I will," he responded, and walked over and sat down on the overstuffed chair, then picked up the phone.

"This is Davis. Can I help you?"

"Jim, Ben Stratton. Alice asked me to call and tell you to get back here posthaste. All she said was to tell you they found Giddons, whoever he is, and he is dead in Atlanta. She said you would know what that meant. We have already changed your schedule, and an Air Force jet is waiting for you at Yakota. How soon can you get there?"

"Probably in about two hours in this traffic."

"That long. We will send a chopper for you from Yakota. You know where to pick it up?"

"Sure do. About a ten-minute walk through the terminals. I will see them there in fifteen."

"Roger that Jim. I will notify Yakota."

"Thanks. On my way."

"Out here," said Stratton, who then dialed up Yakota to get the chopper in the air.

Davis started walking over toward the General Aviation area where a small Air Force detachment, just short of that part of the field, stood up for just such emergencies. He was there about ten minutes when he heard a chopper in the distance. He was on his way home, and in style. In about ten hours, he would be in DC, looked forward to seeing the Capitol, knowing it meant the drudge of DC work life. How wrong he would be this time.

Washington DC *Alice Sawyer made several calls to her contacts at the Department of Agriculture, arranging for O'Neal to join the staff of the*

Cooperative Programs Branch, which was working with Will Johnson on his cooperative project in Elias. When she notified O'Neal, he arranged to go over to Agriculture, about six blocks away, and process in through their human resources office. That gave him an identity and a badge for his surveillance.

The Cooperative Programs Branch is located out in College Park, Maryland, near the University. O'Neal drove out there to meet the senior staff, and get a briefing on his role as a liaison with local community groups, asked a lot of questions, and was introduced to the rest of the liaison staff, who did not know his real persona, nor his purpose for joining the group. Now, all he had to do was wait for the next meeting with Johnson, at which he would be introduced as his new liaison and, hopefully, gain his confidence.

O'Neal's introduction to the staff identified him as a community specialist, one who had spent the last several years overseas working with various Agency for International Development projects. Since several of the staff had AID experience, this made the transition easier, especially since O'Neal had, at one time, done some investigations on AID and knew their routines and locations.

The following morning, O'Neal arrived early in College Park, ready to start his new assignment. He went to the third floor of the building and found the office where he would work; stopping for a cup of coffee in the small dinette the agency had for its employees.

"Hey, you must be new here?" said a man standing by the coffee pot, and extending his hand. "I'm John Betts, and we will probably be working together."

"Glad to meet you, John Betts," responded O'Neal. "I'm Tom O'Neal, a new member of the liaison group. I understand I will be working with a new project in West Virginia that starts today."

"Great Tom. Then you will be working with me. I have the Middle Atlantic area from Maryland to North Carolina, and inland with Tennessee, Kentucky, and West Virginia. A lot of farmland, and a lot of folks who want to start cooperatives for their products." Betts stood staring at O'Neal, and then added, "You know, you look familiar."

Tom O'Neal took a deep breath and waited to see if there would be more.

"Did you ever work for AID?"

"I did actually, in several places. Last assignment was in Botswana about six years ago."

"I thought so. I was with AID in Mali at the time. They had some problems over there, didn't they?"

"Sure did. We had the FBI, and everybody else from State and AID, on our necks for months. It eventually blew over when they found they didn't have anything really wrong, though a station chief did get moved."

"I remember that now," returned Betts. "Something about contracts, wasn't it?"

"Yes, it was," answered O'Neal. "Three contracts, as I remember, went to friends of government officials. It turned out that these guys actually were the best bidders for the contracts, but the station chief was reprimanded for using poor judgment."

"Oh, well, too bad. Those things happen. In any case, welcome to the team Tom. We have a guy coming in from West Virginia today. Is that your first case? I have been out for a few days, so I'm trying to catch up."

"Yes, it is. Bill Jones, I guess he is your assistant, assigned the case so that I could get going."

"Good. I like it when people dive in. We have too many requests, too few people, and too little time; and that doesn't even touch the lack of funding for most requests. This one, though, had some powerful friends, including a Senator, who pushed to get it approved. It went through quickly. Today is the second meeting with their representative, a Will Johnson. He seems like a likeable fellow; easy to work with so far, and I think you will find him interesting."

"Really, in what way?" asked O'Neal.

"He comes from an area that was heavy into both coal and farming; mixed groups including a large Amish population, and they are eager and pushing to move fast to get this going. They have already had several local and regional sales, and have done well. Now, they want to move toward expanding their area, and are looking to see what we can do to help. The meeting this morning will hopefully flesh out what we can do for them." Betts looked at his watch and continued, "Well, it's about time. Better get a refill, and we'll walk down to the conference room. Again, welcome to Cooperative Programs Tom."

O'Neal nodded, and took some more coffee, as did Betts, and they left the dinette headed for a conference room where Will Johnson and his small group waited for them.

Elias, West Virginia Sammi was cleaning up in the restaurant, getting ready to open, when the phone rang. He picked it up and heard a familiar voice.

"Sammi, Assalam Alaikum. How are you today?"

"Alaikum Assalam, my friend, I am fine. What can I do for you?"

"As All'ah wills, I have something I need you to do. There is a couple, living in Delaware, who will be coming to your area. I am instructed to tell you that the woman is to be placed in Will Johnson's house as a housekeeper, and the man is to work in your restaurant. They will arrive within days. Prepare for them."

"May All'ah please forgive me for what I say, but how am I to do that? I barely have enough customers for one person, and Mister Johnson has no need of a housekeeper."

"Convince him of the need. For the man, you will receive enough each month to cover his wages, and a place for him to live. He will come with the money you

From a Vantage Point

need to make it happen. They will be your kinsmen, who need a place to stay and work. Explain that to Johnson and make him agree. The woman named Sira will say she is from Lebanon, the place of his birth, and from a village close to that of his parents. They will have much to discuss. It will be done."

"As All'ah wills," responded Sammi wearily, knowing it was futile to argue. He had a week to figure out how to do what he was told.

"May All'ah reward you with good? I will contact you further to see how they are doing." Sammi heard the phone click off, and hung up his own phone. The feeling of dread he experienced when the other man visited quickly returned, and he started cleaning tables to try and reduce his fear.

Over the Pacific Ocean Jim Davis sat comfortably in one of the ten seats in the Air Force executive jet taking him back to the United States. He shared the flight with an Air Force three-star general on his way to Alaska, their next stop.

"Well, Mister Davis, it seems I have you to thank for getting on this flight today," said the General, looking across the aisle at Davis.

"I don't know about that General. It is probably the other way around, but, in any case, we are on our way. You get off in Alaska?"

"Yes, I do. I'm on an inspection visit to some units above the Arctic Circle. What about you? This is unusual to say the least. We seldom get civilians on these flights."

"I have to be in DC soonest. I'm an air marshal on special assignment. Not much more to tell, other than the summons to the great capital city."

A steward came up to where the men sat across from each other.

"Can I get either of you something? We have both food and drinks on board, so I can probably make anything you might like."

"Sure," responded the general, "Get me some good bourbon on the rocks, would you sergeant?"

"Yes sir, right away. What about you sir," added the steward, looking at Davis.

"I think some coffee would be just fine," responded Davis.

"Coming up for both of you," responded the steward, as he turned back toward the galley to fill the orders.

The steward returned with their drinks, eventually served them dinner, and left the two to discuss whatever they chose. Over the next few hours, before they arrived at Elmendorf Air Force base in Alaska, they had a wide and varied discussion on several topics of interest to both. At Elmendorf, the general departed, and the flight left for the US with Davis, and two families heading to Washington to visit with their spouses recently arrived from Afghanistan, now at Walter Reed Medical Center. Davis read his book, eventually fell asleep, and was awakened by the steward as they arrived in the airspace surrounding Andrews Air Force Base in Washington DC.

Agriculture Department, Washington DC Will Johnson walked into the building confident that he had his plan in place for the cooperative arrangement with Agriculture, and that they would approve and fund the expansion. He had worked weeks on his presentation and was ready.

"You must be Will Johnson," said the man at the reception desk with his right hand extended.

"Sure am," responded Will, shaking his hand.

"I'm Tom O'Neal, and will be your liaison officer here with the program. Let's go upstairs and get going, shall we?" O'Neal motioned toward the elevator, then walked over and pushed an 'up' button. The door opened almost immediately.

"Don't expect this fast service every time Will," added O'Neal. Most of the time they just do not work this fast. Today we got lucky."

Will laughed as they entered for the short trip to the third floor. As they arrived, a small bell sounded, and the doors opened. O'Neal led the way through glass doors opposite the elevator to a well-lit conference room where several people already waited for them. Near the end of the table in the center, Will saw two men seated, and assumed they would lead the group. As they entered, the others in the room also took their seats, leaving spaces for Will and Tom O'Neal.

"Well, I think we can begin," said the one man at the head of the table. "I am John Betts, as most of you know. Will, I'm the director of the Atlantic Region, which includes West Virginia. You have already met your liaison, Tom O'Neal, and the rest will introduce themselves as we go around the table."

"Our meeting today," Betts continued, "Is to discuss a proposal by the Elias, West Virginia Farmer's Cooperative for grant funding to expand their offerings, and consider what they might be able to contribute to the Agricultural Sharing Program in the region. Will, why don't you start with your statement and presentation?"

"Thank you, Mr. Betts," responded Will. "I am happy to be here today to suggest that the farmers in my area of West Virginia have a lot to offer through our cooperative, which we have already started up, and are currently working to provide food and other farm products to an area of roughly 100 miles around our center town, Elias. We want to expand further, but we need assistance in that regard, and that's why I am here today."

Will continued to speak for about ten minutes, showing slides of various farms, and the temporary shelter for the cooperative, pointing out that it was already overflowing with produce and needed expansion, or perhaps a larger building. Most of the audience seemed to listen intently. Thanking the group for their attention, Will returned to his seat and waited for the next steps.

From a Vantage Point

"Good presentation Will," said Betts, who looked around the room, and the others seemed to nod in agreement. "All right, who has questions?"

"Mr. Johnson, Tim Sickle here, with the Adjustment Service. Let me get right to the point. What will happen if we decline to fund your organization?"

Will thought for a moment, taken aback from the direct question, and then offered a response.

"Well sir, I guess we will attempt to find other funding, grow more slowly, but we will grow larger over time. The intent of the grant is to help us do that sooner, and perhaps better than we can do quickly for ourselves."

"Well, OK, so let us say we give you the money. What assurances do we have that it will be used as expected, and who will do the monitoring?" asked another person at the table.

"We have a volunteer board, and expect to hire a professional manager. We also expect to have your liaison actively involved in oversight to help keep us on track," retorted Will, beginning to sense some animosity in the group.

"Those are good steps," interjected Betts. "I'm sure we will see more about the organization over time. The critical question is when you can begin to expand, and what do you intend to offer in the Food Sharing Program?"

"We are already in operation, responded Will although we are still very small, and contributions to the food sharing programs can come at any time, when you tell us what we have that you can use, and where to send it. I assume that will be part of the duties of Mr. O'Neal."

"Correct," answered Betts. "Are there any other questions for Mister Johnson?" Betts looked around the room, and saw no indication of further questions. "All right, then. Mister Johnson thank you for coming in. We will let you know shortly about the grant. I expect within two weeks is probably a good estimate."

"Thank you, sir," responded Will Johnson. "I will wait to hear, and thank you all for your time and effort on our behalf." Will rose and started to leave the room. Tom O'Neal joined and they walked to the elevator.

"Are these people for real?" asked Will.

"Have Faith Will. I thought the meeting went well. Sometimes people have a habit of playing Devil's Advocate and seem rough, but they are just doing their job. I'll let you know as soon as a decision is made."

"Thanks Tom. Good to meet you, and I look forward to hearing from you. Well, I guess it's back to Elias and the co-op. Have a great day."

Will left feeling he had not accomplished what he wanted to do today. As he entered his rental car to return to National Airport for the trip home, he gradually built up some anger over what he perceived to be the disinterest of the program people for his project, but he decided to wait and see the response from them.

From a Vantage Point

At the airport departure lounge, Will reviewed his presentation, and the questions he was asked, trying to fathom where he might have gone wrong in his presentation. He was sure he did something to somehow ire at least one of two of those in the room, but he could not figure it out. Let it be, he kept telling himself, and his other 'self' argued they just did not understand the importance of what he and his friends were doing. All he could do now is wait and see the results.

Later, sitting on the plane in a window seat, and looking out over Washington, he shrugged his shoulders one last time; glad to be going home to West Virginia.

At the meeting in the conference room which followed, O'Neal argued strongly for approval of the project, and seemed to be supported by Betts and one or two others. There was opposition as well, and Betts ended the meeting saying the project package would go out for formal review, with comments expected, and the deadline was 10 days for completed responses before decision. The group nodded, and slowly left as the meeting ended.

Jalalabad, Afghanistan. Abadi awoke with a start; hearing gunfire which appeared to be very close. Suddenly, two men crashed through the front door of the small house. He knew both of them.

"As All'ah wills, Abadi, my friend, you are safe. We had great fear for you, and your master. Is he safe? The government security people are looking for you both house to house. You must leave now."

Just at that moment Hakim emerged from the small room they used as a bedroom, gun in hand, wondering about the commotion.

"Assalam Alaikum, honored friend. We have come to give you safety out of the city. The police look for you."

"Alaikum Assalam, my friends. Thank you for your thoughts. We need to leave. Abadi, gather what we have and we will be gone. Have we a way out of here safely?"

"Just for a short time," responded one of the men, looking out of the doorway keeping guard. "The troops are only three streets away. We must leave now. We will take you over to the street to our underground passage to the edge of the city where you will be safe. There, in the cavern are horses to take you away as quickly as you can ride. We cannot afford to have a car move you for fear of the drone. There were two attacks just yesterday from the Americans."

"Abadi, are we ready?"

"Yes, Hakim, we are ready," answered Abadi, with two packs over his shoulders and another in his right hand. "Let us go swiftly, or we will surely be caught." There was a great sense of fear in his voice, although he trusted his master, he was still afraid.

From a Vantage Point

"The Americans will pay for this," muttered Hakim as they left, with the two men who came to them on either side of the group as they crossed the street, entered another home, and went down into the basement. There one of the men, moved aside a rug, which covered a doorway, and opened the door with a large key he had on a neck chain.

"Come into here," he said, as he pointed the way for both Hakim and Abadi. "We will be safe soon." The men entered the tunnel, and the man with the key relocked the door, and then placed a large iron bar across the doorway to secure the door even more.

The tunnel was high enough to walk, and supported in some places by wooden columns and cross-braces. They found out later those braces were placed where the street was overhead and the tracks of the cars on the one-lane paths could absorb pressure from the weight. This was a lesson learned from the Vietnamese on their Ho Chi Minh trail where they frequently outwitted the Americans in an earlier war in Southeast Asia. Now, it was used to great effect in many places; here in Afghanistan as it had been before in Iraq and the Sinai Desert, and in other places in the Middle East and Africa where insurgencies were learning from each other how to fight the infidels.

After nearly an hour, they again approached a door. This time, one of the men who brought them to the tunnel walked over to the edge of the doorway, and opened a small space where an optical device looked out on the room, much like a hole door eyepiece, and he could see there was no one in the room on the other side. He carefully opened the door, and started to peer through to confirm his view, and then waved to the others to advance.

"It is safe here, "He said, "This takes us to my kinsman's barn where there are horses. It is at the edge of the city, and you can depart in safety among the others who will be riding out into the desert. You should wait until the sun goes down, when there will be many returning to their villages in the cooler night light, and then depart among those who support you."

"Thank you, my friends," responded Hakim. "Abadi and I are in your debt. As All'ah wills, you will have a great place in heaven." Hakim shook hands with both and embraced in the eastern way, then the two departed, leaving Hakim and Abadi to wait for dusk.

Meanwhile, the Afghani Security Forces continued to try to find Hakim and whoever was with him. They had been alerted by an anonymous phone call from someone who said he saw Hakim and another on a boat along the river, and then again on horses headed toward Jalalabad. The security forces knew that Hakim had several houses in the neighborhood, but not which one he might be in presently, so they and their American advisors decided to scour the neighborhood, house by house, to find him. Hakim would hear of the call later from one of his people, and the two men on the boat with him earlier in his trek into Afghanistan would disappear, never to be seen.

Hakim and Abadi left the city in the company of a small caravan travelling toward Kabul, through a small village just outside the city. They would be safe until their next stop.

Washington DC Jim Davis arrived at the Department of Homeland Security, showed his badge and credentials, and was escorted to the offices where Alice Sawyer waited. As far as the main security force was concerned, he was still a suspected person, and Alice wanted it that way for a while, at least.

As he stepped off the escalator which took him to the Mezzanine where Alice's office was located, she was waiting for him.

"Jim, good to see you. Come this way." She waved off the security team, and they went back down the escalator to the lobby.

"Ok, so what is happening here Alice? I understand you found Giddons dead. What about Hakim? He asked as they arrived at her office and went inside.

"Let's discuss this in the conference room, shall we?"

"Sure, Sorry, I just got excited about being right. That doesn't happen often these days, it seems."

"Jim, I know you have gone through a lot, but everything is panning out here. We did get notification that Giddons died of an apparent heart attack on a plane headed for Atlanta. You had him spotted. We could not do the positive ID bit well enough to stop the plane. We have no idea where Hakim is right now, although there are rumors."

"What rumors?"

"Well, we got some intel that he went to Pakistan and then up river toward Afghanistan and was in Jalalabad. We lost him there. We think he got out of the city in one of the caravans that often go through there. The Afghani security and our own Special Ops could find nothing."

"What about the other guy—Johnson?"

"Nothing really brewing there either. He was in DC a couple of days ago, on a business trip. We have one of our people watching him, but there is nothing to indicate he has any real relationship with the other two, except the old social stuff when they were deserters. He is pitching a farming cooperative to Agriculture, and he seems sincere, at least according to our man in the Program. We put Tom O'Neal over there to watch him. You remember Tom? He was in your class at Quantico."

"Sure, Tom is a good man."

"He is assigned to be Johnson's liaison with the AG program undercover. When Johnson returned to West Virginia a couple of days ago, Tom followed a

From a Vantage Point

day later, and is now in the Charleston USDA offices. We will keep a close eye until we can complete an in-depth assessment."

"So, what do you need me here for Alice? I was enjoying a few days in Japan."

"Actually Jim, I brought you back here to send you to Kabul. I have an office set up for you down the hall, with all the intel from Khartoum, and what the IC people can provide, and I want you to go over it with a fine-tooth comb. I want your assessment of what Hakim is going to do in Kabul."

"Why Kabul?"

"Because that is where he will go from Jalalabad. You know him and his people, and you know how he thinks. There is nowhere else for him to go except Kabul, so he will go there. What he will do there, and how it will impact something he plans here in the States is what I want you to find out."

"That's a big order Alice."

"Yes, it is, but you start today. Go over to Langley and see a lady you already know. Her name is Sarah Minihan."

"Wait a minute, Sarah Minihan, of Bernie and Sarah?"

"Sure is Jim, Your old classmate. I have arranged to get you cleared to Langley, and the car leaves in about 45 minutes. Go have something decent to eat, and then go over to Langley and see Sarah. I want you two working together on this."

"Done and happy to do," Jim smiled at the prospect of seeing his friends. Alice gave him the room number where his office was located, and waved him off to get something to eat before he departed for his reunion.

Elias, West Virginia Will Johnson was glad to be home. Sammi was at the airport in Charleston waiting for his call to pick him up at the terminal. Not knowing the exact arrival time, Sammi had parked in the parking lot, and walked over, cell phone waiting for the call. When it came, Sammi walked over to the baggage area to meet his friend.

"Will, it is you. Welcome home my friend," Sammi waived excitedly as he first caught a glimpse of Will waiting for his luggage.

Will waved back, and Sammi literally ran over to where Will stood, and hugged him. Sammi waited until Will got his baggage—a single box with his materials for the meeting—and they left to go toward the parking garage, and eventually home.

"Well Sammi, what has been happening in good old Elias while I was gone?"

"Not very much, Mister Will. One thing, though. I hired two people for the restaurant, but one of them I want to use in your home as a part-time housekeeper, if that is all right with you. She is very good at what she does, and came with references from a family in Delaware. You should meet her, and see

From a Vantage Point

for yourself, but I think it would be good to have someone other than me, during the times you will be gone. What do you think?"

"I know nothing about her, but let's talk about it more at home. I certainly could use someone, if this work with Agriculture and the cooperative works out, so it sounds good to me. Tell me a bit about her."

"She is young, and will be married in the future to her intended, who will be working in the restaurant. She is from Lebanon, and he is from Iraq. They came to this country two years ago, and have been working for a family in Delaware. She is a good housekeeper, and a good cook as well."

"Anything else I should know?"

"She is from your own country of Lebanon as I said, although I am not sure from what part. I believe she is Muslim, although she could easily be Christian such as yourself. I think you will like her."

The two men got to Sammi's car, entered it, and Sammi started to drive out of the parking lot, stopping at the booth to pay the toll, and then they sped along the airport road toward the interstate and home. During the trip, they spoke little, and Will dozed off for a short while, obviously tired from the trip.

In a little less than an hour they were pulling into Will's drive.

"We're home," Will said with an obvious air of thanks for the end of a long trip. He and Sammi still had a lot to discuss, along with the others in the cooperative board, but right now, all he wanted to do was sit on his sofa, watch the news, and drink a beer.

"Will you need anything this evening Mister Will? If not, I will drop you off, and go to the restaurant. Call me if you want some dinner, and I will have it sent over."

"No Sammi, I think whatever is in the fridge will be fine. Let's get together tomorrow over our usual breakfast and talk about the trip and whatever else we need to catch up on."

"I will have your breakfast waiting, if you call me Mister Will. Come anytime."

Will got out of the car as Sammi popped the trunk, and took his bags. He placed one of his carry-ons over the pull of his luggage piece, and started for the house, both hands full. At the door, he reached into his pocket, took out a key chain and opened the door, then turning to wave to Sammi, who drove away. Will was home, and happy to be there. He looked forward to a quiet evening with his thoughts.

CIA, Langley, Virginia *Jim Davis drove out to Langley and the CIA Headquarters, leaving downtown through Constitution Avenue, down to the State Department and then over the Roosevelt Bridge toward the George Washington Parkway, turning off at the exit just beyond State Route 123 into the entranceway to the CIA Complex in McLean Virginia. He knew the route well,* having been part of several task groups which included the CIA. More importantly, Davis started his career, as with so many others, receiving a scholarship from a CIA fund designed to prepare college students for a CIA analyst career.

Davis's class at CIA included several now senior CIA managers, including the Director of Foreign Operations, Bernie Minihan, with whom he served in Istanbul, Turkey before he was injured in an operation. He would have been retired for disability, but instead he chose to join the newly formed US Sky Marshal Service, organized in the early days of the fight against skyjacking by insurgent groups in several Middle Eastern countries opposed to Israel. He had been with the Marshal Service ever since, and worked around the world, now specializing in newer forms of terrorism, bringing him again into contact with his old colleagues in CIA and the intelligence community. Bernie and his wife Sarah were old friends and he was looking forward to renewing that relationship.

Cleared through the main gate, Davis drove up the road toward the CIA main building, named after former President George H. W. Bush, and found a visitor parking space. Luckily, it was near the front of the building, so the walk was less than the usual further lot on the campus.

Entering the front door of the building, Davis found Sarah Minihan waiting for him, with her usual big smile.

"Hey Jim, so glad to see you," bubbled Sarah, as she gave him a big hug. "Here is a badge for you. Let's go this way. That badge, by the way, will get you into most places in the building, just in case you want to do some visiting while you are here."

"Thanks Sarah, there are a couple of people I would like to see, but let's get on with what we need to do first."

"Ok, Jim," Sarah responded, "You always were one for business first." She laughed a bit, and they started up the escalators to the Mezzanine, where they could take some elevators to offices on the other side of the building.

From a Vantage Point

Chapter 27 Sleeping Giants Awaken

Elias, West Virginia Will slept badly his first night at home. First, he relived his trip to Agriculture, questioning himself and his approach, but finally deciding that it was too early to be self-critical; rather, it was important to look at the emerging opportunity for what it was—something evolving and expanding for the community. He seemed satisfied at that prospect.

More ominously, Will continued to lapse into dreams about his trip to Sudan, and ever-increasingly his boyhood in Lebanon during the sectarian civil wars. Virtually every night, he returned to much the same set of dreams, and they awoke him each time in a sweat.

Most often, his first vision was of the woman in Khartoum whose home had been bombed, and several of her family killed or wounded in the attack. He could hear her in his dream clearly condemning the United States for their use of these 'bringers of death', as she called the drones. In her arms was a young child, mangled and bleeding, near death, with no one there to help her prevent the death. Gradually, this vision changed, becoming yet another scene, this time in his small village in Lebanon, with another war but a similar result. He saw his mother holding his youngest brother in her arms, crying disconsolately for anyone who would help her save his life.

Again, as the scene faded, and re-emerged, he saw a small cemetery, and an open grave, with a small white wooden cross off to the side of an open hole. His father and mother are lowering a small wooden box into the hole, and dropping several small flowers and dirt into that hole, before beginning to cover the box with soil. When they finished, the small cross was placed over the grave, and they walked quickly away, as they could hear the roar of planes in the distance, coming again to bomb their village.

Yet another vision often came after the others; this time of the great murals in the Museum in Doha showing the mistreatment by the West of those professing Islam, only in this case, his view of the walls of showed Christians undergoing the same fate. By the time of this last vision, Will often awoke with a start, and a cold sweat, wondering why people would go out of their way to unnecessarily mistreat those of other faiths—especially those who bore no ill will, and were usually unable to defend themselves.

Sitting up in bed, unable to return to a restful sleep, reviewed again his meeting at Agriculture, trying to fathom why the assembled team might not, or even would not fund his project. His presentation was good, his style was down-to-earth and direct, and he answered all their questions honestly. But the thought still nagged him that the project was not going to be approved. He had no real reason to feel that way, but often nagging impressions have a way of becoming reality.

'Perhaps it could be that we are out in the middle of nowhere, just dirt farmers?' He asked himself several times.

'Perhaps they do not think we can produce?' Was another question in his mind? To that, he answered, *'but we already have the numbers they need, and what we can reasonably contribute over that amount.'* Nothing was making sense here, and the more he thought and rethought his meeting over and over, the less his pessimistic thoughts made any sense.

Finally, he decided to rest as best he could, and discuss it further with Sammi and a couple of the others in the morning at the restaurant. He needed answers, and they were simply not coming. He lay back down and tried to rest his eyes, finally dozing off until nearly 6AM, when he decided to get out of bed and prepare to go to town to meet Sammi. He wanted to be there early, before the usual morning crowd, so they had time to talk without interruption.

Early morning is a great time to travel into town; only the tractors and other horse-drawn vehicles of the local Amish community are generally on the road, and even they stay well to the sides to allow others to pass. Will waved at several as he proceeded along the two-lane road toward Elias.

Arriving at the edge of town, Will looked down Main Street and saw only a couple of pickups parked; one at the store and one in front of Sammi's. He knew the truck at the store belonged to Jim Flood, the Mayor, and from the wire and posts in the back of the truck bed, Will assumed he was fixing fences on his farm. As he drove down toward Sammi's restaurant, Jim came out of the store, saw Will's car and waved. Will returned the wave, as he turned right to park in the space next the other truck with Delaware plates.

Sammi came to the door when he heard Will parking. "Look who is up early this morning?"

"I know," responded Will. "I never sleep well on my first night home from anywhere."

"Well then, come in and have some coffee. I just put some on," Sammi explained.

"That's a plan," responded Will, getting out of his car. In seconds, he was in the restaurant, and at his favorite table. He grabbed a local paper on his way past the register area, and sat down waiting for his coffee.

"Black as usual?" asked Sammi, more rhetorically than in expectation of an answer. He put a cup and saucer down, along with a couple of rolls, and then sat down himself.

"How did the trip go?" Sammi continued, "Good or bad? Do we get the grant?"

From a Vantage Point

"Not sure, Sammi," answered Will, as he started to relate the meeting. "I did meet our new contact, a guy named Tom O'Neal, who seems nice enough. He certainly gave the appearance that he wanted us to be in his grant group. I also met his boos, and got the same impression. It was the review meeting that has me up in the air."

"OK, so tell me what happened?" Will related the details of the meeting, and the questions asked around the table.

"Sounds like they have reservations, Will. Perhaps this is not as firm as we would have figured. Is there another meeting coming?"

"Don't know. We will just have to wait. Something is not right though. Just not sure what it might be."

"That's too bad, but I must admit a lot of circumstantial stuff seems to be coming up just about now."

"Like what, Sammi?" asked Will.

"Well, there were these two guys in here a few days ago, while you were gone. I assumed at first they were looking around to validate our application, but they seemed only to ask questions about you rather than the cooperative."

"What kinds of questions?"

"Well, like how long you lived here; did we know about military days; who your family was, you know questions like that."

"That's interesting. What did you tell them? Who else did they talk to?"

"We, at least me, had little to tell them; only that you are a good neighbor and a good customer. I told them you were the real leader of this cooperative, and that this was good for the area. Every time I steered them to the project they steered back to personal questions on you. It was really weird."

Will sat back, a bit amazed, and then his expression changed as he realized they were zeroing in on his overseas time and his desertion from the Army; something for which he received amnesty from the president of the United States. He quickly tied the meeting in DC to the local experience and began to wonder if someone was questioning his loyalty.

Before he could say anything else, two people came up to the table. Both were young, and they stood over near Sammi.

"Will, this is Hassan, and this is Sira, who have come here from Delaware, where they have been working for a cousin of mine. They want to earn enough to get married, and buy a small farm, so he sent them to me hoping they could find work. I took them in, feeling that for now, they could work here, and she perhaps as your housekeeper, and, when the cooperative gets bigger, we have four hands to help. What do you think?

"I remember now," Will responded, "Sammi tells me you come from Lebanon Sira. My father and mother came from Lebanon, as I did I when I was very young."

From a Vantage Point

"We both do," responded Hassan. "We came to America because here we could get married. I am Islam, but she is Christian. In our country, that would not do at all for either family. So, we came here to be together and live our own lives, away from the constant fighting." Will was surprised at Hassan's comment, since Sammi had told Will Hassan was from Iraq, but gave no hint of his questions.

"I come from the village near Jdita. It is very small,' offered Sira, seeming to be very shy. "There is nothing there for us but fighting."

"My family came from that District as well, Sira. Welcome to America. You will find us very different here."

"It does not seem so, sir," responded Sira. "We heard the secret police come and ask about you, and we wondered."

"Sira, they were not secret police," said Will, "We have no such people here. We do have police who come to ask questions occasionally, but they do not do in secret. If they return, I will show you."

"I hope to be wrong, sir, especially if I might have offended you," answered Sira. "It is hard for us to get used to your ways, but we will learn." Sira cracked her first smile.

"Yes, we will," added Hassan. "I hope to live here, and we both hope to be part of the community, if you will have us?"

"I think I can speak for the community on this Hassan. You are both most welcome, and you will better understand our ways after a time. It took me time to do so as well."

Will turned to Sammi and said, "Sammi, I think I do need a housekeeper. How about she comes over three times a week to start, and we'll see if she can make something out of the shambles in my small house. Will that work for you both?"

"Yes sir, it will," responded Sammi.

"I would love it," added Sira.

"Good, then you can start tomorrow morning. Let's say you will come Tuesday, Thursday, and Saturday morning after breakfast. I come to town on those days and generally have breakfast here, so I will pick you up, and take you back to town later in the day. How is that?"

"Oh, very good sir. Thank you."

"Then it is settled. I will pick you up tomorrow morning for your first day. Now for some breakfast. What's good here today Sammi?"

CIA Langley, Virginia Exiting the elevator, Sarah and Jim Davis took a left and then a right toward a long corridor with a sign stand in the center of the entrance marked 'RESTRICTED – VALIDATED BADGES ONLY" Sarah swiped her badge and Jim did the same on a badge machine on the left wall. They continued down the corridor until they reached a door simply marked with a room number. Sarah

From a Vantage Point

inserted her ID badge into the lock slot, and the door lock clicked to allow her to enter. She turned the knob and entered the office with Davis.

"This is my hovel, Jim," said Sarah proudly. "After all the years of working at the cubicle, it's nice to have some real privacy. Davis looked around the room at her desk and small table, along with a myriad of pictures or her, Bernie, and the kids on the credenza behind the desk. She walked over and sat at the table. Piled high on the table were files, most with security markings.

'That's some pile you have there," said Davis.

"That pile is going to be yours for a while Jim," responded Sarah. "I dug up everything we had on Hakim and his group. Most of it is older, but the top of the pile is the latest we have, including his recent trip to Afghanistan via Pakistan. You will see that he gets where he wants to go with the dedicated help of the Pakistani ISI, who then dutifully report to us on his trips. Imagine having an intelligence service that is itself a double agent—or should I say double agency?"

They both laughed, and Jim sat down, looking at the pile.

"That is a lot of work. Do I use this table?"

"No Jim, I can make some office space available for you. This is definitely not cubicle work. You are cleared for all of it, and we will read you in after lunch on some of the stuff not in the files. Just as a formality though, you do understand that, as a former field officer, you are still subject to the non-disclosure provisions of the security act and our regulations?"

"Understand that well," responded Davis, "Now, let's get to the important stuff. How's Bernie and the kids?"

"Bernie is fine. You'll see him for lunch. We thought you might like to have lunch in the private dining room. The kids are doing just fine. One is here at the day care, and the other is now in first grade over at a local Catholic school. She is a constant fountain of energy; just the opposite of her younger sister."

"I expected that. The oldest is a Bernie, and the youngest is a Sarah. Why would I not be surprised? Both sharp as a whip, I bet?"

"Yes. How long are you going to be in town? We want to have you over for dinner so the kids can meet their absentee godfather."

"You pick the evening. I will make sure Alice does not have something else in mind for me to do."

"Good old Alice. She almost knocked me off my feet when she called the other day. She usually speaks to Bernie or one of the higher ups. This time, when she called me and then she mentioned you, I forgave her immediately for not calling more often. We used to get together all the time, until she joined the high-and-mighty club. At least on the phone, she still sounds like her old self."

"She is, really, Sarah. She just gets paid more these days. I don't even get to see her all the time either, even when I'm in town, and she is supposed to be my boss. That's the way it is, I guess."

From a Vantage Point

"Probably so, but I liked it better when she was still the secrecy instructor at the Academy. We spent a lot of time together. That's how I got the job with Rex. It was her recommendation. Otherwise, I would probably be out in some forgotten station wondering when I would see the US again. Well, so much for reminiscences, let's get to work." Sarah started to show Davis the files. She explained what they contained, and the order in which they were in the stack. Davis noted the date order, so getting them out of order was nearly impossible.

Their review took nearly two hours. Sarah looked up at the point they were nearly through the pile, and saw the clock on her desk said 12:15PM.

"Jim, we better get down the corridor if we expect to have lunch with Bernie."

"Great. Good place to stop. We can come back after lunch. I'm famished."

"Me too, so let's go eat."

Elias, West Virginia Finishing his breakfast, Will waved to Hassan for one more cup of coffee before he left to return to the farm.

"Hassan, how you like Elias so far?"

"It is very nice, sir. The people are all friendly, and especially Mister Khan, who has been so nice to us," replied Hassan.

"I'm glad to hear that. You let me know if I can do anything for you, or Sira."

"I will sir, and thank you again for employing her. She is a good worker, as I am sure you will find out quickly."

"I'm sure she is, Hassan," replied Will, going back to finish reading the paper. In a few minutes, he stood up, left a tip, and started to walk through the front door. He turned back for a minute, saw Sira, and waved to her saying, "See you tomorrow morning Sira. Be ready for a day's work."

Will went home to the farm, and came back the following day for breakfast and to pick up Sira to bring her to the farm. He showed her where the cleaning supplies were kept, and which rooms really needed cleaning more than others. He gave her the freedom of the house and farm. He brought her out each morning that she worked, and brought her back to Sammi's each evening. Within a week, it was clearly obvious she was exceptional in her work; the house already looked 200 per cent better, and she was considering flowers to put around the front entrance. Will was pleased.

CIA Langley, Virginia Sarah escorted Jim Davis to the Executive Dining Room, and asked if Bernie had yet arrived. The manager standing at the doorway indicated he had, and allowed them to enter. They quickly found Bernie at a table, as he stood waving to them.

"James, you old fool. How are you?" asked Bernie, as they both hugged like long-lost cousins.

"Not bad Bernie, not bad. Thanks for letting me spend some time with your better half. She is so methodical, it is still really scary, even after all these years."

"Sit down. Tell me, what have you been doing?"

"I am still officially working for the Sky Marshals, although I spend less time with them these days than I do with Alice. She keeps me running around the world. Had me arrested and brought home in chains from Sudan. Other than that, I lead a very quiet life."

"I heard about that. We almost had Rex do the same thing to us in Istanbul, though. You have to live a little once-in-a-while."

"True. We wanted the two we were following to think I was their pigeon, and it seemed to work. I came home, officially under investigation, and the two men moved out of the country. Now we have one of them dead in Atlanta, so I am chasing clues. What about you, though? How have you been?"

"Would it do any good if I told you I still don't like being chained to a desk? I spend more time investigating paper than I do anything else. When Rex died and Bridget retired, I got the Special Ops job, and they brought in Sheila from New York FBI to be Director, Operations. You remember Sheila? She used to be Rex's assistant, long before either Bridget or Sarah."

"Sure do. She got a lot of press on the drug deal in Norfolk. She made a real mess of at least one New York family. If I remember well, a bunch of them, including their boss, went to jail for long stretches."

"That's true. There are still some trials pending, mostly in Norfolk. So, tell me about this current situation. Why do they have you involved?"

Jim Davis related the facts as he knew them, including the trip Will Johnson made to Sudan to see his old war buddies; and how, when Johnson came back to the states, both Giddons and Al-Azahir disappeared from the country. He stopped at the point where Giddons had a heart attack on an airplane headed to Atlanta.

"I remember this guy al-Azahir, Jim. I approved a drone strike against him in Khartoum some months ago. He has been a major supplier and gun-runner for al-Qaeda for some time now. He started during the Fatool days as a small-time money mover and gradually moved up in the Pakistani side of the enterprise. Worked out of Yemen, moved to Sudan and Afghanistan, and then back to Sudan. I had not heard his name in a long time, until the request for the strike came across my desk."

"That's right Bernie. Jeff Namers had him under his watchful eye; he was actually using al-Azahir's own cousin Fatima as the eyes and ears in the organization."

"OK, so what happens now?"

"Alice asked me to bring myself up to date on the case," responded Davis, "Then I go to Pakistan, and eventually on to Kabul to try and figure out his plans.

If he moved Giddons to Atlanta, he had a reason. These people just do not go on vacation five thousand miles away. We also have eyes on their friend Will Johnson, a farmer in West Virginia. We have a plant over there working with the Agriculture Department, but the suggestion is that this guy is simply a fellow deserter, and not involved."

"Fellow deserter?" responded Bernie.

"Yes, the three of them were drafted, and eventually deserted. They did some mercenary work in Europe and the Middle East, but eventually Johnson came home under the Carter Amnesty Program, moved back to his father's farm and has been a model citizen since, as far as we know."

"Well, it sounds like you have everything under control. How can we help? We are somewhat limited by the law in this area, at least domestically."

"That is why I came over; to read the files and bring myself up-to-date. Sarah has been a great help."

"Good, now let's have lunch; not talk about work; and just enjoy ourselves for a few minutes."

"Sounds good to me," answered Davis. Bernie passed a menu to he and Sarah, and the waiter stopped over a minute later to take their orders.

Kabul, Afghanistan The large moon of the Afghani sky was out in full cycle. As Hakim looked at it, it seemed to him to be an omen of the success in America. His plan was to disrupt the upcoming American inauguration, and send a message that the United States, even under a new President was vulnerable to the will of All'ah. It would not be easy, but Will Johnson would help them do it.

Hakim had never cared for Will Johnson; to him, Johnson was simply a pawn in a larger task. That task was to teach the West a lesson on the right of Islam to gain back its rightful place as the leading influence of the world, through peace if possible, but through violence if necessary. Any means to that end was the will of All'ah. The Qu'ran was the guide to follow. Hakim would follow the Qu'ran in that effort, and by all means possible.

Toward that end, he had stimulated friendships with both Johnson and Josh Giddons. He intended to use them for whatever purposes he chose as his means to achieve his goals. In the case of Johnson, he never realized that goal, but now it might be possible. As for Giddons, he had nurtured Giddons soul, thwarted only by the weakness of his heart. He still had Johnson, and resolved to use him to achieve his ultimate purpose.

The first step was to convince Johnson that his best future was to show that he could do the will of All'ah, and to lead a massive assault on Washington. He would show the world that Islam was the object of perfection in the world, and that those who opposed Islam would perish.

Hakim remembered the first time all three men had arrived in Kabul. They had delivered supplies to a camp operated by Bin-Laden in the hills, and stayed several days to enjoy the city. Then, it was relatively bland, since the Russians had driven most of the people from the city into the villages, but the food was still excellent, and they loved the people, the music, and atmosphere of this remote outpost. It was the Russians they hated, and then the Americans who followed them into occupying the country under Bush.

Now, it was time to start the next steps of Hakim's plan, and to do that he needed to renew an association with another of the old leaders of the movement, one who was expected in Kabul any day.

Elias, West Virginia Will picked Sira up as usual, and they drove back to the farm along the winding road in relative silence.

"You are quieter than usual today Sira. Is there anything wrong?" asked Will.

"No sir, I enjoy my work, especially working for you. It is just that I had a letter yesterday from my cousin in Lebanon. As you know, we are Christians. The villages in which we live are surrounded by Muslims. They come into our villages and take our crops and our goods, and then go away, often leaving many injured in their tracks. We cannot defend ourselves, and the police do not defend us either. We thought that when the Government brought in the Americans to help train our police, and allow some Christians to be policemen, things would get better, but they have not."

"My cousins," Sira continued, "Say that a week earlier, that is three weeks ago now, some thugs came into our village and took all of our icons. Two men, one of them my uncle, tried to stop them and were beaten. My uncle was unconscious for three days. After they left, the police came with their American teacher, and they would not even try to get the men. The American told them not to get involved, and they listened to him. Now, we have nothing. It makes me sad. The thugs told my family if we would become Muslim, all of this would stop. Several in the village have already done so. I cannot help them here."

"That's too bad. It should not be happening. I thought the Government was Christian?"

"It is supposed to be, but they are influenced greatly by Hezbollah. Anything the Hezbollah leader wants, they do. The difficulty is that Hezbollah gives the people more than the Government. Some villages get food, clothing for the children, and extra money to use in the markets. The Government gives us nothing. What they get from the Americans, they keep in their own pockets."

Will saw the road to their farm ahead, and turned off onto the farm road that would take them to the house. He wished there was something he could do for her, but had no idea how to ask, so he remained silent. They drove the last of the distance to the farm house, and she went quickly inside to start her housecleaning chores, as soon as they stopped, rushing from the car to the house. Will, delayed for moments as he turned off the ignition, thought to himself what an interesting person Sira was; strong despite family problems, but equally strong in wanting a new life for herself. Then, he remembered she and Hassan were engaged, and it was not his place to replace Hassan in consoling her.

CIA Langley, Virginia Jim Davis and Sarah Minihan finished having lunch with Bernie, although it ended a bit abruptly as Bernie's phone rang, and he had to leave early. The two finished, and left the dining room to return to her office and the pile of documents. When they entered, Davis went right to the small table and picked up the newest file, then asking, "Sarah, I have been thinking through lunch about Johnson."

"What about Johnson bothers you, Jim?"

"What if Johnson is simply a pawn here? We are all looking to eliminate him from contention as a possible terror cell member, but what if he is not a terrorist to begin with? What if Hakim is trying to recruit him instead?"

"That's an interesting point Jim," responded Sarah. "He has the connection to them, but it is possible that he has no political ties, and they were just friends; at least in his mind. If that is the case, then what is the plan here?"

"I can understand wanting to recruit him for something," said Davis, "But what is that something, and how would they do it? Moreover, how would they put him in play? They have no direct contact, and now that Giddons is dead, they have to be changing their plans somewhat. I think the answer here is, unfortunately, in what Giddons was here to do, and now he is dead and will not be telling us."

"Well Jim if we accept that premise, then there must be a contact somewhere that creates the link between Will Johnson and Hakim al-Azahir. If you find that link, you will find the plan. Where do you want to start?"

"OK, so let's consider first those in his environment; the people near where he lives and works. Do we know anything about them? Is there anyone in and around him that might be the contact with al-Azahir?"

"That's a question which Alice and her team need to pursue. You know our limitations in domestic investigations. I can tell you that there are several immigrants in Elias, one of them the owner of the restaurant, a man named Sammi Khan who might fit that profile. Again, Alice's team will have to pursue that. We can give you what we have from overseas intel in our files."

"Thanks Sarah. That starts me in a new direction. What about the files here?"

"Already on their way over to Alice's file repository. You can get them there, or come back anytime you wish. Just give me some notice, and I will get your secure space to work with them. I will keep them in our safe for the time being to make retrieval easier."

"That's great Sarah. I think I will go back to town and work there. That way I can get my requests into the hopper a bit easier in person. Thanks for everything."

"It's my pleasure Jim. I hope this gives you what you need. Will you be staying in town long enough to come over to dinner?"

"Sure, just let me know. I expect to be in DC for at least a month, with some small side trips. Anytime is fine. I would love to see the kids."

Davis and Sarah both rose and started toward the office door. They walked back along the corridor toward the elevator, where Sarah stopped.

"You know the drill, Jim. Swipe the badge at the outgoing turnstile, and put it in your pocket. I had it made good for six months so you can come and go as you need. You feel free to come by anytime. It is always good to see and old friend." Sarah hugged Davis, and the elevator door opened to take him back to the Mezzanine and the exit. In five minutes, he would be back on the drive, and headed down the George Washington Parkway toward DC.

From a Vantage Point

From a Vantage Point

Chapter 28 The Plan

International Airport Kabul, Afghanistan The sleek white private jet cruised easily from the runway across to the general aviation area, where a fuel truck waited to begin refueling. A small pickup truck with four guards sitting on benches in the back was just behind it. As the plane came to a stop, the men jumped down from their benches, and quickly surrounded it. The fuel truck operator started to refuel the plane, as if it was to take off again immediately. The exit door to the plane opened, but no one left the plane for the tarmac.

In a few moments, a small passenger car emerged from a side road between two service buildings, turned in a wide arc toward the plane, and stopped just short of the exit door to the plane. A man stepped out and climbed the stairs, disappearing into the passenger cabin, followed by the closing of the exit door. The plane made no effort to depart.

Inside sat a very tall man in a flowing white gown. He wore a deep red tarboosh on his head, with a gold colored tassel hanging to the side. He sat reading the International Tribune as the man entered, wearing round, horn-rimmed glasses on his face, and smoking a cigarette in a long, French cigarette holder. He looked up as he heard footsteps.

"*As Salamu Alaikum wa rahmatullah wa barakatuhu* (May the mercy, peace and blessings of All'ah be upon you), my friend Hakim?" said the man without rising. He motioned the man to the next opposite him.

"*Awa Alaikum Salam wa rahmatullah wa barakatuhu* (And may the peace. Mercy and blessings of All'ah be upon you) Amid Fattoulah. How was your trip?" asked Hakim.

" The flight went well. I am here for just a few moments to speak with you before I go to Islamabad on other business. When I received your message, I knew it was time for us to meet. Tell me what I can do for you."

"And how is the Imam?" responded Hakim.

"The Imam is well, and sends you his blessings. He misses you at his table, but we both know it is not safe for you to be with him. He speaks kindly of you often."

"His health is good?"

"It is. Now he worries only about his flowers and his friends. So much has changed over these past years; he is happy tending to the needs of the brothers. He leaves others to the sacred work, as All'ah wills."

"My brother, did you hear of the untimely death of Giddons?"

"I did. To All'ah we belong, and to Him we return. Our brother Giddons was not of our faith, but All'ah looked kindly on him as he toiled for us. There were

From a Vantage Point

prayers for him, and the Imam wanted me to say that our friend remains in his prayers."

"Amid, I have a plan for an embarrassment to the apostate in Washington. Soon, he will no longer be President, and it is time to show the Americans that we are still strong and able to inflict pain on them as we did in New York and the Pentagon years ago."

"What is it you suggest, Hakim? What is it you wish from me or the Brotherhood?"

Hakim began to explain how he proposed an attack on the center of Washington during the upcoming inauguration for whoever the new president might be. What he intended to do was to bomb the inaugural parade route with small missiles, which could be launched from hotel room windows. He explained the role of Josh Giddons in the attack, although that was no longer possible. Hakim also explained how he intended to use Will Johnson, another friend who had recently visited them in Sudan.

Amid listened intently, asking questions periodically, but giving no impression of his approval or disapproval. The conversation went on for over an hour, until Amid eyed his wristwatch and indicated it was time for him to leave.

"You have an interesting idea, my friend," Amid said to Hakim. It will need much planning, but it can work, if handled correctly. I can help you there, depending on when you propose to put it into action."

"We have one years and three months, not more Amid. Everything must be in place well before the inauguration, and the planning must stretch out enough to keep it below any discovery level. I must replace Giddons with someone else, and need time to bring Will Johnson over to us. It will take that long, but not more."

"Very well. I will give you my blessing on this, but it must be done correctly. We cannot afford to have this to fail. You must see it does not."

"I can make it happen Amid. Your confidence is most appreciated."

"*Masha All'ah* (As All'ah wills). We will talk again soon, Hakim. I have thoughts on how it can be done. Right now, I must leave for Pakistan. Thank you for coming."

"*Insha All'ah* (As All'ah wills), we will be together again soon Amid." Hakim rose from his seat and departed the plane as the exit door lowered for him. As he reached the ground and started to walk away, the door closed, and the engines began to start in preparation for takeoff. The guards surrounding the plane returned to their truck, which then waited for the plane's departure.

Elias, West Virginia Sira had been with Will for nearly three months, and had done wonders for the farmhouse. The small garden area outside was now showing all the blooms of late summer. She seemed happy enough, did her housework, and often went out to walk for a short time in the field near the barn.

One day, as Will was repairing a part of the fence at the corner of the barn, Sira walked by and stopped to see what he was doing.

"How is it going, Mister Will?" she asked.

"I'm just patching the fence Sira. That way the cows will not get out, and it needs doing before the fall when the bad weather starts to set in. How are you? Are you happy here?"

"I am very happy, Mister Will. I enjoy my work, and I rest easier since I received another letter from my cousin, a few days ago."

"How are they doing?"

"Now, they are doing fine. My uncle is well again. He has decided to become a Muslim. It is important to him. He has been studying with the local Imam, and brushing up on his Arabic. He learned some in the village school when he was younger. My cousins are converting as well."

"How will that make things better?" asked Will.

"It already is, Mister Will. They get extra food from the village food bank, established by Hezbollah. They treat their own better than the rest of the community. Almost all my small village is now Muslim."

"What about your own faith? Do you not believe in God anymore?"

"We believe, but to call him All'ah is a small thing if it means living better. Speaking Arabic brings the community together; all become better off, and even the Government treats us better. It is the belief in God, whatever his name might be that is important. Not to believe in any God makes no sense, so we believe, but in a different way."

"Well I guess that works, but it seems to me that belief in God is something to itself, and not dependent on food or other things. Perhaps I am wrong?"

"Mister Will, it is often those who treat you well that become important to you. The Christian government is supported by the United States, who care little for people; only their own feelings of world power. They do not care about those of us who have little. Instead, they care about corrupt governments who hurt and prevent us from bettering ourselves. The money they give to the government goes into Swiss bank accounts, and into their big mansions and estates, not to feed the poor and the homeless. That is not Christian; that is simply stealing from their own people."

"I do not know about much of what has happened in Lebanon in the past years; I left with my parents as a small child and have not returned. I am mostly American today, and my father's country is in the past."

"That is too bad, Mister Will. The books you brought back with you from your trip you should read. They tell of the poverty and the anxiety of the people; your people."

"Perhaps I should Sira. Right now, I need to fix this fence, but we can speak again if you wish. I do not forget my heritage, only that I do not really know my past."

"Your past is sometimes as important as the present, or even the future, Mister Will. You have a heritage, and your people and their hurting is important. I need to go back to the house to finish my tasks, but I would be happy to discuss this further with you, if you wish."

What Will did not know is that Sira had been receiving letters, not from her family, although the addresses seemed that way, but from friends of Hakim, who were orchestrating the information she was filling Will's mind with, as they slowly started to try to bring him around to being one of them. The most recent letter instructed her to speed up the process because they would soon have a use for him. This is what she was beginning to do.

Will, without perhaps realizing it, was falling more and more under the spell of this young woman. Sira took every opportunity to get into discussion with him on the plight of the people in the MIddle East, and what support the United States was providing in that effort. More importantly, she recognized early on that he was somewhat infatuated with her, and used that as well to try to bring him to their point-of-view. She needed some special event to bring him across the abyss to their perspective. What would it be was still uncertain.

Department of Homeland Security, Washington DC The trip back from Langley was just in time to avoid the beginning of the afternoon exodus from Washington, and Davis found his travel into the city much easier than he expected. The offices Alice and her staff used were in the Ronald Reagan Building, an International trade building in downtown near 14th Street. Davis took the George Washington Parkway to the Roosevelt Bridge then headed down Constitution Avenue toward the center of the city. The Reagan Building had ample parking, and several slots were for visitors to the Federal offices, so he had no problem parking underground.

Coming up to the main rotunda, Davis took an elevator to the second floor, and walked through reception toward Alice's office. The door was open as usual, and he walked in to find Alice and two of her technicians poring over maps and message traffic.

"Back already Jim," asked Alice as she looked up to see him in the doorway.

"Got what I needed, and all of their information is now on your server. I can work on it here. Saw Sarah and Bernie, had lunch with some great conversation, and now I'm back. End of story."

"OK, come look at what we have," responded Alice.

"Here are several messages from Afghanistan. Two relate to phone messages over a satellite phone from Hakim al-Azahir to the United States. The other is a message from the same phone to Cairo, Egypt. The name is unknown as is the number. The only identification we get is to someone named Amid."

"You got no last name, just the name Amid? Is that right?"

"Yes, it is," responded Alice. "Why is that name important?"

"It might be important if that person is Amid Fattoulah, the number two for Amoud Tabriz. You might know his more familiar name Fatool. Bernie and I used to chase him around Europe, and Bernie chased him once to Boston, his home town."

"I remember that," offered Alice. "I thought Fatool had retired and the syndicate he headed was broken up."

"Not really, Alice. Some parts were eliminated; the personal stuff in the drug trade Fatool ran for Bin-Laden went to one of al-Zawahiri's people after Bin-Laden's death; but the rest went to Amid Fattoulah. If anything, Amid is even more ruthless than his old boss, who, I understand, still lives in his place in the old quarter of Cairo. That is one dangerous man. Where did you get all this stuff?"

"Actually, from the NSA, Jim. The local people in Islamabad managed to get a SATCOM phone to Hakim before he left on his trip across the hills to Jalalabad and eventually Kabul. One of his own people, a man named Abadi, works for Pakistani ISI, and has his confidence. The phone was rigged to emit both signals and allow capture of the messages. As they came in, they came here."

"Does CIA know?"

"Not sure. They will eventually, of course, but right now, I am more concerned with the importance of the messages. One of them mentions Will Johnson."

"In what way Alice?"

"See for yourself," Alice said, handing Jim the message.

> ***AL-AZAHIR, HAKIM** Telephonic traffic from KABUL*
>
> *JSOC operative (local) met subject at Peshawar. Travelling with subject, and embedded configured satellite phone with subject as planned. Subject believes phone provided by Pakistani Intel svc. Three messages to date (transcripts follow)*
>
> *Jalalabad (00:26AM) Two calls, both to unknown name – USING KASSIM SAID as ALIAS. Travel update only.*
>
> *Operative SALEEM met subject on Khyber River crossing. Provided second secure phone (Modified with ATK20)*
>
> *CALL TO KABUL –Discussion on death of GIDDONS in Atlanta Hospital and plans to use another for undefined mission in US*

> JALALABAD – Call to AKRAM KARIM – Plan to send two people to the US to contact JOHNSON – No names, but mention of SAMMI at a restaurant. Discussion of incident in South Carolina—al-Azahir responsibility.
> REQUIRES DOMESTIC REVIEW – Route to DIA, DHS, JTCC. With complete transcript

"This is very interesting, Alice," said Jim Davis. "On the surface, it looks like Johnson is being used here. Frankly, I'm not surprised, but we need to see the transcript. In the meanwhile, we need to figure out what is happening, and how these three are involved. Has Tom O'Neal seen this message yet?"

"About an hour ago," responded Alice. "His comments were about the same as yours. I have already spoken with DIA, and they are leaving the situation to us. I'm not worried about JTCC at this point since I sit on that anyway. Let's just concentrate on how to fashion some next steps."

"OK, so can you get Counsel to go to the Court for a tap?"

"Already in progress, Jim. I expect a quick decision there. We have something live and one of those judges will act this afternoon, I expect."

"Good. What records do we have on the three people, this Sammi, and the others?"

"We have a load of information on Sammi Khan. Here is the file on him. Frankly, we know nothing about the other two. Our guys are looking at that right now. There do not seem to be payroll records on any other employees, so we are sending in a 'state health inspector' to look at the place tomorrow morning; surprise visit. The excuse will be a request from Agriculture for a quick review. That will tell us if other employees are there or not."

Elias, West Virginia Sira worked diligently on a new room on this current visit, taking on the cleaning and renovation of Will's office on the first floor opposite his bedroom. Working to neaten and dust his bookcase, she rearranged the copies of the Islamic magazines Will brought home with him from his trip to Sudan to be sure he could find them easily. Sira had found them on her first cleanup of his office, and knew Will had barely touched them—judging at least by the dust covering the top of the small pile she found on a side table. As she completed her dusting and cleaning, it came to her that this might be another opening to speak to Will, typing it once again to their families and villages in war-torn Lebanon. So, while walking out in the barnyard one day a week or so later, she brought them up in the hopes he would take the bait and read them further. She used this opportunity as he drove her back to the restaurant on what was otherwise an overcast and dismal day, with both saying little initially as the pickup drove along the country roads. "Mister Will, I started to clean up in your

From a Vantage Point

office today. You will find it neater and free of dust, at least. I did not want to disturb very much, but if you will tell me next time what to clean; I will add that to the list of work to do."

Will was surprised, and somewhat offended that she took it on, but then changed his mind.

"Very well, Sira, I will show you if you wish to add that to the list. I pretty much know where everything is in there, but it could use an occasional dusting. We'll work on that next time."

"I am happy to do it, Mister Will. I placed your Arabic-English magazines in your bookcase. Could I borrow them sometime to help Hassan keep up his Arabic?"

Will had completely forgotten about the magazines. He replied," Oh those. I got those in Sudan when I visited some friends. Of course, Hassan can borrow them if he wishes. They are mementos of my visit, so I would like them returned at some point. If they will help him, I would be glad to lend them."

"Thank you, Mister Will, I will make sure Hassan keeps them well and returns them."

Please feel free to borrow them. Some are in English, but there are some in Arabic. I am not sure how I got those; I thought I took only the English versions, but with some others mixed in the pile. Take them when you wish."

Later that evening, Will went looking for the magazines himself, and found them neatly on the shelf of the bookcase where he left them, all neatened up, dusted, and in order. He looked through and found the English copies, picking one up to read later that evening, just to see what they contained.

He opened the one on top of the pile. It was a magazine titled 'Inspire', and looked at the contents. What he found simply amazed him. The articles were incendiary, to say the least, and clearly written for those who considered themselves Islamic extremists. He found an article by a man named Shaykh Abu Basir calling himself the leader of al-Qaida in the Arab Peninsula, who claimed that the United States was responsible for everything bad happening in the world. The Arab world, or at least parts of it, simply rose to oppose the United States and its killing regime.

Will shook his head in disbelief. There was a recitation of many events, some from the American perspective, and some from the Islamic perspective, all of which discussed killing innocent people. He read avidly, still disbelieving, but deciding to do further internet research to seek the truth, whatever that might be. He read slowly, and actually ended up reading the article twice, underlining what he wanted to search further, but eventually fell asleep in his easy chair, the magazine dropping to the floor, where it stayed for a couple of days, until picked up by Sira on her next visit.

From a Vantage Point

Downtown, a man in a grey windbreaker, and dark slacks walked into Sammi's Restaurant and waited to be served. Sammi walked over with a menu.

"Welcome to Sammi's Restaurant, sir. Please come this way."

The man took out a set of credentials, and showed them to Sammi. "Ted Corbett, State Health Department. Is Mister Khan in?"

"I am Sammi Khan, sir. How can I help you?"

"Just an unannounced visit, Mister Khan. As you know, the State Health Department does these visits periodically in the smaller towns. We noted you have not had a visit for some time, and I was in the area and decided to come over and get your periodic visit out of the way."

"Welcome," responded Sammi, who put down the menu on a nearby table and turned to say, "What would you like to see first, sir?"

"Let's go look at the kitchen, shall we?" They walked toward the kitchen doors and entered the kitchen area. Corbett saw Hassan preparing food on a preparation table.

"Taking up his clipboard, Corbett took out a pen from his pocket and started writing. "Who has the Food Manager's certificate?"

"I do, sir. It is on the wall," responded Sammi, pointing to a small bulletin board with the certificates for the restaurant displayed. Corbett walked over toward the board.

"I see it there. Thank you. I also see the current health certificate, the certificate of occupancy, the fire marshal inspection, and your health department license. All up-to-date, and in good order. That gets those out of the way."

He turned and faced Hassan saying, "Is this your employee?"

"It is sir."

"Can I see a food handler's certificate on him please?"

"We have none yet, sir. He is a new employee, and the test is not yet given."

"I see. When did he come to work?"

"Two weeks ago, sir."

"What is your name?" asked Corbett of Hassan.

"Hassan, sir," he replied.

Turning to Sammi, Corbett asked, "Can I see his employment folder and work certificate?"

"Yes, sir. It is right over at my desk." Sammi walked over to his desk, looked through the pile in his inbox, and handed Corbett a folder marked HASSAN SINGH. Corbett took the folder, looked through it, and made some notes on his clipboard.

"Any other employees, Mister Khan?"

"No, just Hassan and myself. We are a small restaurant, and this is a small town."

From a Vantage Point

"All right then, let's look through the restaurant. We'll start in the kitchen and work through the building."

Corbett and Sammi spent the next forty minutes walking through the restaurant, looking at the kitchen, the storeroom, the outside and then walked through the main seating area. Periodically, Corbett took notes on his clipboard.

"Well Mister Khan, the restaurant looks good. You need to get the food handler's certificate for Hassan. Remember, you only have thirty days after employment to do that. Clean up outside a bit in the trash area, and remember to have the old grease taken away on a schedule. Otherwise, you are good to go. See you in about six months."

Corbett extended his hand to Sammi, shook it, and walked out of the restaurant toward his car parked outside.

Heading down toward the interstate, Corbett called a number on his hands-free smartphone. It rang several times before it was answered.

"How did the inspection go Tom?" asked Alice Sawyer.

"No problems here, Alice. He thought I was a real inspector. We better be sure to get the report filed with the State in case he checks."

"No problem. What did you find out?" Asked Alice.

"All I saw was one additional employee. His name on the records was Hassan Singh. He claims to be new. And only employed here for two weeks."

"We'll check that out, Tom. No evidence of anyone else?"

"Nothing I could see Alice. Sammi Khan was very outgoing. Singh was a bit more reserved, but neither seemed to have anything to hide."

"OK, Tom. Take it easy driving back. See you tomorrow."

"I will enjoy the scenery Alice. See you tomorrow morning." Corbett hung up the phone, and started to look out the windows, while carefully navigating the winding roads, taking a leisurely trip back to the big city.

Enroute from Kabul, Afghanistan Amid sat back in his seat, the Tarboosh gone along with the newspaper. Instead, another person was sitting opposite him on the executive jet, a small, thin man with a pencil moustache.

"What do we do with Hakim?" asked Amid to the other person sitting there, looking out the window.

"I am not sure Amid. I worry that this will end up the same as the last fiasco we employed him to arrange. Now that Giddons is dead, there will be increased attention to him. It is bound to happen."

"We cannot take this on ourselves, Khalil. I fear we have no choice but to either cancel the plans, or let them go on with Hakim. If we do, and they go badly, we may not have another chance."

"Do we really want another chance Amid? Why not simply let the thoughts of America go for now? We will have time in the future."

"As All'ah wills, Khalil, we will have. Provide Hakim what support he needs discreetly, but do involve us directly. If he succeeds, then so be it. If he fails, it is the last time. I will say no more on this."

"As you wish, Amid. I will issue instructions."

As their flight continued onward out of Afghani airspace, Hakim was returning to his house at the edge of the city. Once there, he and Abadi, who waited for him in the car while he spoke to Amid, sat down in the small living room to discuss their plans.

"We must move quickly, Abadi. I sense that Amid is not in favor of our plans," said Hakim, as they sat to talk.

"Why do you feel that?" responded Abadi.

"He said little, and seemed to have his mind elsewhere. Amid is usually more talkative than he was today. Even after I asked about the Imam, he seemed to have his thoughts elsewhere, even though he usually speaks of him in flowery terms."

"So, what are our options then?"

Hakim thought for a moment. " Do we know how fast it might be that Johnson comes around to our thinking? Is it even possible?"

"I am not sure. If anyone can do it, Sira and Hassan would certainly be the ones. If they cannot have him see the light of the Prophet, may the peace and blessings of All'ah be upon him, then no one else surely could. I will speak with Sammi Khan to get a report today."

"Good, then let me know if we can adjust our plans."

"I will do that right away," answered Abadi, as he rose to go make the call to the US on his satellite phone.

Hakim had carefully arranged this small house to ensure privacy, including the use of jamming devices so that others could not capture conversations. The satellite phones he possessed, however, contained special devices to capture information from those phones, even if jammed. Only Hakim knew the one place in the house where the jamming devices had no effect; that was in the back near the door to the outside garden.

When Abadi left to make his call to the United States, Hakim rose to do the same. Taking his backpack, he reached into a pocket and felt two satellite phones, then a third, a burner phone, which he had not previously used. The number on the phone was from an Afghani company, and he decided to use for a call within Kabul. He dialed the number and waited for an answer.

The phone buzzed and, on the third ring, gave him yet another dial tone. When Hakim heard that tone, he dialed another number and again waited for an answer.

"Yes Hakim, what can I do for you?" came the voice on the other end of the line.

From a Vantage Point

"I need you to do something. I am sending you a picture of a man. Use your skills well."

"As you wish. I will do it. When do you need the result?"

"Within a month. Can you do it?"

"I can, but it will be close. If there is a change I need to know."

"As you wish," responded Hakim, hanging up the phone. Hakim sat back down on the small sofa, wondering if the plans he made would actually work out and create the kind of public response he wanted from his demonstration of power. Only time would tell.

DHS Washington DC Slowly pieces of a puzzle were beginning to emerge, but there were still too many holes to see the complete image. Alice and several of her staff sat in the large conference room, looking at two white boards, brought together to hold the information they knew thus far. On the board, on the left side, was a photo of Will Johnson, another of his farm in Elias, and still another of the downtown business area. Below the downtown photo was one of Sammi's Restaurant.

Some crudely drawn lines below the restaurant picture linked to a small list; right now, only Sammi and Hassan Singh were on the list, with a question mark below the names.

To the right, in the middle of the white board, were four photos, two each of Hakim al-Azahir and Josh Giddons. One of the photos for each was their military photo, and the others were taken later in Khartoum by the CIA. Under Giddons Photos was the writing "DEAD" in red dry-marker ink. Under Hakim's picture was written in red "KABUL"

Further to the right of the board was a photo of Amid Fattoulah, with a large red question mark below the picture. A black dotted line went from Amid over to Hakim. The same was true of the dotted lines from Hakim and Josh to Will Johnson. In green ink, below Hakim's picture was the name "ABADI."

Alice Sawyer spoke first.

"OK, so what do we have here? Do we have anything to add from your visit, Tom?"

"Let's see, Alice. This guy Hassan Singh is from Pakistan. I saw his work papers at the Restaurant, and checked on him when I returned. It seems he came from Pakistan to work in Delaware. He stayed there some weeks, and then apparently decided he wanted to go to West Virginia. He applied for a change in his work permit, with a new sponsor—Sammi Khan. Immigration approved the change, and he moved less than a month ago to West Virginia, where he is employed at Sammi's Restaurant. Completely legit as far as we can determine right now."

From a Vantage Point

"We also checked on another angle," said one of the others at the table. "Both Khan and Singh come from the same city in Pakistan, and both went to the same university in Islamabad."

"Interesting," responded Alice. "No family relationships?"

"None that we know of, Alice. Neither has a file with any of the intel agencies, other than the immigration stuff. They appear to be clean."

"My gut reaction to that is simple; virtually no one coming from that part of the world has a completely clean record. There are skeletons in everyone's closet over there. Let's find them if they exist. Get our own people in Islamabad to do a complete check. Anything else?"

"The question mark under the restaurant Alice," said another of the staff. "I looked over the inbound manifests from Immigration around the time Singh came to the US. It turns out there were two people who came from Pakistan to work with the employer up in Delaware. Hassan was one, and a young woman came later, about three months later, and was picked up in a similar inspection by a local health department."

"Her name was Sira Suleiman," he continued. "The records here are very scant, but she appears to be a Pakistani, but claims to be from Lebanon in other documents. She attended the same university as the other two, and we have no record of her leaving the country. She left Delaware about a month ago as well, but left no forwarding address. Unlike Hassan, she is now on the ICE pick up list."

"All right. Let's assume they both went to West Virginia. How do we confirm that?"

Tom O'Neal spoke up quickly. "Alice, I'm going to Elias tomorrow to see the cooperative on a review visit. I can discreetly be on the lookout for an out of place young woman."

"Good idea, Tom." answered Alice. "That might be it for now. Let's get more background on her as well from our people over in Pakistan. Thanks guys. Keep the board updated as more information comes in." Alice rose to leave just as Jim Davis arrived and asked to see her.

"Let's go to my office Jim. No need to keep these people occupied on our conversation. Thanks again everyone." Alice and Jim Davis left and walked the short distance to her office and closed the door.

Elias, West Virginia Will had just finished doing some chores in the barn when the phone rang.

"Will, this is Tom O'Neal. How are you doing?"

"Just fine Tom. What can I do for you on this bright, sunny day?"

"Well, I called to say that we are close to a decision, and I would like to make a site visit first, before I make my recommendation to the board. Do you think

From a Vantage Point

you could get a few of the members together in the next day or so, and let me know when and where to meet?"

Sure, Tom," replied Will, "Happy to. I think you will find your recommendation much easier with some on-site knowledge of our plans and current operation. Let me get back to you by the end of the day. I am going to town this morning, so I can poll the members on a good time to sit down with you, and give you a tour."

"That will be just fine. Personally, I think you have a good chance at approval here. The visit just gives me more actual information to provide the board."

"No problem. We would like to have you see our progress, and perhaps get some suggestions on improvements that would be recognized by the board. Thanks for the call. I will get back this afternoon."

"Great, Will. Look forward to the call." Tom hung up first, and then Will put the receiver down as well, feeling a bit better about their chances.

Within a few minutes, after making some tea for himself in the kitchen, Will called Sammi and asked if he could gather together several of the members for a meeting in two days at the restaurant, perhaps in the early afternoon. Sammi indicated he would, and Will called Tom O'Neal back to say the meeting would be in two days at Sammi Khan's Restaurant downtown at 2 PM. He invited Tom to come early for a tour of the farms, and a visit to their small processing plant.

Following the conversation, Tom O'Neal called Alice Sawyer to update the status, and tell her about the impending meeting. Alice was pleased, since this was a perfect way for O'Neal to view Will Johnson close-up. That was what they needed.

Alice arranged with her people for small cameras—one for O'Neal's car, and one which looked like an Agriculture lapel pin. With the pin in place, O'Neal could send streaming audio and video back to the DC office, and the staff could make some observations on their own without fear of discovery. Now, all they had to do was wait for the meeting.

Kabul, Afghanistan *Hakim woke early for the busy day he had ahead. Abadi had a call to make. He had not reached those he needed the day before, and he wanted to be sure to complete his task today. Hakim needed to visit another friend who owned a warehouse and did shipping for Hakim on occasion. This time, it would be Hakim shipping instead of things arriving for him from elsewhere. Leaving a note for Abadi, Hakim took the car and headed off for midtown for his friend's offices. The trip took about twenty minutes, since Hakim knew the side streets where he avoided the traffic jams so common in Kabul, even during the wartime conditions.*

Near the building where his friend did business, an alley between two buildings concealed a small parking area in the rear. Hakim liked to use this small lot, both for its safety, and the exit in the rear in case of emergency. Today,

From a Vantage Point

he pulled into the lot, finding it empty, and chose a spot to park near that emergency exit. Then he walked back through the alley to a small, side door on one of the buildings and entered, finding a short corridor through the ground floor with a similar door at the other end. Once on the other side of the building, near the exit door, he turned right and into an office marked "PRIVATE – Arkanon Enterprises."

The company was owned by Heraklos Pentopolos, a thief, murderer, and astute businessman. He was a mercenary like Hakim, working for anyone who paid him for his work. Several years earlier, during the Russian occupation, he was selling information to the Russians, and stealing from their warehouses to sell to the Mujahidin. Later, he sold goods stolen from the Russians to Bin-Laden, and was paid with money the United States sent to the Mujahidin to buy arms—also from Pentopolos.

In recent years, Pentopolos settled down in Kabul as a trader, a middleman for others who traded in arms and other goods, providing a way to move and launder money floating freely throughout the country. That is how he met Hakim.

"May I help you sir," asked a young woman at a desk just inside the door.

"I need to see Heraklos," answered Hakim.

"I will see if he is available. May I have your name?"

"Kassim Said."

"Oh, Mister Said, Mister Pantopolos has been expecting you. Let me tell him you are here."

"Thank you," came the response from Hakim.

In just a few seconds after the woman buzzed the intercom to announce Hakim, a large burly man came through a door with a broad smile on his bearded face.

"Kassim, please come in. I am happy to see you," said the man, pointing the way through the door to an inner office. Hakim walked through and Pentopolos followed, closing the door.

"Welcome Hakim," he continued. "How can I help you, my friend? You have not come to Kabul in a long time. I miss you."

"You miss my money, old Greek fool," responded Hakim.

"Yes, I do miss that too. But it is true, I do miss you. What is it I can do for you today?"

"I need something special."

"Anything for you. What is it you need from me?"

"A set of packing cases, specially made. I have drawings for you, and I will need them delivered in the United States within the month. I will give you delivery instructions, and a list of what to pack in them. They will be going to Atlanta, Georgia in the United States.

"For you, anything, my friend. Do you have the drawings?"

From a Vantage Point

"I do. Let me show you what I want." Hakim took a small group of hand-drawn pages from his pocket where he had folded and placed them before leaving the house. He gave them to Pantopolos, who looked them over, with a somewhat quizzical expression on his face.

"Can you make them for me?"

"Of course, but they are very odd. What will you use them for in the United States?"

"That is not for you to know. You only need to build them, and fill them with a list of parts I give you."

"Very well, my friend. I will do what you want. These are not difficult to make. Do you have any special needs here?"

"No, only that they pass customs for entry into the United States."

"That will be easy. I make them look just like shipping cartons for a salesman. That is what you want, is it not?"

"Yes, exactly. Make them sturdy, with handles on the end as I have shown, so they will look like salesman's cases."

"Good. You will take payment from the fund."

"I can do that. Shall we agree on a price?"

"You set a reasonable price, and I will accept it. Make sure it is reasonable."

"How many do you wish me to make?"

"I will need two, exactly as I have shown you. Six more are being sent to you from Khartoum. You will alter those to this drawing as well."

"I will make then. Anything else I can do for you today?"

"No, I must be going. I need to meet Abadi, and we have other things to do."

"How is my friend Abadi? Is his family well?"

"All is well with all of them. Let me know by the usual means when you are ready to ship and I will tell you what to pack and where to ship."

"I will Hakim, I mean Kassim. You will hear shortly."

"Good. I look forward to hearing from you." Hakim started toward the door, opened it, and went back to the outer office. Pentopolos followed him, they shook hands, and Hakim left to return by the corridor where he arrived.

Elias, West Virginia Tom O'Neal's message said he would arrive in town about 10 AM to meet with Will Johnson. Since it was Sira's normal cleaning day, Will drove into town early, had breakfast, took Sira back to the farm, and then headed again toward town to meet O'Neal.

Sira started her normal cleaning routine, leaving Will's office for last. She was in no hurry, since she knew Will would not return until after the meeting, probably about 5 PM, and perhaps even later. She cleaned through the living room, then the kitchen, where she stopped for lunch, and then on into Will's bedroom to make up the bed, and gather bed clothing for the wash. Her final stop before Will's office was the garden, where she watered the few flowers remaining, clipping stalks on others, and raking a few of the growing numbers of leaves off the flower garden area for Will to pick up later.

It was nearly three o'clock before she finally reached the office to dust and straighten up. As she entered the room, she looked around quickly and noticed a magazine on the floor. She walked over and realized it was a copy of 'Inspire'; one of those she left on the bookshelf. She thumbed through and realized Will had been reading it, with the underlining and side marks, and she wondered how much he believed what he read.

Taking the magazine and opening it to an article on American bombings in Lebanon, she placed it on the easy chair seat cushion so Will was sure to see it later. The bombing had occurred many years earlier when the United States first invaded Lebanon, but that did not matter as much as his seeing what she would later describe to him as 'American Aggression'.

Meanwhile, Will waited anxiously for Tom O'Neal to arrive at the restaurant. Both he and Sammi were pacing as they saw a car pull up out front with DC plates and Will recognized O'Neal.

"Well, here we go Sammi. It is apparently show time," said Johnson.

Tom O'Neal walked through the door of the restaurant and saw Will Johnson waiting for him. He extended his hand as he approached. "Hi Will, glad we could get together."

"Same here, Tom. It is always better to see first-hand. Glad you can make it. This is Sammi Khan, my friend and co-conspirator on the cooperative project." Will turned to Sammi, on his right side, and O'Neal extended his hand to Sammi as well.

"Glad to meet you Sammi. I hope to get to know you better, especially if we will be working with each other."

Same here, Mister O'Neal. Does that mean we are approved?" Sammi smiled as he asked the question.

"Not quite yet, but I have every positive feeling you will be, and shortly."

"Come, sit down, and have something before we give you the tour," said Sammi, pointing to the table where Will normally sat.

"Just some coffee for me Sammi," responded O'Neal, "And please call me Tom. Most of my friends do."

"Coffee coming up Tom," answered Sammi, waving to Hassan, who was looking through the door to the kitchen at the new arrival. He had not expected this visitor, and Sammi had not told him of the possibility. Hassan was concerned, especially after the prior arrival of the health inspector a day before.

"It was a great trip out here," offered O'Neal. "The country is beautiful, and the rolling farms make you want to move out this way right away. Just beautiful."

From a Vantage Point

"It is a great place to live and work Tom, with none of the hustle of the big city; just open and honest people. They just want to be friends, and live the way their families have for generations."

"Your family has owned a farm here for a long time, Will?" asked O'Neal, already actually knowing the answer.

"My father bought the farm with the help of a missionary group years ago, when he fled the first Civil War in Lebanon. He made his way here with my mother and I, and we have lived here ever since. Both my parents are buried in a small plot on the farm."

"I'm sorry to hear they are gone Will, but it's good you have kept it up for them."

"I have, with Sammi's help. We'll go by there today to see it as we look over several of the farms, and the small processing center we have on a nearby farm."

"I look forward to that. You both have done a lot of work thus far, and the reviews are good. That will make it much easier to get your expansion grant approved."

"The coffee should be coming out. Let me go look and see what is holding it up," said Sammi, rising and moving toward the kitchen. "I will be right back with our coffee." He walked through the kitchen doors to see Hassan waiting.

"Why have you not brought out the coffee, Hassan?"

"Who is that person Sammi?" came the response.

"He is from the Department of Agriculture, you fool. He is here to see the cooperative. Is the coffee ready?" Sammi walked over to the coffee urn, where three cups waited for the coffee. He poured the three and placed them on a small tray.

"I will take them myself," he added, he picked up the tray and walked through the doors back into the main dining room and over to the table where Will and Tom sat waiting.

"The coffee had just brewed a new pot," said Sammi, as he placed the cups in front of each of the other men, and then placed the tray to the side to take it back to the kitchen later.

"I know Sira is at the house, but is Hassan not working today Sammi?" asked Will.

"Yes, he is. He is in the kitchen peeling potatoes for the lunch and dinner. He forgot to make the new batch of coffee, so I did it. He is a good boy, but still needs to learn a bit about organization. He does well most of the time." Sammi sat down with the other two, and the conversation quickly moved back to the cooperative.

An hour later, the three men were in Will's car headed for a tour of the local farms and the collection center, where they saw volunteers taking in late crops, milk, and other products for further processing and distribution before sale. O'Neal seemed impressed and the three returned to town for the meeting with other officers of the cooperative. At that time, Tom O'Neal discussed what he needed to complete the review and approval process and answered questions for nearly an hour. Following the meeting, and a short review with Will Johnson, he departed for DC later in that afternoon. Will and Sammi stayed at the restaurant for a short discussion after the other had left.

"Sammi, I think this went extremely well. O'Neal had to be impressed."

"I agree Will," Sammi responded. "The question now is when we will hear. It is getting late in the season, and pretty soon we will have some fall produce, but will them be down to mostly milk and cheese. We may not be able to ramp up until spring; even adding a building is impossible once the snows start."

"I know Sammi. I will keep at it to get them to give us a decision. Now I need to get back to the farm. By the way, Sira is doing extremely well. I am pleased you came up with the idea. The house is two hundred percent cleaner than we used to keep it. Thanks."

"My pleasure, Mister Will. She also has said she is happy with the arrangement. It will continue to work out. She is a hard worker."

"All right. Out of here and back to the grind. See you later, my friend."

"You as well, Will. Later."

Will went out to the car to return to the farm, pick up Sira, and then return to drop her off, and pick up some things at the store he had ordered with Henry just after the meeting. It would be ready for him then.

Tom O'Neal started the drive back to Washington not in any particular hurry. He had gone about five miles when he decided to call Alice Sawyer to debrief his trip. He loved his hands-free capability on his smartphone, and used it often on his trips. This was no exception.

"Call Alice Sawyer," O'Neal said aloud to no one in particular. The earpiece in his right ear responded with the sounds of dialing a number, and then a voice coming on the line.

"Alice, Tom O'Neal here."

"Hey Tom, how is the trip going?"

"Worked out well. I am on the highway coming back to DC. Good opportunity to see Johnson close up."

"What is your impression then?" asked Alice.

"Seems like a straight up guy to me Alice. Liked by the town people. Very direct in admitting his family came in from Lebanon, and seemed ready for questions that are more personal as if he had nothing to hide. Met with his group as well, and visited the farms. Very impressive."

"OK, so what do you propose here?" asked Alice.

From a Vantage Point

"We need to look at a couple more things, and then we might be finished here. Could you have your guys look at someone named Sammi Khan, who owns a local restaurant here, and any employees he may have?"

"Sure Tom," she responded, "I may have some info on that already. Let me look. Here it is, Sammi Khan, also an immigrant, came in on a legit visa, and now has a green card. His restaurant is small, does well, and he has passed every vetting he went through. There is only one other employee we know of; his name is Hassan Singh. You may have met him today. We are still checking on him. Anything else?"

"Not exactly right, perhaps on the people, Alice. Will mentioned someone named Sira, who was working over at the farm. I believe she also works at the restaurant. Anything on that?" Tom asked.

"That's interesting Tom. We had some information on a woman named Sira. She was with the guy Hassan in Delaware, but disappeared afterwards. Any other information on her?"

"Just the one reference Alice. Nothing more. I can follow up on my next visit if you wish."

"Let's do that. We need to nail Sira down, if she is a potential baddie, Tom."

"OK Tom. See you in DC. Thanks for the call," she continued, then hung up the phone.

Alice Sawyer put a note on her scratch pad to ask her techs to do another review of the restaurant, and get back to her quickly. She wanted to settle the Sira question and move on.

Kabul, Afghanistan *Pentopolos looked at the diagrams Hakim left at the office. The shipping boxes looked like many other he built over the years. This set of boxes would be about 12 inches deep by 20 inches wide, with lockable covers on each. Inside, the boxes divided along the edges with an inside wall about 4 inches all around the box. The smaller spaces divided into sections with movable inserts made of thin wood. Pentopolos estimated the boxes would take about three days to build, paint and finish, then cover with an aluminum outer skin to look like footlockers, with carrying handles on each end.*

Calling in his workers, he gave them the drawings and set them to work building Hakim's boxes. He had no idea when they would be delivered, or where, but he also knew Hakim well; these boxes were not designed for casual shipping. They must be well made, and able to carry well. He carefully reviewed the plans with the workers before sending them off to start on the project for Hakim.

Hakim returned to his house to find Abadi still on the phone with their comrades in the United States. Abadi was in another room, but the periodic shouting brought concern to Hakim that not all was well.

Finally, Abadi came into the living room and sat down opposite Hakim.

From a Vantage Point

"These people are very difficult to work with Hakim. They think because they are over there in America, and we are here, they do not have to listen."

"What happened Abadi? Why are you so angry?" asked Hakim.

"I spoke with Yassin, the pig. His people have done nothing to work with Will Johnson, to bring him to the light. We are no further than we were a month or more ago."

"That is a problem, Abadi, but all will be well. Did you tell them to speed everything up?"

"I did but they will not do it. He sent the woman up there, and she spends her time cleaning his house, but he has not changed his views. I told them to try harder."

"Good. So then, what was the shouting about?"

"Johnson is working on his venture with his farmers, and he has started to get into contact with the government people. They think this is bad, and they have slowed down their work out of fear. I told them the government people are Johnson's cover and they should welcome that. They are scared."

"Give them time Abadi. Wait a day or two and call them again. They will see your point-of-view eventually. It is important that they start putting more pressure on Johnson, but he also needs to work with the government people. He needs to be going to Washington if our plan is to work. They need to encourage him, but to turn him to us as well. The woman should be able to do that."

"I understand sir. I will try again in another day. What else can I do?"

"Have patience Abadi. All will be well. He will do our work for us when the time comes. All'ah wills it."

Elias, West Virginia it had been a long day and Will Johnson was tired. After dropping off Sira, and picking up his groceries and other items at the hardware store, Will took the trip back to the farm, made himself some tea, and went over to sit in his chair near the door to his office. On the seat, he found the magazine he had dropped a couple of days earlier, picked it up, and sat down. At first, he intended to put it on the small side table and then changed his mind and started to read it again.

The interview in the magazine with this Shaykh Abu Basir hit him in the face with two conflicting thoughts. First, why was the US involved in some of the events discussed, and second, why might they be bombing innocent people in Yemen or elsewhere? The apartment of his friends had been bombed while he was in Khartoum and that strike put many innocent people out of their homes, including at least one who might be a relative from Lebanon.

Will wanted to read more about what was said in the article, and why the bombings were occurring. He listened to the news as did most people, but the story contained here was different. As someone who had been in the military,

From a Vantage Point

and understood the dangers of war, he was nonetheless conflicted—not because of the deaths directly, but because of the decisions on how those deaths occurred. He simply did not know, and wanted to know more.

Will leafed through the rest of the magazine quickly, recognizing some names, such as Bin Laden and others, and knew the magazine represented the terrorist view. His conflict was not with them versus the US, but on the rightness of the campaign. He had not felt this way previously and he wondered why now?

Putting down the magazine, Will turned on the news and found that the international news had just begun, and the reporter was recounting parts of the ongoing battles between the governments of Iraq and Syria with this new group called ISIS, which had been in the news for weeks. At one point, the reporter made mention of the group al-Qaida in the Arabian Peninsula as another name for ISIS, and he picked up the magazine again to find that Abu Basir was a leader of that group. Looking to the front cover of the magazine, Will realized the data of publication was in the summer of 2010.

Now even more curious, Will went to the computer in his office, opened the browser, typed in Abu Basir's name, and found that he was the leader of an al-Qaida group who was killed in a drone strike in June 2015, just after Will's visit to the region. The Wikipedia page showed a picture of Abu Basir and looking at it, Will realized a picture at the apartment of his friend Hakim included this same man. Suddenly, the bell rang in Will's head, 'The bomb that struck the apartments might have been a drone. Could it have been after Hakim and Josh?"

He continued to search, finding other articles on Abu Basir and others in the ISIS movement since his untimely death. He found two men of particular interest to him, both from his old village in Lebanon, who had gone over to the Islamic States, as ISIS preferred to call itself.

It took a just a short time for Will to realize that not all of those working for ISIS were Islamic, although many had converted from other religions, including some from the area where he and his parents lived in Lebanon years earlier. What Sira told him about conversions now made more sense.

As Will continued to search, he decided to see what might come up if he used 'Hakim Al-Azahir' as his search item. What popped up on the screen amazed him. There were over 100 items on Hakim, some mentioning his friend Josh Giddons as well. One item, from INTERPOL, the International Police Organization, had Hakim on its wanted list for numerous crimes, including smuggling of goods and drugs for al-Qaeda, arranging several major bombings and assassinations, and suggested that he was responsible for an airplane explosion off South Carolina two years earlier. Will remembered that crash, and the subsequent investigation that involved drug smuggling and the Norfolk Naval Base in Virginia.

From a Vantage Point

    Sitting back for a moment, amazed at what he read Will was now sure that the attacks on the apartments where they stayed in Khartoum were aimed at Hakim and Josh, his friends. Will thought about why the US did not simply send people in to arrest them instead of doing so much damage and killing as he has seen with his own eyes in the neighborhood. This kind of killing made no sense to him, and it had injured and killed some of his own people, his Lebanese people, who did nothing wrong.

    When Will decided to stop his searches, and go to bed, he did so with a sense of confusion on why his own government would do this type of killing. He resolved that he would speak with Sira, and discuss his feelings with her to see where her thoughts lay on these things.

    That night, the dreams returned in full force, only this time he was on his family's small farm in Lebanon and trucks were coming down the road spouting fumes and blowing dust high into the air as they came ever-closer. The family looked out, saw the caravan, and Will's mother told the children to go to the root cellar and stay there until she came for them. All three children did as they were told, and had just closed the door over in the corner of a small building where they kept their goats and sheep, when they could hear the trucks stopping, and the stomping of men climbing off the rear of the vehicles.

    Several shots rang out and the children feared for their parents lives. Loud voices were heard, as the men in the group spread out, looking over the house and other buildings on the farm, and then returning to the front of the house.

    Suddenly, several shouts, and then cries in pain filled the air, followed by several more shots. Then, there was quiet and the sounds of engine motors starting. In a few moments, the children could hear more sounds of the trucks pulling away from the house, yet they waited as they had been told, until their mother came for them.

    It seemed like an eternity before the children heard their mother's voice, and slowly, at her insistence, they raised the small door that separated them from her. Looking up, Will could see her waiting, and she had much blood on the front of her simple dress. He rushed to leave and went over to hug her tightly.

    "It is all right children," his mother said quietly, "It is all right. Come out, You are safe now." Will could see she had tears in her eyes. As they climbed from their safe place, and entered the yard, they could see that the house had been ransacked, and their father was in a chair in front of the house, also covered in blood, with a large open wound on his head. He was holding a cloth to it, but it was easy to see the size of the serious wound, a view that Will never forgot.

    Will had dropped off Sira at the front of the restaurant downtown as he usually did following her work at the farm, then waited to see her enter the restaurant before he drove off. On this evening, there were a large number of customers in the restaurant as she entered, and she moved quickly through the

From a Vantage Point

seating area to the kitchen to see Hassan. Sammi was also there, setting up several plates for customers.

"Sira how was your day?" asked Hassan, working over at the dishwasher.

'It went well, I believe. Johnson is beginning to show interest. He was reading one issue of Inspire several times, making notes on some pages. I told him I would be happy to explain things to him, but he was busy fixing a fence. I will work on him on my next visit."

"Good. Would you like some dinner?" asked Sammi. "We made a lot of food today. Take what you wish," he added, as he loaded up a tray to take out to his customers.

DHS, Washington DC Tom Corbett sat in the small cafeteria, eating lunch with two other members of Alice Sawyer's team. They had just begun when Tom O'Neal walked in, grabbed some food, and walked over to their table, claiming the empty seat.

"Well guys, what's new with you?" asked O'Neal, as he pushed the plates around on his tray before starting to unfold his napkin.

"You tell us, my friend," one of the men responded.

"How was your trip to beautiful downtown Elias, Tom?" asked Corbett.

"Interesting," O'Neal responded. "Really interesting. I think one of these days I am going to retire to a small town just like that. It is out in the woods, not near anything big, with lots of trees. Just what I would like to see, and watch the grass grow from the porch of a log cabin house."

"Sounds like going from the very fast lane, to the slowest right lane on the interstate to me," responded Corbett. "But then, it has to be better than fighting traffic and idiots in the Nation's Capital."

"Exactly," answered O'Neal.

"Tom, did you get anything out of the visit?" asked one of the men sitting with Corbett.

"Well, yes and no, is probably the answer. Yes, I did get a better feel for Johnson, and no, I did not get any smoking gun out there. He seems to be pretty clean to me. What about you Corbett? Anything on your visit?"

"Not much more than you saw. Somehow, I just cannot rid myself of the feeling that there is something else there, though. Everything seemed too pat. I also agree that Johnson is not some radicalized terrorist, but the whole community atmosphere is lacking something. There is another angle out there. I just cannot put my finger on it."

"Are you sure you are not wishing for something, Tom?" asked O'Neal.

"I honestly don't know," came the response. "There is some part of the puzzle missing. I just feel it, but have nothing to back it up."

From a Vantage Point

"Well, let's just eat lunch and try to figure that out later, I guess," answered O'Neal, looking down at his food, now getting cold. "I go back there in a week or ten days. Perhaps something will turn up then."

"Could be, I guess," said Corbett. "We still need to figure out who the woman Sira is. None of us has actually seen her, and there are no records to show she is even there. That may be the missing piece."

"Could be," answered O'Neal. Could be." He started to dig at his salad, and the conversation winded down as the men began to devour their lunch.

Elias, West Virginia Will woke to the alarm going off at 6 AM. He clicked on a television remote by the side of his bed. As the TV came on, the news was in progress.

"This is Alan Griffin, Eyewitness News, WCHS-TV in Charleston. For those of you who are just tuning in, we have an update on a three-car crash on Interstate 77, and a fire on a small farm just outside of Elias. First, let us look at some national news. From Atlanta, we have a report of a death on a flight coming into Atlanta-Hartsfield two days ago. There is this report from our sister station WSB-TV, and our reporter Jim Greene. Jim, what can you tell us about this curious case in Atlanta?"

"Good morning Alan. This is certainly a curious case. It involves the death of a passenger on an incoming Delta flight from Seattle two days ago. The passenger, a Joshua Giddons, apparently had a heart attack on the flight, just before it landed at Hartsfield, and the plane made an emergency landing, met by paramedics on the tarmac. They revived Mister Giddons but he died enroute to Mercy Hospital. We still do not have medical information, and the information on Mister Giddons is scanty as well."

"It seems that Mister Giddons came to the US from Canada," continued Greene, "but took a car from Vancouver to Seattle, and then boarded flight east. It was on that flight that he came down ill, and eventually had cardiac arrest. Normally, the security people are giving us more information by now, but everyone is very closed mouth at the Airport, and at TSA."

"Any particular reason?" asked Griffin.

"We are getting rumors that this guy Giddons was traveling under the name Atherton, and he entered Canada as a British citizen, on a British passport. He then flew from Montreal to Vancouver, and stayed some time there before driving down to Seattle. He claimed to be some kind of sales representative, but we cannot confirm that. That is about

From a Vantage Point

all we know right now, but we expect to hear about a press conference later today. Will let you know."

"Thanks Jim. Now, more international news with reports from both London and Baghdad when we return. Alan Griffin for Eyewitness News."

Will sat upright in bed, incredulous about the news on his friend Josh. He had no idea Josh was coming to the states again, and wondered why. The best he knew was that Josh's family lived in the Midwest, and not in the Atlanta area. It was confusing. He made a mental note to himself to continue to follow the story over the next couple of days to see what information came out.

Getting out of bed, Will went to the kitchen to make coffee. Just as he started to put the grounds in the coffeemaker, the phone rang.

"Mister Will, this is Sammi. Did you see the news?"

"I did," responded Will, thinking Sammi was speaking of his friend Josh. It is too bad."

"Yes, the Akins farm buildings are totally gone. They were to be a big part of our cooperative."

The message shook Will into reality. He remembered the news station speaking about a fire outside Elias.

"Sorry Sammi, I thought you were speaking about something else. How much damage did the Akins' have?"

"Everything in the buildings is gone. We are starting a drive to help them."

"Do they need a place to stay?" asked Will. He knew there were only the three, father, mother, and young son now that the oldest had left to go to college.

"They are staying with the James family right now, but they will need a place to stay while they rebuild."

"Please tell them they can have the small cottage over in my pasture. It is clean and neat, and they should be comfortable there."

"Thank you Mister Will. I thought you might do that. What other news was bothering you?" asked Sammi.

"A friend of mine died of a heart attack on a flight to Atlanta. I did not even know he was in the country."

"My deepest sympathies, Mister Will. I heard that report, and wondered if it was your friend."

"It was, but we need to wait for more information, I guess. I have no idea where his family might be, nor do I have a way of getting to our other mutual friend; the man he lived and traveled with in the Middle East. For now, I guess I will just have to wait."

"Please let me know if I can help somehow. You are my friend after all."

"Thanks, Sammi," responded Will, "You are indeed my best friend. Talk to you later."

From a Vantage Point

Sammi hung up the phone and motioned to Sira to come talk to him at the small table he occupied near the kitchen door. She walked over and sat down.

"Sira," Sammi said quietly as she sat, "you may have an opportunity here. Mister Will has found out that his friend Josh Giddons is dead in Atlanta. He saw it on the news just this morning. There may be an opening for you here, to engage in more conversation with him on his feelings."

"Perhaps Sammi, perhaps this is the time to start really bringing him around. When I go over there tomorrow, I will express my sincere sympathies, and try to get him to talk. He was reading a copy of Inspire the other day, and had underlined some things in one article. That is interesting as well."

"It is, and you can pursue it, but I want you to understand something. Mister Will is indeed my friend, and you will not cause him unnecessary harm. We will do as we are told, but I want it to be something he wants to do, when we find out what they want him for. Do you understand?"

"Yes, I do Sammi. You realize, of course, that I do not work for you in this, but for the Brothers. I receive my instructions from them directly as do you. Where there is conflict, I must follow my instructions from the leader. However, I am told to follow your instructions as well. This is a conflict for me."

"That is fine, but you do understand I have a say as well."

"I do," she responded, as she rose and went through the kitchen door to speak to Hassan at the dishwasher.

DHS, Washington DC. Alice Sawyer looked through her secured net e-mail inbox and found the e-mail she had been waiting for all week.

INTER-DEPARTMENTAL ONLY

SAWYERA, HS-101

SUBJECT: RECORDS SEARCH, SINGH HASSAN & SULEIMAN, SIRA

SINGH, CITIZEN PAKISTAN, BORN IRAQ, [DATE] FAMILY FLED TO PAKISTAN AT ONSET OF DESERT STORM. FATHER MEMBER OF THE HUSSEIN REGIME. ATTENDED COLLEGE IN PAKISTAN. WANTED BY INTERPOL (ORIGINAL NAME HOSSANI) APPROVED FOR EMPLOYMENT VISA [DATE]. TRAVELLED TO DELAWARE ON [DATE] AND EMPLOYMENT TRANSFER TO WEST VIRGINIA [DATE]

SULEIMAN, SIRA, BORN LEBANON [DATE] APPLIED FOR VISA, BEIRUT, WITH FAMILY (DENIED). FAMILY NEVER LEFT LEBANON. SIRA TRAVELED TO

PAKISTANT FOR COLLEGE, THEN DELAWARE ON WORK VISA, FOLLOWED BY ISSUANCE OF GREEN CARD. EMPLOYMENT TRANSFER REQUEST [DATE] TO WEST VIRGINIA APPROVED [DATE]. INTERPOL INDICATES TRAINING IN BIN-LADEN TRAINING CAMP IN PAKISTAN IN FIREARMS AND EXPLOSIVES. NO LETTER ISSUED.

ACKNOWLEDGE
JONESJ IC-21

As Alice looked at the message, she wondered about the implications, especially there was adverse information on both persons, yet it seemed, at least in the case of Sira, she was being shielded.

Responding, Alice asked for more in-depth information, hoping that there were enough records in either or both countries to settle her concerns. For now, she had to wait.

From a Vantage Point

Chapter 29 Condolences

Elias, West Virginia Will Johnson picked up Sira in her usual spot in front of the restaurant at 7:00 AM, avoiding what little traffic came into town just a short time later, and they headed out to the farm.

"Mister Will, Sammi told me about the death of your friend. I am truly sorry. I know what it is to lose friends, especially in unexpected situations."

"Thank you Sira. Josh was my friend. We were in the Army together, and travelled the world as well. I had just seen him in Khartoum only a short time ago. It my first vacation in many years, and gave me a chance to renew my friendship with him."

"Sammi did not say how he died. Was it sudden?" she asked, already knowing the answer.

"Yes, apparently, it was. He was on his way to Atlanta from the West Coast, and had a heart attack on the plane as it approached the airport in Atlanta."

"Really, that is very unusual. Was he ill?"

"Not that I know of, Sira. He was very healthy, at least when I saw him last. We travelled all over and he had no indication of being ill."

"That is curious then. I wonder what gave him the heart attack?" responded Sira.

Will though for a moment, and then asked, "Why would you say that Sira? People have heart attacks all the time, and in situations that are even more curious. I have no reason to believe he was ill, or something else happened to him."

"I meant nothing, Mister Will. It is just my nature from living in the Middle East so long. Over there, at least, sometimes people come down with illnesses as if by magic, and die for no reason. Later, it is found that the secret police have killed him. Of course, that does not happen here in America. I must remember that. I am sorry if I made you upset."

"No Sira, you did not upset me. Perhaps there is something to his death. I don't know. I will just have to wait and listen to the news and see what they say."

"Of course, Mister Will. I hope everything is perfectly natural, so you do not feel badly about it."

The two drove quietly toward the farm, as Will pondered what Sira said. He thought about the drone strike, and the other things he heard and saw during his visit, and began to wonder if there was more to Josh's death than a simple heart attack. He had no way of knowing, of course, but that did not stop him from thinking about how some of these pieces might fit together.

Trying to break the silence, but not wanting a long conversation, Will hit the button for the radio to hear the morning news.

From a Vantage Point

"This is WCHS-Radio, 580 AM on your dial. The news and radio talk station everybody listens to in Charleston. This is Jimmy Ray Jones with the rush hour news."

"We want to follow up today on a story that broke two days ago in Atlanta, which has taken some interesting twists overnight. We reported on an airplane passenger death on a Delta Airline flight from Seattle to Hartsfield-Atlanta. That death has taken on an interesting turn when last evening, without much apparent warning, the US department of Homeland Security swooped into Mercy Hospital with a court order, taking the body of the dead man, Joshua Giddons, and then moved it to an unannounced location."

"We don't know why the transfer," Jones continued, "Nor do we have much more information on Giddons; only that he is apparently a person of interest for the FBI and DHS. Our sources in Charleston tell us that Giddons is alleged to be involved with some terrorist group in the Middle East, and the Government wants to know why he was in the US. We do understand he was traveling on a false passport with the name Atherton. We expect more information later in the day. Stay tuned to 580 for more news, after this message."

Will sat listening to the brief news piece, and immediately thought back to what Sira had just said. Now he was completely confused.

"Mister Will, are you sure there is nothing else going on with your friend? It seems like the Government has a big interest in him," said Sira.

"Not sure what is going on Sira. Here is the road to the farm. Let's worry about the work we need to do, and worry about Josh later." Will turned off the radio, and drove the last few yards to the house. Both exited the car, Will going to the barn, and Sira to the front door of the house.

US Embassy, Khartoum, Sudan The phone was ringing as Jeff Namers entered his office.

"Who the hell can that be?" said Namers at the top of his voice. "I'm not supposed to even be here until tomorrow. Who wants me now?"

"Namers," Jim said as he picked up the phone and put it to his ear.

"Jeff, this is Fatima. Do you have a moment to talk?"

"Sure Fatima. I have not heard much from you lately. What can I do for you?"

"It is what I can do for you, my friend that is important, I believe. I heard yesterday from my cousin Hakim."

From a Vantage Point

"You did? Where is he? Half the world is looking for him," responded Namers.

"That I am not completely sure, but I believe he is in Kabul, or close to there. One of my shipping people saw some equipment being shipped to Kabul, to Arkanon Industries."

Arkanon does not sound familiar. Who are they?"

"Arkanon is a company owned by a pig named Pentopolos, a Greek who does business with the Taliban. He and Hakim worked together for the Mujahidin and Bin-Laden."

"So, why is this so unusual? Everyone worked for them in the old days."

"It is only when Hakim is involved do we get orders from them for anything. The company is really a front for Hakim; Pentopolos just runs it, but wants people to think he owns it."

"All right then," responded Namers, "So you have orders from Arkanon for shipment to Kabul. How does that directly link Hakim to all this?"

"The order was for six packing cases to be refitted in Kabul by Arkanon. We have done that business before. They get refitted in Kabul and sent on to somewhere else; only after they have been filled with things Hakim wants to ship."

Namers began to take an interest in the conversation as his mind began to think what packing cases could do to hide something else.

"When is this stuff shipping Fatima?"

"It goes out tomorrow by air to Kabul," she answered.

"From where?"

"From our warehouse," came the reply.

"Good. I will be over to look at this stuff. Can I get in there with no one seeing me come in?"

"Come to the back of the building. Be here at noon. My uncle always goes to prayers before noon. No one else will be here but me until after one o'clock. That will be a good time."

"I will be there at noon. See you then," Namers said, hanging up the phone.

Namers quickly left his office to go down the corridor toward his telecommunication center to see one of his people. The idea was to place homing devices on one or more of the packing cases, to track them, if they could. The only question was finding a device small enough to do the job, and not be detected.

Elias, West Virginia *Will spent the morning working on fences, patching a hole in a small barn roof, and preparing for the coming fall. Soon, it would be time to take in the winter hay supply for the cattle, and he cleared space on the loft in the barn to hold the many hay bales he needed to store. All through the*

From a Vantage Point

morning, he kept thinking about Josh and Hakim; their free-living life style, and now Josh's death. He could not help himself in wondering if there was more to it than the news was saying. Even the news reporter this morning on the radio said that Homeland Security was saying very little. He remembered as well, the bombing in Khartoum that could have meant the death of all three, except that they were away in the villages at the time the bombs dropped.

The idea the he could be killed by his government, even accidently while they tried to kill his friends, made Will very angry. Who were these unnamed people, Will thought to himself? What right do they have to send out a drone and kill someone, especially an American citizen? What ever happened to the idea that the Government was supposed to protect its people, not kill them the way he and his friends were nearly killed, however allegedly guilty they might be?

By lunchtime, Will was tired; both from the work he did through the morning, and the deep thinking about his friends. He needed to sort out all his feelings, but he had no idea how to do that.

"Well Sira," asked Will as he came through the front door, finding her dusting in the living room, "How did your morning go?"

"My job here is easy, Mister Will. Once I went through the house cleaning the first time, it is now more dusting and straightening out that is needed. How is your day going?"

"I got a lot of work done this morning myself. Now I feel ready for the coming winter. There is still a lot to do, but at least the major things are starting to get done. About a week more, and I should have everything in order. I hope so, because I really need to move on some things for the cooperative as well."

"I am glad to hear that Mister Will. Work will also help you take your mind off your friend for a while," Sira said, with a simple smile.

"All that certainly does help," responded Will. "Sira, let me ask you a question. Why do you think people, or even governments, have to act the way they do?"

"What do you mean, Mister Will?"

"Well, you know, I went to visit Josh and another friend some time ago in Sudan. While I was there, the building they were living in was bombed, some said by an American drone. It trashed the place. I never got my stuff out. There was nothing left to get. We all could have been killed at the time, but we were out sightseeing at the moment of the attack."

"You were lucky, Mister Will. Many people have been killed with those drones, sent by the United States military into several countries. They do not seem to care who they kill, and later try to say they tried to protect the innocent. Let them tell that to the innocents who are killed or injured by their bombs. No, they do not care, and America is not the only country doing that. The Israelis and others do the same thing, day after day."

From a Vantage Point

"Sira, I know we come from different worlds, but I really want to believe that the military tries to be exact on who they target. These drones are supposed to be precise."

"That may be true, Mister Will," Sira responded, "I am certainly not an expert here. I only know what I read in the news reports. If the building has others in it, even families of those who are targeted, they are still dead. You have been here in this country and have forgotten perhaps what happened in your own country in the past. Your family left during a period of fighting, just as mine experienced, but we could not leave. We had to hope every day we would not be killed."

"I can understand what happens overseas, but not here," said Will, seeming frustrated.

"But, of course it can, Mister Will. There are many instances where countries have sent people here to kill one of their own. Look at the Russians, the Iranians, the North Koreans, even the Israelis have done the same. What would make you think that the United States, which seems to find killing easy overseas, would not also do it here?"

Will had no immediate answer. He thought about Josh being taken away from the hospital, and now he began to grow doubts about how he died.

"I need to think about this more. Let's have lunch and change the subject for now."

"As you wish, Mister Will, I do not want to make you sad or angry," responded Sira, who went to the kitchen, to prepare sandwiches for lunch. She returned a few minutes later, and they sat quietly, eating their food, while Will pondered his thoughts.

Khartoum, Sudan Jeff Namers came well prepared to ensure that the boxes shipped to Kabul were trackable. His team provided him with micro-sensors, shaped like the heads of nails with a barb to embed in wood, capable of emitting ultrasound waves that were difficult to detect, but fairly easy to document via satellite. He was comfortable that they would do the job needed, and as he drove to Fatima's shipping office, he hoped this might lead to a resolution of the continuing problem of Hakim and his network of terrorists.

As Fatima told him, he pulled his vehicle behind the shipping office and parked inside the enclosure, away from the exit to avoid any notice. She met him at the door and they went inside.

"Fatima, you are just as gorgeous as ever," said Namers, as they entered the building, and headed for the shipping area.

"Jeff, you are a complete, what do you call it, a bull shitter, but I love it," Responded Fatima.

"This is the set of boxes they want shipped," she continued, moving over to the wall where six boxes made of wood sat there, almost like small coffins.

From a Vantage Point

"What do they want these for?" asked Namers.

"Well," she said, "They are made of cedar wood. These have very thick fibers, and very dense. They are difficult to x-ray or anything else by normal means. I think they expected to have them pass through customs with perhaps a simple scan which would show nothing."

"We can fix that," responded Namers, taking out a small package from his left pocket. "Let's see what this does," he added as he took out a sheet with several microdots, placing one on each end of a box, near the corners and down toward the bottom. He took out a small scanner from his pants pocket and waved it over the t boxes. Finally, he took out the sensors shaped like the nail heads, and placed them on the outer packing cartons.

"This will do just fine. Now ship them to Kabul. We will follow them as they travel, and then be able to locate them once they leave their packing cartons."

"Are you sure, Jeff?" asked Fatima.

"It's the best we can do here, Fatima. Ship them, and we will hope they do the job."

"OK, they go out today," she responded, "How about some tea?"

"Love some."

They walked out of the shipping area toward the office where she had a large pot of water brewing for her tea. Pointing toward the small table over at the side of the office, she took two cups from a small shelf and placed them on the table. Then she took some loose tea, placed it into Aluminum steepers, and placed them in the cups. Finally, she poured hot water into the cups.

"This is fancy Chinese Oolong Jeff. We get it periodically from the shippers. It is real Chinese tea; not the stuff you get in the bazaar. Try it. You will like its flavor."

Namers and Fatima sat there for a long while, drinking tea and discussing their relationship. Namers revealed that the agency was now willing to put her back on the payroll. She refused, saying that her information was free to him because she believed in him. He knew they had reached a new plateau in their relationship, but wished that Jim Davis had been there to see the change.

Elias, West Virginia *Sira worked through the rest of the rooms in the house, cleaning and neatening the place as best she could. She now knew that Will Johnson was beginning to have doubts about himself, his relationship with his friends, and even his feelings about his government. His doubts about the policies of the US Government could be magnified, and that was exactly what she wanted to happen. The question now was how to expand on that quickly enough to push him into a position of working the plan Hakim hatched for Washington DC in the coming Presidential Inauguration.*

Sira sensed that Will still needed time to sort out his thoughts, but she also knew his own doubts would help in that regard. She would respond carefully and softly to his expressed concerns, while encouraging him to express them freely to her so she could seem to respond with compassion and understanding.

Will worked through part of the afternoon, coming back to the house about 3 PM, just as Sira was finishing her dusting. As he walked into the living room, she smiled, and he returned it, thinking how glad he was that she had come to town, and was now taking care of his home. The place changed dramatically after her arrival, cleaner, brighter, and a place to enjoy.

"Sira, how about you finish early today, and we both go to Sammi's and have some dinner?"

"That would be wonderful, Mister Will. Perhaps you can relax a bit, and be less tense."

"Do you really think it shows?" Will asked.

"Yes, it does Mister Will. You should not carry so much misery on your shoulders. My father always used to say that only God must carry the weight of the world alone."

"Funny, I remember my father saying something similar," responded Will.

"It is an old saying that actually comes from the Prophet, may the peace of All'ah be upon him, and it goes, 'each person is responsible for himself, and those around him, but do not take all their cares and worries upon yourself. Others must carry their own misery on their own shoulders. Only All'ah carries the worries of the world on his shoulders'. It is a wise saying."

Will thought for a moment on what she said, and responded, "Sira you are a very astute person for someone your age. Have you considered going to college and improving yourself?"

"I would like to do that Mister Will, perhaps some time, but for now, I need to earn a living to stay here in America. As you Americans say, first things first."

"Well said. Let's get ready to go to town, shall we?"

"Of course, I have just two things to finish. It will take about ten minutes."

"That gives me time to clean up a bit, and change my shirt," said Will, moving toward his bedroom. "See you in a couple of minutes."

Sira smiled, and went back to her chores waiting for Will to signal he was ready to leave.

It was closer to fifteen minutes before they left the farm, but Will seemed in better spirits than the morning, and Sira knew he needed further prodding. Just as she was ready to speak to him, Will turned on the radio.

"This is WCHS-Radio, 580 Am on your dial," said the voice on the radio after completing an ongoing discussion with viewers. 'This is Viewpoint with Jimmy Ray Jones, and we just heard from Maybelle on the new gun control measures the Governor is trying to get the State Legislature to pass. Let's hear from another listener on the live, shall we? This is Jimmy Ray, who do we have?"

"This is Bobby, Jimmy Ray, and I think the idea of gun control, when we have all these ragheads running around with guns and bombs, is just plain stupid. We need to protect ourselves and taking our guns away while these people have them is not right; it ain't American."

"Well then Bobby, what do you think we should be doing?"

"We need to get rid of all these damn mosques, and send these people back to where they came from. Hell, those idiots in Washington want to bring even more over here to do damage, and they expect us to roll over and greet them while they shoot us and molest our kids. It ain't right I say."

"Thanks for your feelings, Bobby. We have one more on the line before we go to the news. Who's next?" asked Jimmy Ray.

"Jimmy Ray, this is Jackie speaking."

"Welcome Jackie," answered Jimmy Ray, "What do you want to add to this conversation?"

"I think this is the Government people's fault. We need to stop killing people in the Middle East, and bring our boys home. We need to stop sending these drones out to kill, because the Government doesn't have the guts to go get the bad guys. Hell, I was over there twice, and now this administration has given everything back. It's disgusting is what it is. Like the other guy said, it ain't right."

"What do you propose then Jackie?"

"I say either go in there and kill them all, get the leaders and do what has to be done, or get out and leave them to themselves. Let them kill each other all they want. Stop acting like cowards and sending in those drone things to kill our own people as well as anyone else in the way. That's what I think."

"Thanks for your comments, Jackie. That wraps up the discussion for this afternoon. We will continue after the news on the crisis in the coal industry."

"In other news today, this afternoon, Homeland Security has given out some more information on that guy

From a Vantage Point

we reported on in Atlanta earlier this morning. A DHS spokesperson said that Giddons was on the Interpol want list, along with an associate, and entered the US illegally using a false identity. They had no comment on his death, other than to say, another autopsy is ongoing by an undisclosed team or location, and that further information would be made available in due time," Jimmy Ray continued.

"We do have information, as yet unconfirmed, that the man Giddons was some kind of soldier for hire in the Middle East, associated with al-Qaeda and other organizations. Interpol has been trying to get him for over three years at the request of the US Government. I guess we will have to wait to see what happens here."

Jimmy Ray went on with other local and national news, and both Will and Sira listened quietly as they neared Main Street. Will pulled into a parking spot in front of Sammi's. They both went inside, Sira to the kitchen, and Will took his usual table near the door.

Khartoum, Sudan "Fatima, what is your take on why he wants these boxes?" asked Namers, looking over at her sipping her tea.

"I have no idea, Jeff. You can get boxes like these virtually anywhere. We get them for packing loose items; things that people want, but you do not have exactly the right sized box to pack it in. The cedar wood is good; it's hard; and it lasts. These boxes will last probably forty to fifty years. I really have no idea why he wants them."

"Well, there is not much more we can do than follow them wherever they go. I made that a bit easier," responded Namers, as he again took the small device from his pocket and turned it on to check that the sensors worked. As he moved the small device close to one of the dots, the machine buzzed to show activity.

"Good, it works," continued Namers. "The device we use to actually follow these things is larger, more powerful, and it can track at large distances through a satellite link. This should do what we want. When are you shipping?"

"Probably today," came the response. "We will pack these with the outer case as I showed you. We have space in a large cargo container going to Kabul via Islamabad, this evening. I will make sure they pack with other things in the container. That will get them to Kabul tomorrow afternoon, and probably picked up by our shipping agent there later in the day. Arkanon will get them the following day by truck."

"That gives us time to follow the trace on them. Thanks Fatima. I owe you one."

"Happy to do it Jeff. I was worried for a long time that you might think I was not in your camp. Hakim burned me and I will not forget it."

"Let's talk about that for a moment. Why do you think he burned you with us?"

"He was not after me," replied Fatima. "He had figured out Jim Davis, and the relationship we had. He thought we were lovers and that was blasphemy to him, in his twisted version of Islam. We were not lovers, but we were very good friends. Do you know why?"

"Not really," responded Namers.

"Jim Davis started in CIA with you; you were both in the same class. Jim came to the Middle East long before you, and worked in Istanbul. There he met my father, and my uncle. They had a small shipping business, working for Amoud Tabriz. "

"Ah yes, Fatool. Those were the days when he was active."

"Yes, Fatool gave them business, just like Hakim gives business to me. The difference is that Fatool had his own ethics, and treated people well. My kinsman Hakim is an animal who forces what he wants. Jim Davis arranged to have my father and uncle leave Istanbul just before a big operation took place; the one in which Jim was injured.

I was young then, but I remember when he came to the house and told both men they could go home. The three of us, my father, my uncle, and myself boarded a government plane, and went to Pakistan, where the CIA arranged to bring us into Khartoum, and set us up in this business."

"Everybody thought it was Hakim who did that, but it was the CIA," Fatima continued. "Even you did not know that. It was Jim Davis and his friend Bernie Minihan who did that. I am grateful for them, as I am for you. Jim and I are still friends, and always will be. That is the story."

"I never knew that Fatima. Much of your early history is closed; only a few people get access to your family files. I simply assumed the stories were correct. In a way, I am glad I did not know. Treating you differently might have caused you and your uncle some real harm."

"That was the way it was supposed to be Jeff. I am only telling you because you will keep my secret."

" That I will. That I will," said Namers as the two walked back toward the rear door. "Now, let's go get Hakim," said Jeff as walked through the rear door into the sunlight.

On the drive back to his office, Namers thought back to the days when he, Davis, and Bernie Minihan roamed through Europe trying their best to bring down Fatool's empire; stymied at each point by the Egyptian's political connections. Even the Red Letter Issued by Interpol was never enough to bring him down.

From a Vantage Point

When he retired to live on his villa in Libya, law enforcement around the world took a collective deep breath.

Fatool moved from his villa during the "Arab Spring" which brought down the Libyan regime and simply vanished from the world scene. The intelligence community let him live quietly, confident he would not be a threat in the future. They relied on his word, and he had not broken it since.

Elias, West Virginia A dark blue sedan pulled up next to Will Johnson's car outside Sammi's Restaurant, and two men in suits and overcoats came into the restaurant. They looked around quickly and started to walk over to Will Johnson's table.

"Mister Johnson? I am Special Agent Burke, and this is Special Agent James, FBI. We need you to come with us please."

"What is happening here? Am I under arrest?" Will asked.

"No sir, you are not under arrest. We need to ask you some questions, and would like you to come to our office."

"You can ask me what you want here. I'm about to have lunch."

"That will not do sir. Please come with us now," responded the agent.

"Can you tell me what this is about?" asked Will, looking bewildered.

"Happy to advise you at the office sir," came the response.

"Where are we going?"

"The Charleston office sir," the agent answered as Sammi came out of the kitchen and saw the two men with Will.

"Sammi," shouted Will toward the kitchen door, "Please call Elmer and tell him I have been taken by the FBI to Charleston. I need his help."

"Who is that gentleman sir?" asked one of the agents.

"My lawyer. OK, if you insist, let's go. Elmer will follow us to Charleston. I will tell you nothing except my name until he is in the room with us, and I can find out what this is all about."

"Sorry you feel that way sir, but we have our orders." The two men led Will out to their car, placed him in the back seat, and entered their car, driving off toward the Interstate.

Sammi rushed over to the phone to call Elmer Sites, the local attorney for most of the town.

"Elmer, this is Sammi. Two guys from the FBI just came in took Will Johnson away to their offices in Charleston. Can you go help him?"

"Of course, Sammi. Do you know what this is all about?"

"No Elmer," responded Sammi, "They just took him and said they would tell him what this was about when they got to Charleston."

"All right, I am on my way. I should get there pretty close to when they do. The Federal Courthouse is the same building, so I can get a writ quickly if I need it."

"Thanks Elmer," said Sammi, hanging up the phone. Then he turned to the customers, who were all sitting waiting to hear what was happening.

"Go back to having lunch folks. I don't know what is going on but Elmer is on his way to help Will. Let's just wait until we hear from them before anyone gets excited." People started to sit back down, although it was clear that the room was tense and anxious.

Homeland Security had asked the FBI to pick up Will for questioning when they looked over the personal effects of Josh Giddons and found Will's name on a piece of paper, and the words 'Sammi's Restaurant'. When they came from Charleston, they had a photo of Will, It was a coincidence he was at the restaurant; saving them having to look further. The agents considered their actions to be normal practice, and had no idea of the effect on the mind of Will Johnson; already anxious over the death of his friend.

The men drove in silence down the Interstate to Charleston, arriving at the Federal Courthouse about forty minutes later. They parked in a reserved space in front of the Courthouse, and took Will to an office on the second floor, where they left him sitting at a small table with three chairs around it.

Elmer Sites arrived about five minutes later, entered the courthouse and asked for the FBI offices. He was told to go to the second floor, took the elevator up the second floor, and stood before a receptionist desk.

"My name is Elmer Sites. I am the attorney for Mister Will Johnson. He was just brought in here. I want to see him immediately."

"Sorry, Mister Sites, but that might be difficult. Agents are interviewing him."

"Not without my attendance, they are not, let me go up to see Judge Smith and get a writ. Tell them I will be back within five minutes."

"Yes sir."

Attorney Sites walked up the stairs to the chambers of Judge Smith, spoke to his clerk, and was back at the FBI offices in less than ten minutes.

"Young lady, this is a writ from Judge Smith. No longer a request, I demand to see my client, right now." The woman took the paper, and excused herself, walking through a door into the inner offices. About a minute later, Special Agent Burke walked out to the reception area.

"Mister Sites, can I help you?"

"You have the writ from Judge Smith. I demand to see my client right now," was the response from Sites.

"Of course, sir. Mister Johnson is not under arrest. We just need to ask him some questions. He decided to wait for your arrival. The writ was really not necessary."

"Of course it was, Agent Burke. Your employee refused to let me enter, saying you were interviewing my client. That is illegal, and you know it."

"I can assure you Mister Johnson has said nothing to us. In fact, we are waiting ourselves for someone from Homeland Security to come over before we start any questioning. Right this way, and I will show you where your client is located." Agent Burke opened the door, and the two entered the inner offices, walking toward a room marked 'Interrogation 1'. Inside sat Will Johnson.

"Will, how are you doing?" asked Sites as they entered the room.

"Everything is fine, Elmer, except of course for why I was shanghaied here by this guy and his partner. I still have no answers," Will responded, looking at Agent Burke.

"The ball is in your court, Agent Burke. Tell us what is going on here, or my client and I walk. Of course, if you choose to arrest him for something, that is your problem. I will walk back upstairs to see Judge Smith, who has agreed to wait around, just in case I need him. What is it going to be?"

"Sir, we need a few questions answered, that's all. There is nothing sinister here."

"OK, so nothing sinister here. Two questions come to mind; why not simply ask them in Elias, and what are the questions? If you want patience here, then I want to know what we are facing here. Simple swap of information"

"Mister Sites, I can tell you this. Homeland found Mister Johnson's name, phone number, and a message on a piece of paper on a dead man in Atlanta. They asked us to detain him for questioning. That's all I know right now."

"When do you expect them to arrive?" asked Sites.

"Don't know," came the answer from Agent Burke.

"Then we are going home. I will make Mister Johnson available in Elias at my office any time you need him for reasonable questions. I will not have him waiting around for some unknown reason, for people who could arrive anytime, and then find this is simply some wild goose chase. The bottom line is either arrest him for something or we are leaving. Any questions?"

"No sir. Mister Johnson is free to leave with you," responded Burke, opening the door. "I do suggest he stays available as you indicated. DHS will be coming to see him."

"Fair enough," responded Sites, and he and Will started to leave. Just as they reached the door, a large man entered ahead of them.

"Who told you to leave Johnson?" asked the man.

"I did," responded Elmer Sites, handing the person his card. "This is my client, and he is Mister Johnson to you. I need to see some identification, by the way."

"Sure. Ben Thorne, Homeland Security. You have to leave, Mister Sites. This is a classified interview."

From a Vantage Point

"Will, say nothing further. I will go back up to Judge Smith and ask for an immediate hearing."

"Do what you wish sir. Mister Johnson, take a seat."

Elmer Sites left to go to see Judge Smith, who issued another order for the Homeland Security people to come to his office to explain. The big man did so, and returned quickly.

"You can go Johnson," he said as he entered the room. "Don't breathe more than twelve times a minute though. We will have you on constant surveillance."

"Will, let's go home, shall we?" The two left the room, went through the outer office door, and down the stairs to the main floor. As they walked through the doors to the street, two men standing to the right side of the door started to follow them toward Elmer Sites' car. Clearly, they now had a team tailing their movements.

DHS Washington DC Tom Corbett rushed into Alice Sawyer's office with the news.

"Alice, we have a situation on our hands."

"What's that Tom?" she replied.

"The Atlanta office retrieved the body from Mercy Hospital, along with what little effects there were. They found a note with Will Johnson's name and number on it, so they told the local DHS people to go get Johnson for questioning. They sent an FBI team out from Charleston, and the team took Johnson to their FBI offices, followed quickly by his lawyer, to wait for our people coming in from Atlanta."

"So, what's the problem here? I would not have done that, but it's done. What else is going on?"

"Johnson's lawyer, a Mister Sites, went to a Federal judge and got a writ releasing Johnson, after he was ordered out of the interrogation room by one of our people, who decided the interrogation was classified."

"He what? Who was this fool? This could ruin everything. Get me Atlanta on the phone."

Alice spent nearly twenty minutes on the phone with DHS-Atlanta. She did most of the talking, and whomever she spoke with in Atlanta did most of the listening. Tom could hear her tell them to take the tail off Johnson, and work out something to get his information. It was not a pleasant conversation for the person on the other end of the line.

Finally, she hung up and looked back at Tom Corbett.

"Everything is back on track, Tom. They now understand the ground rules. A team will go to Elias tomorrow to speak with Mister Johnson. All we wanted to know was why the note was in Giddons' pocket. Nothing more sinister. These people are idiots."

From a Vantage Point

"No comment Alice," shrugged Corbett, as he left to return to his own office.

Khartoum, Sudan. Jeff Namers entered the embassy grounds and drove to his usual parking space. Stopping the car, he sat for a moment to think about where this latest turn of events was leading. Fatima was shipping some interesting packing cartons, boxes which could be purchased anywhere locally, to Kabul for a company doing business with Hakim. The boxes serve no apparently useful purpose, other than to provide a means for shipping small items.

As he left the car to travel the short distance to the entrance and his office, it came to Namers that he had seen this type of box before. The question was where? The answer nagged at him all the way to his office, and then later as he met with his small staff, which he had quickly called into his office.

"Ok guys, let's think about something," said Namers, as he started to draw a box on his whiteboard. "What would you want one of these boxes for?"

"Wow," responded one of his men? "I can tell you if this is well-built, I would sure like to get one for my power tools. I could put my circular saw in the center and all the attachments in the pigeon holes around the edges. That's a great box, whoever is creating it."

"Well, if it were me and I wanted to ship something I didn't want people to see, I would put something bulky in the center, and then surround it with things that are difficult to x-ray," said another. "Of course, I could also take out the dividers and line the box with something to prevent the x-ray from even penetrating."

"That is true," said a third, "But that would be a big red flag, almost assuring inspection, at least here in the US on arrival."

"Agreed," answered Namers, "But what about if it were being shipped in an even larger crate—a CONEX for example, which was already lined and sealed?"

"Then you have a problem Jeff," responded Charlie Irving, the security officer, "Even minor insulation with something like Aluminum, for example, would dull or obstruct something in the center of the box, packed in a CONEX, or another type of shipping container. It would be almost impossible to examine."

"All right then," said Namers in reply, "I have microdots on the boxes, and several of your sensors Charlie. I put the sensors on the outer shipping boxes. If these go into CONEXs, can we monitor the bugs?"

"I think so Jeff," responded Irving.

"OK, then let's get our surveillance into gear. Charlies, you need to arrange a net to follow the shipment. It goes out today by air to Kabul, via Islamabad. Let's see how well we can follow the trail here. We may lose a couple of bugs in the transfers, but we may luck out."

"Sure, I can do that," responded Irving. "Need about ten minutes, and a blessing to set up the next. Will the ambassador give it to us?"

From a Vantage Point

"I will take care of that. You just get the net configured."

"Will do Jeff," responded Irving, as he left the room. Namers gave a few other instructions on things he needed done, and the rest followed out to their own spaces, leaving Namers alone, looking at the drawing on the wall, still unable to remember the context of the boxes.

Kabul, Afghanistan *An open-back utility truck with the name Arkanon painted on its left door waited at the customs post for the arrival of the morning flight from Islamabad. The driver sat patiently looking out at the runway with what someone could call a blank stare. He was told to meet the flight, speak to the customs people, mention his boss Pentopolos, and pick up a large shipping crate. His instructions were to deliver it to another shipper in town, near the airport. That company would unpack the shipping crate, and give the driver two smaller boxes to bring to Arkanon.*

Finally, coming down through the clouds over the hills surrounding Kabul, a plane drifted lower toward the runway, landing on the east runway and moving quickly toward an off-ramp and the arrival area. The driver sat up from his resting position; started the truck, and moved slowly over to the customs ramp entrance where the guard listened to his story, and waved him on toward a parking space near the unloading area for the customs service.

It took nearly an hour for the unloading of the plane and the actions of the customs inspectors to release the shipping crate. A small forklift brought the crate over to the truck, and placed it on the flatbed. The truck driver closed the rear gate of the truck, reentered the cab, started the engine and drove through the customs gate toward downtown.

At Arkanon, the phone rank and Pentopolos picked it up to answer it.

"Yes, this is Arkanon, how can I help you?" He quickly recognized the voice of Hakim al-Azahir on the other end of the line.

"My man is at the airport now picking up your shipment Hakim. Have patience. We will get it this afternoon, and the men are waiting to build them to your drawings. We will have them done in two days."

"Good," responded Hakim. "In two days, then, I will call again with instruction on what you are to do with the boxes." Hakim hung up the phone, as did Pentopolos, who went back to reading the book he was enjoying before the phone call interrupted his thoughts.

Another two hours went by before the truck containing the two shipping cases arrived on the truck from the airport. The driver backed the truck into the loading dock and went inside, dropping the keys on the desk, and leaving the office without saying a word.

"You two over there," said Pentopolos, "Go get the boxes off the truck and let's get to work. We have only two days. The men responded, and brought the boxes into the warehouse, placing them on a long table. Inside were the yet smaller boxes; simply wood with covers. They did not seem worth the effort Hakim was making over them. Pentopolos learned years earlier not to question Hakim, but to do what he was told. He would do that now, and get the boxes finished and out of his warehouse. Inside each box was several pieces of varied length wood—the same kind used to construct the outer shell. They were wrapped in packing paper, which the men removed, placing the pieces on the long table next to their respective box.

The men looked at the drawings and quickly went to work. On a table opposite the boxes was a metal-bending machine on which they fashioned thin metal pieces to fit both inside and outside of the boxes. Then, using the wood strips that came with the boxes from Khartoum, they created the inside set of walls and dividers which created small bins around the edges of the boxes. This was not easy work with basic tools, and they worked into the night to complete the first box; intending to complete the other the following morning. Only after they attached handles to the sides of the first box did they stop work, close up the warehouse, and leave for their homes.

Pentopolos came in early the next morning; he wanted to be there before his workers to see their progress. He was impressed with the first shipping crate; it was exactly what Hakim described, fit well, and was sturdy for long shipping periods. He looked at it, and the other ready for completion today, again wondering why Hakim needed them. These were the types of crates which could be acquired almost anywhere. Why build them from scratch?

Playing a hunch, Pentopolos went to his office and returned with a sensor scanner, passing the instrument over each of the boxes. The unfinished one gave off a strong signal, so he passed it over the crate again; the same signal appeared a second time. Pentopolos looked closely at the sport where the beep emanated, and saw a very small flaw in the wood. Looking closely, he noticed it was not a flaw at all; it was a sensor device. Using a small knife on the table near the box, Pentopolos dug into the wood and extracted the sensor. It fit on the edge of his finger.

Thinking quickly, Pentopolos scanned the finished box again as well, and received no signal. Finding a small sensor, Pentopolos removed it, then re-attached it to another box, one going out into the mountains in the next few days. He also scanned each of the other boxes, and found several more sensors; some he placed on other packages going to various places, and in two cases, he simply removed them and wrapped them in paper to dispose of them later. Deciding to keep the whole thing to himself; he did not want to hear an angry response from Hakim, but also reminded himself to tell Fatima, so she would know she had problems over in Khartoum.

From a Vantage Point

As the morning progressed, the workers gradually came into the shop and began to fashion the plates for the other crate. Pentopolos watched as they cut then placed the metal sheaths, which would cover the wood. He made sure to tell one of his workers to test both crates again with the sensor device before preparing them for shipping. The most important parts of the crates, the inner walls, and the dividers were the last fabricated. These took the most time since the pieces were small, and had to fit exactly so the covers would close snugly. When both crates were complete, Pentopolos had the workers place them on a shelf to the side of the warehouse, awaiting the call from Hakim on shipping arrangements to the United States.

Elias, West Virginia The phone rang early at Will Johnson's farm. He picked it up and Elmer Sites was on the other end.

"Will, it's Elmer. Hope I did not wake you?"

"No, Elmer, I was awake. What can I do for you today? Thanks for getting me out of that mess yesterday."

"No problem, Will. That 'mess' is what I am calling about actually. I just got a call from the Homeland Security people in Atlanta; they are coming up here to Elias to ask some questions they say they need answered. I told them 2 PM in my office. Can you be here then?"

"Sure Elmer. Any idea what they want?" I'm completely in the dark here."

"Something about someone named Josh Giddons. Do you know him?"

"Sure do. We were in the Army together years back. What about Josh? I heard on the news he was dead."

"That's what they are working on. They have some questions for you. I spoke with the director down there, and he profusely apologized for your treatment yesterday. The FBI over-reacted, they said. Are you willing to meet with them?"

"Sure Elmer, I have nothing to hide. Two o'clock at your office?"

"That's it Will. See you then. Come a few minutes early, and we will talk" Elmer hung up, and Will got dressed to go have breakfast, still wondering what was happening.

As the morning progressed, Will worked out in the barn, moving more hay bales and cleaning out the stalls. He kept thinking about Josh and Hakim, and wondered why the FBI treated him the way they did. *I'm not some kind of criminal or terrorist,* He asked himself. *Why me, and what did I do to get them hauling me away. That's just not right,* and even worse in front of my friends. The more he thought about the prior day, the madder he became, and the more he resented the treated he received at the hands of the FBI agents.

Will decided to have lunch at the restaurant before he walked across Main Street to Elmer's office next to the store. He wanted to speak to Sammi first, and really did not want to make lunch for himself.

From a Vantage Point

Starting the drive toward town Will could see a helicopter flying in circles above Elias; eventually circling lower as it went over downtown. After a couple of circles, it stopped, and Will assumed it set down on the emergency pad near the fire station.

"Must be the Federal people coming in," Will said loudly to himself in the car. Then it occurred to him that these people just might mess up the work he was doing on the cooperative. He needed to discuss that possibility with Elmer and Sammi. Another thought also came to him as well. Would these people be at the restaurant when he arrived in town? He would have to wait to see.

The drive seemed shorter today, but Will chalked it up to faster driving. Soon he was on Main Street and found a space to park just down from the restaurant. He walked the short distance, and entered to find Sammi at the door.

"Mister Will these guys at the first table just came in riding a helicopter. They are both wearing guns. Be careful," said Sammi, ushering Will to a table near the kitchen door.

"Thanks, Sammi," responded Will, "They are here to ask some questions about Josh's death. They came here because I refused to talk to them when they hauled me to Charleston yesterday. Elmer got me out of that. It should be interesting today."

"Why can't they let that poor man die in peace? These police, they pick and pick, and destroy people's lives for no reason<" said Sammi, obviously upset.

"It's OK Sammi. I have nothing to hide. They can ask all the questions they want, and intend to at Elmer's at 2 PM. First though I want some lunch. What's good today?"

"For you Mister Will, everything is good. I will make whatever you want myself," responded Sammi, breaking a smile.

"Thanks again, Sammi. How about some coffee and I will look at the menu?" Sammi walked back to the kitchen and brought out a small pot of coffee, placing it, a cup, and a napkin on the table in front of Will.

"Enjoy," offered Sammi as he started to walk away. When he did so, one of the government men stood and started toward the table where Will was pouring his coffee.

"Are you Mister Johnson?' the man asked.

"I am. What can I do for you?"

"I have some questions for you," the man responded.

"At 2PM at my lawyer's offices across the street. Ask what you want then. Right now, I am having lunch."

"All right, if that is the way you want it," said the man, as he walked back to his table, and making a short comment to the other person with him. They picked up menus from the table, and Sammi came over to them to take their order.

Will picked up his own menu to look at the specials, saying quietly to himself, "Those guys have a lot of balls."

Sammi gave Will ample time to decide on his menu choice, but finally came over and sat down with Will, dropping the menus he carried on the table.

'Mister Will, those guys seem really pissed off at you," muttered Sammi through his teeth. "They were not happy when you refused to talk with them. One even said that he understood how the FBI felt, and that they ought to haul you off to Charleston again to 'get to the bottom of this', whatever 'this' is."

"Sammi," responded Will. I wish I knew myself what 'this' is," raising his hands like a set of quotation marks. 'They obviously want something about Josh, but their bullying will get them nowhere with me. A little courtesy goes a long way."

"It sure does, Mister Will. What was Josh doing that was so bad?"

"I really do not know Sammi. I get the feeling they were in trouble with someone though. The news report on CHS said he was on an Interpol list and associated with al-Qaeda, among others. I guess they think I might be involved since I know him."

"How much do you really know about him, Mister Will? Could he be doing these things?"

"It's possible, I guess," responded Will. "It had been years before I heard from him, or my other friend Hakim al-Azahir. We were in the Army and eventually travelled in Europe and the Middle East for a while before I came home. They were guns for hire, and when we got together, we did training for the Palestinians for a long time. Eventually, I came home and they went to Yemen, Sudan, and eventually Afghanistan. That's where I lost sight of them for a long time. I was really surprised when Josh called this last time, and invited me to visit them in Qatar. We had a great time, but really didn't talk business."

"Just before we left," Will continued, "The building we were living in blew up from a bombing. They said it was a drone attack. All I know is that we were sightseeing in the country when it happened, and we found new living quarters when we returned. I lost everything I took with me, and came home shortly after. That's it, the whole story."

"That's terrible, Mister Will,' answered Sammi. 'Those bombing hurt real people, innocent people, and they happen over there virtually every day, from what I read in the papers."

"It was interesting, Sammi. I met a woman at the bombing site who said she came from my old village in Lebanon, and had lost everything, including her family in the bombing. How she could live through that I will never know. I was very young when the war broke out in Lebanon, and it was soon after when my father and mother took me to America. I never really knew what this kind of war was like, and don't want to now."

"It is a terrible thing, Mister Will," responded Sammi. "I watched my village burn to the ground, and saw many people killed, only because they did not like Israel or the United States. We were bombed constantly, and little was left. What we had was very little other than the clothes we wore. When the Red Cross and others came, the Americans would even bomb their buildings, and later claim that terrorists were there. No one came to prove; they simply accepted the word of the Israelis and the Americans. If you did not accept it, you moved away. There was nothing else. Only the Palestinian organizations and some missionaries tried to help. That is how I came to America and started the restaurant."

"Let me get you some food, Mister Will. What will you have," continued Sammi, taking a pad and pencil to write down the order. Will looked again at the menu and ordered a hamburger with cheese, fries, and a milk shake. Sammi went off through to the kitchen to start making the orders for Will and the other men who ordered earlier. Later, coming out with the food for the agents, Sammi noticed a stack of the *Elias Courier* on the stand by the cash register, and brought one over to Will to read.

Will picked up the Courier to see what the latest news contained. There were the usual births, deaths, and the farm prices. One wedding was announced, and two farms were up for sale outside town. Otherwise, there seemed to be nothing special or out-of-the-ordinary.

On page 3, Will noted another article on 'town happenings', including a short piece on him. Seeing it made him particularly upset as he read:

> *"The town was in an uproar late yesterday morning when word started going around time that two men claiming to be Federal agents came into Sammi's' Restaurant, met for a short time with our own Will Johnson, and took him out of the restaurant, claiming they were taking him to the FBI Offices in Charleston."*
>
> *"While the agents claimed that Will was not under arrest, he was placed in their car and driven out of town toward Charleston, with Elmer Sites following close behind. The Courier now knows that a Federal judge ordered Will's release from the FBI, and he returned to Elias later in the afternoon with Elmer."*
>
> *"There is no word on what they wanted; nor did the FBI have a comment when this reporter called to inquire."*

From a Vantage Point

This is ridiculous, thought Will. These people believe in me, and to be hauled off for no reason makes things even worse. Then he remembered what Elmer had told him on the way back from Charleston the day before, "Will, you have nothing to hide, and the people here believe in you. Don't forget that; the people believe in you. Make them proud."

Sammi arrived with Will's food, and a plate for himself, and they both sat down to enjoy their lunch. Will looked over periodically at the Federal agents, and muttered to himself that he hoped they choked on their food.

Khartoum, Sudan Fatima sat in her office sipping on strong Egyptian coffee, enjoying a brief few moments before the bustle of the day began. Her solitude was interrupted by the ringing of her cell phone. She looked to see the name and saw it was Pentopolos. That was odd, she thought to herself. Why would he be calling me? She answered the phone.

"This is Fatima. How can I help you?" she asked.

"This is Pentopolos. I want you to know the boxes have arrived, and in good order. However, there is a small problem."

"What is that, Pentopolos?" Fatima responded.

"There was a listening device embedded in the wood of one of the boxes. I took it out and threw it away. Is there something I should know about?"

Fatima thought quickly before responding. "There is nothing to it, Pentopolos. So many things are strange these days. I do not wonder that someone put something into wood here in this cesspool of spies and followers. Do you wish me to send you a replacement?"

"No that will not be necessary my dear," Pentopolos responded. "Everything is under control. The call was more of a warning than anything else. I wanted you to know, and the situation stays with us. Neither of us needs the wrath of Hakim."

"I appreciate the call Pentopolos. We will check more closely here in the future. I will tell my men to be very careful."

"Thank you, Fatima. It has been a pleasure speaking with you." Pentopolos hung up, and Fatima sat to think about next steps. She would call Jeff Namers, but first she had other important business to attend to.

Elias, West Virginia. Will Johnson looked at his watch and saw it was one-thirty PM. He waved to Sammi to get his bill. Sammi walked over to the table.

"There is no bill, Mister Will. It is on the house for you."

"Thanks, Sammi, I owe you one," smiled Will as he rose to leave, dropping a five-dollar bill on the table, and placing a salt shaker over it.

Walking across the street, Will stopped to say hello to a customer outside the store, and then walked to the right to the door way marked 'Elmer Sites,

From a Vantage Point

Attorney-at-Law'. He walked through the doorway and up the stairs to Elmer's office, knocked, and walked inside. Elmer was waiting for him.

" Feeling better today Will?" asked Elmer.

"Honestly, I still feel pissed off to be honest Elmer. Whatever that crap was yesterday, I do not understand, nor do I appreciate being treated the way I was by the FBI. "

"I understand Will," responded Sites, "Just roll with it for now until we find out what they want. It makes no sense to seem angry or refuse to cooperate. It could hurt your cooperative. Effort."

"That is what really bothers me Elmer,' answered Will, "I don't care how they want to treat me. I'm a big boy, but the possibility they could do something to hurt the community is really chicken shit to me."

Let's just hope it does not go that far, Will," opined Sites, "We have no real idea what they want, so let's just wait and let them tell us. Agreed?"

"Agreed," responded Will.

They continued to speak for about fifteen minutes, and Will related his experiences with Josh and Hakim in years past, his visit to Qatar and Sudan more recently so that Elmer had the full view of what he knew about Josh.

" Thanks for the update, Will," Elmer said, just as the door received its first knock from someone outside. Sites went to the door, opened it, and found two men—the men Will saw in the restaurant—outside waiting to come in.

"Gentlemen, can I help you?" asked Elmer.

"Yes sir," replied one of the men showing his badge. "I am Agent Cohen, and this is Agent Burke of Homeland Security. I called you yesterday about working with you to question Mister Johnson. We flew in a while ago from Atlanta."

"Come in gentlemen," responded Elmer Sites. "This is Mister Will Johnson. We can go into my conference room, if you wish."

"Thank you, sir," answered Agent Cohen. "That will be just fine. Sorry for the short fuse. We just have a couple of questions really, and can get this over with quickly."

"No problem. Let's go this way. Will please join us. Can I get anyone some coffee or a soft drink?"

All nodded no, and they sat around the conference table ready to start."

"How about you tell us what this is all about, Agent Cohen?" asked Elmer.

"Well sir, it is a bit complicated. Homeland was notified of the death of a person on a flight from Seattle Washington a few days ago. That person tuned out to be a Mister Joshua Giddons. He is wanted for conspiracy to commit terrorist acts on a warrant issued by Interpol over two years ago. He is also wanted by the US military for desertion during the Vietnam War, but has eluded US agents for years."

"I thought all those people were pardoned or something by President Carter, Agent Cohen?" asked Elmer.

"Some received clemency sir, like Johnson here, but you had to apply and be granted it. There were no pardons, only the right to continue to live and work in the US."

"I see. All right, Agent Cohen, please go on."

"Well, we were aware that Mister Giddons had a partner, Hakim al-Azahir, and they were working actively for several terrorist organizations, moving supplies, money, and other resources around the Middle East and into Afghanistan and Pakistan. We were also aware that Mister Johnson here was a friend of theirs, and had recently visited them in Sudan. When Giddons showed up dead in Atlanta, there was a note in his pocket with Mister Johnson's name and number in it, and a notation for Sammi's Restaurant. We would like to know something about that note."

"All right," said Elmer Sites, "Is there anything else you need to know?"

"Not sure, sir," replied the other agent. "We would like to hear about the note first, though, and then ask any logical follow-on questions."

"Seems fair to me gentlemen. What about you Will?"

"It seems OK to me as well. I only wish the goons that were here yesterday who hauled me out of a public place in my hometown to Charleston could have said the same thing, and saved themselves an embarrassment."

"We understand sir," responded Agent Cohen. "That whole situation was unfortunate, and the Agency expresses its regret on the matter."

"Will, let's get on to the questions," said Sites, "Tell them what you told me about Josh and his friend Hakim."

Over the next ten minutes, Will told the agents about his relationship with the two men, his visit to Qatar and Sudan, the drone strike, and his return to the United States. He indicated that he knew nothing about the note, and could only assume that Josh had something in mind, perhaps another visit to Elias, but he really had no idea. Both agents sat and listened, taking occasional notes, and looking back and forth at each other.

"Is there anything else we need to know, Mister Johnson?" asked Agent Burke.

"I can't think of anything I have left out. Is there something you want to ask me? I'm apparently in as much of the dark as you are. I know these guys from military days, and not much since. If you need more, please feel free to come back and ask. My farm is here in town, and, except for occasional trips to DC on a project we are working as a community, I am always here."

"Gentlemen, you can contact me anytime for further information," interjected Elmer Sites. "Anytime, but I expect to get the call, not Mister Johnson. Understood?"

From a Vantage Point

"Yes sir, Mister Sites. We understand clearly. Thank you for arranging this visit. I wish the original contact had been on better circumstances. There was no real reason for how they treated you, Mister Johnson. I can assure you it will not happen in the future." The two men rose to leave, shook hands with both Elmer and Will, and walked from the room, through the outer door, and down to the street.

"Will, that is probably the last we will see of those two, so relax. You did well."

"Thanks Elmer, this has been a real situation. Now, I need to get back to work on the farm. See you later." Will went the same direction as the agents and walked across the street to his car, hearing the engine of a helicopter revving, then rise about the fire station and move forward to the southeast. The interview was over, but Will wondered what was coming next.

Aboard the Helicopter Agent Burke spoke into the set of earphones he put on after entering the helicopter. "Put me through to DHS Washington, will you?" he asked the pilot.

"Can do sir," came the reply. Within seconds, Alice Sawyer was on the line.

"Alice, Jim Burke here."

"Hi Jim, where are you?" asked Alice.

"I took the trip to see Johnson myself, Alice," responded Burke. "I did not want another screw-up on this."

"Appreciate that Jim. What did you find out?"

"I really think this guy knows nothing Alice. He readily admitted to knowing the other two; discussed his trip to Sudan in detail, and how it came about, and offered to answer any further questions we might have. Either he is an accomplished liar and actor, or he is being honest here. I tend to think it is honesty. We can continue to monitor, but there is not much we can do without sticking out like a sore thumb."

"Thanks Jim. I think you have done what I wanted. We will take any further actions here."

"Ok Alice, Happy to help. Out here." The line went dead, Burke turned to the other agent and shrugged as the helicopter flew quickly toward home.

Khartoum, Sudan Charlie Irving set up the capability to monitor the boxes as they left Khartoum, and worked with other stations to follow their trail. It was to be a chain, with a station following the shipments through their space, and then passing off the detail to the next station or listening post until some final location could be determined. In each case, the sending station would notify the next, and also report back to the Khartoum station, which would maintain the travel map. In turn, having notified Langley of the action, Khartoum would read in

From a Vantage Point

Langley Operations on the movements. Langley would then provide appropriate information to the DHS, FBI and other domestic agencies.

It was a good plan of operation, and Jeff Namers said so as it was briefed to him. Gaining the ambassadors approval was a formality, since Namers had kept him in the loop since the situation first started. The current ambassador, a signal officer during Vietnam was actually intrigued by the current state of the art in surveillance; quite different from the capabilities of the 1960s. That made Namers job much easier.

"Jeff, we have the net up and running," said Irving, as he burst into Jeff Namers office, obviously excited. "I make six dots, and four spikes. Is that correct?"

"Sure is," responded Namers, just as his phone rang.

"Hold on a second, Charlie. Let me take this call quickly, and then we will continue. Get some coffee over there if you want," said Namers, pointing to his ever-brewing coffee pot.

"Namers' Jeff said into the phone.

"Jeff, this is Fatima. The package has gone to the airport. Good luck."

"Thanks, my friend. We see the dots on our surveillance map, everything is set."

"Good. I hope you get them. It will make my life, and my uncle's a bit easier. Talk to you soon."

Namers looked over at Charlie Irving. "Charlie, the packages are on their way. Let's get into real-time here, and follow the birds to wherever they intend to nest."

"Will do Jeff. We have this under control. I will notify Langley we are in real-time, and hook them to the Net as well."

"Thanks Charlie. Now, what about two other items we need to discuss." Namers and Irving started to discuss other issues of a more local nature and spent the greater part of an hour in animated conversation.

Washington DC "Tom, come by and see me at your earlies convenience," Alice Sawyer said to Tom O'Neal's voice mail in his office over at Agriculture. She hoped he would get the message quickly and wanted to get together with him as soon as possible.

"Somebody mention my name?" asked Tom O'Neal, less than an hour later at the door to Alice's office.

"Sure did Tom. How is it going?" asked Alice.

"Just fine. Those boys are about to approved the cooperative for its grant program. I got your message, but I was already on the Metro on the way downtown so I waited to get with you in person."

From a Vantage Point

"That's fine Tom. I'm glad they are approving it. You may know we sent two agents out to speak with Johnson, actually twice. The first visit got really screwed up, then we sent Jim Burke out to visit with him again. Burke thinks he knows nothing. That seems consistent with your opinion, so the ball is in your court, working with him on his project to see if we are right or wrong here."

"Got it Alice. We will be working very closely over the next few weeks, so I should come up with a pretty good evaluation."

"OK, go do it. The next few weeks are going to be busy here, as we get closer to the inauguration. You are about all I can spare from the details we are assigned for events in and around DC. You are the eyes and ears. Do it well. Let me know right away if you smell any kind of rat."

As O'Neal left the office, he began to wonder why, if all the investigation so far brought up nothing, and Johnson seemed to be clear of any conspiracy did Alice want to continue pursuing what seemed to a fruitless expedition. Oh well, he thought, we keep trucking until we reach a stopping point.

O'Neal returned to his office over at Agriculture to find that a meeting was scheduled for first thing in the morning the following day to discuss approvals of new projects. He looked quickly down the list and saw the Elias Cooperative on the list.

Elias, West Virginia Sira arrived the following morning and started work as she normally did. Will picked her up at the restaurant, and drove her to the farm, but this morning it was a bit different. It was Sira that was quiet, not Will, and he recognized the difference immediately.

"Is everything all right Sira?" Will said, starting the conversation.

"Mister Will, I do not know what to do. My aunt still lives in our village, and some days ago she was killed by some person who claimed to be a Christian."

"I thought your family was Christian, mostly?" asked Will.

"We were, but many converted to Islam, and now the Christians left in the village are persecuting those who converted. I do not know what to do, Mister Will."

"What would you like to do?" responded Will.

"I am not a violent person, Mister Will, but I would like to kill everyone who bothers my family. We have a right to live in peace. If it is not the villagers, then it is someone outside. Only Hizbollah seems to care about us now that we are Islam."

"What did the police do?"

"They stood and watched as the person came over to her and shot her. She was speaking to a policeman at that moment, but it did not matter. The policeman simply walked away. Now, there is no one from my family in that village any longer. They have all been driven out or killed."

From a Vantage Point

"How can I help, Sira?" asked Will.

"Mister Will, I know you are Christian, but right now I think that Christians only want to kill my people. It is not right that they kill and not be punished." Sira had tears in her eyes as she walked away from him into the kitchen. Will stood for a moment thinking, and then went outside to work in the yard.

Over the morning, Will thought back to the day after the bombing in Khartoum, when they returned from the countryside, only to find the apartment complex destroyed, people walking about in confusion, and the woman, Mariyah Ashkar, who claimed to be from his village in Lebanon. The more he thought, the more he wondered what the world was coming to with innocent people persecuted for their beliefs, and why the US was involved in these things. It made no sense to him.

Pushing into his work, Will tried to refocus his thoughts to other things, but everywhere he seemed to turn the message was the same. When his thoughts turned to the next steps on the cooperative, his thoughts went to the Federal agents who, He was sure, were following his every move, and the possibility they might find a way to stop progress on it.

He thought about Josh and Hakim, and their efforts to work with the Palestinians and others, remembering their efforts to provide supplies to the Mujahidin as they fought the Russians, and providing similar assistance to Hamas and Fatah when Israel attacked the West Bank. Mostly, he thought about his parents, driven from their homes and village by the American attacks during the Civil War, with many killed, not unlike what Sira currently experienced with her family.

Will was becoming confused as his thoughts rambled from topic to topic. This quickly rekindled the mélange of disgust for war and oppression he experienced when he deserted from Vietnam duty. In those days, watching the TV footage of bombings, injuries and death, and the use of large-scale weapons, such as phosphorus bombs to burn and kill civilians, he had become disillusioned. Now, reliving many of those same feelings, and how much he grew to hate his country, feeling that the US was responsible for much of the discord then, he was gradually beginning to see in the conflicts of the Middle East and elsewhere, the responsibility of the US. The more he tried to separate events, and focus his thoughts, the more the woman in the rubble in Khartoum came to his mind.

Just two evenings earlier, he awoke screaming in his bedroom. His dream that night returned as usual to his village, but this time it was not convoy coming to attack; it was two drones with bombs underneath, and they were headed directly for his house. This time, the children were not in the root cellar, they were under the kitchen table, and he could hear clearly the high-sounding wail of the drone coming closer, then dropping its bombs over their home. As he woke, *he could see his mother holding the two younger children as they disappeared in a wall of flame.*

Looking at his watch, Will realized it was nearly noon, and decided to stop for lunch, returning to the house to eat. Sira had prepared a meal for them, which they ate mostly in silence, both keeping their inner thoughts to themselves. It was an uncomfortable situation for Will; something which seemed to be deepening in his mind.

"Sira, how do you cope with the problems you have with the family back in your country?" Will finally said across the table, looking at Sira staring down into her food.

"It is hard, Mister Will," she responded, looking up at him. "I think about them all the time. The trouble they are having is not their fault. It is the fault of the big nations, who interfere in people's lives. It is the fault of those who disrespect religious beliefs. It is the fault of the politicians who look the other way when their people are hurting. It is the fault of those who will not come to help those less fortunate. All these things are bad, I think, and the blame is shared widely, I think." Sira had tears in her eyes as she spoke, and it affected Will deeply.

"So how can people help from thousands of miles away?" asked Will.

"Do what is in your heart, Mister Will," answered Sira. "Your heart will tell you how to help."

Here is a young woman, he thought to himself, many thousands of miles from home, trying to make a living here in the United States, but spending her time worrying about her family back there in the fighting and conflict. He knew about that as well, but only as a small boy. She grew up with it, and escaped from it, or so he thought.

Will began to see Sira in an entirely new light, one of respect and admiration, something that would blossom further over time.

Both went back to eating lunch, then Sira cleared the plates, and returned to her chores she needed to complete for the remaining time she was at the farm today. Sira made a list for each visit, thinking out specific rooms she needed to clean and tidy each time, and followed through on her list, doing a nearly complete makeover of the house in just a short time. Will went into his bedroom and decided to read for a while before going back out to the fields. He sat in his easy chair, and looked over toward the books nearby, eyeing the magazines on the top of his reading pile, noticing these were some of the magazines he brought from Sudan.

Picking the top one up, he leafed through the first few pages, and noticed an article discussing US bombing and drone attacks in several places in the Middle East, including several down into Africa in Sudan. Seeing this, he started to read, and found that the article listed a number of attacks over several years, and the numbers killed and wounded, including many women and children.

At first, he paid more attention to the numbers of terrorists killed, but gradually turned his attention to the numbers of innocent people also killed. Will read several articles in the magazine, then picked up two others; reading more articles in those, until he threw them on the floor near his easy chair, and rose to leave the room to return to work.

In the 'education' of a homegrown terrorist, what was beginning to happen to Will is common. First, someone places small thoughts into the mind of the person, encouraging him or her to seek more information. Then, when the person does go looking, the information they read will often determine their next steps. In this case, the first information Will read was from the Islamist Radical perspective, and now, in seeking even more information, should he do so, it will be to validate what he has already read. Subconsciously, the person begins to listen, read, and feel the pain expressed by the other radicals, aided by someone guiding the process in the background—in this case Sira, the housekeeper. Interestingly, according to some psychologists in the field, the religion practiced is not as important as the feeling of oppression the person feels for others.

Spending the rest of the day out in the fields eased Will's mind a bit. He tried to concentrate on what needed repairing and upgrading before the worst of winter set in, and tried to deal with his mixed feelings on his perception of the status of the cooperative, getting a bit worried that the time for decision was clearly approaching, but he had yet to hear a decision. He returned Sira to the restaurant late in the afternoon, stopping to have coffee with Sammi, but then returned to his farm for the evening.

Sira had prepared a small dinner with salad and chicken for Will, leaving it in the refrigerator so that he could warm the main plate later. He opened the refrigerator intending to take out some white wine, but decided he would have dinner early, do some reading after the evening news, and then go to bed at an early hour. As he expected, the dinner was delicious, the wine very cold, and the news more of the same he saw daily; ISIS, terrorism, and a faltering economy.

Scanning the news for any mention of his friend Josh, it seemed the story had simply dropped from notice. He watched a bit of the national news, seeing that there were outbreaks in several countries against refugees and other immigrants from the Middle East, and that several countries were investigating damage to mosques and religious schools in Muslim neighborhoods, including several in the US. Will wondered what made people think the way they do, and why people could not just live peaceful lives. Finally, he went toward his bedroom, dropping down into his easy chair, where he picked up the magazines he threw to the floor earlier in the day.

The first magazine had a huge picture of Osama Bin-Laden on the cover, and inside the story of bin-Laden's death. As he opened it to read, the first thing he noticed was the number of people across the world with comments on Bin-Laden's death, most calling him a martyr to their cause. Will paid little attention to who was writing, only that the messages seemed to be consistent.

As the evening progressed, Will leafed through several of the magazines, all in English, with Arabic titles, such as "Dabiq", and "Azan", along with several others. While they seemed to represent differing aspects of the Islamic resistance—Jihad—their tone and information was remarkably consistent. Moreover, each copy was very well printed on glossy paper with amazing photographs, showing that each had been professionally produced. Will was impressed that these groups, usually called bandits and terrorists in the press, must have some wealth to be able to produce such magazines.

Each story highlighted some attack or military activity of the US, some also showed activities of several other, mostly European nations. In turn, each copy also highlighted attacks by various Islamic military forces and the reasoning behind the attacks, such as the USS Cole, several embassies, and first airplane and then drone attacks on specific leaders of Islamic resistance groups. It was made clear to anyone reading these magazines that for every attack by the West, ISIS, al-Qaeda, and others were prepared and capable of exacting a response. *They are powerful people,* thought Will. *If they can do this, they can do something similar here when they wish, just as they did on 9-11.*

Most of the vitriolic reporting was concerning the US, and its involvement in trying to kill Islamic leaders. What Will found interesting was an article by Bin laden in one journal where he (bin-laden) described why he opposed the US; ranging from defiling his native Saudi Arabia, and supporting the oppression of its King, to supporting Israel and other nations fighting for All'ah.

He learned some new terms, such as Ummah, the people of Islam, and the differences between the Sunni and the Shia---causing the great rift existing for centuries—mostly over the successors to Muhammed. It seemed reasonable to him that people should fight over religion if they chose—after all, the Christians had persecuted the Jews and the Muslims for centuries—creating the Inquisition and burning many at the stake throughout Europe. The Crusades of the 11th Century and after trying to take back the Holy Places in the Middle East—now Israel and Jordan—but were beaten back. Many of the countries, including his own Lebanon, lived long after that with splits in their religious population, but together until outside influences, such as the Europeans and later the American interrupted their lives.

Again, as with other causes of radicalization, people read what they think may be the truth, add to it from their own 'knowledge' and begin to rationalize without having a real grasp of the issues involved. What they see is often truth,

From a Vantage Point

but only part of the truth, and they know only what they read. If there are other issues involved, such as the experiences of both Will and Sira becoming co-mingled, the skew to the 'truth' becomes even more suspect, but real to person and gradually increasing in importance. They continue to read or listen to others, not for more objective information, but to confirm their fears or concerns. Where there is a pliable person, such as Will, interacting with an antagonist, such as Sira, and eventually others, the person adopts a view that may cause them to take actions they would normally reject.

Looking toward the clock by his bed, and realizing it was nearly 11 PM, Will dropped the magazines back on the pile near his chair and took a remote control from a side table—turning on the local news just as it was to switch to the national coverage.

'This is WCHS-TV News, Charleston, West Virginia. Reporting tonight is Jonas Spath, in for Alan Griffin, and this is the news," Will heard as the channel came on the TV.

"In world news tonight, the latest bombing in Europe, this time in Germany has so far caused 11 deaths, and over 100 wounded in an attack on a restaurant crowded with people attending a wedding party. We also report on the continuing saga of the man who died on a plane coming to Atlanta. That story and a number of others in this evenings news."

"Let's go to Atlanta first and the story on a plane passenger, now identified as Joshua Giddons, who died enroute to Atlanta from Seattle just two weeks ago. We have reported several times on this story, but each time it seems to get even more complex.," continued Spath, "And it is continuing to do so."

"Our sources now say that Giddons belonged to a terror group based in Sudan. He was a deserter from the US Army during the Vietnam War, eventually settling in Europe and gaining Sudanese citizenship about ten years ago. Since his desertion in the early 70s, he and several associates established a network of mercenaries, and supplies feeders to opposition groups, including al-Qaeda, and now the Islamic State."

"Sources tell us that Giddons came to the US through entry into Canada with a false passport, calling himself James Atherton, a British salesman, eventually traveling west through Vancouver and down into the United States. The reason for his trip to Atlanta remains clouded; we have no idea why he was here or what his intentions were. His family lives in another part of the country and he has no known relatives in the Atlanta area."

"The case is being handled by the DC-based Joint Terrorism Task Force Organization. Normally it would be conducted by the Atlanta-based section, but the case has been kicked upstairs, in a manner of speaking, for some unknown reason, probably because, as our sources tell us, he had very high-level contacts and responsibilities within the emerging Islamic State-ISIS. We will continue to follow up on those leads, but for now, this case remains a deepening mystery."

In Other news," Spath trailed off, and Will stopped listening, using the remote to turn off the TV.

"My God, Josh, what were you and Hakim involved in?" he screamed out, with no one near to hear. "Dead is not the way to deal with things." Will went to the kitchen and made some tea, brought it into the bedroom, and sipped it slowly, then put the cup on the night stand and rolled over to go to sleep, confused even more by what they said his friend had done.

That evening, as always, his dreams returned, this time in a series of vignettes of the times he, Josh and Hakim traveled around Europe and the Middle East after their desertion from the Army. In one, they were on a train crossing the French Alps, when suddenly, out of the clouds, came a large drone that zoomed over the car in which they rode, swooping off over the mountains. In another, the three were on a dusty desert road, going toward a village, when another drone swooped in and buzzed their automobile. This time Hakim took a rifle from the rear seat and started shooting at the aircraft, which shot back, covering the trunk of the car with bullets before leaving.

In vignette after vignette, the plot was the same; a drone trying to kill them and their fighting back as best they could. For Will, it was a very rough night; he awoke three times before finally getting some rest, just before dawn.

From a Vantage Point

Chapter 30 Dreams

The same scenario began to play itself out each day over the next several weeks. In each case, as he drifted toward sleep, tired from the day's work, and even more so from the reading and news he saw and heard, Will had difficulty closing his eyes, His emotions taking the better of him, thinking about his friend Josh, dying alone in Atlanta, and now the subject of news broadcasts arguing that he was some kind of traitor to the US, and wondering what had become of Hakim was too much for a person to comprehend. Will always did have a somewhat fragile temperament, and tended to dote on things otherwise unknown or curious. Now, he wondered what Josh was doing in the US, and why he had not contacted him, or even let him know that the trip was planned. That bothered him more than the news. It was a case of friendship and trust.

Will often drifted into sleep recalling the trip to Qatar and Sudan, the magnificent buildings, the people, and sights and smells of the Middle East. While he dreamt of these, his mind wandered at will toward the more macabre, on death and destruction, with most of it being caused by his own country. The world was no longer the same.

In one of these reminiscences, Will and his two friends were in an automobile, travelling along the streets of Doha, enjoying the views, the mix of ancient and new building styles; on their way to the great Museum of Islamic Art in the harbor. Will again heard Hakim saying, "I love coming here (to the museum) because it teaches me something new about my religion each time I can get here," and Josh's admonition not to try to convert Will—that it was a social visit only. He saw the exhibits they passed through during their visit in his sleep, including one exhibit where large photos of the aftermath of coalition bombings in Iraq, Afghanistan, Sudan, and Yemen, were posted along a corridor titled 'The Muslim Holocaust', along with others showing the bombings of the USS Cole and American Embassies in several countries, these labeled 'retribution.' His dream was not real, of course, but it was what he chose to remember.

Soon, a panoply of other visions entered his head; his life as a young child in Lebanon; the sight of the early groups who ravaged his village; the smell of smoke and burning bodies; and a host of other visions sped by as Will tossed and turned in his sleep.

Then his mind changed directions, as he returned to his visit with Josh and Hakim, now in Khartoum, and the places they visited as they toured the city and countryside; coming back to the apartment and the damage to the area. He saw in his mind the women, picking through the refuse for personal items, crying all the while as people were removed from the collapsed buildings. He thought he

From a Vantage Point

could hear the buzz of a drone as it passed over and dropped yet another bomb, killing many of those in the area around him, but leaving him untouched.

He saw the woman who said she was from his village in Lebanon, wailing over the loss of her husband and yelling at Will, calling him an American killer and spitting on him. Finally, he saw his backpack in the wreckage; the one he had worn throughout his trip, sitting in the rubble, ripped to shreds and useless.

Suddenly, Will's mind changed direction again, and he saw the fields of his farm, and saw himself walking with his father over one area they had plowed and seeded for the spring crops. One moment it was clean, well-cared for rows, and the next two men in a truck were driving through their rows, twisting and turning, and laughing, as they yelled to both to go home to their own country and leave America to the Americans.

Other similar scenes continued through Will's mind for nearly three hours, before, in a sudden start, he saw the face of his friend Josh in the rubble in Khartoum, burning with the fire. Will had no way to get him out, and simply ran around attempting to find a way in; a way he knew did not exist. He began to wake as one last scene came to mind; Josh on an examination table in the morgue, looking straight toward the ceiling, unmoving, and a faint blue tinge to his body. Will seemed to be looking down at Josh's face and, as he looked into his eyes, Josh opened them suddenly and stared at Will almost absent-mindedly, then said, "Will stop being someone who doesn't care about his past. Make a difference, and see the real world."

Will woke with a start, sat up in bed, realizing he was sweating profusely, looking pale as he had been visited by a ghost. He looked at the clock, realized it was not yet 4 AM, and tried to fall back to sleep, with no success. For the next two hours, he lay in bed wondering what the dream meant and was confused.

Suddenly, all the reading he had done, the memories of his visit to his friends, and the discussion he had with Sira all began to make a kind of sense. Will had been repressing his past; living for today, and forgetting that he and his family had been persecuted as well. While they were Christians and not Muslim, mistreatment began to replace religion and his feelings returned to the woman in Khartoum—the one who claimed to be his kinsman, and the horrible situation she was placed in by the American missile or drone strike.

Whatever the damage, it was damage to his people, and his friends that mattered. His feelings blasted into his consciousness, and his revulsion for what his country had done to innocent people began to outweigh the rightness or wrongness of the acts.

Dressing to go downtown to have breakfast at Sammi's and pick up Sira, he wondered once again why Josh was in the country, but had not contacted him. There must be something, some reason, he thought to himself. Shrugging his shoulders, he finished dressing and headed toward the car for the trip to town.

Will was turning the key in the door lock when the phone rang. He looked over quickly to see who was calling and saw it was Tom O'Neal, and he reached over to pick up the wireless phone.

"Tom, I hoped I would be hearing from you," said Will, "You have good news, right?"

"I sure do Will," Responded O'Neal, "Your grant was approved yesterday afternoon. You need to be coming to DC for a while to get this thing moving. Can you be here tomorrow?"

"Sure can," responded Will, "Just tell me the time and place."

"Good. Expect to be here for a couple of days, and we will get everything moving. Where do you usually stay?"

"Not sure. That past couple of times I came, I stayed at the Alexander downtown near the Treasury."

"Great hotel, Will. I used to stay there myself when I first came into this town, and they always treated me well. Do you want me to make a reservation for you?"

"No," responded Will. "I will do it myself. I'm about to go down to Sammi's and pick up my housekeeper, but I will do it when I get back. They usually have rooms."

"OK, then let me know and I will meet you for drinks later in the afternoon after you arrive. Plan to stay about three days. That will give us enough time to get everything signed, and a plan in place to execute the grant. Good for you?"

"Sure is. I have the authority of the board to act, so we are set to go, Tom."

"Then I will see you in a day or so, Will. Bring a copy of the board minutes with the authority to act. We will need that."

"Sure will, Tom, and thanks for all you did for us."

"No problem, Will, see you soon."

O'Neal hung up the phone and Will placed the wireless back on the stand and went outside, closing and locking the door, and heading toward his car. It was the first time in a couple of days that he felt a bit better about both his project and his feelings for all his other worries. Climbing into his car, he headed downtown to Sammi's.

Washington, D.C. Tom O' Neal clicked off his phone, then made a second call—this time to Alice Sawyer to report on his call with Will Johnson.

"Alice Sawyer, May I help you?"

"Alice, this is Tom. Got a minute?"

"Of course, but just that. I was almost on my way to a meeting. What's up?"

"Agriculture approved the West Virginia project. Will Johnson is coming this way for a few days on the day after tomorrow. Looks like we are moving forward."

"Great, and not too soon Tom," responded Alice," "We have been getting rumblings through CIA of something brewing with his old friend Hakim al-Azahir. Not really sure anything here involves him, but it pays to be vigilant for a while. Any idea where he wants to stay in the District?"

"Says he usually stays at the Alexander."

"Ok, then, I will have one or two of the guys get in contact with the Alexander and see if he stays in the same room, or what he normally does. We might luck out and get some intel from a peep."

"Sounds good to me. I can come over tomorrow to come up-to-date before he arrives, if that works for you."

"Sure. The one you want to see is Carl. He has been keeping up with this the closest. You two need to share info directly instead of through me anyway. Feel free to work with him and his staff for anything you need."

"Thanks Alice. See you and the staff tomorrow." Tom hung up, and went back to his pile of papers on the desk. After all, he was supposed to be an action officer.

A steady stream of information had been coming from various places in Pakistan and Kabul, and the Homeland Security people, working with two Joint Terrorism Task Forces had been gradually developing an idea of what Hakim was doing. They still had no idea about any specific event, but they did know much more than they had guessed just a month ago.

A series of calls had come into the Atlanta area, via Pakistan, to a contracting firm outside Atlanta. This firm, Horizon LLC was a small firm, mostly composed of former special operations people with jaded pasts, who were known to occasionally do work for both sides. Some of their 'consultants' were on the no-fly lists, and others were under investigation for various shady dealings, mostly in Pakistan.

Over the past month, fifteen calls had come in; twelve to Horizons, and three to its CEO Ralph Freitag. Curiously, only first two were recorded; the rest, including those to Freitag came through garbled. It was a while before the Homeland people realized that Horizon had put a block on the calls at first, they encrypted them to make them seem garbled. The calls to Freitag's home were nonsense. There again, it took some time to realize that the calls, which started after those to the company itself, were pre-recordings with nonsense messages. Even what little they could hear in the early messages made little sense.

What DHS did not know is that Horizon LLC was being used to retransmit messages elsewhere. The process was quite simple; a call would originate in Kabul, be routed through the Pakistani Security Service to their contractor Horizon, and then routed again to a final destination. All quite illegal, and all impossible to trace without giving away the intercept tap on the lines connecting

From a Vantage Point

the two locations to DHS. That left DHS, and the FBI for that matter, mostly in the dark on what might be transpiring.

This protection had been set up by Hakim and his people, using their contacts in the Pakistani Security Service. Hakim needed a secure way to discuss his plans with his cell leads, and developing a false trail, while not hard to do, kept the intelligence people in the US off his real trail.

Now Hakim was working diligently to put his plan in place. He sent Josh to the US in part to give the DHS and FBI another trail to follow. He knew the likelihood of Josh being discovered might be high, but he needed that effort to give him time to complete his plans. Josh would be missed, but like many others such as Fatima, he was, in the end, expendable for the cause. More importantly, Josh knew so little that even if he was caught and interrogated, he had little to tell. He could say he was to meet someone in Atlanta, and Hakim had even mentioned Horizon once or twice to put that name in his head; another wild goose chase for the authorities.

Hakim did have a real plan, and it involved a small cell outside Atlanta whose members lived in four neighboring states. Not more than two of them ever got together at any one time, and none knew who the other members were, beyond the one or two they were allowed to meet. Everything the cell did was designed to get Will Johnson involved in the plot. Hakim's plans would take time, but in his mind, they would leave an even greater impression on the American government than the bin-Laden's airplanes on September 11, 2001. His plan was to disrupt the next inauguration, and perhaps kill the next President of the United States.

Elias, West Virginia "Morning guys," said Will, as he walked into Sammi's Restaurant, looking around to see that several of his friends were there having breakfast. Will took a morning paper from the stack on the counter by the cash register, and walked over to his usual table and sat down. Sammi, who heard his arrival, came out quickly with coffee.

"Good morning, Mister Will," smiled Sammi, "How are you today, my friend?"

"Very well," responded Will, who began to stand as Sammi poured the coffee. "Listen up everyone. I heard from the Department of Agriculture this morning before I left the farm. Our project was approved. I go to DC tomorrow to work out the paperwork and get us going." Will smiled as the group in the restaurant clapped and Jim Flood, the Mayor of Elias came over to pat him on the back.

"Great job Will," said Flood in his best political tone, "The community is proud of you. I just know this will be a big success and make us all rich."

"Maybe not rich Jim," responded Will, "But at least we now have a good, broad market for our produce and the other things our people make. We won't

From a Vantage Point

have to rely on a few tourists for a livelihood. This could get big, but let's get it going first."

"You're right Jim. Go get it done. We'll have a meeting next week to work out what you want us to do.," said Flood. "Go and make us proud." Flood patted Will on the back again and shook his hand before he went back to the booth where he was sitting. Will sat down as well, and Sammi was waiting with a menu.

"What will it be today, Mister Will?" asked Sammi.

"Give me a minute will you Sammi? I want to think about what I want. Maybe something different today."

"Of course, Mister Will. I will come back when you are ready," answered Sammi, as he walked back toward the register counter where a customer was waiting to pay his bill.

"Thank you for coming in," said Sammi to the customer, "Come back again soon." The customer smiled and left. Soon, others were doing the same, and by 9:30 only Sammi and Will remained.

"Quiet now until lunch Sammi."

"It sure will be Mister Will. Have another cup of coffee; Miss Sira will be a few minutes. She got a late start today. I will chastise her severely."

"Not necessary, Sammi," answered Will, "Everyone has a late day sometime."

Kabul, Afghanistan "Hakim, the information you asked for," announced Daoud, a computer person in his office, "The American Government has announced the agreement with the cooperative in West Virginia led by your friend Johnson. They put it on their website just a few minutes ago."

"Good," responded Hakim, "Continue to monitor what they publish. We want to know everything they say."

"As you wish," responded Daoud, who went back to his computer screen.

Hakim picked up his satellite phone and dialed a number, waiting with the buzzing sound until he received an answer.

"Are you ready to begin your task?" asked Hakim.

"We are," responded the person on the other end of the line. "I spoke to Sammi just this morning and the project your friend Will Johnson was working on was approved and it will soon be time to bring him in closer to our desires."

"Good," responded Hakim, "I want that to happen quickly. We do not have a lot of time. The Americans will be swearing in their president in just a short time—three or four months—and we need to be ready. What have you prepared?"

"Sammi is ready to push Johnson forward, and we are also ready to support the event in Washington. We have recruited people there to do our bidding, and we expect that we will have no problem bringing Johnson to us. We need to be assured he is with us. All depends on him. He will be with us, if you do what you

From a Vantage Point

are expected to do with your people. Make sure of it," shouted Hakim. "There will be no errors here."

"There will be no errors Hakim," said the cell leader. The call ended quickly and the cell leader put his phone down, and his head in his hands, not sure that he could deliver on his promises.

Finishing the call, Hakim went to the warehouse in Kabul where he did most of his business, and found two men looking at the boxes delivered by truck earlier. Pentopolos had his men drop the boxes off, telling the men at the warehouse that this was a special deal for Hakim. They took the boxes and put them on a shelf near the entrance, waiting for Hakim's arrival to tell them what to do with them. Soon, it would be time to make the boxes into something Hakim could use to achieve his goals.

Meanwhile, in another part of Kabul two other men were also working hard at fitting together what appeared to be pieces of plumbing pipe, white PVC pipe of varying lengths, which they were carefully putting together, making sure they fit well. Each of the pieces fit into others, and when completed, their creation resembled a pipe about three feet in length, with a similar PVC or plastic box at one end.

When their assembly was completed, the men added a set if legs to the pipe which were adjustable, allowing the pipe to go both up and down, and could be tilted at various angles. The men carefully moved around the various dials on the legs, raising and lowering, then slanting the pipes to see that all the mechanisms worked.

When they completed their tasks on two of these pipe sets, they quickly, disassembled them, wrapped them carefully in cloth, and placed them in a large box on the floor of their workshop. The had been instructed to wait for further instructions, so they sat down on nearby chairs and began to read newspapers; hoping that the call would come quickly. They did not have very long to wait for that phone call.

A cellphone in the pocket of one of the workmen rang, and he reached to answer it, walking over to the side wall of the warehouse as he did so.

Washington DC Tom O'Neal strode into Alice Sawyer's offices, stopping to say hello to her secretary, and ask if she had seen Carl that morning. When she responded that he was in the coffee area just moments ago, O'Neal walked toward the back of the suite, and found him there speaking to another staff member.

"Carl, how goes things?" he asked as he walked up to a large man, with a large coffee cup in his hand, and a lanyard around his neck with a wad of badges in many colors. This was Carl Quint, analyst extraordinaire; the man who seems to know a bit about virtually everything.

"Good Tom," replied Quint, "Haven't seen you in a while. Been hiding from your ex-wife, or just hiding?" Carl Quint always had an interesting greeting for everyone he saw.

"No, I have been working on a case you seem to have an interest on—Hakim al-Azahir. Sound familiar?"

"Sure does Tom. Let's go to my office, shall we?" Carl turned in a split second from his usual outward and funny demeanor to more inward and deadly serious.

"Show me the way, then" answered O'Neal, ready to move, having poured a cup of coffee for himself.

The two men walked down the corridor toward the back wall of the suite, and through a door, into an office that was one of the most over-crowded, messy, and loaded with stuff he had ever seen.

"Throw something on the floor from one of the chairs, Tom," said Quint. "Make yourself comfortable."

"Are you sure Carl," responded O'Neal, "I can stand."

"No, not necessary. If you dump something on the floor that I need, I can find it later. Don't worry, just make yourself at home." O'Neal dropped a pile of books and articles on the floor next to a chair, and sat down, then took a gulp of coffee.

"So, you want an update on Hakim, huh?" asked Quint.

"Sure do. We have been following a guy in West Virginia that is a friend of Hakim's and trying to figure out if he is involved in some plot. That got worse when another friend died in Atlanta."

"I know about that. Will Johnson, and Josh Giddons—the two war deserters who became friends. This is what we know so far," started Quint. "We know they were in Dubai and Sudan together, officially on a holiday, and that Johnson had been invited to go during a surprise visit by Giddons to West Virginia. We think it was a setup to get Johnson involved again with the other two. The three men, after deserting from the Army, had spent a couple of years working mercenary gigs in the Middle East and Africa; spending some time in the camps in Afghanistan as well. Johnson eventually returned to the US, got clemency under the Carter Administration program and turned good guy, running his father's old farm in a little town in West by God Virginia."

"There are a few more things you need to know, perhaps," observed Quint. "We have been in contact with the CIA station in Kabul. They tell us through their informants that Giddons and Hakim were not exactly equal partners. True, they acted like they were, but Hakim always considered himself the brains, and Giddons the worker in the team. Hakim is a curious personality. He only lets people into his domain to a certain degree, reserving the critical information to himself. He may have been using Giddons, or even Johnson for some purpose of his own."

"One thing we are pretty sure of," continued Quint, "The CIA sources in Kabul are sure that Hakim was planning something big in the US. One of their contacts, a cousin, said that Hakim was always talking about doing something even more horrific than the Twin Towers; something which would make what he called a 'scar on Washington even bigger than the Pentagon.'"

"Do you have any idea what, and how Johnson might be involved?" asked O'Neal quizzically.

"Not a clue right now, Tom," came the reply. We are putting pieces of a big puzzle together, and all we can see is the key, and the tops of a couple of trees, with no box top to help."

"So, what can I do then?" asked O'Neal.

"Just keep a watch, Tom. Look and hear. Frankly I don't think Johnson is our man, but we have to be sure. Get as close to him as possible. Get close to his friends and his associates, and listen. We are doing the same in other areas as well. Sooner or later, we start to see the picture; we just want to see it before it is too late to change it."

"Thanks Carl. Let me go see if Alice has a minute, then I go back to my 'other' job." O'Neal shook Quint's hand and walked out of the office, heading down the other end of the space toward Alice's, and saw the door was open. He looked in.

"Good day lady. Got a minute?" he asked

Alice waved him in and he went over to sit at a chair near her desk, to the side of a small round table.

"Glad you came in Tom," said Alice, "I assume you and Carl spoke?"

"Sure did Alice. This is an interesting situation—the puzzle Carl calls it."

"That it is Tom. As I'm sure he already said, look and listen. We need to rule him out or in. I could really use you back here."

"Alice, I would like nothing better. I am bored to death playing Agriculture Agent. Any thoughts on how long this might last?"

Khartoum, Sudan *The analysts in the secure communications area had located the boxes which Pentopolos created in his workshop and followed their journey to Kabul. Only one of the sensors had not registered; the others sat quietly and gave off a green light on the video screen when the analysts periodically pinged them. There was no more activity, since the sensors were programmed to identify themselves only when they were being moved. For now, this was sufficient.*

A group of three men monitored other communications. Having the sensors in place gave them the ability to identify other communications at those locations. Every phone call was identified and documented, even the burner and satellite phones could be traced with these methods. While it was not possible to identify who made the calls, it was possible to a limited extent to know who received the calls. During the last several days, the group identified a number of calls, including those to Pentopolos, and just an hour ago, one from the Kabul offices of Hakim to his cousin Fatima. When they reported their find to Charlies Irving, the lead analyst, he took it directly to Jeff Namers.

"Jeff, I've got something you need to see," said Irving, as he walked into the office. Just as he did so, the phone range. Jeff waved Charlie to a seat, and answered the phone.

"Jeff Namers."

"Jeff, this Fatima. How are you today?"

"Just fine Fatima," he responded, "What can I do for you?"

"It is what I can do for you, my friend," she replied, "I just had a call from Hakim. I waited an hour and called from another phone in the marketplace."

"Thanks. What did he have to say? Let me put you on speaker. Charlie Irving is here and needs to hear as well." Namers hit the speaker button on the desk set.

"OK Fatima, all set," added Namers, sitting back in his chair.

"Jeff, he called just an hour ago, and seemed excited about something. He kept talking about his friend Giddons being dead, and he would not be able to bury him properly. He really sounded down, if someone with no personality could be that way."

"Tell us what he said, if you can remember enough of it?" asked Namers.

"Well, he started by asking how our family was, and that he was in Kabul on business. He thanked me for the boxes from Pentopolos; he had received them just yesterday, he said. I asked what he would use them for, and he said something about toy chests, and then changed the subject."

"Toy chests, that's interesting," said Irving, adding, "Has he ever talked about toys before?"

"I don't remember that. No, wait, I do remember just once, when we were both doing work for bin-Laden. He called the weapons he was buying for him his 'toys'. Perhaps he spoke about them at other times, but I don't really remember."

"Fatima, what kinds of weapons were you shipping then?" asked Namers, already really knowing the answer, which he wanted Irving to hear.

"We shipped a lot of rockets other hand-held things—he knew all the names. We just packed and shipped for him. He loved to play with the mortars, running around the warehouse pretending to be firing them. I think he really enjoyed the sounds or something."

"Jeff, we need to get to Pentopolos' offices and see if we can get the original drawings," Offered Charlie Irving.

"I agree Charlie. Fatima, do you happen to know when Pentopolos is there alone?"

"Only on Friday's Jeff. He does little business on Friday, and mostly does not even come in to the shop. All of his people have the day off, since there is usually no shipping on Friday there."

"All right then. I need to have the guys in Kabul get a look around his warehouse on Friday."

"Charlie, you need to be prepared to get in there on Friday morning," responded Namers, "We'll get some of our locals in Kabul to watch the shop to be sure he is not there, while you and one of our guys goes through the place. Not more than thirty minutes—tops. I will notify our station chief in Kabul right away to be prepared to help."

"Understand Jeff. We can be in and out before that."

"Great, then that's the plan."

"Fatima, thanks for the heads up, and the info," said Namers.

"For you, anytime," answered Fatima, as she clicked on the speaker button to end the call.

"Let's do it Charlie. We need to see if we can get copies of the plans to those boxes."

Both men quickly realized that a set of curious wooden boxes with side pockets could easily hide storage for a set of mortars. The real question was what he intended to do with them, but first steps first—get the plans to be sure. Meanwhile, they would continue to monitor the sensors to be ready to move quickly should whatever Hakim had planned did not go off before they were ready.

Washington DC Tom Corbett walked into Alice Sawyer's office and quickly saw her in a heated conversation with Jim Davis. He had not seen Davis since going to Sudan, picking him up, and returning him to the US earlier in the year. He wondered a bit why Davis was now with Alice instead of on suspension.

"Come on in, Tom," said Alice, as she saw him in the doorway. "You know Jim Davis," she added, waving her right hand toward Jim, sitting at a chair near her conference table.

"Sure do," responded Corbett. "Surprised to see you here."

"Not so surprising Tom," offered Alice," "We set up that situation in Sudan to get him back here, and have whoever tried to finger him think he had destroyed Jim as an agent. Jim has been doing some things quietly since, but now we really need him if we are going to continue putting the puzzle together. Sit down and let's talk."

Corbett sat next to Davis at the table, and Alice moved over to join then, carrying her coffee with her.

"Now, Jim, you had some questions?"

From a Vantage Point

"I sure do Alice. I still think we have a big part of the puzzle missing here. Something is just not right on what we have so far. A question for Tom," added Davis, looking over his left shoulder toward Corbett, "Tom, when you went to West Virginia on your inspection, you visited Sammi's, right?"

"Sure did Jim," Corbett answered. "A funny duck, though. He said he had only one other employee other than himself—a guy named Hassan. Everything we knew was that Hassan and a woman named Sira were in Elias, but no evidence of her, at least in the restaurant."

"Could she be working somewhere else?" asked Davis.

"That's possible, Jim," responded Alice. "The guy who would know that is Tom O'Neal. We have a lot of Tom's working here, by the way. Sometimes it's difficult to keep them straight. Let's get him on the phone and see what he knows." Alice dialed a number and O'Neal came on the line.

"Alice, let me close the door, and we can talk. The three heard his chair creak as he rose to go to the door, and then a noise as it shut. Another creak and he was back at his desk. Alice, meanwhile, had put him on her speaker.

"OK, what can I do for you Alice?"

"Tom, I have Tom Corbett and Jim Davis with me. We have a question for you."

"Shoot. I'm good at answering questions," responded O'Neal.

"Was there a woman at the restaurant when you were last there?" asked Alice.

"Sure was. Her name was Sira, or something similar. Will Johnson told me he shared her with Sammi. She cleaned his house part of the week, and spent the rest working at the restaurant. I got the impression she was close with the owner's other employee at the restaurant. I don't remember his name exactly."

"Hassan," answered Corbett," Is that it?"

"That's it, Hassan, Tom. I remember now."

"Well that adds a piece to the puzzle Tom. Thanks," said Alice. "By the way, when is Johnson due in here?"

"Tomorrow evening," offered O'Neal.

"How about I just happen to meet him at his hotel bar, Tom. He should remember me from Khartoum, and we can have a drink and a discussion?" asked Jim Davis.

"That might be good, Jim. He will be staying at the Alexander off 14th Street. He says he stays there when he comes to town. Not sure why. It's a nice hotel but still a bit far from Agriculture at the other end of the Mall," answered O'Neal. "I could meet you there as well, if you like."

"Let's do this," said Davis. "What time do you expect to meet him?"

"About five PM in the bar."

From a Vantage Point

"OK then, you meet him at five PM, I will arrive about six and happen upon you two in the bar."

"Good, that will work. See you then. Maybe with two, we can get more information. Anything else you need Alice?"

"Not from me Tom. Either of you have more for Tom?" Both nodded negative, and Alice said goodbye then hung up the phone.

"You two need to work together on this," said Alice. "I have a feeling something will be coming down and we need to be ready. He may have nothing, but he may be able to give us a link to someone or somewhere else. I am particularly concerned with those two others, Hassan and Sira, and what role they have in tis. Get me some answers."

"One more thing before you go," added Alice, "We got a Patriot Act order from the FISA Court for the phones of Johnson and the restaurant. The guy Hassan apparently is living there in a room. When we find out where Sira is living, we'll put a tap on that place as well. Now go and do good things."

Both Jim and Tom Corbett rose to leave at the same time, and Jim replied, "We will work the issues Alice. This should be either interesting or deadpan boring, but we will work the issue." They walked out of the office together, and Alice returned to her desk where the phone had just started to ring. She looked at the caller ID and decided to let it go to voicemail.

Kabul, Afghanistan The voice the workman in the warehouse heard was Hakim's, but it seemed different somehow.

"Are you ready with the products?" asked Hakim.

"We are," came the response from the workman. "Where do you want us to deliver them?"

"To my office, and quickly." Hakim ended the call as quickly as it started, leaving the workman somewhat astonished. He walked over to the others.

"Something is happening," he said to his two laborers, "Hakim's voice is very tense. I am really afraid here."

"What did he tell us to do," asked another of the men.

"We deliver to his office at the other warehouse, and quickly he said. Is everything ready? I assured him it was."

The two workers shook their head in agreement, and started to pack up the parts in large sacks for the trip across town. There, they assumed they would finish the assemblies, and prepare the pipes for shipping. All they wanted to do now was get this job finished.

Elias, West Virginia There was nothing in the Elias Courier that caught Will's attention this morning. There were the usual lists of births, deaths, marriages, and the short, mostly farm-oriented stock reports, but little else. The high school

From a Vantage Point

was having an art fair, and the 4-H Club was planning the annual exhibition and sale. Will did notice a seed sale at the hardware store, and made a mental note to go by and see what they had in stock. Otherwise, it was coffee and his usual eggs, bacon, and pancakes that took up much of his attention.

Sammi came over and sat down, looking a bit concerned, and Will put down the paper to see what might be the matter.

"A bit down in the mouth today Sammi; is everything all right?" asked Will, concerned.

"Everything is all right, Mister Will. Well mostly anyway," responded Sammi, "I worry about my family with everything going on in the mountains these days.

He, like his family, had started working on the railway between the cities in Pakistan and those in Afghanistan years before. Sammi was lucky; he managed to come to the US to work on an American railroad, but left their employ after getting hurt, and established his restaurant. The rest of the family remained behind, although Sammi did provide remittances for them periodically. He was never sure whether they received the money, since he sent it commercially rather than through the traditional Muslim banking system, but he did occasionally go into Charleston where an agent would forward his small amounts. Those he respected, and his family periodically responded that they had received his money.

"The Government and the many drones and other attacks make it harder for my family," Sammi continued, "They still work for the railroad outside Lahore, and just two weeks ago one of the trains was blown up in a drone attack. One of my cousins worked on that train. It is horrible to be here, in the country which does the blowing up back in my country, and try to be a loyal American."

"I understand my friend," responded Will, "When I was in Khartoum, I met a person—an older woman—whose house had been bombed in one of those attacks, and we were probably related as well. She was left with nothing, and no chance to get out with anything. The friends I was visiting told me that often there is no warning; just a few seconds of high-pitched sounds that alert people one of those bombs is coming. You try to get out, or far enough below the surface, then hope someone finds you before you are dead. That is no way to live, even over there where bombings are so common. These are still people."

"Most are peaceful, Mister Will. They do not want war either—they are just in the middle of two groups who want to fight. They can do nothing about it, except hope to live. Sometimes, I just want to go home and help defend them, but I have no way to do that. They are on their own."

"There must be something you can do Sammi? What about the relief organizations?" asked Will.

"Mostly, they are foreigners as well, Mister Will. Some try to help, but one side or the other knows they are there, and either stay away from them, especially if they have fighters among them, or blow them up as well. It is just the local people who most feel the power of the United States.

My uncle wrote me a letter a short time ago, and said that he has come to hate the Americans—even those in organizations who have come to help them after the attacks. He calls them double-faced—they say they care, but refuse to condemn their own government for the things they do. That is not right. People stay away from them and do not trust them."

"I will tell you," Sammi continued, "A short time ago, someone came to me and said they were recruiting people to oppose the United States, and wanted me to join them. I said no, and told them to get out of here. Sometimes, I regret that. I become so excited by my feelings that I want to do something—anything that might help my people."

"My God, Sammi," shouted Will, "Did you report that? If the government found out, you could be in trouble."

"No, I did not report it, Mister Will. I would be in trouble, and could be deported since I have not yet become a citizen. I have one more year before I can take the oath as an American. I want to do that, but my mind becomes more troubled all the time. I don't know where to go or what to do sometimes."

Will was curiously silent when he heard the news Sammi had given him on his contacts. He remembered what he read in the magazines at the house, and how there were numbers of cells in the United States, looking for those who would join with them to oppose American involvement in the Middle East and elsewhere. Will wondered if this contact was for one of those groups.

"Be careful, my friend," said Will, "Don't get caught up in something that is too big to get out of later. Trust me when I say that you are as good an American as anyone—with or without citizenship. Do what you think is right, but think carefully before you make this kind of decision. I am glad that you sent them away. This is not for you."

"I know that Mister Will," responded Sammi, "But sometimes things are so hard." Sammi shook his head as he rose, took the plates and cups off the table, and started for the kitchen. "More coffee Mister Will," he asked as he turned slightly before going through the swinging doors.

"Sure, I will have some," answered Will, shouting after Sammi went into the kitchen.

Before Will could say anymore, Sira came through the doors, put down a fresh cup of coffee, and said, "How are you today, Mister Will. Have some coffee and we can go to the farm whenever you are ready."

Will looked at the coffee, picked up the cup and started to drink, saying, "Just a moment Sira. Good morning to you as well." Within five minutes, they were on the road back to the farm.

From a Vantage Point

Will spent the rest of the day going over his presentation notes, and preparing questions he needed to ask at Agriculture during his trip. He would leave mid-morning tomorrow and arrive in Washington by mid-afternoon. His reservations at the Alexander Hotel were made, and he expected to meet Tom O'Neal later in the afternoon in the bar. He hoped he had covered everything needed for the trip. As he usually did, though, he would think of something—hopefully not critical—during the ride somewhere between Elias and Interstate 66, when it was too late to return home.

Khartoum, Sudan The secure phone rang in Jeff Namers' office several times before he picked it up and answered.

"Namers here"

"Jeff, this is Rick Cartwright in Kabul. How are you?"

"Great Rick. Doing just fine. How's life in the danger lane?"

"Ok right now, but the fighting season will be coming quickly. This is the pause before the semi-annual storm, I guess, but that's not why I called?" Cartwright was always to the point, with little side conversation.

"Well then, shoot," responded Namers. "What can I do for you?"

"More likely what I can do for you, my friend," came the counter. "We have been getting a lot of local chatter here about your old friend Hakim. Both of his warehouses are working; we understand he is here in town, although I must admit a bit more covert than usual. We think something big is starting on this end. Anything on yours?"

"Rick, we know that several packing cases were fabricated for him here, and then shipped through Pakistan to Kabul. We have no idea at this point what they contained, or what they might be used for, but we do have several sensors tagged to them. We also know his friend Giddons is dead in the US—heart attack, and he is now apparently working alone. Beyond that I have no clue. His footprints here are as scarce as they are there."

"That's not good. I called to ask a favor."

"What do need friend?" responded Namers.

"We are getting a lot of chatter here, cells and sat phones going out of the country and into the ether almost immediately. Can your guys give us an assist here? I don't want a security check to go through the usual channels here, it is too porous, and too unsecure, if you know what I mean."

"What have you found already?"

"We catch a message and it goes out over an odd sat connection controlled by Pakistani Intelligence. From there it is scrambled and simply disappears."

"OK, sounds like we can help you there. My guys will set up a link to your surveillance capability and we'll do the trace. You need to give us an alert when something comes in, and we will pick it up then using our intercepts on those

Pakistani satellites. When you pick up another call, we should be able to do an in-out on the call and at least take you one more step, perhaps more."

"That would be a great start Jeff, thanks," answered Cartwright. "We'll let you know. By the way, the assistance you wanted for a look at Pentopolos's warehouse is all set for Friday. Is Charlie on the way?"

"Sure is, Rick, He left last evening. Should get there with a day to spare to brief you all," answered Namers.

"Great. Since all is well, I'm out here." Cartwright hung up his phone, and Namers made a note to set up the connection with his communications team.

Over the next several days, the communications teams in Khartoum and Kabul created the intercept connections needed to trace calls utilizing the satellite node managed by the Pakistanis. Within the week, several calls emanating from one or another of Hakim's known associates, including one from Hakim himself were intercepted, their trail followed, and the link to Horizon discovered.

Once they realized that the calls were being routed from Horizon through the ISI communications network managed by Horizons, it took only a short time to discover the inter-connect to the DHS server. That meant DHS information was vulnerable. More importantly, when it was realized that the DHS link gave them access out into the commercial phone grid, both Namers and Cartwright knew they had major problems.

First, they could not go beyond the DHS network without their investigation becoming known, and since Horizon was a DHS contractor, they had to be concerned with the possibility that someone at Horizon might discover their surveillance and simply switch their connections. Neither was an acceptable option. It was time to call in the cavalry—Alice Sawyer.

From a Vantage Point

From a Vantage Point

Chapter 31 Nightmares Again

Will and Sira worked through the day, he in the upper pasture, and she in the house, seeing little of each other than over lunch. Even the meal was different; Will was very quiet, still thinking about his discussion with Sammi earlier that morning, and how similar they were in their family experiences, and the immense damage being done in the Middle East, at least some of it by the United States. Will knew from his military training that the US was there for a purpose—to help the various governments to rid themselves of large terrorist groups. At the same time, why, he asked, did it have to be the US, with all their immense power, and from his reading, he knew there had been so many mistakes, with people killed who were complete innocents.

His own family had been harmed greatly by raids, in part supported by the US, causing his parents to leave their country and travel overseas; the same was true of Sammi, and he was sure, many others. Too many more were killed or injured by bombs, mines, drones, and so many other kinds of weapons, and so many people were innocent bystanders to a wart they did not ask for, or could not avoid.

Will tried constantly to think of other things. The US had been good to him, and forgave his desertion years earlier, but he still came back to the same thought; why would the US do this to innocent people?

About mid-afternoon, he saw three of his cows outside the fences. Quickly moving over to where there was a break, Will went through the hole in the fence, bringing his cows back to his portion of the field, then shooing them into the pasture so he could fix the fence. He was just about done, looked at his watch and realized it was after 3:30 PM, and knew he needed to get back to the house to take Sira back to town. Driving along the dirt roads that separated his farm from his neighbor, Will thought how pleasant and quiet it was here in West Virginia. He hoped that everyone in war-torn places could eventually come to enjoy the please and quiet.

As he reached a bend in the road, he suddenly heard the screeching of two jets, probably out of the Air National Guard Station at Charleston, and their streaks through the sky brought him back to the reality of concern on the Middle East.

"God, why can't we be a peaceful nation?" shouted Will himself in the cab of his truck. "Why do we have to be the killers of the world?" The darkness which had previously taken his mind returned as he approached the house.

Sira waited on the porch. "You are later this evening, Mister Will," said Sira, as Will opened his drive-side door and moved to the other side of the truck to open the passenger door for her.

"I am Sira. Sorry, but I had things on my mind, and time got lost." Sira looked at him with a puzzled look as she entered the truck.

"Is there anything I can help you with, Mister Will?" she asked as she settled in and locked her seat belt around herself.

"Not really Sira. I have a lot on my mind. It seems that you and Sammi both have recently experienced the pain of war and terrorism, perhaps from different angles, but the result is the same. In fact, it is not much different from what my family and myself went through some years ago."

"You told me some things, Mister Will. I remember that your family was driven out of Lebanon with other Christians, just as my family was, and that caused great pain. By the time this pain came to me, it was the other way around. Hizbollah had taken over parts of the country and provided protection and food for our people. It was the Christians then who resented what those who were left received from their enemy. Personally, I think both sides are terrible. They have no concern for the people, just themselves, but I must admit, if I had a choice, it would be Islam. Their sense for the people is better," she said as she folded her hands in front of her.

"Do you really mean that?" asked Will.

"I do," Sira continued. "They seem to care about the people more, not their religion. If I had to go back, I would help them because they helped my family."

Sitting there quietly, thinking about his own situation, and what Sammi had said earlier that morning. Will knew he needed to ask more questions of his friend, and would do so after he returned from Washington. For now, he tried to smile and make it seem that he truly understood Sira, even though he was not quite sure.

Pulling up in front of the restaurant, he turned off the engine, got out of the truck, and moved to the other side to open the door for Sira, who got out quickly. She started to walk into the restaurant, but turned and said, "Mister Will. Do not be fearful of your thoughts. Practical people find practical solutions, even if they do not think so at the time." She waved as she went toward the front door.

"Sira, remember, I will be in Washington for the next three days. Sammi will bring you out to the house, and take you back in the evening."

"I remember, Mister Will. I will take good care of it for you as usual." She waved and went inside. Will went back to the driver side of the truck, got in, and started the engine. Soon, he was on his way back to the farm where Sira left the dinner she prepared for him.

Will parked his truck near the barn, since he would be using his automobile the following day for his trip to Washington DC. Entering the house through the side door near the barn, he came to the living room and almost absentmindedly turned on the TV to the news.

[Reporter] "This is WCHS-TC, Charleston bringing you the evening news. I am Allie Aldrich, sitting in for Jonas Spath this evening, and we have a lot going on around the world today, so let's get to that right away."

"President Obama was in London today attending an economic conference, and took the opportunity to hold a press conference for a large group of reporters outside the conference center. Guarded by a large contingent of US Secret Service, Scotland Yard, and local British police, the "Bobbies", Obama seemed to be dwarfed more by security than reporters. His two main topics did not mention economic concerns, but instead dwelt on climate change, and rising opposition to Islam.'

One reporter asked about the atrocities against Christians and Christian holy sites in Iraq and Syria, and received an unexpected response."

[Obama] "Perhaps it is time that some of the Christians rose up themselves, supporting our efforts to combat terrorism by joining our coalition. You cannot expect us to defend everyone everywhere with only our own resources."

[Reporter] "The murmuring among the reporters was evident and the reaction from the President clearly showed he had misspoken. A few minutes later one of the President's spokespersons tried to take the statement back, saying that the President meant to say that Christian leader support for the coalition could be better than it was. The reporters were clearly not impressed with the explanation."

"In other news, there were two bombings in Afghanistan this morning, in two local villages outside Kabul. The Taliban quickly surrounded the villages to provide aid to the inhabitants. Loudspeakers were blaring out that the bombings were American drones, and that no Taliban were in the area during the bombing.

First estimates, so far unconfirmed, were twelve people dead, mostly women and children, and over fifty wounded. The Red Cross was allowed in along with Doctors Without Borders to set up makeshift hospitals for the injured."

"Later in the afternoon, the US Command announced the bombings, claiming that some Taliban leaders, so far unnamed, were in one of the villages, then escaped to the second village, necessitating strikes against both.

From a Vantage Point

Doctors Without Borders Spokesperson Olav Torgenson, pointed out this was the fourth such strike in local villages over the past two weeks, and the Americans had yet to document a single Taliban leader. Torgenson indicated that there were now over sixty dead, and nearly twice that wounded from what really seems to be sloppy American intelligence work."

"In the local news, a former student at the University of West Virginia was arrested by the FBI as he attempted to board a plane to Germany yesterday afternoon. He had purchased a ticket taking him from Charleston to Atlanta, and then to Germany, where another ticket waited for him to take him to Syria.

When arrested, he spoke briefly in response to a shouted question from our reporter at the Airport, saying he was a Christian going to fight with ISIS to protect his people, both Christian and Islamic.

Meanwhile, an FBI agent, speaking on condition of anonymity because they were not officially authorized to speak, indicated that this was not the first former student wanting to go to the Middle East in the mistaken belief that ISIS would protect anyone, much less Christians. That word, the person said, does not seem to be sinking in."

"Elsewhere..."

The news report droned on with other local and national news, but Will remembered that he had dinner waiting, turning the channel with his remote control to a music station. Going to the kitchen, he opened a bottle of Pinot Grigio wine, and poured some into a stemmed glass. Then he went to the refrigerator, found the meal Sira had carefully wrapped in plastic wrap, removed the wrap and placed the plate in the microwave to reheat it. He took the glass of wine to the living room, placing it on the table aside his chair then sat listening to the music and thinking absently, until he heard the bell of the microwave tell him dinner was ready.

His first thoughts were of Sira, whom he thought was an interesting person, an excellent cook, and a great housekeeper. He was glad that Sammi had suggested her when she arrived in town, and her work has been most helpful since. She had endured so much in her own country, and now was here, enjoying the freedom Americans enjoy. He also thought for a moment how lucky he was to be here on the farm with his friends nearby, and the cooperative about to begin

From a Vantage Point

its operations. The community had accepted his family from the beginning, and he returned their courtesy in many ways.

Everything was working out well, he thought for a fleeting moment before his awareness returned to the problems facing his friends. As he listened to the music and sipped his wine, he thought again in quick order about Josh and Hakim, Sammi, Sira and Hassan, and the myriad of people he called his friends.

Eventually, the fateful bell rang and Will knew his dinner was ready. He opened the microwave, looked at the plate Sira prepared as he removed it, and then placed it on the counter. He found a chicken breast, some vegetables, and some yellow rice, with mushrooms and herbs, just the way one of the restaurants in Khartoum had prepared it when he was visiting there. Taking it back to the living room, he placed it on the side table, remembering he forgot a napkin, and he walked back into the kitchen to take one from the counter. Now he was ready to enjoy his meal.

Will continued to listen to music as he ate, reviewing the things he needed to do in Washington, and what remained to be done on his farm, before they could open the cooperative on an expanded basis. He had the fences to reinforce along the north side of the farm, and new planking for the hay bale storage area in the barn. He also had a livestock show coming up for new stock he needed badly. Finishing his meal, he placed the empty plate on the side table and returned to his thoughts. The more he thought, the more his mind began to wander, and eventually Will fell asleep in his chair.

Sitting up sharply, he looked around and found himself in a chair, but not in his living room. He wasn't sure exactly where he was, but the noise which woke him sounded a bit like a car backfiring. Within seconds, he realized that the sounds were gunfire. Then, he heard a loud rap on the door of the building, and the sound of a boot kicking the door in.

In front of him stood four men; each of them carrying a large rifle, and wearing what looked like some sort of military clothing of a type he had never seen before. One of the men strode over to where he sat, reached out his right arm, and grabbed Will by the shirt front, pulling him to his feet, then slapping him across the face.

"Christian pig, who else is here with you?" the man asked.

Before Will could answer, he was slapped again across the face and started to fall. As he did so, the man kicked him in the stomach and hit his head with his rifle butt. Will went unconscious.

"Wake up," the man who appeared to be the leader kept saying as Will began to revive. "Listen Christian, we want to know who is here with you. If you do not tell us, we will burn everything around you—with you and anybody else in it. Talk or die, it is your choice," he added, holding Will up to prevent him falling back to the floor. As he stood there, Will realized he had seen the uniform before—in Khartoum. It was the same uniform the security police wore that he had seen in his travels around the city.

"Look what we have here Akim," said another of the men in uniform, dragging a young woman into the house. It was Sira. "I found her hiding in the barn," the man added.

"Was there anyone else?" asked the leader, looking at Sira and her now disheveled clothing. She obviously had been attacked by at least one of the men, but seemed to be holding her own.

"No one Akim, just her. We looked carefully as you ordered."

"Good, then burn the barn," the leader responded. Two of the men left and soon the smell of burning hay and wood filled the air.

"You have one hour to be out of here Christian. If you are not gone by then, we will return and kill you in this place." The man holding Will released him and Will fell back to the floor.

"Take the woman with us," said the leader. "She is of no use to him, but she is to us. We will make a good Muslim out of her. Put her with the others, the ones who claim to believe in the Great One, all praise is due to him. We will sell them all to one who is more devout than them."

The he turned back to Will and said, "One hour, Christian. No more. You will be gone when we return, or you will be dead."

Pushing Sira out of the house and into the yard, the men left, but not before one of them had pushed his rifle butt harshly into Will's stomach, knocking him to the floor, and then laughing as he left. Sira's screams could be heard clearly as she was thrown into a truck and driven away. Two other pickup trucks followed down the dusty road from wherever they were.

Will rose slowly, feeling the pain from both assaults, and walked slowly to the doorway. Outside he could see where he was; it was the farm where he was born and lived until his family was driven away during the Civil War.

In the distance, he heard more gunfire, and then two other trucks coming down that same road. As they got closer, he feared for his life, and thought it might be more of the same.

"Are you all right mister?" asked one of the men in the first truck stopping in front of the farmhouse.

"I am fine, a bit beaten up, but fine," answered Will. "Who are you?"

"We are members of the Christian militia. We have come to save you," responded another man in the new group. "What did they say to you?" asked yet another.

"They told me to be gone within the hour. They would be returning and would kill me if I was still here."

"Well then, the answer is simple; you must leave. We cannot defend you. When you leave, we will take over the house and fight with them if they return.

Pack up and be gone if you want to live," said one of the men. This one looked the most hardcore of all the men, as if he was not sure even which side he was on. They were obviously looking for a fight with the others, and his farm would be destroyed if necessary to have that fight.

"You cannot stay, Mister. You must leave if that is what they have said to you," said the man who appeared to be the leader. "We are not enough to defend you. You must leave."

Will returned to the house to get a few things, and emerged again to face the men in the trucks.

"Which way should I go?" he asked.

"Go this way," said the leader, pointing in the opposite direction from that where the first group had gone with Sira. "Go that way if you want to be safe."

Will started to walk along the road, coming eventually to a rise where he could look back over the farm and see what was happening. Only a short time had elapsed and he saw another group of trucks coming down the road and stopping at the farmhouse. A man emerged and Will recognized him immediately. It was the leader of the group which first broke into his house. The leader shook hands with the person who told Will to leave.

"Those bastards," said Will to himself, "They were working together. As he watched, another of the men grabbed Sira from the truck bed and threw her on the ground near the leader who last told Will to leave. Then one group returned to their vehicles and drove off. The leader of the second group grabbed Sira and took her into the house.

Screaming at the top of his voice, "These people are not Muslims, they are my own people," Will pounded his fist against a nearby tree, bloodying his knuckles, and then sitting down in front of the tree with his head in his hands.

"Why are my own people doing this?" he asked. His only reply was the screaming he heard in the distance from the farmhouse. They were Sira's screams, and he could only imagine what the men were doing to her. Will closed his eyes, trying to drive the sounds from his brain.

Suddenly, the sounds disappeared, and Will opened his eyes again but saw a completely different scene before him. He was no longer sitting under a tree, but against a large rock. In front of him was a field and beyond the field was a large town. Lying everywhere on the field were many men and women, lying mostly face down and covered with blood. Two men were walking with obvious difficulty away from the field. Will rose and walked forward to meet the one closest to him.

"What happened here?" he asked.

"There was large group," said the man in reply, "Pilgrims I think, on their way to Mecca. When they arrived here, artillery in the town started to fire on them,

From a Vantage Point

killing a large number. Then, the planes started to strafe the field, killing many more. Only a few of us survived, those who were covered by other bodies."

"Really, who was doing the strafing?" asked Will.

"Your people," a second man responded, as he came close to Will and the other man, "The planes had a big white star inside a blue circle, with red and white stripes on the sides. It was your people," the man said again. "We were doing nothing, but trying to get along on our trip to Mecca for the Hadj. The people in the town were Christians and they refused us everything. They told us to leave so we did, but the planes caught us in the field. We had nowhere to hide. All of my family was killed," the man said, as he started to walk away.

"Where are you going now?" asked Will.

"On to Mecca," responded the man, "It is my duty to the Most Holy. That is all I have left." Slowly, he walked away as Will looked again over the field of the dead.

As Will shook his head, he could barely hear a clock chiming, and, as he looked toward the town to see where the sounds came from, his whole body jolted and the sight of the field passed.

Sitting up with a jolt, he realized he had fallen asleep, and had another of the increasing bad dreams. The sound of the chiming was his alarm clock telling him it was five AM, and time to get up if he was to finish a few chores before going into Washington. The dream was so vivid in his mind that, unlike most of the others he experienced, he remembered every part of it, and the thoughts it brought troubled him; even more so than those he had experienced several days earlier.

As he rose shakily from his chair, Will realized the clothing he still wore was damp with sweat, and he headed to his room and then into the bathroom for a shower. He turned the shower head to a beating pulse, and stood there trying to shake the dreams so he could begin his day.

Washington DC Alice Sawyer sat in her office going over the message traffic from the late evening before and found a cryptic message from Jeff Namers in Khartoum:

> *"Alice, need to have about thirty minutes' time tomorrow morning. URGENT*
> *Jeff*

What is this all about, she wondered. Just as she was about to respond to his message, her secure phone rang, and she answered it.

"Alice, this is Sarah Minihan, got a minute?"

"What is this about you CIA people today," asked Alice. "That is the second ominous-sounding request I have had today, and it isn't even eight o'clock AM yet."

From a Vantage Point

"Sorry about that Alice, but I received a call from Jeff Namers in Khartoum last evening, and we had a long conversation. I know he sent you a message that he wanted to talk, and I wanted to bring you up-to-speed first."

"Fine with me Sarah. This is unusual at best. What's happening?"

"Let me just give you the brief intro Alice. Jeff and his counterpart in Kabul, Rick Cartwright, have been following Hakim al-Azahir as you know. Cartwright managed to locate some traffic moving out of Kabul toward the US, and he needed some assistance from Jeff's communications people to triangulate and decrypt the message traffic."

"That's not unusual, Sarah. We do that for several agencies around the globe," responded Alice.

"True, Alice, but it's the path of the message traffic that has us concerned. Hakim makes a call that bounces off the satellite node owned by the Pakistani Security Service, encrypted. The bounce lands at a server farm owned by Horizon LLC. You may know the name."

"Oh God," exclaimed Alice. "You can prove all this?"

"Sure can. I'll let Jeff and Rick fill you in on the particulars. That isn't all, however."

"What other bad news then?" asked Alice

"The traffic apparently goes from Horizon's servers, maintained for the Pakistani ISI to one or more servers they maintain for you guys, from which it goes to commercial services. Since we don't have access to your secure services, the trip stops for us at your contractor. That's what Jeff needs some help with. He can fill you in on all the gory details. Let me add this as well to the mix. We found out that Hakim al-Azahir ordered some strange packing boxes through his cousin living in Khartoum. Jeff managed to get some sensing devices on the boxes, before they were shipped to Kabul for completion.

A few days later, he and Rick Cartwright in Kabul managed to get some people into the place where the boxes were delivered, and apparently completed, getting a look at the original drawings. While we are not one hundred percent on this, we think these boxes are designed to hold weapons—maybe mortars, which could be shipped into other countries undetected. Our concern now is that they are destined for here. Jeff can fill you in on this as well."

"Thanks Sarah. Of course, you have my complete support. If Horizon is directly involved, I will have them shut down by evening."

"Speak with Jeff first Alice, if you would. I think he and Rick have a plan for trying to get end-to-end. That might be complicated, and we can't obviously be involved because it is domestic, but we will give you every assistance we can if we are asked."

"I will give them any support I can Sarah, you can be sure of that. If you or someone else would like to link in to the video telcom, that can be arranged."

From a Vantage Point

"As a matter of fact, Sarah," continued Alice, "If we could do the video telcom from Langley, that would be much better. That way, we have no leaks to anyone here, if there is a mole at DHS. Can you do that?"

"Sure, happy to Alice. Let me schedule it for later this afternoon. With four time zones, someone will be up in the middle of the night. I'll get back to you after I speak with Jeff and Rick."

Great, now on to the important stuff. How are the little ones?"

"Both great. Not so little anymore. Rex is five and goes to the day care here. Sally is three and stays at home with her nanny until she is ready to come here. The other one, Bernie is fine." Sarah laughed, and Alice joined her.

"Will he ever grow up, really?"

"Probably not, Alice, but we can always hope. He is so great with the kids, though. It's a joy having him home most of the time and not away. He misses the travel, but the kids keep him happy, especially Rex."

"Bernie still misses his mentor, doesn't he?"

"We all do. We had the hope with them living literally down the lane from us that we would have a lot of time after his retirement to enjoy time with them, and Rex adored the kids. His death was a shock."

"For me as well," responded Alice, "He was my friend for so many years. I find some reason to miss him every day. In this business, that is easy. Look, I should go. My staff meets in about ten minutes, and I will wait to hear from you on confirming the video conference. See you in Langley this afternoon. I get to see the kids, and maybe I can take you and Bernie to dinner."

"He would love that Alice. Talk to you later."

Alice hung up the phone, looked over at a picture on her credenza showing Rex, Bernie, and herself in Istanbul in front of the Haggia Sophia Museum. Then she grabbed her notebook and headed off for her morning staff meeting.

Through the rest of the morning, Alice met, first with her staff to confirm the arrangements for Will Johnson's visit the following day, and their plan for continuing surveillance of him and the others in Elias. As they planned, Tom O'Neal would meet with Johnson at the Alexander for drinks later in the afternoon, and Jim Davis, who secured a room at the hotel would happen upon them in the bar during happy hour. Together, they would try to assess where Johnson stood.

Following the staff meeting, Alice did some quiet research on Horizon and its relationship with the Agency. She knew Ralph Freitag, the CEO and had worked with him on several operations when both were with the CIA. Looking through the security files, she noted that several of his people had problems securing security clearances, mostly due to mixed records in government and private industry, although there was nothing in the record to indicate any caution tags on their contracts with DHS. Nonetheless, it was time to be vigilant, especially if Namers and the CIA had the kind of evidence Sarah Minihan indicated.

Sarah called and left a message about one o'clock PM that the video conference would be at five o'clock, and Sawyer left for Langley about three o'clock, giving her enough time to get out the George Washington Parkway before the major portion of the rush hour mess. Her credentials quickly cleared her thorough the Langley gate, and a visitor parking space awaited her outside the Bush headquarters building. Sarah met her in the lobby.

Kabul, Afghanistan The small, red car sped quickly along the narrow streets of Kabul, headed toward the warehouse district near the International Airport. Inside, Hakim thought about the next steps in his plans for an attack on Washington DC. As he weaved in an around traffic, crossing intersections and nearly hitting several pedestrians, he worried that there was something wrong. He had no real reason to worry, nor had he received any information from outside the country that the plans might not be progressing as he wished, but in his head, he felt more than the usual anxiety. Every facet of the plan had gone well to this point; the weapons would shortly be shipped to his people in Atlanta, and his effort to have a scapegoat—Will Johnson—was progressing as well.

"What have I missed," Hakim kept saying to himself quietly, "Something is not exactly right." Then a thought hit him; it wasn't that something was wrong, rather it was that everything was going exactly according to plan. In his business, everything seldom goes according to plan; something inevitably goes wrong, but thus far that was not the case.

He carefully went over every facet of his plan again, but putting his finger on something out of place was elusive. When he got to the warehouse, he would call Atlanta and check. For now, all he could do was move forward, get the weapons on their way, and bring the parts of the puzzle together as planned.

Ahead, Hakim could see the warehouse where his office was located. He pulled along the side of the building, parked in the back, out of sight of the main street, and entered the warehouse through the side door. His men were waiting for him. The weapons had arrived a bit earlier, and the workers were fitting them into the boxes as Hakim had told them to do. When the packing was finished, the boxes would be sealed after being filled with other items in the main compartments, and sealed for shipping.

One of his trucks would take them to the airport and check them in at cargo shipping. Later that day, the boxes would be on their way to the United States. Hakim's contact at Afghani Customs would clear and stamp the boxes as inspected, then get them into the large shipping containers for loading on the aircraft that would take them, first to Germany, and then on to Atlanta. There, they would be met by another of Hakim's people, who would clear the boxes for

From a Vantage Point

delivery. Since only about 5% of commercial packages are inspected at entry points in the US, having his packages cleared without visual inspection was a routine matter.

Satisfied that this part of his plan was working, Hakim went to his office on the back side of the warehouse floor, and went inside, closing the door behind him. He sat at his desk and pulled out a phone from his desk drawer, checking to be sure it was a new, unused one. Turning it on, and making sure that it was completely charged, Hakim then dialed a number and waited for an answer.

CIA Offices, Kabul, Afghanistan Rick Cartwright and his communications specialist sat looking at a large flat screen on the opposite wall. Suddenly, a green blip appeared near the International Airport. The communication specialist looked at another screen at his desk, noted the phone number, and the routing stated. He took out his own phone, dialed a number, and then entered a code. Within seconds, the large flat screen lit up with many other green points, each blinking, and each having a number next to the blip.

Someone had started a phone call from Hakim's warehouse and it was looking for an outbound traffic route. Then, two yellow blips appeared on the screen, both near the Airport, and both having a steady light. The call was connected to an outbound connection with the Pakistani Intelligence Agency and was being routed to the satellite for transmission.

Cartwright's phone rang, and he answered it, still looking at the screen. "Cartwright, can I help you?"

"Rick, this is Jeff. We have the call and are following it."

"Thanks Jeff, this may just be our chance here."

"I hope so. It could not have come at a better time. We have a conference call with Alice Sawyer and the crew at Langley in just shy of an hour. Let's see what we will be able to tell them, shall we?"

"Love it," responded Cartwright, "I want this guy, badly."

"So do I my friend. So do I."

The two men watched the screens in their respective offices as a line extended from the green blip on the screen and travelled first to one of the yellow blips, then the second, and seemed to momentarily disappear. Suddenly, the screen refreshed itself, with a larger map, now showing the line moving from the yellow blips to another site, located just over the border in Pakistan, then shoot westward.

As the line moved, the screen image grew larger and larger, until it showed virtually a world map. The original green blip was now a tiny speck, and the line extended through several other blips in Europe until it reached across the Atlantic Ocean, stopping on the east coast of the United States.

The communications technician, who had been monitoring the movements and collecting information, yelled over to Namers.

"Jeff, we have them. The current state of the call is Atlanta, Georgia, and the IP address for that location server is Horizon LLC."

"Great work guys. Now, let's see if we can get an off-net trace," responded Namers, loud enough for both his staff and that of Rick Cartwright to hear.

The technician pulled up another screen, connected to Langley, and in seconds, began to map the routing of the call. From the Horizon server, the call was transferred to a Homeland Security server in Atlanta, then pushed through to another server in the same server farm. It went off the government net to a local number in suburban Atlanta. The call was recorded as soon as the person at the receiving end picked up the phone.

"OK Rick, we have what we need. Let's go talk to the powers-that-be. You have the connection. See you shortly."

"Will do Jeff, and thanks."

From a Vantage Point

From a Vantage Point

Part 5 Working the Plan

Chapter 32 Approaching the Edge

The trip to Washington seemed to go quickly this time. There was less traffic than usual, the day was bright and sunny, and a recent rain cleared the air of the usual pollen. Will Johnson left a bit after ten AM for the five-hour trip refreshed from his shower and ready to meet the people from Agriculture and get his project moving. He rose early that morning, packed his bags, reviewed his papers, and felt he was prepared for the day. He could get on the road with his head clear and enthusiastic that his dream was about to come to fruition.

Sammi was bringing Sira to the farm this morning, he thought to himself as he ate—something he prepared himself, thinking it just was not as good as when she does breakfast, or even what he would eat at Sammi's downtown. This morning, it would have to do. He was placing his breakfast plates in the sink just as he heard a car outside, and then front door open.

"Mr. Will, are you still here?" he heard.

"In the kitchen, Sira," came his response. He heard her footsteps as she came to the kitchen door.

"You are not yet gone to Washington?"

"No, I will be leaving shortly. I want to miss the heavy traffic into Washington, so leaving about ten is the best to do that."

"OK, well good luck on your trip," she answered, as she took an apron from the back of the kitchen door, put it on, and started to look around to decide where to start cleaning today.

Will smiled as he moved through the door from the kitchen to the living room, took his papers, and bags and started toward the front door for his car

"Mister Will, do you need a lunch for the trip? Asked Sira.

"No Sira, I think I will probably stop along the way in Virginia."

"All right. No lunch. Have a great trip," Sira said smiling as Will went out the front door.

Washington DC The telecommunications area at Homeland Security was huge, with a 72' screen for the main presentations, and at least eight other screens working in tandem with displays of information. This morning was no different. Alice Sawyer and several of her staff, along with others from The Department, the CIA, and the FBI were in the room as several of the screens began to light up as connections were made and the familiar faces of Jeff

Namers in Khartoum, Rick Cartwright in Kabul, and others logged in. The main screen was programmed to change views as people spoke.

In the center of the room was a large oval table, around which sat Alice and her people, Sarah Minihan and two others from CIA, and the rest of the staff. Alice looked around the room, introduced those with her to those on the screen, and started to ask questions almost immediately.

"Jeff, let's start. What did you and your people find?"

"Alice, let me show you," Namers answered as the screen changed to show the same images he and his staff had seen earlier. "This is a tape of the progress of a call from Hakim's warehouse in Kabul, through a link to the Pakistani Intelligence Service, and then another PI relay link, out to one of their satellite links, and then down to a location in Atlanta, Georgia. That end link is the server farm at Horizon LLC."

"You are absolutely sure on this?" asked Alice.

"Absolutely," Namers responded.

"Rick, are you sure it is Hakim on the other end?"

"We are Ms. Sawyer. The call went from a SAT phone we have registered to the PI offices in Kabul, the ones which legally don't exist. We also know that the node on the satellite is one registered to the Intel Services. No one else uses it."

Alice looked around the table, saw Tom Clement, one of her communications people, and asked, "Clem, where did it go from there?"

"Glad you asked, Alice. I just pulled the log. The call went from server XC—11-6, Node 6, to the off-net node, then out to a node they maintain for us in a separate server farm—same building, different server farm. When it reached us, it dialed out back to Atlanta, to a commercial number. We are getting Verizon to give us that information as we speak."

"Jeff, tell us what you know about Hakim's latest adventure," asked Sarah Minihan.

"Not a lot Sarah, but what we do know is that Hakim had some packing boxes created in two phases, with an interesting configuration. The originals look like common packing boxes, but were altered in Kabul. It looks like they had side sections added, just large enough for something round and angular, perhaps one and one-half to two inches wide, with several parts. The inside walls are lined with some thin brass or lead."

"We arranged to put some small sensors in various places on the boxes in Khartoum, before they were shipped, so we could track them. We lost a couple of those, but we do know where all six boxes are at present."

"Where is that?" asked Alice.

"All six are in Kabul," answered Rick Cartwright. "We expect them to be shipped in the next day or so from the looks of the work being done in that building. We also intercepted part of the telephone conversation between Hakim

From a Vantage Point

and someone else, on that same SAT phone, by the way. Listen." Rick pushed a button at his console and the rest of the groups heard the audio clip.

> *"Be ready," said a voice, presumed to be Hakim, "The equipment is coming in a few days. You know what to do with it, Remember D—889—9126–A"*
> *"We do," answered a voice on the other end, "We are ready for it. By then, we will have the other one ready as well."*
> *"Good," came the response, and then a dead line.*

"Have we confirmed the voice?" asked Sarah Minihan.

"We have," responded Namers, "Our contacts here have listened to the tape and confirm it is Hakim.

"What do we make of the last statement about the 'Other one ready'?" asked Alice.

"Not completely sure there, Alice, but it can only be one of two things; first, they have another shipment with other equipment coming from somewhere else, or they have someone getting ready to use whatever they are sending."

"Educated guess here?" asked Alice.

"We think they are talking about a person using whatever they are sending," responded Namers. "Our primary contact here, Hakim's cousin, seems to feel that Hakim wants to make an even bigger statement than bin-Laden. That will take a lot of firepower, and someone able to do the work.

"OK, so we have danced around it long enough. What is your guesstimate here?" asked Alice.

Rick Cartwright responded, "Both Jeff and I agree that we think the boxes will contain some type of mortar or breakdown RPG—something aimable, which can also be hidden well. Perhaps they are developing something in plastic that can be mounted and assembled in place. That's about as close as we can guess thus far."

"Then we need to know more quickly," responded Alice. She looked around the table to the legal counsel. What do you make of this Aaron?"

Aaron Shapiro was a very experienced lawyer, and a very experienced operative. He thought for a minute, and then said, "Alice, I think there are three things to do here. First, we need to go to FISA and get a warrant for Horizon. We need to do it in a way we don't necessarily tip our hand on this. Perhaps it is time to do a periodic inspection of their facility for security purposes, and then just happen to find a weakness in their system. Not enough to close them down—we want to continue monitoring their transmissions—that's the purpose of the warrant—but we get to go in and look closer."

"Second," he continued, "We need to put a similar tap on our own out lines, and we need to find who gave the approval for the link. I will bet it was buried in some change order with Horizon. We need to see who authorized it, and what justification."

"Third," said Shapiro, "We need another order from FISA for a domestic tap on the final destination line. We want to know who they are, what they do."

"Good Aaron," responded Alice, "Do that today. I want to be on this post haste."

"Understood," responded Shapiro, taking notes.

"Sarah, this is obviously a joint thing. I hope we can continue to work with your people until this is done."

"Absolutely, Alice. I already have the OK for a joint effort."

Alice looked again down the room and came to her FBI contact, Tim Feeney. "Tim, think about how to get the Atlanta Task Forces capability; working on this without upsetting the apple cart. I know that they use the Horizon communication. Let's give them some alternate comms for this effort, something outside the usual server farm. Can you do that?"

"Sure Alice, I can make that happen today.

"All right then, we have a plan ladies and gentlemen. Let's make it work." The screens started to go dark and people signed off, and some of those in attendance got up to leave, with Sarah and Alice left at the table.

"Sarah, I really have a weird feeling on this. Something major is about to happen, and we are totally unprepared.

"I agree Alice. I have the same feeling myself. Let's just work the issues and see where it goes." Sarah rose to leave herself, and added, I will brief Bernie. You have our full cooperation here. Just let us know what you need." She patted Alice's shoulder as she left. Alice remained, looking at the now-blank screens, and wondering where her plan would take them.

Over the next several hours, a flurry of activity occurred, mostly a result of decisions made at the earlier meeting. The FISA Court was asked for the warrants, and quickly issued them, taking the additional step of securing the requests on their classified docket. A Presidential Decision Memorandum was requested, authorizing assets of the Central Intelligence Agency to work in cooperation with a special task force to link the domestic and overseas intelligence-gathering activities. Verizon Communications was served with a National Security Letter, followed by yet another search warrant for the files involving the number dialed in Atlanta, along with a request for a phone tap on the line. Luckily, the FBI anticipated it being a commercial line, and all lines controlled by the company were placed under the order.

Internally, Alice Sawyer and her staff briefed the Office of the Inspector General at DHS on problems with Horizon, asking that no formal investigation be started until the National Security issues had been determined and defused; the IG agreed, and a member of that staff was also added to the task force. Constant monitoring for future calls was put in place, linking Kabul and Khartoum to the surveillance net.

Elias, West Virginia Sammi's Restaurant has an odd configuration; it is long but relatively narrow, rectangular in size. As a customer walks through the door, they faced a row of booths ahead, and turning to the right, the cash register, then more booths down the right-hand wall. In the center of the room are six tables, four down the center and two at the left end of the restaurant, near the door to the kitchen, which separated the booths from those tables. Anyone coming into the restaurant could see all the other customers from anywhere in the restaurant.

Sammi and Hassan were cleaning up tables from the small morning rush for breakfast as the woman walked into the restaurant and sat in a booth near the cash register, along the right wall, away from the door. Sammi went toward the table, picking up a menu on the way at the register, meaning to give it to his new customer.

"May I help you," Sammi asked, handing her the menu.

"Yes, I think I will order lunch. You are serving lunch now, aren't you?" the woman answered.

"We are, Ma'am, that we are," responded Sammi, looking toward Hassan, giving him the eye to get to the kitchen to be sure the stove was hot and clean for lunch.

"Give me a moment to look at the menu, if you would," said the woman, taking the menu from his hands. Sammi bowed slightly and walked back toward the kitchen door, then going through to the kitchen.

"Who is she?" asked Hassan.

"Don't know. I have never seen her before. She wants lunch." Hassan nodded, and started to scrape down the grill, and get ready for an order. Sammi walked back out into the restaurant, and toward her table. The woman looked up, and waved to him to tell him she was ready to order.

"I will have a tuna salad sandwich and a garden salad as well, please. Do you have iced tea?"

"Yes ma'am, we do," responded Sammi. "Would you prefer sweetened or unsweetened?"

"Sweetened will be fine, with lemon," answered the woman, handing Sammi the menu.

From a Vantage Point

Sammi wrote the order down on his pad, ripped off the sheet, and started back toward the kitchen to give Hassan the order. She stopped him midway.

"When you deliver the order, tell Hassan to come out here. I want to speak with both of you."

Sammi's face drained, and his pulse quickened.

"Yes ma'am," he responded, and pushed his way through the door, giving Hassan the order and telling him to come out."

"Hassan will be right here, in a moment," Sammi said to the woman. She nodded, and he sat down on a bench opposite her.

"Who are you?" Asked Sammi.

"It does not matter who I am," she replied, "Only that you and Hassan understand what is required of you by the one who is our leader in all. He expects you to do what is required of you, at your own peril." Sammi looked toward her and saw immediately the steely grey eyes of someone who was very determined. Before he could respond, Hassan came out of the kitchen, wiping his hands on a towel, which he threw over his should as he sat down next to his boss.

"Now that both of you are here, tell me how you are doing," said the woman.

"What is it you want to know about us?" asked Sammi, incredulous at her question.

"Everything is moving along," responded Hassan, "Slowly, but moving along."

"Will this person do our bidding?" she asked.

"I believe he will," said Hassan, "He needs more urging. We have to be careful how to do that, since he is so involved in this cooperative project, and that needs to stay on track first, if we are to be successful." It became clear to Sammi that Hassan knew a lot more about the interactions with Will Johnson than he realized.

"Do what urging is required. He must do what we want him to do," came the response.

"What is it that he must do?" asked Sammi.

"You have no need to know. Only those directly involved will know more details. That is to keep our people safe," said the woman in response. Sammi realized he was into something over which he had no control, and for which his own life was in great danger.

"We will do as you wish," said Sammi, with a resigning sigh. "What is it you suggest we do to speed up the process?"

"Whatever you need to do," was the only response. "Now, it is time for my lunch. I will be back in one week; I expect progress by then. I will return as many times as necessary, or someone else will, to assure success. Now, get me my lunch. Take this cell phone as well. I may wish to contact you through it." As Sammi considered her face, he saw the steely eyes sharply focused and

From a Vantage Point

determined. He knew he was too deeply involved to get out, yet he still knew virtually nothing. He was simply a pawn in a larger game. He told himself he would speak to Hassan later, after she left.

Hassan brought out her lunch a few minutes later, refilled her tea, and asked her if she required anything else. The woman did not answer his questions, instead started to eat her salad. Knowing he was going to get no more information, Hassan returned to the kitchen.

When she finished her meal, the woman stood up and left the restaurant, walking down the street on both sides, seemingly interested in the old buildings, especially the hardware store, into which she walked to buy a small token take back home with her.

Sammi waited nearly three hours after the woman left before he approached Hassan in the kitchen where he was washing dishes from the lunch meals.

"Hassan, I have been good to you and Sira. I let you live here, and made sure you were protected. I agree to go along with something, I am not sure about, but I trusted you. Now, this woman comes in and treats me like I am simply a slave to push around. What is happening here?"

"Sammi, my friend," answered Hassan, "I am truly grateful for you and your friendship. You have treated us well and All'ah, may he be praised forever, will shine his blessings on you for it. I am afraid to tell you very much about what is to happen. I can only say that you must trust me, and you will not be hurt in any way. It is on Sira and myself to complete this deed, and on our own lives that this will occur. I cannot tell you more, for fear that your life will be in even more danger."

This was not the response Sammi wanted to hear, but he knew in his heart that it was all he could expect. He would listen closer, and remember. For now, all he could do was protect Hassan and Sira as best he could. They had become part of his family, and he feared for them.

Horizon LLC, Atlanta, GA The following morning the security office at Horizon received a call from DHS security than an unannounced net security inspection would commence 24 hours later in accordance with the provisions of their contract with the agency. Horizon was used to these periodic inspections, although they, like most contractors, wished they had more notice to prepare for them.

The procedures were standard; a team would arrive and take over administration of the dedicated circuits and servers and for a short period; the logs would be reviewed, including the listings of routed calls, and a review would be conducted of the servers themselves. Any discrepancies would be noted in a report, along with the comments and responses of the Horizon staff and management. All they could do now is wait for the team.

From a Vantage Point

Alice Sawyer arranged for two members of her staff, including her comms specialist Tom Clement to accompany the team to Atlanta, giving them specific instructions on which servers, nodes, and calls she had an interest in, and to make sure that these observations were included in the report, but among enough other minor comments they would not be flagged to any other type of investigation.

The team arrived promptly at 9:00 AM at the front lobby of Horizon. Their arrival in three black extended vans with government plates was impressive; as was their entrance into the lobby, where they met Ralph Freitag, the CEO and Eric Quigley, the Chief of Security.

"Welcome to Horizon, gentlemen," said Freitag, looking around the team to be sure there were no women in the group. Seeing one in the back, from the FBI he later learned, he added, "And ladies as well. I hope you enjoy your stay. This is Eric Quigley, my chief of security who will work with you during you time with us." Freitag motioned to the security personnel at the entry desk to show them where to sign the guest logs. Each did so, showing their credentials first, then signing in and receiving a security badge.

The group moved over to the elevator bank, where some entered the first car with Freitag, and the rest to another car with Quigley, all destined to arrive about the same time on the tenth floor of the building where the executive offices were located.

"Right this way," said Quigley, as both groups left their elevators and stood in the atrium. "Your space we designated for you is right over here," he added, pointing to a doorway near the elevators. They all entered and found a large office, with several desks, computers, and communications.

"We really did not know what you might need. The computers are on a separate network set up for you. I will show the person you want to designate as the administrator what the permissions are, and you can change them at will to what you desire. Same for the phones. All the phones are on a separate trunk line not connected to the company servers. Again, you can decide what you want to configure it to suit yourselves. We are happy to assist in any way we can."

"I know you will want to get settled before we start to meet, so how about we get together in an hour in the main conference room. It's two doors down on the right. Is that enough time?"

"Sure, it's fine," said one of the team members. That's about what we need," he added. "See you in an hour. Quigley left the room, and the team started putting backpacks and briefcases on desks. Tom Clement started to look at the computers and phones to see what he needed to do to secure them. He would get with Quigley later for that. Right now, they had their cell phones and laptops for immediate needs.

From a Vantage Point

The team, chief, Rich Alcorn, turned to the group and made some simple remarks; "Team, we need to work smartly and fast. I would like to be out of here in three days, if possible. Each of you already knows what they need to review, and those who are new to the team will work with other, more experienced people. Look at everything, but don't waste time on nothing. This is a security review so let's review security. Everybody understand?" Most of the team nodded, and they started to organize, knowing they would be in their first session in less than an hour.

In Freitag's office, he and Quigley sat on a sofa and easy chair to the side of his desk. Neither of them had known about the security inspection; they learned as everyone did, from the single call. To Freitag, at least, that raised a flag and he was concerned.

"Eric, with them starting today, they won't get very far for the first day, but this evening I want a maximum effort to go over everything; look at logs, and check out security well. I want to know if there are problems before they do, not afterwards. You understand?"

"Sure Ralph, we can do that, but it will show in the logs."

"I really don't care about that. I think we have nothing to hide, and I just want to be sure. When they ask, I will cover my concerns here. When can your staff start?"

"This afternoon, Ralph, if that is what you want."

"No, wait until they stop for their first day, then put your people to work. We don't get that much traffic at night, so they ought to be able to cover a lot of ground."

"Will do Boss. If there is anything out there, we will find it. Any idea why this particular time? Has there been any odd traffic lately?"

"Just a bit of an increase out of the Afghan-Pakistan area, but not a real lot. I will have that reviewed along with several other areas tonight, first thing."

"Do that, and cross-overs from our farm to theirs. See if there are any suspicious items there as well."

"OK Ralph, I have my marching orders. We'll get it done," answered Quigley, as he rose to go back to his own office to get ready before the first conference in less than 30 minutes. Freitag sat on the sofa as Quigley left, thinking to himself, but not coming up with answers.

Approaching Washington, DC Will Johnson drove along through the countryside and on into the edge of the city, enjoying his ride and looking forward to his meetings the following day. He felt good about this visit; approval meant everything to his community, and he had a lot to pay back for their acceptance of him and his family over the years. For the first time in weeks, he felt that success was literally around the corner for his project.

From a Vantage Point

Stopping along the highway after he crossed the Virginia-- West Virginia border, he took an early exit, finding a local restaurant next to a gas station. He needed gas, making this a logical point for him to stop. He filled the tank then pulled over into a parking space near the restaurant door. Going inside, he looked around to find a small table or booth where he might sit after he ordered food. There were many in the nearly empty restaurant.

Arriving at the counter, he looked at the menu, and a young server stood by the register waiting for his order.

"Can I help you, sir," she asked. Will looked at her, realizing she was probably not much more than sixteen; a high school student working part-time.

"Sure," answered Johnson, looking at the menu. "I will have a number three, with a medium coke and tater tots, and a small salad."

"Coming right up sir," said the young server, going toward the back to get his order. She returned in just a minute, and said, "We just finished cooking the items in the specials so they are really fresh. Please enjoy. Is there anything else I can get you?"

"No, not really," answered Johnson, as he pulled out money to pay, and looked toward seats while waiting for his change. He noticed a family sitting off to the right side, and thought that might be a good place as well. Will enjoyed children and their antics in a restaurant. It was a young couple with two children, both girls, who were sitting between their parents eating dry cereal from the bowl, piece by piece. Most of it, however, was all over the table. They were pushing some around and clearly enjoying themselves. The father looked frustrated, and the mother was trying to keep the table cleaned up as best she could.

Will dropped his tray at the next table and sat down, placing his coke on the side of the small tray, and prepared to start eating. He turned to the mother, who was closest to him, and said, "Good morning, you have two lovely daughters." The woman seemed to shy away, but the man spoke up instead in reply.

"My wife does not speak English sir. We are from overseas she speaks only Arabic. I speak English. We love our daughters. The one next to her mother is Mariyah, and the other is Miriam."

"They are beautiful, and they seem to be having fun," responded Will.

"They are," answered the man, "We have recently come here as refugees, from France where I have cousins. We intend to make a new life here in the United States."

"Welcome to my country then," responded Will, "I too was an immigrant and have lived here now for many years. My family came from Lebanon during the civil wars. There are great opportunities here."

"That is amazing, sir. We too are from Lebanon, although we were driven out during the battles between the Christians and those of our faith. We are Muslim,

From a Vantage Point

Shia Muslim. They took our farm and burned it, giving us just a few minutes to get out. We took only ourselves and some clothes for the children."

"All around us as we drove off in our car was burning," he continued. Along the way to the town, we saw other farms burning, and many people joining us on the road toward the town. My children are young; they will not remember, but I will not forget what the Christians did to us."

"Are you sure it was Christians?' Asked Will.

"Sir, with respect, a man who wears the Cross of Jesus around his neck to me is a Christian," answered the man with complete disdain.

"I understand," said Will in return. "You have a great burden to bear. Where will you live?"

"We are driving to Tennessee. There I have another cousin who will take us in. He has a small business fixing cars. I can help him do that. I am good with cars, and I can learn. We will do all right in America. I think." The man turned, looked at his wife and children, and then back to Will smiling. "I have everything I need."

Will and the man continued their conversation over lunch, and then, as he got up to leave, he turned to him and said, I am sorry that people of my religion were uncaring for you and yours. That is not the way it should be. I wish you every happiness." Will smiled, extended his hand to the other man and shook hands with him then turned to depart. As he went out the door toward his car, Will turned once more to look at the family sitting there having breakfast. At least they were alive and free, he said to himself.

What Will did not notice was another person, a woman, sitting in a booth on the opposite side of the restaurant reading a newspaper. She looked over at the two men conversing periodically and then back at her paper. The steel grey eyes were absorbing the scene with great interest.

Hotel Alexander, Washington DC Entering the wide doors of the Alexander Hotel, a man with a large briefcase, and a suit bag over his right shoulder walked quickly toward the main desk.

"Good afternoon, my name is Davis, James Davis. I believe I have a reservation with you for three nights."

The man at the desk looked at him, then down to an arrival list on the desk, and responded, "Yes, we do have a reservation for Davis. My I please see some identification and a credit card?"

"Of course," said Jim Davis, as he pulled out his Government American Express and his Virginia Drivers' License.

"Thank you, Mister Davis," responded the clerk as he returned the items, and offered a card for him to sign. "Will you be needing parking for your car?"

From a Vantage Point

"No, I just came by cab from the airport. What business I have this time will not require a car. Thanks for asking."

"Part of our service to our customers, sir," answered the clerk. "Your room number is 1210. I can have the bellhop take your bags to your room, if you wish."

"Just the suit bag, thank you," was his response. The clerk waved for a bellhop, who took Davis' bag and started toward the elevators after receiving a small tip from Davis.

"Where is cocktail lounge?" asked Davis.

"Up the main staircase toward the left, you will find the afternoon lounge open. The main lounge will open after four o'clock," came the response.

"Great, thanks," said Davis, picking up his briefcase and starting toward the stairs, where he would be joined eventually by his soon-to-be partner for this adventure. In just an hour or two, the next stage of learning more about Will Johnson would begin.

As Will anticipated, it was nearly three o'clock in the afternoon before he would reach his destination downtown in the District. For the most part, he had interstate highways all the way. Starting with Interstate 64 near Charleston, he came East to Interstate 81, north on 81 to Interstate 66 East, he had wide highways to speed his journey. Will also enjoyed getting off periodically to stretch his feet, and find food in small restaurants rather than the interstate exit types, so that added some time to his overall trip. He made it to Interstate 66 just after one o'clock, and knew the two-hour trip he had left would mean even more traffic the closer he came to the city.

Interstate 66 was an interesting road; it simply stopped at the border of the District—never having been finished or connected to another road never built. Today, he would get off at the last local freeway exit and head downtown. Sometimes that took almost as long, at least in his mind, as the trip down the interstate. Eventually, he would end up on 14th Street and find his hotel near the Treasury Department.

One of the truly great American sights is the drive into downtown Washington, D.C., with its curious mix of monuments, government building and commercial space. Most of those who live downtown do so in large apartment buildings, interspersed among the other building so they are not overly noticeable. One that is, the Watergate Complex, where the great political break-in on the 1970's caused the downfall of President Nixon, is on the parkway path from Interstate 66 into downtown. That's the route Will prefers because it gets him into the area where he stays quickly, and with minimal stop lights and pedestrian traffic.

Turning off 14th Street, having wended his way through the numbered and alphabetical street maze which is the city, Will found himself at his destination,

From a Vantage Point

the Alexander Hotel. He pulled up out front, where a doorman waited, took his car keys, and helped him with his two small bags into the hotel lobby, dropping them with a bellhop as Will went forward toward the registration desk.

"Hi, I'm Will Johnson. You have a reservation for me?" asked Will as the clerk behind the desk looked up at him.

"We do sir," responded the clerk. "Welcome to the Alexander," he added, passing Will a registration card with his name and information already printed on it. "Please sign at the bottom, and indicate your automobile information. I will need a major credit card from you. Also, will you be using our valet service? If so, please fill in the information at the bottom."

Will completed the required information, pulled a credit card from his wallet, and handed both back to the clerk, who then imprinted a credit card slip and the registration card with his credit information, then handed the card back to him.

"Everything is in order, Sir. I hope you enjoy your stay." The clerk motioned to the bellhop, handed him the room card, and said to Will, "The bellhop will bring your luggage if you wish sir. Your room number is 1322. Is there anything else I can do for you?"

"Everything is fine," responded Will. "I think I will go to the lounge." He handed a tip to the bellhop, who turned toward the elevators with his luggage as Will started up the main staircase to the lounge. He walked to the left to the afternoon lounge, knowing the main lounge was not open, and hoped that there would be room at the small bar for him.

Walking into the dimly lit lounge, Will did see three seats at the bar and walked closer, then stopped. Ahead, on the corner was Jim Davis, the guy he met on the plane to Middle East. Looking a bit shocked, Will walked over and sat down next to him, then turned to face him.

"You're Jim Davis, aren't you?" Will asked.

"Certainly am, Will Johnson," Davis replied, "Good to see you. I thought you lived out in the woods of West Virginia. What brings you to the big city?" asked Davis.

"I have a meeting later, and again tomorrow here with the Agriculture people. How are you doing?"

"Doing just fine. I flew in today for a couple of days with a client, then off again to the world of Asia. First stop Korea, then Japan."

"Great to see you. Let me make a quick call, and we can talk if you have some time."

"Sure can," Davis replied, "Just sitting here nursing this drink before I figure out where I want to go for dinner."

Will stood and walked over toward a table, pulled out his cell phone and dialed Tom O'Neal's number. "Tom, its Will Johnson. I'm in town, at the Alexander. Just checked in."

From a Vantage Point

"Great Will, I can be there about five o'clock. Will that work?"

"Sure will Tom. Amazingly, I just walked into the lounge and found someone I haven't seen in a while. His name is Jim Davis, a world traveler, and we will sit catching up until you arrive."

"Good, then five o'clock Will. I look forward to seeing you. Enjoy." O'Neal was glad he had met with Davis first. The plan was working perfectly.

"See you then, Tom" answered Will, then hanging up. And walking back to the bar stool he left earlier. Davis, still sitting with his drink in hand overheard most of the conversation, and was sure that the plan he and O'Neal had was working out well.

"I have a guy from Agriculture I have to meet at five o'clock, Jim. You are welcome to join us if you wish. We are going to have a drink and discuss a bit about tomorrow's meeting," said Will as he sat back down on the bar stool.

"Let's see how that works out," responded Davis. "I don't want to intrude in your important conversation."

"No intrusion," retorted Johnson, "Happy to have you. So, what have you been doing?"

"Travelling mostly, Will. My work takes me everywhere. If I had a wife and family, I would have been divorced long ago. I enjoy travelling though. The sights and sounds in different places are awesome."

"They can be harrowing too," responded Johnson, "After I last saw you, and my friends and I went on to Khartoum, the building we were staying in was blown up in the middle of day."

"That's too bad. Any Idea why?"

"Well, I didn't know it then, but apparently these two were involved in some kinds of terrorist activities, and someone went after them. It's too bad really," said Will.

As Jim Davis was about to respond, the bartender came over. "Drinks gentlemen? Perhaps some munchies? "he asked, handing them a small menu. "We only have a few things here. The main lounge opens in less than an hour. They have a larger menu."

"This is OK," responded Johnson, "Think I will have a beer on tap, an IPA will be fine. What about you Jim?"

"Same for me," Davis responded, handing his menu back to the bartender.

"Coming right up gentlemen," the bartender responded, walking over to where he kept the chilled glasses. He took out two from a chilled reefer and started pouring one of the taps on his bar. In less than a minute, two beers on coasters were sitting in front of Will and Jim.

"Give a yell if you need anything else. Oh, do you want me to run a tab?" asked the bartender. Will pulled out his credit card. "Sure, run it on this," he answered, handing him the card.

From a Vantage Point

"Will do," came the response as the bartender walked over to his register to swipe the card.

"Thanks Will," said Davis, "Appreciate the hospitality. How is it going with you? The farm OK?"

"We are having a great year, Jim," answered Johnson, "Now the cooperative a bunch of us have been organizing for a couple of years is starting to bear fruit. Agriculture approved us about two weeks ago, and the meeting tomorrow is to iron out details. That will give us the Fall and Winter to work out what we need to do in the West Virginia end, and give them time to help us get into markets along the route toward DC. A win for both, I think,"

"Sure sounds like it. Do you have enough farmers willing to participate?"

"Virtually everyone in the valley is working with us, and several further out also want to contribute. We will establish at least two central locations for the people to deliver what goes into the cooperative list, and then there is the delivery. We still need to work that out completely."

"Well, you do have some time during the off-season to get out the kinks. When I come back in the spring, I expect to visit and see a success."

"Jim, you are welcome anytime. Come and stay at the farm and meet our people. I think you would really like them; just common, ordinary farm people."

"Did I tell you that I came off a farm in Iowa, Will? Left there to go to college, and only go back periodically, but farming is still in my veins. At least once or twice a year, I go back to help with the gathering and hay baling. It gives me a renewal of my roots. I love the clean air, and the good people."

"Then you know how much this means to us out there in the valley. This is our way to get some of what we produce out to other people, perhaps some who could not afford fresh produce for their families."

"That's a noble thing to do Will," responded Davis.

"It isn't noble to want to pay back what you owe people for taking care of you when you needed it Jim. When my family came to the US, we had nothing, and ended up with a good farm, good friends, and a feeling that we belonged again, as we had in Lebanon."

"You never told me you were from Lebanon, Will."

"Really, I usually tell everyone sooner or later. Yes, we had to leave during the earlier civil wars between the Christians and the Muslims—north versus southern Lebanon. I was very young and a good humanitarian group arranged for us to come here. We have lived here, in a small town in West Virginia ever since. It's called Elias. You probably never heard of it."

"Ever thought about going back, Will?"

"Not really, Jim. Who knows if I still have family there, but the people here are really my family now. I got stupid in the Army, deserted during Vietnam, and

From a Vantage Point

then got into the Amnesty Program. The government helped me get back on my feet, and I appreciated that. I grew up. I'm happy here with my friends."

Elias, West Virginia Sira walked into the restaurant as she normally did, took off her pullover and walked into the kitchen where Hassan waited.

It's about time," said Hassan, seeing her coming through the door, "I have been waiting for you."

"Don't be so excited Hassan," she replied, "I am only just a few minutes late. Why are you so excited?"

"A woman came to the restaurant this morning; a strange woman who wanted to speak to Sammi and myself."

Sira looked at Hassan and saw the look of fear in his eyes.

"And what did this woman want?" she asked.

"She wanted to know how we were doing in bringing Johnson around. That's what she wanted," came the response.

"Anything else?" asked Sira

"Just that we are to speed up what we are doing. They want to move soon. She made it very clear that we are not moving fast enough," said Hassan. As he spoke, Sammi walked into the kitchen.

"Good morning Sira," said Sammi, smiling, and then handing an order to Hassan. "Easy over on the eggs for Mister Jules, if you will please, Hassan," said Sammi, then turning and walking back out to the restaurant.

"What does he know?" asked Sira.

"Very little, and he asked me about her. I told him he was better off knowing little for his own sake. He seemed to accept that."

"Good," she responded. "What do we do next?"

"You need to get closer to him. He trusts you, and listens to you, from what you have said to me. You need to convince him that what we want him to do is good."

"Just how do you expect me to do that quickly?" she asked.

"Do whatever you have to do. Play up to him if you need to. Go to bed with him if you need to. Make him believe that his cause is our cause and get him to do what we wish. That is what you need to do," responded Hassan, somewhat testily. "She will come back next week, and expect progress. Do it. She even gave me a phone if I needed to call her." Hassan showed Sira the phone, almost making it seem to be a weapon.

"You know what you are saying Hassan?"

"I do," he responded. "If we are killed for not doing the work of the group, we will be no better off. We must do what they wish, and use any means to get it done, and ourselves out of the way. Do you understand that?"

From a Vantage Point

"Yes, I do," she responded in a low voice. "I will do what you wish." Hassan could see she had tears in her eyes, as she turned and walked out into the restaurant where she met Sammi.

"Is everything all right Sira?" Sammi asked.

Sira wiped the tears from her eyes, and responded, "Everything is fine Sammi. Just an argument, that is all. They happen on occasion. I will be fine." Sira picked up a washrag from the bucket near the door to the kitchen, then started to wipe down tables in preparation for the lunch crowd. None of the three said very much from that time on, all thinking about the morning's events.

Hotel Alexander, Washington DC Will and Jim Davis continued their conversation for the next hour, discussing some of the sights he had seen in Doha and Khartoum. Will was impressed that Davis was a real-world traveler, and Davis, in turn became more convinced that Will was no terrorist. Davis looked at his watch as he picked up his drink and saw that it was nearly five o'clock and turned to Will to excuse himself to go to the restroom.

As Davis left, heading toward the rest rooms in the corridor, Will ordered another drink and looked at his own watch, seeing it was very close to five o'clock and looked around to see if Tom O'Neal was anywhere near the bar. He spied O'Neal coming up the stairs and waved as O'Neal turned toward the bar.

"Hey Will, good to see you, my friend," said O'Neal, extending his hand to Will as he came near the bar.

"Good to see you as well, Tom," responded Will, pointing to a chair on his right. "Saved this for you." Both men laughed, realizing there was no one else at the bar, except the bartender.

"Can I get something for you, sir?" asked the bartender. "I'm Jake. Glad you are with us this evening."

"Thanks Jake. Sure, let me have a vodka martini straight up with an olive."

"Coming right up, sir. Shaken or stirred?"

"Shaken is fine, no vermouth."

"Just the way I like it myself," answered Jake, as he went off to make the drink.

Jim Davis walked back to the bar and sat on Will's left. He looked up at the TV screen in front of them and asked, "Anything earth-shaking since I left Will?"

"Haven't been watching Jim, but let me introduce you to Tom O'Neal. He works for Agriculture, and is the coordinator for my project."

"Glad to meet you Tom O'Neal," answered Davis, extending his hand across Will toward O'Neal.

"Same here," responded Davis, "Jim Davis is my name. Glad to meet you."

The three men had light conversation over the next hour or so before deciding they would stay together and have dinner in the hotel. They discussed

From a Vantage Point

the potential for the cooperative, travel and mostly baseball. All three seemed to enjoy themselves immensely.

As the evening stretched out, Davis gave up a couple of yawns, and eventually decided it was time to go to his room.

"Well guys, this has been great, but for a traveler, it is time to get some sleep. I hate to break up the conversation, but I am gradually becoming dead on my feet. Enjoyed the evening. How about letting me pick up the tab here?"

"Not necessary, Jim," answered Will, "It's my party. I'll pay."

"No Will, I insist. I really enjoyed myself this evening." Davis took out a credit card and put in on the table for the waiter to pick up. Waiters have a way of arriving just as credit cards appear, and was soon back with the bill for Davis to sign, which he did, adding the tip, and putting his card back in his pocket.

Rising from his chair, Davis said, "Thanks again for the great evening guys. Hope we get together again in the future." He shook hands with both Will and Tom O'Neal and started walking away from the table toward the corridor to reach the elevators near the stairway. Will and Tom both rose as well, with O'Neal also saying good evening, and followed Davis out the door. Will indicated he would have another drink before going to his room.

Davis entered the elevator and went up to his room on the 12th floor. O'Neal went down the stairway toward the lobby, and then toward the front desk.

"Hi, I'm Mister O'Neal. I understand you have an envelope for me?" said Tom O'Neal.

"We do sir," responded the clerk, handing Tom the envelope with his name on the front. O'Neal felt it and found the key card inside. "Thanks," he responded, walking away and back toward the elevators near the stairway. In less than two minutes, O'Neal was up at Jim Davis' room, ready to discuss their mutual concern.

Atlanta, Georgia The Downtown Boxing Club wasn't downtown, and it wasn't exactly a boxing club; it acted more as a meeting place for a range of people who generally tried to avoid the law. The place was owned by a man named Sam Oakley, a local promoter, who spent some time in the Army in the days when the military still supported boxing and wrestling matches for the troops. Oakley had this large warehouse down near the Atlanta-Hartsfield Airport. Part of it was used for shipping coming in through the airport, and part was fashioned into a gym on the first floor, and office space above it.

One of the larger offices, on the second floor just above the gym was once occupied by Tabriz Shipping of Cairo, Egypt, although it had long been replaced by another company, called simply Near East Imports, owned by an ex-patriot from Iran, who left as the 1979 revolution grew in force, and the followers of the Shah left the country in droves.

For this man, Jalil Radan, there were two worlds in which he lived. The first was as an importer of fine good from the Near and Middle East. His goods included rugs, clothing, furniture, art, and even religious goods used by the various sects in their mosques and prayer houses. Well-known as a charitable man, he had a large family; his wife was a Syrian Druze, but he brought his children up Christian. He was a frequent contributor to local community events, especially at the large Maronite parish in Atlanta, where his children went to school, and to the local universities, where he often donated ancient art items for their collections.

In his other life, Radan had been a loyal follower of Amoud Tabriz—known to most of the world as Fatool—a legend in the world of terrorism, and now retired. When Tabriz Shipping closed, Radan purchased the office space and its furnishings, and many of the contracts Tabriz held moved over to this new company. Radan had several long-time loyal employees and they protected him well. He needed that protection. After the retirement of Tabriz, his successor, Amid Fattoulah, met with him, working out an agreement to represent another group in the US, one led by Hakim Al-Azahir.

While he occasionally shipped goods for al-Azahir, Radan's real job was to recruit immigrants and others for a few cells in the states in and around Georgia, and serve as a conduit for the instructions al-Azahir might provide for actions he was undertaking. Oakley had also done work for al-Azahir and his boss many times, including blowing up a plane over the marshes outside Charleston, South Carolina, nearly causing the complete collapse of the cells Radan formed. However, the FBI never got close enough to them, mostly because they concentrated only on one local group, spending little time trying to trace other threads beyond Charleston.

Another of the actions Radan was working on involved a new scheme for al-Azahir; one created to attack Washington DC during the upcoming presidential Inauguration. These were grand plans for al-Azahir, still evolving, and designed to make an even bigger statement than that occurring on September 11, 2001 in New York and Washington. It was Radan's job to recruit the local people, train them, and get them ready to act on al-Azahir's command.

His instructions were that everyone recruited had to be an American citizen, with impeccable credentials, no police or government record, and public ties to the community. Those requirements made recruiting exceedingly difficult, but Radan managed to create three small cells, one in Washington DC, one in Atlanta Georgia, and the last in Charlotte, North Carolina.

Al-Azahir also expected Radan to convert one of al-Azahir's friends, a guy in West Virginia, who had once been part of al-Azahir's working group in the early days. Like al-Azahir, he had been a deserter from the Army, fled the country, but eventually returned and was now a respectable farmer in West Virginia.

From a Vantage Point

What kind of man, Radan thought, *would try to turn his own friend to do his dirty work?* As he sat thinking about Hakim al-Azahir, he quickly knew exactly what kind of man that would be, shrugged his shoulders, and decided to continue working on other aspects of the upcoming action.

Radan shook his head slightly to turn to the present, and looked around his office to the two others who sat in his office discussing that same upcoming action.

"What does Samira say about the one in West Virginia?" he asked one of the men sitting in front of him to his left.

"She reported visiting the restaurant and speaking to Sammi and Hassan, telling them to speed up their work on Johnson. As she was returning to Washington, she also saw Johnson on the road at a restaurant at a truck stop."

"Did she get into a conversation with him" Radan asked.

"Yes, she did, and photos as well with her cell phone. She sent them to us," replied the man. "She took Said and his wife and children with her on the hope she would see Johnson as well. They did meet on the road and Said claimed to be Shia persecuted by the Christians in the same part of Lebanon we know Johnson's family came from. They had a long discussion. Samira sat off to the side from them where she took her pictures."

Then Radan turned to the man on his right and said, "Good, Do you think his meeting yet another family with his background could have effect?"

"It may," replied the man, "We continue to follow the plan. Is there anything else you need now?"

"No," Radan responded, "We have someone coming here to Atlanta who will join our group shortly. I will tell you when. Tell Samira to be prepared for them and find them a place to stay."

"I will Radan," answered the man.

"Good, then go and do what you need to do. I need to go downstairs and watch a new fighter." The three rose from their seats and walked through the front door of the office, closing the door behind them. All three went down the wide stairs to the first floor. Radan stayed to watch a new fighter in the ring and the other two left by a side door.

At the Alexander Hotel, Washington DC "Come on it," invited Jim Davis, as Tom O'Neal walked through the door. "Grab the chair over there, and let's talk about this evening."

"It was certainly interesting, Jim," responded O'Neal. "I must say though that I really don't know what to think at this point," he added, as he sat in the Victorian style chair in the corner of the room.

"It was interesting conversation, I agree," answered Davis, who took a corner of the bed as his perch. "Personally, I think this guy is clean. We spent over an hour together before you arrived. Our conversation was very forthcoming; he pointed out his days on the other side of the law, and his interest in getting his cooperative idea working. Sounds to me just like an honest farmer who wants to make good. What about you Tom? You have had more contact with him than me? Do we need to be chasing this guy?"

"Jim, I think the jury is still out on that, although my impressions of him are close to yours. If he were not involved with al-Azahir and his late friend Giddons, I would agree completely with you." O'Neal stood up and walked over toward the small refrigerator in the room. "Would you like something? I have virtually everything in here that is cold, and expensive. What is your pleasure?"

"Just a bottle of water Tom. That will be fine for me." responded Davis, who then added, "What is the plan for next steps then?"

"Well, I have him for the day, or at least part of it tomorrow as we go over the eaches for his project. I will take him to lunch and see what else comes up. Will you be available about the same time tomorrow?"

"Sure, I'm in town for at least a week. Let's meet here if you want, down in the bar?"

"Works for me Tom. You're welcome to stay and watch a ball game if you wish."

"No, I think it's time to get on the road to home for me. See you tomorrow then." O'Neal rose to leave and Jim Davis joined him at the door for a quick handshake, then O'Neal headed for the elevator.

Elias, West Virginia Sira sat in her room, restless and unable to sleep. She knew she was facing a great dilemma. On the one side, she was betrothed to Hassan; they had been for some years, and they expected to marry in the future, once they earned enough money to become self-sufficient. Sadly, that option was made worse by their decision to follow to Hakim al-Azahir and his terrorist groups.

Hassan and Sira, having met al-Azahir in Pakistan, while they were in school, became enamored with his views on violence as a means of bringing Jihad, and the return of the Muslim Caliphate. They went through training in Pakistan, the in Afghanistan, before Being sent to the United States. Sira was dedicated to her task, and to Hassan, but she was also afraid—that something would happen to them, and that they might not ever live a normal life under al-Qaeda. Hassan, on the other hand was more rabid, more prone to violence and rash acts, which, she feared, would eventually get them into trouble with the authorities, and defeat their purpose.

At the same time, the other side of her dilemma was becoming more important to her. She truly liked Will Johnson, and wanted nothing to happen to him. He had been good to her, as had Sammi, and she felt so comfortable and secure when she was on the farm working, and sometimes just sitting and listening to his future plans.

The difficulty for her was trying to have both. She either had to do what al-Azahir wanted, or she and Hassan could lose their lives, and Will Johnson's as well. There seemed to be no way out of her dilemma.

Another difficulty for her was the woman Sammi and Hassan described to her, who had visited the restaurant while she was at the farm working. It seemed they were describing her kinswoman Samira. They grew up in the same town; Samira was very strong willed, and most of all very dedicated to her cause. Sira needed to find out more about the plans, so she decided to call her on the cell phone Samira had given them, try to pry more information from her, and perhaps even get her to back off somewhat. She would do that tomorrow. Tonight, she would try to sleep.

From a Vantage Point

Chapter 33 The Net Widens

Alexander Hotel, Washington DC *Will Johnson woke from a deep sleep, perhaps the first good night's sleep he had in several weeks, and looked forward to his meetings. Whether it was the travel or something else, he did not have his usual round of nightmares; instead, his dreams were of some of the good times on the farm, including several where Sira played a large part. In one scene, Will was milking cows, and Sira tried to help, getting more milk on herself than in the dairy bucket, with both laughing and enjoying their time together.*

Looking at the clock by his bed, Will realized he had barely an hour before Tom O'Neal would pick him up outside the lobby, so he had to hurry. Rushing to get a quick shower, then dress, he was in the lobby with a bit of time to spare, so he entered the dining room, saw they offered a buffet, and found a table to eat quickly. He made it out the front door just as O'Neal arrived.

"Hey Will, got here just in time, I see," said O'Neal, rolling down his passenger side window.

"Sure did. Thanks for picking me up, Tom."

"No problem. Easier to get you there than to try to give you directions through the city early in the morning." Will climbed into the car and they were off toward their meeting at Main Agriculture off Pennsylvania Avenue at the Mall.

"Well, I hope you are in for a long day. We have a lot to discuss, and several meetings to attend to get this project of yours moving, Will," announced O'Neal.

"And this is probably the first of many," responded Will.

"It sure is,' retorted O'Neal. "It sure is." The drive down from the Alexander went well, and they were turning into Pennsylvania Avenue, and off toward Agriculture quickly. They went down an alley between buildings and O'Neal parked in a spot marked for the Agricultural Adjustment Service, took out a placard from his glove compartments, and put it on the window as well. "To make sure they don't ticket or tow," announced O'Neal, as he started to exit the car. Johnson followed, and they went toward a side door close to the car space.

O'Neal looked at his watch, saying, "We have a lot of time. Meeting does not start for twenty minutes. Do you want some coffee first?"

"Sure," answered Will, "I never turn down coffee in the morning." They headed toward a small coffee shop in the basement, which had two tables where they could sit for a few minutes.

Elias, West Virginia Sira woke early from her fretful sleep. She had tossed and turned most of the evening and into the night wondering what she would say to Samira when she called. Finally, she decided to simply ask about the plan, and see if she could get more information from her kinswoman. She was not sure of the response, but at least she could try.

Going down into Sammi's, she checked to be sure the men were in the kitchen cooking, and then went over to her purse and pulled out a cell phone along with a small slip of paper from her right pocket, and dialed the number on the sheet. She heard the ringing and then a voice came on the phone.

"Who is calling?"

"It is me Samira, your cousin Sira. I need to speak with you."

"You were told to call here only in a dire emergency. What is it that you want?" responded Samira.

"I am confused cousin. I do not know what we are supposed to do, or why we are doing it. How am I to convince this man to do what we wish if I do not know what that is?" asked Sira plaintively.

"It is not for you to know everything little one. It is only for you to obey. Do not call here again, unless it is necessary." Sira heard the click of the phone as Samira hung up, and she burst into tears as it happened.

"What am I to do now," she asked herself, "How am I to do this?" She hung up the phone, brushed her eyes, and walked toward the kitchen. Going through the swinging door, she could see Sammi and Hassan busy making biscuits and other things for the morning breakfast. Hassan saw her first, and walked over to her.

"What is the matter with you Sira? You look like you have been crying. Tell me what bothers you."

"Hassan, I am so confused. I do not know what to do."

"Come with me Sira. We will go into the restaurant to speak with each other." Hassan put his hand around her shoulders and led her back through the doors from the kitchen to a booth on the other side of the restaurant. They both sat on the same side of the booth.

"Now, tell me what is the matter," asked Hassan.

"How am I to bring this man over to us if we do not know why he is to turn, or what he is to do? How am I to convince him of something I do not know myself?" Hassan turned toward her and was about to begin to speak when he heard another voice.

"Yes, tell us both what is happening here," said Sammi, who had walked from the kitchen into the restaurant area. "Tell us what we are supposed to do."

Hassan was speechless. He did not really know he should or could say, so he decided to give both the true story of their task.

"Sammi, we both are part of a group working for a man named al-Azahir, Hakim al-Azahir, who is a very bad man. He and his friend Josh Giddons work for a very powerful lord in our country, who is trying to create large damage in the United States."

"Giddons," responded Sammi, "I know that name. He is the man who died in Atlanta, the friend of Mister Will. "

"That is true, Sammi," responded Hassan, "Mister Giddons is a friend, or was, of Mister Will. He was coming here to get him to work with them on a plan to do damage during the upcoming presidential inauguration in Washington. Now, he is dead, and it is up to us to convince Mister Will to join the cause."

"What is it he is to do?" asked Sammi.

"There are to be explosions along the parade route on Inauguration Day which will disrupt the ceremonies," Answered Hassan, "Mister Will is to do that from his hotel room along the Mall. He is to stay at the same hotel each time, and in the same room, so people will be used to his coming and going. He will be provided with the means for the attack. Then he is to go to Canada."

"That is an amazing tale, Hassan. How did you expect to do that?" asked Sammi. "What did you get us into here?" he continued.

Sammi looked over to Sira. "Are you a part of this as well? Was it you who was to convince Mister Will to do this?"

"Yes," said Sira quietly, as a low sob rose in her voice. "I was brought here to do it, although I did not know all the details as Hassan has said."

Sammi rose from the table, turned to go toward the kitchen, and stopped and turned back. "Say nothing about this. We will speak more of it later. Right now, we must get breakfast ready. Both of you to the kitchen."

DHS, Washington DC. *The communications map on the large screen lit up as the call from a burner phone in Elias, West Virginia to Atlanta, Georgia went through. The staff recognized that its origination was in Elias, as they back-traced the call. Perhaps this finally gave them the link they needed to figure out who and what was to happen.*

It took only minutes to zero in on the location called, then retrieve the message text. The Atlanta phone was the same one receiving messages off-line from the Horizon servers. They could not tie the call directly to Sammi's Restaurant. That would come later, they thought. For now, they would continue to monitor everything they could coming out of Elias.

One of the staff members literally ran down the corridor to Alice Sawyer's office when they linked the call, completely forgetting she had a direct line to their office. In this case, it did not matter—they wanted her to enjoy their search and discovery as quickly as possible.

Alice shared their excitement when the analyst ran into her office, disrupting her meeting, and shouting out the news. These were her people, and she appreciated their excitement.

From a Vantage Point

Alice quietly dismissed her meeting, apologizing for her staff's excitement, and walked backed down to the communications area to see what they had discovered.

Department of Agriculture, Washington DC Tom O'Neal and Will Johnson entered the building, going toward a bank of elevators which would take them to the third floor and a conference room. As they entered, Will realized there were several others there already.

"Looks like the house is full, Tom" said Johnson, as he looked for a seat with his name on it around a large table. He found it on the other side of the room, with Tom O'Neal sitting next to him. On the table, in front of his seat, were several large binders standing on their edges. As Will looked quickly at the titles, he realized they were rules and regulations for the program, along with a binder containing his original proposal to Agriculture.

"Well, shall we begin?" asked the man sitting about center table to the right of Johnson, "For your benefit, Mister Johnson, I am Jack Tapscott, director of the Community Projects Office, which will be setting your cooperative up as a partner in this food for the community program. Welcome. For the rest of you, this is Mister Will Johnson, Director of the Elias Cooperative, a community organization in West Virginia that provides produce to surrounding areas, and petitioned to become a part of our program. That petition was approved two weeks ago, and this is the first meeting to determine how they will fit among the rest of the ongoing projects."

"Before we get into the rather dull business of discussing lettuce and beets, Mister Johnson, do you have a few words to say to the team?" continued Tapscott.

"Thanks Mister Tapscott. I am happy to be here today to represent the farmers and merchants in the Elias, West Virginia area, and we look forward to working with you all in the future. We grow a lot of produce, and produce large amounts of other goods, such as furniture, and preserved goods that we look forward to having others come to know as quality purchases. We appreciate the faith you have in us thus far, and we look forward as well to convincing you that your faith is returned by us in cooperative efforts. Thanks for the invitation to be here today."

"All right then, let's get down to business," responded Tapscott. For the next three hours, the group at the table discussed the items Elias Cooperative could provide, the delivery rates, and expected first deliveries. As they made changes, Will noted them in the binder he picked up in front of his place at the table, so that his delivery schedule in the proposal could be updated.

The group broke for a short time for lunch, which the Agency had brought in from a caterer, and then worked hard through the afternoon, stopping just before

From a Vantage Point

four PM, leaving Will with several pages of changes and updates he would need to make before his cooperative could begin providing their produce and goods.

As the meeting broke up, both Johnson and O'Neal went toward the door after shaking hands with Jack Tapscott then headed for O'Neal's car.

"Quite a day, Tom," said Will as they left the building for the small parking lot where O'Neal's car was parked.

"Sure was," responded O'Neal, "You have a lot to do before you are open for business. Are you going to be able to get all this done, and be ready for late Fall?"

"Sure Tom," answered Will, "Our first orders through the Winter are milk, cheese, and eggs, primarily, along with some Christmas trees and wreath materials. We can do all that, and still be planning for the broader list in the Spring. This is a great opportunity for our people, and we will make it work."

"I thought you would, Will. My suggestion is that we meet every week to ten days for the next couple of months, to assess the timelines you set. Think about perhaps a day and a half each week to begin with, and then we can stretch it out perhaps later. Same days each time. You might try to work something out with the Alexander and see if they have one of those low rates they give to the sales people and others who come to town frequently."

"That's a good idea, Tom," answered Will, "I will do that when I get back. Let's say Tuesday afternoon and Wednesday morning every two weeks. Would that work for you?"

"Sure Will, that will work just fine. That way we can be consistent."

"Great," responded Will, "Want to join me for dinner?"

"Just might do that," answered O'Neal, "It sure beats driving back out into the country after a long day. Let's head for the Alexander, shall we?"

The men reached the car, entered, and O'Neal swung out of the exit to the lot, waving his credentials, and they were quickly out on 14th Street, headed uptown toward the Alexander.

Tom and Will went back to the Alexander and sat in the bar to have dinner, discussing the events of the day and the promise of the newly-expanded cooperative. Over that time, they discussed a wide range of topics as well, including the efforts the Johnson family made to come to America and settle on their farm, Will's desertion from the Army, and his later return from Europe to face the Army. As they sat, Tom became even more convinced that Will Johnson was not a terrorist.

Finally, as the time neared nine o'clock, Tom looked at his watch and announced it was time to go home. When the bill came, he insisted on paying for the evening, and told Will he looked forward to seeing him at their next meeting. That reminded Will that he needed to discuss his frequent trips with the front desk; something he did that evening before going up to his room. The hotel clerk *assured him that the room was blocked for him every other week on the same days, and to please call if he would not be coming.*

Sammi's Restaurant, Elias, West Virginia Sammi sat in his chair amazed. He was also part of Hakim al-Azahir's network, and his job was to become Will Johnson's friend. That job he had done well, but he never knew that there was another use Hakim had decided on for Johnson. For some reason, he thought he was to protect Hakim's friend, but now knew he was to coerce Will into committing a crime.

Listening to the two others, he realized how deeply involved they all were, remembering the earlier visit of the man as well whose voice he knew but had never met, the one who encouraged him to take in Hassan and Sira. These events, and others, now came into better focus; Sammi was being used like the others, and feared for all four of them, including his friend Will.

"What would you have me do, Hassan?" asked Sammi, looking sadly toward his cook.

"We must convince Mister Will to do what they want, Sammi, for his sake, his life, and our own as well," Hassan responded, "They are very strong and we are weak. They can kill us at will."

"No, we should go to Mister Will and to the authorities for help," responded Sammi.

"We cannot do that, Sammi," interjected Sira, "They have people everywhere. They will find out, and they will kill us." She burst out crying as the last of her words came out, and she buried her face in her hands.

"Sira is right, Sammi," added Hassan. "They know everything, and they will come for us. We have no choice but to do what they say." Hassan looked directly into Sammi's eyes, and both men knew he was right.

"All right. What do wish of me then?" asked Sammi.

"Just keep doing what you are doing. Be his friend, and act no differently. Sira and I will deal with bringing him around to what they want," was Hassan's response.

"Sira, we have only little more than four months until the time," continued Hassan, "You will need to get closer to Mister Will, and encourage him even more. Can you do that?"

"I am not sure, but I will try," came the response, through her continuing sobs. As she answered his question, Sira rose and left the kitchen, going out into the restaurant. Sammi looked through the door and saw her starting to wipe tables and prepare for lunch. Shrugging his shoulders, he turned from Hassan and went through the swinging doors to help Sira with the lunch preparations.

Sammi walked around the restaurant straightening chairs, and adjusting condiment items on the tables, working around Sira for several minutes. Finally, they reached the same table.

"Sira, come, sit down for a moment," he said as he waved her toward a seat at the table.

"You have begun to feel something for Mister Will, haven't you?" Sammi asked, as he looked at the young woman sitting at the table with reddened eyes, now looking down at the table.

The expression on Sira's face changed dramatically as Sammi spoke to her. He could tell that what he said was true, but waited for her to say the same.

"I do feel for him," she answered quietly, still with her eyes down. "What can I do? He is a good man. He deserves better than this from his so-called friends. He is a simple man, with a big heart. He does not deserve what they want him to do."

"When Hassan and I came here, we were in love. We wanted to get away from these things and eventually marry. Now, I see that his own concern is for himself. He is weak and cowardly, not strong like Mister Will. What will I do Sammi? I cannot see him hurt."

"We will find a way to keep him safe," Sammi responded, taking her hands in his on the table as she held her rage, "We will not let them do this to him if we can stop it. Now, dry your eyes and we will get ready to open our doors. We will talk again, but you must let me know if you hear more from Hassan. Will you do that?"

"Yes, I will," Sira whimpered in response. Then, she took a small tissue from the rack on the table, and started to wipe her eyes. "Oh, Sammi, what did I get myself into?"

"Nothing that cannot be fixed, Sira. We will fix it together," Sammi answered, knowing in his own heart that he also had just broken with al-Azahir and his group. His own life would be in danger if he tried to stop them.

Sammi stood up, walked around the table, and patted Sira lightly, then kissed her on top of the head. As he moved over to the register, making sure everything was ready for the lunch customers. He knew his life had changed, but he felt better about himself than he had in a long time.

DHS Washington DC Six people sat around the table in Alice Sawyer's office, all of them very pensive. Two were from communications; one from the Counsel's office, together with Tom O'Neal and Jim Davis.

"Ok, so we have a phone call from Elias, an unknown phone, and unknown location, and only a guess really that it is actually from anywhere in Elias. Am I correct here?" asked Alice Sawyer.

"Well, yes and no," responded one of the communications people, "Actually, we do know that the call bounced off a tower just outside Elias, on its way to Atlanta. Aside from some of the local farmers, most of whom have satellite phone service, the limits of that tower really mean the call probably came from Elias. Locating the actual phone will mean getting the records of the transmits sent through the tower. We have already checked for the number in our listings and we can say it is not an Elias exchange number, nor is it a number from a cell sold in the local area. Might want to call it a burner phone, if you wish."

"What I wish," retorted Alice, clearly irritated, "Is that we find out who made the call. If we need to get the tower records, go get them."

"I'm afraid that is not as easy as you might make it Ms. Sawyer," responded the person from the Counsel's Office. "Without a search warrant we won't get the records. Since these calls originated within the US to another US location, we need a search warrant before we can do anything further, like a wiretap when and if we get the location. I can start that process, but we will need specifics to convince a judge we have some level of probable cause for the search."

Alice looked out toward the rest of the attendees and said, "All right then, make it happen. I want the warrant issued, and the data secured so we can move on this. It seems like every time we think we know what direction we are going in and who the bad guys are the situation changes. Tom, your guy could not have been involved, because he was in DC, but who else could be playing here? We need to find out, and quickly."

"Alice, I will be meeting with Johnson every week for the foreseeable future to work out his cooperative effort. I can keep him under control, and get into his skin over time, but I still think he is not involved, at least directly. What I worry about is that there are people in the background who want to manipulate him, and we need to find out who they are."

"Good point, Tom," said Alice. "How do we get to specifics folks?"

The room stayed silent until one of the communications people spoke up.

"Ms. Sawyer, we could send someone out to do a survey on the phone capabilities in the immediate area. We might just get them to give us information if we said we were reviewing the capabilities for the cooperative to respond quickly to changes in demand. Doing a review might give us numbers and locations of phones, but it would have to go through Agriculture to be authentic."

"Tom," asked Alice," can that be done?"

"I will work the issue following the meeting Alice. I do not see why not," responded O'Neal. "Agriculture has been very responsive. They should go along with a local survey rather than something through the mail. Eye contact information seems to be better for what we need. I will need some people to do that, though."

"I will get four or five agents experienced in this kind of data collection Tom. You just get the approval for it. Let me know if I need to get involved."

"Sure will Alice. This should not be a problem, though," answered O'Neal. "We can start in the next day or two. I can notify Johnson they will be coming to do the survey. That will give us a level of authenticity."

"Good Tom," said Alice, "Go do it."

"Anything else?" Alice continued. Hearing nothing, she waved them off and the group quickly left, leaving only O'Neal and Jim Davis.

"So, give me your honest opinion guys," asked Alice. "What do we have here?" Davis spoke first.

"Alice, I am probably the most distant to the situation among those involved. I think you have someone in Will Johnson who never intended to get involved with these people, but did, and not from a terrorist perspective. He thinks they are friends. Not a good situation to be in these days, but I simply do not think he is a terrorist."

"I have to agree with Jim Alice. Everything I see does fails to shout out terrorist, or even someone who has considered it, at least lately. Johnson ran with these guys when they were all deserters and had wide eyes for adventure. He gave that up long ago, as far as I can see. He bears watching, but I do not think he is a terrorist," added O'Neal.

"OK," responded Alice, "What if we have a person in unwitting training here? We have seen that before in several instances, in the US and Europe, where someone perfectly innocent eventually gets turned. What if we have this going on here? What do we do about it? How do we find his trainers? Most importantly, how do we find out what is planned for him to execute when he does turn, if he does?"

"I want the three of us to get together tomorrow morning. Just us and no one else. I want to go over every inch of what we know, every piece of information, every trip, every possible scenario. I want to know what we can expect: Let's keep working, and figure out what is really going on here." Both men nodded their agreement.

"Alice, you might need to talk to the Sky Marshal Service. I have flights starting tomorrow that won't work into your schedule."

"Consider that done Jim. You stay here and work with us on this."

"Thanks. See you tomorrow." Davis rose and left the room, leaving only O'Neal.

"Tom, this is one of the craziest and most exasperating cases I have worked in all my years in intel and now in Homeland Security," said Alice, looking at her friend.

"I understand Alice," responded O'Neal, "There are no common points, no common denominators on which to make even some possible determinations. It

From a Vantage Point

is like working on a diagram in quicksand. We will get through it, though. My feeling is that we are just not looking in the rights places for the right people."

"Probably that is the case Tom," Alice responded, "But tomorrow that all changes. We need a path and enough understanding to fix this. See you tomorrow morning."

"Right," responded O'Neal as he stood and left the room, leaving Alice the only person at the table. She banged her hand on the table top then left herself, returning to her office as she had before with not enough answers to make any real decisions.

Tampa-St. Petersburg International Airport, Florida "British Airways flight 2167 arriving at Gate 92," blared the loudspeaker in the operations area in Airside F.

"All right people," said a supervisor, "It's time to play dodgem cars. Let's get ready to receive 2167. Send out four five baggage trams, and have two trollies ready for the packed shipping. This thing is in from London, if my mind is still working. It will need complete resupply and fuel. Let's get to it."

As with most airports, at least the larger ones, crews are assigned to specific flights to make sure that everything in loading, unloading, and resupply are done according to fixed procedures. That way nothing is forgotten that needs to be done. In this case, the crew numbered about 15, aside from the fuel drivers and catering staff. As soon as the supervisor said go, the crew moved into position near the terminal, called 'Airside F' at Tampa International, and moved toward their vehicles and wait for the arrival and docking of the flight. As soon as the engines were shut down, the crew moved into action, opening the stowage areas, and quickly starting to offload the luggage and other loose cargo; the pre-crated cargo would wait until everything else had been off-loaded.

Usually, the pre-packaged cargo was already marked for other locations. Today, there were five of these large aluminum crates, and all were moving from Tampa to Atlanta on a follow-on flight. The crew will off-load them and move them over to the gate where they are re-loaded on another plane and be on their way to that destination, often in hours.

Aboard the aircraft, the crew had prepared for arrival at Tampa and, since they were coming in from London, the passengers had been provided US Customs Declarations and had the opportunity to fill them out before deplaning and moving toward the Customs Inspection Area.

"Ladies and Gentlemen, welcome to Tampa International Airport. We will be docking at Gate 92 today in the International Terminal. You will be able to retrieve your luggage and proceed to the Customs Area within the Terminal. Thanks for flying British Airways with us today. The flight crew and myself all hope you enjoyed your flight, and will select British Airways again soon for your next

From a Vantage Point

journey," said the Captain, and they began to taxi toward Gate 92, and their final stop for the day.

"Ma'am, how long is the Customs check if you have nothing to declare?" asked the passenger in seat 26E as one of the flight attendants walked by, picking up loose trash and empty coffee and juice cups.

"Perhaps 30 minutes' sir," responded the flight attendant, "But that really depends on the volume they have coming in. There are four flights from London alone during this time of the day, so it may take a while."

"Thanks, I appreciate that," the man retorted, sitting back in his seat and returning to the book he had been reading. The attendant continued down the aisle toward the galley.

It took nearly fifteen minutes for the plane to dock at Gate 92 before the passengers began to disembark. Airline personnel were at the jet way and the corridor linking the gate to the Terminal, ushering the passengers toward the Customs area, where they could pick up their baggage and proceed through the Customs inspection process. That went surprisingly fast, with most of the passengers getting through in less than forty-five minutes. Once through the line, they could then proceed toward the exits and transportation to take them to their destination in Tampa.

Outside the secure area, a man waited, holding a sign saying simply, "Mr. John Day". He wore a dark suit, such as might be worn by a limo driver, and he waited near a pillar, occasionally leaning on it for support. He stood straight as the crowd began to emerge from the door leading to Customs, and within a couple of minutes, a man approached him.

"I assume you are here for me?" asked the passenger.

"If you are Mister Day, yes sir, I am here for you."

"I am," Day responded.

"Please come with me sir. My vehicle is waiting at the curb."

Day followed the man with the sign, and, as they exited the terminal, Day could see a large van with a driver waiting. On the side of the van, a sign on the door stated, "Privacy LTD." As he approached, the side door opened, the man with the sign, told him to enter and sit in the center section. Day climbed into the van, the driver threw the sign in the trash can nearby, and entered the passenger seat on the right. The door closed quickly and the van drove away from the terminal, toward the Airport exit road and downtown Tampa.

Inside the security area, one of the security monitors was watching the scene as Day left Customs, found the man with the sign, and started to leave the terminal. For some unknown reason, he pushed a button to get a photo of the man and the driver, and then moved on to other screens. Only later in the day, looking over the several photos he had taken did the security monitor remember a notice some weeks earlier from Homeland Security asking about a man

From a Vantage Point

arriving at an unknown airport; an American who would look like a businessman. The monitor had no idea why he might have remembered that particular notice, but he had, and went looking for it.

When he found the notice, and comparted it to the notice, he took both to his supervisor.

"Ken, take a look at this pic I took of a guy coming in earlier today. He was picked up by a man with a van and it just happened to hit me to push the button. Then, I remembered a notice from DHS," he said, as he handed the photo and the notice to his boss. "Look at these two photos. They could be twins."

"Sure could," answered his supervisor, "Let's send them on to TSA and let them sort it out. Be prepared for questions over the next couple of days."

Sammi's Restaurant, Elias, West Virginia Will Johnson walked into the restaurant and sat down as if he had not been gone for a couple of days. On the way to his usual seat, he picked up a menu and, as Sammi walked out of the kitchen he greeted his friend in his also usual cheery way.

"Sammi, how about some lunch for a hungry man?" asked Will.

"Of course, Mister Will. Welcome back. How did your meetings go? Is everything on track? What do we need to do next?" Sammi spouted out in quick succession, not giving Will a chance to answer.

"Whoa, Sammi," responded Will, "One question at a time. Yes, the meeting went well. Tom O'Neal has been great, and we are on track. I expect several more meetings over the next several weeks, but we are going to need to be ready to start providing fall and winter produce, and then go great guns in the spring. It was a great meeting, but right now I want to get some lunch."

"Of course, Mister Will. Right away. What would you like? Some coffee first?"

"Yes, coffee would be great." Sammi went over to the side condiment area to bring the coffee urn. In the meanwhile, Sira heard Will's voice, and ran out of the kitchen, saw him, and ran over to sit at his table.

"Mister Will, I have missed you. I kept your house very clean, but I am glad you are back."

"I am too Sira. I missed you all, even if it was for just a couple of days."

Sira pushed over at the table as Sammi returned, filled Will's coffee cup, and then sat down himself. Both were obviously happy about his return, and they wanted to hear everything.

Transportation Security Agency, Tampa International Airport *The Transportation Security Agency (TSA) has the overarching responsibility for security and safety at the Nation's airports. In most cases, when something out of the ordinary happens, such as a passenger on the no-fly list, or someone acting suspiciously, the TSA is immediately notified, and the incident is* *investigated, the data added to their database, and contributes to an overall profile of the safety and security of that location.*

"Hey boss, something weird here," said Dick Usher, a DHS communications tech at the Tampa-St. Petersburg DHS Office, as he walked into his boss's office. "We have a photo from the TSA security office showing a guy who died in Atlanta nearly a month ago."

"That's interesting. Let me see what you think you have," came the response. Usher turned the photo over to him, along with a copy of a circular DHS distributed nearly sixty days ago, asking offices to be looking for a guy named Josh Giddons. "So, what am I seeing, and what is important here?" he asked.

"This guy Giddons died on a flight coming into Atlanta last month. Positive ID. This guy could be his twin brother. He came in earlier, was met by a limo driver, driven off in a van from curbside. The van turned out to be a rental."

"Ok, so I have a guy who is dead that has a twin brother," responded the supervisor. "What am I supposed to do with it?"

"Look closely boss. This guy looks exactly like Giddons, mole on his neck and all. A duplicate."

"All right. Get the tapes and let's look at it. I think there is nothing here but a doppelganger, but we'll look at it."

"Right boss," said Usher, as he left the office to make the call to get the tapes.

Tampa, Florida The van with John Day entered the downtown area and headed for the Sunrise Inn, a small motel nearby. There, the driver pulled into the parking lot, near the end of the building and stopped.

"Here we are," said the man who held the sign at the airport, "This is where we will stay for the next couple of days. Then, we leave for Atlanta." The man opened the door and stood out on the side of the vehicle, then opened the side door for his passenger to leave the van.

"Any idea why we are staying here, asked Mister Day?"

"The boss told us to, that's why," came the answer. One of the men, the driver, took the bags from the back of the van and they started toward Room 104. "Inside," said the driver as he unlocked the room. "This is now home, at least for a few days."

Sammi's Restaurant, Elias, West Virginia "So tell me, Mister Will," asked Sammi, "What happens next?" Sammi had a smile on his face for the first time in two days, and it was clear that he was happy that Will had returned.

"Well, the committee approved everything we suggested. They are anxious for our produce and other products, and the pricing scheme is also approved.

From a Vantage Point

They will help us enter other farmer markets, and they will also buy some part of our output for their assistance programs. Virtually everything we produce each season can be sold through the agreement. There is still a lot to work out, and I will need to make several frequent trips back to Washington to iron out details, but we have a deal with them."

"We owe a lot," Will continued, "to our friend Tom O'Neal who really shepherded this through for us. He has been so amazing, and made things seem simple. Once everything is done, we need to get him out here, and have a party in his honor. Right now, though I am incredibly hungry for some of your food Sammi. I missed it. The hotel food is nothing close."

"Coming right up, Mister Will," answered Sammi, standing up to go to the kitchen.

Sira stopped him, saying, "I will go Mister Sammi. You stay and talk to your friend." Sira pushed over from her seat to the aisle and stood, turning toward the kitchen where hopefully Will's food was ready.

"What did he say?" asked Hassan as Sira entered the kitchen. "Tell me all."

"He said he had a good trip, the cooperative was approved, and that he will be going back to Washington to finalize the details," Sira responded, starting to pick up the food Hassan had prepared to take it out to the restaurant.

"Good. Humor him, and get on his side. We want him to go to Washington so that everything falls into place."

"I know that Hassan," answered Sira sarcastically, "You leave him to me. I will make sure everything happens that needs to happen." She scowled again at Hassan as she left with Will's food.

"Here you are, Mister Will," beamed Sira as she put down her tray on the next table, and started to pick up the food plates. "Just like you like your lunch. I will bet it is better than the hotel food you had. Everything is better here," she continued, as she placed everything in front of him, then pulled up a chair and started to sit down at the end of the table.

"Sira, you have customers," admonished Sammi, as several people had come in to the restaurant that she had not noticed. Turning around, Sira picked up the tray, and leaned it by the wall near the kitchen, then walked over to the customers, took out her pad and pencil and, saying hello, started to take their orders.

Johnson looked at all the food and stopped momentarily trying to decide what to eat first. Sammi had ordered country ham, grilled potatoes, cole slaw and rolls. He buttered a roll, and then started to eat the ham.

"Sammi, I have missed the food," as Sira said. "There is nothing like your cooking."

"Thank you Mister Will," Sammi responded, "We missed you as well. You are my best customer, and the one who gives me the best compliments, but it is Hassan who cooked your meal."

"How is Hassan?" Will asked.

"He is fine. He stays busy and people come in just for his food. Some come two times a day now. It is amazing. The numbers are going up and we are making a profit. I am glad."

"I am glad as well my friend," responded Will, "You have worked hard, putting up Hassan and Sira even when the volume was down, and now that things are better they seem happy as well."

Will continued to eat and in between bites brought Sammi up-to-date on the agreements. Hopefully, after their next meeting in Washington, it will be time to have another meeting of the whole cooperative group. There will be enough information then, Will thought. He and Sammi agreed they would bring together the smaller group on the weekend to hear Will's report on his progress. For now, lunch was the most important topic.

Sira looked through the window in the door to the kitchen, watching Will and Sammi speaking while waiting for the food for her customers. Several times Hassan tried to speak with her, but she seemingly paid no attention to him. She concentrated instead at the man at the table eating lunch that she was quickly falling in love with, knowing that could be trouble for both on them.

Sunrise Inn, Tampa Florida The three men sat watching television in their small, cramped room. One periodically rose, went to the side of the closed drapes to look outside, as if waiting for someone, and then sat back down at the edge of the bed and resumed watching whatever was on the TV. The other two occasionally had small conversations about the TV show, but there was little real interaction between them. Finally, Mister Day decided to break the ice.

"Any idea how long this foolishness will last?" he asked.

"Until the boss tells us to do something else," came the reply.

"Just who is this BOSS?" asked Day.

"You do not need to know, Mister Day. You only need to do as you are told, until we can get you off to Atlanta. That will happen when the boss says so, so watch your TV and be quiet," said the man who had picked him up at the airport. Day resumed watching television.

"How about I go get some food?" asked the driver.

"Good idea," responded Day, "I am famished. How about some burgers and fries?"

"No one goes anywhere until the boss says so," came the response again. "We stay here until he calls." They all went back to their television show.

From a Vantage Point

Ten minutes later, there was a knock on the door. The driver rose and looked through the keyhole. "It's the boss," he announced, turning the lock to open the door.

A tall man walked into the room. He was lanky, wore a brightly colored Florida shirt and a Panama hat. In his hand, he carried a small sack.

"Gentlemen, here is lunch," he announced. "Enjoy." The sack contained six hamburgers, and several orders of French fries, along with napkins and condiments. He tossed the bag on the bed, and sat in a chair to the side of the room. The driver grabbed the bag and started passing out the burgers. They were quickly gone, along with the fries. The bag went in the trash with the other refuse and wrappers.

'This is the plan gentlemen," said the boss. "You are all going to Atlanta today. I want you on the road within the hour. I need you there by tomorrow evening. That means you do not have to rush, but you do need to move along. When you are about 50 miles from Atlanta, you will call me on this cellphone." He handed a cell phone to the driver.

"This number is registered to none of us so it will be safe to use," he continued, "I will give you an address to deliver Mister Day, and then you will return. You will use that phone only once, and then destroy it. Do not just throw it in a trash can, break it up or smash it. Do you understand?"

"Yes," responded the driver, "I understand. It will be done as you ask."

"Good, now finish your meal, and then get on the road. The bill here is taken care of. You do not need to check out. Goodbye Mister Day. Have a good trip"

"But sir," started Day. He was cut off quickly.

"No questions, because you will get no answers. You are to do as I said. Go to Atlanta. All will become clear there."

"Yes sir," responded Day, somewhat embarrassed.

The boss rose from the bed and walked toward the door, opening it and closing it as he left. He said nothing further, not even goodbye to his men.

Kabul, Afghanistan Abadi looked over at his leader Hakim al-Azahir, who seemed engrossed in a map of the United States laid out before him on a table.

"Your mind and heart seem to be so occupied these days my friend Hakim. Is there something I can do for you?"

"No Abadi," responded Hakim, as he looked toward his friend. "Everything is coming together as it was planned. In a short while, the Americans will understand that Islam is still strong and that Jihad is to be feared just as it was under our beloved bin-Laden, may All'ah protect his soul. We will strike a blow they will not soon forget."

"He continues to be great in the eyes of the prophet, as you carry out his works, Hakim, The Almighty One is protecting his soul through you."

390

From a Vantage Point

"You can do one thing for me Abadi. Go and see Pentopolos. Get the plans I gave him for the boxes he created, and bring them here."

"As you wish Hakim. I will go right now." Abadi walked from the side of the room to the doorway and quickly left through a rear entrance where his car was parked. Driving out into the main streets, he arrived at Pentapolos's workshop in a bit more than ten minutes. He parked on the side of the building and went quickly inside, where Pentopolos was at his desk in the warehouse.

"What brings you here Abadi?" asked the businessman and terrorist supplier.

"Hakim sent me to collect the drawings he gave you on some boxes you prepared for him. I am to bring them back to him."

"No problem," responded Pentopolos, "They are right here in my cabinet. He walked over to a tall wooden cabinet, lifted the glass door, and started to retrieve the plans. Then he stopped.

"Someone has been in here," shouted Pentopolos. "Only I have been working with the plans, and placed them here. Someone unrolled them, and then rerolled them in a different way. Someone has seen these."

"Hakim will not be pleased," responded Abadi, "Give them to me so that I can return them." Pentopolos did so quickly, as if they were danger. "I will tell Hakim what you have said. He will decide what to do," added Abadi, as he strode through the door to the warehouse back to his car. He could see Pentopolos pacing around the room as he left.

Hakim had returned to his map after Abadi left. He thought about the plan he created and how it would work. The boxes built in Sudan and shipped to Pentopolos in Kabul had been completed here, and refitted to take additional equipment which Pentopolos fabricated, then shipped through a circuitous route through Europe and on to the US. Their ultimate destination was Atlanta, Georgia. They would arrive in plenty of time to be tested prior to their use.

Picking up a satellite phone, Hakim dialed a number and waited for a response.

"Yes, how can I help you?" came the response.

"It is I. Is all ready?"

"Yes sir. The boxes have arrived and additional fittings are being made. The men have arrived from Tampa and we will be ready."

"Good," responded Hakim, hanging up the call. Now, he would wait patiently for Abadi to return, which took only a very short time.

Abadi rushed into Hakim's office, seeming out of breath.

"What is it Abadi? Has something happened to you?"

"Not to me my friend, to Pentopolos," he responded.

"What happened to Pentopolos? I see you have the plans, what has happened?"

"Pentopolos says that these plans were seen by others, and then replaced in his cabinet. He is sure of it." Abadi handed the plans to Hakim.

"All the drawings are here, Abadi. Someone must have seen them and then replaced them. Is Pentopolos absolutely sure they were handled by others?"

"Yes, he is. They were handled by his men to make the fabrications, but then he placed them in the cabinet, which he unlocked in front of me. He says they had been unrolled, and then rerolled differently from what he had done."

"Calm down Abadi, everything is fine. If someone looked at them, they would see plans for boxes and inserts; nothing else. All is fine," said Hakim, trying to calm down his friend and associate. In his own mind though, Hakim was worried. It would not be difficulty to figure out what the designs might be used for, and he had taken precautions to prevent just such an occurrence. Now, Pentopolos had made a critical error.

"Abadi, close up here and we will go to have lunch," offered Hakim.

"If you wish," came the response. Abadi locked the cabinets, and secured the windows, checking everything himself.

"We are ready Hakim."

"Good, then go to the car. I want to wash my hands first and then will be out to go with you."

Abadi left and Hakim started to walk toward the small toilet room they had, stopping to take out his own cell and say a few words into it, before going to wash his hands. In a few minutes, they were on their way to the center of town to have lunch.

Three days later, a body washed up on the shore of an inlet to the Kabul River. The body was unrecognizable, and had obviously been brutalized, the throat cut, and the eyes crushed. Dental records later identified the body as that of Pentopolos, who had been reported missing by his wife, not having been home nor arrived at his warehouse for three days after the visit of Abadi.

TSA, Tampa International Airport As the screen lit up in the conference room, the videotape began to run showing the arrival of The British Airways flight from, London. Three different views came on the screen; first, a short view from a camera in the jet way which panned the departing passengers; the second in the arrival terminal near Customs where the passengers picked up their luggage and started to move toward the waiting lines at Customs; and a third view showing passengers leaving customs and heading for the main terminal and the transportation area. The two men saw the departing passenger identified by the TSA security officer, and they both agreed that it looked very close to the photo they had on the late Josh Giddons.

"Let's access the Customs data and get the passport information on this guy," said one of the men to the other.

From a Vantage Point

"No problem," replied the other man, as he typed a few codes into his computer and found the passport and visa records for the passenger.

"This guy's name is Anderson, Joseph Anderson," announced the man looking at the screen. "He departed from Cairo two days ago, on a flight through Rome and London, then on to The U. S. Tampa is shown as his final destination. The address we have for him is 1610 Ivanhoe Avenue. That's over on the west side."

"Ok," responded the person who was evidently in change, "Let's get a field team out there and find out what we can."

"Will do, the other agent answered, "typing a few lines into his computer screen. "On the way shortly, boos."

"Great, now what else do we know about this guy? Reason for coming to the US? Prior visits? Citizenship? What do we know?"

"Not much really, was the response from the agent at the screen. If the information here is to be believed, the guy has never traveled before, is a British citizen, and completely unknown to anyone other than our own Customs today."

"All right, as a starting point, let's assume this information is a fraud and we have a person arriving who might not need to be here. If that might be the case, why is he here, and how is he involved in something? We need to set someone up the chain involved here. Who signed the poster on Giddons?"

"Alice Sawyer in DC at DHS Headquarters," came the reply.

"Really. Alice only does high-level stuff. Let me get her on the phone and let's see what she may know." The agent opened a small book on his desk, looked over several pages, and then picked up the phone and dialed a number. It rang several times before it was answered.

"Alice Sawyer, how can I help you?"

"Ms. Sawyer, this is Al Crandall at TSA, Tampa. We have a situation here I need to discuss with you. Have a minute?"

"Sure Al, what can I help you with?" Alice answered.

"I am sending you three stills of a passenger who arrived early this morning from London on a British Air flight. You should have them in your inbox in a second or two."

"Got them now. Opening the file," said Alice, then added 'Oh my God. Al, stay on the line will you. I want two of my people to come into the conversation."

"Yes, Ma'am, I sure will." Crandall heard her yelling to someone to bring in two others whose names he could not hear. As each entered the room and looked at the screen on Sawyer's desk, they all said about the same thing.

"Al, you still with me?" asked Alice.

"Sure am, Ma'am," he responded, "What do you think I have here?"

"Well, first of all, I think you already know that this person is a doppelganger for a man we know is dead in Atlanta."

"Sure do, but this is too close to be coincidence, isn't it?" Crandall replied.

"It sure is," Alice agreed, "Where is this man now?"

"He was picked up by a van after he cleared Customs, and was driven off. We have an address for him, but frankly I do not expect him to be there. I have a team out to check."

"Good work. I don't expect him to be there either, but we do need to confirm what we can. Send me what you have on this guy. Better yet, I will have one of my people in Tampa connect with you within the hour. We need to figure out where this guy is, and quickly."

"Thanks Ms. Sawyer. We will wait for your guy to make contact, and collect up what we have on him."

"Actually, thank you Al. You may have given us a real break on a major case here. Let me get with my staff and we will get back to you to complete the loop. Thanks again," said Alice, as she ended the call.

The TSA team went to the listed location and found only an old abandoned school. There was no one on the property, not even a watchman, just a sign with the number of the realty company. The team leader called back to Crandall, and they returned to the station. With their report, Crandall provided everything they had to the DHS agent who arrived at his office, took what they had and then left. The TSA people went back to their normal duties.

The DHS agent sent everything he received to Washington on a flight that left an hour later. Within four hours, the materials, including the custom declaration for 'Mister Day' were being examined by the lab. The person was not Josh Giddons, but he did turn out to be a minor criminal named Walter Burns, who had dropped off the radar some months earlier with Scotland Yard and Interpol looking for him, in connection with a jewelry heist in London. He had escaped the country just before detectives raided his flat in Huston, was seen for a short time in Cairo, and then dropped off the map. Now they knew he was in the US. The question was why, and how did he become a duplicate of Josh Giddons?

CIA Station, Khartoum, Sudan The secure phone on Jeff Namers desk rang twice before he picked it up.

"Namers," he said into the headpiece.

"Jeff, this is Alice," came the reply. "We had something amazing occur yesterday in Tampa Florida at the Airport. A passenger arrived on a flight from London with the name John Day."

"Really," responded Namers, "Am I supposed to know that name Alice?"

"No, but you might know the name Walter Burns," she said.

"Now that name I do know. Virtually every police and investigate agency has been looking for him for some time on an Interpol warrant. Where is he?"

"Jeff that is the question of the day. He arrived in Tampa a few days ago, using the name John Day. The queer thing here is that he has apparently had plastic surgery, and now looks like a clone of the late Josh Giddons."

"No kidding," Namers responded. "Where did he fly in from?"

"From what we see, he boarded a flight in Cairo to Rome, then London, and British Air to Tampa."

"Okay," answered Namers. "We tracked him from London through Germany and on to Cairo where we lost track of him. As far as I know, he never left Cairo. That would mean a good plastic surgeon in the city. There are only a couple that could do that kind of job. One of them, a Doctor Sameer used to do work for Fatool in the old days. I thought he had retired long ago. The other one, a Doctor Ahmad Faisal had a private practice in the old city. He may still be doing some work. Do you want me to send someone over to Cairo to check it out quietly?"

"Technically, I should ask the Embassy in Cairo."

"Sure, you should, but I can do that for you, and either go myself, or send someone I trust to do a search and recon. I will work it out with the Ambassador and he will call Cairo."

"All right, Jeff. That approach will save me weeks of coordination. We really need the information."

"You got it Alice. Call you back when we get something in the next 24 hours or so."

"Thanks Jeff, I will wait for your call."

Namers kept his promise and went to see the ambassador, who made a call to his counterpart in Cairo, while Jeff called his own CIA counterpart, explaining the situation. Both agreed it was more possible for Namers to get the information quickly, since he knew his way around Cairo, and the people possibly involved. By the time the two ambassadors had agreed, the plan was already in place. Jeff also called Langley to let Sarah Minihan know the situation. She agreed as well. The operation was on.

Going down the corridor to his communications staff to let them know his plans, Namers was stopped by his lead analyst who updated him on the boxes Hakim had ordered shipped to Kabul, telling Jeff they had been placed on a plane overnight bound for Cairo. It seemed that everything was happening in Cairo this week.

Elias, West Virginia It was great to be back on the farm, thought Will Johnson, as he walked in the early morning down the path from the house to the barn. Even though he was only gone a couple of days, Will truly enjoyed the farm he and his father had built. When his father bought the place, it was run-down, badly needing massive repairs, and it was far out in the countryside. That meant hauling everything in a small pickup truck from Elias out the nearly ten miles, and making multiple trips on many occasions. He could only help his father part-time as he had school, and then college, and a stint in the military, but every time he eventually came back to the farm. When his parents died, Will made a commitment to keep the farm active, and he had been dedicated to that task for many years.

Now, he had the opportunity to pay back the community for their help in achieving his dream. The cooperative had been a joint idea among several of the town's citizens, but Sammi and Will had led the effort, along with the mayor since its beginning. Their efforts had finally paid off, and Will wondered how he would do both—operate the cooperative and keep his farm running as well. It was true that he had Sammi on occasion, and now Sira to help, but in the back of his head, he thought about hiring someone part-time, or even full-time to live on the farm and help work the fields, especially if the cooperative really took off as he expected.

Will looked at his watch and realized he would be late in picking up Sira, so he cut his walk short, and headed for his truck. Driving through the country roads, he came to Elias in about fifteen minutes, and pulled up in his usual space in front of Sammi's Restaurant. Early in the day, most of the residents who came to town early had 'their space', and people would not park where a fellow citizen usually parked. In Will's case, that was the space right in front of Sammi's front door.

As he arrived, he could see Sammi looking out the window, probably wondering why he was late. Will waved as he exited his truck, and quickly went inside.

"Sammi, sorry I'm running late this morning. Decided to walk a bit of the farm and lost track of time."

"No problem Mister Will. Sira has been waiting patiently for you. She is in the kitchen I think."

"Sammi, what would you think if I were to try to hire someone to live at the farm who could be the caretaker? With all these trips to Washington and the cooperative becoming busier, perhaps it is time to take some of the burden off you, and that way we could deal with the business? What do you think?"

"Mister Will, that is certainly a possibility. If you wish I will look for someone. I think it is a good idea. We are both busy having someone there constantly is probably good."

Will sensed that Sammi might have some degree of hurt feelings, and did not want to press the issue.

From a Vantage Point

"Let's wait a bit and see how things evolve before we take a major step. I was just starting to think about it, and I don't want to move too quickly." Now Will saw the shine come back to Sammi's eyes and expression.

"That is a good idea, Mister Will. Let us think on it first. I will go find Sira for you. Some breakfast first maybe?"

"Absolutely," responded Will, sitting down at his usual table near the register.

On Interstate 75 approaching Atlanta, GA

The drive from Tampa to Atlanta is direct; Interstate 75 connects just outside the Tampa International Airport and goes directly northwest toward downtown Atlanta, nearly 500 miles away. On a good day, with a couple of stops, the trip takes about 9 hours. With three men in a car who do not necessarily want to be together, that time may seem like an eternity.

"This is one of the most unexciting roads I have ever seen," said Day from the rear seat to the others in the car with him.

"Well then, I guess that is too bad, since it is the only road we have to get where we are going," responded the driver, not even looking back.

"Where are we going?" Day asked.

"I told you before, you do not need to know until I decide to tell you. Shut up and read a paper or something," answered the driver. The other man in the car with them looked back toward Day from the passenger seat but said nothing.

About ten minutes went by and a sign on the side of the road said 'Atlanta, GA 52 miles'. The man in the passenger seat finally spoke, saying, "Well, I guess we better call the boss. It looks like we are getting close."

"Yeah, you better do it," the driver responded.

"Looks like Atlanta then," said Day.

"Great, you can read signs," answered the driver. "Now you know, so shut up and let me pay attention to the road."

The other passenger in the front pulled out the cell phone he was given and dialed a number. The phone rang several times before it was answered.

"We are about fifty out of Atlanta boss," said the man into the phone. "What do you want us to do?"

"How is Day doing?"

"He is a real pain," came the response. "Like a small kid in a car."

"Well, put up with him. When you get to Atlanta, go to the Omni Downtown and drop him off. He has a room confirmed for him all paid up for three days. Tell him to go to the room, order room service, but stay in the room."

"Anything else?" asked the man on the phone.

"Just tell him to shut his mouth, and look at the scenery," responded the Boss.

From a Vantage Point

The drive continued along Interstate 75, as it wended its way northwest toward the city, becoming Interstate 85 in South Atlanta. They stopped only once for gasoline and something to eat, with the two men gradually wondering if they would ever get to the city. Finally, on the horizon, they could see the outline of the tallest building in the city along with increasing housing developments and small shopping exits. They aimed toward one of the largest of the buildings, knowing that the downtown center was where the Omni Hotel was located—the end of their journey.

Wending their way down the Interstate to the exit taking them to Marietta Street and the CNN Center, where the Omni was located, the men became quiet, taking in the tall buildings and myriad of streets and exits, fearing they would miss the entrance to the hotel.

US Embassy, Cairo, Egypt. Jeff Namers looked at the Embassy, coming up the short drive, and remembered the times he and Bernie Minihan had bounced from Istanbul and Lisbon to Cairo chasing Amoud Tabriz and his associates. He often felt let down now that his arch-enemy had retired, leaving the affairs to his cousin and protégé Amid Fatoullah. He thought to himself that he wanted to visit the older part of the city, if he had the opportunity and see the old offices of Tabriz Shipping; he wondered if Amid still ran the many businesses out of that location, or had departed for elsewhere. His name seldom came up in discussions these days, but that did not mean we was no longer dangerous. Namers knew better than that.

Right now, his primary concern was the boxes fabricated by Pentopolos on orders from Hakim, and what they were to be used for somewhere in the US. Two of the sensors placed in the boxes during their fabrication were unaccounted for, and he assumed they were discovered. The question now was where they were shipped to, and to whom. He intended to find out quickly.

Namers entered the Embassy through the side security entrance, showed his credentials and was validated for entrance. As quickly as the US marine validated his entry card, the marine said, "Sir, the Chief of Station will be down immediately. He asks you to wait. You can go into the side reception room if you like."

"Thanks Sergeant," Namers replied, seeing his stripes, he walked across the corridor and was about to enter the reception room when he heard a voice behind him say, "OK Namers, why are you here, and why wasn't I told? Namers turned, and saw his friend Dan Victorino, the CIA Station Chief standing there with his arms folded across his chest.

"Oops, Dan," replied Namers, "We must have forgotten to do our due diligence, but this was a fast, emergency trip. I'm doing some work for DHS. You remember our old associate Alice Sawyer. They have a problem, and we have

From a Vantage Point

been working it for some time. Let me fill you in quickly because time is really of the essence here."

"Just busting your chops, Jeff. Both Alice and Sarah Minihan called about this trip to be sure you would not forget. You still have friends in high places. So, what is so critical that yours truly has to come here myself?" The two men started walking down the first-floor corridor, toward a more secure place where they could talk. They went through a door toward a small garden, where they sat on a stone bench.

Namers related to Victorino what he knew to date on the situation, the death of Giddons, and the traffic that indicated Hakim was planning some big event in DC near the coming Inauguration. He told of the packing boxes created by Pentopolos, outfitted somehow, and then moved to the airport in Islamabad. The last signals they had were the arrival in Cairo, but two boxes were missing, and it was assumed the sensors had been discovered and removed. Namers pulled a piece of paper from his pocket with the signal codes and handed it to Victorino.

'We need your help here Dan. We need to know when the boxes arrived, if they were delayed, and where they were shipped. Can you get us that info?"

"Consider it done, Jeff. Nothing moves in or out of Cairo in anything commercial that we don't know about. Might take a few minutes, let's go see what the boys have for us." Dan rose and pointed to a door on the other side of the garden. Namers followed and they walked inside to what looked like a World War II intelligence bunker, with all kinds of equipment, and staff in garments that looked like they had been worn for a week. The air was not exactly rosy either.

Victorino handed the paper to one of the computer operators.

"See what you can do with this Sam. This man needs information right away. He is a friend of Bernie Minihan's, but do it anyway."

"Right away boss. How is that old fart anyway, now that he has given up doing real work?" Sam asked.

"Guess he is OK. By the way, for some of you, this is Jeff Namers, station chief in Khartoum. He says both Bernie and Sarah are fine, but while you are at it check your watch and wallet. Meanwhile, let's get to this and see what we find."

Sam sat down at a console, started typing and quickly turned toward his boos. "These boxes came in from Islamabad as part of a shipment five days ago. The shipment was six boxes, and four were shipped to the US through Rome, and the other two were stored in container storage at the Cairo Terminal. Now, looking at your sensor data, it appears that two of the boxes, those in storage here, can be pinged. They have your sensors. That leaves the other four. Since they are already out of Rome, I can't ping on those." I already have someone checking on the two boxes in storage. We should get a report on them shortly."

Thanks Sam," responded Namers. "Dan, I need a secure line to call Langley."

From a Vantage Point

"No problem," can the response. "Use that phone over there on the last desk." Namers walked the short distance, picked up the phone, and, when the operator came on, he gave her a number at Langley Operations. Sarah answered.

"Sarah, this is Jeff. We have four of the boxes on their way to stateside. Two have sensors. They shipped Cairo to Rome, and on to the US."

"Tampa International," yelled Sam from the other side of the room.

"Tampa International is the arrival point Sarah. Will you see what you can find?"

"Sure Jeff. It will take about ten minutes."

"Great, I am in Dan's ops center in Cairo."

"Call you back then as soon as I have an answer," responded Sarah, who promptly hung up the phone.

"Answer in about ten minutes," said Namers to his counterpart Victorino.

"Good, then let's go get coffee." Victorino started to turn and said, "Sam come get us when Sarah Minihan calls. We will be in the Ambassador's small dining room."

"OK boss. Am I allowed in there?"

"You are today, just don't steal the silver," Victorino laughed as the two men left.

Elias, West Virginia Will and Sira drove along the country roads approaching the farm. They said little to each other during most of the trip. Will was occupied with his concerns on being gone so often on his frequent trips to Washington, and Sira was deeply troubled with the idea that she was to turn Will into a terrorist.

The idea of turning him previously had never been a real concern for Sira. She was trained to do exactly that, and the only reason she was brought to the area was because she was very good at that type of task. Since her arrival, however, something had happened. She began to see Johnson in a very different light. Not that she wanted to at first; after all she was expected to marry Hassan, and looked forward to that day. They had known each other since childhood, and both families expected their marriage. When Hassan went off to join al-Qaeda, she quickly found a way to join him. They trained together for exactly these types of actions.

Gradually however, as she met and then began to work for Will Johnson, she realized that he was good man, and being led toward something that would probably get him killed, if not by the Government, then certainly by other terrorists, who would not want the story of their actions to get out. The situation with her own cousin proved that to her. She began to look at Will in a new, more protective light, and that feeling of protection soon blossomed into love. She had no idea if he felt the same way but it did not matter to her. She wanted only to protect him, even at the risk of harm to herself. The real question was how to do that and possibly protect both from harm.

Sira overheard the conversation between Sammi and Will in the restaurant and Will's suggestion that he probably needed someone full-time at the farm during the period he would be travelling back and forth to DC. She began to plot in her mind how she could approach both and make it possible that the full-time person would be her. After all, she was the housekeeper now, even if part-time, and extending that, and living at the farm should be a simple extension of her current duties.

Gradually the thought came to her; it would involve extending her time at the farm each time she went out to clean, until it became obvious to both that she should simply live there. In addition, she would subtly encourage Will in that direction, while reducing her work at the restaurant. The more she thought about it, the more she agreed with herself that it was the exact thing to do.

Over the next several weeks, Sira worked her plan, trying not to make it appear to be something premeditated on her part. She continued to report that her time with Will Johnson, especially the times where she worked on the farm later than usual, was designed to bring him around to Hassan's constant demands that he would agree to do their bidding in DC during the inauguration. She also made the same statements to Sammi, both to support him, and reduce the possibility that he would be hurt in the inevitable exchange that might occur if those in Atlanta found out about her plan.

Will Johnson for his part made the trips to Washington DC like clockwork, on a schedule he and Tom O'Neal agreed on during their early visits; sometimes altering the dates somewhat when it was not possible to have other needed Department of Agriculture staff present for their discussions. Johnson, on Sira's suggestion, also worked out an arrangement with the hotel to stay in the same room each time, whenever possible so that, if needed she could call him directly without having to get the hotel switchboard to find him.

Sira did not tell Will Johnson about her plans; instead she led him along slowly to make the plan seem to be working. When the people from Atlanta would periodically check on his status in DC, he would be in the same room, meeting the same people, and travelling directly between the farm and the city, returning directly as well after his frequent visits.

On one occasion, someone stood in the lobby of the Alexander, and asked a hotel staff member who he was, pointing at Will Johnson, as was told he was "Mr. Johnson", one of their frequent customers. The report went back to Atlanta that their plan was apparently working.

From a Vantage Point

Chapter 34 Connecting the Dots

CIA Operations Division, Mclean, Virginia Sarah Minihan looked up from her small, glass-enclosed office out toward the cubicles of her staff, and saw several looking over the board last used by Jeff Namers on his recent visit. She wondered was happening, and decided to walk into the main part of the office to take in the conversation.

"OK, so we have a total of ten of the twelve sensors Namers' people set out, and some idea where they are headed," said one of the analysts as she approached.

"Sure, but look at the scatter, here Joe," responded another, "They are going in all sorts of directions. We have no idea what they are attached to, except, of course, these three here," the person continued, pointing to three pins on the board. Sarah looked over to the board and saw the three pins were in Tampa, Atlanta, and locally in Washington D.C.

"What have we got here, guys?" Asked Sarah, as she reached where the others were discussing the information on the board.

"Well Sarah," answered one of the female analysts, the senior in the group, "We have been tracking the sensors placed in several boxes sent from Kabul to Islamabad, and eventually shipped out from there. Initially, we thought they might be going to the same place," she said as she pointed to a scatter diagram on the board, "But it appears from this chart, the boxes actually moved along several paths."

"Some shipped from Cairo and headed toward Europe, then here to the US. Others shipped from Islamabad to other destinations in Russia and China. Oh, and one went to London as well. That leaves us without much more good information than when we started." She gave Sarah a somewhat puzzled look, as she turned from the board back to where Sarah stood.

"Not really," Sarah responded. "What you have to do is go back to the original information. We know from other intel that there is something cooking here in the US around the inauguration. So, let's assume for a moment that the indicators we have here in the US might be real, so we need to confirm what they are. I would look at what we have locally, domestically, and then circle out as things move to see where everything ends up."

The analysts looked around among themselves, and then the female analyst asked, "What happened if we send the domestic agencies out on a royal goose chase?"

"Let me worry about that," responded Sarah. "Package up what analysis you have and let me send it over to DHS. They will do the legwork to see what we have. It is basically a win-win, they check it out and if we are right, they move in.

From a Vantage Point

if the other sensors start moving toward the US, we can expand the search and reconnaissance as needed." The analysts nodded their agreement, and Sarah started back to her office, thinking that this new section, with equally new analysts had a lot of learning to do.

Sitting at her desk, Sarah dialed a number on her phone, then hit the speaker button while she waited for the connection.

"This is Namers," she heard from the speaker. "It better be important at 3AM."

"Jeff, It's Sarah. What are you doing at home at 3AM?"

"Hi Sarah, I do come home occasionally. What's up?"

"We have been following your sensors from here. They are scattered all over the world, but there is a concentration on the East Coast. My people are following those, and getting Alice and her people into the loop. We will continue to follow the others, but it looks some may have been separated from their original boxes."

"That is possible, Sarah. My contact in Khartoum said she received a call from Pentopolos that he found a sensor, and then a second. Those are totally unaccounted for. It seems reasonable he may have found others, and re-attached them to other shipments going elsewhere."

"That was my feeling, Jeff, and why I told the staff to concentrate on those in the US and one that seems to be wending its way toward us."

"What else is happening to muddle things over there?" asked Namers.

"I spoke to Alice yesterday," she replied, "But, of course, I seem to speak to Alice every day, in these times. Their surveillance of anything related to Will Johnson seems to be moving along. They still do not believe he is involved. There was one weird thing, though. Someone came into Tampa a few days ago, who could be Giddons' doppelganger. A perfect image. Unfortunately, they saw it too late, and the guy had left the airport. He was picked up by the proverbial man with the sign and drove off with him. DHS has some info on the car and are trying to follow it. They know it headed north, on I-75. The cameras on that route are spaced far apart, so they may have a problem tracing it. We wait and see on that.'

"The real concern though is why, at this particular time, someone this close to a dead man's face should be coming into the country. Our people are tracing where he came from. He used the name Joseph Anderson."

"That is interesting, Sarah. When Bernie and I were traipsing around Europe and the Balkans, I often used the name Joseph Anderson myself. Wonder if that is connected."

"Who knows," retorted Sarah, "Let's just take this a step at the time. We might catch him and eventually find out."

"OK, anything else, my dear. Otherwise, I am going back to bed."

From a Vantage Point

"Have good dreams, my friend," answered Sarah, as she hung up the phone, and then sat back in her chair. She made a mental note to speak to Bernie about Joseph Anderson.

A small village outside Kabul, Afghanistan Along the side of a dusty, dirt road sat a beat-up Range Rover that looked like it was over twenty years old (and probably was). Inside sat a driver on the right front seat, his right elbow out the window, with a pair of ear buds in his ears, connected to a cell phone. In the rear sat a man in Afghani dress wearing sunglasses, but reading a magazine.

To their rear, a cloud of sand was rising in the distance; meaning that a vehicle of some type was approaching. The driver looked out the window into his rearview mirror, banged on the door to gain the attention of the passenger, and quickly reached for an AK-47 Assault rifle nestled between his legs.

"Settle down Saleem," said the man in the rear seat. "That should be the one we are waiting for these last two hours." The driver looked into his rear window, and soon saw a much newer Range Rover, this one in a bright green color, lumbering down the dirt road. In just a couple of minutes, the Range Rover came up to where the first vehicle waited, and parked on the opposite side of the small road.

As soon as it stopped, the man in the rear of the green Rover stepped from the vehicle, walking toward the other side of the road. The passenger in the other vehicle did the same.

"As-salaam 'Alaikum (Peace be upon you), Amid," said the man from the first vehicle as he arrived near the center of the road.

"wa 'Alaikum as-salam (And with you), Hakim, my friend. How are you?" responded the man from the green Rover. This man was very tall, probably over six feet five inches, wearing an Arab Keffiyah draped over his more-western clothes, as a westerner would wear a scarf, and a bright red fez on his head.

"How was your trip," Hakim continued.

"My trip from Cairo was uneventful, Hakim, at least until I was told that there were problems with your plan for Washington. You will tell me its status so I can decide what we will do next." Amid, although usually a very reserved man, was clearly anxious about Hakim's plans.

While they were exchanging greetings, Amid's driver was removing a small table, two chairs, and a large canopy, which he set up behind Amid's Land Rover. When he finished, he simply walked back to his vehicle, entered, and sat there patiently without expression. Amid and Hakim moved over under the canopy and sat on the chairs provided for them.

"Well Hakim, tell me, how is your plan proceeding then?"

"Most everything seems to be following our plan Amid. I did not expect the death of Josh Giddons."

From a Vantage Point

"Josh was a good man. May he rest in Allah's arms. What else has not followed the plan?" Amid asked again.

"Our people are telling us that the man Will Johnson is coming over to us. We placed people in his town, including a young woman to work in his house. He seems to take to her, and she is our best effort at coaxing him to do our bidding. He has this project, a food cooperative, and goes back and forth to Washington DC often enough that he is recognized where he goes, and has arranged to stay in the same hotel room each time he travels. That room has a wide window view toward the big mall the Americans have from their Capitol to the monument to George Washington, their first President, an obelisk."

"My plan is to have the equipment we need fitted to some special cases and sent to the United States, where it will be carried to Washington and delivered in Johnson's name. There will be three specially made mortars, which can be disconnected and then up by the windows in his room, and aimed toward that mall during the inauguration of the new president. Our aim here is not to kill the new president but to make the point that we can, and anytime we wish," Hakim continued.

"What happens to Johnson," asked Amid.

"I do not care what the Americans do to Johnson," Hakim responded.

"But, was he not your friend? Did Giddons and Johnson not both desert from their Army, and then come to us to work? Why would you not care?"

"If he is truly one of us Amid, then he will be prepared to die for the Prophet. Johnson will die a martyr."

"Hakim, what if he does not die, but is arrested. What is your plan for that?"

"If he is arrested, he will be sent to their prison in Cuba, and there one of my people, our people, will assure his death."

"What of the others who have worked with him?"

"They also are expendable Amid. To be sure, I will have our people from Atlanta, Georgia take care of that."

"All right Hakim, now let us get to the problems. One of my contacts in Interpol tells me that a man was recognized in Tampa Florida arriving on an airplane from London. His face was that of Josh Giddons. The Government agents are tracking him now. They know he has gone to Atlanta and a search has been ordered for him. What is the meaning of this?"

Hakim clearly looked startled as he responded, "The man was made to look like Giddons before Giddons' untimely death. He was to come to the United States to work in the background in Atlanta to confuse the Americans. When I sent Giddons to the United States, through a long route, he also was on the way to Atlanta when he died on a plane enroute."

"All that I understand Hakim," Amid replied, "But now he is a hindrance. With his face, he is being hunted and cannot be useful. Also, since the police officials

From a Vantage Point

are looking for him in Atlanta, the rest of the people there are also in jeopardy. You need to tell them to eliminate the problem and get the police and Federal agents to stop their searching before they uncover something we do not want them to know."

"One more thing," added Amid, "These boxes you created and had shipped. The American CIA knows about them as well, and the man you had make them suddenly is dead in a river. That calls even more attention to what you are doing. The agent from Khartoum, Namers is a very experienced man. More importantly, he is a close friend of another agent called Minihan, Bernie Minihan. You do not want either Namers or Minihan, or both, involved here, although it appears from what I hear that you have already involved yourself at least with Namers."

"If this plan is to succeed, and it must, you will be careful, patient, and above all discrete; even more so than usual. You are normally much more cautious Hakim. Return to that state. I have business for two days in Kabul before I return to Cairo. If we need to meet again, then so be it, but you assure that this project I have given you is successful. Do you understand?"

"I do Amid. We will be successful. Thank you for the opportunity."

The two men rose, and as they did Amid's driver emerged from the Rover, walked to the rear of the vehicle, and started to remove the table, chairs, and finally the canopy, placing them in the rear compartment of the Rover. Amid started to walk toward the vehicle, and the driver opened the door for him. Hakim, in turn walked across the road toward his own vehicle.

No more words were said; the driver entered Amid's vehicle, started the engine, and turned around in the sand, then speeding off quickly back toward Kabul. Hakim waited a short time, observing the rising dust, and then did the same. The two men would not see each other again.

CIA Operations, McLean Virginia Sitting at the small side table in her office, Sarah Minihan was multi-tasking, concurrently reading her inbox and talking to her husband, Bernie Minihan. They were loudly interrupted by a knock on the door, and the vision of a young woman bursting in with a pile of papers in her hand.

"Sarah, I have." her voice trailed off as she saw that Bernie was also in the room. "Sorry about barging in Sarah," said the woman, Sophie Taggart, a relatively new analyst. "We just got two important pieces of information you really need to know."

"OK Sophie, come on it. Let's make this a crowd. What do you have?"

Bernie sat there somewhat amused. He thought back to when Sarah joined the Agency, and the first time she did the same thing to him and his old boss, Ramsey. Just like Sarah, this young woman turned beet red from

From a Vantage Point

embarrassment, then quickly recovered, as she sat down at the table to present what she knew.

"Two things, as I said," Sophie started, "First, we had Interpol chase down the sensors for the boxes outside the US. Only one of the sensors was attached to something even closely resembling the diagrams Jeff Namers provided. DHS managed to get images of the boxes here in the US as they shipped. Here they are." Sophie put photos of the boxes on the table for both to see. She also showed several others taken by the Interpol agents. It was clear that two of the boxes were very different from the others. They looked to all be made of the same wood, but created for very different purposes.

"Well then Sophie, what do you think these boxes, the ones here in the US are to be used for?" asked Bernie.

"In my view, they do or will contain something like a small mortar; something that can easily be dis-assembled and put back together quickly." She responded so confidently that Bernie and Sarah were both impressed.

"What makes you think that will be the case?" continued Bernie.

"Well, if you look at the construction of the boxes, they have several side compartments, those on the long side could easily hold parts of the mortar tube, and the side sections could hold the mortar rounds."

"OK, so if I buy that, how do these get through customs without some scanner showing the mortar in pieces?"

"Easy," answered Sophie, "Create the parts on a 3-D camera; fill the rounds with light explosive, and put just enough lead lining in the boxes to blur, but not obscure completely what is inside, I would pack the center of the boxes with other routine things, like a salesman's kit, and it should pass most detectors.

"That is a very plausible scenario, Sophie. Let's explore it some more. What about your second item?" asked Sarah.

"Not sure how important this is Sarah, but look at these pics taken yesterday by one of our satellites. She placed six photos on the table, having picked up the others. As Sarah and Bernie looked over the photos, Bernie's eyes lit up.

"Sophie, where were these taken?"

"In the desert about five miles outside of Kabul. The image specialist thought it odd to have two Land Rovers on either side of a small road, with a tent or canopy behind one. Why would anyone picnic in that place?" answered Sophie.

"They weren't picnicking Sophie," responded Bernie, "Look at this one Sarah," said Bernie, pointing to one photo.

"That person, my dear is Amid Fatoullah. Old and valued adversary. So, first, why is he in Afghanistan this time of year, and second, why is he with Hakim al-Azahir?" Two interesting, and possibly fateful questions.

"Sarah, I have to go back to my office, but keep me in the loop on this. You may have something even bigger than Alice thought."

"Sure Bernie, see you later this evening at home." Replied Sarah. Bernie rose to leave and turned to Sophie.

"Good work Sophie. You may have put some pieces to a puzzle here. Keep it up." As he finished, Bernie Minihan walked out the door, and turned left to go down the corridor to his own office.

"Sit down for a minute, Sophie," asked Sarah. "You impressed the boss today. Feel good about that. Bernie is not known for passing out too many compliments, especially to junior staff. You did well. Now, let's figure out what you have here.

Department of Homeland Security, Washington DC Looking ahead at a very large screen, Alice Sawyer saw multiple views, purposely shaped as a puzzle piece, each of which represented a unique, but probably related problem.

In the upper left were the pictures of Hakim al-Azahir, Josh Giddons and Will Johnson, the friends from wartime days, one of whom, Giddons was now dead in Atlanta. To the right was the drawing of a packing box, a peculiar packing box, with multiple compartments. The originals were built and probably outfitted in Kabul, then shipped out, some to the US, and others, possibly to other places.

The lower left displayed pictures of three people; those who worked most closely with Will Johnson. Sammi, the restaurant owner and his two employees. DHS and other agencies involved knew little about any of the three.

Down in the lower right were several ongoing video feeds with the morning international news. In the center was one solo shot of a man named Joseph Anderson; below him a picture of the Horizons LLC building in Atlanta, a DHS contractor.

Alice sat looking at the large screen for some time, until people started to file into the room, taking seats along a long, curved table extending out from the screen area. Alice continued to stare at the screen until one of the staff began to speak.

"Alice, I believe everyone you asked for is here." Looking a bit startled, Alice looked toward the voice and responded.

"Thanks Joe. I appreciate all of you coming over here today, especially you Sarah. Coming cross-town into traffic is mind-boggling. Well folks, look at the screen. Each of your agencies have put parts of this puzzle up there on display. The question is what does this all mean? How does the puzzle fit together? If it does, and I certainly think it does, what do we need to do about it"

"What intel we have," she continued, "From the chatter, and other sources, something is planned for the inauguration period. That is why your people are

From a Vantage Point

here from the Inaugural Committee, Bill. You need to be read in on this particular threat."

"Could you wrap the threat up in a thirty second elevator speech for me Alice?" asked Bill Donohue, security director for the Inauguration Committee.

"Sure Bill, happy to," responded Alice. "The CIA Station in Khartoum followed information some weeks ago, demonstrating a plan for an attack in DC about the time of the inauguration. We do not know what kind of attack, nor do we necessarily know who is planning it, although we do believe strongly there is an al-Qaeda connection out there. I will discuss that shortly. What we have right now is pieces of a puzzle. "

"One piece is in the upper left of the collage. One of these is Hakim al-Azahir, a protégé of Amid Fatoullah, one of the kingpins of both the Brotherhood and the Egyptian part of al-Qaeda. Some of you in the room who have been around a while might remember Amid's old boss Fatool, Amoud Tabriz, now retired we think. Amid was recently seen in Kabul and met there with Hakim. One connection here with many to go."

"Another piece of the puzzle is the diagram in the upper right which shows the construction of packing boxes, contents unknown, but some apparently on their way from Kabul to Atlanta. Sarah, you know a bit more about some of the boxes. How about chiming in here?"

"Sure Alice, happy to. Our people tracked the boxes, inspected the warehouse where they were built, and attached sensors, which DHS and NSA are tracking along with us. We have a scatter from the sensor pings, which might tell us that some were discovered and simply placed on other packages; we are tracking those now and trying to get a visual inspection to see what they are."

"One of our people visited the warehouse where these packing boxes were built, and discovered a 3-D industrial strength copier, capable of producing large parts, or smaller ones which fit together to form larger objects. That seems to fit with the design of the boxes. They could be assembling plastic parts, capable of fitting together, but, with minimal lead inside coating, could pass through out scanners at entry points."

"We know at least two boxes arrived in Atlanta several weeks ago, empty when they arrived in Tampa, and forwarded from Atlanta for delivery here in the DC area."

"We got the call," Roger Doucette of the FBI reported. "We sent two agents down to the international cargo area at Reagan Airport to look at the boxes. They were scheduled for pickup by a delivery service tomorrow. They are still empty,"

"The FBI will have whoever picks up the cartons covered," Doucette added.

"Thank you, Roger. The other two guys in the pics on upper left are Josh Giddons, now deceased and Will Johnson, a farmer from West Virginia," continued Alice Sawyer. "These guys were Army deserters in the 70s, although

Johnson eventually accepted the Carter Amnesty Program and has led a stable life since. The other two continued as mercenaries and runners for al-Qaeda. Johnson went to the Gulf and then to Khartoum recently to meet with them, after Giddons paid him a visit in West Virginia last year."

"Johnson is working to create a farm cooperative through Agriculture. We have someone over there watching him, but everything we have right now says he may be an innocent here. Not taking chances though. That leads to the three in the lower left, also in West Virginia. One of them, a man named Sammi owns a restaurant, and the other two work for him. We are not yet sure how they are involved with anything, but it is curious that one, a man named Hassan recently came from Atlanta, and his girlfriend, named Sira soon followed. All are expats from the Middle East over the past few years, and all have virtually uncheckable backgrounds. Again, Atlanta seems to be a player here."

"Bolstering that is the man in the middle of all this, who calls himself Joseph Anderson," Alice continued, "But who is Joseph Anderson, and why is he here? Why does he look like a match to Giddons, and why is he on his way to Atlanta? There are a lot of questions here, and we need to figure out the answers to each of them."

"Finally," said Alice, "How does Horizons LLC, in Atlanta, play in all this? Once we realized some of the overseas traffic was going through their servers, we put a short leash on them; stopped directing our classified stuff through them, and have our own people supervising their operations that relate to us, DHS, and any other federal agency with contracts that utilize their services. Is there a connection here?" her voice trailed off as she continued to look avidly at the large screen.

Swiveling in her chair, Alice looked toward both sides of the arched table, and said, "We need answers people, and we need them fast. I am not going to have to tell the Inaugural committee that we do not think we can assure the President's safety in his own capital city. We need to put this puzzle together in some logical way and figure out the game plan here. We need to do that now."

"All right, so let me suggest this plan", responded Roger Doucette of the FBI, "We are following the boxes. We will follow but not arrest right now. We want to know where they go, who receives them, and what they intend to do with them. Arrests can come later. Our Atlanta agents will find this guy Anderson, and do the same with him. If he is there to contact a cell or group, we need to identify them all."

"NSA can lock down Horizon LLC, and do the necessary overseas traces using our own authority from the Court under Section 207 Alice," piped up the representatives from that agency. "We probably have much of the metadata right now, and fleshing it out with warrant authority ought to give us what we need to start identifying a strand from overseas to here."

"Alice, we can help with continuing to pursue the other overseas sensors," added Sarah Minihan. "The CIA teams in both Kabul and Khartoum have this under control. Our officers in other cities can easily find out what and where the other sensors have gone, and if they are relevant."

"Right now, I think we need to keep all this under deep wraps," responded the representative from the Inaugural Committee. I need to brief the chair of the committee, and he can decide if we need to brief the President-elect or one of his senior people, but we would certainly prefer nothing came out prematurely on this. It would really make a mess of the inauguration ceremonies and public events. I will work with you Ms. Sawyer to decide what level of disclosure is appropriate."

Others quickly joined, each taking a piece of the puzzle, and agreeing to contribute their agency's assets to trying to solve what was really, at this point, a pile of Jell-O.

"Thanks, all. We will meet again in five days," Alice responded, "That will give you time to marshal your resources and get them on the ground. I want to emphasize, however, that a call anytime is appropriate. Do not wait until the next meeting if you have something critical to add." The attendees all nodded their agreement, and some started to leave. Sarah Minihan sat with Alice for a few moments as the meeting slowly dispersed.

"Well Sarah, what is your take on all this?" asked Alice.

"Well," began Sarah, repeating Alice, "I do think you have a puzzle here, which will eventually show the map of Atlanta. The question is whether Atlanta is the hub of activity or simply a portal. My guess, based on what we know now, is Atlanta is a staging point for whatever is coming to DC during the inauguration. There is probably a rather large cell there, with tentacles, such as the people surrounding Will Johnson in West Virginia."

"Ok Sarah. If that is the case what do you see as the plan here?"

"Alice, I think you have the pieces in place. You need to lock down Horizon with as much discretion as possible. My hunch is there is a mole or two there who have hacked a server, but the company itself is probably clean." We will find the mole when we crack the cell."

"What about Johnson?" Alice asked.

"I think Johnson is being manipulated by two guys he thought were long-time friends, but who went further to the dark side, and want to take Johnson with them to use as a front man in their operations. One of those is now dead. The other will probably only get one shot during the inauguration, and are using Johnson as a logical surrogate, if they can figure out how to turn him. That is probably the job of whoever has been designated to do the job in West Virginia.

The people in West Virginia might be your weakest link in the chain. If you can, you might get an order to monitor the lines from there, and try to snag anything going to Atlanta, or nearby. My hunch is that very few people in that small town would be calling there, and it might provide you a way to tie some of these things together. If NSA can get you two-way traffic, you could get a link, and perhaps even the link through Horizon that you want."

"That makes a lot of sense Sarah," answered Alice, "You and I think so much alike. I knew you would say little at the public meeting, but I was hoping you had something in the back of that pretty head of yours. I can see why Rex thought so much of you."

The mention of the name Rex brought a momentary tear to Sarah's eyes. It was Rex Ramsey that brought Sarah into the Agency, gave her a chance to rise in the Operations Directorate, and, in his inimitable way, made sure that she and her husband Bernie Minihan met and eventually married. Rex was their surrogate father, their mentor, and their friend, as he had been to Alice Sawyer. His sudden death affected them all in so many ways.

"All right then Alice, how can we really help? You know our legal limitations, but I want you to know that we will stretch the law as far as we can to help in this. We do have some domestic assets in agencies that could be assigned 'special work' if needed—through the agencies where they are embedded, of course. We will take care of the overseas work I mentioned in the meeting, but anything else we can possibly do we will. As soon as Bernie heard about Amid being involved, you could literally see his temperature rise. He still loves the hunt, where it comes to that gang."

"Right now, the best thing you can do for me is follow the overseas threads Sarah. I need to know when and if any of those threads start wending their way toward the US. Those sensors are our only eyes to these people right now. Get me anything you can on what these packages, whatever they look like might be used for, and stay close.

I would especially love to know if the possibility exists if boxes might be arriving with no sensors attached to them. Having you next to me at the table is a lot more comforting that one of those stodgy FBI people with their procedure-bound rules and actions. I need someone who can, I hate to say it, 'Think out of the box". Whoever created that trite phrase, by the way? I worry these days there is no one working inside the box, whatever the box might be. Thanks for diving in here. You and Bernie are my mainstays."

"We appreciate that Alice. By the way, what are you doing for Thanksgiving? If you wish, come over to our house and celebrate with us. You haven't seen the twins, and the other two will run you ragged, but we would like to see you."

"You know, I will do that Sarah. I was thinking this morning what I would do. I really do not want to travel while all this is going on, so Iowa is out this year. I would be happy to come over. What can I bring?"

"Just yourself, Alice. Bernie has decided he wants to do the turkey this year in the deep fryer he bought two or three years ago, which has been sitting in the garage. Come and watch the fun as the great spy turns chef." They both laughed, and then Sarah added, "I have to get back to Langley, but I will keep you updated. Anything we get will go over the link we established last year. It doesn't go through Horizon so it should be OK. Will have the guys test it this afternoon, and will let Everett over at NSA monitor it to be sure we don't have a connection we don't want listening in."

"Great, I will wait for the confirmation. Thanks again my dear. You are so often my lifesaver." Sarah rose to leave, as did Alice, and they embraced, Sarah turned toward the doorway, waved one last time, and departed for Langley. Alice did likewise, walking down the short corridor to her office, stopping at the communications office to tell the staff to expect the check on the secure link to Langley.

From a Vantage Point

Chapter 35 Breaking the Conundrum

The concept of the puzzle struck each of the attendees at Alice Sawyer's meeting differently. In many ways, the idea of a puzzle was not much different from what the various agencies had been dealing with since the attacks on September 11, 2001. It took a long time for the more traditional law enforcement agencies to realize that they were dealing with people whose entire though process was asynchronous—they did not think in established patterns, but from what was in their heart and mind at any particular moment. This seemed to be no different.

Many of their planners, such as Hakim al-Azahir, were well-educated, and understood the technicalities of what they planned. They were not people who simply struck out and cared not for the consequences—they designed their acts to effect consequences, which would create fear and anxiety in those whose lives were affected. The numbers of casualties were less important than the effect of their acts. They wanted to make a statement, one that would drive actions on the other side in a way that the terrorists desired. Breaking that course of events was what would stop the terrorists—at least temporarily, until another plan was developed by others.

Alice Sawyer knew she had to determine how the 'puzzle' pieces fit together—that was the key to stopping at least this effort. The question was how to do it, and which actor was the most important. Right now, she had no answers, but the team she put together would find the answers she needed. Her principal concern was finding those answers in time to prevent disaster.

National Security Agency, Ft. Meade, MD Arriving at the main parking lot, Eldon Zambino showed his pass to the guard, who checked his parking permit sticker as well, then waved him into the secured lot. Zambino found a space, parked and locked his car, heading across the short distance to the main entrance to the Agency building, where he worked each day as a branch manager in the Central Security Service (CSS). His branch's mission was to provide the technology and capabilities for data interception, primarily for the Armed Forces, but also occasionally for other Government agencies, such as the FBI and DHS.

Zambino returned from the meeting with Alice Sawyer's task force, excited about the prospect of putting into operation some of the ideas he had developed over the past few months, on linking specific data to specific situations, trying to stay within the legal requirements of his guiding statute, The US Patriot Act, and the ruling of the FISA Court. Sometimes in the past that had been an onerous task, since much of what the Agency does is at the very edges of emerging law and practice, and going over a line was disastrous, especially if, as had

From a Vantage Point

happened in the Snowden case, it becomes a public relations nightmare. Zambino wanted desperately to avoid another Snowden case.

Coming to the turnstiles at the entrance, Zambino swiped his badge, then headed toward the elevators, taking him up to the 7th floor, toward his office.

He had already called ahead, and his small staff waited to receive whatever tasking he received at the Sawyer meeting. As the elevator rose toward the top floors of the building, Zambino began to prepare an action plan, one designed to get quickly to the information he needed. That staff could secure the data quickly, and send them on their way toward giving Alice Sawyer answers.

Exiting the elevator at his floor, Zambino stopped first at the office of Legal Counsel, went in and asked for his contact in that office. A short stocky man came up to meet him.

"Well Eldon, what can I do for you today? What exceptional twisting of the law can I create to help you, is probably more to the point?"

"I do have a request Ned," responded Zambino, "Just left a meeting at DHS and they need some data and analysis. Got a minute to discuss it?"

"Sure Eldon, come this way," responded the attorney, pointing to his office to the left side of the larger office space. They walked the short distance, entered his office, and closed the door.

"Now, what is it you need me to do Eldon?" the attorney asked.

"Ned, I really need to know is, can we legally do a sweep of the metadata over the past three months within a circle covered roughly by West Virginia, DC, and the Atlanta area to see if we have calling patterns that match a specific set of circumstances, are we covered under the Act?"

"Well, yes and no," answered the attorney, "Yes we can do it under Section 207 authority, but we would have to file with the court, and have those specifics ready. Conversely, the Court has begun to look more closely, so the reasons need to be reasonable, and potentially lead to uncovering some form of plot. What do you have here?"

Zambino outlined the situation as explained by Alice Sawyer, pointing out the circumstances in Elias, West Virginia, along with the information known that seemed to be emanating from the Atlanta area, and the small amount of intelligence that alluded to a potential attack in DC on Inauguration Day.

"Will that do it Ned?"

"Sure enough. I can get an approval on that. You set everything up, use what you told me, and give me a plan format. I will submit to the Court. We should have an approval by this evening, if I can find one of the judges available, and he is willing to hear my submittal. I would have preferred on this one to go to Judge G, but she is out of the loop for a week. I'll get one of the others to do the deed. It should go through though. Be ready."

From a Vantage Point

"Thanks Ned. We will be ready," Zambino responded as he rose from his chair and started to leave. "Thanks again Ned, you do good work for me."

"I know. Just don't get me in trouble by starting on your crusade before we get the approval. Now, get out of here. I have work to do."

Zambino walked a bit further down the corridor until he arrived at his own office space, entered through a door with no indication of what was behind it. Only a small sign on the left side indicated a room number, nothing else. Inside, there were large monitor screens around the walls and on desks. In the center was a large conference table, with eight staff members sitting around it, smaller screens in front of them, and multiple discussions going on around the table.

"Morning, gang. I see we are busily protecting the world from whomever our enemies happen to be today," Zambino said, as he announced himself to the group.

"Right," responded a young female sitting toward the end of the table furthest from where Zambino stood. Seeing an empty chair, Zambino sat as the conversations faded away, and everyone looked toward him for their expected instructions.

Washington Field Office, Federal Bureau of Investigation, Washington DC
Similar things were happening in other agencies around the city following the Sawyer meeting, perhaps none as active as what began to transpire at the FBI. Roger Doucette, on his return to the DC Field office, co-located with the Washington Area Terrorism Joint Task Force, went immediately to see his boss, Deputy FBI Director Richard Peabody to relate the issues and assignments from the meeting.

"Come on in Roger," announced Peabody, seeing Doucette in the doorway, starting to knock to gain his attention. "How did the meeting go?"

"Well I think, boss. It was certainly high-powered, at the least. There were people there from several agencies with acronyms you never see at these think sessions." Doucette tried as best he could to organize his thoughts and lay out the events of the meeting, but soon became hopelessly lost, trying to organize what he heard, and failing miserably. Peabody gradually became agitated.

"Roger, you have me completely confused," announced Peabody. "You are speaking so fast, and moving around on topics so much, my head is beginning to hurt. Let's start at the beginning and move onward from there."

"Ok boss," responded Doucette, "I'll start again. As you know, I went to a meeting called by Alice Sawyer over at Homeland to discuss an emerging threat. That's my job as the emerging threat analyst at the JTF. Ms. Sawyer laid out a complex scenario that is also so confusing," Doucette continued before Peabody stopped him.

"First, who else was there besides Alice Sawyer?" Peabody inquired.

From a Vantage Point

"Well, there was Sarah Minihan from CIA, Doucette said for the second time.

"You said Sarah Minihan was there? What was her role?"

"Well, I'm really not sure of that. She seemed to be acting more of an advisor to Ms. Sawyer. She really said very little, except about some of the overseas details, and a bit about a guy named," Doucette stopped to look at his notes, "Ah, here it is, Amid something-or-other. That was the name."

Peabody's face went ashen, and his hand shook visibly as he wrote on his scratch pad.

On the road toward Elias, West Virginia The weather was clearly going from bad to worse as Will Johnson drove along the last fifty miles toward home. The weather channels in DC had predicted some rain, followed by a cold front that would deliver sleet by the evening. As usual, they were wrong, at least in the countryside. Rain tuned quickly to sleet and then to snow in just over an hour. It was currently coming down at what seemed to be about an inch an hour, but the farther he drove toward home, the heavier it seemed to become, causing his windshield wipers to strain.

Will thought about many things as he drove toward home. The scenarios were the same as they had always been; his days in the desert in the Arabian Gulf, and then Khartoum with his friends. He thought about the damage he saw from the bombing that destroyed Hakim and Josh's home, and he thought about the people who were harmed by what Hakim told him was an American drone attack. He also thought back to his childhood, and the attacks on his village, the injuries to his family, and their forced departure from Lebanon.

These were dark memories for him. He seldom remembered, or even tried to remember the early days in Lebanon. He was happy in the United States, and never stopped loving the country which took him and his family in as refugees, even after he deserted during the Vietnam War; regretting that later, and quickly committing to the Carter amnesty program.

One lingering thought bothered him. In his own mind, Will considered the failure of the US to help innocent people in their drone attacks, and their continuing support of regimes whose only purpose was their own preservation and not that of the people, really bothered him. It was not just that the drones were unmanned, but that they could not be so precisely navigated to prevent damage, injury, and death to anyone else in the immediate area. No country should be doing those things. Equally, he understood that some collateral damage was probably unavoidable, but not to the extent that he had seen. Will did not really understand diplomacy and politics, only pain, suffering, and deprivation, much as he had experienced in his early youth, and all these thoughts returned vividly to his mind as he drove toward home.

From a Vantage Point

Finally, he saw the entrance fence to his property ahead, and pulled into the drive taking him toward his house. He knew the route by heart, as did his car, which seemed to turn along the way without much direction, even in the snow-covered path, until he reached the front doorway. Instead of pulling into the garage, Will decided to simply leave his car at the door, took his bags from the rear seat, and walked toward the front door, not even locking the car.

Inside, Sira waited. She had prepared dinner, and was at the door with a cup of his favorite tea as he entered. Dropping his bags and taking the cup, warming his hands, Will was grateful. He had noticed that Sira seemed to be staying longer, and frankly he appreciated that, and her company. Tonight, it was clear she would stay at the house; he was not going to risk taking her back to the restaurant.

Sira had the same idea. She prepared a hot meal for his return, making soup and other simple things that would warm him and help him to relax after the journey through the snow. She called Sammi earlier and told him she would stay in the guest room for this evening, and Sammi agreed. An hour later Hassan called, and wanted to know why she was doing this. She said simply that the weather was not worth taking the chance to come back to town. He seemed satisfied with the answer.

Now Sira was prepared for Will's arrival. This was her night to make him comfortable with her, even make him desirous of her staying at the house permanently

Interpol Headquarters, Lyon, France Jacques Saucier, the duty officer had dozed for a few moments in the otherwise dull evening, when suddenly, the large screen in front of him went ablaze with light and a message appeared.

"Who the hell is sending a message at this hour," Saucier said to himself, as he looked at the clock on the wall, realizing it was 2 AM, Lyon time. Looking at the screen, he realized the originating country was the United States, and the agency, the US Central intelligence Agency was the originator.

"What do they want at this hour," Saucier said again, mostly for his own benefit, since there was no one else on duty at the time.

0705Z PRIORITY CEN INTEL AGENCY PUSH TO DIRECTOR

FROM: MINIHAN, OP-1
SUBJECT; ASSISTANCE ON SEARCH

CIA REQUIRES ASSISTANCE ON SEARCH FOR POTENTIALLY LETHAL ARTIFACTS.

From a Vantage Point

REQUEST CONFERENCE CALL (SECURE) AT 1400HRS VIA SECURE VIDEO LINK.

CONFIRM

MINIHAN

"Now who the hell do I route this to?" Saucier asked himself, thinking quickly it had better go to the front office. He looked on his log to see who the duty officer was in the Secretary-General's office, found the name and number and made a call.

The phone rang and then an obviously groggy voice came on the line, "This is LeParc, and it better be important," came the voice on the other end.

"It is sir," responded Saucier, "this message just came in." He read the message to LeParc, who asked it be read a second time, and then LeParc said, "Send me a copy immediately, and another to my cell phone. I will notify the Secretary-General." The phone went dead, and Saucier did as he was told, then going back to his interrupted sleep.

LeParc, who was at home when the call came, was sitting in a chair in his den as he heard the message, rose and went to his office immediately. He lived in an apartment not a mile from Interpol Headquarters. In the ten minutes, it took to get there in the early morning, LeParc heard his phone ding, and expected that was the message sent from communications.

As he entered the Interpol building, he went straight to his office and turned on the large screen that nearly covered one side of his desk. The message was there. He read it at least three times, and then pushed a button on his phone connecting him directly to the Secretary-General, who was also at home.

"Mister Secretary, a message has come in from the US CIA,"

"What does it say LeParc?" the Secretary-General asked. LeParc read it to him.

"Arrange the hookup. If Minihan is excited about something, it must be non-trivial. I do wish the Americans would realize the rest of the world is not on their time. I will be in the office in about two hours," the Secretary-General indicated, before hanging up the phone.

LeParc looked at the message again, and started arranging the linkup on secure video services with the Americans for later that day. It would be a very long day for LeParc and his staff.

Kabul, Afghanistan Hakim al-Azahir left his meeting with Amid Fatoullah with a growing sense of dread. As he approached the city, Hakim wondered who and how Amid had so much information on his operations, since he was not overly

From a Vantage Point

sharing, preferring to keep much of his activities far under the radar. Yet Amid knew virtually every aspect of his plans, including some obvious references to the Atlanta cell, their activities, and their lack of success.

Now, Hakim had an even bigger problem; what to do with Joseph Anderson. That decision had to be made, and quickly before everything blew up in Hakim's face.

Hakim drove straight to his warehouse, parking his Rover behind the fence, and entered, finding only two men working.

"Where are the men?" he asked. One of them turned and responded.

"We are alone here today boss," answered the worker.

"Why now?" asked Hakim.

"We thought you were dead, boss," responded one of the workmen, "Every time Amid comes to Kabul someone dies, and we knew he was meeting with you."

"How did you know that?" Hakim asked.

"Because he came here looking for you, boss. Amid does not come looking for people he likes. They come to him. We are glad you are alive."

"All right. Tell the others I need them tomorrow morning. Have them here early. We have work to do."

"We will do that boss. What do you need today?" asked one of the workmen.

"Tell me where all the boxes were shipped; those that Pentopolos created, and any others," ordered Hakim.

"That is easy boss," responded the workman who had been speaking, "Two went to Cairo to be shipped to the United States. One went to Damascus, and will go overland to Ankara, and then to the United States. The other three, were sent to three other locations, one each day," the man said. "I will get those sheets to tell you the cities, one was in Canada, that I remember."

Hakim knew the first two had arrived in the United States, through Tampa, but now worried about the third. Was it the one without the sensor and could it get through without detection. The other three were simply decoys, designed to make the boxes harder to trace.

"The box going out through Damascus," Hakim asked, "Was it the one with the equipment in it?"

"It was," both men answered together.

Hakim knew he had to contact his person at Interpol; they had to be involved by now, and he wanted to know to what extent he had real troubles, especially if Amid was watching. He removed his cell phone from his pocket and dialed a number. The phone rang several times before it was answered.

'How can I help you Hakim? Came the voice on the phone.

"The packages we spoke of several days ago," Hakim answered, "Have they been tracked down yet?"

From a Vantage Point

"Only one that was going through Damascus and on to Ankara. That was identified by our people yesterday, and marked for international tracking," came the response. Hakim immediately hung up, fearing that his call was being traced. In fact, it was, and his person at Interpol was arrested about two hours later. Hakim was in trouble, far more trouble than in the past, and he knew nothing about the extent of the surveillance on him. That knowledge would come later, as he tried to contact his agent, and received no answer.

INTERPOL Headquarters, Lyon, France As Central Intelligence had requested in their message, two things happened within hours; first, once they had received the sensor information, tracking started on where the boxes containing the sensors had travelled. Second, Interpol also started to monitor communications between the warehouse Hakim maintained in Kabul, and any calls emanating from that office. It took them only a short time to intercept a call from a cell phone at that location, and the recipient at the Interpol field office in Kabul.

Interpol management had assumed for some time that Hakim had a mole in their offices, and now they had proof. The man was arrested and confessed everything, including the information on the sensors in the boxes, and how several had been discovered and placed in other cartons to delay the discovery of the real shipments.

Acting on that information, Interpol began to segregate the information they were pinging on the sensors, and identified three shipments, the two already delivered in the US, one more on its way through Kennedy International in New York, and three more that seemed to be circling from place to place in Europe. The circles seem to be moving west toward the Atlantic, and the INTERPOL team would continue to monitor them as well. Now they could begin to work with their US partners in the CIA and DHS to isolate any potential problems.

On a second front, INTERPOL analysts used their extensive contacts with the major telcom companies through Europe and Asia to trace calls from Hakim's known offices, drops, and his known associates. It took only three days to secure cooperation with the Kabul Constabulary to raid Hakim's warehouse; the one where the shipments left for other parts of the world. When they entered, they found another 3-D printer, one similar to that found at Pentopolos' workshop. The printer was seized, as was the data still stored in the printer. Within minutes, the data was transferred to Lyon for the analysts to decode and review it.

It took about an hour to have the information decoded and an initial analysis completed. One of the analysts on duty took it to LeParc, who read it, and immediately picked up his telephone, calling Sarah Minihan at CIA.

"Sarah, this is LeParc," he spoke into the phone, "I have some interesting information for you." LeParc described both the arrest of Hakim's mole in Kabul, and the raid on his warehouse where they found the 3-D printer. He also described the data contained on the printer.

"We have decoded the data, and it is a program with dimensions for a collapsible mortar, capable of discharging a round of about ten inches long, with about two pounds of C-4 explosive. There were several test runs made, and some of the discarded parts were still in the warehouse. What do you make of that?" LeParc asked.

"Well Augustine, that is an interesting turn of events. We have two of the boxes under surveillance at Reagan Airport in DC. They both came in empty. The FBI is going to monitor where these go, but they have instructions not to intercept. We want them to get to wherever they need to go, especially now with the information you provided. I will let Alice Sawyer over at Homeland Security know what you found out."

"The other thing, Sarah," added LeParc, "was the mole in Kabul. We had long suspected there was one, especially after we found one here from the Fatool days. More important to this is the stream of messages going out from him to Cairo and other places. When we arrested him, it was officially for other reasons so that Hakim would not immediately suspect we were on to him."

"Appreciate that Augustine," Sarah responded, "What are your next steps? Wait, let's do this. Let me connect your secure line to both mine and Alice's, and let's sort this out together. Do you have the time right now?"

"I do," LeParc responded.

"OK then, let me put you on hold for a moment and get the connection made." Sarah quickly asked her secretary to get the connection made.

"Augustine," Sarah said as the line came alive a few moments later. "I have Alice Sawyer on the line as well. Let's go over the warehouse quickly, bring Alice up-to-date, and then move on, shall we?"

For the next thirty-five minutes, Sarah in her office as was LeParc, and Alice in her conference room looking at her huge screen went meticulously through what each knew and decided on some next steps.

The Johnson Farm, Elias, West Virginia Will had parked the car in front of his home instead of nearer to the garage. With all the snow continuing to fall, it was not worth the struggle later, especially in taking Sira back to town after dinner. In his own mind, he thought to suggest to her to stay for the night, eliminating the need for another trip. He had a large guest room, which had been his room while his parents lived, and when he moved into the larger bedroom some years back, he converted his own room to a guest room, although he seldom had visitors. The last person to do so, in fact, had been Josh Giddons.

As he pulled up close to the front door, Will saw Sira through the window, walking between the kitchen and the dining room with plates and other things for

From a Vantage Point

the table. 'Great', he said to himself, 'Hopefully she will have something hot and ready to serve.' He parked the car, opened the door, walked to the other side, opened the rear passenger door, and took out his travel bag. Then he closed the door and walked toward the house, pausing only to see if there had been mail.

"Sira, I'm home," Will announced as he entered.

Sira came out of the kitchen, walked over to him, and gave him a short hug. "I am glad you are home, Mister Will. I was worried about you for the storm outside."

"It was not an easy drive this time," responded Will. "Tell you what; how about you stay here this evening in the guest room. The storm is pretty miserable, and only God knows how long it will take to get to town."

"Thank you, Mister Will," she responded. "I thought about that myself, but it would be presumptuous of me to ask. I hoped you would though." Sira smiled, as she turned to go to the kitchen for more things for the table.

Within a few minutes, Will had taken his bag to his bedroom, removed his coat and sweater, and put another pullover on before returning to the living room. Sira had just finished setting the table for dinner, and everything was now ready. They sat and enjoyed their first meal together in nearly three weeks.

"Well, how did your trip go?" asked Sira, beaming at Will. "Did you do everything you wanted?"

"We are moving along well, Sira," responded Will. "By the way, the idea you had on trying to get the same room really worked out well. It is very convenient, and I get a great view of Washington. One of these trips I will take you along to see Washington, and you can see for yourself."

"Oh, I do not know, Mister Will. How would I explain that to Mister Sammi? He might think badly of me."

"You just leave Sammi to me Sira. Trust me, he will understand." Will ate some of his food, and drank some of the tea Sira had prepared. He was glad to be home, and especially glad he did not have to go out again this evening. He just wanted peace and quiet; hopefully for of the evening news, and then his bed.

FBI Headquarters, Washington DC "Amid Fatoullah? Was that the name?" asked Peabody quickly. "We will continue shortly Doucette. First, I have something to do right now. Stay here." Peabody rose from his desk and walked to the door. "Amy'" he said to his assistant, "Get me Alice Sawyer, and Sarah Minihan at CIA. Put them both on my secure line, will you?"

"Sure boss, right away," she replied. It took only a few minutes, while Peabody got some coffee and returned to his office just before his phone rang. He picked it up quickly, after his assistant yelled through the door that the call was secure. He knew who was on the other line, and pushed the speaker button.

From a Vantage Point

"Good morning ladies. How are you both today?" asked Peabody. "I was sitting here with Roger Doucette, and your names came up in the conversation. I just knew I had to get the information directly, so what in the hell is happening?"

"Richard, this is Sarah. How are you?" she asked quietly.

"Just fine Sarah, and how are you Alice?"

"Great, Richard," she replied.

"So, what do we have here that has your fingers all over it?"

The two explained the entire scenario, with Alice doing most of the talking, except where the CIA connections in Khartoum and Kabul were concerned. Alice went point-by-point, including the surveillance of Will Johnson, the situation with Giddons in Atlanta, and the travels of Hakim through Asia, ending with what they currently knew about a Giddons lookalike in Atlanta, a set of boxes in Boston, and everything else they knew to throw into the conversation.

Richard Peabody listened intently, taking notes, and finally, as they finished, asked a pivotal question.

"OK, so who is going to mention Amid Fatoullah?"

"Well Richard, I should have chimed in on that, but I know how excited you get when those names are mentioned. I thought you might like the big picture first," answered Sarah.

"Thanks for the concern Sarah, but the mention of this guy does give me goosebumps, and head pain. Will we ever be rid of the Fatool gang?" Peabody asked, somewhat rhetorically.

"Richard," interrupted Alice and quickly changing the subject somewhat, "We do have some things we need FBI help on. We want to find a guy named Anderson who came in through Tampa two weeks ago, and eventually headed for Atlanta, where he disappeared. That person may be the key to this whole scenario."

"Wait Alice," responded Peabody, "What makes him so important?"

"Richard, this guy is the exact twin-brother image of the dead guy, also in Atlanta, Josh Giddons, a friend of two other guys in this plot, Hakim al-Azahir, you may know of him, and a Will Johnson in West Virginia. We are not sure of the connections, but it sure is interesting to have two men with the same face, one dead, and one alive in Atlanta."

"What else do you need from me Alice?" asked Peabody, as he took some notes on a small notepad.

"Right now, I think we have everything under control Richard. Two of your agents are watching two suspicious packages which came in from Cairo. They fit into the plot as well. Agent Doucette can explain that situation. We do not want to apprehend, just watch and follow. We need to know what happens to the boxes; where they go, and if they suddenly disappear as well. There may be another box or two coming in to the country, but we will let you know on those?"

"What's the importance of the boxes?" asked Peabody.

"We think they are intended to be fitted with some kind of explosive weapon or instrument to be set off during the coming inauguration Richard. We can't verify that yet, but they came from a warehouse in Kabul outfitted with a 3-D printer, and plans for something looking like a mortar."

Peabody kept taking notes, putting comments on the margins for the offices that needed to be involved.

"And this guy Anderson, what is his importance, other than the face?" asked Peabody.

"Well," interjected Doucette, "In addition to having the same face as a guy who died enroute to Atlanta some time ago, Josh Giddons, a partner with this guy Hakim al-Azahir in Kabul, there is the possibility he may be linking up with a new cell we don't know about in Atlanta. It certainly seems that way. The guy comes into the country from abroad with a need for support by someone, and we have a photo of the person who picked him up at Tampa International, and then drove him to Atlanta. Smells like a cell to me."

"That cell, if it exists," continued Doucette, "May be linked as well to another guy, in West Virginia, who was a friend of this Giddons character."

"And his name is Will Johnson if I might guess?" interposed Peabody.

"Sure is. How did you know what?"

"Well, let me tell you a story before we get too far," answered Peabody. For the next several minutes, Peabody told the story of Johnson, his past, and his 'altercation' with Peabody's agents recently in Elias, West Virginia, something Alice already knew in detail.

"We need to be careful if we have to deal with Johnson, Roger. No more screw-ups there," responded Alice, "I do not want us to have to deal with the judge again on that situation. It was at my request they went to pick him up. They just bungled the job on bad information from my own people in Charleston," continued Alice.

"Ok, so I need to involve Boston, Washington, Charleston, Atlanta, and perhaps Tampa on this one," responded Peabody. "That's a lot of manpower on some guesses Alice. Are you sure enough to bet on this?"

"Yes, I am Richard," said Alice Sawyer, "We have to be on this. The Inauguration is too important to let intelligence like this slip though unchecked."

Peabody sighed, and answered, "You are right of course. I will go see the Deputy, and get the allocations. Thanks to you both. Sarah, how's Bernie and the kids?"

"Everyone is fine Richard. You know, we are only fifteen miles away. Would love to have you come over for dinner."

From a Vantage Point

"I promise I will Sarah. This new job is just sucking up all my time. My own wife introduces me to the kids every time I get home, if they are not already in bed."

"I know how you feel Richard. Let's try soon, though. Come out, and let the kids run around. We have lots of space." The three spoke for a few more moments, then the call ended. Peabody looked over at Doucette.

"I sure hope you realize how deep we are in this Roger. A lot of the work will fall on you, you know."

"I understand boss. By the way, who is this Sarah Minihan anyway? She is one of the sharpest people I have ever heard."

"That she is," replied Peabody, "That she is. That woman is married to the Deputy Director of Operations at CIA, an acknowledged senior analyst in her own right, and was my partner in New Orleans some years ago, on a complex case, also involving this guy Amid Fatoullah. I was on loan from the Boston office then, before taking it over. She is very methodical, makes no guesses, even educated ones, on anything, and always has facts to back up her statements. Glad you had the chance to meet her. Now, what part do we really play here? Let's get down to a plan, shall we?"

"We need the West Virginia Field Office, and the Atlanta Office to do what?" continued Peabody.

For the next thirty minutes or so, they discussed what needed to be done, and by which office. Once they agreed, Peabody got on the phone to all the involved offices to read in the Special Agents-in-Charge, and told them Doucette would follow up in writing. He also pointed out that anything they received was to be funneled through Doucette.

The plan began to move. Within hours, there were agents fanning out in Atlanta trying to determine where this guy Anderson could be hiding. All they had were the pics from the security cams at Tampa International, and some footage from cameras along I-75, but it was enough to begin digging.

National Security Agency, Ft. Meade MD Zambino looked at the monitors behind the table, which reflected the data his analysts were reviewing on their own screens. He waited a few minutes, perusing the data himself, and then announced, "Gang, we have a job to do for Homeland." Everyone looked up and waited.

"Homeland thinks there is a situation going on in an area bounded by West Virginia, DC, and the Atlanta area. We are going to find out if that situation has a factual basis and, if it does, who is playing the game here."

"Eldon, what do you want us to do?" asked the same woman who commented earlier on his arrival.

'That is the easy part," began Zamboni, "First, we need to establish links with the major repeaters in an area from roughly Charleston to a smaller town, Elias, in West Virginia. We want the metadata on calls, especially those emanating from Elias going to DC and down toward Atlanta. The second task is to set up a similar sweep in a circle, starting perhaps fifty miles around Atlanta. In the Atlanta situation, we need overseas calls, calls from the West Virginia and DC areas, especially calls that ping on Horizon LLC in Atlanta. The third task is to tap a selected set of servers at Horizon LLC, a Homeland contractor, for anomalous calls overseas, or from overseas, especially from Afghanistan, Pakistan, or Sudan."

"Whoa, Eldon," said one of the other analysts, "That is a lot of metadata. Will we have cover from FISA and our own counsel?"

"In the works now," responded Zamboni. "Let's begin to set up the parameters so that when we get the writ, we are ready to power up. For the present, I do not want to use our wire taps directly to the telecoms; use our alternatives though through the tower sweeps. Everybody understand?" The staff nodded, and Zamboni put out the assignments, with two analysts on each task and three on the Horizon surveillance.

"We need to be ready by late afternoon," added Zamboni, as he rose to leave the table. "I'm going to brief the boss man on what we are going to do. Any questions or problems?" There were no responses, so Zamboni continued his way, leaving the room, and walking further down the corridor to another office where his chief of section would probably have a lot of questions. Following that session, he also needed to get the request format completed so the Counsel's office could go to the Court for their approval.

Two hours later, Zamboni was back in the Office of Legal Counsel with his completed and signed request for the warrant to collect and analyze the data he described in depth. Zamboni was careful to point out that this was being done in conjunction with Homeland and the FBI, who would share the metadata for the ongoing investigation. He also carefully pointed out the role of the CIA in securing overseas data which might be linked to that same investigation. Having been burned several times with his requests, Zamboni was being overly cautious this time, and for good reason. The Agency had been pilloried following the Snowden disclosures, limited by the FISA Court, and the White House on what it could collect and maintain, and his request carefully described exactly what they wanted, how they would handle the data, and its eventual estimated disposal date.

"This looks good, Eldon," responded Ned, his counsel, after perusing the document. "I have one of the judges waiting for this. Sit here for a moment, and let me see how fast this goes." The lawyer took the document, placed it in his fax

From a Vantage Point

machine, and dialed a number. The machine scanned the documents and beeped to indicate it had been sent.

"Now we wait," said Ned, "Hopefully not for long." True enough, in about ten minutes the phone rang. From the Caller ID, Ned could see it was from the Judge's chambers where he had faxed the request. He picked up the phone.

"Sir, this is Judge O'Neill's Office. The judge has signed your request, with a single caveat."

"What is that?" asked Ned.

"You have 90 days to collect limited data as described, and then you must come back to the Court for an extension. You have 180 days to establish a case or destroy the data."

"That is close, but it will work," Ned responded. "Please thank Judge O'Neill for me."

"Well, you have your order Eldon, go do it," offered the lawyer, "Just do things right and I will be happy."

"Thanks Ned," was the response, as Zamboni literally ran down the corridor to his own work area, opened the door, and shouted in, "We have a go. Let's get working on our data collection."

From a Vantage Point

Chapter 36 Disrupting the Plans

The Johnson Farm, Elias, West Virginia "Sira, you are an excellent cook. This is one of the best meals I have had in years, especially considering I eat so many meals at Sammi's." Will sat back in his chair, looking tired but contented, sipping his tea and looking over at Sira on the other side of the table.

"Thank you, Mister Will. I try to do my best. Sometimes it is hard, but here, with all that you have, it is easy to make wonderful dinners and other meals as well. Back in my country, it was truly hard to learn to be a good cook, since we had so little, and what we could grow or buy was often stolen. It was hard."

"I certainly understand, Sira. I'm glad you had the opportunity to come to America and see that everything does not have to be hard."

"That is true Mister Will," Sira said, "But I still worry about those back in my country. They have nothing but war and robbers, and the West does nothing to help them, except make big speeches in the United Nations. After their speeches, nothing gets better." Sira was hoping to coax Will into a political discussion and he seemed to be biting on the suggestion.

"Sometimes," responded Will, "It is equally hard for outsiders to have a real impact, and especially if they are from the West, without a real understanding of Middle East and other so widely varied cultures. When I went to the Persian Gulf and then on to Sudan last year, it was so obvious that there was a wide disparity in those with wealth and the poor. I remember visiting a village where the mud huts were worse than those in my own country of Lebanon. Yet, there were people living in palaces only fifty miles away."

"In Khartoum, I watched the results of a bombing of an old area of the city, with numbers of people killed, and the apartment in which my friends were living destroyed along with many others. People walked the streets with nowhere to go," added Will, looking over at Sira.

"It is true, Mister Will. These things happen, and when you look at it, it is usually the West that has sent bombs and drones to kill innocent people. I will not say that my own people have not done the same, but when they do, it is because of religion and tribal differences. The Americans and others have simply sent in bombs for political reasons, killing women, children, and destroying large places. That is not right."

"Life is not always fair," responded Will, looking at Sira. "People kill and hurt for many reasons, not always logical, by the way. I know little of Islam, other than what I learned from my travels and my friends. When I visited them last, we went to a museum in Dubai. Along the walk were murals of the history of Islam, and the killings and destruction caused by the Prophet Muhammed in his quest to gain Arabia. Later mosaics along the walls spoke to the expulsion from Spain and

From a Vantage Point

much of North Africa, and how the Christians conquered Europe and drove them back once again"

"I know that Mister Will, but did the mosaics show what the Christians did over history. Using force to drive Islam out of Spain is one thing, but the Inquisition and its unnecessary destruction and killing, and the later Crusades went far beyond that. Islam has a history too, and it should also be respected. My family died because of those who believed that only Christians had a God, and everyone else was a blasphemer and could be killed. Is that right?"

Will thought for a moment, and then replied, "No, it is not Sira. It is always better than people live together and in peace than in constant fighting. In this age, the constant fighting seems to take over from that desire for peace."

"But the politicians all want peace, they say," replied Sira, "Just their type of peace, and everyone else has to live as they wish it. Is that fair, or right?"

"No, it is not Sira," Will said, "People should expect better from their leaders, on all sides."

"But how does a person tell their leaders they object to the way they are treated?" asked Sira. "A person like me or you have no real influence, unless you choose to make a loud voice to be heard."

"That is true, Sira," retorted Will, "Sometimes, you just should speak loudly, even protest to be heard. We can do that in the United States, but in some other countries, it would be illegal. We can shout from the rooftops, if we choose, and hope that politicians hear us. Sometimes, getting people together to speak loud enough means we really will be heard."

"Well then Mister Will," said Sira, as she rose to start collecting dishes to take them to the kitchen, "Maybe it is time to do what you call shouting from the rooftops. With a new group of politicians coming into office in Washington, it is perhaps time to tell them what they need to hear."

"Perhaps so," answered Will, "Perhaps so. Politicians always listen to the loudest, it seems."

"Well then, we need to speak loudly," said Sira, as she completed collecting the dishes and then walking toward the kitchen. "Perhaps so," she muttered again as she left the room.

Will Johnson picked up his coffee cup from the table and moved over toward his easy chair in the living room, turning on the TV as he passed to listen to the news.

Sammi's Restaurant, Elias, West Virginia Hassan walked out through the swinging door to the kitchen and faced Sammi, who was wiping tables.

"Sammi, where is Sira?" he asked.

"With this weather, she will stay at the farm this evening. It is too difficult to travel between the farm and the town. She will be fine with Mister Will."

From a Vantage Point

"Why was I not told that this would happen?" retorted Hassan.

"Because her call came in just a short time ago, Hassan. I looked at the weather, and told her it was all right to stay at the farm. What is your problem with that?" Sammi asked.

"I must be kept informed, Sammi. I am responsible to my people in Atlanta, and they will not be happy. I must call them to let them know."

"Do what you wish Hassan, and tell them as well that I gave permission for her to stay. If they wish to argue with me, let them do so. I look forward to the argument." Sammi threw the rag he was using to wipe tables into a bucket on the next table, and walked slowly over toward the large window near the cash register. Looking outside at the quickly falling snow, he turned back to say something else to Hassan, but Hassan had returned to the kitchen. "Piece of shit," Sammi said quietly and low enough that it would not reach the kitchen.

Hassan stormed into the kitchen, sat down at the small desk near the food reefer, and pulled out his cell phone, dialing a number and waiting for an answer. While he waited, he thought about what he would say.

"What is it you want, Hassan?" asked the voice on the other end of the live. Hassan knew it was the woman he and Sammi met earlier in the restaurant. "What do you need from me?" she asked again.

"I want to tell you Samira, that your kinsman Sira may be moving to the Johnson farm. She is staying there tonight because of the storm, but I have fear she will want to do it permanently."

"If that is so, let her do it. What is important now," said the woman's voice, "Is that the man does what we wish him to do. She will be better able to perform her task at the farm. Let her do it."

"But we are betrothed?" responded Hassan into the phone, standing up as he did so.

"Betrothals are not as important as the duty Hassan. You and she will perform your duty; everything else takes second place. Do it, and let her do what she must." Having said that, the woman hung up, and Hassan stood there for a few moments trying to comprehend the situation, and finally put the phone back in his pocket. "What must be, must be," he said to himself. "The Great One allows it, "he continued to mumble, as he walked over to the preparation area to begin peeling carrots and potatoes.

Sammi, hearing the conversation Hassan was having in the kitchen, became even more alarmed. While he also had been recruited for this cell, although early on he did not know that was the case, he had become involved, and regretted he had not said more to Will Johnson, or even the police. Now, he had to deal with Hassan, who was out of control, and Sira, who also had second thoughts. The question was what to do, and how. He decided that he would speak to Will Johnson at the first opportunity, when the others might not be within earshot.

From a Vantage Point

National Security Agency, Ft. Meade, MD. The team worked diligently to set up the metadata capture, working through the night until they could test connections. Once everything was in place, it was a matter of comparing calls to see if there were matches. They fully expected it to be a long process.

Suddenly, the screen lit up with pings. A cell phone originating in Elias, West Virginia made a call to Atlanta, Georgia. The metadata was captured as it passed through a repeater tower outside town high on a local hill, travelling on its way to a downtown Atlanta location. The team captured the information and set the system to continue monitoring. In the meanwhile, the metadata dump went to Eldon Zamboni for a decision on next steps.

As soon as Zamboni saw the metadata, he decided to call Alice Sawyer with what he had.

"Alice, this is Eldon Zamboni over at NSA. I may have something for you." Eldon explained the metadata, the time it was recorded, and the to-from information on the data pair. Alice wrote down what he provided, then called in one of her own analysts, and asked for the specifics on the owners of the phones.

"Thanks Eldon," she responded, "I will get back post-haste."

It took about an hour to match the location receiving the call. The phone was registered to an old boxing club downtown, owned by an Iranian ex-patriot, Jalil Radan. The outgoing cell phone used was purchased three months earlier in Elias at the hardware store, and registered to a man named Hassan Singh. Alice recalled the name, but could not immediately place it. Suddenly the memory came back; this Hassan Singh was one of the employees at Sammi's Restaurant.

Alice called Eldon Zamboni back. "Eldon," she said quickly. "We have a good hit on the Atlanta number. Your staff needs to continue to monitor Elias, and to pay close attention to everything come from the area of the gym owned by Radan, the location of the Atlanta phone, monitor those calls, especially any going or coming from overseas, and get that information back to Homeland as quickly as it comes in."

"Yes Ma'am," responded Eldon, "Do you want us to make the link with the service providers?"

"No Eldon, we will do that from here. We have different routes we can go to get the specific information we need, based on your FISA court approval Thanks for everything thus far."

When Alice hung up from Zamboni, she called Richard Peabody next. "Richard," she started to say without introducing herself, "We need to." Peabody stopped her.

"Alice hold on a second. Let me get Doucette in here."

From a Vantage Point

"Sure, I probably should have called Roger first, but this is a critical piece of information for you all."

"No problem Alice, here he comes now," responded Peabody. Alice could hear someone coming into the room. "OK, ready now Alice," Peabody continued.

"We received information from NSA just about an hour ago, on a call from Elias to Atlanta. Hassan Singh made a call from his cell phone to a small gym in downtown Atlanta, owned by a guy named Jalil Radan. Here is the address." Alice read the address and phone number information she had to the two agents.

"The call lasted only a couple of minutes," Sawyer continued, "We are asking the service providers to get us a domestic tap, based on approval of a FISA Court request today by NSA. We notified the judge we are associating with the request. That gives you free reign to have access to the information as well. Could you see what your agents can do with it? We don't want any arrests right now, just monitoring and surveillance."

"No problem Alice," answered Peabody. "That address rings a bell though. Roger, do we have anything going on there?"

"Actually, boss, that's very near the area where we lost track of that Anderson guy when we first followed the trail to Atlanta from Tampa."

"Good, then let's keep a close watch. Put a team over there if necessary, and look out for the possibility of finding Anderson. Anything else Alice?"

"Looks like we have some pieces coming together, Richard. We just need a bit of luck now, I think. Let's keep talking," responded Sawyer.

"Later Alice," answered Richard Peabody, as he hung up the phone.

"Roger, let's let Atlanta know what we know, and alert Charleston to be ready to move into Elias if needed. Lets' go back over what we know about this restaurant as well. I have a meeting in a couple of minutes. It will take about thirty, and then let's get back together in the conference room."

"Will do boss," answered Doucette, as he rose to leave, taking his notepad with him.

Doucette made the calls, both to Charleston and Atlanta to bring them up-to-date on the situation, letting them know that action might be necessary. In the case of the Atlanta office, his discussion with the Special-agent-in-charge resulted in a small, but discrete dragnet to try to find Anderson.

Doucette forwarded what he had, and asked that the Atlanta agents try to find additional video footage from local sources that might extend their trail. He also decided to call the Tampa Field office in the hope that additional footage in and around the airport might become available that would help them in their search. Now, all Doucette could do is wait for any results.

From a Vantage Point

The Johnson Farm, Elias, West Virginia Sitting in his easy chair facing toward the television, Will took the remote control, turned on the set, and pushed the channel button until he found his favorite news channel.

"This is Allie Aldrich, WCHS-TV, sitting in this evening for the news hour. We have several stories brewing this evening. First, plans are already underway for the inauguration ceremonies, both in Charleston, and in Washington, D.C. First, here in Charleston, we have Alan Griffin, Capitol Hill Reporter with the latest. Alan, what are the plans for Inauguration Day?"

"Thanks Allie," responded Griffin, "There are multiple events planned in conjunction with the ceremonies for the new governor. A little more subdued this time than in the past, but it is expected to be a well-attended series of events throughout the city. First, of course, is the inauguration itself, on the main steps of the Capitol, presided over by the Chief Justice. The Governor-elect will, as in the past, ride up to the Capitol building along the main street, with the West Virginia National Guard and the State Police lining the sides in salute. We understand the official State Bible, from the Archives will be used this time. As you know, the bible was used to swear in every governor since the state split from Virginia during the Civil War."

"Following the ceremonies, the new Governor will return to his motorcade for a parade through downtown and later in the day, the parties and balls will start, the largest one at the Arena is expected to have over one thousand people, many of whom have paid large contributions to earn one of those tickets. All in all, it is expected to keep the city lit well into the early morning. Back to you."

"Thanks Alan. Which ball will you be attending?" asked Allie.

" I'm going to another ball, at the Armory. They are calling that the Young People's Ball, and several local country groups will be playing to another packed house. How about you?" Griffin asked.

"I'm here in the studio part of the evening Alan. Then several of us are going over to the Arena to broadcast from there. The Governor is expected to speak at about ten o'clock, and WCHS-TV will be covering it. Thanks for the report, Alan. Enjoy your evening."

"Now," Aldrich continued, "We have a report from Jim Smead of Eyewitness News on the doings in DC at the upcoming presidential Inauguration. Jim, are you there?"

"Sure, I am Allie," responded Snead. "The city will be gearing up for a massive display for the new President. There is a total of nine balls, all in the evening, following two parades and the inauguration itself. It seems to be a Washington tradition building that there is a

From a Vantage Point

main parade, and an anti-president parade, not along the same route, but close on Inauguration Day. There will also be several demonstrations along the streets and the Mall, but the Capitol and Park Police say they are limiting permits, and will closely control all demonstrations. With the animosity built up from the elections, as always seems to happen these days, you can expect that the demonstrations will be loud and hard to control."

As Smead spoke, there were multiple views of past parades and demonstrations, including several which became violent. As the scenes raced across the screen Sira came into the room, and sat opposite Will on another chair facing toward the TV. She seemed rapt in attention to the demonstrations and violence.

"In any event, Allie, there are thousands of extra police, National Guard and other law enforcement and protective personnel, along with fire department and security support planned to make sure that nothing serious happens here. Time will tell, of course, but the planning continues feverishly to try to prevent damage and injury. As you know, several terrorist groups have threatened to disrupt the festivities, and Homeland Security is equally bound that these efforts will not occur."

"Has Homeland started briefings on what it thinks might possibly happen Jim?" Allie asked.

"No, but they issue frequent bulletins, publishing do's and don'ts for the public, and lots of background information on possible terrorist activity. They continue to say there is no known specific threat, but they always say that. We have no way to know at this point what their plans are, or who they are planning to prevent from whatever might happen. Not a lot to go on, but we still have nearly sixty days until the inauguration."

"Do they really think there will be trouble in Washington, Mister Will?" interrupted Sira.

"While I do not want to see anyone injured, perhaps something like that would be a wakeup call for you Americans, like September 11th."

" That would not be a good thing, Sira," answered Will, keeping his eyes on the TV screen as he spoke. "Having people die, innocent people, is not what the inauguration is all about. It is about the transition of power in the country after a free election."

"What is different when the American Government sends in their planes and drones and kills innocent people? Is that allowable, or is it

From a Vantage Point

just because the American are powerful enough to do it?" asked Sira, also looking at the screen.

Just then, the screen images started to change and showed Allie Aldrich at the news desk. "In other news," she began, "There were multiple attacks by coalition forces on targets within Syria, also in the Mosel Valley area of Iraq. The Iraqi forces have been fighting steadily to reenter the Mosel Valley over the past two months, aiming to take the city back from ISIS. American and allied jets pounded positions in several bombing runs. It is unclear what the number of casualties might be, although an ISIS source indicated that numbers of women and children were killed and wounded."

In Syria," Aldrich continued, "Similar allied strikes attacked positions around Raqqa, while Russian Jets attacked both Aleppo and surrounding villages. The Russians claim they are attacking ISIS, but independent observers indicate a very different story, with major damage being done primarily to opponents of the Assad regime. More on the fighting on the eleven o'clock news."

Aldrich then went on to the local news and that gave Johnson an opportunity to go to bed.

"Sira, I think I will turn in," said Will, rising and moving toward his bedroom. "You have everything you need in the guest room. I will see you in the morning," Will added, as he started to walk through the door to his bedroom, closing it behind him as he moved through it.

"Good night, Mister Will," responded Sira. "See you in the morning. Thank you for letting me stay tonight."

"No problem. Happy to have you," was Will's final response as he closed the door behind him.

Downtown Boxing Club, Atlanta, Georgia Jalil Radan walked in through the front door of the boxing club, something he seldom did, preferring the side entrance hidden from the street, and asked for Sam Oakley. The employee sitting behind the small entrance desk saw that Radan was excited about something.

"I need to see Oakley, and right now," shouted Radan at the man. "Where is he? I will go find him myself," he continued.

"Won't do you any good, man," responded the employee, not moving from his seat leaning against a wall. "He ain't here, and I don't know where he is or when he will be back. Anything else you need right away?" the employee said with a lot of sarcasm.

Radan looked at him, shook his head, and started to walk up the stairs to his office. "When you do hear from him, I want to see him. Understand?"

"Sure mister," came the response, equally sarcastic.

A short time earlier, Radan had received a call from his associate Hakim al-Azahir in Kabul; a call that excited and frustrated Radan to no end. Hakim spoke of his meeting with Amid, without mentioning him by name, and what he expected Radan to have done with the man who looked like Giddons in Atlanta. This man, Anderson, simply had to disappear, since the use of his services was no longer required. Radan understood what that meant, although he did not clearly understand all the ramifications of the call. He ended his brief conversation telling Amid he would take care of everything, and now had to rely on Oakley to do just that.

National Security Agency, Fort Meade, Maryland A series of pings were sounding loudly throughout the small office and the two analysts wondered if these were related to previous intercepts earlier in the day. One looked at his screen and realized the pinging was due to calls being made through a secure sever at Horizons LLC.

"Hey Jim, look at this?" said one man to another, who walked over to where the screen continued to ping. "A call going out between Atlanta and a cell overseas. The software is trying to resolve both addresses, but this thing is bouncing all over the world and back." Both men could easily see that the call was being routed through multiple connections and intercepts, and was still chasing it from router to router.

Then, the screen went momentarily dark, and, when it refreshed, both analysts could see that the origin was somewhere in Kabul, Afghanistan, and the destination in Atlanta.

"All right then," said the analysts at the screen, "Let's get the to-from information. The server is already recording the call." Typing a few keystrokes, and entering an access code indicating they had authorization for the data collection, it took only seconds to show that the destination of the call was to a place called Near East Imports, and provided the phone number and address. More important, the server it used at Horizons LLC was one of those under contract to Homeland Security.

"We better get the Zambino in here," added the analyst, "He will want the FBI over there pronto, I will assume." The other analyst picked up the phone on his own desk, dialed a number reaching Zambino, who then literally ran down the corridor to their office space.

"What do you have guys?" asked the boss, excitedly.

"A call is in progress, from a place called Near East Imports going to Kabul, Mr. Z, responded the analyst. "We can't get the info on the cell, so it is probably a burner, but the origination is in Kabul. The tape is running on it now."

From a Vantage Point

"Good, bring it up on the speakers." One of the analysts tied in the phone conversation. What they heard was a foreign dialect neither of the analysts knew, but Zamboni's eyes lit up.

"Boys, this is a dialect of Pashto," offered Zamboni. 'One is saying to the other that someone named Anderson needs to disappear, and quickly. This needs to go to Homeland and the FBI." Zamboni walked over to a phone and dialed.

"This is Alice Sawyer," said the person on the other end of Zamboni's call.

"Alice, this is Eldon Zamboni at NSA. We have a call between Atlanta and Kabul, going through one of your servers. We have the call monitored. They are speaking in what appears to be Pashto. I understood enough to say someone wants someone else, named Anderson to disappear. Mean anything to you?"

"Sure does. Where did the call come from?" asked Sawyer.

"Kabul," came the response, "To a place called Near East Imports in Atlanta." Zamboni gave her the address. Alice hung up quickly, after saying thanks for the info, and telling them not to shut down the line. She pushed another button on the phone set and called Richard Peabody to let him know about the situation in Atlanta, gave him the address, and asked that they go and pick up Anderson. Now she had to wait and hope they had the man before he disappeared.

Will Johnson Farm, Elias, West Virginia The howling wind outside his house, seeming to go in swirls around the building awoke Will Johnson with a start. He looked over to the clock on his nightstand and saw it was nearly 3 AM, It was not unusual for this type of wind in the valley during the late fall, but it was strong enough to knock over several tools Will have left earlier in the week, before he left for Washington, that blew over, making an even larger racket than normal.

Knowing he was not going to go back to sleep easily, Will decided to get up and go to the kitchen for some tea. As he left his room, he noticed that the door to the guest room opposite his bedroom was open, and then looked over toward the couch. Sira was wrapped up in a blanket asleep on one end of the couch. Walking over toward her, he saw that she was fast asleep, and decided to try not to wake her, but to carry her to the bedroom and place her on the waiting bed. He picked her up easily, and started toward the bedroom, with her barely stirring.

Walking slowly, he entered the bedroom and went over toward the left side of the bed, where he had turned down the cover earlier in the evening, then placed her on the bad. As he started to move the covers, she began to stir, looking up at him as he moved to cover her with the blankets.

"Mister Will, I was comfortable on the couch."

"Sira, the bedroom is for sleeping, not the couch. Now, go back to sleep. We have a big day tomorrow." As he reached down to pull up the covers, she tried to sit up slightly and they came close to each other, looking into each other's eyes. She sat up a bit more and kissed him.

"Mister Will, you are a wonderful man," she said, and lay back down, continuing to lock onto his eyes. "I know no one else like you."

"You are a wonderful woman as well, Sira. Now, go to sleep."

"Mister Will, please stay here with me, she said softly."

Will did not know how to respond. His feelings for her had been repressed, but now they began to stir.

"Sira, what are you saying? This is not how it is supposed to be," responded Will.

"Let us think more about it tomorrow. For tonight, will you stay with me? I want you very much." She looked even more deeply into his eyes, and Will felt his resistance crumbling. He climbed into bed as she pushed over into the center, and covered them both with the blankets and coverlet, Sira moved closer to him, placed her arm around his chest, and closed her eyes. Will felt the warmth of her body, and, in his heart, was glad that they finally realized their feelings for each other.

Will awoke at about 5 AM, just as a rooster in the yard began to crow, sending the rest of the birds in the trees surrounding the house into a fit of chirping on their own. Looking over toward his right, he also saw Sira sleeping quietly, and tried to rise from the bed without waking her. In that regard, he was not so lucky, as she started to stir about the same time, turning to look at him and smiling. She was first to speak.

"Good morning, Mister Will. Did you sleep well?" she asked.

"I did, and yourself?" he responded, "But now I have to get moving. I have a lot of work to do today, and only a couple of days before I have to go back to Washington."

Sira started to rise herself, but Will added, "Stay in bed for a while. I will get myself some coffee. You rest a while. It is still very early."

"But you need breakfast if you are going to work, Mister Will. I will make some for you." As she climbed out of bed, Will saw that she was still naked, and suddenly marveled at what a beauty she was. He smiled again, and watched as she grabbed her robe from the floor by the bed, and rushed for the bathroom. Once inside, she turned on the water to the shower, dropped her robe, and stepped inside.

Sitting back down on the bed for moment, Will thought about the prior evening, and the depth of their lovemaking. He was obviously in love with her, and her response said she felt the same way. He knew she was betrothed to Hassan, but not completely sure of what that meant. For now, he could only bask in the wonderful feelings that came with new love. Everything else could be sorted out later.

Sira, feeling the warmth of the shower, was working through a dilemma as well; one concerned with her feelings for Will, and her obligations, both to Hassan, and to the Movement. She knew that everything could not come out well for them, but what could she do to at least try. For now, it was still her duty to lead him along and get him to agree to do what her leaders wanted' her own personal opinions mattered much less. She wanted to be strong and do her duty, but her heart was beginning to tell her otherwise.

Newsroom, WGCL, Atlanta, GA *"This is WGCL News, Atlanta with the early morning news. We start today with the story of a massive shootout at the Downtown Boxing Club on the East Side early this morning. The shootout was precipitated by a raid conducted by the FBI."*

"This is Jim Shubo," the reporter continued, *"This morning's raid, according to an FBI spokesperson, was to serve a search warrant on the owner, one Sam Oakley, or "Big Boy' as he is called in the neighborhood. That warrant, issued last evening by the federal Court downtown, alleges that the Boxing Club is a front for a terrorist cell here in the Atlanta area. There is still no description or name for the group, but at least one source close to the investigation says the alleged group has links to the Muslim Brotherhood."*

"We do not know, at this point who the FBI was looking for specifically. What we do know is that, when the FBI agents from the FBI Atlanta office, along with several from Homeland Security attempted to enter the building about 7:00AM this morning, shooting quickly broke out from inside. One FBI agent was taken to a local hospital with what has been called minor injuries."

"There were apparently several people inside the Boxing Club, and some attempted to flee through a rear entrance. Three men and a woman reached the short alley next to the club, heavily armed, where they were met by a phalanx or Federal agents, supported numbers of Atlanta PD officers. When they started firing, the law enforcement personnel returned fire. We now understand that all four were killed. Their bodies are still at the scene."

"At the main entrance, about twenty minutes later, a similar firefight broke out, as six men and two women, also heavily armed and wearing body armor, attempted to leave, resulting in both deaths and injuries on both sides. The FBI Spokesperson described the firefight at the front this way." (Pan to FBI Agent).

"I am FBI Agent Anne Harding of the Atlanta FBI Field Office. This morning at approximately 6:45AM, the FBI and the Department of

From a Vantage Point

Homeland Security arrived at this location to serve a search warrant issued by the Federal Courts. When agents attempted to enter, they were immediately met by both small arms and assault rifle fire, and took protective action to ensure that they themselves and any local bystanders were protected. A group inside attempted to leave through a rear entrance, exchanged fire with agents and local police, and all were killed."

"At the front entrance, Agents propelled two smoke grenades, and two tear grades grenades through front windows. Within seconds, the doors opened, and a total of eight people attempted to exit, wearing heavy body armor and firing automatic weapons. Agents and local police returned fire, killing two and wounding the others. The wounded do not have life-threatening injuries and are being transported to local hospitals."

"We have no further information for you at this time, except to say that the building has now been secured, and there is no further possible danger to the public." (Pan back to newsroom)

"That is what we know now: two separate but related firefights at the Downtown Boxing Club, with six people dead, and six injured. The crime scene is secured and the coroner is expected to take away the bodies shortly. Meanwhile, there is an arrest warrant for Sam Oakley, who was not at the club, and two other men supposedly working with him."

"More as we get more information. In other news, as Atlanta wakes up this bright morning, let's go to the weather first, and then to downtown local happenings. This is Jim Shubo WGCL news."

The FBI confrontation at the Boxing Club, and the subsequent search of the premises provided a wealth of information; far more than simply confirming a terror-related cell in the Atlanta area. The information gathered in the offices on the second floor also showed a far larger network, one which received, processed and managed large holdings in the metro area, like the Boxing Club, and the relationships with numbers of firms who received goods and sometimes services from Far East Trading Company.

The owner of Far East Trading, Jalil Radan, was not there when the FBI entered, and an alert was issued that he was wanted for interrogation. Moreover, information was also found linking the trading company to the ports of Charleston, Miami, and New Orleans, along with several overseas ports and organizations.

While the agents were not yet sure of the importance of the information they found, that would be analyzed later by the Terrorism Task Force, they quickly

From a Vantage Point

became aware that both the boxing Club and the trading company were not what they seemed on the surface. The building, and an adjacent one connected to it through the basement, were sealed off, and police details posted to prevent entry of anyone outside the investigation. The focus became one of finding Radan.

In all the initial commotion surrounding the shootout, it went completely unnoticed that two men went to the basement of the boxing club, opened a door in a dark corner, and walked down a short corridor to another door, leading them to a stairway in another building. Once in that building, the men quickly left, turning to see the police converge around the boxing club, reached their car and quickly drove off. The club had been warned by telephone that the FBI was coming. These men would get the message back to Hakim al-Azahir that they had been compromised.

Nearly a week would go by before forensics teams discovered a body in the shallow cement floor in the building next to the Boxing Club. That body was removed to the Coroner's morgue for examination, and later found to have a curious resemblance to an earlier morgue client—Josh Giddons.

Newsroom, WGCL, Atlanta, GA Jim Shubo sat as his desk, looking at the monitor as he reviewed the footage of the morning shootout at the Downtown Boxing Club. The station was lucky that it had a cameraman in a mobile van near the scene, along with one of the junior reporters. Atlanta had a lot of local happenings overnight, and all the mobile crews were busy. This one, though, gave WGCL the only virtually complete live stream of the entire event.

Curiously, the station would normally monitor police channels for routine news, and they had this morning as well. What was different, though was the number of police units starting to congregate at a specific location. The station news director took the opportunity to reroute one crew to that location, and found a gold mine for news. The cameras shot live, and streamed it uncut to the newsroom, eventually having it land on Shubo's screen.

After doing the 7:30AM initial story, Shubo scanned for any possible updates. He contacted all his usual people in the Atlanta PD, and those he had in some of the Federal offices. This event seemed different to him. The FBI and DHS were saying nothing at all, as if the event did not exist, and his Atlanta PD people indicated they were told by higher-ups to say nothing to anyone. Somebody put a lid on the story. Shubo saw that as a challenge; he would find out and air the real story here. Now he had to figure out where he could get the information he needed.

Shubo's break came earlier than he expected. It was nearly ten when his phone rang and a garbled voice said simply, "the name of one of the women killed in this morning's shootout is Samira Suleiman. On the terrorist watch list."

From a Vantage Point

The phone ID said only 'unknown person'. It was followed a few minutes later by a text message to his cell phone, saying the same thing, and adding only 'interested' as a name, and, as before, no phone number.

At least that gave Shubo a lead.

Along I-75 South Radan sped south in his Volkswagen Passat, stopping briefly after he left the area of the Boxing Club to drop off the other man who escaped with him, This person had no record of any kind, and the police would not chase him. Radan gave him several thousand dollars and simply told him to disappear. With no family, that would be an easy task.

Now, speeding south Radan needed to think. He needed to find a safe-haven, which would enable him to contact Hakim and tell him what happened. Radan also needed to protect his own life. He was not sure what Hakim might do, and he was unaware of many of the other members of the cell, since these people did not report through him to Hakim. Better to move south toward Miami, where he knew several other traders, some of whom could enable him to escape or at least hide from the authorities.

What Radan did not realize, in his haste to escape, is that his cell phone in his pocket was on, but in sleep mode, and it could be traced, the calls recorded, and his escape route determined by the authorities.

About eight miles south of Atlanta, Radan felt it was safe enough to call his friend and benefactor. He pulled off at a visitor center overlooking some scenic view, and parked a short distance away from the others, far enough that he could make a call and not be heard. Taking the phone out of his pocket, he dialed an international number. The phone rang for a few seconds and then a voice came on the speaker.

"How can I help you?" the voice said, in English, but a decidedly Arabic tone.

"This is Radan," he said in response. "I need to speak with Hakim."

" Who told you to call here? There is no Hakim here?"

'You must tell Hakim I need to speak with him. He can call me at this number. It is very important." All Radan heard in return was the click of the phone, ending the call.

What do I do now, Radan said to himself? *I will sit for a short time and he will call. That is it, I will wait.* He waited over thirty minutes before the phone rang, and he picked it up.

"You fool," came the message, "You were told never to call. Why have you done it? What has happened? Did you do as I told you?" came the questions in quick staccato.

"Yesterday, the Boxing Club was raided by the FBI," Radan responded. "They shot or killed most of our people. Only myself and one other escaped."

"Is the other one with you?" asked Hakim.

"No, I left him in Atlanta. He is not known and will fade into the city. There is no way the government can find him or link him to us."

"He should have been killed," responded Hakim, "Never leave loose ends. What about the other one."

"He was taken care of as you asked. He will never talk to anyone."

"Good. Now, I want to you to drive south to Miami. You will go to an address you know and see Malik. He will have instructions to get you safely out of the country. Do you understand?"

"Yes, Hakim. I understand," responded Radan, "I will go to Malik."

"Destroy the phone, and never call this number again, on pain of your own death." With that admonition, Hakim hung up, and Radan sat staring at the phone. Finally, he opened the door to the car, climbed out, and placed the phone on the ground under the left front wheel, and re-entered the car. Thinking better of his actions, he retrieved the phone, turned it off, and threw it in the back of the car, where it now nested under the front seat. Backing out of the parking space, Radan returned to the highway and again drove south, headed to Miami Florida and safety.

Newsroom, WGCL, Atlanta, GA The noon news hour was rapidly approaching and Shubo was still without a real updated to his story. So far, he had re-written it three times, but you can only go so far with few facts. Earlier, a message appeared on his screen reading:

> *"The name of one of the women killed in this morning's shootout is Samira Suleiman. On the Terrorist watch list"*

There was no name on the message, only 'Interested'.

Shubo started searching for the name Samira Suleiman, and found out quite a bit. She was apparently on several watch lists, including that of Interpol, which was seeking her on an international warrant for a bombing in Beirut several years earlier. The Interpol letter indicated she might be in the US, but did not specify anything further.

Born in a village outside Beirut, Lebanon, she became involved with Hizbollah, was used as a courier for their efforts, and served as a go-between for Hizbollah with the Muslim Brotherhood in Cairo and Libya, working with someone named Amoud Tabriz, a shipping agent and merchant in Cairo.

Entering the name 'Tabriz Shipping', Shubo found he owned Tabriz Shipping Company, a dealer in oil and other commodities. A little more digging and Shubo had his link. Tabriz Shipping had offices in the Boxing Club, owned the property, and rented it out to Charlie Dale.

From a Vantage Point

The Boxing Club had originally been a warehouse, converted into a boxing club. 'What a great cover,' Jim said to himself, as he started to rewrite his story to meet the news deadline. As he did so, he waved over to the news editor to come and read over his shoulder, to get a quick approval to release it. A tap on the shoulder told Shubo he had the green light.

Nearing the end of his rewrite, Shubo called both the FBI offices and Homeland Security for comments, but reached only a stone wall, and a sense of irritation that he knew as much as he did.

FBI Atlanta Field Office, Atlanta, GA No sooner had Anne Harding, who did double duty as the information officer for the field office, hung up from speaking to Jim Shubo, that she walked down the short corridor to the Special-Agent-in-Charge's Office to notify him of the call, and the fact that some of the story would shortly be out on the wire.

"How did that happen?" came the inevitable question.

"Not sure sir," Harding responded, "Only a few people knew the identity of the woman killed, and they were mostly over at the coroner's office.

"Find out who leaked the information and get back to me."

"Yes, sir," responded Harding, as she headed for the door and the short trip back to her own office.

Three agents were at the Coroner's office within 20 minutes, and within the hour after their arrival, using a small room in the Coroner's office they converted to an interview room, they had determined the five people who would have had access to the information on Suleiman. These people were interviewed one-by-one but came up with no culprit. Harding, who had accompanied the other agents, listened carefully to each of the interviews and, in her mind, the person probably responsible was a female forensic technician named Isabel. Harding asked the supervisor working with them from the Coroner's office to bring her back to talk to her.

When she was called, Isabel returned to the interview room, and waited outside for Harding, who opened the door and asked her to return to the table in the center of the room. Harding sat opposite her in a similar chair to the one on which Isabel sat waiting.

Looking over the file already composed from the first interview, Harding looked up and asked, "Your name is Isabel. Is that correct? Isabel Fuentes, I believe?"

"Yes ma'am, it is," Isabel replied.

"You had access to the records of the woman brought in earlier today, identified by a tag with the number "4"?"

"Yes ma'am," came the reply.

"Was it not you who identified the deceased?"

From a Vantage Point

"It was ma'am; from the Interpol database. They had fingerprints on file," responded Isabel.

"All right, you identified the deceased, and entered the information into the coroner's records. Is that correct as well?"

"Yes ma'am, it is correct. I printed the information on the fingerprint match and added it to the coroner record. I do that with every identification I do."

"Were you aware that this was a 'sensitive' case, and that the coroner's office was under strict orders not to release any information on any of the deceased?"

"Yes, I was ma'am. We were not to release any information. I entered the document and put the record back into the locked file cabinet to keep it safe."

"Did anyone else have access to the cabinet in your office?"

"Only the coroner, ma'am," came her response.

"Help me out here Isabel. If only you and the coroner had access to this file, how could information on deceased number four get out? Let's go back over the steps you took. Tell me what you did."

"Well, Ma'am, I took the fingerprints with the electronic pad and plugged the pad into the computer over in the corner of the autopsy room to see if I could get a match. I was surprised that one came back in just a couple of minutes. I hit the print button on the computer to print the screen page, as I was taught to do, and went to the file cabinet to get the autopsy record. I put the record on the desk, and the printout of the fingerprint match inside it."

"OK, what did you do next?" asked Harding.

Isabel thought for a moment and then said, "Well, I had to go to the bathroom really bad, so I locked the door to the corridor, and went to the small bathroom adjacent to the autopsy room. When I came back, in a minute or so, I picked up the record, clipped the fingerprint document to the record, and walked over to the file cabinet, placed it in the file, closed the drawer, and locked the file. I have the key here." Isabel showed Harding the key attached to her Employee ID tag on a lanyard around her neck.

Harding looked at the key and asked, "Could anyone have entered the autopsy room while you were in the bathroom?"

"I don't think so ma'am. I would have heard someone come in, I think. The door sometimes sticks and it makes noise when you open it." Harding made a mental note to check on the door.

"All right Isabel, Thank you for your help. I might need to ask some more questions later, but do appreciate your cooperation." Isabel rose to leave as did Harding, and they both exited to the corridor outside the interview room, Harding going toward the autopsy room to check out the squeaky door.

As she entered the autopsy room, Harding noticed two cameras on the walls near the ceiling. 'I wonder,' she asked herself, 'could these have been on beyond

From a Vantage Point

the autopsy?' She determined to find out. In the meanwhile, she called the Atlanta FBI office to report they could not determine who might have been the leaker, but still had several leads to follow-up on before their return.

Newsroom, WGCL, Atlanta, GA "This is WGCL," intoned the announcer as the clock struck 11AM. "Here with the news, and a special update is Jim Shubo, in the news room."

"This is Jim Shubo with more on the developing story on the shootout at the Downtown Boxing Club earlier this morning. Recapping our earlier story, there was a major shootout between Federal and local law enforcement and a group inside the Downtown Boxing Club on the East side. Two groups attempted to leave the building after the FBI arrived with a search warrant at about 7AM, with one trying to escape from the rear and the other on Front Street. Neither attempt was successful and, so far there have been at least six dead and six wounded among the group, with one FBI agent wounded, but expected to recover."

"The situation has turned a biz bizarre, as WGCL has learned that one of the dead, a woman named Samira Suleiman was on the terrorist want list, and the subject of a request by Interpol, the International Police Agency, for arrest regarding a Middle East bombing in Beirut, Lebanon several years ago. She has been in hiding since, and rumored previously to be in the US."

"What makes this case even more bizarre is that the building is owned by a company, Tabriz Shipping of Cairo Egypt, a firm with known ties to the Muslim Brotherhood organizations in Egypt and Libya for many years. The building, originally a warehouse, was later converted to the Boxing Club, but Tabriz continued to keep offices in the building until just last year. Our sources could not confirm that Ms. Suleiman was directly connected to Tabriz or another group. Oakley, the manager of the Boxing Club is still missing, and himself the subject of an arrest warrant."

"We reached out to the FBI and Homeland Security for their comments on our information, but both agencies declined any comment. We will keep you apprised of developments in this still-developing story. This is Jim Shubo for WGCL news. Up next, The Local news with Aaron Deal."

FBI Atlanta Field Office, Atlanta, GA Listening to Anne Harding on the phone, Tom Arnold, the Special Agent-in-Charge knew he had a major problem. Dialing a number on the phone on his desk, Arnold waited for the line to ring, and when he

From a Vantage Point

got a response said, "Rich, this is Tom Arnold in Atlanta. We executed the warrant this morning on the Boxing Club to a hail of gunfire. One of our guys down, not serious, but six dead and six wounded on the other side."

"Wow, amazing but not entirely unexpected Tom. Have you kept it out of the news?" responded Richard Peabody.

"That is the reason for the call Rich. We locked it up, but a leaker, probably in the Coroner's office gave out the info on Samira Suleiman to a reporter at one of the media outlets here. He called earlier trying to confirm, but we declined comment. Expect it to hit the national wire by 11 AM."

"Crap," responded Peabody, "That is just what we don't need. With some of those wounded, we would have had a chance to find out the extent of the cell activity. Now, we blow the cover. Any chance we find out who the leaker was?"

"I have three of my agents working that right now Rich. I would suggest though that this needs to go up the flagpole so no one is surprised in DC."

"Going to do that as soon as I hang up, Tom. Keep me up on what you get. Try to keep this as low a profile as you can, for as long as you can. We really need to figure out where the tentacles of this mess go."

"OK Rich, out here.'" answered Arnold, as he hung up the phone.

FBI Headquarters, Washington DC Richard Peabody sat back in his chair, looking at a makeshift whiteboard on the far wall, littered with items on the investigation thus far. The latest piece of news from Atlanta was only partially good; they still had some of the alleged cell alive, if wounded in the shootout. Now, he realized, they had to move quickly. Turning to his intercom, Peabody asked his assistant to get a connection to Alice Sawyer.

"Alice, this is Richard. Have you seen the latest from Atlanta?"

'Yes Richard," she responded, "Just minutes ago. How is your agent?"

"He will be fine, an arm wound, as I understand it. We still do not have Dale, but we do have six in the hospital, most with relatively small injuries. We should be able to start interviews tomorrow or the next day. What worries me now, though, is the announcement of the name of one of the women by an Atlanta station.

They claim to have received the information from someone in the know—and that can only mean the coroner's Office, but we interviewed everyone there, and no real leads. One woman, responsible for the files, claimed she left it out on a desk while leaving for an internal area bathroom, with the outer doors locked. My gut reaction is she leaked it somehow, and we are continuing to pursue it. Regardless, the information is out, and we have to assume al-Azahir and his people now know we busted up their cell."

From a Vantage Point

"I agree Richard," retorted Alice. "We need to get the NSA FISA Court order extended to cover more space in Atlanta. That might bring up a contact between her and someone else."

"Will you do that, or shall I?" asked Peabody.

"I am going over to NSA shortly to a meeting. I'll start the ball rolling there."

"Thanks Alice. Let me know what else you need from here."

The two hung up simultaneously, and Peabody decided to call Sarah Minihan to let her in on the latest news.

Peabody and Sarah Minihan spoke for nearly 30 minutes. Sarah agreed to ask the Kabul staff to monitor calls from the suspected al-Azahir locations to the US, and let Peabody and Alice Sawyer know immediately if any calls were made. That way, Alice's staff monitoring the Horizon servers in Atlanta could do the domestic trace. She also asked Peabody to send the names of those killed or injured from the cell, hoping that running the names through the Agency's own internal watch list, she might add some information Peabody could use.

On the way to Sammi's Restaurant, Elias, West Virginia The lunch crowd was slow today. The county fair was still in progress, and many of those who usually came to town were out at Caskill's Farms where the Fair had been held for many years. Will stopped first at the farm, as he came to town, bringing Sira with him. They were a bit uncomfortable during the drive, with both remembering the experiences of the previous evening. In their own way, they would work out what they felt, and how they would react in the future. For now, both decided to repress their feelings until they had the opportunity to work out their own perspectives on the future.

As they approached the Caskill Farm, Will turned on the radio to hear the latest news. He picked up WKCJ-FM, which was in the middle of its late morning news.

"And in the national news today," the reporter announced, "There was an interesting situation in Atlanta, where the FBI and other federal agencies, trying to execute a search warrant at the Downtown Boxing Club on the East side of Atlanta, ran into sustained gunfire from occupants. At the end of the shootout, six were dead and seven injured, including an FBI agent. Our sources in Atlanta tell us that the FBI refuses to comment on the incident. One of the dead has been identified as Samira Suleiman, a Lebanese, wanted for terrorism by Interpol. Not much more is known at this point, but it is interesting that it follows by only a few weeks the mysterious death of two others, one here in West Virginia, and one in Atlanta. More later as we get updates from our sister station in Georgia.'

Sira gasped audibly.

Will turned to her and asked, "What is the matter? Do you know her?"

"Yes, she is my cousin. I don't know why she was killed. The Lebanese Government has been trying to blame her for a bombing in Beirut five years ago, but she was with me in Europe at that time. Mister Will, why are they trying to kill off my family?"

"Who Sira?" asked Will, really knowing the answer.

"It is the Americans Mister Will. They do these things for their own political aims, and do not care what happens to families or even countries. They are just as much criminals as anyone they charge with horrible crimes. When they kill innocents, it is 'collateral damage', but when others do the same it is terrorism. Who is right? I do not know. Explain it to me." Sira was clearly upset, and Will really did not know what to respond. For several minutes, there was an awkward silence, as Sira sobbed quietly in her seat.

Arriving at Caskill's Farm, Will stopped the car, and went over to the passenger side to open the door for Sira. As she moved to leave the car, he swept her into his arms, and whispered softly, "We will get through this. Everything will be fine." She hugged him closely and then she looked up at him. Will could see the fear in her eyes.

"We'll just stay a few minutes," Will said quietly, as he closed the passenger door, then turned back to where she waited for him. Putting his hand on her shoulder, they walked together toward the fair. True to his word, they walked quickly through some of the exhibits, stopped to discuss the cooperative with several of the farmers attending the fair, and after about 30 minutes went back to the car to go to Sammi's. That trip took another 20 minutes, driven mostly in silence.

Department of Homeland Security, Washington DC Alice Sawyer had a quandary. Now that the situation at the Boxing Club in Atlanta happened, she quickly needed to make other plans to contain whatever the cell involved was planning, and make some fast links, in any, to what was happening in DC and West Virginia.

She still had no hard facts. Everything reported seemed to indicate that Johnson at best was a dupe like others in the past. She had nothing to show, no evidence he had been turned, even partially to make him a suspect in something—whatever it might be. Nonetheless, her instinct said that all these happenings were connected. The difficulty was proving it.

Standing up from her desk, she walked to the outer office and asked her assistant, "Sally, Is the Johnson team in the building?"

"Yes Ma'am, they all are, unless, of course, they stepped out for lunch."

From a Vantage Point

"Ok, then let's ring them all up for a meeting in my office in an hour. Also, would you please get me Sarah Wright, I mean Minihan, at CIA." She had never completely changed her thought to accept that Sarah and Bernie were married. She always thought of Sarah as the independent one.

"Sure will Ms. Sawyer. Right away."

"Thanks," replied Alice, returning to her inner office, and back to sitting at her desk looking at the white board on the wall across her office. *There has simply got to be a connection here*, she thought to herself. *What are they?*

Just short of an hour passed as the three men critical to the discussion arrived at Alice's doorway. The first to arrive, Tom O'Neal, Sally found over at Agriculture, and he quickly came uptown. The next to arrive, Jim Lawson, had only arrived back in town from a flight to Mexico, which arrived at Dulles Airport at 7:00 AM. The final member, Rich Alcorn breezed in right on time from his office down the hall. They all took seats around the table in front of the White board, and Alice came over to join them.

"You have all undoubtedly heard about the FBI raid on the Boxing Club in Atlanta? Asked Alice. The men nodded quickly.

"Alice, I have to say," piped up Jim Lawson, "It did not sound like there was a lot of planning that went into that raid. Either that, or the FBI has a leak. These guys knew the Mounties were coming, and were ready." The guys laughed at the reference to their Canadian counterparts, known for 'getting their man'.

"The raid went as planned, Jim," responded Alice. "What went wrong was the leak of the name of the woman to the press. We have tried to chase that to the ground, but no success yet."

"What do we know about this woman, Alice?" asked Rick Alcorn. "There has to be something, some connection, some small link that we can follow here. The rest of these people were all unknowns. They had no records, and they came to the US from widespread locations. Only the woman and one other of the deceased even came from the same country."

"Alice looked up at Alcorn, asking, "What country Rick? I saw nothing in the reports about any two having common stats. Where did you get that information?"

"Got it from NSA Alice, it seems this Samira woman, and another of those killed in the alley, a guy named Abdool, were from a small village in Lebanon, later moved to Syria in the 80's, and eventually took different paths to the US. Both entered legally, have worked quietly in Atlanta, with nothing coming on the radar until now."

Alice's eyes lit up. "Where in Lebanon Rick?" she asked.

When he told her the name, she stood, walked over to her desk, and picked up two files. She opened the first and started to read.

" Hassan Singh, waiter and dishwasher in Sammi's Restaurant, lived in the same village in the early 80's." Taking the other folder, she read, "Sira Suleiman, also known as Sira Hassan, is also from the same village. I can understand similarities in names, especially Suleiman in Lebanon, but could these people, Samira and Sira, be related and if so, have we established the connection here?"

"Then there is the question of Hassan Singh," she continued. He also had a relationship with that village. Is there yet another connection?"

"Tom, when is Johnson due back in town?" she asked, looking over at him on the opposite side of the table.

"Next Tuesday, is his next visit Alice," responded O'Neal.

"OK then, let's push up the heat a bit," said Alice. "When he comes in, you will have a moment with him, and show him a report we will prepare on the possible links, and its possible effects on his cooperative. Nothing too serious, just a few asides on perception, but make sure he has a few moments to see and read the report. Let's see where that takes us."

"I can do that easily. We will have a lot of time together. Anything else?"

"Try to find out what the relationships are among them, Tom. Is there a link between Sira and Hassan? Is Sammi, the owner involved? Mostly, look for the expression responses you get from Johnson. That might tell us more than we think. I want to try to wrap this up quickly, now that we know something is moving."

"Jim," Alice continued, "Let's get an up-date on these packing boxes moving toward DC. Get the CIA and FBI updated on the latest there, and the expected delivery and location. We want to watch those closely. No slipups."

"Understand Alice," came the response from Lawson.

"Rich, anything on phone or computer traffic that needs our attention?"

"Things are very quiet Alice, at least since that one call from Elias to Atlanta. These people live in their own little isolated world. They don't often make calls outside their own neighborhood."

"That's good for us, though," Alice retorted, "Calls and messages stick out like a sore thumb. Keep on watching that, just in case."

"Anything else I need to know about gentlemen?" she asked, looking around the room. "If not, then let's get on with it." The small group rose slowly from the table and started to disperse, except for Rich Alcorn, who lingered a bit.

"Something else Rich?" asked Alice.

"There is one thing Alice," Rich began, "The phone traffic in and out of Horizon is still spotty, but slowing. We have kept ears to the server doing most of the message-passing, and it seems like what we are getting is mostly minor chatter. These guys, whoever they are, are moving their location. I would bet on it."

"Any idea where or who?"

"Not yet, but we broadened the boundary, and asked NSA to check some things as well, primarily to let us know if something off-the-wall pops up with an overseas origination that should not be where it is coming in, just to see if we hook something."

"Any bites yet?"

"Just one," said Alcorn, "It was a relay call from Kabul to a phone server in Quebec that acted as a bounce into New York, then Atlanta. They are getting us the metadata. We'll look and see if we want to put an ear to it."

"Good. Keep me informed, especially if we need to request any FISA action. The court is taking a far stricter approach these days, as you know."

"Will do. That's it," answered Rich Alcorn, and he waved as he left to return to his own cubicle down the hall.

Alice sat and looked at the board for a minute or so, and then returned to tackle her inbox.

Sammi's Restaurant, Elias, West Virginia The long, quiet ride ended as Will Johnson pulled into a space in front of Sammi's. Sira opened the passenger door quickly, and ran inside. Will could see through the restaurant window as she ran up to Sammi, who quickly embraced her, patting her back. As Will entered, Sammi looked over at him, with eyes that said everything about Sira's feelings of loss.

Finally, Sira backed away from Sammi, tears still streaming down her face, and she rushed through the door to the kitchen.

"She will be fine, Mister Will," said Sammi. "Her cousin was with her when she came to this country. Samira was probably the only family she had, other than her betrothal to Hassan."

Will looked up at Sammi with a questioning look on his face. Sammi knew immediately that this was new information to him.

"Mister Will, come and sit down. If have to tell you a story." He waved Will toward his usual table, and then sat down opposite him at the table.

"Sira came from a small village in Lebanon, just like you. During the Civil War, she and her family, along with their cousins went to Syria to escape the fighting. They were Muslims in a Christian area."

"Sira told me some of that Sammi," responded Will.

"Then let me go on," retorted Sammi. "Eventually, Sira and part of the family came to the United States, and lived in Atlanta for a time before coming to Delaware, where she worked in a restaurant like this. Her childhood friend Hassan came later. He knew the family had gone to Delaware, and he too began to work in that restaurant, which is owned by a kinsman of mine. They came here because my kinsman became ill, and his business declined, so he asked me to take the two of them in. They came here together, and have worked well here in our community."

"Later," Sammi continued, "She met you and became your housekeeper. She thinks the world of you, and has been incredibly happy keeping house for you. She and Hassan, in the meanwhile have grown apart. Their childhood betrothal in the old country has less meaning. She believes in freedom to do what she wishes, and has become more independent, something the Muslim faith does not take kindly to in women. It was better for her when she began to stay at the farm, avoiding the arguments with Hassan. She is a bright woman, Mister Will, with her own views, her own attitudes, and her own feelings. She is becoming American."

"The news that Samira is dead hurts deeply. They were close, even though physically far away. Samira stayed in Atlanta and got involved with some people there who have a dark past. I do not know everything, but this I do know; Sira has been afraid for her for a long time. She does not know her feelings right now, except for those of a hot-blooded Muslim who believes in the words of the Qu'ran that retribution comes to those who injure and kill kinsmen. Be careful, Mister Will."

Will was puzzled by the last statement, but did not know how or what to respond.

"How can I help her?" asked Will. "What can I do to make her life easier?"

Sammi thought for a minute, with his hands together in a prayer position, the tips touching his lips, and then looked up and said, "Mister Will, that girl is in love with you. I do not know how you feel about her, she loves you. If you feel the same, take care of her." Sammi started to form tears in his eyes, and continued, "You are both like my children." Then, he stood, and walked toward the kitchen saying, "I must get lunch started. Will you have your usual breakfast, Mister Will?"

Will nodded, and Sammi walked through the doors to the kitchen. Almost immediately, Will could hear a loud argument going on in the kitchen in Arabic—he assumed it was with Hassan, and then a woman's voice added to the cacophony as well, quieting everything down.

Kabul, Afghanistan Hakim al-Azahir paced up and down in his small office, trying to figure out what had happened in Atlanta. The call from Radan, his man in Near East Imports, had only said there were deaths and some captures. Who died? Who was in police custody? Radan was obviously trying to escape south, and Hakim had to decide what to do with him, now that he was no longer useful. He could make that decision as Radan reached Miami and the safety of that cell.

From a Vantage Point

As he paced, he heard a phone ring in the warehouse. Looking around, since he knew none of his men were there, he tried to find the phone. Then, he saw an older phone on the wall, and he moved over toward it while it still rang.

Picking it up, and simply listening, he heard a voice say, "I need to speak to Hakim right away."

Pretending, Hakim answered, "He is not here. What do you want with him?"

'This is Hassan," came the response, "I need to speak with him. When will he return?"

"I know no Hassan," said the voice, really Hakim, "What do you want of him?"

"I am in trouble and need him," said Hassan. "How do I get him to call me?"

"There is no Hakim here. I do not know how to get to him. What kind of trouble are you in with this Hakim?"

"Do not mind. I must have the wrong place," said Hassan.

When he finished, it was obvious the call had ended from the other side.

Hakim began to fear the worst. Never in all his dealings, had he been uncomfortable in his position. Working first for Fatool, and then Amid, he had always been clearly in charge of situations, yet now, it seemed that his current plans were completely falling apart. He could not bring failure to Amid; that would mean his own death, or at least disappearance. This plan had to succeed, even if it meant that Hakim had to take the chance and go to America himself to complete the planning.

Department of Homeland Security, Washington DC Rich Alcorn's eyes widened as he saw the alert message pop up on his screen.

> *[Heading Deleted]*
> *Rich:*
> *Call we think from al-Azahir came across the pipe through Quebec and New York to Elias, West Virginia. The number is 681-555-5679. Amazed he took the same route twice. Good hunting*
> *Abe*

Forwarding the message to Alice Sawyer, Rich Alcorn added:

> *Alice:*
> *This just came in from Zamboni at NSA. Can we ask them to confirm this number in West Virginia? We might have gold here?*
> *Rich*

Alice Sawyer picked up the phone, dialed a number, and waited.

"Zamboni, can I help you?"

"Eldon, Alice Sawyer. The message you sent to Rich. We need the meat. How long will it take?"

"Alice, I knew you might call back soonest. The number is a burner phone, used in Elias, West Virginia, but originally purchased in a mall outside Wilmington Delaware about a year ago. The buyer paid cash, and uses it seldom. Hasn't even used up the time allowance since it was purchased. Mostly incoming calls, and even those are countable on one hand."

"OK Eldon, can you get me anything else?"

"Sure can, Ms. Sawyer," came the reply. "I can't go back too far, but we have the latest conversation on record, since the phone was tagged. It is on the way to you as we speak. Watch your e-mail."

Within seconds, an e-mail message popped up on Alice's screen. It read:

Attached.
Zamboni.

The attached file read:

"Good morning. Are you well?"

"Yes, I am Hakim. I am glad to hear from you."

"Say nothing more that indicates us. What is your condition there?"

"Sorry. We are still working on the subject. The other people have moved the woman to his house, and she is working on him, but I am not sure how successful she is. She does not seem to be sincere in her task."

"Who allowed her to go to his home and live there?"

"I did sir, but at the urging of the owner there."

"Do what you think is right, but he must be turned. He is a very strong-willed person. I have known him for many years, and he is not easy. He was not years ago when we first met, and he is probably not now. He must be turned. It is critical to our efforts. Make the woman work harder."

"I will do what I must sir. "

"Good. It must happen quickly. We are close to our deadlines and I must answer for them."

"I understand fully. It will be done."

"It will mean your life if you do not. Do you understand well?"

Hassan gulped, and answered, "I do sir."

Then, the phone clicked off.

In Elias at the restaurant, Hassan put the phone in his pocket, and went back to work, thinking he had to have a serious discussion with Sammi over the situation later in the day.

Alice Sawyer read the message over three times before she forwarded a copy of it to Rich Peabody at the FBI Washington Office.

FROM: Alice Sawyer, CIV, DHS, AZ
TO: Richard Peabody, AIC, WASFLDOFC FBI

SUBJECT: Surveillance on Elias, WV

Rich:
Just received from NSA, on an official request. Do we want to move now, or wait for more? Advise.

Alice

Now, it was time to wait to create a plan. Hopefully, both would agree in a very short time. Alice had even more concerns than she did before the message traffic and her meeting with the staff.

Sammi's Restaurant, Elias, West Virginia "I heard your conversation with the pig," yelled Hassan. I should kill him for bedding my betrothed. He deserves to die, the Christian. He is a pig."

'Hassan, calm down" exhorted Sammi. "This has been coming for a while, and it may work in your favor. You care less about Sira, you care only to please that leader you follow in Kabul, or wherever he happens to be. She is doing what you wish, and what is in her heart. That is not an easy task."

"I do not care about her wishes," responded Hassan in a loud, shrill voice, "I care that she is insulting me and my family. If she were still in Lebanon, she would be killed, and that would be it. He is a pig and defiles her as he wishes. That is not our way."

"It may be Hassan," answered Sammi, "but she is doing what you told her to do. You cannot have it both ways."

Hassan looked at Sammi with blood-red eyes, and responded, "You are a pig as well. You deserve to die for your blasphemy." Hassan took up a carving knife

From a Vantage Point

and started toward Sammi, who inched backward toward the swinging door, stopping just before it.

"Kill me if you think you can, Hassan, but you do yourself nothing in return. My death means your cover is no longer useful, and the police will drag you in as a common criminal. If that is what you want, then try to kill me."

Sira, hearing what was going on from the small bathroom off the kitchen, opened the door and walked out into the preparation area, her eyes red from crying.

"What are you doing Hassan? What will this accomplish? Are we to finish this in this way? The truth is that I do not love you, but I have a duty to complete my mission. I will do that in a way that works, or I will not be successful, and the Brotherhood can do what they wish. I am no whore as you would say, but I do not love you. You are a cruel and inconsiderate person, who cares only for what you wish. That does not include me. You are not my owner. We were betrothed early in life when you were a different person, as was I. Neither of us is the same person today."

"You cannot talk to me that way," answered Hassan.

"Of course, I can," responded Sira, "This is America and we are adults. Now quiet down, and we will figure out what we need to do. Understand though, if you harm Will Johnson, I will kill you myself, and you know I am capable of doing that easily."

Hassan looked her in the eye, and visibly calmed down, eventually walking away to chop carrots for the lunch menu. Sammi smiled at her, walked out of the kitchen to greet the first customers for the lunch hour.

Moments later, Sira followed Sammi out into the main restaurant area, hearing the first customers coming in for lunch. She looked much better than when they arrived, but it was still clear, at least to Will, that she was upset—not herself. She walked toward his table and smiled as she passed by to take a customer order.

Later, she stopped by the table, and asked, "Is there anything I can get for you Mister Will?"

"No, I am fine Sira, and please stop calling me Mister Will. Will is just fine,"

"Oh," she responded, smiling. 'Of course, and I thank you. Will you be staying until after lunch?"

"Yes, I have to get some things at the hardware store. Is there anything we need for the house?"

"Nothing I can think of, except maybe some washing soap for the dishes, if he has that," she responded.

"OK, I can take care of that. I will be back in a while, and wait until you are ready to go home."

From a Vantage Point

Sira heard the word home and winced a bit. She still had to try to get him to do Hakim's bidding, but it was getting harder all the time.

"I will be here and ready to go about two o'clock, Will," she said, using his first name for the first time. She felt proud.

Will said nothing about the conversations in the kitchen he overheard, feeling that it was a subject better discussed back at the farm. Finishing his coffee, he rose from the table, put some money down for the breakfast, and walked out to go across the street to the hardware store.

Sira looked out through the window to the kitchen and followed him with her eyes as he crossed the street.

Operations Directorate, Central Intelligence Agency, Langley, VA Sarah Minihan walked into her office after a meeting to find a closed folder sitting in the middle of her desk with a large sign attached to the front cover saying, **"IMMEDIATE ATTENTION"** emblazoned in large red letters. Sitting down, she opened the folder and started to read. One paragraph particularly interested her. It read:

> SULEIMAN, SAMIRA, Lebanese, 46 yrs. old, wanted by INTERPOL in connection with a bombing in Beirut. Known associate of AMOUD TABRIZ (aka AMOUD FATOOL) and more recently employed by JALIL RADAN, manager of Near East Imports, Atlanta. Near East Imports actually owned by AMID FATOULLAH, presently running Tabriz Enterprises.
>
> Present location of RADAN not known, and presumed to be at large. None of the artifacts submitted by FBI Atlanta linked to RADAN. Last indication was that he was in US.
>
> Other artifacts not linked to known overseas operatives. Cell phone discovery still in progress

FBI Headquarters, Washington DC Richard Peabody was away from his desk at a meeting when the message from Alice Sawyer arrived. It was nearly an hour later before he could glance at it using his cell phone e-mail, and stopping to read it twice, he was not sure what to tell her on next steps. The message gave enough information to order an arrest of both men, Hassan and Sammi, but was that a wise move?

Hitting a button on his phone, he could hear it dialing a number, and then a voice came on.

"Richard, I see you received my message," stated Alice Sawyer, "Any advice on next steps?

From a Vantage Point

"Hi Alice, "he responded, "Most of the time it would be easy. The answer would be which one of us goes out and arrests the two of them in Elias. In this situation, though, there is a real question."

"What's that Richard?" Alice Asked.

"Do we want to leave it alone to play out some more, or do we want to make an arrest, either flushing out more of the cell, or possibly drive it even further underground? Either way, it does seem that Johnson might be an innocent dupe here."

"Perhaps there might be a middle ground Rich," Alice retorted, "We could shake them up a bit, perhaps send in an agent or two to ask questions, and see where that takes us. What do you think?"

"Might be the right move here Alice. How about you send two guys they have not seen before up there. The last episode with my guys from Atlanta was too heavy-handed."

"I agree Rich. I know just the guys to send. Thanks. Talk to you later." Alice hung up the phone and hit an intercom button, then asking, "Mister Alcorn, please come by. We have to talk."

A few minutes later, Rich Alcorn walked through the door to Alice's office, strolled over to her side table, and sat down, cup of coffee in hand. "What up, Alice?" he asked, in his usual slang.

"Rich, I have a job for you," answered Alice, "In Elias. Interested?"

Alcorn's ears perked up as he heard a name that seemed to dominate virtually every conversation over the past few weeks.

"Hey, field duty. Of course, I am interested. Looking at the same four walls in my very small office every day gets old, very old."

"Rich, you have been here five years," Alice threw back at him.

"I know, it got old a long time ago. What do you want me to do?"

"This is the plan," Sawyer started, "I want you and the girlfriend, the one in your office I'm not supposed to know about, and I want you both to take a trip to Elias. This must be a special trip. I need you both to drive into town as visitors stopping for lunch. Go to Sammie's Restaurant and enjoy a meal. Walk around town, visit some of the stores and simply ask a few questions."

Alcorn was sitting on the edge of his chair, clearly interested, even excited about getting out in the field. "This sounds too easy Alice," responded Alcorn, "What is really going on here?"

"Rich, I want to plant some subtle seeds here. Let it be known that you know about the prior FBI visits to meet with Johnson, and that you have a few friends in DC who happened to mention the story when you indicated you might stop there on your two-week trip through part of the Appalachians. Make something else up if you want. I need to put some concerns out there. No pressure, and no push off, just lay a few seeds. Buy a few local things, and then drive away. We want to see what that does."

"OK Alice, that seems easy enough. How about I go out there tomorrow?"

"Perfect Rich. Put it all on your expense account—within reason, of course,

"Sure Alice, happy to get out. We'll go first thing in the morning."

"Good, keep me in the loop, but, again, be discreet and not pushy."

"Me pushy Alice? I don't know the meaning of the word," smiled Alcorn as he rose to leave. "By the way, do we get to stay somewhere overnight?"

"Get out of here," yelled Alice, laughing out loud as he left the room.

The following morning Rich Alcorn and his friend left early, dressed as tourists and driving an old van with North Carolina plates. It took them about three hours to reach Elias, and their first stop was, as expected, Sammi's Restaurant.

Sawyer had one more card up her sleeve, and she called Tom O'Neal right after Rich Alcorn had left. They spoke nearly fifteen minutes. Now, she could wait to see if results would follow.

Elias, West Virginia Will Johnson finished his breakfast and left the restaurant, starting to walk across the street toward the hardware store. Walking in, he saw that several neighbors were shopping, and he stopped to speak with each, as he headed toward the counter where Henry Gates, the store's owner, was watching the group, arms crossed, and a serious look on his face.

"Morning Harry," said Will as he approached the counter. "Looks like the start of a busy day."

"Perhaps," responded Gates, "If it stays busy. Have you got a minute, Will?" Gates asked.

"Sure Harry, what's up?"

"Well, I'm not sure actually," came the answer. "Two people, a couple actually, were in town a day ago, and they seemed to be asking a bunch of questions."

"What kind of questions?" Asked Will.

"Well, not so much questions, although they had some. It was more like they were putting out information."

"What kind of information Harry? This is beginning to sound sinister," said Will in response.

'Will, this guy and a woman came into the store and looked around. They bought a couple of small things and when they came up to pay, they started asking questions. The guy made a comment that they had friends in Washington who told them to come visit. When I asked about his comments, he replied that his friends knew people in the FBI and they were investigating the town. He mentioned the day the agents came to see you as an example. We all know you Will, and what the FBI was doing, but is this all over with you and them?"

Johnson looked shocked, and finally answered, "Harry I have no idea what he might have been talking about. The situation with my two former friends is dead and buried. There was nothing to it to begin with, and there is nothing now. Where this guy found his information is beyond me." Will sounded clearly frustrated.

"Will, you are our friend. None of us believe any of this government crap. The real shame here is that some outsider came to town, and started making noise. Leave it alone Will. Just continue to do the good things you are doing. We all support you," responded Harry, who came from behind the country to pat Will on the shoulder, and then move over to where a woman was looking at bolt cloth.

"Thanks Harry. I appreciate you all very much," said Will as he started to leave, shaking his head in disbelief at the last conversation. When he reached the door, he looked up and down the street, viewing the stores and buildings of his friends, and wondered what was happening now. In his mind, something had to be going on, and somehow, he was in the middle of it.

Why are they still bugging me? Will asked himself that question over and over as he walked along the sidewalk away from the hardware store, then crossed over and walked up the other side, heading back toward Sammi's.

As he passed the newspaper on the way to Sammi's, Will heard a voice from inside the newspaper office calling to him. He walked in to find Fred Loomis, the editor looking at a bulletin board on the side wall. Fred kept clippings for other areas and the DC papers on the wall for people to read, and occasionally to copy, filling a space in the news.

"What's new Fred?" he asked, walking inside toward that same board he often perused when he came to town. "Anything important in the clippings?"

"It isn't the clippings that are important today, Will," Fred responded. "Today's news just might be you."

"That's pretty cryptic, Fred," Said Will in response. "What have I done to merit anything newsworthy?"

"Will, two people came in a day or so ago and wanted a copy of the paper—the one that had the article about the FBI coming looking for you. They said they had a friend in DC that collected stuff on his terrorism investigations. I offered that we had no terrorists in Elias, but that didn't change their minds. They wanted a copy of the paper, if I had one, so I dug it out and they went back to their car and drove off. It had North Caroline plates, if I remember correctly."

"Anything I need to know that you might want to tell me Will?" said Fred, nearly laughing. I remember the day those two FBI strong arms came to town, and then flew off roaring away in their big black car. Thought that was long over."

From a Vantage Point

"It is Fred. These guys are chasing windmills. From what I read, they never give up. Anyone can come in and lay down lies and great stories. I have lived here for years, and you all know me. Have never been a terrorist, and have no desire to be one. You can print that if you like."

"Didn't want to get you upset Will," said Loomis, "You know I have to ask. It's my job. That doesn't mean I must believe everything I hear—I just need to ask. Your word and your hand has always been gold with me. This is one of those stories that stays buried."

"Thanks Fred. With the cooperative just coming up we don't need—at least I don't need bad, unproven publicity right now. You will be the first to know if I decide to go terrorist."

"Thanks Will," responded Loomis, "I will hold you to it too."

"OK Fred, you do that. Right now, I should get Sira and go back to the farm. I have two fences to mend, and three cows to milk. I will check to see if any of the cows are terrorists."

"You do that Will," laughed Loomis, and Will turned to leave. "Good to see you, my friend."

"Good to see you too, Fred," answered Will, going out the door, and turning toward Sammi's.

By the time Will arrived at Sammi's, he had gone from irritated to incensed. *Who the hell were these people spreading their crap around town and making insinuations?* Will thought. *Why now, and why about me? I answered their questions.*

Walking into the restaurant, Will sat at a table and was still speaking to himself as Sammi came from the kitchen.

"What is the matter, Mister Will?" Sammi asked.

"Sammi, have you heard about two people who came to town a day or so ago, asking questions about me and the FBI?"

"I did Mister Will," he responded, "But I decided not to say something, since the thing was so stupid. They came first to have lunch here, and then walked along the street. I heard from Fred Loomis, and he heard as well from Henry at the hardware. I do not know where else they may have gone?"

"What did they look like Sammi?" asked Will.

"Oh, two young people in an old beat-up van. They looked like they had been hiking or camping. They said little while they were here, but the woman, very young and pretty, seemed to be looking around for something. You know, sometimes you just get a feeling about someone? In this instance, I got the feeling she was looking for something. Who knows what."

As Sammi finished talking, Sira came out of the kitchen and walked over to where Will sat.

From a Vantage Point

"I am ready to go if you are, Mister Will," she said, looking over at Sammi as well.

"Sure Sira," will responded, "Let's head for the barn. It is much more peaceful there than town today." Will rose from his chair, and he headed toward the door with Sira, both turning and waving to Sammi as they left.

"*What a nice couple they could be*, thought Sammi. *If only they could be left to themselves and not have such a large sword hanging over them*, Sammi continued silently, shrugging his shoulders as he returned to the kitchen.

Chapter 37 Closing the Loop

US Department of Agriculture, Washington, DC Tom O'Neal paced back and forth in his office, thinking about the call he received from Alice Sawyer, trying to decide how to handle her request. Finally, he decided to simply comply, even though he disagreed intensely with its possible results.

Walking over to his desk, O'Neal dialed a number and heard a response.

"Will Johnson here, how are you Tom?"

"Great Will," responded O'Neal, "I wanted to call for a couple of things, the most important being your schedule over the next few weeks. The inauguration is approaching and I wondered what your trip schedule might be like until then. There will be a tremendous increase in visitors and that will be a problem."

"Tom, I have my reservations made for the next two visits. That will take us up to the week or so before the Inauguration week. I will drop you the schedule in a text message and you can tell me how that will fit. I'm out in the barn, so I don't have my calendar in front of me. I also have reservations for the three days of the Inauguration-day before, day of, and day after. Thought I just might like to see one of these myself. We don't have to get together, but I would guess most of you Feds will be off anyway."

"Sounds good to me Will. I hate coming into town on Inauguration Day, with all the politicians, and would-be politicians around. You enjoy yourself though."

"Will do Tom. Anything else on your agenda today?"

"Well there is one thing, Will. Someone from Homeland Security came by the other day asking about the cooperative project, and how you and some other town people were involved. Seemed to me they were asking about several, but really zeroing in on you. Any idea why?"

"Tom, this is the second instance of someone asking this week, and, to be honest, it is really beginning to piss me off." Will told him of the visit of the couple, and his feeling that it was linked to the prior visits of the FBI to Elias weeks before. Will had told O'Neal of those visits, and this latest conversation simply reinforced O'Neal's view that Johnson was an innocent dupe.

"OK Will, I think I understand. Their visit does not affect your effort. I need to make a note for the record, but let's just continue as we have been working, and not let anything get in the way of progress here. See you in a week or so." O'Neal hung up as did Will Johnson.

Later in the afternoon, O'Neal called Alice Sawyer to report the conversation, and Alice simply said thanks.

From a Vantage Point

Sammi's Restaurant, Elias, West Virginia Soon after Will and Sira left the restaurant, Sammi pushed his way through the doors into the kitchen and walked over to where Hassan was preparing vegetables.

"Hassan, there are problems rising with the task," said Sammi. "People are coming through town and raising the issue there are terrorists here. They are trying to draw in Mister Will, and that means trouble. What do you suggest we do?"

"I heard you talking to Mister Will Sammi. We move on, but must go faster to get him to do our bidding. There is no room for failure here. It must be done, and Sira must work faster. We have only weeks left." Hassan went back to chopping his vegetables, as if the solution had been found.

"Hassan, this is serious," Sammi screamed at the top of his voice. "We cannot hide your intentions much longer. Your leader is sticking your neck out to get it chopped off just like those carrots. What are you going to do about it?"

"Calm down Sammi," retorted Hassan, "We need to keep our senses, and not get so excited we make mistakes here. You must calm down. Leave this to me. I will make this work. Right now, leave me alone to think."

Sammi pushed through the doors from the kitchen roughly, leaving Hassan to his chores. Within seconds, Hassan pulled out a cell phone to make a call. To do so, he walked over toward the storage room so Sammi would not hear him. Dialing a number, he waited patiently for an answer. The phone rang several times before it was answered.

"Yes," said the person on the other side of the line.

"This is Hassan. I must get a message to Hakim."

"You may wish to do that, but it is not possible. You should not be calling. The group in Atlanta has been broken up by the FBI, and several are dead. I alone escaped, the others were arrested. I have no way to get to Hakim, and cannot help you. You are on your own. Do not call this number again." Then, the phone went dead.

Hassan stood there speechless for several seconds, then threw the cell phone in the trash. *What do I do now*, he thought? *If Radan is compromised, what about us?* Hassan, for the first time, began to panic. He remembered Sammi's words that Hakim would leave him to his fate. Hassan would not let that happen. He must do something, and he must also continue to try to succeed. That way, whatever happened, he would be ready.

Then, he remembered another phone, an unused one upstairs in his room which he had been given before his travels to the US, but since left packed away. He could use that phone to call Hakim directly. Without thinking, he went up to his room, found the phone, and placed it in his pocket before returning to the kitchen and his vegetables.

From a Vantage Point

Department of Homeland Security, Washington DC "Alice, we lit up a light on the board," said Rich Alcorn, as he literally ran into her office. "It's amazing," Alcorn continued, "This is the second ping on this phone, and the same one we got the voice from NSA. Pretty stupid, I think."

"Will they give us the voice this time?" asked Sawyer.

"Sure will. It's covered by the request to the court. Might take a day or two to get it, but Zamboni will provide it."

"Good. Let's stay on it, and confirm it twice." Alice Sawyer looked back to her papers as Alcorn rose to leave. "Back when I get the info, Alice." He waved, but she was reading and paid little attention to his leaving.

As Alcorn came into his own office space, the two others who shared that space with him looked up to see his reaction.

"Keep on the monitoring guys. It seems we may have hit pay dirt. Let's be sure to catch anything else. These guys' days are limited," smiled Alcorn, sitting down at the huge monitor in his own space. "Now, let's isolate the guy on the other end in Atlanta." Alcorn started typing on his keyboard, watching the large screen change, and seemed to zoom in on a section of a small town outside Atlanta, Georgia.

"Looks like this guy was scared after the phone call from Elias," continued Alcorn, "He's moving south on I-75 South at high speed." Alcorn Picked up the phone, looked at a list of numbers and dialed one.

"This is Alcorn," Rich spoke into the phone. "Click on the intercept I am sending, and follow it. You can ping the phone number and get a plate from one of the cameras on I-75. Then, get the State Police to stop the guy and hold him for the FBI. I'm calling Atlanta FBI right now. We want this guy alive."

Alcorn dialed another number from the list, waited a few moments, and then identified himself to the person answering the call.

"This is Richard Alcorn at DHS HQ. As you are aware, we are working with the Joint Terrorism Task Force on cell identification in the Washington-Atlanta area. We have a suspect moving south on Interstate 75 who is wanted as a potential suspect in a recently broken terrorist cell in Atlanta. Georgia Patrol has been contacted to identify, locate and stop the suspect. They will call you to go get the guy, and we would appreciate your assistance in doing this, both for our investigation and yours. We want this guy alive. He has a connection with the recent bust at Downtown Gym. Appreciate the help. Please let me know when you get him."

"Sir, this is Agent Arnold, the Agent-in-charge. My men linked me in. Can I assume this a part of the investigation headed by Assistant Director Peabody?"

"Yes sir," responded Alcorn, "We need to nail this guy, and get him alive if possible. We are assuming he is armed, and might try to take his own life if an apprehension is attempted."

"OK, so we will coordinate with Georgia Patrol and make this happen. Thanks for the heads up. I'll let you know when the dominos fall on this guy."

"Thanks Agent Arnold. Call me for anything you need."

"No problem, out here," came the response.

Within the hour, the Georgia Patrol identified the vehicle and stopped it about 50 miles south of Atlanta. The person driving, a man later identified as Jalil Radan, was taken alive after a short gunfight with the officers in a visitor outcrop on the interstate. They notified the Atlanta FBI office, and agents drove to the scene, took Radan into custody, and then back to Atlanta for interview. At the outset, they had no idea how important this man would become in their investigation.

On the Road, Elias, West Virginia "You are too quiet this afternoon, Will. What is the matter?"

" I have a lot to think about Sira. Everything seems to be happening at once. What about you? What was the fight in the kitchen at Sammi's all about?" Sira looked at Will, suddenly realizing he had heard the conversation with Hassan, but she wondered how much.

Perhaps this is the time to push, thought Sira to herself. *But, how do I explain it to him?* She thought.

Suddenly, her eyes welled with tears as she turned toward the man she was beginning to love, and said slowly, "Will there is something I must tell you."

"I thought you might," he responded, looking at her. "So, what is so bad that you have tears in those beautiful eyes of yours?"

"Hassan and I came here months ago, to do something, a bad thing. We were sent by someone you know well, your friend Hakim."

"Really, how is Hakim involved, and what?" Will asked.

"We were sent to get you involved in an event during the coming inauguration. Hakim wants to show that Americans hate their own country. That is why we were sent—to push you into the plot he has created. There is a group he owns in Atlanta—that is where we came from—and that is what was invaded by the FBI days ago. That raid killed my cousin Samira, and several others. We heard about that yesterday."

"So, this was a plot by my friend to get me to do something in Washington to disrupt the inauguration?"

"Yes Will, it was."

"You all were using me to get me to switch sides against my country?" Will's voice rose as he was visibly affected by what he had just heard. "Is that all this meant to you? What did Sammi know about all this?"

"Sammi is only partly involved Will. He came here legitimately, but knew Hakim many years ago, and was drawn in just to have a place for others to go

From a Vantage Point

avoid detection, like Hassan and myself. Sammi is a wonderful person, and a really nice man. He should not be doing this."

"What about you Sira? Has all of this been simply an assignment for you?" As Will spoke, he pulled over to the side of the country road and stopped the truck. Looking over at Sira, whose eyes had reddened and was clearly distraught, he added, "What about you Sira?"

"Oh Will," she sobbed, "I never expected to fall in love with you. I don't want you to be hurt." She covered her eyes and face in her hands and cried uncontrollably.

Will waited a few moments, and then asked, "What do we do now?"

Sira looked up, and answered, "Will I do not know what to do. I do not want you or Sammi to be hurt, but I am afraid of what Hakim will do to us if his plot fails. He is a very bad man, one with no soul."

"All right. Let's take this one step at the time. We will work this out somehow. Right now, let's get going to the farm. I need to do some work and some thinking." Will turned to Sira, reached his arm over behind her, and drew her to him. "Trust me, we will find a way through this. He kissed her on the forehead, and took his left hand and started to brush away some of her tears.

"Will, I am so sorry for what pain I have caused you. I never wanted this to happen."

"It's all right Sira," Will responded, "We will get through this and you and Sammi will be safe. I may have to do some things that seem to support Hakim, as if he were still my friend."

"You must be careful Will. He is truly a bad man," answered Sira.

"I know that now," Will responded, then repeating, "I know that now. It will be easier to deal with him knowing what you just told me. Dry your eyes and we'll go home." Saying that, he started the truck, pulled out on the highway, and headed for the farm.

Al-Azahir's Warehouse, Kabul, Afghanistan Hakim knew from the phone call with Hassan that his project was in deep trouble. First, hearing from Radan about the discovery of the cell at the Boxing Club, and the deaths of the cell members, and now the fear Hassan clearly had in his voice, told Hakim he needed to do something, and quickly. He had little time.

Hearing a commotion outside in the storage area, Hakim left his office to find two of his men engaged in an argument with another person, clearly an Arab from his dress, but unknown to him.

"Hakim is not here," said one of his men. "He will not be in all day."

"Where is he then?" asked the stranger.

From a Vantage Point

"We do not always know where he is going, or where he has been," responded another of Hakim's men. "For that matter, we do not know you. Who are you and what do you want with our boss?"

"That is none of your business," responded the stranger. "I speak only with Hakim."

"If you wish to speak with Hakim, you may wait a very long time," answered one of the men, "He comes and goes on his own schedule. We report to him, and not the other way around. He does not see everyone. Why should he see you?"

"Again, that is none of your business. I have come a long way, from Cairo, to see Hakim, and I expect you will find him and tell him to come here to see me, at his peril if he does not." Saying that, the man stormed out, but not before turning once more and saying, "I will return in two hours. Hakim had better be here then."

The two workers stared at the man as he left, then turned to hear Hakim come out from behind a stack of cartons.

"Hakim, did you hear?" asked one of the workers. "That man has the dark eyes of the Evil One."

"He is a *Shayṭṭān*, Hakim, a worker of **Iblis**, the Great Evil One who is a friend to those without faith," said the other, in great fear. "What do we do?"

"This man is my problem," responded Hakim, "Let me deal with him. You both have been loyal to me above the others. Even Radan has gone over to the other side," he added with sadness. "Above all the others, Radan was my true friend, but now he must be punished. I will deal with that, and you will continue as before. I will protect you against harm from this *Shayṭṭān*."

Hakim turned to go to the office, went inside and closed the door. Taking a cell phone from his bottom drawer, he dialed a number, and then three additional digits when he heard a tone. Getting a new dial tone, he dialed a number in Miami Florida.

"Can I help you, sir?" came the response from the phone.

"Listen quickly to my voice," was the response from Hakim. "The brothers in Atlanta have been compromised, and one of them, a brother, is coming to you. Greet him, and send him on his way to the Holy One, may His name be praised forever."

"I understand, my brother. It will be done." Having said that, both hung up at the same time.

Hakim sat as his desk, wondering how he would handle the mysterious man looking for him. He had to think fast with less than two hours before he returned.

The shadowy man returned to the small inn where he was staying, eventually making his own call, this time to Cairo.

From a Vantage Point

"Yes," said the man on the other end of the call, "What do you have to report? Have you seen Hakim?"

"No Amid, I have not," the man responded, "His men said he was not there, but I felt the coward was there, behind some boxes, listening."

"I would not be surprised. Hakim is a brave man, but, at the same time, a coward with those above his station. What message did you leave?"

"I told his men two hours."

"Good, be there promptly, and tell me if he is not. This act of his does not help him. Be prepared to take over if necessary. Use any resources in Kabul you need. You know who to contact. This latest project in the United States must either work or be stopped in its tracks before we lose valuable people. My sources tell me there has already been a violation of one group in Atlanta. This cannot happen again, Ali."

"I understand. What you wish will be done."

"Good," responded Amid, "Praise to the Holy One that you will be safe."

"I will be safe, at least from Hakim, if All'ah wills. I will call when all is done."

The men ended their call and it was now clear to the shadowy one what must be done.

FBI Office, Atlanta, Georgia Radan sat in the interrogation room looking small and fragile, staring around the walls, waiting for someone—anyone—to come in and speak with him. The FBI agents let him sit there alone for over two hours before they made any overt move to speak with him. Instead, they observed him in shifts from behind a wall with a very large screen mirroring the scene in the interrogation room.

Finally, a man walked into the room, then another. One sat in a chair opposite where Radan was shackled to the table, and the other stood over by a corner near the door, and both simply stared at their prisoner.

"Mister Radan," said one of the agents, looking at a folder in front of him to see the prisoner's name. "I am Agent James Kelly, Federal Bureau of Investigation, and this is Agent Arnold. We are both from the Atlanta office of the FBI." Kelly showed his credentials. "Do you know why you are here?"

"Have no idea," responded Radan. "Why don't you tell me why you have taken an innocent person traveling south on vacation, and brought me here to this dungeon."

"Glad you asked that question," answered Kelly, "Let's look at your record, shall we? You have a very impressive history. Started out early as a bomber, only you were arrested before your car bomb went off in Cairo. That was at age 14, it says here."

"Since that time," Kelly continued, "you are known to have attended al-Azhar University, although you did not graduate; worked with al-Qaeda in Yemen and

473

From a Vantage Point

then attended a desert school run by bin-Laden in Afghanistan. Following that, you returned to Cairo, and were involved in several other bombing attempts in Europe. Interpol has you on a Red-Letter Arrest alert, but you left Europe for the US, where you settled in Atlanta, eventually running Near East Imports for Amoud Tabriz in the same building as the Downtown Boxing Club, raided yesterday."

"Finally," said Kelly, "You were seen at the club, left either just before or during the incident yesterday, and escaped in your car. We tracked you through your phone, you were arrested by the Georgia patrol, and here you are, back in Atlanta. How was your trip on vacation?" Said Kelly, with a sneer.

"Radan," said Arnold over in the corner, "Let's cut this short. You have two choices here. The first choice is that you come clean on what you were doing with your cell here in Atlanta, most of whom, by the way, are now dead—six at the scene, and four more since in the hospital. The other two will live, and one is already singing loudly."

"Of course," added Arnold, "You can take what is behind the door at option number two. You get a free trip to Guantanamo to join your compatriots. Of course, in that case we make sure they know you told us everything we wanted to know. That might not go well for you. We cannot protect you every moment of the day, even in solitary. Choice is yours. Which do you prefer?"

"Pick well," added Kelly, "You only get one chance. What will it be?" he asked with a sneer.

Radan sat staring at the two men. His first impulse was to refuse to do anything, but he also knew well that there were ways for Hakim and others to get messages into Guantanamo, and he would surely be dead. On the other hand, he had virtually no team to rejoin—they were either dead or injured for the most part, and his 'trip' to Miami was probably nothing but a cover by Hakim to get him there and have him killed.

"All right," Radan responded, "I will tell you what you want to know."

Chapter 38 Creating an Image

Johnson Farm, Elias, West Virginia As they pulled into the yard from the dirt road to the farm, Will and Sira knew they needed to create a plan to protect themselves as well as Sammi from the possibility of retribution from Hakim, or even Hassan. They discussed it on the road, but still had a lot to decide that evening at the farm.

Will stopped the engine and walked around to open the door for Sira so they could enter the house. His instincts from years of living on the farm told him that someone or something was watching them. Looking around, he noticed a small glint in the woods to the left of the house across the short field from the main house. He wondered who it might be; the Federal agents who had been investigating in town, or someone else, perhaps even Hassan. He decided it was not worth the effort. If someone wanted to observe them, that was their right.

Entering the house, and closing the door, Will whispered to Sira, "There is someone over in the woods watching. I'm not sure who or why, but stay close to the house for the time being until things become clearer. Understand?"

Sira walked over to the window to the left of the front door, and looked out toward the woods through the small slit that separated the window curtains, trying to see something without moving them too much and giving an indication that she knew someone was out there.

"I see nothing Will, but I am not good at these things," she turned and said to Will.

"Don't worry about right now," he responded, "Let's just act normal, and let them identify themselves if they wish. We have done nothing wrong, and don't need to be hiding or worrying." Will tried to keep Sira's attitude up, even though he was deeply worried himself.

"Let's have something simple for dinner," said Will. "How about I cook for a change. You go sit in the living room, put up your feet, and I will be server this evening."

"I cannot let you do that," she replied, "It is my task to make the meals and do the work here, not yours."

"OK, then let's make this an exception. Pretend it is your birthday, and I am doing this as a gift to you."

"But it is not my birthday, Will. Not for another month."

"I might forget then," said Will. "Let's pre-celebrate it tonight. Just sit and enjoy the evening. Put your feet up and relax."

Sira thought to herself that she should not be doing what she was doing. It was her place to do the housework and cooking, not Will's. That was how she was brought up. But then, she thought, if Americans can do this, why cannot I?

From a Vantage Point

She started to put her feet up on a large hassock near the chair on which she sat, and suddenly felt good about it.

I love America, she said quietly to herself, and then added, *and I love Will Johnson even more.*

Meanwhile, Will was in the kitchen, looking through the refrigerator for ingredients to make dinner. He selected some chicken to grill on the small stove grill, some vegetables, and some yellow rice in a bowl in the refrigerator. *This ought to work*, he said as he started to organize his efforts. Soon, the chicken was on the small grill, seasoned with a rub of salt, and other seasonings with a bit of lime, the vegetables were in a saucepan about to boil, and the rice was in a pan covered by a Chinese wicker steamer.

"Dinner in about 20 minutes," yelled Will from the kitchen. He looked out through the small window on the counter, peered out into the living room, and Sira smiled, as she watched television, with her feet up on the hassock.

"This American way of doing things is something I could get used to," she answered Will.

"I hope so," he answered from the kitchen.

Later, after dinner, Will and Sira sat on the sofa watching the television shows. Little was said between them until Will asked, "Do you know what Hakim's plan is, Sira?"

"I know very little, Will," she responded, "I am to get you to your hotel on the morning of the Inauguration. That is all I really know. Hassan knows more than I. Within our group, the knowledge is split so that if anyone is captured, they will know little of value."

"Hassan has said nothing, then?"

"Only a small bit. There is to be some kind of great explosion, or something— bigger than New York, he said. What that is he never told me."

"How would they know about my hotel?" Will asked.

"When we first arrived, you were speaking with Sammi one day, and discussing how you were going to get the same room each time that you had on your first visit. You described the front view, high up. Hassan and I heard the conversation and he reported on it to our contacts in Atlanta."

Will thought back to the days when he, Hakim and Josh were traveling around the world, working as mercenaries. They were in Nigeria on a mission for someone, and their job was to blow up a motorcade. They chose a room high in a hotel, with a view of the street. They set up three mortars to blow through the windows and land on the motorcade. That time, it worked, and the person they were hired to kill died along with several of his bodyguards.

"Sira, I think I know what Hakim intends. He has done it before," exclaimed Will. "Now I know what I have to do this time."

From a Vantage Point

Department of Homeland Security, Washington DC The staff meeting had been droning on for nearly forty-five minutes, when Alice Sawyer's cell phone buzzed. She looked at the screen. The message said, 'NEED YOU RIGHT AWAY. ALCORN'.

"Gentlemen," said Sawyer, "I am needed in the situation room. Let's reconvene about 1300 hours. I want decisions today on these issues." Alice rose to leave, and she waved to one of her assistants to come to the door with her.

"Cindy, get hold of Rich Peabody and see if he has time for lunch."

"Yes ma'am," came the reply.

Sawyer walked out of the meeting room, and down the corridor to her own office, where she knew Alcorn would be waiting.

"All right Mister Alcorn, what was so important that you thankfully dragged me out of an incredibly boring meeting?"

"Alice, several things, as it happens," answered Alcorn, "Several IMPORTANT things."

"Ok," responded Alice, "Give the really important first, and then everything else you think might be important."

"Where shall I start," retorted Alcorn, "Let's see, first, there was another cell phone call out of Elias, this time to Kabul, Second, we lost our location on the boxes after they were picked up in DC. Third, One of the two guys who we now know escaped from Atlanta has disappeared, but the other was just picked up south of Atlanta by the FBI. Where would you like to start?" asked Alcorn, a bit sarcastically.

Alice Sawyer Sat Up in her chair and momentarily lost the words she wanted to say.

"Sorry Rich," she finally said," let's talk about the boxes first. What happened?"

"They were picked up by a freight company, Davis Fast Freight, who had orders to deliver them to the Post Office at Union Station. When we got there, and chased them downtown, the boxes had been moved to the Brentwood facility in Northeast. Shortly after, they disappeared from the radar. A postal supervisor said they were loaded to a commercial CONEX for sorting."

"Well, what does that mean?" she asked.

"That means they loaded the boxes into a storage box that was probably either lead or aluminum-lined, and moved out into the yard at Brentwood for later sorting and delivery. It also means the boxes probably had a fixed delivery date that is still a bit off in the timeline."

"Not good information there, but let's keep looking for them to come back on the radar."

"Now, what about the two men in Atlanta?" she continued.

From a Vantage Point

"We have good and bad news there," Alcorn responded. "The good part is that the FBI has this guy named Radan, and he is beginning to sing like a bird. He has only limited information, but even that is more than what we have now."

"OK, do we have people over there listening?"

"We do, Alice. Cohen from Charleston, and one of our guys in Atlanta are over there taking notes."

"Good, now for the phone call. What is happening there?"

"That was really what I expected you to ask first. NSA intercepted a message going out from Elias, or close by, from a cell phone previously unknown, but purchased in Pakistan some months ago. One call was made to the warehouse owned by al-Azahir, and apparently, he answered the call himself, spoke for a minute or two, mentioned the name Hassan, and then hung up."

"Let me get this straight," she responded, "Someone calling himself Hassan made a call to Kabul to someone he called Hakim. Is that right?"

"Sure is Alice."

"These guys are really running scared Rich. I think it's time to ratchet things up again. Make sure we get the message traffic from Zamboni, and I'll let Peabody at FBI know. He can get a warrant for Hassan the dishwasher. Let's see what that does."

"OK Alice, I'll get the transcript shortly and forward it to you. Better yet, I'll have Zamboni send it directly."

"Good, any other good news?"

"Nope Alice, that's it. You don't need to hear the bad news," Alcorn laughed, as he started to return to his own office.

As he left, Alice Sawyer was already on the phone to Rich Peabody, and within the hour a Federal Judge issued orders for the arrest of Hassan Singh. The warrants indicated that Hassan was involved directly in a terrorist plot with a known, highly dangerous terrorist, Hakim al-Azahir, and mentioned Sammi as a possible co-conspirator for allowing terrorist activity in his establishment. Curiously, the FBI did not ask for Sammi's arrest.

The arrest of Hassan was planned for the following day. As would normally be the case, the local police were notified of the warrant, and the execution time, asking for their cooperation and assistance. The chief notified the Mayor, who made the mistake of telling Sammi confidentially of the pending arrest, but made no mention of the co-conspirator angle. Hassan overheard the remarks. Within minutes, he was up to his room, collecting the small amount of possessions there, and quickly ran out the back door to his car, speeding away down the state highway.

FBI Atlanta Office, Federal Building, Atlanta, Georgia Tom Arnold, the Special-agent-in-charge of the Atlanta FBI Office sat in the observation room next to the

From a Vantage Point

Interrogation room holding Radan. The questions from the two agents thus far were mostly on peripheral issues, designed to ensure that this suspect was really who he said he was, and where in the organization he stood. Gradually, the agents moved closer to the activities of the Boxing Club.

"All right, Mister Radan, let's talk a bit about your company at the Boxing Club, shall we?" asked one of the agents.

"You ran an importing company. Is that right?" asked the second.

"Yes, I do; that is, yes, I did," answered Radan.

"When did you start to operate the company?"

"About five years ago. The previous owner wanted to sell it, and he sold it to me. I was his shipping agent before that."

"Who are you referring to, Mister Radan?"

"The previous owner was Amoud Tabriz of Tabriz Shipping. Over here, he called it Near East Importing. I left it that name. It was easier than changing it."

"What did you import, and from whom?" came the next inquiry.

"Mister Tabriz left me with several companies he was doing business with, and I was able to keep them, I import grains, cloth, and some near east furnishings."

"Anything else?" asked one of the agents.

"Occasionally, his company will send boxes or goods, just for trans-shipping in the United States or Canada. We act as his agent in that."

"You said 'we', Mister Radan. Do you have other employees?"

"Yes, I have several workmen, and an associate, a Mister Fatoullah,' Radan responded.

"Where is Mister Fatoullah now?" one agent asked.

"I do not know. Both of us were gone before your agents raided the Club."

"Mister Radan, let me give you a second chance on that question. We have one of the survivors of your group, and he has stated clearly that you and another man were there, but escaped through the basement as the raid started. Is that true?"

Radan looked at the two men, both of whom had serious expressions on their face, and responded, "It is true. I was there, and did escape with Mister Fatoullah. Where he went after we eluded your men, I do not know. He walked away as I was getting to my car to leave Atlanta.

"Where do you think he might have gone?"

"I do not know, sir," answered Radan. "He had only worked a few days at the company. He came to me and asked for a job. I had not even time to complete his employment papers before the raid. I can really tell you nothing."

"Where did he come from?" asked an agent

"From Egypt, I think," answered Radan. "He had an accent that seemed Egyptian."

"Where are you from, Mister Radan?" asked the other agent.

"My family is from near Giza, in Egypt," he responded.

"Did you and Fatoullah know each other before you hired him?"

"No, I did not," came the reply.

"How did he come to you, then?"

"He came thinking Amoud still owned the company, I think. He knew the name," answered Radan.

Arnold listened carefully to every word Radan spoke, but the hairs in the back of his neck told him the man was lying. How do we prove it, he wondered?

"OK Mister Radan,' asked one of the agents, "Did you have people in other cities who reported to Atlanta?"

"What do you mean, mister agent?" responded Radan.

"I mean what I said," came the terse reply. "Did you have people in other cities?"

"We were not told who else was in other cities, only those we worked with at the club."

"Then why were you speeding south out of the city?"

"I wanted to escape," came the reply.

"Why south? Why not north, or west?"

"Because I got on the ramp near where my car was, and it was going south," said Radan in response.

"Mister Radan, I have two more questions for you," said one of the agents, "But let me be very clear. So far, you have told us nothing we did not already know. If you continue to evade giving us answers, your next stop is Camp Alpha. As I said earlier, in your case, we will make sure the guests down there know you cooperated with us. That should make you very welcome."

"What do you want to know," responded Radan, slipping slightly down in his chair.

"First, who do you work for?"

"I am responsible to Hakim al-Azahir, a brother."

"What do you do for him?" asked the agent.

"I do what he wishes me to do," came his response.

"Give me an example," asked the other agent, feeling that there might be more to the conversation.

"We had a man come to us some weeks ago from Cairo. He had been made to look like someone else, but when he came, we no longer had a use for him. I was told to make him disappear."

"How did do you that?" asked the agent, following up quickly.

"He went to sleep, and was placed in the ground under the Boxing Club."

"Jesus Christ," said the agent, "You mean you killed him and then buried him in the building?"

"He was not the first, and will not be the last undoubtedly," came the answer from Radan.

Arnold, on the other side of the wall from the interrogation room, quickly picked up a phone, and sent a team of agents, and an Atlanta Forensic team to the Club to look for bodies. They would report back within the hour the discovery of three decomposed bodies being taken to the Medical Examiner for potential identification. One of the agents told Arnold that he was amazed about the last they found; he looked just like the guy Giddons who was already there in the ME's coolers.

The two agents interrogating Radan started to walk from the room. As they reached the door to leave, Radan shouted out, "What will happen to me now?"

"Mister Radan," answered the agent still in the room, "We have a lot more questions for you. Just sit there and think about answers before we come back." Then, the agent turned, and went through the door, closing it as he left. Radan was left, handcuffed to the table bar, alone.

Johnson Farm, Elias, West Virginia Will and Sira fell asleep on the sofa, sleeping soundly until early the next morning. Sira awoke first, getting up to take a shower then start breakfast. She let Will continue to sleep, covering him with a blanket, and trying to move around as quietly as possible.

When they arrived at the farm, neither could know that Hassan was in the grove near the house, watching for their arrival. When he left Elias, he headed down the state highway to the small road leading out into the farmlands, and eventually to Johnson' farm. There, he hid in the wooded area near the house, and observed them as they arrived, and entered the house. When he was sure he would not be seen, he came closer and looked through the large picture window into the living room, as they spoke after entering. Then he watched Will move toward the kitchen, and Sira sit down on the couch.

Hassan had been to the farm many times since Sira started to show she wanted to stay there instead of her room at the restaurant. His jealousy inflamed him, not because he loved her, but because his family beliefs said she was his in betrothal, and could belong to no one else. He hated Will Johnson for what he had done to take her away from him.

That hatred now became even more pervasive as Hassan realized his predicament in not having Johnson come over to their plans for the upcoming incident in Washington. He knew in his heart that Sira had not persuaded Johnson, but was instead covering her feelings for him. Regardless of his thoughts, he knew that the action had to be taken, and he would somehow force Johnson to participate in it as Hakim desired.

From a Vantage Point

As the lights went out in most of the house, Hassan crept closer, seeing Sira and Will gradually fall asleep on the couch, she fell over toward him, and he wrapped his arms around her.

"I will kill them," muttered Hassan, looking through the living room window. "He will die, no matter what he does, and she will return to me." Hassan thought about shooting them immediately, since he had a small caliber pistol in his pocket, but then remembered the need to have Will alive, and slowly walked away from the house, returning to his car, parked on the other side of the grove.

As Hassan drove back to town, he lost control of his patience. Pulling the cell phone from his pocket, the one he took from his room earlier in the day, he started to dial a number, and hoped he remembered it correctly.

'Why have you called here," said Hakim, answering the call. "What do you want?"

"Hakim, this is Hassan. I cannot control Johnson, and Sira is not doing what she must. What do I do?"

"You are a fool Hassan. You have put the Brotherhood in danger by your calls, and your whimpering. I will tell you later what I want you to do. For now, I will handle Johnson." Then, the phone clicked off.

Now, Hakim had a double problem, and probably a triple problem, all related. He had to deal with Amid, who was already concerned his project was off its track and would fail, bringing dishonor to the Brotherhood. He was also concerned that he had no backup in Atlanta to continue with the plan, since most were either dead or in custody, except Radan, who was headed, he thought, for Florida. Hakim's third problem was the inability of the local people, Sammi, Hassan, and Sira, to deal with Will Johnson, a major difficulty, and one which could not easily be fixed. The immediate question was what to do to fix what he could.

Department of Homeland Security, Washington DC Alice Sawyer walked into her office as the direct phone line was ringing. She walked over and picked it up.

"Alice," she heard quickly, "This is Rich Peabody. We got the warrant issued and will be picking up Hassan tomorrow morning. Already notified the locals, and asked they keep everything under wraps. We will get him first thing in the morning."

"Good Rich. I'll let Cohen in Charleston know. Would appreciate having him along for the ride, if you don't mind."

"Not a problem," responded Peabody, "I'll let the SAC, Charleston know so he is not surprised. Those two know each other well. I think they still go fishing occasionally."

"Good. We still have a lot of holes here, especially on what the major play will be, but I think we are getting closer. These guys, or at least Singh, is really scared right now. He must know we are on to him, or at least that someone is. I just wish I knew what the real position of Johnson might be. Guess that will come with time."

"If we must," she continued, "our next step is to grab the restaurant owner. He and Johnson are really close, and that might jar loose more action. For now, I just want to keep the pot boiling. We have enough evidence to charge Hassan right now. The rest, let's keep on a closer leash until we see what happens."

"I agree Alice," responded Peabody, "It makes no sense to overly tip our hand unless we have to."

"Do we know any more about the location of the boxes?" asked Peabody.

"Not much, I am afraid, Rich," she responded, "We followed them to delivery at Reagan National. A delivery service picked them up, dropped them off later at a post office near Union Station, and the PO took them to Brentwood for sorting and delivery. Someone there stored them in one of the CONEX's in the yard for sorting, and they disappeared, probably due to the metal in the boxes preventing the signal from getting through. We'll find them as soon as they exit that storage box."

"OK," retorted Peabody. " How will you handle them when they magically reappear?"

"Rich, that's the easy part. We have a team at Brentwood full-time, ever since the Anthrax scare a few years ago. We have enough people out there to handle whatever might happen. As soon as the sensors start giving us information, our people will be following the trail wherever it leads."

"Good enough for me Alice," responded Peabody. "Sure, you don't want to go to Elias yourself to see the action?"

"Not me, Rich," she answered, "Been there, done that for too many years. Now, the younger guys get all the fun," she laughed. "Talk to you later," she added, as they ended their call.

A short while later, Alice Sawyer notified Anderson Cohen in the Charleston Office of the plans for the raid and arrest at Elias.

Al-Azahir's Warehouse, Kabul, Afghanistan The shadowy man from a day earlier walked through the wide entrance to the warehouse, and the three men working looked up, saw him enter, and began to shudder. One ran quickly to the office to tell Hakim he had arrived.

"Hakim," the worker said hurriedly, and in fear, "The Shayṭṭān has returned. What do we do?"

"Leave him to me and go back to work," answered Hakim. "When he asks you, send him to me."

The worker returned to his place with the others, and the man came up to them, as he expected.

"Where is Hakim?" the man demanded.

"He is in the office," one of the workers answered. "Just as you asked, he is here."

"Where is the office?" the man inquired.

One of the men pointed to the doorway on the side of the warehouse to the right of a group of packing boxes. The man started in that direction, walking quickly toward the doorway, then entering and closing the door behind him. Hakim sat behind the desk reading some papers.

"Hakim," the man said.

Hakim looked up and responded, "Ali, I did not know you were here. My men only said that someone had come, but did not give your name."

"That is because I did not give it to them. My time here is short, but Amid directs me to tell you he is displeased. This plan of yours is falling apart. What do you intend to do?" it was obvious from the tone of his voice that Ali was expressing the words of his own leader, Amid Fatoullah, and Hakim knew that.

"Ali, I will shortly be going to America to work out the details myself. If you wish, you could accompany me to show you that this plan will work. I would be happy to call Amid to arrange it if you wish."

"I do not need you to arrange my affairs, Hakim. It could be well for us if I were to go to America with you, but first, how will you accomplish your mission by going there?"

"Only I can bring Will Johnson to the state where he will do what we wish. The others cannot do it. I must go to him and convince him he is to do the will of the Great One, all praise to him."

"How would you do that?" asked Ali.

"Johnson has been putty in my hands for years, since we were in the Army of the Americans, and after as we travelled together. When he is with me, he is my servant. He will do what we require."

"And if he does not?"

"Then, I will kill him because we cannot have the plan discovered."

"How will you get to America?" Ali Asked.

"By the same route I sent Josh Giddons, my other late friend. Through Canada, and then to the United States. It is all arranged. If you wish to go with me, I need to arrange for you as well."

"I will go to America, Hakim, but not with you. Unlike you, I can travel freely in the United States. I will see you in Washington, and I hope to see a glorious end to your plans, a very glorious end, which I can report to Amid." Ali stressed the name of Amid with a cold stare at Hakim, and turned to leave.

"How will I contact you in Washington Ali?" asked Hakim.

From a Vantage Point

"You will not," he responded, "I will contact you when I need to do it." Ali walked from the room, stared at the workers once more, and then left the building as he had come in, though the wide bay doors.

Hakim sat at his desk wondering the meanings of the conversation he just completed with Ali. One thing was certain, Amid was not pleased, and sending Ali to the United States was an ominous sign; only one would return.

From a Vantage Point

From a Vantage Point

Chapter 39 Into the Jaws of the Lion

Johnson Farm, Elias, West Virginia Will Johnson awoke with a start, hearing the telephone ring, but then it stopped.

"Will, you must answer the phone," exclaimed Sira, as she entered the living room, "It is Sammi, and he is anxious about something."

"All right, Sira" Will answered, "Give me the phone." Sira handed Will the wireless phone, and walked back to the kitchen, where she was preparing breakfast.

"Sammi, what is going on?"

"Mister Will, something terrible has happened," shouted Sammi into the phone, "The police and government people, they are coming to arrest Hassan this morning. What do I do?"

"First, calm down," answered Will, "Then call Elmer and tell him what you told me. What time are they coming?"

"About ten o'clock I think. That is what the chief thinks as well. He told me last night."

"All right, then, call Elmer, and we will be in town in a short while." Looking over at the clock, and smelling breakfast, Will added, "About 9:30 I think."

"Thank you, Mister Will. Please be careful, and so must Sira," said Sammi, obviously distraught.

"Just take it easy Sammi. We will work this out. See you in about ninety minutes." Will clicked off the phone, and rose to walk toward the kitchen.

"Sira, Hassan has been discovered. The police are coming to arrest him this morning. Do you want to come to town, or would you prefer to stay here?"

"I will come Will," she answered, "But after we have breakfast. Then we will go." She tried to smile, but it was obvious she was upset over Hassan. "He is my friend, and was my betrothed. I owe it to him and his family to be there for his troubles."

"I understand and respect that Sira," answered Will. "I just wanted to be sure you were comfortable with that. Not knowing what they want, or even if they are looking at you as well, or even Sammi, I might bring you to town and leave you at Elmer's office, at least until we see what is really going on."

"That will be fine Will, for the moment," said Sira, "Sammi will need help with the restaurant when they take Hassan. I will share time as I have done before."

"We'll work everything out Sira, don't worry about that. For now, let's just get through today, and that starts with breakfast before we go to town."

"It's ready Will. I was just waiting for you to awaken, and I didn't want to disturb you. Instead, the telephone did." Sira smiled, and Will suddenly forgot about breakfast in a wave of love for her.

From a Vantage Point

During the nearly 30-minute drive to town, Will thought a great deal about what was happening, how he would protect Sira and Sammi, and what could possibly happen with Hassan. He also thought a great deal on how this might affect his cooperative venture, especially since he had only recently had the discussion with Tom O'Neal on the questions from Homeland Security. Will felt he could trust Tom, but was not sure how he could help in this situation. As they neared the town, Will put most of this out of his mind, driving down Main Street, and parking over near where Elmer Sites' office was located.

Will helped Sira out of the truck, and brought her up the stairs to the office. Elmer was still there.

"Elmer, how goes it?" asked Will.

"I assume you have heard from Sammi, Will," answered Elmer. 'This is turning into a real goat screw. How many spies and terrorists do the Feds think we have here anyway?"

"Not sure Elmer, but I have a favor to ask before you leave. Could Sira stay here while the Feds are in town? I don't think we need another immigrant the Feds just might decide to take along when they get Hassan."

"Happy to oblige Will," responded Elmer. "Sira, you know Gladys, my secretary? You two can pass the time while the two of us go across the street and figure out what is going on. Gladys, why not find some tea and whatever else is around for Sira."

"Sure boss," responded Gladys. "No problem. Sira and I speak all the time, at least when she is over at the restaurant. Let's go see what we have in the fridge, and make some tea." Sira smiled at Will as the two men turned to leave.

"That is some woman, Will. I hope you see in her eyes the same thing I do. That woman is head-over-heels in love with you."

"I know Elmer, and the feeling is mutual. We just have to get through this mess. We need to speak later, by the way." Elmer looked quizzically at Will.

"Sure, no problem, Will. Anything in particular?"

"No, we just need to update what you know, just in case," Will responded. The two men left the office, and started to walk across the street, when the caravan of black SUVs came down the street, stopping in from of Sammi's. The first person out of the lead van was Agent Cohen from DHS.

"Agent Cohen," yelled Elmer Sites, "Looks like we do some more business today, my friend."

"Guess so, counselor," he responded, "Hopefully in a better frame of mind than in the past."

"I think so," Elmer responded, "Let's just get this over with so the towns' people can get back to what they really need to be doing."

From a Vantage Point

The federal agents in the small caravan disembarked from their vehicles, with several going toward the restaurant, and others covering the sides and rear entrance. Agent Cohen, an FBI Agent, Elmer Sites and Will entered the restaurant, and found Sammi waiting for them.

An FBI agent went up to Sammi and said, "Mister Khan, I am Special Agent Richardson of the Charleston FBI Office. Please ask your employee Hassan Singh to come into the restaurant."

"I would be happy to, Mister Agent Richardson, but he is not here. I do not know where he is. He did not come in to work today, and his room upstairs is empty."

"Where is his room?" asked Richardson. Sammi pointed toward the kitchen.

"He lives in a room upstairs. Stairs in the kitchen go up to the second floor."

Richardson waved to two agents to go through the kitchen and secure the room. In less than two minutes, one was back in the restaurant telling Richardson there was no one in the room.

"Do you have any idea where Singh might have gone Mister Khan?" asked Richardson.

"No sir. He said nothing to me last evening. We closed the restaurant and he went to his room. I went home to my own room down the street."

"When was that sir?" the agent asked.

"About nine o'clock sir," came the response.

"OK," said Richardson, turning to one of his agents. Let's put out a BOLO on Hassan Singh. Get a good description from Mr. Khan, and say arrest on sight."

"Mister Khan, do you know if Singh had a weapon of any kind?"

"No sir, I do not think so."

"Better say possibly armed," Richardson added to his directions to the other FBI agent. "Let's make that a wide search. Who knows where he may have gone?"

"Mister Khan, are you sure he wasn't tipped off about the pending arrest?"

"Well, that is possible Agent Richardson," answered the Chief of Police. I did provide Mister Khan with a private advance on the pending arrest. I guess Singh might have overheard. I did look toward the kitchen to make sure no one was here last evening, but I could have missed it. Sorry if this complicates your task."

"No problem Chief," answered Richardson with a sigh, "We'll get him. He can't have gone very far. Let's just get the BOLO out and see what we find."

Richardson turned to his people, and said, "Let's check around town just in case he is somewhere in the vicinity, and make sure the State Police have his information. We have a photo from his immigration paperwork. Mister Khan, you don't perhaps have anything more recent?"

From a Vantage Point

Sammi thought for a moment, and knowing he did have a photo of both Hassan and Sira, responded, "No, I do not think so. We do not take a lot of pictures here. I will look in my desk and see, but I don't think so."

"Thanks Mister Khan," responded Richardson, "We really don't need it, but if you do find one, give it to the chief, and he can send it to us."

"I will, sir," Sammi said in response.

"All right folks. There isn't much else we can do here. Check the town, and let's go back to Charleston. Chief, if you do see him, let us know. Would be great if we came back to find him in your jail."

"I will have my own men scour the town and the surrounding area, Agent Richardson. I'll call the county sheriff as well, and we'll put teams out to see what we can find."

"Thanks. Appreciate the effort," responded Richardson, obviously disappointed at not getting an arrest.

Within thirty minutes, the caravan was wending its way out of town, back to Charleston, but without a prisoner. As they reached the end of Main Street, and started for the State Highway, over in a clump of trees, Hassan watched, his car hidden by the foliage, and he breathed a sigh of relief that he was still free. Just as they were leaving, Anderson Cohen came over to Will, standing near the door of the restaurant with Elmer, shook his hand, exchanged a few words, and left to join the rest of the agents. Entering the van, and closing the door, he waved to Will, now standing in the doorway.

As the last of the convoy pulled away, Will and Elmer said goodbye to Sammi, and started back across the street toward the law firm, as Elmer asked, "Now, what is it you wanted to talk about Will?"

Department of Homeland Security, Washington DC Rich Alcorn had refreshed the screen at least fifty times over the past 4 hours, waiting to see if a CONEX at the Brentwood Postal Facility would finally be opened, the boxes Alcorn wanted would visualize on the screen as their sensors could again emit their signals. So far, no luck, but Alcorn knew it would change. He just had to wait, be patient, and vigilant. Sooner or later, he would get the signals he wanted that would alert them to where the boxes were headed.

The question of the boxes had interested Rich Alcorn since he first heard about them in one of the early meetings at DHS. Alice Sawyer asked, meeting after meeting, for ideas on how they could be used, but no one really knew what to respond. Then, about a month ago, the copy of the plans for boxes, apparently drawn by Hakim al-Azahir, and found in the workshop of Pentopolos in Kabul, arrived through CIA channels.

From a Vantage Point

The boxes were an interesting design of wood with some shielding designed to lessen, but not completely obliterate the material stored inside. They were built 18 inches high by 16 inches wide, with a larger central space, and smaller compartments along the edges. An interesting design, but confounding as to how such a box, or boxes, could be used.

Alcorn looked again at the two rough drawings of the boxes. Suddenly, it came to him. Rich Alcorn had been an artilleryman in the Army. More specifically, he was part of a mortar platoon. That platoon carried their weapons in large packing boxes; the 'foot' on the side of the box, the pipe sections in the center, and the ammunition along the alternate sides. Those boxes were much larger than the drawing here would indicate, but what if these boxes had smaller versions of a mortar, perhaps even made of lighter material, for a one-time use.

Looking at some of the other material which had arrived from CIA, Alcorn noticed a description in a report Jeff Namers had written on his incursion into the Pentopolos warehouse. In that report, Namers said, *"It was particularly interesting that, over in a corner, stood both a lathe and an early model 3-D printer. We found nothing in the warehouse where either of these tools might be used, or had been used, on projects in this location."*

That was it!

These guys were making one-time use mortars, probably in heavy plastic or PVC, and the boxes made it easier for them to travel, said Alcorn to himself. Then, his short-lived bubble burst, as he continued to look over the CIA material, and realized the boxes were shipped empty.

Why ship them empty? He asked himself, and answering as well that *empty meant they left the country easily. If that were the case, then where could they have gone and picked up the plastic mortars, packed them away, and re-shipped them to the US?*

Now it was time to trace what they knew of the boxes.

Again, looking at the Namers reports, Alcorn saw that eventually two boxes were shipped to the US, with a delivery destination of Atlanta. Four others, including two with no sensor contact, were shipped to other places around the world. All six were accounted for in the reports.

Something is wrong here, mussed Alcorn. *We have two boxes with sensors, which apparently were shipped empty to Atlanta. When they arrived in Atlanta, they never left the airport. Logic says they are still empty, but they were re-shipped to DC, and then ended up in the Postal Service as well. Why go to so much trouble for two empty boxes?*

Re-reading Namer's report, Alcorn saw the note on the two boxes, shipped out through Cairo with no sensors discernable.

From a Vantage Point

Where did they go after Cairo? He asked himself. According to the manifests, they were delivered to an address in the old city which was the main office of Near East Shipping and Export.

Alcorn knew that name, or at least something close. The company in Atlanta, in the boxing club building, was Near East Imports.

Could these two be the same? Alcorn asked himself.

As he sat there thinking, the phone rang, and Alcorn reached over to pick it up, hitting the speaker button instead of having to cradle the phone and try to continue reading the Namer's report.

"Alcorn, can I help you?"

"Rich, this is Anderson Cohen from Charleston. How are you today?"

"Fine Anderson, You were with the team to go pick up Singh. How did it go?"

"Not well, I am afraid," Cohen responded, "We missed him. He had somehow heard we were coming, probably overhearing the local chief of police, and skipped. The FBI have a multi-state BOLO out on him now."

"Alice will not be pleased?" Alcorn retorted, "Very much not pleased. Please keep us up on how the search goes. Are you planning on keeping someone there?"

"The FBI special agent discussed that with the Chief, a bit loudly I might add, and the locals will cover the town in case he returns."

"OK, I guess that is the best we can do. Thanks for the effort Anderson. I'll let Ms. Sawyer know."

"Appreciate that Rich. You saved my skin today. I owe you one."

"No problem Anderson. Go home and enjoy the rest of the day. Out here," Alcorn said, as he clicked the speaker off, ending the call.

Karzai International Airport, Kabul, Afghanistan *The Karzai International Airport, now jointly used by both the Airlines servicing Kabul, and the International Security and Assistance Forces (ISAF) operating in the country, is located quite close to the city, and has undergone extensive modernization over the past several years. It is the principal airport for both domestic and international flights, and has significant general aviation capability, mostly with border countries, such as Pakistan. Arrivals and departures occur throughout a twenty-four-hour day, although on religious holidays, and during the winter season, the numbers of flights markedly declines.*

Three men, in western-style suits entered the main entrance of the International Terminal, and were met, as they approached the check-in area for KAM Airlines, by the security officer in uniform. Each had an official passport, which the security officer requested, and they were then escorted from the main check-in lines through a side door, leading to the security area. They passed quickly through the small office, and exited through another door out toward the

From a Vantage Point

tarmac, where they climbed up the side stairway to a waiting jumbo jet, headed in less than an hour to Cairo, Egypt.

While this type of service happened frequently for governmental and diplomatic personnel, these were not ordinary government travelers. They were not government employees at all, although their passports stated differently. Akram Karim and his brother Ahmad, along with Kassim Said had tickets taking them first to Cairo, Egypt, and then through Frankfurt, Germany and Lisbon, Portugal to Boston, Massachusetts. Their papers indicated they were advisors to the Afghani Ministry of Trade, and their mission was to attend a meeting in Boston related to the wool industry.

The three men sat aside each other in the front section of the aircraft, the one near the window reading an Afghani newspaper, and the man near the aisle listened to music, while the man in the middle sat simply staring ahead, as if in deep thought.

"Kassim," said the man near the window, whose name was Akram, "We are flying. Now the world is before us."

"Yes," responded Kassim, "We are on our way to Cairo. There, all is arranged as well." Then, Kassim went back to his thoughts.

Kassim Said was Hakim al-Azahir, but the other two men were told to refer to him only as Kassim, the name on his passport. It took several payoffs to ensure the security officials would not watch them too closely at the airport. Hakim had friends within the Ministry of Trade, and it was through him they secured official passports, and avoid the long lines, sometimes overseen by the ISAF. They should do as well in Cairo, if Amid, his leader, did not intervene. Once they were free of Cairo, they could relax. Their passports were genuine; their backgrounds and pictures matched the official Afghani Government records, and they should have no trouble going through their other stopovers before they reached America.

Suddenly, the man near the aisle, Ahmad Karim, sat up and turned to Kassim saying, "Kassim, the news is saying the American police and Interpol are looking for Hassan Singh. They tried to arrest Hassan yesterday, and he escaped their grasp."

"Speak softly Ahmad," responded Kassim. "All is well. We do not need him if that is the will of All'ah, may he ever be praised. Go back to your music and let me worry about our trip."

"All right Kassim, if that is what you wish," Ahmad answered.

"It will be a long flight," Kassim said to both, before Ahmad had restored his earphones. "We must be careful and quiet in the meanwhile. No one can discover our trip, or all is lost."

Hakim grew even more worried about his trip, now that he knew about Hassan Singh. He tried to rest his eyes, but his mind was moving in too many directions to relax.

Sammi's Restaurant, Elias, West Virginia "Don't worry, Will, all of this is going to work out," said Elmer Sites, his attorney, as they reached the sidewalk in from of the restaurant. It seemed that every day something new was happening in this small town that usually had nothing more than an occasional speeder.

"I know Elmer," responded Johnson, "It just seems that I can never put my past behind me, and now even my friends, or those I thought were friends, are involved. I just want to keep the cooperative idea going, but every turn is some new delay."

"Have some patience, boy," said Elmer, "Things are really going to work out for you, and that lovely young lady you are stashing over in my office. Isn't it about time, you went over there and got her. I'll be back over after I see Sammi for a moment."

"Wow, in all this, I almost forgot about Sira," exclaimed Will, "I better get over there right away. She must be frantic by now."

"And don't tell her you forgot about her. Women don't like to hear that," smiled Elmer, as he turned to walk into the restaurant.

Will walked up the steps two at a time, getting to the second-floor landing in seconds, and then just a couple of steps to Elmer's law offices.

"Oh, Will, Is everything all right?" asked Sira, as she rushed over to him.

"Everything is fine Sira," he responded, "Hassan escaped some time before the law arrived, so there is a warrant out for his arrest. Otherwise, everything is OK, except maybe for Sammi, who right about now needs two staff members to wait tables so he can cook for the lunch crowd. Feel like waiting tables?"

"Let's go," she answered, "I feel like a lot of work today."

As they walked down the steps to the street, Will and Sira could see a crowd gathering in front of Sammi's. They crossed the street and went up to the doorway on the side of the crowd. People saw who they were and stepped aside. Inside, the place was mayhem. All the tables were full, and people were waiting patiently to get their orders taken.

"Thank God, Mister Will. Can you and Sira help please?"

"That's what the cavalry is here for, Sammi. We'll start right away. Sira, you take one side and I will take the other."

"Sure Will, but what is 'cavalry'?" she asked.

Several patrons laughed, and she became embarrassed.

"Don't worry Sira," said Will, "These people are not laughing at you, they are laughing with you. Why should you know what cavalry is? It's the help coming to take orders. We're the cavalry." Sira looked at Will and started laughing as well.

From a Vantage Point

"I better start to learn new words, I guess," she responded, as she put on an apron, went to the cash register area, and took two pencils and two pads, giving one of each to Will. Then, they started down the tables taking orders.

Sira and Will spent the day with Sammi, working through the long lunch that turned into dinner, as people from all over town came to show their support. Sammi spent part of the day with tears in his eyes, hoping he could somehow later repay their kindnesses, and their support. Every time Sira would come to the kitchen, he claimed he had cut more onions, but she knew better.

Finally, it was after ten o'clock, and the last customers left the restaurant. Will turned the 'OPEN' sign to 'CLOSED' and the cleanup started. Sammi and Sira cleaned the kitchen, putting away the large pots and pans, things Will washed as he fed plates and utensils into the dishwasher. It took them over an hour to clean up the restaurant, sweep it down, and get ready for the morning.

"We are out of here, Sammi," said Will, looking toward Sammi and Sira.

"Thank you so much Mister Will," he responded, "I thank you from my heart. You saved me today, and I will not forget it. And you too, Sira. I thank you as well. Now, take him home. You both look very tired."

Sira looked at Will, then said, "We are, both of us. We will be back tomorrow to help again, so you can stay open." Will nodded in agreement.

"Thank you both, and now go home. It is late, and you have a long trip." Sammi pushed them toward the doorway so he could close and go home as well. Will and Sira walked through the doorway, and out into the street and then up toward his truck. Sammi closed the doors of the restaurant, and turned out the lights as they crossed the street.

Department of Homeland Security, Washington DC Rich Alcorn walked along the corridor separating his area from Alice Sawyer's office. Reaching the doorway to her suite, he breezed in, waved to her assistant, and started to walk into her office, when her assistant stopped him.

"Sorry Rich. You can't go in right now. She has a delegation from the FBI in there. They just arrived, and it might be a while."

"OK, but you might want to tell her I'm out here and do need to see her on the boxes issue. Please call me when she is free."

"Sure will, but, as I said, it might be a while."

"That's OK. I will be in my office." Alcorn waved as he turned and started leave. Just as he reached the door to the corridor, Alice came out of her office and said, "Rich, just the person I need. Come on in."

Alcorn entered behind Alice and saw the room had several other people, including Richard Peabody, the Assistant Director for Counter-Terrorism with her.

From a Vantage Point

"Gentlemen, this is Richard Alcorn, my right-hand man and general nuisance genius. Rich, I think you know some of these guys." Alcorn introduced himself, saving Peabody for last.

"How are you, RP?" He asked, extending his hand.

"Good Rich, and good to see you. She keeps you hidden most of the time."

"And for good reason," Alice interjected. "If I let him out too often, he might find greener pastures somewhere else."

"Rich, grab a seat. I assume you have something you need to tell me, and we want to ask some questions as well." Alice pointed to a chair near her at the conference table.

"Well," started Alcorn, "I think we now know a bit more about the boxes coming here. They have bugged me for weeks, since we first learned about them, and something just didn't seem right."

"Like what?" asked Peabody.

"Well, first, why would anyone send a set of boxes through a public shipping process which are empty. In addition, since the senders knew that some had sensors for tracking attached, but did not remove them, you have to ask what their plan really might have been."

"I traced all the boxes we know about, six of them, four with sensors, and two without sensors. Two headed directly for the US, and the other four went into other directions. Of course, we could trace those with sensors, as I said, and two arrived here, empty, and are still, as far as we know, at Brentwood."

"But then," Alcorn continued, "I began to think about the other two—those without sensors, and what happened to them. At the same time, I began to surmise to myself—what about the possibility of there being more than six boxes? I looked through the file the CIA sent over, and noticed the equipment in al-Azahir's warehouse. There was a lathe, a 3-D printer, and a table saw over in a corner, along with lots of wood piled along the wall near the saw."

"Could it be, I said to myself, that there might be more than six boxes, and whatever number more that were built might also be on the way to the US?"

"When I saw the lathe and the 3-D printer, looking at those pictures, there was a small amount of PVC pipe on the ground, but still visible in the photo. What could happen if the boxes were intended to carry a weapon? How about a PVC-built small mortar, capable of one-time use, and sending out shells with enough force to do some damage? It doesn't have to be major damage, just enough to make a point."

"The PVC, if it's thick enough, could be shaped on a lathe, and the mechanisms for firing created on the 3-D printer. The plans are readily available—all someone could do is go to a Patent Office to get the patent design drawings, or even copy one a terrorist might already have. You use it one time and simply walk away."

From a Vantage Point

"Rich, you have outdone yourself with this one," responded Alice Sawyer. "There is still the question of getting all of this into the US."

"Not really," interjected Peabody, "Plastic, PVC, is harder to scan, and if all the parts are made of something similar, and then broken down into parts, placed in a fitted box, and shipped, the terrorists only have to worry about the possibility of discovery at some customs point. The lack of sensors throws them off track—the intelligence and customs people are looking for something that beeps, not something in a non-descript box. In addition, of course, is that simply packing them with other goods coming in even further reduces the possibility of finding them. We only actually search about five percent of cargos these days; I think that's right, or at least close, Alice. This is a very possible scenario."

"OK, I'll buy that," retorted Alice. "What about the shells?"

"Just as easy," answered Peabody. "You get them here in the US. We have small mortar rounds going missing from the military all the time; some reported, and some not. What we need to find is the local source, an armory, or a commercial arms dealer, or even a museum."

"If we accept this scenario as a possibility," asked Alice, "Does this mean we have been looking in the wrong direction here?"

"Perhaps so," came the response from a woman's voice. Alcorn looked around the room, and, over at the corner of the table sat a lone woman in the room."

"For those of you who have not previously met her, this is Sarah Minihan. She works at Central Intelligence."

"If what we know now is true, then Hakim al-Azahir works for the Tabriz organization, some of you may know it as the Fatool Organization. Tabriz is retired, but his associate Amid Fatoullah is still in charge, and this scene fits well with their methods. Create a large smoke screen, keep the opposition occupied, and work your real plan outside the light of day. They have been doing this for years, and we don't always catch them in time."

"The boxes you have at Brentwood, if they are indeed empty, are probably part of that smokescreen, designed to keep you occupied while whoever is working the effort on their part is doing something completely different. The real questions here seem to be 'what' and 'where', before you can get to 'when', although, based on what we know now, it seems reasonable as well to say they will target the Inauguration."

The others at the table started buzzing with side conversations, and several looking down at the file folders in front of each, trying to come up with a response.

"All right, let's come back to order here," said Alice Sawyer. "Thanks Sarah for your insights here. For the record, I want to point out I asked Sarah to come this morning, not to participate in this operation, but to express her own professional views on possible scenarios. She is eminently qualified for that task, and I appreciate your taking the time to be here. Anyone have questions for Sarah?"

"Ms. Minihan, If this were your case, what do you think the next moves will be?" asked one of the men sitting at the table.

"Well, that is a hard question," said Sarah. "Listening to the earlier briefing, it would seem to me that al-Azahir has no choice but to send someone to oversee his plan, or to come himself. You have crushed the Atlanta cell, have its leader in custody, and now the guy Hassan Singh in Elias is on the run. He is of no value to al-Azahir as a fugitive. Unless he has other players, he can bring in quickly, he will probably have to come himself, and that is obviously dangerous."

"Frankly, as Mister Alcorn has said, I would be looking to determine the reality here. What boxes, if any, play in the scenario? Are the boxes in Brentwood real, or simply a diversion? If they are a diversion, then do any boxes play in the scenario? What plans can you make to determine if al-Azahir is on his way, or are others? If he or others are coming, where would they go?"

"One final question for you," Sarah Minihan added, "If the Inauguration is the target, and the boxes are real, and the boxes would hold some type of weapon or bomb, where would they do the most damage, physical or psychological? If this were our case at the Agency, these are the questions we would be pondering right now."

The room stayed totally quiet as Sarah Minihan finished speaking. Slowly, those around the table seemed to come out of a stupor, then start asking each other questions, as they had a short time earlier.

"Sarah, it seems you have put a stake in the ground for these people. Thanks for coming. Any comments from the rest of you?" Alice asked, looking around the room.

Richard Peabody, who had been sitting next to Alice, rose and turned around to face a white board behind him on the wall. "We have four things to worry about here, the simple interrogatories, WHO, WHAT, WHEN, and WHERE." As he spoke, he wrote the four words on the white board in large letters at the top, spacing them out across the board.

"We have a pretty good idea, at least in a general way, on the WHO," he added, as he underlined the word. "We can make a reasonable assumption that it will be people involved with al-Azahir and his cells, like the one in Atlanta. One of those people is in our interrogation room in the Atlanta office, singing like a bird, afraid of being sent to Guantanamo. He gave us two things, the WHO, as I mentioned, and the WHEN, Inauguration Day, he said as he underlined WHEN on the board. We do not know much about the rest to fill in the board. That is what we need, and quickly."

From a Vantage Point

As Peabody sat down, Alice took his place at the white board, filling out the name of al-Azahir and a question mark under WHO, and 'Inauguration Day' under WHEN. "Let's assume for a moment that Mister Alcorn is right about the boxes. Let's say they will or do contain a weapon for creating explosions or other kinds of havoc. How do we locate and disarm that possibility?" Alice entered 'Boxes', 'Weapons', and 'Disarm or neutralize under WHAT, and then 'Washington DC' under WHERE. "That is the map we start with guys, and we fill in the blanks from there."

"Rich Alcorn, your people work solely on the boxes, what they can do, where they are, and where they are going—all of the boxes. Sarah, if you could help with footage from Kabul and the air freight operations there, and in Cairo, we would be most appreciative. Your guys have been working that angle, and we need to continue filling in that perspective. Can you help there?"

"Sure Alice, answered Sara, "that's no problem. I'll get it cleared with Bernie, and we'll notify Kabul, and the anti-terrorism team in Khartoum to assist."

"Great, now for the WHERE aspect, Richard Peabody, can your staff work on the guy in Atlanta, and anybody else in that cell still alive, and get as much as you can get on the timing and location. We need to find a string to follow that will take us beyond Atlanta into the DC area. There must be more people here who are involved—beyond that guy Hassan Singh you all just tried to arrest in West Virginia. We need a break there."

"Good. That leads us to the most critical part, the WHAT," said Alice. "There are a lot of 'Ifs' already on the board. If they are anywhere near correct, we have something going to happen in DC on or around Inauguration Day. The description Rich Alcorn gave us might indicate a possible mortar attack, and that means relatively short range in the area at or between the Capitol and the White House. At least for now, that seems to be the most logical area for whatever they have planned.

We have the Metropolitan Police and the Secret Service, but will probably need even more officers for the planned events. We can't just put anyone in the streets or on the rooftops, we need people trained to observe and act. You folks from the Secret Service need to be putting everyone you can on this, and coordinate with any other law enforcement entity you need, but get intel on what is rumbling in the street. Somebody should be saying something. There must be something out-of-the-ordinary that doesn't ring true. We need to find that 'something'."

"What authority do we use for all this, Ms. Sawyer? There are a lot of lines to cross here," asked one of the men sitting on the far end of the table.

"For now, we will use the statutory authority covering inauguration protection," she responded, "If we need something stronger, and beyond arm-twisting, I will go to the secretary for an order. Will that work for you all?" Most nodded or said nothing.

"All right then, let's get at it. Rich Alcorn will be my delegate for this adventure. If you cannot get to me, call Rich for whatever you need. Thanks for coming. Rich Peabody and Sarah, could you all stay a moment?"

Most of the group rose to leave, some still shaking their heads and wondering among themselves what this action was all about. Sarah Minihan walked up to where Rich and Alice were standing.

"Well Alice, I think you have a full hand here," offered Sarah. 'And you too, Rich. This is not going to be an easy win. We'll help how we can, but we are a bit limited here."

"I know that Sarah," responded Alice, "But you have the foreign intel we need badly. Whatever you can give us will be appreciated immensely."

"Seems like a bit of New Orleans all over again, Sarah," said Peabody, "What did the great Yogi say, 'Déjà vu all over again'?"

"Only this time we are not dealing with Fatool or even Amid," responded Sarah, "Those guys we eventually figured out and could counter. This new generation, like al-Azahir, don't have the thought processes, or experience the other two had in spades."

"Rich," asked Alice, "If you were someone like al-Azahir, what would your plan be?"

Peabody thought for a minute, and then responded, "I would probably try to create panic on Inauguration Day, perhaps using these mortars Rich Alcorn described in a high arc from a hotel, aiming them to land at or near Pennsylvania Avenue during the parade."

"Why there?" asked Alice.

"Well, look at what you have on Inauguration Day. There is no way anyone can get near enough to the Capitol to disrupt the actual swearing-in. It is possible, I guess, that someone could attack the motorcade as it comes up to the Capitol, but that would not have as great an impact, and they are more in the open, smaller footprint, and harder target to zone in on. No, I think they want to make a big public relations splash more than kill people, and that means putting some rounds into or near the inauguration parade. They don't have to do anything but lob the shells in a high-enough arc to get them to the street. We need to be looking for high points in hotels or tall buildings for the terrorist effort."

"I agree with Rich, Alice," said Sarah in reply, "This is a public stunt as much as an attempt to do damage. These people are smart; they will go after the easiest target that gets them news time on an important day, like the Inauguration. That would be my hunch."

From a Vantage Point

"We all agree on that," answered Alice. "That's why this plan needs to ferret out Hassan Singh, and quickly, and we need to get this guy Radan to sing even louder. What about the others who lived from the shoot-out Rich? Anything on them?"

"No Alice, they were low-level types, doing what they were told. We did get the info on the body in the basement that turned out to be a likeness of Giddons, al-Azahir's associate, and we are still trying to figure that one out, but these guys are simply doofers, they do for the boss whatever he wants."

"OK, so we have to push hard to find Singh. He may be our only real lead with information here. Thanks to both of you. We ought to get together more often, and without the need to be discussing terrorists, when we could be talking about kids," added Alice. The three started to walk toward the door.

US Embassy, Kabul, Afghanistan "Hello, this is Rick Cartwright, Commercial Attaché. I am out right now, but please leave a message and I will return your call. Thanks."

"I can't believe this," said Jeff Namers, CIA Chief in Khartoum, Sudan. "The guy leaves a message tape when he is out of the office," Namers continued, speaking with his hand over the phone, and looking over at two of his staff in his office. "I better think about that instead of the drivel the government puts on there for you." The men sitting there both laughed.

"OK, then, we will talk to Cartwright later," he told his people, "We have to figure out what to do about the call I just received from Sarah Minihan and Alice Sawyer of DHS.

"What did they want?" one of the men asked.

"What else. They wanted to know the whereabouts of Hakim al-Azahir, of course. I might have him move in with me here in Khartoum so I always know where he is," said Namers sarcastically. "Seriously guys, Langley is worried that Hakim is running, perhaps toward the US. Put out your feelers to see if he has started his run. I would start at Cairo myself, since he might look to the Fatool people for his health and safety. Let's see what we can find. I will continue to call Cartwright to confirm that he is not in Kabul."

"Will do, boss," they both said in unison, then turning after saluting, and going out the door of Namer's office.

Cairo International Airport, Egypt The public-address system blared in Arabic and English for the arrival of several flights, including one from Kabul, the one Hakim and his men flew from that city.

"Arriving from Kabul, KEM Air Flight Number 42, at Gate 6. This flight will be on the ground for forty-five minutes before proceeding to Frankfurt, Germany. All passengers arriving on the flight destined for Cairo will depart for the Customs

Inspection area, and those continuing will stay on board, inside or in the secured area. Passengers boarding this flight for Frankfurt, Germany, should proceed to Gate 6 for check-in."

"I think I will stretch my legs in the terminal," said Kassim (his assumed name) to the men on either side of him. "I will be back shortly, unless you choose to join me, of course?"

"No Kassim," answered one of the men, "We will stay on board, "he added, looking at the other man with them.

"So be it, then, I will return," Kassim noted, as he rose to leave with the man on the aisle also rising to let him out of the row, after which he quickly walked the short distance to the door and the jetway.

As he exited the jetway, two men with the name 'Kassim' on a piece of cardboard waited. One of the men he knew as Amid Fatoullah's bodyguard. He walked over to where they stood.

"Hakim, I wish it was good to see you. We are to take you to see Amid." With that, both men turned toward the central walkway, and Hakim followed. They went a short distance to a door marked, 'Employees only' and held the door for Hakim to enter, then they followed.

Inside, sitting at a small table, drinking Turkish coffee, whose aroma filled the room, was Amid. "Well, Hakim, it seems you are traveling to America. Shall I be pleased, or shall I be displeased?"

"As I told Ali, and I am sure he told you as well Amid, I am going to make sure our plans are carried out."

"Be careful of your talk Hakim. Be sure who you speak to in a sarcastic voice. I am not one of the peasants who work for you."

"My apologies, Amid. My comment was not intended to be offensive," answered Hakim. "There have been some problems, and I am going to make sure everything is fixed and is done the way it is expected."

"I know of the problems, Hakim. We have spoken of some of them before, but now it seems that your plans are falling apart. This project must succeed, even if you are to do it yourself. Do you understand me?"

"I do Amid," responded al-Azahir, "I have never disappointed you, and this will not be the first time."

"Good, then we understand each other Hakim. Do this well, or do not dare to return." Amid rose from his seat, and walked from the room. As he did so, he turned and said to his men, "Take him back to his plane, and be sure he enters it and does not get off." Then, Amid left the room, his brightly colored caftan flowing around him as he walked out the door.

The two men walked back to the plane with Hakim, saw that he entered, and one of the men stayed in the gate to be sure the plane took off with all their passengers, then returned to where Amid waited with the other man.

From a Vantage Point

"Make sure that the security people in Frankfurt know that Hakim is on the plane. I do not want him arrested, just the knowledge that he is departing for the United States. How he deals with staying out of the hands of the police there is his problem. Tell Ali that Hakim is on his way as well, and to stay clear of him until he hears from me."

"Have our people in the United States keep Hakim under close watch," Amid added, "I want to know everything he does, or tries to do." The man nodded and all three walked away into the terminal.

Johnson Farm, Elias, West Virginia The pickup truck bounced along the dark, dirt road leading up to the farmhouse. Each time it hit a bump, Sira stirred a bit from the sleep which overcame her shortly after they left the restaurant, and started down the state road toward the farm. Finally, they reached the front door, Will Johnson turned off the motor, and left the cab, going to the passenger side to waken Sira, and get her into the house.

He opened the door slowly, and then nudged her softly, saying, "Sira, we are home. It's time to go inside." Sira moved slightly, and barely opened her eyes, looking toward Will.

"Are we at the farm?" she asked, not realizing Will just told her that same thing.

"Yes, Sira, we are. Now, it's time to go inside," he repeated.

"All right. Let's go inside," she repeated herself.

Will helped her to the house, closing the door to the pickup, and walking along the short path to the house, where he opened the front door to the house, and took her inside. Without stopping, he guided Sira along toward her bedroom, picked her up in the room, and placed her on the bed, pulling down the covers with one hand as he did so. Then, he turned out the light and closed the door.

It had been a very long and anxious day for Sira, and tomorrow might not be any better. Will returned to the front of the house, clicked his keyring to lock the pickup, and then locked the front door. He still worried about whoever had been over in the tree grove, and did not want to take chances. Going next to his own room, Will was asleep himself within twenty minutes.

The next morning, Will awoke first, looked at the clock and saw it was 6:30 AM, and decided to get up and make breakfast. He looked in on Sira who was still asleep, and continued to the kitchen, looking in the refrigerator for breakfast food. Over the next twenty minutes, or so, the house filled with the aroma of coffee, pancakes, and other items that both he and Sira liked.

"Good morning," said Sira, now in a bathrobe, rubbing her eyes, and looking at all the food Will was cooking. "We will never eat all that," she added.

"You might not, but personally, I am famished," he responded. "Go sit down and I will bring breakfast."

Hassan had been staying in a small shack in the woods near the Johnson Farm, which had been used years ago as a toolshed, and was still loaded with rusty reaping tools. Piling them to the side, Hassan used two blankets he took from his room at the restaurant as his bed, He also found a small kerosene lamp, and a rusty kerosene can, which still contained some fluid. Afraid that the liquid might either be something else, or even more volatile over time, Hassan instead used a small flashlight on his keychain for what light he needed at night. He spent every waking hour creating more hate in his mind for both Johnson and Sira, hoping for the opportunity to exact his revenge on one, or preferably both, of them.

On the second day, he was nearly out of the food he also took with him, and thought about how to get more without being discovered. He also needed gasoline for his car, since the tank was only a quarter tank full. Remembering that there was a town in the opposite direction from Elias, about twenty miles down the road, he decided to wait until late afternoon, and drive in that direction, where he was much less likely to be recognized.

Meanwhile, using a set of binoculars, he tried to keep watch on the farmhouse, without drawing attention to his presence. Over the next several days, that would prove to be more difficult, as the sun drew lower on the horizon, and the possibility of a reflection off the glass of the binoculars became possible. He wondered to himself almost constantly how long he could hold out.

Will Johnson took the food he prepared to the table where Sira was already sitting, and then remembered he forgot the milk. Walking back toward the kitchen, he happened to look out through the living room window, and thought he momentarily saw a glint in the trees. Shrugging it off, he entered the kitchen, went to the refrigerator, and returned with a pitcher of milk, poured some into the two glasses, and sat down next to her at the table.

"Well, dig in," said Will to Sira, smiling. "This food is for you, you know."

"I am impressed," she responded. "I expected to go to Sammi's for breakfast, and then work."

"Not this morning. We will go to Sammi's, and shortly, but first you get a Will Johnson breakfast."

Sira reached for two pancakes, and then the syrup. She ate both pancakes in just seconds.

"For someone who was amazed at the food, you sure ate those fast," exclaimed Will.

"I was hungry after all, I guess," she answered. "These are very good," she smiled.

"I do good work occasionally," responded Will. "Be nice, and I will cook more, so you can watch TV," he laughed.

From a Vantage Point

"You are making fun of me now."

"No, not really. I enjoy having you here, and making breakfast is one of those ways I can say thank you for what you do." Will grasped her hand and she turned hers over so they were truly holding hands.

"Will, what are we going to do about this mess?" she finally asked. Both knew they had to discuss it sooner or later, since they were both so directly involved.

"I have some ideas Sira, but right now my first concern is protecting you and Sammi. I might have to do some things I do not want to do, but everything will come out all right. Trust me."

"I do trust you Will, but I also do not want you hurt. Perhaps the best thing to do is to go to the authorities and simply tell them what has been going on."

"In time Sira," he replied, "But I have a plan that will make all that unnecessary. Now, let's finish breakfast and get ready to go to town to help Sammi."

They finished their breakfast, and did eat most of what Will had prepared, then took the dishes to the kitchen, promising each other to do them when they returned. Sira ran water in the sink to let them soak, then they both went to get dressed for town.

Will was already in the living room when Sira came out. She walked over to him and said, "I'm ready to go." She started for the door, but Will stopped her and put his arms around her, drawing her into him.

"I'm not quite," he said, as he leaned over and kissed her. They kissed for several seconds, and then separated. "I love you, you know," added Will, still holding her in his arms.

"I know," Sira answered quietly, "And I love you too." She put her head against his chest and simply stood there in his embrace for several seconds before standing straight and saying, "Now we have to go. Sammi needs our help."

"Yes Ma'am," responded Will, following her out the door to the truck.

US Embassy, Kabul, Afghanistan Rick Cartwright looked out the door of his office and asked the secretary to get him Jeff Namers on a secure line in Khartoum. She made the call, and they yelled into his office.

"Mister Namers is on the line, Rick."

"Thanks. Please make sure I am not disturbed for the next thirty minutes or so."

"Will do sir," she responded.

Picking up the phone, Rick spoke, "Jeff, how are you doing. Got your message, and two of my boys just returned with some news you might want to hear."

From a Vantage Point

"What's that, Rick?" Namers responded.

"Apparently, Hakim is on the move. There is no one at his warehouse; the place is padlocked on all sides. We checked the airport, and one of our informants said he thought he saw Hakim with two of his henchmen board a flight this morning. The manifest for the KEM flight to Cairo did not have him on board, but it did have Kassim Said on the manifest, along with two others who fit the descriptions of his associates. We hacked the security footage at KEM's gate, and sure enough, al-Azahir and two others boarded the early flight to Cairo. They should be there by now."

"Thanks Rick. That is interesting news. Back to you later."

As soon as Namers hung up, he asked his secretary to get his counterpart in Cairo, Dan Victorino, on the line.

"Dan," said Namers into his phone, "al-Azahir is on the move. We understand he came in on a KEM flight from Kabul, with a stop in Cairo. Can you confirm that?"

"Interesting you should just happen to call Jeff. We got information less than an hour ago that Amid Fatoullah, our friend, was at Cairo International meeting a KEM plane. He had two of his men escort someone from the jetway to a private room for a discussion, and then back to the plane. One of his men stood guard to make sure the passenger departed."

"I asked for the footage," Rick continued, "And it just came in. I'm looking at it now. Here is the jetway tape, and, oh well, sure enough it is Hakim with two other men on either arm. They take him out of the jetway and over toward a door marked employees, and they go inside. Streaming ahead a bit, out comes Amid Fatoullah, looking a bit pissed off, and a bit later out comes Hakim, still escorted, going back to the plane. He doesn't look very happy either. Unfortunately, we have no audio in that room, so no idea of the discussion."

"Where is the KEM flight going Rick?" asked Namers.

"From here to Frankfurt, and then on to Lisbon, Jeff."

"Where after that?" Namers asked.

"Don't know Jeff. The flight ends there, and we see not further travel for Mister Said. Is there a reason for them to stop in Lisbon?"

"Nothing I know of. When do they land?"

"About two hours left until they reach Frankfurt, I estimate, assuming no headwinds. You have time if you want to stop them."

"No, I do want to make sure we keep them under surveillance, though. I can handle that. We have an Air Marshal in both cities who can provide the info we want. Thanks Dan."

"No problem Jeff. Out here." Victorino hung up his phone, shook his head, and commented to another staff member, "Well our friend Hakim is on the move,

From a Vantage Point

and working with Amid Fatoullah. That is some combination. Remember Namers in your prayers tonight. He will need it with those two."

Namers made the necessary calls to both Frankfurt and Lisbon, finding out that Jim Davis was in Lisbon, and would wait there for Hakim's arrival. He cautioned Davis not to venture too close to Hakim for fear he would be recognized. All everyone could do now was wait to see how this drama unfolded.

Sammi's Restaurant, Elias, West Virginia Sammi was already running around trying to put everything in place when Will and Sira arrived.

"Thank God you are here, Sira," he said. "I have to cook, and set tables, and get ready for customers. We also have reporters coming in. I don't know what I will do."

"Calm down, Sammi," offered Will, "We're here now, and you go cook. We will get the restaurant ready. We already had breakfast, so you don't have to worry about us."

"Thank you, Mister Will, and you too Sira. I don't know what I will do," mumbled Sammi, pushing his way through the swinging door to the kitchen, then making a bunch of loud sounds with pots and pans.

Sammi started cooking the items he thought they might need, scrambled eggs, bacon, sausage, and mixed a batch of flour for pancakes. Finally, he put a bunch of breakfast rolls in the oven, which he received from the wholesale truck, already formed, but not browned.

Will and Sira put out the silverware and napkins, along with placemats, and then changed the sign from 'closed' to 'open' and waited for the early customers. They did not have to wait long.

The first one in the door was Elmer Sites, and he quickly said, "Smelled the bacon and eggs, and knew you were about to open. Must have breakfast early. We have the travel judge today, and he likes to start early."

"No problem, Elmer," answered Will, "Sammi is about ready. The usual?" Elmer always had a plate of scrambled eggs, sausage, and some rolls, with coffee, and a large glass of water.

"Coming right up, almost," responded Will, writing his order down to take to Sammi.

Several others also entered the restaurant, and Sira told them to take any table they wished, and started to walk around to take their orders as well. Within thirty minutes, the restaurant was full, and Will and Sira could hardly keep up, taking orders, getting them to Sammi, and returning with their food.

One of the customers, a farmer from just outside town asked, "Boy, you could sure use some help here. My daughter is visiting for a while. Would you like her to come help during busy hours? She worked in a restaurant in Tennessee for four years, and knows a lot, and she will not be going back to school until the

From a Vantage Point

spring semester, so she has time to work, and really want to if she can find something."

"Sure, said Will and Sira in unison. "Have her come in tomorrow morning," added Will. Sammi would be happy to hire her.

"You make my life happy Will," responded the farmer, "She really would like a job, and you know there are very few in town these days. This will help out a lot."

"No problem," said Will, running between tables. "She will really be doing Sammi a great favor."

Everyone laughed. Will made himself a mental note to tell Sammi he had just hired a new employee for him.

Over the next three hours, Will and Sira took orders, bussed tables, and delivered food. It was nearly eleven o'clock before the crowd abated, and they could reset for lunch. By then, he wished he had asked the farmer to have his daughter come in today instead of tomorrow.

When they had a moment to stop and sit, Will got some coffee for him and Sira, and they just sat, looking at each other, saying little, but feeling a great deal. Finally, Will came out of the haze he was in as his phone was ringing.

He looked at the name, and told Sira, "I have to take this on the cooperative," as he waved his phone in the air. Then he rose and walked outside, phone to his ear, and engaged in a conversation lasting about ten minutes. When that conversation ended, Will remembered he had not called the Alexander to tell them he would not need his room this time, so he made a quick call to reconfirm the dates for next month at the Inauguration time. The reservation clerk assured him his room would be available, but to please call on a cancellation, since they were booked full, and could resell the room.

When he returned, Sira was finishing the table settings, and replacing the placemats for lunch.

"Everything all right Will?" she asked, as Will entered looking a bit serious.

"Everything is fine Sira," responded Will, "Just some cooperative business with the Agriculture Department. They want to have a one-day meeting tomorrow, so I need to go to DC. Could you work with the new girl, and make sure everything is OK with Sammi? I will drop you off early on my way out of town, and can pick you up on my way back from DC after the dinner rush. If I get back early, I will just stay and have dinner at Sammi's."

"That will be fine, Will," answered Sira, still a bit puzzled on the call, since Will usually shared any information on the cooperative with her.

Lisbon Portela International Airport, Lisbon, Portugal Jim Davis has come into Lisbon on a routine international flight two days ago, and that would give him at least five days before another flight, if the normal procedures were

From a Vantage Point

followed. However, in this case, a message had come to his manager that there was a 'sensitive' matter needing his attention. That meant his alternate bosses, the CIA, needed his attention. It could be anything, but he assumed it was really DHS matters, and he silently cursed Alice Sawyer for his delay.

"Passenger James Davis, please pick up the red phone along the wall of any concourse for a message," Said the loudspeaker in both English and Portuguese. The massage repeated itself several times.

"This is Davis," he said, into the corridor phone, "What can I do for you?"

"Mister Davis, let me patch you through to the caller," answered the operator.

"Sure," he answered.

"Jim," came the voice on the phone, "This is Jeff Namers. Hakim is in transit, from Kabul to Lisbon. He cleared Cairo after spending some time with Amid Fatoullah, and is on his way to you. We have cleared your flights, and you need to observe, but not apprehend Hakim in Lisbon. He is coming in on a KEM flight. The details are coming to your cell phone. We want to follow him, but not apprehend. Our guess is that he is headed for the US. We have no info on that, and you need to fill in the spaces. Any problems?"

"Good to hear from too, Jeff," he answered, "Last time we were together I was being arrested and hauled off to the US. Love our relationship. So, Hakim is on the move, and suddenly I am the pillar of freedom, or whatever. What do you need from me?"

"Sorry you feel slighted Jim, but we had to get you out of the country before he learned that you and Fatima had a line of information going. It took us a while to settle that down, and get her back in good graces with her cousin. Now, he has something working over the period of the inauguration.

Our bet is that he is coming to the US to fix a botched-up plan, and we really need to keep eyes on him. Your schedule was changed to put a Sky Marshal on the fight to the US that he would not recognize. We need you to tell us what flight. The guess here is that he changes identity in Lisbon, and goes out with his two people under other names. We need you to work that issue."

"Sure Jeff, happy to oblige a friend," Davis responded sarcastically. "Just tell me what I need to do."

"We need to know what he does in the airport, after he gets off his KEM flight, and what flight he picks up there in Lisbon. We have nothing on him as Kassim Said, and we assume he will use another name to get on a plane to the US. Get us what you can Jim. We have no one else even close to keep tabs on him and his two travel buddies."

"OK Jeff," I can do that for you. Can I go up and punch him in the face if I have the chance?"

From a Vantage Point

Namers laughed, and responded, "Would really prefer not Jim. Pick another time, if you really want to do it." The two passed a couple of more pleasantries, and Davis asked about Fatima before they closed the call. Davis looked at the arrivals list, and saw he had about five hours before the flight arrival, and went off to have lunch and catch up on his paperwork.

Hakim and his men spent their time from Cairo to Frankfurt mostly dozing off or reading. They seemed to have no idea they had been seen and followed onto their flight by an Air Marshal, who sat about five rows behind them. None of the men left the plane during the ground time at Frankfurt; instead, they sat in their seats, along with many other passengers, so there was nothing to indicate Hakim was being followed.

When the plane took off, the Air Marshal started reading a newspaper, then a magazine, eventually dozed off himself for the three-hour trip to Lisbon.

From a Vantage Point

Chapter 40 Boxes Everywhere

Rich Alcorn was what most people would call a driven employee. Graduating from Carnegie-Mellon University in Pittsburgh, Pennsylvania in computer science, Alcorn had developed into the resident nerd-genius at DHS headquarters, eventually moving over to the staff assembled by Alice Sawyer in counter-intelligence operations.

Sawyer's team was not a normal team in any way. She selected the very best people for their skills, their intelligence, their willingness to think outside the box, and their desire to prove each other wrong as often as possible. It was a pleasant relationship, competitive, but the result was always the same—when a critical situation arrived, they melded into one person to solve the problem. That was their strength, and that was their capability to achieve success. No other team in DHS had the record these people had, and Alice kept them on their toes.

In this situation, she needed them at their best, and they responded, and especially Alcorn.

Alcorn did not have a 'normal' desk in his office space. In fact, he had no desk at all. On the walls were three large monitors, each over 30 inches wide. They were connected to a state-of-the-art computer, called a quad processor because it had four separate computer processing unit (CPU) chips on its motherboard, enabling it to manage three different major tasks at a time, and still perform routine computer tasks with the fourth processor. To the left of the computer, atop a short side table, was another large black box containing an array of additional memory drives, giving Alcorn the ability to store and use over twenty terabytes of data, including video.

Instead of a desk, Alcorn had a draftsman table, the kind of table used to create plans and blueprints, only, in his case, it was a combination of desktop and bulletin board. Slightly raised on the far end, the lip on the bottom of the table held his keyboard, and above it he could post pictures, papers or anything else he wanted to see quickly. On the left side of the table, attached to the end, was a small plexiglass square, attached to the table by a bracket. This small square Alcorn used to operate his mouse. Anyone who wandered into his office usually marveled at the lack of furniture, and the concentration his sparse, but amazing, computer configuration gave him efficiency. As some would say, Alcorn was 'the nerd's nerd'.

"Do you have something for me, Rick?" asked Alice Sawyer, walking into his space.

"Sure do, Alice," he responded, "It's time for a picture show. Grab a piece of my table. I think you will find this interesting." As he finished, the large screen directly in front of them popped up a warehouse scene.

From a Vantage Point

"What am I looking at Rick?"

"This is one of al-Azahir's warehouse in Kabul, run by his associate Pentopolos. Pretty dismal, and mostly boring, since it apparently does little business that we know of," said Alcorn. "But, let me show you this, courtesy, by the way, of the Afghani Security Service." Alcorn smiled, but Alice looked a bit puzzled.

"Of course, they don't know I took their tapes," added Alcorn, "but then, they are our allies most of the time. These snippets go back weeks, to before the first boxes arrived in Kabul. In this first piece, you can see the arrival of a truck, covered with a tarp, back up close to the warehouse, and notice the wooden boxes being off-loaded. We know from our CIA friends in Khartoum that six boxes were fabricated there, and shipped to Kabul. Count 'em—all six coming off the truck."

"OK, so we have six boxes, and they are entering Pentopolos's warehouse. You can see the date-time stamp at the bottom," Alcorn continued. "Now, look at this snippet. Here comes the truck again, this time with its tarp folded back and empty. Two men open the door to the loading dock and start bringing out boxes— the same look as the ones that went in earlier, and they lay them on the dock to load into the truck. Eventually, they come outside, take the boxes from the loading dock, and place them on the floor of the truck, pulling the tarp over them. A minute or so later, a driver comes out and moves away with the truck going to another destination."

"OK, so what am I supposed to be seeing here?" asked Alice.

"Let em go back a few frames Alice," answered Alcorn, "How many boxes on the dock?"

Alice counted in her head, and sad, "Oh crap, there are eight, not six. They made two more boxes at the warehouse."

"Right," responded Alcorn. "Now, let's move the tape forward some more, shall we? Here is the truck coming up to the general aviation area at Kabul Airport. Again, he pulls up near the dock, and pulls back the tarp. You can still see eight boxes, right?" Alice nodded.

"Then, the driver unloads six of them on the dock, hands the person there some paperwork, pulls his tarp back over the truck and departs. A few minutes later, he arrives at another shipping point, and drops off the other two boxes. We have been chasing only six when we should have been chasing eight."

"Great work, Rick," said Sawyer, "How do we chase the others?"

"Same way we got this far. The Afghanis are paranoid over security, and they have cameras all over the place. It took a while, I found two cameras, one inside each shipping point, and all it took from there was to follow the paper trails. We know where the six original boxes went, and now we know where the other two ended up. They were both put aside for three days, and then shipped through

Islamabad, Frankfurt, and eventually on to the US. They arrive in New York, JFK Airport to be exact, for eventual delivery, via UPS to the Alexander Hotel, Washington DC, under the name of a Mister Will Johnson. This is a scheduled delivery. The papers say deliver early morning January 19th."

Alice Sawyer sat there simply amazed. She said nothing for nearly five minutes, simply looking at the screens and obviously in deep thought. Coming out of her thoughts, she responded, "Rick, you are a genius. This is what we have been waiting for. If the agency had medals, you would get one for this. Now, I have something solid to go on. Thanks. Stay close, we might need more of your 'investigative thievery' shortly." Still in a bit of a trance, Alice went back to her office to plan next steps.

Sitting at her desk, she realized she had voicemail, clicked the button and listened.

"Alice, this is Anderson Cohen. I have a couple of hunches on this guy Johnson. Could you give me the OK to pursue quietly for a few days? Call me and we can discuss. Thanks."

Lisbon Portela International Airport, Lisbon, Portugal Jim Davis sat unobtrusively near the gate where the KEM flight from Frankfurt would arrive in about thirty minutes. Reading the *International Tribune,* on a forthcoming conference hosted by China under its Silk Road initiative to extend trade and extend globalization of myriad economies, Davis was fascinated by the extent to which China was emerging as a global trading leader, rather than the partner it had been for many years. One thing Davis had learned from his years of international travel was the principle that if you wanted to lead on the global stage, you had to have a plan, and execute it well.

Over the past several weeks, as the Chinese Government brought out its initiative, over 20 nations indicated their willingness to participate, and it seemed that the new Silk Road could easily have as much impact as its medieval ancestor achieved in bringing the East to the West. Only time would tell, of course, was it did make interesting reading for someone removed from its politics.

Davis prepared for the arrival, working with the Portuguese Aviation authorities, making sure all security cameras around the gate were in working order, those along the corridors to the other concourses, and that several security officials out of uniform would assist in monitoring Hakim and his associates.

He had been careful to indicate to them that, despite the Interpol Red Letter apprehension request, the US Government wanted only to monitor his activities during the pass-through, and coordinated with INTERPOL and the aviation authority management to make sure this approach was understood.

From a Vantage Point

The arrival board changed, noting the arrival of the KEM flight—ten minutes early—and Davis spoke into his ear bud letting others working the arrival know, then sat back reading his paper, waiting for Hakim to depart the plane.

Once the plane docked, and the door opened, passengers started deplaning quickly, walking along a short jet way to the gate, where airport personnel waited to direct them to their next destination. This was the easy part for Davis, since the airport employee standing at the end of the jet way was a member of the security force. She knew what Hakim looked like, and made sure she would intercept him as he deplaned, walking up to him and his associates and asking, "Sir, do you have a connecting flight I can help you with?"

Hakim said nothing, but one of those with him said, "We are going Alitalia to Boston. How do we get there?"

"Sir, there are two flights on Alitalia this morning. Which one will you be taking? They are in different parts of the concourse."

"We are taking the 11:35 flight to Boston," he responded.

"All right," she answered, "That will be Gate 22 in the Second Concourse. Have a great flight."

"Thank you," the man mumbled, and they moved off.

Davis waited until they had cleared the immediate area before he spoke into his ear bud, saying, "We know they are headed toward Alitalia. Let's make sure of that, and then get the airline to tell us what names they are traveling under. We better get that info after they check-in to be sure we have the right people."

"No problem, Mister Davis," came the response. "We have them in sight, and they are going toward the second concourse"

"I have them in view," announced a second voice. "They are entering the second concourse, and headed together toward gate 22. We have an officer down that way."

Minutes went by before the security team heard anything else. Then the ear buds crackled again.

"The three subjects checked in at Gate 22 for the flight to Boston. There are three names, on the manifest. The one you want is Amoud Said, and the other two..." Davis lost attention on the other two, but paid close attention to the name Hakim used.

"Thanks to all. Let's just make sure no one gets off the flight before it departs. I will let the sky marshal on the flight know who he has aboard."

Thirty minutes later, the doors closed, and the flight departed. Hakim and his men were on board, and now the interest shifted to their arrival in Boston, Massachusetts.

Department of Homeland Security, Washington DC "Anderson, this is Alice, returning your call. We do need to talk about Johnson. What is your suggestion here?"

"Alice, thanks for calling back. I share your concern that there is more going on here than simply Hassan Singh. Since I was in the sort-of local area, I thought perhaps doing an occasional visit to Elias, and making it clear I am watching, might be beneficial. What do you think?"

"I agree Anderson. We do need to keep up a presence, at least an informal one, so go ahead, if you think that might be a positive action here. Just be careful though. We found out just this morning that Johnson is involved with something, so I worry that he might get spooked if we push too hard." She shared what she learned from Rick Alcorn on the arrival of the boxes in DC just before the inauguration, and made it clear she was now less willing to count Johnson out as a conspirator.

"We have to consider that all he has been through, the visit to the Middle East, the people surrounding him in Elias, and anything else in his background that may be contributing to his choices, Johnson may have been turned, and we have to be prepared for that. Even if he claims he is not, we should take precautions, just in case the opposite turns out to be true. Understood?"

"Sure is, Alice. I will keep you up on what I find out."

"OK. Work with Tom O'Neal to coordinate information and actions. Tom has the lead here, and has been working with Johnson under the cover of an official at Agriculture. Let's be sure you are both on the same sheet of music."

"Will do Alice. Thanks for the chance here."

"You're a good agent, Anderson. Do well here. Talk to you soon," said Alice, as she hung up the phone.

Alice clicked off the phone, and quickly dialed another number, this time calling Tom O'Neal.

"Tom, this is Alice. Come by and see me when you can," she said into the phone, leaving a message on his voicemail.

Later that afternoon, about two-thirty PM, O'Neal came by Alice's office, walked in and sat down by her small conference table. Alice looked up at him.

"Tom, we are getting closer to January 20th, and some pieces are starting to come together," she said, looking up. "What have you heard or seen lately from Will Johnson?"

"Not a lot, Alice. We spoke on the phone, discussed the rush that normally accompanies the Inauguration, and I suggested perhaps one more meeting, and then he could make his next visit in early February, after all the festivities are over. He let me know he was coming to town for the Inauguration, though. Said he had never seen one, and wanted to see the hoopla."

From a Vantage Point

Alice looked up, concerned. "He did?" she asked. "Will he be staying where he usually stays at the Alexander?"

"Probably, they know him there, and he likes his room. I assume he will be. Any problem with that?"

"Tom, I want to let you in on some info I received just this morning." Alice patiently went through her meeting with Rick Alcorn, the movement of the boxes, the two additional ones he found, and the information they were on their way to Boston, and then DC. Last stop, she indicated was the Alexander, the day before the Inauguration, addressed to Will Johnson.

"No shit," exclaimed O'Neal, "I would have given my career that Will was not involved."

"He still might not be, Tom, but we have to do due diligence here, answered Alice. "When is he coming to town?"

"Next week," offered O'Neal. We will be discussing a distribution plan. What do you want me to do?"

"First, have you spoken with Anderson Cohen yet?"

"Sure did, about an hour ago."

"All right. You arrange your meeting with Johnson, and I will work with Cohen to make a small search of the farm while he is gone."

"That will work," responded O'Neal. It must be quick, since this one is a 'come-in-the-morning, leave-in-the-evening' type meeting. It starts at ten AM, so he will be leaving the farm by 6:30AM, but the meeting ends at 3PM, so he will be home by six. Can Anderson work on that schedule, coming from Charleston?"

"I hope so, Tom. He will have to."

"I'll try to do what I can to keep him right up to the last minute. That will give Anderson a bit more time."

"Thanks Tom. That will help."

"Anything in particular you would like to find, Alice?"

"Not sure Tom. I just hope this guy is innocent. I share your feelings on this. If he isn't, though, we will have to move quickly to clean it up. We cannot have the Inauguration interrupted in any way. The crazies that march are bad enough, without having to worry about someone who would like to bomb the city."

"Understand Alice. We'll take it a step at the time. I'll get with Anderson on it."

"Ok Tom," Alice responded, "Let's hope for the best, but be prepared for the worst." O'Neal shook his head as he rose to leave, not quite knowing what to say. He had truly come to believe that Will Johnson was a victim, and not a conspirator. Now, he would have to wait to see the truth.

Johnson Farm, Elias, West Virginia It seemed to both Will and Sira that their days were being consumed with trips to and from the farm, mostly to help

From a Vantage Point

Sammi, but leaving little time for themselves. Tomorrow, Will would go to Washington, early in the morning, and return late. Sira would not have any quality time with him at all, but she adored him for many reasons; among them the fact that he is so giving to others, even at the detriment to his own enjoyment.

As they left Sammi's for the trip home, both were tired; it had been a particularly busy day, but it also had a ray of sunshine in it, when one of the farmers announced her daughter would like a job for the next few months, until she returns to school in the new year.

Both Will and Sira were tired but happy, as they saw the road into the farm and realized they were finally home. Normally, Will would shut down the engine of the pickup, then go to the other side and open the door for Sira. Not tonight, however. Sira was out of the truck and heading for the door as soon as the engine shut down.

"Whoa," yelled Will after her. "Slow down."

"I want to get into the house, get into the shower, and get my feet up," responded Sira. "This has been a hard day. I hope you understand Will," she added as she turned the key and entered the dark house, turning on the lamp to the left of the door and she went in.

By the time Will entered, and turned on more lights, Sira was already in her room, and headed for the bathroom. Will sat down after he turned on the evening news, and started to relax himself. He realized the local news was on, and wanted something more exciting than the local farm prices, although they were important to him, and took the TV remote, changing the station to the national news. Eventually, he got up, went to the kitchen, poured himself a glass of white wine and returned to the couch.

Sira came out of the bathroom, wrapped in a robe, her hair wrapped as well in a towel, and went off to the couch where Will sat, dropping to the couch, and snuggling close.

"Now, I am much better," she exclaimed. "My body aches all over."

"I know how you feel," answered Will, reaching over and kissing her on the forehead. "My turn next," he continued, "But first a bit of the news. Would you like some wine?" She nodded yes, and Will rose to go to the kitchen to get her a glass of the white wine he was enjoying.

"We have an early day tomorrow, Sira," Will said, as he sat back down, placing her wine glass on the coffee table before them. "We have to be up and out by 6 AM, so I can get on the road."

"I know," she responded. "Just a bit of the news, and then off to bed. I will sleep well tonight."

Will nodded, and sipped some wine, and they sat watching the evening news. Perhaps thirty minutes later, Will stood, held out his hand to Sira, after

From a Vantage Point

turning off the TV with the remote, and she grasped it, pulling herself to her feet. Together, they started to walk away from the couch, and Will gently tugged for her to follow him. They walked together toward his bedroom, closing off the lights in the room, and walking in the dark to his room, closing the door as they entered.

Six AM came early, especially when you are tired from the day before, but they both woke at the same time when Will's alarm clock went off. Sira moved first, starting to get out of bed when she realized the towel from her hair and her robe were on the floor by the bed. She was still wrapped in Will's arms and, as he began to move as well, she escaped his grasp, reached for her robe, and rose to her feet, picking up the towel as well.

"Will, it is six o'clock. We have to move if we are going to Sammi's and you are going to Washington for your meeting."

"I know Sira," said a still half-asleep Will Johnson. "Getting up in a moment." She shrugged her shoulders and started for the bathroom, near her own room, leaving the bathroom off Will's room for his own use. That would save them time. By 6:30, they were ready to go, locked the house securely, and started down the farm road toward the state highway on the way to Sammi's before Will continued to Washington and his meeting with Tom O'Neal.

Sammi's Restaurant, Elias, West Virginia Will and Sira arrived in town, but had trouble finding a parking space near the restaurant. People were already arriving for breakfast. They parked over by the hardware store, and walked across the short distance, asking people to move so they could enter. Most, knowing Will, readily smiled and moved.

"Sammi, what is happening here?" asked Will, as he walked in and saw all the tables filled, and Sammi running around taking orders. "Why are all these people here so early?"

"Mister Will, I really do not know. Everybody just showed up."

"Ok Sammi, you go in the kitchen. Sira and I will take orders, and get them to you."

"Oh, thank you, Mister Will," answered Sammi, running for the kitchen. He knew he had pots on the stove, and others waiting, bacon in the oven, and sausage on the grill. He had to get there to prevent everything from burning.

Sira took two pads, and started taking orders, giving one to Will as he came close to her. "Let's get to work, I guess," Said Will, smiling at her, and walking to the other side of the restaurant. "I only have a short time, but I can at least get you both going before I leave."

"Mister Will," yelled Sammi from the Kitchen, "Come in here and eat before you have to go on the road."

From a Vantage Point

"Just a minute Sammi," he answered, taking a few more orders that he could bring with him.

"Sit down, Mister Will," ordered Sammi, pointing to a small table in the kitchen. "Eat before you go on the road to Washington. You must eat. It will be a busy day."

"I will," responded Will, "Just what I wanted too," he added, looking at the plate of food already on the table, along with a cup of coffee. Will wolfed down his food quickly and prepared to leave, but not before Sira came in with more orders, saw Will eating quickly, and walked over to him, kissing him on the head.

"Eat slowly, the people in Washington will expect that you might be a bit late."

Just about finished, Will looked up at her, grinned, and said, "You are really beautiful when you are angry, you know." Sammi smiled as he saw the two looking at each other, but then went back quickly to the grill, where the sausage and home fries were about to burn.

A few minutes later, Will rose from his seat and started out into the restaurant, went over to Sira to say goodbye, and walked out across the street to his truck, and started the trek to Washington.

At the farm, a sleek, black sedan drove up toward the front of the house, parking over toward the barn, and a large man got out, walking toward the house. He took a set of tools from his pocket and turned the lock to enter, moving quickly inside, and then relocking the door.

The man looked left and right, deciding to walk first toward his left, where the kitchen and Will's bedroom were located. He paid little attention to the kitchen, but did go into the bedroom and look through his closets and drawers over about twenty minutes. Returning to the living room, the man looked over the bookcase to the side of the room, and then the corresponding one on the other side of the front door before walking down the small corridor toward what he guessed was the guest room. Finding nothing on interest there, he returned to the living room, looked at the listing of calls from the wireless phone, taking note of several numbers, and started back out through the front door.

The man had started toward his car when he saw a glint in the trees nearby, and started toward where the brief light had shone. As he entered the margin of the small wooded area, someone attacked him, trying to ring him to the ground, hitting him several times in the chest and head.

"Federal agent" yelled Anderson Cohen to the assailant. Then, he recognized who had attacked him, and shouted, "Singh, you are under arrest, then lunged at him. Hassan Singh, glanced off the lunge, and moved to the side, hitting Cohen on the side of the dead, stunning him momentarily. Realizing that Cohen was stopped, at least for a few moments, Singh ran toward his car, sheltered in the woods, got in, and raced off before Cohen could reach him, unfortunately not getting a plate or good description.

Cohen took out a handkerchief, held it to his head at the point where Singh had hit him, and started back to his car. Once inside, he grabbed the radio, identified himself, and put out a bulletin describing as best he could Singh's car, and the fact that he had assaulted Cohen. Within minutes, two police cars from Elias, one the chief, and the other from the Sheriff's department arrived on the scene.

"Are you agent Cohen?" asked the chief.

"I am," Cohen responded, pulling out his badge and credentials.

"What are you doing up here?" the chief asked.

"I was in the area going back toward Charleston, and decided to see for myself some of the scenery, and the farms, Chief. I wondered if Singh might still be in the area, and it appears he was monitoring Will Johnson's house."

"Do you need some medical attention, Mister Cohen?" asked one of the sheriff's deputies.

"No, I'm fine, Just a scratch," answered Cohen. "Chief, could I see you for a moment?"

The two men walked to the side, away from the others who arrived. "Chief, I would appreciate that any mention of this event be kept close hold. I don't want people to start thinking that Johnson is in any way involved with Singh, and I don't want Singh to be overly rattled to the point that we lose any track of him. Right now, it seems he is staying in the area, at least for now, and that is better than having him on the loose in a wider area. Do me a favor and make sure this does not get out very far. I know it was on the air, but please try to contain it any further."

"I can certainly do that Agent Cohen. Sorry for calling you mister a few minutes ago. What about the FBI?"

"I'll take care of that when I submit my report this afternoon Chief. Will send you a copy as well. Here is my card in the Charleston office, please let me know if you see this guy again."

"Sure will, Agent Cohen," said the chief, card in hand tipping his hat in salute. "Better get that head taken care of though, he admonished. "Don't want to get it infected, or worse."

"Thanks again Chief," added Cohen, as he started to walk back to the sedan. "How am I going to explain this to Alice," he wondered out loud to himself.

Once he was out of town, and on the State Road, Cohen pulled over at an overlook and stopped the car. Taking out his cell phone, Cohen called Alice Sawyer.

"Alice, this is Anderson Cohen. Just left Elias."

"Great Anderson, anything interesting?"

From a Vantage Point

"Yes and no," he responded, "No, at the Johnson Farm I found nothing that would link him to anything, except perhaps his cooperative. Yes, I found Hassan Singh, at least for a few moments."

"A few moments?" asked Alice.

"Yeah, he was hiding in the woods off in the distance from the house. I saw something up there and went to look. Didn't call the locals for help since this was to be discrete look-see. Singh came out of the woods at an angle and sideswiped me. He got away in a beat-up old car before I could stop him."

"Are you all right Anderson?"

"Sure, Alice. The most damaged is my ego. I have a small scratch on the side of the head, but it's nothing. I did call in the locals. Talked to the Chief to search for Singh. He agreed to keep my visit discreet. I told him I did not want any more publicity that might hurt the town or Johnson and his friends."

"Good move. Now get back to Charleston, and get that head looked after. I'll let the FBI know in DC. You tell their agent in Charleston. We need to try to get Singh, and alive."

"Sure will, Alice. Thanks for being understanding."

"Anderson, we have been together too many years for me not to know how good an agent you are. Singh must be pretty fast to get you sideswiped. Send in your after-action report."

"Today, this afternoon, Alice. Out here."

Alice Sawyer pushed another button on her console and gave Richard Peabody what information Cohen had provided, then looking up at her clock, decided to go to lunch.

Logan International Airport, Boston, Massachusetts The Alitalia jumbo jet had been in a holding pattern for nearly twenty-five minutes before the flight attendant made an announcement on the public-address system.

"Ladies and Gentlemen, again, welcome to Boston's Logan International Airport. We are about to pull up to the International Terminal. Sorry for the delay, the plane at our gate had difficulties that needed correction before it could depart. Thankfully, it was a small adjustment, and they have moved off toward the runway. The pilot will taxi the aircraft toward the gate, and that few yards will be aided by a tractor so that the pilot can turn off the engines. Sorry for the short delay, and, again, welcome to Logan International Airport. The current time is approximately 9:45 AM. Attendants please secure all equipment and cross-check."

Hakim and his two associates were in row 7 on the right, giving them a good view of the front of the plane. He noticed the attendants starting to collect the last of the breakfast dishes and paper, along with anything else the customers

From a Vantage Point

wanted to give away. They were beginning to lock up the cabinets, preparing the plane for restocking once they were at the gate.

"Be careful here," Hakim said to his two associates. "This is a big airport, and I know already we have a sky marshal on board. Do nothing to make anyone suspicious." Both men nodded in return.

"What do we do in Boston, Sir?" asked one of the men.

"We are not staying in Boston," came the reply. "We will take the public train to the city. There, I have friends who are waiting for us. All is prepared for us."

Another of the men asked, "If we are not staying in Boston, why go to the city?"

Hakim did not answer directly, just saying, "All will be obvious to you later. For now, be patient, and careful."

As the plane taxied, then was pulled to the gate, Hakim retrieved his bag from the underneath area of the seat in front of him. On the flap of the bag was the US Customs declaration he needed to clear the arrival Customs area, and enter the United States.

Taking his carry-on bag from the overhead compartment, Hakim stepped into the aisle of the plane, followed by his two associates, and departed through the forward door to the jetway. They walked through the jetway with the rest of the passengers into the main concourse and down toward the baggage area. There, they were met by a man with a sign labelled 'Amoud Said and party'.

"I am Mister Said," said Hakim as he walked up to the gentleman. "These are my associates. I assume you have transportation for us."

"Yes sir," the man responded, "Let me get your bags for you. Do you have luggage tags?"

Hakim handed him the tags from the boarding folders, and the man went off to get their luggage with a small rental cart, returning about ten minutes later.

"I believe we have everything, sir," said the man. "Please come this way. I have transportation for you to the hotel."

The two men with Hakim looked puzzled. Hakim had said they were not staying in Boston, but it seemed they were after all. The three walked along with the man pushing the luggage toward the exit door, where a large white van waited for them.

"This is for us, Sirs," offered the man, "I will put your luggage in the back of the van. Hakim and his two men climbed into the van, Hakim sitting in the front passenger seat, and the other two in the second seat. Once in and settled, they waited for the luggage to be loaded, and the man who met them, apparently also the driver, closed the side door, and climbed into the driver's seat.

As the van started to move along the exit road toward the tunnels which would take them into the city, the driver turned slightly as said, "It is good to see you sir. We have been waiting for your arrival."

"Is everything prepared?" asked Hakim.

"Yes sir, everything you asked is ready for you."

"Good. Take us through the city, and make sure we are not being followed, and then take us to the place you have our rental car so we can be on our way."

"Another of our people picked up your car this morning, sir," answered the driver. "It is waiting for you." The man drove through the tunnels to Boston, and started to drive through the city streets, going up and down along several streets to be sure they were not followed, and then headed for Columbus Avenue in the South End. The van drove through the streets of the South End, eventually ending up on the hill above Columbus Avenue, near a large school. Along the street were numbers of three-decked houses, common in Boston

"We have lunch for you if you wish, Sir. You and your friends before you leave. The rental car is good for a week. That will give you plenty of time to go wherever you need. It is registered to one of our friends, and no one will know it is for you."

"Good, I am hungry, and I assume my friends as well. The plane food is terrible, and mostly inedible. We will be glad for a good meal." The other two men with Hakim nodded their agreement. The driver turned off the engine of the van, and hopped out, going to the passenger side, to open the front door for Hakim, and slide the panel back to allow the others to leave.

"I will leave your bags in the van sir," said the driver. "When you are ready to leave, we will move them to the car for you."

"That will be fine," answered Hakim, as they walked up to the house. Once inside, they realized the apartment was really an armed camp; several men, and two women were in the rooms, and large numbers of small arms and automatic rifles were clearly evident.

Hakim and his men sat down to lunch, enjoying the first real halal meal they had eaten in days, and enjoyed the company for the short time they were in the apartment. Hakim went off, at one point, to speak to the driver in another room and, when he returned, announced to his men they would be leaving shortly after they ate the meal.

By mid-afternoon, the three men, Hakim and his two compatriots, were in a small red sedan headed south on Interstate 95 out of Boston. Driving quickly through Rhode Island, and then into Connecticut, they marveled at the highways, trees, and farms that dotted the highway—very different from their own country. By evening, they had stopped to fill the gas tank, and were well south of New York, following the directions the men from Boston gave them, and down toward New Jersey.

Hakim sat on the passenger side of the car, reading maps given him by the men in Boston, and acted as the navigator for the other two men with him, who took turns driving. They followed the route down Intestate 95 until they were just

From a Vantage Point

above New York City, cutting over on Interstate 80 and then down Interstate 95 toward Philadelphia, their next stop. Although this was a busier route than they could have taken, Hakim felt with more traffic, they could more easily blend in than might be possible on a less-traveled route. He had an address in Philadelphia, and used a new cellphone he received in Boston to locate the address in the city.

In Philadelphia, they changed clothes, identities, and picked up another car, leaving the one they had to be returned to Boston. While he was here, Hakim made one phone call, had lunch, and then returned to the highway, headed for Baltimore, Maryland.

On the road to Washington DC It was a beautiful morning coming through the hills on the way to the Interstate, and eventually toward Washington for his scheduled meeting at Agriculture. Will Johnson left early, knowing there would be traffic, and he was not disappointed, arriving just before 10 AM at the Agriculture Offices in Silver Spring, Maryland, as requested by Tom O'Neal. O'Neal was waiting for him in the parking lot, having just arrived himself.

"Great to see you Will," said O'Neal, walking over to Will's car just as Will was exiting.

"Same here, Tom. You mentioned a busy day today. What do you have in mind?"

"We need to finalize some of the distributions plans, Will. Many of the Farmer Markets, and our own crop purchase people like to make their plans in late January early February for the spring. I just want to be sure you are ready. We might not be all day, but I will guess we will be at it most of the time we have. There is a great place for lunch close by, and we can relax for a time before meetings."

"OK, let's get at it. Lead me on sir," said Johnson, pointing towards the building. He followed O'Neal to the entrance, signed in, and they headed for the elevators.

"How are things going in Elias, by the way?" asked O'Neal nonchalantly. "Any more snoopy Feds?"

'Things have slowed down a bit, Tom, and probably will stay that way, now that they have caught, or at least tried to catch one of the workers in the local restaurant."

"Really, what happened there?"

"Not sure, really Tom. The police are a bit closed mouthed on it, but from what I have heard, this guy working for my friend Sammi, named Hassan, might have been a mole or something. He escaped before he was caught, and is still on the loose, as I understand it. Who knows what will come of it, but everything seems to be quieting down."

From a Vantage Point

"I'm glad of that Will," responded O'Neal, "We don't need bad publicity any more than necessary. By the way, you have one or two farmers doing primarily beets and radishes, don't you?" said O'Neal, neatly changing the subject.

"I do, Tom. Two young couples outside town love to grow tubers. They are even trying a strain of potato this year. They claim it is insect and borer resistant. We'll see what they get."

"Good, because if it works out, they will have good prospects for the farmer markets, at least from our stats from last year. Those tubers sell well, and consistently." The two men walked into the building, signed in, and went off to the right, through glass doors to a conference room. Inside were several others, some of whom Will knew from previous meetings.

As they entered, Tom O'Neal's phone rang. He looked at the number on the screen, and turned to Will.

"Will, I need to take this call. Go on in. You know many of those in the room. Introduce yourself to the rest. I will be back in just a minute," he added as he left through the glass doors, phone to his ear.

"Anderson, what brings you to call me on this bright, sunny day?"

"Tom, I just spoke to Alice, and I wanted to let you know about something as well," Cohen started, "I was out to the Johnson Farm today looking around. As I was leaving, I found Hassan Singh in the woods away from the house. It looks like he had been staying there in the woods since he escaped. A lot of litter around the area. My guess is that he was observing the house."

"Any indication that Johnson was letting him stay there?" asked O'Neal.

"Nothing, Tom. I don't think Johnson knew he was out there, and there was nothing in the house to indicate he had been staying inside. He had an old car parked back in the tree grove; probably living out of it."

"Sounds like you didn't get him," said O'Neal.

"He blindsided me Tom. That's why I think he was staying in the woods. He took off in an old, beat-up car. The police are looking for it now." Cohen and O'Neal spoke for a few more minutes, then hung up, and O'Neal returned to the meeting, which was just starting.

The first part of the meeting lasted two hours, discussing all kinds of possibilities for Will Johnson's cooperative venture, and several others, also represented at the meeting. They broke for lunch about 12:30 PM, with Will and Tom O'Neal going down toward the University for lunch at a small Italian restaurant. They made mostly small talk, enjoying veal piccata, and a glass of white wine. O'Neal's mind lay heavily on his discussion with Cohen earlier. Finally, he changed the conversation from growing patterns in West Virginia back to the events in Elias.

"Will, one thing I wondered, changing the subject a bit. What about the woman that came to town with this guy Hassan, what was his last name, Singh?"

From a Vantage Point

"Her name is Sira," responded Johnson. "She is mostly my housekeeper these days, although she does work in the restaurant a couple of days a week. Those two came to Elias pretty much together, and Sammi took them in. They were, at one time, going to be married, but, from what he told me, Hassan was very abusive, and she broke their engagement off, some weeks back."

"Sammi and I try to watch over her," Will added, "Hassan still gets very angry with her. Hopefully the authorities will eventually get him, and that part of her life can be over. I must admit, I enjoy having her around the house. She stays at the farm most of the time, doing the housework, and some of the other chores. That way, there is someone around during the times I am gone."

"Don't you worry he might come out there and bother her?"

"Of course, that is a problem, but she can take care of herself very well. She might be small, but she packs a wallop. The other day, I was in the barn, and she had called me for lunch at least three times, according to her, and she came out to get me. Punched me in the chest so hard, I lost my breath. It hurt for two days."

"I see," responded O'Neal, "She must be some woman?"

"She is Tom. I trust her with everything. She is keeping the books for the cooperative, and goes to town once a week to work with the local accountant. He is teaching her simple bookkeeping, and she is picking it up fast."

"That's great Will," responded O'Neal, now thinking back to his conversation again with Cohen. *I wonder*, he mused to himself, *Is this why Singh was in the woods? Trying to get her back, or even do harm to either or both?* He reminded himself to call Cohen back to discuss that issue later after Johnson left.

Will and Tom returned to the Agriculture offices for the last part of the meeting, which took another two hours, closing at just before 3:30PM. As they walked out, O'Neal started a brief discussion.

"Well, the meeting went well Will, and I think the staff, and some of the others look forward to working with your group. That's good, since some of them have been at it for a long time. The next meeting, by the way, is in February. I'll send you the date and time, same place."

"Thanks, Tom," responded Johnson, "I'll be coming up to the inauguration in January, and will be staying at the *Alexander*, if you happen to come by. You might even get a chance to meet Sira; I promised her a trip to DC to shop, and might as well give her the chance to see a new President. She is starting citizenship classes in about three weeks at the high school, and that would be a good experience for her, I think." O'Neal made another set of mental notes to be sure Cohen knew he and Sira were coming to DC.

"Great. I hope you enjoy yourselves. As I think I told you, they give the Feds off because they don't want us in town during the festivities, and the traffic is abominable. Chances of my coming into town during that period is negligible. See you in February."

The two shook hands, and O'Neal started to walk away toward his own car. Will put the materials he received at the meeting in the truck behind the seat, and got ready to leave for the trip home. As he fished in his pocket for the truck keys, his cell phone rang. Will looked at it and saw that it was an unknown number. He decided to answer it, just in case it was from Elias.

'You know who this is," came the voice from the phone.

"What do you want Hakim," responded Johnson. "You and I have nothing to discuss."

"Exactly the opposite, my friend. We have much to discuss, and you will listen. I will tell you when it is time to hang up."

"Really? Why would I care what someone from, by the way, where are you? Why would I care what you might have to say?"

"Will Johnson, you know I wanted you to be part of a plan Josh and I created to impress the Americans during the upcoming Inauguration. It was to be our payback for all that we suffered not being able to come to America for so long. We will still do that, although now that Josh in no longer with us, you will take his place?"

"You are crazy Hakim. There is no good reason for me to get involved again with you, or your insane plans. Don't call me again."

"Before you hang up Mister Will Johnson, you better listen to me. I have come to America to finish my plan, and you are part of that plan. If it means killing you, destroying your farm, or even your town, or that woman you stole from Hassan, I will do what it takes to make you do what I wish. If you do not believe me, then risk the consequences."

As Hakim finished, he hung up the phone. Will stood there incredulous, wondering if what Hakim said, that he was in the US, was true, and if he would do what he claimed. Now, all Will could do is wait, and see if Hakim called back. In the meanwhile, it was time to return home.

Homeland Security, Washington DC Several lights started flashing in tandem on the center screen on Rich Alcorn's desk. Noticing they were all around Brentwood, Alcorn picked up the telephone, and told the agents stationed at the Postal Facility to go and check out the boxes. They were in two CONEX's, across a short interspace from each other, off to the right side of the shipping area.

It took about two hours for the agents to return his call, and their report was not exactly what he wanted to hear. The three boxes were empty, and it appeared they were in the same condition as they were when fabricated in Khartoum, before shipping to Kabul.

"Another dead end," said Alcorn out loud, although no one else was close enough to hear. "Well, that's three out of the way," he added. That meant all six of the original boxes could not be a part of whatever was planned for DC during the inauguration.

"OK," said Alcorn, continuing his personal conversation, "If the first six are phonies, then the boxes coming through from Reagan Airport have to be the real ones, unless there are other we don't know about." Alcorn shook his head, and continued, "But that is not possible either. We watched the tapes, and scanned all the shipments from that warehouse. The two going to the *Alexander* hotel have to be the real thing."

Alcorn walked down the corridor to Alice Sawyers' office, and found her on the phone. Listening to the voices, he realized it was a conference call between the FBI, Tom O'Neal, and Alice. He walked in and sat down.

"Rich," said Alice, "There is nothing whatever to link Johnson to this plot. If he is involved, I am more convinced than ever he is an unwitting, or involuntary participant."

"If that is so Alice, why is this guy Hassan staying in the immediate area of his farm? It isn't logical given the circumstances," responded Rich Peabody. "Something is missing here."

"I also would like to believe that, Rich," answered Alice Sawyer, "and I am not sure myself why these circumstances have come together. Tom, you met with Johnson today. What's your feeling here?"

"Alice, I think we have an affair of the heart here," responded O'Neal. "Will did not come right out and say it, but he has Hassan's girlfriend living at the house doing his housework. According to him, she broke up with Singh some weeks ago, and then moved to the farm. She has been there since."

"Think about this scenario," O'Neal added, "Arab couples don't simply 'break up', they are betrothed from childhood. They are expected to marry, and the woman is expected to be subservient to her betrothed and/or husband. That is clearly not the case, and, if she were back in the Middle East, she would be stoned, and certainly if she decided to live with another man, regardless of how innocent. These people do not put up with those things."

"I agree, Tom," said Peabody. "Here, we are working with people who are fanatical, in their faith, and in their politics. Above all, they are traditionalists, and they expect those with them to adhere to the rules, Islamic rules, on which they were raised, regardless of where they might be. This guy Singh must really hate Johnson, and, if he does, we have a problem brewing that we have to watch closely."

"Rich, one of my men, you know him, Anderson Cohen, was out at the farm yesterday and ran into Singh, getting bonked on the head for his efforts, and

Singh escaped besides. We have the locals looking for him, but he now has a new hiding place, and it will take time to locate it."

"I saw that on the reports, and spoke to the Chief in Elias, Alice. We are making sure that story is buried so we don't spook Singh any more than necessary. We will get him, but, as I said, it will take time."

"I know that Rich, and I know your guys, and the locals are doing the best they can. We are up against a deadline here, and I do not control that deadline. My bosses are not about to go to the White House, and say, 'no inauguration'. They expect us to stop whatever is happening, and quickly."

"Let's go back to facts here, guys," added Alice. "We know something is brewing; we know it will happen, we think, in DC, during the Inauguration. We think it has something to do with Johnson and others in Elias, and, unfortunately, we also know that Hakim al-Azahir is either in the US, or on the way. Those are the facts we know right now."

"In addition, we have a lot of 'think so's' that seem to point to the facts, but we are not sure. Somehow, I believe Rich Alcorn just came in with one of those 'think-so's'. Rich, What are you waiting to tell us?"

"Hi guys," Alcorn answered, "Alice, We have now ruled out the boxes in Brentwood. They were empty, and not even fabricated according to the diagrams al-Azahir made. That means all six boxes made in Khartoum are decoys. There have to be others out there, and my guess, and it is just a guess, is the ones coming through Reagan Airport, and off to the delivery service are the real boxes."

"Where are they headed, Rich?" Asked Peabody.

"Eventually, the *Alexander* Hotel, just a day or so before the Inauguration," came the response.

"Wow," interrupted O'Neal, "Will Johnson and his housekeeper Sira, Singh's old girlfriend, will be in DC during the Inauguration, and I believe he told me they were staying at the *Alexander* Hotel."

"Oh God," retorted Alice Sawyer, "the plot thickens. We need a plan for close monitoring of the boxes, Johnson, and anybody else who comes anywhere near him. We can't let him not arrive; that would arouse suspicion. We have to let it happen and be sure he does no harm."

The Johnson Farm, Elias, West Virginia The light was fading quickly. The sun was down behind the hills, and the residual light was casting large shadows through the countryside near the Johnson Farm. Along the edge of the woods, a solitary figure in dark clothes was moving from tree to tree, until it had reached the edge of the clump of trees, surrounded by scrub bush. The figure went behind the bushy area, looking to see if any movement occurred in the house or

From a Vantage Point

the barn. Satisfied, the dark figure started across the short space of open land separating the clumped bushes and trees and the corner of the barn.

Hassan Singh took a significant chance coming back to the place where he had almost been arrested by the federal agent, but, having watched all day, and seen no movement in or around the house, he figured the chance was worth the effort.

The short distance from the barn to the house was hidden by a hay wagon, which Will Johnson used to bring in the bales of hay in the fall, for storage in the barn, providing feeding for animals during the winter. Now, it simply sat there, with its only use being concealment.

Hassan climbed over the low railing on the side of the house, and stayed close to the outside wall as he approached the doorway. Weeks earlier, he had stolen Sira's key, and had a duplicate made at the hardware store, telling the owner that Sammi needed a duplicate key. Now, he could use that key to enter and leave Will and Sira a message; one that said they were not safe from him.

Rummaging through the house, in no apparent order or plan, Hassan simply upturned some things and handled others, leaving then slightly off their original location. He wanted Sira to realize that someone, and he hoped she would realize it was him, had been in the house and disturbed it with his presence. After about thirty minutes, Hassan left the house and the farm the same way he entered, driving away in his car, without lights on, until he was well down the state road, and out of the area.

Will had been driving nearly two hours and decided to stop for a short break at a roadside stop. He went in, got a cup of coffee, and decided to call Sammi's to let them know he was on the way home. The phone rang and was soon answered, but it was Sira, rather than Sammi who answered.

"This is Sammi's Restaurant, can I help you?" she asked into the phone.

"You certainly can" came the response.

Sira's eyes lit up, a smile on her face, as she responded, "Will. It is you. Are you on your way?"

"Yes, I am Sira. About an hour out. Just in time for dinner. Is the place busy?"

"It seems to be busy always, Will. I have become too used to the house, where everything is quiet. How were your meetings?"

"Great. They are very interested in many of our crops, particularly the beets, radishes, potatoes, and the corn, of course. We should have a great association with the farmer's markets. Many of them were at the meeting, and looking forward to working with us."

"That is good, Will, but when will you be home? I miss you," she whispered into the phone.

"In an hour or so," he answered. "What's for dinner?"

From a Vantage Point

"Whatever you want," she beamed. Sammi walked over to where she was talking at the register. "Hold on a minute, here is Sammi."

"Will, this is Sammi. How did your meeting go?" he asked.

Will spent a few minutes on the details, telling Sammi about the various things that were discussed. "Glad the meeting is over," he said, "I'm tired."

"We are waiting for you Mister Will. I will have a big dinner ready for you, and Sira cannot wait to see you. She has stars in her eyes."

"Be there shortly, then. I should go and get back on the road. See you soonest." Will hung up, and went over to get gas for the truck, then got back on the road toward Elias.

Hassan drove quickly down the state road toward the Interstate, intent on leaving the area. However, a member of the Sheriff's detail saw the beat-up car, recognized it from the description the DHS agent published, and took off after it in chase. The two cars went about five miles down the state road before Hassan veered off into a field, with the Sheriff's car chasing him. About half-way through the field, Hassan stopped the car, pulled a gun out from under the seat, and turned to fire at the officer.

The sheriff's deputy, seeing what was happening, removed his pistol from its holster, and, as Hassan raised his weapon, the deputy fired three times from the window of his car, hitting Hassan in the chest. When the deputy arrived at the Hassan's location, he was on the ground bleeding profusely. The deputy called in the shooting, but, twenty minutes later, when the emergency vehicle arrived, Hassan was dead.

As the Sheriff's car pulled up in front of Sammi's Restaurant, and the officers left the car to walk over to the Police Department, Sira looked out the window and wondered what was happening. Shortly after, two other police vehicles arrived, and then a dark colored sedan, from which three men in suits emerged, all walking toward the police department.

"Something is going on," shouted Sira to Sammi, who turned around from the register, "Over at the police department," she added, pointing out the window. As she did another vehicle came down the street, this time a pickup truck.

"Sammi, Will is home," she shouted out smiling. This time, everyone in the restaurant looked as she ran to the door to greet Will Johnson.

"What's happening over at the police department?" asked Will as he walked in the door.

"We don't know yet Mister Will, but welcome home. All these people and cars just arrived a few minutes ago. Perhaps soon, we will know something," answered Sammi, going back to his register.

From a Vantage Point

Will came in and sat down at a table near the front, and Sira quickly brought him a menu and sat down opposite him. "How was the trip Will? Did everything go well?" she asked, pleading for information.

"It did," responded Will, "They want our goods, and want to help us get them to market. As I said quickly on the phone, I think we have a winner here."

"When do you have to go back there?" asked Sira.

"Well, not until February, but I thought perhaps we might go to Washington in January, to see the Inauguration. What do you think?"

"Oh, I don't know what to say Will. I have never been there, and never seen such an event. Tell me about Washington. Will there be a large crowd? What do I wear?" Sira pummeled Will with questions one after the other, obviously excited.

Will placed his hand on hers, still holding the menu, and responded, "Anything you wear will be just fine Sira, except the apron, of course." They both laughed.

Before they could say anything else, the police chief walked into the restaurant, looked around, and went over to Sammi, speaking with him for a few seconds, and then going back out the front door.

Sammi walked over to the table where Will and Sira were holding hands, and stopped in front of it, saying softly, "Sira, the police found Hassan a while ago, in a field off the highway. He started to fire at a deputy sheriff, and was shot. He is dead." Sammi had tears in his eyes as Sira rose and went over to hug him. As she did so, tears began to fill her eyes as well. Regardless of what he was, Hassan was still their friend.

Will stood, and took Sira from Sammi, walking her through the swinging doors to the kitchen. There, she broke out in sobbing, saying softly, "He was my betrothed, my family, and I could not be there for him. Will, was all this necessary? What have we done?"

Trying to console her as best he could, Will put his arm around her, not saying a word, but just being there in her moment of grief. He knew it would take time for her to heal, and he wanted even more to be with her and help her out of this sad situation. They stood in the kitchen for several minutes, simply embracing, before Sira broke away, saying, "I have to go back to work, Will. Sammi needs to come and cook, and people are still coming into the restaurant. We need to help him."

"Don't worry, Sira, We will take care of Sammi," Will responded, thinking not just of the present, but what would eventually occur in the future for both Sammi and Sira.

As the evening progressed, more officers and sheriff's deputies, as well as three FBI agents came to the restaurant for something to eat. For most of them, Sammi and Will took the orders; they left Sira in the kitchen to cook the meals,

From a Vantage Point

giving her some breathing time from the stories the officers and agents were telling, and re-telling.

Will tried to learn as much as he could from the conversations, finding out about the shoot-out in the field off the state road, and that Hassan started the firefight with the Sheriff's deputy. Hassan's body was being taken to Charleston for autopsy. Will knew eventually someone would be inquiring about his family, and knew he needed to discuss that with Sira. For now, better to let this situation settle; they could worry about details later.

It was well after 10 PM when Sammi finally flipped the sign on the restaurant door, closing for the night. His last customer, a sheriff's deputy, came over to get coffee, and some food for those in the police department offices who were still writing reports, and working on the shooting. They had been joined earlier by several members of the State Police Forensics and shooting teams, whose job it was to document the event and recommend any action to the State's attorney, if needed.

Will thought to himself that this was not exactly the homecoming he wanted or expected. Things had been so cheerful earlier in the day, and he and Sira had started discussing a trip to Washington for the Inauguration. Now, everything was up in the air, and they both drove home in the pickup with their minds filled with thoughts of joy, and hurt, and questions about what could have been different.

For Sira, thinking back to earlier days, when she and Hassan had been happy—the days before Hassan joined with Hakim al-Azahir and began to walk down the road of terrorism, although Hassan called it 'Pride in my Heritage'. Gradually, he drew Sira into the web, and they both went to take training in the camps in Sudan, then Yemen. She became a better marksman than him, although Hassan excelled in planning and bomb-making. Over time, both moved into the cells, first in Sudan, then Syria, and then coming to the US to work in Atlanta and Delaware.

Their job was simply to work and wait—wait for the call that would tell them to act. That call came when they were told they were moving to a small town, Elias West Virginia, and would work in a restaurant for a man named Sammi Khan. In this town was another man, Will Johnson, a friend of Hakim al-Azahir, and one who had been in their business, but managed to escape it, coming back to the US and working a farm in this small town. Hakim wanted him back, for something he planned in Washington DC. Sira and Hassan would get him to do what Hakim wanted.

Unfortunately, those plans did not exactly work out. Now, Hassan was dead, Will knew about the plans, and she had fallen in love with Will Johnson as well.

As Will managed the darkness on the State Road, and then the twists and turns of the dirt road toward his farm, he too had a mind filled with questions, and a dilemma. He wondered how all this excitement over Hassan might affect

From a Vantage Point

his relationship with Sira, whom he knew he deeply loved. He worried about Sammi, and how it would be possible to keep his friend out of trouble. He wondered as well to what extent Hakim could do harm to him or especially Sira.

The dilemma he faced was what to do about Hakim and his 'plan'. Should he simply go along, and hope that an opportunity arises to defuse whatever Hakim had in mind? Should he go to the authorities in town and tell them what he knew? Should he do nothing, and hope for the best? In life, he knew, there were no easy answers. His dilemma was which solution would be best for him, and his life here in Elias.

As the truck pulled up outside the house, Will noticed a small light on in the living room.

"Sira, did we turn off all the lights this morning as we left?" he asked.

"I did, Will. I am sure of it," she responded, thinking for a few moments, then adding, "Yes, I am sure of it."

"There is a light on now. Stay here in the truck, and lock the doors after I leave," said Will, reaching behind the cab seat, and taking a tire iron from behind it.

"Lock the doors, Sira."

Will approached the front door, felt the door knob, and realized it was unlocked. He slowly entered the house, and walked into the living room, then the kitchen. Finally, he entered his bedroom, looked around, opened the closet and bathroom, and did the same in Sira's room before coming back to the front door.

"You can unlock the doors now, Sira," said Will, banging on the driver-side window. "No one is in the house." Sira unlocked the truck, then opened the passenger door. She swung her legs over and started to leave the truck as she asked, "Are you sure, Will?"

"Yes, Sira, everything is all right now. Close the door, and I will lock the truck for the night. Let's go inside," he added, as he used his electronic key to lock the truck.

When they entered the house, Sira was the first to speak, as she looked around the room. "There has been someone here, Will. I can tell. Things are out of place from where I had them. I know it." She walked around, then went to her room to look around there, returning in just seconds.

"Will, Hassan was here, today."

"How can you tell, Sira?"

"A picture of us, the only one I had. It was on the bureau, and now it is gone. Only Hassan would know of the picture, and now it is gone. Hassan was here."

"If that is the case, we do not have to worry anymore about a burglar, Sira. Look around and see if anything else was taken. We'll let the police know in the morning."

From a Vantage Point

"All right, Will, I will look, but I am still scared," she answered, as Johnson was walking over to the front door to lock it for then night.

"Tomorrow, when we go to town, I will go to the hardware store, and get new locks, and some deadbolts for the doors. That ought to make things somewhat safer."

"All right, Will, I guess." she responded, as her voice trailed off. Will noticed she was still trembling a bit.

"You come and stay with me tonight. Don't worry about protection. I will take a tire iron to bed with us, just in case." Sira looked over to him, and put on a small smile, then went to the kitchen to get some orange juice, something she liked to have before bed. Coming out into the living room, she walked over and kissed Will on the cheek.

"You are my protector, Mister Will."

"That I am, my dear," he answered, "That I am."

From a Vantage Point

From a Vantage Point

Chapter 41 Chasing Ghosts

Interstate 95 to Baltimore Hakim and his men, armed with their new identities and another car, a non-descript Ford in a dull grey finish, left the house in Philadelphia for the next leg of their journey. This time, they were headed down Interstate 95 south to Baltimore, Maryland where a small motel, owned by one of Hakim's people awaited them. That would be the base of operations for their upcoming event in Washington DC.

"We have been driving for over an hour, sir," said one of the men in the back. "Will we be stopping soon for a rest room maybe?"

Hakim looked at his map from the front passenger seat, trying to figure out a good place to stop. "Soon, we will stop soon," he replied, then went back to his map, looking for the exit marked on the map the men in Philadelphia told him was the location of the motel. He saw that they had to go through Baltimore, then south, and eventually get off on another road to reach their destination near the Baltimore Airport.

Finally finding the mark the man had made for him, Hakim announced, "We still have a way to go, but we will stop along the way so you can get rid of all that American soda you drank in Philadelphia."

"Thank you, sir," the man in the back of the car replied.

"When we get to the place we will stay, I will be gone for a time," said Hakim. "I need you to stay in the rooms they will give us, and speak to no one. These people are our friends, but we do not know if they are being followed by police here. Understand?"

"We understand," both men replied in concert.

Taking out a cell phone, Hakim dialed a number and put the phone to his ear as it rang.

"Good morning, this is Nights Inn, may I help you?" came the message from the phone.

"Yes, I need to speak to Joseph Day," said Hakim. He could hear the man on the other end of the phone cough, then put down the phone, and walk away.

"This is Mister Day," he heard in a few seconds, after someone picked up the phone. "May I help you?"

"I will be at your inn within two hours. Is all ready for us?" answered Hakim.

"Everything is in readiness," responded Mister Day, sounding a bit anxious. "Will there be anything in particular you need?"

"No, just the three rooms. We will order from your room service, if there is one."

"Sir, we do not have a restaurant here. There is one next door. The menu will be in your room, and I can have one of my people get food for you. Will that be satisfactory?"

From a Vantage Point

"Very much so. That will do," responded Hakim.

"Is there anything else, sir?" asked Mister Day.

"Nothing more. We will be there soon," responded Hakim, hanging up the phone, and throwing it out the window, well onto the grassy area beyond the road.

"All is ready for us, gentlemen. We will be there soon. For now, take the next exit. There is a gas station, and restrooms there for you to use. We need to move quickly. Do not delay here." The driver saw the exit, and moved to the right to take the off-ramp. At the bottom of a short hill, he came to an intersection. Hakim looked both ways, saw a small gas station with a store, and told the driver to go right. They pulled into the station, and into a parking space in front of the small store. The men in the back left the car quickly, one heading for the rest room, and the other for the store.

It took about ten minutes for the three men to get back on the road, headed toward Baltimore, and a motel called the Night's Inn. The three men would stay there until their plan had been accomplished.

Johnson Farm, Elias, West Virginia Will slept poorly the night of his return. He kept the tire iron close to his bed, just in case it was not Hassan, but someone else, who was entering the house for whatever reason.

Looking to his left, Sira was sleeping soundly, wrapped in blankets, and huddled into a cocoon. He fell asleep almost as soon as she entered his bed, and he kissed her on the side of the head and let her sleep. Sira was working hard, trying to help Sammi out, and the announcement of the death of Hassan hit her hard as well. When she climbed into bed, she spoke softly, saying good night to Will, and drifted off quickly into a deep sleep.

Will remained awake for a period, thinking about many things. He thought about his friend Josh, and wondered if the death of Josh was simply another action of Hakim. They had seemed to be close for so many years, yet Will thought of the many times Hakim had done thinks the other two would not have agreed to, but had to accept.

Now, he thought as well, of the last call from Hakim, telling him he had to work the action, and, if not, others would suffer. That was pure Hakim, in Will's mind. But this time, Will was not going to be simply a follower. He would deal with Hakim as he had to, especially if it affected Sira and Sammi, but he would try to make sure they were protected, even if it meant he had to do something he really wanted not to do.

As the morning sunlight arose, Will got out of bed, and went to the kitchen to make coffee. He was still thinking about how he would deal with Hakim. It was 8:30, as he looked at the kitchen clock. Will never arose this late, except for today.

From a Vantage Point

He had just started to make the coffee when the phone rang. As always, He looked at the name on the phone power unit, and saw it was 'unknown caller'. He had to decide what to do, but answered the call.

"My friend, I told you I would call back. It is Hakim," said the caller.

"What do you want Hakim," responded Will.

"It is not what I want, but what you will do that is important, my friend."

"Please do not call me your friend, Hakim. Anyone who would use people for their own violent ends is not my friend. You should know that this is not me," answered Will.

"Violence for an end is the Will of the Most-High, Will. It can be no other way. The infidel must be destroyed."

"Why must everything you do not believe in be destroyed Hakim. That is not what the Qu-ran says," responded Will.

"Who are you to interpret the Qu'ran, infidel?" retorted Hakim. "You are a Christian, one who must be used or destroyed if you do not bend to the will of the Most-High."

"Was Josh an infidel, Hakim? Did he really have to die to make you happy that you are following the crazy tenets of a violent Jihad?" Will was trying as best he could to make his case for stopping whatever Hakim had in mind before it was completed.

"Your friend Josh was a good man, Will. He did not believe, but he understood, something you never did. Josh had a heart condition, and was dying. I sent him to the United States hoping he would get care, but he died on the plane. That is not Jihad, that is mercy," answered Hakim. "He was my friend as well, you know."

Returning to the original question, Will asked, "All right, let's get back to what we started to talk about. What do you want Hakim? What is it you think I will do for you?"

"I will not speak of that now, Will Johnson. I will meet you on your Interstate 81, at one of the things they call visitor centers on the map. I will choose a place, and we will discuss what you will do. After we discuss it, you will do it as I ask."

"What if I do not, my so-called friend?"

"You will do it, because you want your friends to live in Elias. I will call back to tell you when and where Will Johnson." The phone went to a signal, telling Will Hakim had hung up.

"What an incredibly vile, and stupid man," Will said to himself, going back to making the coffee. "I called him a friend, and he treats the world like crap. Josh was a friend, but he is not." Will slammed down the cover on the coffee bin box, and silently swore to himself that he would bring Hakim down, whatever it took.

Nights Inn, Maryland The men with Hakim were amazed at the sights, driving through Baltimore, as they had been in Boston and Philadelphia; neither had been to the United States before, nor had they seen such tall buildings and huge, modern homes and offices.

Now, they were again headed on Interstate 95, eventually coming to its intersection with Interstate 195, the road which would take them east toward their destination. The motel, a small one with only about twenty rooms, was off a side street near the Baltimore International Airport, and catered to those coming from the Middle East. The rooms were generally full of recent arrivals, who might stay a day, a few days, or even longer, as they arranged for housing and transportation toward their new communities.

Hakim often used this motel when his people came to the United States. The owner was willing to look the other way, ask few questions, and accept small bribes to forget to register or remember some of his patrons. That fit well into Hakim's plans, and the owner was rewarded well for his assistance.

As they drove up to the motel, a man was standing outside, apparently waiting for someone. Hakim's driver started to pull up to the front entrance, but the man standing there waved them away, saying, "Go around to the side. The immigration people were just here. You do not want to be seen."

Hakim waved to the driver, to go around the front toward the side of the motel. There, another person waited, a woman.

"Come in sirs," she greeted, as they stopped, and Hakim left the car to walk toward her.

"As Salaam Alaikum," offered Hakim to the woman in greeting.

"Wa Alaikum Salaam," she responded. "We have been waiting for you, with the hope you would not arrive too quickly. The Immigration agents have been here just today. We did not want you to be caught with them. Come in." She waved the three men, who had now come together near the door, to enter.

"Your car will be safe here," she added.

The men walked inside, and were greeted by the man who had been in the front.

"As Salaam Alaikum my friend Hakim," said the man, touching his hand to his forehead and bowing, in the customary greeting gesture.

"Wa Alaikum Salaam," responded Hakim, adding, "May the Prophet shine upon you for your good works."

The man gestured for Hakim to come forward to the front area of the motel, and his men and the woman followed.

"Welcome to Night's Inn, sirs. I hope your stay here will be fruitful. As you asked, we have three rooms for you, each next to the other, and there are doors connecting each to the other. As you saw when you entered, next to our motel is a very fine restaurant. I have provided menus for you in your rooms. Order

From a Vantage Point

anything you like; it will be delivered, and there will be no bill for you. Is there anything else we can do for you?"

Hakim looked at the two people, and asked, "Who is this woman?"

"My apologies, sir," answered the motel owner, this is Fatima, my wife. We both work here, and either of us can help you at any time, any hour. All you need do is call and indicate what you wish."

"Thank you," responded Hakim. "Our rooms?"

The man handed Hakim and his men their room keys. "We must register you sirs, especially with the immigration people here. Do you have passports?"

All three handed the man their passports. He took them, and entered them into the register one-by-one, and then turned to them, "I will keep these in the safe, as is required sirs, until you leave."

Hakim nodded, and asked where the rooms were located, and Fatima showed them how to get there, asking the three to follow her back toward the side door, but then turning right into a corridor just inside. The rooms were along the corridor on the inside, one after the other.

"Thank you," Hakim said to Fatima, "All is well here. Could you send me some tea?"

"We have some very good tea, sir. I will brew it fresh right away and bring it to you."

"That would be good," Hakim responded, turning to open the door to his room, and then stepped inside, closing it behind him.

Hakim waited for Fatima to bring him his tea. In the meanwhile, he looked at the maps he received in Boston, and tried to determine where he could meet Will Johnson in the next few days along Interstate 81, going south along the boundary line between Virginia and West Virginia. He wanted someplace which would be open, yet discreet, and where he would not be recognized. Also, he needed someplace where he could observe for a time before Johnson would arrive, to be sure he did not come with others trying to arrest him.

Looking at the map on the table in front of him, Hakim started marking places; first Elias, east of Charleston, and then their own location in Baltimore. He traced I-95 south toward Washington DC, and then I-66 West to I-81 That would take him far to the west of Virginia. Taking I-81 South, he would eventually reach I-64, then driving along I-64 to the West, they would come to White Sulphur Springs. In that place, there was a state Welcome Center. Hakim remembered that these places always had numbers of people; they could easily hide their discussions with Will Johnson. Hakim felt he had the route and the place, but he had no computer to verify his plans.

Leaving his room, Hakim took his map and went to the office. The only one there was Fatima, the wife of the owner.

"I have need of a computer. Do you have one I can use?" Hakim asked.

From a Vantage Point

"Of course, Sir," she responded. "Use this one on my husband's desk. It needs no password or anything to use."

Hakim sat down at the desk, started typing on the keyboard after bringing up a web browser, and soon found the information he needed on the West Virginia Welcome Center in White Sulphur Springs.

"That will work well," Hakim said aloud, but to himself. "That will work very well," he repeated, then took his map and stood up, preparing to leave the office.

"Was the tea satisfactory, Sir?" Fatima asked.

"It was," Hakim responded. "Thank you for your courtesy." He left the office, headed for his room, banged on the doors of his two associates, and told them he wanted them to come in 15 minutes, then went to his room to call Will Johnson.

After they spoke, it was just a few minutes before he heard a knock on his door. His two men entered Hakim's room to discuss their coming trip.

Department of Homeland Security, Washington DC "What do you mean you have no idea where our subject is?" screamed Alice Sawyer into her phone, discussing the loss of surveillance on Hakim al-Azahir at Logan Airport in Boston.

"You had a Sky Marshal on the flight, a raft of TSA employees on the ground, all of whom should have been keyed into the arrival of a major terrorist, and you lost him in the crowd? Tell me how that was possible?" she continued to scream. Virtually everyone on the third floor could hear her, and little other work was being done as she took the DHS Boston manager over the coals in her own inimitable way.

"What have you done to try to locate him?" she asked, quieting down a bit. "Have you checked your cameras, and have you checked those of the Port Authority, the local police, and virtually every supermarket in the city? What have you done to locate my man?"

"Ma'am," the manager responded, "We know he went toward the baggage area in the International Terminal, picked up his bags, and was met by someone with a name card looking for Kassim Said. When he had the other two men traveling with Said, they went outside and over the walkway to the parking area, got into a white van and exited the Airport, heading for down town. We followed them through the tunnels, and into the North End, the Italian section of Boston. There, they moved around a lot, we lost them several times, and finally started across the road under the expressway and disappeared. We have no local cameras there at the underpass."

"So, what happens now? What is your plan?" asked Alice. "We pay you to have contingency plans, don't we?"

"Yes Ma'am. We have people monitoring every possible camera along the major routes fed by the underpass road. We did see the van briefly, we think it

From a Vantage Point

was the van, going off toward the South End, and picked up another white van later, heading toward Dorchester. The last camera we monitored that had a white van at about that time was heading toward the South Boston tenements, and, in those narrow streets, there are no cameras. This is the neighborhood of Whitey Bulger and the gangs. No one records down there for very long."

"All right, so we think he is in Boston, somewhere in Boston, or maybe even not in Boston. It is logical that the van will disappear shortly, and they will use some other mode of transportation. Do what you can, and we will try to do something from here." Alice slammed the phone into the receiver, obviously miffed at the setback.

Rich, I have a job for you," she said, walking into Rich Alcorn's office down the corridor from her own. "I want you to find a needle in a haystack, and right away."

Nights Inn, Baltimore, Maryland "We will meet Johnson in four days-time," said Hakim, "Until then, we will plan out what we will do as we go south, and what we must do when I meet Johnson. Look at this map," He told his two men, "Here is where we are now, and here being where we will meet Johnson," Hakim said, pointing to the map on the table.

"We must be careful," he continued. "We do not know if Johnson will bring in the authorities. Therefore, this is what we will do. I will arrange for another automobile, which I will take to the meeting place. You two will take the vehicle we have now, and you will go to Elias. There, you will go to the restaurant owned by Sammi Khan, and you will bring Sira to me. Let no one stop you."

"We understand," answered one of the men, looking at the other. "We will bring her to you."

"No, you will meet me at this point," responded Hakim, pointing again to the map, at a location just north on I-81, about 40 miles east and north of the meeting place in White Sulphur Springs. "It is an open parking place off the highway that many people use to visit the scenery on the highway. You will wait for me there, with her."

Both men nodded again, and Hakim continued, "Now, ask the woman in the office where to get good food. What is on the menu in the restaurant nearby is not fit for us. Ask where they eat."

"Yes, sir," said one of the men, who went out the door and down the hall, returning a few minutes later to say, "There is an Afghani restaurant or sorts down the road about a mile, they say. It is not truly Halal, but it is owned by a brother who cooks well."

"Good. Did you get directions?" asked Hakim.

"Yes," the man responded. "She gave them to me, and wondered if we wanted them to go to get the food for us."

From a Vantage Point

"No, we will go ourselves, since it is not far. We can all use the air of the mountains."

The three prepared to leave, two of the men going to get a coat for the cool weather, and Hakim pulling on a sweater made of Afghani wool that was very warm. They went through the side door to the car, and drove around the motel to get back to the street, then turned left onto the local road, heading for the restaurant.

Department of Homeland Security, Washington DC Using every trick he knew, and hacking into several systems he was probably not allowed to enter, Rick Alcorn started to try and find his terrorists. Over a period of ten hours, through the night, Alcorn took the biometric data from the videos at Logan Airport showing the three men, and started trying to find a way to identify them along the major routes between Boston and Washington, DC. He made several assumptions, the most important being that three men, with no experience in driving in the US, would attempt to stay to the largest highways. That way, he reasoned, they could blend in with other travelers, reducing the potential for their discovery. He was right, they did blend in, and finding them was very much like Alice's description—finding a needle in a haystack.

Alcorn had his first piece of luck when the biometrics of one of the men matched a man about to go over the George Washington Bridge in New York City. The man craned his head outside the rear car window, and the bells began to ring. It was one of the terrorists. They were driving in a white car, a rental car, and Alcorn could see the plate number. It took only seconds to realize it was rented from a small rental agency in Boston. Within the hour, FBI and DHS agents were at the rental place, looking over their rental agreements, and, getting a name, they went to the apartment listed as the rental, finding the white car out front.

Inside the apartment, they found the person who rented the car, and the agents arrested all three men then in the apartment. A forensics team took fingerprints in the car, and validated that Hakim and two others used the vehicle. Looking at the speedometer, they also realized the car had gone nearly 1,000 miles in the several days since its rental. That gave Alcorn a circle extending down toward Philadelphia and Baltimore. He also had a problem; they were obviously no longer in the same car, but where did they change vehicles?

Alcorn posted a large map on the whiteboard across from his desk. On the map, he placed a large green "X" on Boston, and another on Washington DC. Yet a third "X" went on the George Washington Bridge in New York City. It quickly became clear the terrorists were driving directly south on I-95. He wondered what their next stop might be. As I-95 goes south into New Jersey, it eventually splits off into two roads, both similarly labeled, one I-95, and one I-295, with both

From a Vantage Point

eventually coming back together south of Wilmington, Delaware, and on into Baltimore, Maryland.

He started looking for cameras after GW Bridge, but above the split. He zoomed in on several white cars that fit the description of the rental, but then realized it would take too much time. Instead, he concentrated on the cameras at tool booths, aimed toward license plates, and found several hits, confirming his view they were traveling I-95 South.

There were no cameras at or near the split, leaving Alcorn no choice but to review camera footage on both roads. As it happened, both Maryland and Pennsylvania have camera systems for monitoring traffic at intervals along the interstate highways, and Alcorn applied his biometrics to see what he could find. Starting with the direct route, I-295, Alcorn tried, but found nothing as far south as Wilmington Delaware.

Trying the same algorithm on the I-95 traffic, he hit on multiple cameras and soon found the white automobile with the plate number matching the seized vehicle in Boston. That trail took them toward Philadelphia, and the last image Alcorn found was on an overpass camera coming into the city. After that, the vehicle was lost in the local traffic. Alcorn placed a large "X" on Philadelphia.

"Where do I go next," Alcorn asked himself. "Let's leave it alone for a few minutes, and maybe the cloud will clear," he added, moving over to look through some papers in his in-box.

Nights Inn, Baltimore, Maryland Hakim and his men enjoyed their dinner at the small restaurant near the motel. It had an Afghani atmosphere, due to its owners, and had several good dishes on the menu, which they could enjoy. Following dinner, they waited for coffee and an ethnic dessert, Firni, made from corn flour, cardamom and pistachios. It was one of those simple, yet elegant deserts that even the poorest of villagers could make with the simple ingredients, and they were happy to have it on their trip.

"Well, gentlemen," asked Hakim, "How are you enjoying your first trip to America so far?"

"Praise to the Great One, and holy is his name," exclaimed one of his men, "There are so many wonders, tall buildings, and people. It is amazing."

The other remained a bit more silent, until Hakim asked him again, "What have you seen Akram?"

"I see so many things the Prophet, blessed be his name, would never agree that those who are believers should see, or taste, or encounter. This Western world is blasphemy, and ruled by *Shayṭān*. We, the believers, should not be here."

From a Vantage Point

"Have patience Akram," responded Hakim, "We are true believers, and we will do the will of Al'lah, may he be praised, and we will succeed in showing the Americans they are subject to his will. Have patience."

"We will stay here until two days' pass, "Hakim continued. "Then, we will start to deal with Johnson and the American Inauguration. We will make Johnson do what we wish, and will show the country the wrath of Al'lah for their attempts to destroy us, as they continue to defend the pigs of Israel. Let us enjoy our evening; it is the beginning of our holy journey, and we should be glad that we will serve the Great One."

In the morning, Hakim approached the owner of the Motel and inquired about a rental car for his use for several days. The man offered to allow Hakim to use his car, asking why he needed it, since the three already had a car.

"My two men will be travelling separately, and I will require a car to continue my journey. Is this possible here?"

"It is, sir," responded the motel owner, "I can arrange that for you. I have a friend who owns a car lot, and I am sure, for such a man as you, he would be glad to loan a vehicle for a short time. How much time do you think you will need?"

"Perhaps five days, six at the most," responded Hakim. "We will not be travelling far, but will have need of two cars. I appreciate what you can do. Please tell him I would be happy to pay for his services."

"No need," answered the motel owner, "I am sure my friend will let you use one of his cars as a friendly gesture. No money is needed."

"Please let me know. We wish to travel in two days."

"I will, sir. You will be informed promptly," replied the motel owner.

For the next two days, Hakim and his men went over their plans. He showed them the maps and the way to Elias. He also drew them a map of the town, showing where Sammi's restaurant was located, as well as the way to the Johnson farm. Hakim had a good memory, and the others who come to Elias earlier had given him a great deal of information on the town and the surrounding countryside. Now, he could put it to best use.

They agreed on a plan to go to Elias and visit Sammi's, have a small meal, and determine if Sira was at the restaurant. Otherwise, the two men would go to the farm. In either case, they were to seize Sira and take her with them back to White Sulphur Springs, where they would wait for Hakim in a large parking lot at a shopping center.

Hakim, in the meanwhile, would make a call to Will Johnson, and set up a meeting in the Visitor Center parking area at While Sulphur Springs, making sure that Johnson would follow his orders on the attack he planned for Inauguration. He expected problems with Johnson, and having Sira would force him to comply.

From a Vantage Point

If necessary, he would put Sira on the phone to Johnson from the place they had taken her after her abduction.

Department of Homeland Security, Washington DC Alcorn spent hours, meticulously finding cameras along the I-95 route toward Philadelphia, while continuing to have one of his staff members do the same on the route toward Wilmington and Baltimore. They had two possibilities, a facial or body recognition, or a license plate recognition; either one would help their tracking.

His staff member was the first to find something; a man in a red car passing toward Baltimore just south of the merger between I-95 and I-295. He brought his finding quickly to Alcorn, who placed an "X" with a question mark on it on I-95 South.

"That's great," Alcorn announced, "Now, all we have to do is figure out where they ditched the white car. We know from the reports we received, it went back to Boston from Philadelphia, so the change had to occur somewhere in the city. Let's keep looking. Start moving north on I-95 from Wilmington, and see if you can get some captures. I will do the same with local cameras in the city. We meet in the middle."

Two hours later, Alcorn found another camera, at Exit 20 of I-95 showing the white car taking the exit headed into the south of the city, and yet another on South Broad Street, showing the car taking a right onto a city street. Doing a quick search on that part of Philadelphia, Alcorn found that a car chase occurred that same day, with police helicopters making chase.

After contact with the city police, Alcorn reviewed the tapes of the chase, and found a small white car parked at a local address. Zooming in, he noticed the plate—it was the same. He had the location where the cars were probably exchanged, since, just in front was another car, a red one, which matched the description his staff member had for the car going south. The question mark came off the "X" south of Wilmington, and Alcorn made a mental note to get his staff to find the plate number, if possible.

Taking down the map, he walked down to Alice Sawyer's office, put it up on the white board across from her desk, and waited while she finished a phone call.

"What have we here Rick? Alice asked.

"The trail of the terrorists," he replied. "Say, that might make a great movie," he added.

"OK, so show me what you have."

"Well, we know the three men, Hakim and his two fellow bombers, or whatever, came in at Logan Airport, were picked up there, and taken to a location in the city. They got into a small white car and started south, along I-95.

From a Vantage Point

Going through New York City, they ended up in Philadelphia, changing cars there and again headed south; we have to presume headed for DC."

"OK, so we have the route, and we know they went south. What else?"

"We are still working cameras south to Baltimore, and then down to DC. That will take time. We must identify each location, get access, and then search. I have an algorithm that tests for biometrics and license plate, but it still takes time. There is a question, though."

"And that is?" asked Alice.

"What do we do when we find them?"

"We monitor, but not move in. The FBI will do the arrests when they happen. Our job is to locate, and then isolate, if possible. What are your plans for completing the search?"

"Basically, down I-95 and then around DC. Should we extend that?"

"Absolutely Rick. Create a larger circle from Baltimore south, and include I-81 out toward Elias, West Virginia. If Johnson is involved, it is possible Hakim will try to contact him directly, even in person. We need to be prepared for that."

"That was my thought as well, Alice, but I wanted to hear it from you before I put more people on the task."

"Use anyone you need Rick. This is a critical for us. This guy and his people cannot slip through," responded Alice.

"Aye, Aye, Captain," answered Alcorn, Taking down his map, then saluting as he left Sawyer's office.

When he was gone, Alice picked up the phone, dialed a number, and said quickly, "They are coming your way. Get ready," then hung up the phone, going to her in-box looking for a document.

FBI Field Office, Washington DC Richard Peabody arrived for a briefing on the status of the several cases, but was met at the door by a senior agent, who asked for a couple of minutes of his time.

"Sure. We have thirty minutes before the briefing starts," answered Peabody, "What's on your mind?" he asked, as they walked into the main area of the field office.

"Well, Mister Peabody, we have quite a bit of traffic, requests for information from local law enforcement, and, frankly, some hacks into mostly security services, cameras, and sensors along the east coast, generally from Boston, south. It seems to be emanating from DHS here in DC. We have nothing on the radar for that kind of activity."

"I know about the DHS matter," Peabody replied, "and I want to give them as much leeway as possible on the investigation they are doing on some terrorist activity. Alice Sawyer over at Counter-Terrorism keeps me up on the situation,

From a Vantage Point

and there are several offices, in Atlanta and Charleston involved, but they have the lead in DC."

"Okay, so what do we do?"

"Regarding what?" asked Peabody.

"We are getting calls from the locals. What do we tell them?"

"Tell then it is a National Security matter and classified. If there is a real problem, have the chief or sheriff call me."

"Okay," the agent repeated, "Will do."

Richard looked at him for a moment, and added, "Come to my office tomorrow, and I will get you a brief on the action. Tell your boss that you are the only one in the Field Office to get the info for now. Better yet, I will call him, and ask for you, and say the same. That will keep you out of trouble."

"Thanks Rich, I appreciate it," said the agent in reply.

"Good, now let's go into the briefing and see what your boys have to say about the other cases I came to review." Peabody patted his senior agent on the back as they walked down toward the conference room. At the same time, he made a mental note to call Alice about the latest actions.

Nights Inn, Baltimore, Maryland The time had finally come to put his plan in action. Hakim and the others with him were anxious to get on with their task; sitting in rooms in a small motel was not very exciting for any of them. As he promised, there was an additional car waiting at the side door entrance, parked next to the one they brought from Philadelphia. All that was left to do was check out, have their passports returned, and be on their way toward West Virginia.

Their plan was simple. They would drive south on I-95 to the Washington DC area, and take a route called I-495, a beltway road around DC, which would take them to I-66 west, and on to I-81, where they would go south to their destination. The day before, Hakim had walked down the street to get additional maps for his driver, which he marked well, so there was no question about the route or destination. He marked the way to Elias, and the return to White Sulphur Springs. There, both groups would meet, following Hakim's meeting with Will Johnson.

"Thank you both for your kindness," said Hakim, as he turned in keys. "And to your friend for the loan of the automobile, which we will return as we come back this way. We expect that to be in five days, perhaps six, depending on how fast we finish our business."

"You are most welcome, sir," responded the motel keeper. "We are happy to accommodate our countrymen when we can. We have little really, but we do share what we have. Where will you go from here, if I may ask," then realizing he had probably insulted Hakim.

Looking somewhat sternly at the man, Hakim answered, "We are going down to North Carolina to see some of our friends, who have recently come to

From a Vantage Point

America." Then, Hakim turned and started back toward the rooms, where the men were waiting, and they left through the side door to the parking area. Hakim took the car given by the local dealer, and the other two took the red sedan they received in Philadelphia. It would be a long drive, but they agreed to stop along I-66, at a place called Gainesville, for lunch and to refill their gas tanks.

From a Vantage Point

Chapter 42 Encountering the Devil

John F. Kennedy Airport, New York The Egypt Air flight MS 988, from Cairo, Egypt to JFK was 20 minutes late, not unusual for longer cross-Atlantic flights, especially those through the Mediterranean, subject to significant cross-winds as they enter the Atlantic Ocean free space. The crossing had been uneventful, and relatively smooth, but still somewhat late, causing some passengers a bit of angst on connections.

"Ladies and Gentlemen, please be advised we are a bit late, approximately twenty minutes, and it may take some time to connect to a gate here at John Kennedy Airport. We regret the delay, but we are first in the cue for a gate assignment, and expect to be disembarking in about fifteen minutes. You are, of course, free to use your cell phones and laptops while we wait for a gate assignment, and the flight attendants will provide you your beverages of choice during the delay. We will keep you informed on the final disembarking," said the voice on the public address.

Many of the passengers rushed to their cell phones, as did the passenger in seat 3-E, who dialed a number quickly and waited for a response.

"This phone is currently not active," said the message. "Please leave a voice message, and it will be delivered as soon as the customer powers on their phone. We regret we cannot connect you, but assure you the message will be delivered as quickly as possible."

"Radan," came the response from the passenger, "This is Ali. I am arriving at Kennedy Airport in New York. You must return my call as quickly as possible. We need to speak." Ali wondered why the phone was shown as off, but assumed it was an American way of providing service. Putting the cell phone in his pocket, he sat back waiting to disembark from the place once the airplane was assigned a gate.

Ali did not know the FBI had Radan in their custody in Atlanta. His phone message was recorded, and the Atlanta office asked the New York office to detain the person making the call. They did not realize, of course, the importance of the detainee, only that he had made a call to Radan.

Later, at the gate, Two FBI agents waited for Ali to debark from the plane. As he did so, he was arrested, and taken to the New York FBI field Office for detention and interrogation.

Johnson Farm, Elias, West Virginia As Will Johnson awoke and looked out his bedroom window, he saw snow on the ground; not much, but enough to cover the grass.

From a Vantage Point

"Well, I'm glad the hay bales are out for the cattle," mused Will to himself, "Sooner or later the weather had to start to turn. It has been a very mild winter so far and I guess we should be thankful for that." He showered and dressed, going then to the kitchen to make coffee. He just barely made the living room before the phone rang. He saw from the caller ID it was Sammi.

"Mister Will," said Sammi as Will picked up the phone. "Please stay at home today, it is supposed to snow even more, and I have someone this morning who will help in the restaurant."

"Are you sure, Sammi?" Will asked. "Sira and I can easily come in with the pickup."

"No, Mister Will," responded Sammi, "Henry over at the hardware store, his wife Ellen is coming. They live upstairs of the store, so she walked across the street to help. You can stay home if you wish. Come in for breakfast or lunch, but come when you wish. We will be fine here."

"All right, Sammi," answered Will, "We will probably come in for lunch. See you later then."

Will hung up the phone, and started toward the kitchen to make his coffee, having the aroma of his dark Arabica beans waft throughout the house in just seconds. As he was pouring the first cup, Will sensed movement in the living room. Looking out through the small service window, separating the rooms, he saw Sira, wrapped in a huge robe. The only parts of her body visible were her head, and the feet. She still looked half-asleep, but walked over to the sofa, and sat down, feet under her at the corner.

"Did you sleep well?" asked Will, looking through the door at her.

"Yes, I did. I slept soundly. You?"

"Like a log. I was tired, and I know you were, in addition to the excitement of finding the house broken into. I'm actually a bit surprised you slept at all."

Will walked through the door to the living room, and came over to sit next to Sira, placing his coffee cup on the side table. "Would you like some coffee?"

"No, Will," she responded, "I will get some shortly. I want to wake up first."

"Take your time. We don't have to go Sammi's today. Henry's wife from the hardware store is going to help at the restaurant."

"But I do need to go to the store to get some things. Perhaps later this morning we can go?" she asked.

"Of course, but just relax for now. We have the whole day."

Will sat on the sofa, and they watched the news and morning shows until nearly lunchtime. Eventually, Sira went to her room to dress, returning with a pair of jeans and a bright plaid blouse, looking ready to go to work on the farm.

"When do you want to go to town Will?" she asked. "Remember, we need to get some locks for the doors at the hardware store."

From a Vantage Point

"I know," he responded, "I also want some of the new locks you can get to secure the windows. Things are changing, I guess. During all the years, I and my family, now you, have lived here, we never thought about locking the house, until recently. Now, even that seems inadequate. Times change, I guess," he repeated. "We could have lunch at Sammi's and then I can go to the hardware store, and you can do your shopping."

"I like that," Sira replied. "First, I will do laundry and some cleaning, then we can go."

Over the next hours, Sira did some cleaning and laundry, and Will looked over the windows and doors to see what he wanted for locks. He was particularly concerned with those windows, and the rear door, which could not be seen from the street. Finished, he went out to brush the snow off the pickup truck, and returned to announce he was ready. Sira smiled, and nodded agreement.

They drove carefully into town, with the roads slick from the snow, but now turning to mush, taking more time than usual, but they had the chance to talk, and discuss some future things. Seeing the main street ahead, Will slowed and turned to Sira, then changed the conversation.

"You do know I love you, I hope?" Will asked, looked over at Sira, while still trying to pay attention to the road.

"Yes Will, it is very clear to me that you love me, and it is also clear that I love you. Now pay attention to the road. There are people on the street ahead. This is a very interesting time for you to ask. Perhaps, it is the locks we need to buy, and you are afraid for my safety? Perhaps you just want to hear yourself say it. Whatever the reason might be, I am glad you asked," she said, patting his right leg and smiling. "No one could be happier than me right now. Do you think Sammi knows?"

"Sira, Sammi has known for weeks. Everyone in town has known for weeks. The only thing they have not done is put up a poster telling everyone who drives through." Will laughed as he finished, and Sira developed a scowl on her face.

"Now you are making fun of me," she responded.

"No Sira, I could never do that. We have a lot to look forward to, and I'm glad we both feel the same way about each other." Will pulled into a parking space in front of Sammi's and turned to Sira, "Ok, we're here. Lunch first, or shopping; which will it be?"

"Lunch, of course. A man always feeds a woman before he sends her off on errands," said Sira, laughing.

"OK, lunch it is, madam," responded Will, stopping the truck and going out and around the truck to open Sira's door for her. "This way to lunch, Ma'am," he pointed toward the front door of Sammi's.

Will and Sira went through the door to Sammi's and were greeted by a big hug from the owner, who escorted them to Will's usual table near the register.

From a Vantage Point

"I made sure this table would stay free for you, Mister Will. I knew you two would be coming in, and it is your table," Sammi announced, pointing to it with a flourish as Ellen Gates, the hardware Store owner's wife came over with menus.

"Sira, this is fun," said Ellen Gates. "I didn't realize how much fun it would be. A lot more so than selling screws and nails, or cutting class. I just might do this with Sammi more often." She smiled widely, and Sira returned her smile.

"Thank you for helping Sammi, Miss Ellen. I really appreciated the extra hour of sleep this morning before Will started making noise in the kitchen, waking me up." Both women looked toward Will, who threw up his hands, admitting his guilt. Then they all laughed.

"I'll come back for your order, Sira. I know what he wants, Sammi already told me. Do you both want something to drink? Coffee? Tea? Orange juice Sira?" Will nodded quickly for the coffee.

"Orange juice will be fine for me," responded Sira.

"Coming right up," came the comment from Ellen, turning to walk toward the kitchen, but moving over to the right of the door, where the coffee and tea machines, and the juices were kept, along with cups and glasses.

When the crowd eased a bit, Sammi came over to sit with the couple, spending some time musing about his days back in the old country, and how the missionary group brought him to the United States, eventually finding him this restaurant, helping him set up and make the restaurant work. Sammi was Will's friend, for a time his only friend in the town, and, as he looked over at both Sammi and Sira, he wondered how all this with Hakim would work out. One thing he knew; he would never mention Hakim to Sammi.

It was Sira who broke up the conversation, saying, "You men may continue to discuss the past, but I need to go to the store to get things we need for today, and the future. You will excuse me, I hope, so I can go shopping."

"Do you need money Sira?" asked Will, wondering how she was going to pay for what she needed.

"Oh no, Will, I will charge it to your account at the store. That is all right?"

Will laughed. "Of course, that is what I was going to say anyway, and get some things for yourself as well."

"All right then, you, Mister Will, need to go to the hardware store, and I need to go to the market. Let's do what we need to do, shall we?"

"She already has you under control, Mister Will," kidded Sammi. "It will get worse when you to marry. Trust me." Sammi laughed, as he rose to go to the kitchen.

"He's right, you know Will," added Ellen, "But I can't think of a better person to put a leash on you." She smiled, picked up their plates, and started for the kitchen, leaving Sira and Will standing at the table, as if they wondered what to do next.

From a Vantage Point

Sira went down the street to the market, took a cart, and started to walk along the aisles, and Will went over to gates' Hardware Store to get his locks, and order some wood for the fences. Henry told him he did not have all the locks he needed; it seemed that everyone was doing the same thing as Will. Henry knew that the hardware store on the outskirts of Beckley, about twenty miles away, had exactly what Will wanted.

Walking down the street after thanking henry, Will went to the market to find Sira.

"I have to make a quick trip to Beckley, to get the hardware I need. Should be back in less than two hours Sira. That will give you time to shop, and I will meet you at Sammi's when I get back. OK with you?" Will asked.

"Of course, that gives me more time to shop, and not rush. Go and do what you must do. Mister Gates did not have what you want?" she asked.

"No, he says he has had a lot of customers coming in looking for this stuff. He found the hardware outside Beckley has what I need. He already sent someone else there today. That's the way it is, I guess. Won't be too long," he offered, kissing Sira on the head, and heading toward the truck. Sira went back to her shopping.

Will drove the distance to Beckley in about thirty minutes, giving himself time to drive more slowly with the icy mush. Coming off the state road onto I-64, Will was able to increase speed and move with traffic, and was soon on the outskirts of Beckley, and the turn off to the small shopping center with the Build-Right hardware. His phone began to ring as he drove down the exit ramp toward the parking area of the store. Stopping the truck, he picked up his phone to see an 'unknown number' he assumed it was Hakim. Pushing the talk button, he waited for a response.

"Will Johnson, how are you?" Will knew the voice immediately.

"What do you want Hakim?"

"Listen carefully. You will be going to Washington the day before the Inauguration. You will stay at the same hotel, in the same room, and you will do all the same things you normally do when you go there. This time, however, it will be different."

"How so?" Will asked.

"Because this time, you will call down to the desk and ask to have packages brought to you. They will be there waiting for you. You will open then, and see the instructions on what to do, then you will do it."

"What is it, I am supposed to be doing, Hakim?"

"You will see from the packages, Will Johnson. Just do what you are instructed, and you and your whore Sira will be safe from me. That I will give you. If you do not do what I wish, you will not be safe, and she will be dead. Her death will be on your head. Do you wish that?"

From a Vantage Point

"You have no way of hurting Sira, Hakim. She is safe from you. She is not your pawn, nor am I, nor was Josh. You use people for what you want, but this time you will not win. You had Josh killed to suit your purposes, but I broke your chain a long time ago."

"Will Johnson, you will not believe, and I really do not care if you do, but your friend Josh Giddons, also my friend died of a heart attack. He had a bad heart, and he knew it. Believe what you wish, but you will do what I wish." Again, as in the prior call, Will quickly heard a dial tone indicating the call had ended.

Will sat for several minutes thinking about what Hakim had said. He left the truck, then returned; he could get the hardware later. Right now, he wanted only to get back as quickly as possible to be sure of the safety of Sira and Sammi.

Sira came out of the grocery store with several bags in a small cart, which she pushed toward Sammi's Restaurant to wait for Will. There was a white car with two men sitting in the front seat drinking coffee parked in a space in front of the restaurant. She passed the car, and started toward the front door of Sammi's with her groceries.

The two men emerged from the car together, one going on either side of her cart.

"Please come with us quietly," said one of the men, gasping Sira's arm, and directing her toward the car. When he did so, the other man came along the other side, and was soon behind her. She could not escape.

"Do not try to make a scene,' said the man who held her arm, "We will simply kill you in the street if you do. Hakim says to tell you that you will come, and your man Will might live for another day."

"Why are you doing this?" asked Sira.

"It is not for you to understand or agree," answered the man on her arm, "It is only for you to obey and get in the car. The man opened the door, and pushed her in.

At that point, the other man entered the front side and turned the key in the ignition, starting the car. As he did so, Sammi, who had been observing what was happening, ran from his restaurant to the car.

"Leave her alone," he told the men, who paid no attention to him. "Leave her alone," he said again, as she was pushed into the car, the door closed, and the second man, entering the passenger side, told him to mind his own business. The car sped off toward the state road before Sammi could call over to the police station.

As soon as they left with Sira, Sammi ran to the police station and reported what he saw. A police car took off after the car, hoping to catch it. Sammi, in tears, returned to the restaurant to wait for Will Johnson to return.

From a Vantage Point

Will drove into town in his pickup, as people gathered on the street. He parked near the restaurant, and was not even able to leave the pickup before Sammi came out, tears in his eyes.

"Mister Will," Sammi sobbed, "Someone has taken Sira in their car, and gone away."

"What are you saying Sammi?" Will asked, trying to make sense of his slobbered speech.

"Two men took Sira," Sammi answered, "They took her in a white car, and drove off. She was crying and looked very frightened."

"When did this happen?" asked Will.

"Just ten minutes or so ago, Mister Will. They were in a car in front of the restaurant when Sira came from the store. They took her, and left the groceries on the sidewalk. As Will and Sammi spoke, the chief of police walked across the street, and all three entered the restaurant, sitting in a booth at the rear.

"Have you found her chief?" asked Will. "What is going on here?" he continued.

"That's what I really need to know, Will. She was taken by two men, in a light-colored car, which my men are chasing right now. Anything you might know about this?" he asked.

"I don't know what to think Chief," answered Johnson. "She was my housekeeper, and, as you know, we have become close. Why would someone want to do this? It makes no real sense."

The police cam the chief wore started to crackle, and the chief listened to whatever was coming in. "Will, it seems they eluded our officers just short of White Sulphur Springs. The officers had them in sight for a while, and asked for assistance from the State Patrol as well, but the car went off on an exit ramp in traffic, and our guys missed them. We didn't have time to get a bird in the air, so all we had was the guys keeping them in sight," the chief added.

"What happens now?" asked Will, as much to himself as to the others.

"We continue to search," responded the chief. "We have the State Patrol, you know the State police, and the various local departments, and the two sheriff departments between here and White Sulphur Springs. One or another will find the car and Sira. We'll get her back. Try not to worry. I'll make sure you are up-to-date on what unfolds. Go home, and let us conduct the investigation. Sammi, I will want to talk to you in a bit, and see if we can get more information on what you might remember." Sammi nodded in agreement, then turned back to Will.

"There is nothing else to do, Mister Will," added Sammi. "I have the groceries and other things Sira was pushing in the cart from the store when they took her. I will put them in the truck for you."

"Thanks, Sammi," responded Will, looking totally confused and concerned. "Not much else to do but go home and wait, I guess." Sammi patted Will on the shoulder, and escorted him to the door of the restaurant. All those sitting at tables looked toward Will as he left. It was obvious how the town appreciated Will Johnson.

Department of Homeland Security, Washington DC Rick Alcorn took Alice Sawyer at her word, and placed three more analysts on the trail of Hakim and his cohorts. They expanded the circle as Alice suggested, and eventually found the red car, with the right license plate, coming south to Baltimore, Maryland. They were surprised when the myriad camera images showed the car going through Baltimore, but continuing south. As Rick looked at the images, he was, at first, surprised, because he expected them to stop, but then realized they wanted to retain their anonymity if possible, and moving south was probably to their advantage.

The questions still unanswered were simple; where would they stop, and what was their ultimate destination? Without those answers, it was impossible to develop a plan to counteract whatever they planned for the Inauguration.

Working patiently, Alcorn and his small team, working with advanced technology, scanned the video of every available camera, Federal, State, and local along the Interstate, extended as far south as the I-495 Beltway around Washington DC. Gradually, the drew a picture of the progress of Hakim and his two men, leading them toward Baltimore-Washington Airport, and the mall motel nearby—Night's Inn.

As ordered, Alcorn notified Alice Sawyer of this latest stop. She called Richard Peabody, and an FBI team swept down on the motel, arresting the owner, and taking him to the Baltimore Field office. They did not arrest his wife, since she was off cleaning empty rooms. She in turn, quickly called their friend, the used car dealer, who promptly reported a stolen car from his lot.

Continuing the monitoring, Alcorn noted that the three men stayed nearly three days at the motel before leaving to resume their journey south. He was not aware, at first, that the car following closely behind the red car driven by Hakim al-Azahir contained his other two men. However, within an hour, the report of the stolen car arrived on the screen. Matching the information to the videos, it became clear the men had split up, with both cars now proceeding south.

FBI Field Office, New York. "All right, let's go over this again," said an agent sitting with Ali Peshar in an interrogation room. "Your name is Ali Peshar, and you are an associate of Amid Fatoullah, a wanted terrorist. Isn't that correct?" he continued.

"I have only to say that I am Ali Peshar, a member of the Diplomatic Corps of Egypt, in this country to meet with members of the Egyptian Government at the

From a Vantage Point

United Nations. I have diplomatic immunity, and I demand to speak to the Egyptian Embassy immediately."

"Mister Peshar, or whatever your real name is. That is a load of crap," said the agent in response. "We have notified the Egyptian Embassy of your detention here, and are awaiting a response on your status."

"Then, I have nothing further to say until my country's officials arrive to secure my release."

The agent banged on the table, then rose, walking toward the door, where another agent had wrapped on the door. Stepping outside, he listened as another agent told him the news he had not hoped to hear.

"Sully," said the other agent, "The Egyptian Embassy has made a formal complaint to the State Department, and State has ordered this guy's immediate release, but they are kicking him out of the country. Get something if you can, but the embassy staff will be here in a few minutes to pick him up."

"No problem," came the response, as the agent walked back into the room, sat down, and looked Ali in the eyes.

"Your embassy is coming to get you. They have a right to take you out of here, but let me tell you this; the State Department has ordered you to be expelled from the country. They can take you where they wish, as long as it is directly to the Embassy. From the Embassy, you go back directly to JFK, where we will watch you leave. Try to do anything else, make a call, or even piss on the street and you will be back here. Do you understand me, mister terrorist?"

Ali fought the temptation to say anything to the agent. Instead, his wry smile said it all. He rose from the table and waited for his embassy people to get him. The agent rose as well, walking toward the door, and slamming it loudly as he left.

The limousine from the Egyptian Embassy arrived in downtown Manhattan about fifteen minutes later, and two men in dark suits entered the lobby, where Ali Peshar and an FBI agent waited.

"He's yours," said the agent, pointed to Peshar, seated on a chair to the side of the lobby.

"Thank you, Sir. On behalf of the Egyptian Embassy, we express our apologies for your inconvenience in this matter. The ambassador wants you to know he will be dealt with, and harshly."

"Of course," responded the agent, then turning to walk back toward the elevators.

"Come with us, Mister Peshar," said one of the men from the Embassy. "We have instructions on you." The two men escorted Ali out of the lobby, into the limousine, and it sped off, heading toward the south end of Manhattan.

Ali became concerned. "Where are we headed," he asked.

From a Vantage Point

"We have instructions to take you directly to Kennedy Airport. There, you will board an Egyptian Government plane, which will take you to Cairo. We are also ordered to tell you, from the Foreign Minister that you no longer enjoy a special status. Future requests will not be honored."

Ali sat back, looking at the building, and then the crossing from Manhattan toward Long Island, and the Belt Expressway, taking them to Kennedy Airport.

Johnson Farm, Elias, West Virginia Will pulled up in front of the house, and turned off the engine, dropping his head on the steering wheel, and breathing heavily, as his eyes began to tear up. "What do I do now?" he asked himself. "Nothing to do but wait for another call from Hakim, I guess."

Leaving the truck, Will took the bags of groceries from the back of the truck, and started for the house. He no sooner had unlocked the door that the phone rang. Dropping the groceries on the sofa, he ran for the phone.

"You have received my message, Will Johnson?" asked Hakim.

"When this is over, I will kill you myself Hakim," said Will is a deep, serious tone. "What do you want?"

"As I told you earlier, you will do what I wish in three days. Until then, I will have the pleasure of the company of Sira, until she joins you in Washington at your hotel. What is it, The *Alexander* that you stay at?"

"You think you know everything Hakim, but you have obviously forgotten we did this thing before, years ago, and it did not work then."

"It will this time, Will Johnson. You will make it work, if you wish to survive with Sira."

"What do I do, then?" Will asked, seeming resigned to do what Hakim wished.

"In good time, Mister Will Johnson. In good time. You will hear from me again, and soon." The dial tome came up, and Will put the phone back on its cradle, sitting down on the sofa.

Later that evening, Will programmed the phone at the farm to ring to his cell phone, so he would not miss any calls from Hakim, wherever he was now. He packed his bag to take to Washington, and closed the house to start his journey, wherever it was going to take him.

Alexander **Hotel, Washington DC** Two men and a woman stood at the concierge desk, waiting for her to complete her phone conversation. As she did, she looked up, and asked, "What can I do for you this morning?"

"Roger Doucette, FBI, and these are two of my agents. We need to see your director of security please." All showed their credentials as the woman scanned the three, then stated, "Sir our Director of Security is in a meeting with the General Manager. Shall I have him come out of the meeting?"

From a Vantage Point

"We would appreciate that very much," came the reply from Doucette.

In moments, two men came out of a side door, one coming up to the agents, and saying, "Hello. I'm Joe Xanaria, the Chief of Security, and this Alfonso Guerrero, the General Manager. How can we help the FBI today?" he asked

"Do you have someplace we can have a private discussion?" asked Doucette, introducing himself to both men.

"We do," responded Mister Guerrero. "Please come this way." He pointed down the hall, and then again to a door, recessed in the wall to make it disappear. Pulling a small device out of his pocket, he clicked it, and the door came ajar. "We use this space for diplomatic and other meetings, where privacy is critical. There are no telephones or other technology in here. It is like what your government people call a 'SKIFF', he said, meaning a Sensitive Compartmented Information Facility. "Our guests, including government people, sometimes have the need for such meetings. We have the President here occasionally."

Guerrero smiled faintly with pride. He pointed the way for the agents to enter, and then pushed a button to close the door.

"Only three people have access to this room; myself, the Security Chief, and my Assistant General manager. We all have security clearances through the Secret Service. You are quite safe, and able to have private conversations here. So, I ask again, what can we do for you?" He pointed toward a small group of plush chairs surrounding a large, low circular table.

"Sir," started Agent Doucette, "You have a steady customer, Mister Will Johnson, who comes here frequently, and always stays in the same small suite, as I understand it."

Guerrero looked over at Xanaria, who answered, "Yes, Mister Johnson is a frequent guest. We understand he is working on a project with the Department of Agriculture. I have met with him several times over drinks myself. A farmer from West Virginia, as I understand it."

"That he is, Mister Xanaria, and as far as we know, he is a good citizen as he undoubtedly is as a customer. Right now, we are dealing with a sensitive situation, one which Mister Johnson may be unwittingly walking into, and we need your help to keep him on our side of the law."

"This is serious, Mister Doucette. The Alexander Hotel does not desire bad situations or bad customers. Please tell me I do not have either," responded Guerrero.

"Your hotel is quite safe, Mister Guerrero, I can assure you of that. Right now, we are looking to some suspicious packages coming to the hotel in Mister Johnson's name. I have both a warrant and a National Security letter, one to look at the packages as they arrive, and the other to make sure nothing of our meeting gets out to anyone else, I repeat ANYONE ELSE, who might even possibly release the information."

From a Vantage Point

"I understand what you are trying to do, Mister Doucette. I was with DHS until I retired a year ago. I believe we can help you here. As Mister Guerrero said, we do not want bad publicity, even unintentionally. Your confidence will stay with us."

"You were with DHS?' asked Doucette. "Mind if I ask which area?"

"Sure, I worked for Alice Sawyer in counter-intelligence. I know well what you are trying to deal with here. Tell Alice I said hello, if she is involved, and I'm sure she is, in this situation."

"Mister Xanaria, let me say this," answered Doucette, "Please go ahead and call Alice if you are at all uncomfortable. I will allow you that one call, and I will forget the slip. I want you both to be comfortable here."

"Thanks Agent Doucette," returned Xanaria, "But my bet is on the fact that you already knew I formerly worked for Alice Sawyer. True?"

"Well, actually, Mister Xanaria, it might have slipped out just a bit." Both men smiled and the general manager sat there, really perplexed.

"What are the next steps, gentlemen?" Guerrero asked.

"We will need to know when three wooden packages arrive, addressed to Johnson. When they do, we want to send a team to look them over securely, then get them back to your mailroom for his arrival. Can that happen?"

"Of course," smiled Xanaria, "Anything for Alice. I hate to tell you how many tough places that woman got me into over the years. Let's have a drink sometime devoted to Alice Sawyer stories. Again, the two men laughed.

"Good, then we will wait to hear from you, Mister Xanaria."

"Please all of you, I'm Joe. We use last names and formality here, but I enjoy the days when simpler forms of address were more common. Let me know whatever we can do." All the agents, then the two from the hotel rose to leave, shaking hands all around, before they went through the door to the corridor.

"Joe," said Guerrero, "I want to know everything they want to do. We cannot have a problem here during our busiest season."

"Understand boss," came the reply, as the two men went back to their original meeting.

White Sulphur Springs, West Virginia Hakim waited in the Visitor Center parking area for his men to return from their task. He went inside the visitor center to look over the maps and literature, asking about low-priced local motels, and found one about ten miles from the visitor center. The woman behind the desk marked it on a map for him. He also went back at least two more time, once for a soft drink and the other to use the rest rooms. He hoped the men would return before the center guards became suspicious and start asking questions.

The guard on duty had become suspicious, and took down the license number of the car, meaning to check it with the State Police, then got busy when

From a Vantage Point

a busload of school children arrived on the scene. When they left, and he had the opportunity, he looked out and the car was gone. He stuck the note with the number in his pocket, and promptly forgot it as he went on to do other things.

The second car pulled up just as Hakim was returning from the rest room. In the back, sitting next to one of his men was Sira.

"We are leaving immediately," he said to the driver of the other car. "Did you have any trouble getting this whore out of their town?"

"No trouble at all, sir," came the response. "She was on the street with a shopping cart. We took her and left the cart. A man came out of the restaurant to try to help her, but we simply drove away."

"That is not good," responded Hakim. "That means we will have to get a new vehicle, or all go together. I will think on it. Right now, you will drive," he told the man driving the other car. "You two will sit in the back. Leave this car here, over in the edge of the place. Wipe it well, but do not take too long."

The driver drove the car over under some trees, took his handkerchief and wiped the steering wheel, the dashboard, and the outer door handle as he left, walking back to where Hakim and the others waited. He climbed into the driver seat, as Hakim had moved over to the passenger seat, then they drove off, back toward the highway.

Sammi's Restaurant, Elias, West Virginia "Sammi, think," said Chief Edwards, "You walked outside to help Sira when you saw her accosted by the men, two men. What was the car like? Did you see a plate number? Think, man."

Sammi sat there, not really knowing what to say. "Chief, I have thought of nothing else since this happened. I did see the car, it was parked in front of the restaurant. It was small and white, with a bird on the front."

"What kind of bird?" asked the chief.

"It wasn't a bird," Sammi responded. "It was a big one of those deer with big antlers." Sammi smiled, having remembered something.

"Like an Elk?" asked the chief.

"Yes, like that ad on TV, what is it, I remember, 'RAM TOUGH', it says."

"A Dodge. It was a Dodge, the chief exclaimed. A small Dodge. OK, now we are getting somewhere."

"What color was it?""

"That I know," Sammi replied, "It was white."

"Great, now do you remember anything about the white car's license plate?"

"It had American colors, red, white, and blue, and a picture on it. It had numbers starting with, let's see "B", and "C", and the last two numbers were "1" and "0". Will that help, Chief?"

563

From a Vantage Point

"You bet it will, Sammi." The Chief picked up his phone and dialed a number. "This is Chief Edwards in Elias. I have a late model Dodge, White, possibly a Maryland plate, starts with BC, and ends with 10. Can you give me anything?"

"Hold a moment Chief, let me see," came the response. "Here we go, Chief. I have a 2010 White Dodge Avenger, Maryland plate, reported stolen two days ago in Linthicum Heights, Maryland. Owner runs a used car lot, said it was stolen overnight while he was closed. Has a flag from Homeland Security on it. Not much else, though. Hope that helps."

"It will, thanks," responded the Chief, looking over at Sammi as he hung up his phone. "Ever see those guys before Sammi?"

"Never, chief, why would you ask?"

"There is something funny going on here. These guys are wanted by Homeland Security, just as your cook was before he was killed. I better call the Feds on this. Thanks, Sammi. You were a great help." Edwards walked out of the restaurant to return to his office. He needed to call DHS.

Crossing Main Street, Edwards thought about all the 'coincidences' occurring in his town. There had been so many reports prepared covering the events of the past several weeks. He continued to think everything seemed to point toward Will Johnson. First, the FBI shows up, hauls him over to Charleston, then they interview him in Elias, with the Department of Homeland Security in tow. Then, there was the issue of Hassan Singh, the cook and dishwasher at Sammi's; this time he disappears just as the FBI wants to talk with him, and then goes on a rampage, first at Will Johnson's Farm, and then in a field along the State Road. His death is still under investigation.

Now, another employee, this time of both Sammi and Will Johnson, Sira Suleiman, gets grabbed on the main street; taken away by two guys in a car with Maryland plates, reported stolen from a used car dealer, in front of Sammi's, as she returned from shopping for groceries to take back to her home at Will Johnson's farm.

As Edwards looked at the reports, seeing the threads—Sammi's Restaurant and Will Johnson, he also saw another thread—immigrants, Middle Eastern immigrants at that, and he wondered how all this was connected. He was beginning to feel the same as some of his officers had mentioned—there might be a terrorist cell in town. Edwards was not going to put up with that for even a moment regardless of what the Feds might say.

Sitting at his desk thinking for a few moments, looking again at the reports on his desk, Edwards picked up the phone, looked for a business card, and dialed the number for Anderson Cohen at Charleston, DHS.

"Anderson Cohen, can I help you?"

"Agent Cohen, this is Chief Edwards in Elias."

"Great day, Chief. What can I do for you?"

"We have another situation here, right up your alley, I'm afraid. One of our citizens, Sira Suleiman, was just kidnapped on Main Street."

"Sira Suleiman, the woman who works for Will Johnson and Sammi Khan?"

"The very same. About an hour ago, with two men in an out-of-state stolen car doing the honors. DMV says there is a flag from DHS on the car. Know anything you might want to tell me?"

"Chief, I need to look at this. You have caught my blind eye here. Let me call you back in just a minute."

"Sure Anderson, I'll be here. Any information I can get would be appreciated. We have people out chasing the car, need more to go on."

"Out here, Chief," said Cohen, as he hung up, and then quickly dialed another number.

"Alice, this is Anderson," he said into the phone before the other person could answer.

"You sound excited, Anderson, what's going on?"

"Two men picked Sira Suleiman up off a public street in Elias, about an hour ago. The locals chased the car, and found out it was stolen, and has a DHS tag on it. Anything I should know?"

"Hold on a second, Anderson, let me ring in Rick Alcorn," she answered, putting him on hold.

"Rick," said Alice, "I'm connecting us with Anderson Cohen in Charleston. He has information you both need to share."

Alice punched two buttons on her phone, and the three were now connection.

"OK Anderson, Rick is on the line. Tell me again what you have."

"Earlier this morning Sira Suleiman was grabbed in Elias. As you both know, she works for both Sammi Khan and Will Johnson. Two men in a stolen car grabbed her on the street. The locals lost them along the state road somewhere. Chief Edwards says there is a DHS tag on the report."

"There is Anderson," responded Alcorn. "If that car is a white Dodge with Maryland plates, it was reported stolen and taken by Hakim al-Azahir and his people up in Maryland near the Baltimore-Washington Airport, and driven south. We have been tracking them for three days now. Where did they lose them?"

"East of Elias, I am guessing, although I will have to go back to the Chief for specifics. The real question here is what we tell them. Agreed?"

"Absolutely," inserted Alice, "We do not want this investigation to get out of the bag until we know what they are planning. If you trust the Chief enough, give him a bare-bones understanding that we are trying to protect Johnson in this. No news reporters, no media; he keeps the information to himself. If he can't agree to that, then we give him nothing. Understood?"

From a Vantage Point

"No problem here," responded Cohen. "I'll call the chief and see what we can do." Cohen hung up the phone and decided to wait a few minutes before calling Chief Edwards back, organizing his thoughts on what to say.

State Road 61, West Virginia Hakim and his men, with Sira in the back seat, headed east on State Road 61, trying hard to avoid the possibility of being identified and possibly captured. Luckily, it was both a weekend, and the day after it snowed; the road had few cars, mostly pickup trucks from the local farms. At Dickinson, they reached the I-64 connection, which would take them back to White Sulphur Springs and beyond. The best thing for them right now was to return to Virginia, and head East, as quickly as possible with their valuable hostage.

Hakim looked back, seeing Sira behind the driver, arms crossed, and looking angry.

" That angry look does you no good, Sira," said Hakim, "Besides, you have nothing to fear, assuming, of course, that your lover does what he is supposed to do." Hakim laughed.

"He will kill you when he gets you," she responded. "You were supposed to be his friend, but you are nothing but a killer, and a coward as a man. You do not even have the courage to face him, a real man."

The other member of Hakim's team reached over and slapped Sira on the face. "Do not talk like that, you whore. You speak of courage, yet, you sleep around, and dishonor your betrothal. Better you should be stoned in the old way, or thrown from the car to die. You are nothing but a whore."

"Hold your tongue," admonished Hakim, "There will be plenty of time later, when we have both this woman and Will Johnson together. Then, there will be righteous retribution for their sins. For now, it is important that she not be harmed. She is a valuable asset for us. Have patience."

Both men went quiet. It was clear to Hakim they did not agree with him, but, for now, they would accept his leadership.

"Now, we have two needs," stated Hakim, "We need to find a place to stay, one that will not care if there are three men and a woman, and we need a different car. As we drive through White Sulphur Springs, we will make a change." At this point, they were about twenty miles from the city, and Hakim thought a great deal on how to arrange for their needs. He looked at the maps they had been given in Baltimore, and turned the map over; the other side contained several rental agencies, and one, A-1 Rentals, offered mini-vans as well. He noted the address, and turned the map over again to see where the place was on the map.

"I think I have a solution," said Hakim, looking carefully. "About five miles ahead is an exit, one which will take us to another state road, Route 60 into

From a Vantage Point

White Sulphur Springs. On that road is A-1 Rentals. We will drive along that road, after we get another vehicle until we reach the Virginia border. There is one of those welcome places over the Virginia border. There, we will stop and leave this car, as we did the other one."

"We will continue on the road to a place called Covington," continued Hakim. "There, we will find shelter for the night. Tomorrow, we go on to Washington to see our plan come to effect. Your destiny will be soon, my friends, and Mister Will Johnson will make it happen."

As they approached the exit into White Sulphur Springs, the car slowed, and the men became a bit apprehensive. They saw lights ahead for a police car, and were worried. Then, as they came closer, they realized there was an accident on the shoulder of the road, and they passed by it slowly, as did other cars wishing to exit at this point. Once they did so, they went down the small grade toward a crossroad, and, as Hakim instructed, turned left toward the city. Just ahead on the right was a fast-food restaurant. There, they parked their car, One of the men went in and purchased food, and, while he was in the restaurant, Hakim went next door to A-1 Rentals and quickly rented a van, using his American Express Card in the name of Amoud Said.

Returning with the van, everyone but a single driver moved over to the van, and the small caravan set off on the State route, seeing that it would eventually flow back into I-64, as they headed toward Covington, Virginia, about 30 miles away, and their last stop before heading to Washington, DC.

Sammi's Restaurant, Elias, West Virginia "Sammi, I'm going after them, whoever they are," said Will, excitedly, as he sat at a table in the otherwise empty restaurant.

"Mister Will," responded Sammi, "Is that wise? You should be here if she returns. She will want to see you."

"Sammi, it is time to be honest with each other. You know, I think, what is happening here. This is something the man I thought was a friend, Hakim al-Azahir, has cooked up, and you, Sira, and Hassan all had parts to play. The only problem was that you and Sira decided not to play his tune. Isn't that correct?"

"Well, Mister Will," responded Sammi, "It was correct. Hassan and Sira were sent here to do you harm, to get you to do Hakim's will. Hassan was a crazy person, but Sira, she had a heart, and she quickly changed her mind. She loves you, Mister Will."

"For myself, I am beholden to Hakim for this restaurant. He made the contacts with the missionary agency that helped me come here to work. When he called, I felt obligated to do his bidding, but then I met you, and realized you were a good man. I had no choice to do what I was told, but now I am afraid for the lady."

From a Vantage Point

"Sammi, I heard from Hakim yesterday. I know what he wants, and I am going to look for Sira, and go to Washington as he requires. I will agree to do what Hakim wishes to get Sira back, and to keep you two from problems with the police. For now, you must trust me; I will be back with Sira. All you can tell the police is that I have gone off to find her. Believe nothing you see in the news or on the television."

"Mister Will, I am very afraid for you and her. That man will kill you both." Sammi had tears in his eyes, and spoke in broken words.

"We will be fine Sammi. Everything will be fine." Will rose to leave, and he and Sammi hugged closely, Sammi wiping tears from his eyes.

"Come back, Mister Will. Come back," Sammi said, as he watched his friend go through the door, and over to his truck.

Department of Homeland Security, Washington DC "Hey Rick, look at this traffic," said one of the analysts working with Rick Alcorn. "We've got one of the cars, it seems."

"Where?" yelled Alcorn from his desk.

"In a visitor center in West Virginia, White Sulphur Springs, it looks like," Came the response.

"Hey guys, look at the center screen," said another of the analysts, putting a current news feed on the screen.

> "This is Allie Aldrich, WCHS Charleston, reporting on some curious things happening in the little town of Elias over the past few days. We hear from reputable sources of two occurences, involving a couple who came to Elias to work several months ago from Delaware."

> "One of these people, a man named Hassan Singh, according to a reputable source, knowledgeable on the circumstances, was the subject of a raid on a local restaurant in Elias. Sammi's Restaurant, a local favorite, employed this man Singh," she continued.

> "The raid, conducted by both the FBI and DHS, did not immediately find Singh, who escaped, hiding out in the woods along the State Road. After attacking a DHS agent, several days later, he tried to escape again, but was cornered in a field off the State Road east of Elias, and was killed in gunfire."

From a Vantage Point

"More curious," Aldrich added, "Was the abduction a day ago of Sira Suleiman, also an employee of Sammi's Restaurant, and allegedly engaged to Singh. She also worked on a local farm owned by Will Johnson, the local food cooperative manager. There is no reason given for her abduction by two men in an out-of-state car. They sped off with Ms. Suleiman, leaving her groceries on the sidewalk. The State police, as we understand it, are investigating."

"We tried to get confirmation from the FBI and DHS here in Charleston, along with the State Police, but all three had no comment. We will continue to update you as further information comes across the news desk. This is Allie Aldrich, WCHS-News. Now for the traffic with Bert Bings."

Before he had even finished listening to her statement, Alcorn had Alice Sawyer on the phone. "Alice, look at the news feed coming in."

"I have Rick. We have a leak in Elias. I told Anderson we would have a problem with the locals. Nothing much we can do now, though."

"We have the car they took off in," said Alcorn. "The Visitor Center in White Sulphur Springs reported an abandoned car in their parking lot. It matches the vehicle reported stolen. One more "X" for the map."

"What do you think you have then," asked Sawyer.

"Probably that they are heading back toward Virginia, Alice. If they have involved Johnson in their scheme, they might have taken the woman as insurance. At least that means they will keep her alive until they no longer have a use for her, or for Johnson for that matter."

"OK then, let's be on the watch for another replacement car. We have to assume they will continue to switch them in and out."

"Sure will, Alice. I have three analysts on this now. We'll find something."

"There goes my budget. You better find something," she responded.

"Hold a second Alice, will you?" said Alcorn, as he saw another of his men waving toward him, then yell some information over toward him.

"Alice, we might have lucked out again," said Alcorn. "A blue van was just rented in White Sulphur Springs, using an American Express card issued to Amoud Said, one of Hakim's aliases. We asked for the security footage, and they are getting it now. They have the new vehicle. The owner said they asked for a Virginia map. When he looked out at the arriving car, it was red, with four people inside, two in front and two in back, one a woman."

From a Vantage Point

"Good. Keep on it you guys. We must keep them in sight. Again, I want no arrest right now, unless they do something really stupid. I really want to catch them in the act, here in DC."

"No problem. We love to chase people here," responded Alcorn, as Alice Sawyer hung up her phone.

"OK guys, we have them in sight. Where are the next places we could see them on camera?"

Alice Sawyer picked up the phone shortly after her call with Alcorn and dialed up Anderson Cohen in Charleston, telling him to shut down any information, including anything to the Chief of Police in Elias.

Outside Elias, West Virginia Johnson's pickup truck sped down the State Road, picking up speed, then realizing he would do Sira or anyone else no good if he crashed. Slowing down, Will saw a pull-off, and stopped to think.

"What would Hakim do in this situation?' Will asked himself, trying to put his mind in Hakim's. "He would avoid any possibility of detection. That means no reads with cameras, or large numbers of police cars. If that is so, then he would certainly stay on the State Road if possible, since it parallels the Interstate, and then get on I-64 at the bend toward White Sulphur Springs. That's exactly what I will do," Will continued to muse.

Johnson restarted the engine of the truck, and moved out onto the road, going a bit slower this time, hoping to have enough luck to find Sira quickly, but, in his heart, he knew the end would come in Washington.

From a Vantage Point

Chapter 43 A Fateful Trip

The *Alexander* Hotel, Washington DC *The bulk mail truck had more difficulty than usual getting into the loading dock area this morning, one day before the Inauguration would have shut it down, just as the Secret Service does with all hotels on, or near the parade route. The two postal workers on the truck had to wait first for a National Foods truck, then a Prince Georges Beef truck to vacate lanes before they could back in the truck to unload their packages.*

Once they did so, both men went to the rear of the truck, one opened the wide door, and both took two-wheel moving dollies in preparation for off-loading the volume of packages they had, primarily for hotel guests. To them, all packages looked the same; some large, some small, some wrapped, and like three arriving this morning, some were wooden cartons. Whatever they were, the route was the same; go through the swinging doors to a doorway on the right marked "PRIVATE'. Inside was the storeroom for packages, which eventually would be moved upstairs to the package delivery area set aside for guests.

Hotel employees moved the packages from the storage area where the Postal Service employees stacked them, needing to register each package on a list containing the name of the hotel guest, room number, and expected date and time of delivery. The hotel employees updated the list twice each day, usually about an hour after the Postal Service completed its delivery.

It was not unusual for packages to stay in the storage area, especially if the guest was arriving more than a day later, but the Alexander, this time of year, was generally full, and room numbers were assigned in advance. The packages for guests not yet in the hotel went to a separate part of the storage room, sorted by room numbers to ease moving them up to the lobby level, and ultimately delivering them to guests.

On this day, hotel employees were already in the room, waiting for the Postal Service people, since they knew there would be many packages, and sorting, moving, and accounting for them would take more time than usual. A clipboard held the names of present and future guests, and the hotel staff quickly started separating the current guests' packages to expedite delivery. As they went through documenting what packages had arrived, they noticed two wooden boxes with the message 'HOLD FOR ARRIVAL MISTER WILL JOHNSON.'

Looking at their list of guests, the two men went through the pages, found the section where names began with 'J', and quickly located a Will Johnson arriving on the following day. In this instance, however, there was a note in the comments section saying, 'Notify Xanaria- Security on arrival packages.' One of the men thought that a bit odd, but the other simply shrugged, put the boxes

From a Vantage Point

aside, and spoke into his cellphone intercom, telling Joe Xanaria the packages he tagged had arrived.

"Where are they?" asked Xanaria, as he arrived at the storage room.

"Right here," answered the workman, pointing to two boxes over in the corner. Xanaria went over to where the boxes were stacked, looked them over, and picked up the side of one with the handle built into the wall of the box.

"Leave them there, and don't move them until I tell you," barked Xanaria, making it clear the seriousness of his point. Then, he turned to go back to his own office on the same floor. Inside, he dialed up Roger Doucette over at the FBI.

"Roger," said Xanaria into his phone, "The boxes have arrived. I had them separated from others in the storage area. When can you guys come, and check them out?"

"I can get a team there this morning, Joe," Doucette responded. "What do they look like?"

"Like two packing boxes to be Roger. Made of wood, with reinforced corners and cover. Sealed shut with nails it looks like, and not very heavy, by the way. I picked one up slightly."

"All right then, Joe, we'll get a team out there shortly. Can you arrange for us to use the loading dock area?" asked Doucette.

"Sure, but do me a favor, will you? Come with an unmarked truck or van, something guests will not recognize or get excited about. The Gm is already on me, and the one thing I don't need is more angst."

Doucette smiled, and then laughed a bit, "Sorry Joe. Of course, we can do that. We get similar requests every once-in-a-while. We have a dark blue, unmarked van for just that purpose. It still has all our equipment, just not the advertising. How about 10:30 AM or so?"

"That's good. I will make sure the dock has a space for you from 10 AM on," answered Xanaria. "See you folks then. Just have whoever comes tell the dock worker to call me when they arrive."

"Good Joe," added Doucette, "I'll be over there myself. We have some logistics to discuss as well. See you then."

Along Interstate 64 As Will Johnson sped along the Interstate, he continued to hope that, somehow, he could stop Hakim, and free Sira from her captors. He knew that would be difficult, yet he had to try.

Johnson crossed the border into Virginia just about thirty minutes after Hakim and his friends. As he drove along, he looked from side to side, trying to see into the cars in the hopes he might find them, but with no success. The men with Sira in the van, along with the other car, had turned off on the exit to Covington, Virginia. Sometime later, Will Johnson passed the same point, keeping on the road toward I-81, and eventually Washington, DC.

From a Vantage Point

Hakim looked at his map. "We will take Exit 14 off this road," he announced to the driver of the van. "Slow down so Akram will see us, and know we are turning off the road." The driver, seeing the exit sign coming up, slowed the van as he moved to the right lane, and tried to see the other car in his side mirror.

"I see him," the driver said to Hakim, "He is behind us two cars."

"Good, we turn at the exit, go down the ramp, and turn right. You will see a sign for a large shopping center on the right. There, we stop."

Alexander Hotel, Washington, DC "Glad you could accommodate us so quickly Joe'" said Roger Doucette, as he left the van, which had pulled up in to the Loading dock area of the hotel. "We really support your assistance on this," he continued.

"No problem, Roger," countered Xanaria. "We want this to come out right as much as you folks do. Bring your team in and let's get busy here."

The FBI team came onto the loading platform through the rear doors of the van. The team pushed a small walkway up from the floor of the van onto the main part of the dock, then emerged one at a time with packs and toolkits.

"Where do we do this?" asked Doucette.

"Right this way guys," responded Xanaria, pointing toward the rear of the dock.

"By the way guys," announced Doucette, "This is Joe Xanaria, the Director of Security here at the hotel, and a retired member of the Counter-terrorism team over at DHS. We lucked out here, be happy."

Each of the team members shook Xanaria's hand as they walked by, two men and two women, in addition to Doucette, who followed along with Xanaria, and they went further into the dock area.

"We are going to the door on the right in the back, guys," said Xanaria, and he and Doucette caught up with the team. Xanaria took out a ring of keys, found the one he needed, and turned the lock to open the door. "Inside at the back are the two boxes we received early this morning."

"Two boxes?" responded Doucette. "Are you sure there are not three?"

"Are you expecting another one Roger?" asked Xanaria, looking puzzled.

"Not necessarily. Some of the information we had indicated there might be three," answered Doucette. "Ok gang, let's look at what we have, shall we?"

One of the team members took the large toolkit he held, opened it, and pulled out a long, rectangular instrument, hooking it to a laptop he placed on the floor, turning both pieces of equipment on. Placing it on the top, right end of the first box, he carefully moved it slowly across the top of the box. As he did, the laptop screen lit up with vague images of what was inside.

"It will take about thirty seconds for the image to normalize sir," the agent said to Doucette. "See, the picture is coming a bit clearer now. It looks like the inside has some kind of covering, probably aluminum or another alloy, so we won't get pics crystal clear, but we will see what's inside."

"I can see that," responded Doucette. "Are those sections of pipe of some kind?"

"They are, sir," answered the agent, "Probably a kind of PVC or plastic. It reduces the image. There seem to be three sections in the box, and probably layers in there as well. In a second, I'll sweep one side left to right to see what the layers look like." The agent was about to do that second sweep, when he saw something else.

"OK, sir, we have something else," stated the agent, "Something more important here. It looks like there are some ammo charges here."

"What does that mean?" asked Xanaria. "Do we have something that will go off in there?"

"Sure do, Sir, but not by itself. We can take care of that when we open the box," responded the agent, as he hit the 'ENTER' button on the laptop, and started to scan the sides. "I'm saving the pics here, by the way."

Eventually, over the next hour, the agents scanned both boxes, making sure no trip wires or other devices were present, and then carefully opened each box, removing the pieces of pipe, and the plastic-wrapped explosives carefully, examining them, and then returning them to their place in the same order.

The explosives were removed, replaced by a small charge of black powder; enough to make a lot of noise, and even shatter a window, but do no major damage. Then, the boxes were carefully resealed and placed back against the wall where they had been placed originally by the dock space workers. Everything was left the way it was for the expected arrival of Will Johnson.

Covington, Virginia "This is where we leave the car," announced Hakim, looking over the vast parking lot in the shopping center. "Take everything, and leave it near a light post, in the center of the lot. These fools will take a long time to find it, with the numbers of customers who come and go here. This leaves a mark for us."

The others did not know that Hakim al-Azahir was born here, in Covington, not Yemen, as he liked to claim. His family came here from Syria during the early 1950s, and Hakim was born in a small hospital nearby. He was an American citizen, by birth. Eventually, he was drafted for the Vietnam War, but deserted quickly, going to Europe to avoid capture, and settling in Sweden where there was no extradition treaty for war resisters.

Eventually meeting up with two fellow deserters, Josh Giddons and Will Johnson, they traveled the world together, mostly in Africa and the Middle East as soldiers-for-hire. Will eventually returned to the US, received clemency, and went back to his family's farm, but the other continued on their quests. This was

From a Vantage Point

Hakim's first opportunity to return, and his desire was to leave the city as quickly as possible.

One of his men moved the car, after carefully cleaning it, and assuring there was nothing left of their personal items, found a tall light pole where he could park the car, then returned to where the rest were waiting in the van. Once inside, Hakim took one last look, closed the side panel door, and they drove off, headed back to the Interstate, toward Washington DC. There, they would meet Will Johnson, who was about to become a terrorist.

Alexander Hotel, **Washington DC** "Well, I feel better now, I guess," offered Joe Xanaria, "At least the bombs are gone. This will be interested to explain to the GM."

"No problem, Joe," responded Doucette, "Happy to go see him with you and explain everything. Right now, I need one more favor, really two. I need to arrange for a room next to Johnson's, hopefully with a door between the two."

That's doable," said Xanaria, "What's the other thing?"

"We will need to put people in the hotel. Preferably, they will be special security people on your staff for the Inauguration—something you usually do, but this time they will be FBI and DHS."

"I can work that as well. We have already hired a bunch of extra staff, but a few more will never be noticed. Right now, my biggest concern is what will happen here Roger? What do you see is the scenario as it unfolds?"

"What I hope, Joe, is that Johnson arrives, goes to his room, and waits for the right time. Eventually, he will ask for the boxes, and they will be delivered—but by two of our people. They will survey who besides Johnson might be in the room, and then leave. That's when we start being concerned by the audio, and the cameras. We want to know exactly what he will do, who calls him, or joins him, and where he expects to go afterward. Johnson will not escape, but I would truly like to get his handlers as well."

"OK, so what do you want from me?"

"I need to make sure that Johnson has no problem getting into the hotel, we have the opportunity to wire his room for sound, and wire the parking lot, as well as other places he might go, like the roof, for sound and video, so we get him in the act."

"Works for me. Let's get that moving," responded Xanaria. "I'll work out each with the GM. You won't have a problem, once I wave the national security flag. He understands that."

Xanaria made certain the room adjoining Will Johnson' was not assigned, as 'Under Repairs', and the FBI/DHS team wired both rooms for sound and video. They also connected the cameras in the garage, and those on the roof to a central communications console in the room next to Will's. That way, they could monitor everything, yet still have a staff concentrated on where they felt the major attempt at damage might occur.

Finally, after about six hours, they were ready. Doucette and Joe Xanaria walked through the various parts of the protective blanket they had laid throughout the hotel, and they were satisfied. Now, it was time to wait for Johnson, and anyone else involved.

It was early evening when Will Johnson's pickup truck arrived at the *Alexander*. As he had done so many times in the past, he pulled into the parking garage first, found a space, and then took his luggage to the lobby to register. The attendant at the garage knew him well by now, and gave him the ticket he needed to turn in at the desk, passing a couple of minutes in small conversation on weather and families. Will truly appreciated how well he was treated by the hotel staff.

Coming up to the lobby, he walked over to the main desk to register. One of the employees was familiar, and greeted him warmly. The others on the desk that evening he did not know.

"May I help you sir?" asked the man in the middle of the desk.

"Yes, I believe you have a reservation for Johnson?" he asked.

"Hello, Mister Johnson. Glad to have you back," said one of the female front desk staff, who had just walked out from the back room. "Staying through the Inauguration?"

"I'll be here for probably three or four days this time," came his answer.

"Please sign the check-in card, Mister Johnson," said the clerk. "Do you have your parking ticket as well, so that we can enter the information for you?"

"Sure do," Will responded, "Here it is," he added, pulling the ticket out of his shirt pocket.

"Thank you, sir," the clerk responded. Somehow, Will felt a sense of difference from other visits 'perhaps it is the season, and the new staff,' he thought to himself, 'But there seems to be a chill today. Wonder what is going on?'

Shrugging his shoulders, he passed it off on the busy season, and looked forward to his visit, even with the problems he had to deal with on this visit. At least he was off the road and in a place where he could hopefully do something to get Sira back.

"We have your usual room, sir," offered the clerk, "This is a very busy season, and your room has a magnificent vista on the capital, the parade, and all the other festivities. I must admit to being a bit jealous."

"Thank you. I love the room, and its view is magnificent."

"Can we send your bags up for you, sir?"

From a Vantage Point

"Sure. I'm going to walk up one to the bar, and have a drink. I'll come back down to give the porter a tip. Thanks for your help." Will waved to the clerk who knew him, and headed over to the stairs to go up to the main bar.

"Well, Mister Johnson," said Dave, the bartender, "Interesting to have you in town this weekend. I know by now you hate the big crowds. What changed your mind?"

"Dave, I just decided to see an Inauguration. Never had had the opportunity, and this seemed like a good time. Is business good so far?"

"Sure is, sir," responded Dave, "This week I will make more money in tips than the rest of the year. Wish it happened more than once every four years, though."

"I understand, my friend," responded Will, "Hopefully, this year will be as good as in the past. With some of the President's we've had lately, it might be better to elect them every two years. That way, we don't have them screwing up as long. But then, that's just me speaking, and even without a drink."

"Your usual, sir?" Dave asked.

"Absolutely, Absolute, Dave," Will kidded.

"Coming right up, sir," came the response, as Dave grabbed the bottle of Absolute Vodka to pour him a good-sized shot, straight-up.

Will sat for the greater part of an hour, sipping his drink, ordering a second, and having a great discussion with Dave, the bartender. Finally, it was time to go to his room.

"Dave, would you send me up a bottle of Absolute, a small one, and put in on my tab?" asked Will.

"Sure, Mister Johnson. Anything for you," answered Dave, who rang it up, and gave the bill to Will to sign. Will added a good tip, and walked back toward the stairs and the main lobby.

Over in the corner of the bar were two people, a man and a woman, seemingly in deep conversation. The real object of their conversation was Will Johnson. As he started to leave, the woman spoke into a small microphone on the inside of a small brooch she wore on her jacket. "The subject is moving. Looks like down to the lobby. The conversation says he is going to his room." *Then, the two went back to their drinks and other conversation.*

Along Interstate Route 64 *Sitting in the back of a closed van is not a comfortable journey. The van Hakim rented was one of those with two inside seats, a window in a side door, but limited access otherwise to a view of the landscape as they traveled. Picking this van, Hakim explained they needed it mostly for transporting a small group to and from a picnic event at a church, just north of Lexington. Hakim counted on his looks; so many other immigrants were settled in Covington over the years, an accepting community, that the owner of* *the rental agency thought nothing of what would usually be a simple rental. The man, after all, used American Express, and it was accepted, which meant he would be paid quickly.*

Hakim assumed all along that his journey would eventually be discovered, documented and followed. In fact, he left clues, including the one which would eventually be discovered in his own hometown in Covington. He expected the Federal people to be bright, and intuitive, but they were not, at least in his mind, quite as capable as himself. For now, at least, he was ahead of them, and, if he could stay that way until Washington, he had a chance of success.

Hakim looked over at Sira, sitting on the rear seat by the wall with no window, and asked, "Why did you fail me, Sira?"

Sira looked over at Hakim and responded, "You are the failure, Hakim. What you do is against our Holy Law. You know it, but you twist everything you do to claim that you are doing God's will. That is blasphemy, and you are surrounded by it, as if you are in a large lake, about to drown."

"Will Johnson," Sira continued, "is a man with virtue, a man with courage, and most importantly, a man who believes in people. His people do not hate him as yours do you, instead, they admire him. It is very hard to change a person with a good soul."

"Do you really believe that Sira?" asked Hakim, "Or are you so inflamed in your passion for him, that you cannot see your way to your duty? You were sent to make sure this man Will Johnson would do as I wished, and yet he does not. He will shortly, but that is because he is a weak man, and cares for you. He cares enough that he will do as I ask simply to save your life. That is a weak man." Hakim laughed as he turned back to watch the road, the added, "And weak men do things they would not normally do."

Alexander Hotel, Washington, DC "Dave, I think I will take my tab, if you please," said Will Johnson to the bartender. "It's been a long day and I think it's time to go upstairs, order some room service, and turn on the TV, as if there were any news worth listening to in this town."

"You are right there, Mister Johnson," responded the bartender, and he punched Johnson's ticket, and printed out the bill. Will added a generous tip, signed it and started to walk from the bar.

"Have a great evening Mister Johnson," called Dave the bartender, as Will walked through the door toward the stairs to go down to the lobby.

Through the earphones, the couple in the corner wore, a voice crackled, saying, "We have him in sight coming down the stairs."

Walking toward the bell captain's desk, Will stopped and asked who had taken his luggage to his room. The man at the desk responded, "It was me, sir. My name is Jimmy. I'm new here."

From a Vantage Point

'Well Jimmy, thanks for taking up my luggage." Will handed the man a five-dollar bill, then said good evening, and turned to go to the desk to get his room key. The clerk handed Johnson his key, and Will started over toward the elevators.

"Oh, Mister Johnson, I see you have some large packages, would you like the staff to get them up to you?"

Will turned, and looked at the desk clerk, saying, "Not tonight, but could you have whatever they are sent up in the morning?" The clerk nodded, and Will stepped into the elevator, pushing the button for his floor. Once inside, Will leaned back toward the wall of the elevator, and thought to himself, 'Whatever is in the boxes, must have something to do with Hakim's scheme. I better play along, at least for now. I'll worry about it tomorrow,' he added in his mind, as the door opened on his floor.

"It's post time," announced one of the FBI agents in the room next to Will Johnson's, as he heard the elevator door open. On a table in the room, a computer screen lit up, showing the corridor, and Johnson walking down toward his room, pull out his door keycard, and insert it into the door slot. Pulling down on the door handle, Will opened the door; as he did so, another screen lit up on the table showing the main area of Will's hotel room.

Wil looked around, went toward the bedroom, saw his bags on the racks, and looked to see that his clothes were in the closet. Coming back into the living room area, he sat down on the sofa, picked up the television remote, and turned on the TV. As the sound began to blare, the audio connections in the next room came alive.

"We have him on HD," said the agent, nodding to the others. "We are good to go." The rest of the people in the room began to laugh, and Doucette took up repeating the agent's speech, saying, "Houston, we are good to go. We have lift-off," then added, "Now all we need is a good orbit." Everyone laughed, but quickly realized they might be heard in the next room.

"Ok folks, we have this under control," responded Doucette, "Let's be vigilant here. We want al-Azahir and whoever he has with him, and we want them in the act. We maintain communication between the three lookout points. You Jed," he said, pointing to the agent monitoring the screens, "Have the point. Everything comes to you, the garage control people, and the roof control people all coordinate through this room, and that's you. We want to know and record every move. When we move in, we have them cold. Everybody understand?"

The agents in the room nodded, and Doucette heard as well from the other two posts, connected by their communications system.

"Everybody keep your buds in, and your brain working. If you do, we break a big operation here. We want no more damage than needed Let's do it."

From a Vantage Point

A-1 Rentals, Covington, Virginia "Are you the manager here?" asked a man, walking into the office at A-1 Rentals.

"That depends on who wants to know," responded the man behind the desk, dressed in a pair of greyish-brown chino pants, and a light blue shirt, with "A-1 Rentals" emblazoned over the left pocket.

"Department of Homeland Security," came his answer quickly, as the man pulled out his credentials and badge. "Anderson Cohen, Special Agent in the Charleston, West Virginia Office. I need to see some records on your recent rental of a van."

"Which van? I have a lot of them," the manager responded.

"Dark panel van, rented yesterday. The person used an American Express Card, a platinum one, first one I've seen, but it went through like crap through a goose. What's the problem?"

"Might be or might not be a problem. I need to see the rental agreement please."

"Sure, right away," said the manager, a bit un-nerved and anxious, wondering what he had done. This was also the first time he ever met anyone from Homeland Security up close.

"Here it is," the manager added, "All in order. The guy had a valid driver license, a credit card, and I rented it to him. Anything wrong?"

"Not sure," said the agent, taking the rental form, and snapping a picture of it with his phone. "Where is this address?" the agency asked.

"That's over in the part of town where we have many recent immigrants. The guy looked like he was one of them; nothing out of the ordinary. I get rentals from them all the time. I must admit, though, I never had one named Said before." The man shrugged his shoulders as if it was simply a normal rental.

"Do you keep your security cameras up-to-date and running?" the agent asked next.

"Sure do. These are set on twelve-hour cycles, on a DVR machine in the back. I date and keep all the discs."

"Good, I'll need the one covering the rental. It will be returned to you."

"I don't know," offered the manager, "Don't you have to have a warrant or something?" he asked.

"You are correct, sir. We do need a warrant; here it is," responded Cohen, handing him the document. "Now, the DVR please?"

"Right away, sir," answered the manager, who opened the drawer of his desk, looked through a stack of discs, and pulled out the one marked the day before. "Here it is, sir. I would like it back, or, if you want to wait a minute or two, I can copy it for you."

From a Vantage Point

"Appreciate that. I'll wait," said Cohen. The manager went to the back of the office and soon brought out a copy of the DVR. "This works," the manager said to Cohen.

"I know," responded Cohen, "Watched you make the copy through the glass. Appreciate your efforts. Have a great day. Is this your card?" Cohen asked, picking up a business card.

"Yes, sir, it is" the manager answered, "Please take it in case you need to talk to me again. I am here every day."

"Great, and thanks again," said Cohen, turning to walk out of the office.

Reaching his car, parked in the rental lot, Cohen picked up his cell phone, called a number, and was soon on the line with Rick Alcorn.

Rick," said Cohen into his phone, "This is Anderson Cohen, and I have some news for you on the van."

Along the Interstate, Virginia "We are nearing someplace called Clifton Forge, Hakim," commented the driver of the van. "Do you have a wish to stop for a few moments.

"We still have a long way to go, even before we get to the roads we need to pass to get to Washington" Hakim responded, looking out the window on the right. "It appears there is a storm coming. We need to move along. If it is rain, that is one thing, but if it is snow, we do not want to be too far west, or we may not make it to our destination today. We will stop along the next Interstate, Route 81"

The driver nodded, and increased his speed a bit as they started to see signs of local towns and other attractions.

Over the next nearly three hours, the van moved along I-64 to the junction of I-81, and then north, toward their ultimate destination, Washington DC. They eventually stopped outside Staunton for some food and the rest rooms, along with re-filling the gas tank, and then got back on the road. It was late afternoon when they reached the interchange taking them East on I-66, where they saw their first signs toward Washington.

Hakim looked at his watch, realized the hour, and hoped they would get to their destination without hitting too much traffic, a bane of the Washington area. He arranged for them to stay in the Northeast of the city, out of downtown, so they could avoid detection.

Department of Homeland Security, Washington DC "Hey Anderson, what's happening?" asked Alcorn, as he picked up his phone.

"Hey, Rick, as I said, I have some news for you on the van."

"Great, what do you know?" asked Alcorn.

"The rental agreement is on the way. Late model, perhaps 2015, with the vin number. Can you use that to pinpoint them?"

"Sure can. Let me pull up the info on the van," responded Alcorn. "Here it is now, dark blue, West Virginia plates, two-door, with side panel. No windows – like a utility. Ah, here is what I want," said Alcorn. "Anderson, this van is new enough I can access its chip, as long as its running, and it seems to be right now. Somewhere around Clifton Forge, in Virginia."

"Coming East, then," answered Cohen.

"Sure is," and that's what we want. Thanks Anderson. We'll monitor them from here."

"Good, I'm going back to peaceful West Virginia. Have a great day."

"Bye friend," responded Alcorn, "You can come visit us occasionally, you know."

"And leave all this peace and quiet?" laughed Cohen. "Not on your life, unless, of course, the government is paying for the trip." They both laughed as they ended their call, Alcorn adding a new "X" to his map before returning to his camera reviews.

Interstate-66, Fairfax, Virginia Darkness had fallen by the time the van crossed the state, and was nearly at the end of I-66, headed into Washington DC. The van made only one more stop during the trip, picking an exit near Gainesville, where there were several fast food places, interspersed with gas stations. The van, and the people inside, needed both. This was their last stop, and one of the men with Hakim bought a large bag of groceries—mostly munchies—for their hotel room, wherever that would be.

As Hakim looked at his map, they arrived at I-495, the beltway around Washington, and Hakim told Akram the driver to go through toward the city, since it was a much shorter distance to their destination. From the ending point of I-66, they travelled a short distance down the George Washington Parkway to its intersection with I-395, and then into central Washington. Following the I-395 signs through the District, they ended up in the large underpass going under several major federal buildings, then up again at New York Avenue in the Northeast.

Akram became confused several times, but Hakim encouraged him to 'look for the signs', and 'stay to right and you will go the right way.' Eventually they reached the northern end of New York Avenue, and there, on the right was the Cascade Motel. Hakim told his driver to pull into the parking lot, which he did. Hakim left the van to go into the motel, where he spoke with the manager, shaking his hand several times, before coming back to where the van was stopped.

He motioned at Akram to roll down the window, which he did.

From a Vantage Point

"Akram, pull the van around to the rear of the motel. Our rooms are there." Having said that, Hakim started to walk the distance himself, going to the left front of the motel and walking down a short side drive, then taking a right. The van followed slowly. Finally, Hakim stopped and walked toward a room; Akram pulled into a parking space in front of the room.

As Hakim opened the side door, he pointed to the building, saying, "These are our rooms, number 121 and number 122. Sira, you will come with me to room 121, and the others will go to room 122. Do not leave once you are settled. No one must see us. The manager will protect us, as he is one of us. Others will not be so kind to you, if they know who you are. Be careful."

Akram opened the rear door of the van with his key, and started to unload the bags the men carried during their trip. Sira, the last to leave the van, carried no bags, simply moving with Hakim toward the door at room 121.

The next morning, Hakim walked out of the room, leaving Sira in the bed, where she had slept the previous night, and tried to figure out the next steps. When they came to the motel, and entered the room, Hakim saw there was only one bed, and despite his feelings that that bed belonged to the man, he opted to give Sira the opportunity to have a sleep night, not knowing what Will Johnson would do, and whether it might be her last sleep night.

"Sira, it is time to meet the world," Hakim announced, as he came back into the room. "We have only one day for Will Johnson to do what I wish, and it is important that you understand the consequence."

Sira looked at him, as she rose from her bed, covering herself with the covers, and responded," Why do you choose to act like an animal, Hakim? What is it that tells you that you need to be unmerciful to people to be important? Are you so insecure in your life that you need to hurt people to be important? This is not Islam, this is your ego," Sira shouted to him.

"Shut up, woman," he responded, "You are lucky you are still alive. If it were my wish, you would have been dead on the street in Elias, a demonstration of the will of Al'lah. Instead, I kept you alive, a whore, and a disrespectful one. Be happy you are not dead. Get up, and prepare for the day."

"How am I to prepare, Hakim, I have no change of clothes. I can only wash and wear what I have. Is that Islam?"

"Hakim threw her a bag. She looked inside and found clothes, traditional clothes, and looked back at him with dismay.

"These are the clothes of a woman in the most extreme circumstances. I will not wear a hajib, nor an all-covering veil. I am not one of your concubines, Hakim," she answered.

"Then wear your clothes on your back, if you choose. It is no matter to me," responded Hakim, expressing his disdain.

From a Vantage Point

Sira went to the bathroom, closed the door, and locked it, hoping that, as she took a shower, and cleaned up as best she could, he would not interrupt her. Entering the warm shower, Sira thought only of Will Johnson, not the predicament she was in.

Hakim took the opportunity to think about his next steps, while she was in the bathroom, and what he needed to do to ensure Will Johnson's acceptance of his demands. Knowing he had only one chance at success, he had to push forward, trying to force Johnson to do what he wished, and then successfully escape. That would not be easy.

Picking up the phone, Hakim looked at a note he pulled from his pocket, and dialed a number. The response came as, "This is the Alexander Hotel, can I help you?"

"Yes," responded Hakim, "Please connect me to Mister Johnson's room."

"We have several Mister Johnson's," said the operator, "Which one would you wish?"

"Mister Will Johnson," answered Hakim, "Please connect me with Mister Will Johnson."

"Please wait a moment, and I will connect you," answered the operator. Then, Hakim listened to music for a moment.

"Will Johnson," said the voice on the phone.

"You are there. I am proud of you, Will Johnson," said Hakim. "You are ready to do All'ah's will, praise be his name forever."

"Stop with the religious dribble Hakim," Will answered. "You could not care less if All'ah appreciates your work or not. You only appreciate the damage you do to others. What do you want?"

"You know what I want, Will Johnson. I expect you to do what you are told, and that is to do what I wish."

"All right Hakim," responded Will, "What is it that you, the phony prophet, wants me to do and why?"

Hakim answered, obviously angered, "You will tell the hotel you wish to have some boxes I have sent to you delivered to your room. Those boxes contain parts and instructions on what you will do. When you receive them, you will unpack them, and read the instructions. At exactly 12:30PM on Inauguration day, you will execute the actions you are told to do. Do you understand?" asked Hakim.

"I will understand better when I get the boxes, and figure out the perverse activity you want to conduct against your own country. I might do it, or I might not. It depends on what it is you want me to do. Otherwise, come and do it yourself," Will Johnson answered.

Sira, meanwhile, had emerged from the bathroom, her hair wrapped in a towel, and a bathrobe around her body.

From a Vantage Point

"Come here Sira," demanded Hakim. "Speak to your lover. Tell him what he must do," spouted Hakim. He handed her the phone, twisting her arm to point out that she was still vulnerable to his wrath.

"Will, it is Sira," she said quickly.

"Sira, are you all right?" Will interjected quickly.

"I am all right," she answered, "Do not do what this fiend wants you to do. Be a good American for your friends." Hakim ripped the phone from her hand.

"If you listen to her, you are both dead, and painfully," Hakim shouted. "You will do what I wish, for the sake of both of you. I will put her in the hotel with you, and if you do not do what I wish, I will send you both to hell. Think well, Will Johnson." At that moment, Hakim cut off the phone.

The agents in the next room recorded everything and sat amazed.

"This guy Hakim is crazy," one of the agents exclaimed. "He is not stable, and the guy next door is a dead man if this action goes south."

"True," responded Doucette, "That's why we replaced the munitions in the boxes. The trouble is, we don't know that these are the only arms. We can't trust this guy al-Azahir, and we have to be watching very closely," he added.

Will hung up the phone, then pressed one of the intercom buttons, calling down to the front desk.

"This is Mister Johnson," he said, "Please send the boxes up we discussed yesterday. I'm ready to deal with them now."

National Security Agency, Ft. Meade, Maryland Eldon Zamboni sat at his desk, looking at a sheaf of papers, more staring than reading. Reaching over toward the side of his desk, Zamboni picked up the phone, dialed a number, and waited patiently for a response.

"Alice Sawyer, can I help you?"

"Alice, this is Eldon. I just received a transcript of some message traffic you might have an interest in reading. I've just sent it over via the secure line, so it should be coming up for you."

Sawyer turned from her desk to her credenza, looked at the computer screen, and pulled out a small drawer with her keyboard. "I have it Eldon. Wow, this is interesting. When did this conversation come over?" She read the transcript through quickly.

> *[Begin Recording]*
> *[Dialing] International Number*
> *[Ringing]*
> *"This is Ali. Give me Amid immediately."*
> *[Pause]*
> *"How are you doing?"*

> "Not well. I am departing for the United States. It will be hours before I arrive. Do you know where Hakim is now?"
>
> "No. He eluded our people in Frankfurt, but we understand he took two of his men with him, and they are traveling together through Lisbon to Boston. Where he goes from there, we do not know."
>
> "I am concerned, Amid, that he is playing us, and we are falling into his trap. What about this man Johnson, the one in Washington?"
>
> "He is a sheep, being pushed to the slaughter, but, if I know Hakim, he will be used badly first, then killed. You must be careful as well."
>
> "I will my uncle, with the help of Al'lah, may he be praised forever. I must go. The plane will leave soon."
>
> "Peace to you, my nephew."
>
> [Dial tone]
>
> [END]

"There is no time or date stamp on this Eldon. When was it transcribed?"

"Three days ago. It just crossed my desk," he responded.

"Great. What do we know about Ali in New York, then?"

"Good news, and possibly bad news," came the answer. "He arrived at JFK in New York on an Egypt Air Flight with a diplomatic passport. He was detained at JFK by ICE, claimed diplomatic immunity, and was vouched for by the Egyptian Embassy to the UN. Later that evening, he was put back on a plane to Egypt, orders of the State Department, and left the country."

"You said good and bad Eldon?"

"Sure. I think he was here to either make sure that Hakim's scheme was successful, or kill him, and stop any further debacles. What little we heard at JFK of the discussion between Ali and the Egyptian Security people was that, and I quote, 'this is the last time the Government will support you in this status. Go home, and stay there,' end quote."

"You may be right here, Eldon. Thanks for the transcript, and the call. I just wish he had said more about Hakim's plans. By the way, why the delay in getting this to us?"

"There was a big delay in getting to all of us, Alice. It just arrived on my desk less than an hour ago, while I was at a meeting. Somebody here is either clamming up, or losing their sharp edge. We'll figure that out in due time. Sorry for the delay, though. I know how much this means. Talk to you soon."

"Have a great day, and thanks Eldon," responded Alice, as they ended the call.

From a Vantage Point

Alice looked again at the message, still wondering what the hold was between Hakim and Johnson. With only a bit more than a day before the Inauguration activities start, she had little time to worry about; she had to focus on preventing what might be a catastrophe.

Cascade Motel, Washington DC Hakim, his two men, and Sira huddled together in Hakim's room to discuss their plans. With only one day left before the Inauguration began, they had to make up for lost time spent trying to convince Johnson to do their bidding, and what part they would play in the events.

Hakim brought out a map from his backpack, and laid it on the bed, opening it as he did so. It was a sketch of the area between the Capitol and the White House, covering both Pennsylvania and Constitution Avenues, along with many of the buildings on the route.

"This is the route," started Hakim, pointing on the sketch with a pen from the hotel, which he picked up from the bedside table. "We have friends who listen, and they tell us that there will be many guards and shooters atop the government buildings along Pennsylvania and Constitution Avenues," added Hakim, pointing with his pen.

"We have Johnson in a room facing the Mall, here," he continued, pointing to the roughed in location. "The men on the buildings will be looking for people on rooftops, and scanning windows to see shooters. We will do no shooting. We will send rockets toward the Mall, and disrupt their Inauguration. That will tell the world we can go and do what we wish."

"When we arrive, we will go to the parking lot behind the *Alexander* Hotel. It is here," he said, pointing to the *Alexander* and the lot next to it on the map. "There is a ramp to take us down to the lower level. There, we will park the van, and you, Akram and myself, will take the box in the van to the roof. The door to the roof is shielded from view, and there is a large front that is high enough to conceal us. We will set up our weapon there, behind the façade. Johnson has instructions to set up and blow his weapons at exactly 12:05PM. We will do the same. All will be aimed toward the mall."

"Once we have fired, we will leave everything, and go back to the door, down to the garage, and drive away. By the time the government people get to the hotel, they will think that Johnson is the bomber, and they will pay no attention to us in our van. We will leave, and drive away to another location. Johnson will be blamed."

"Hakim, what if they block the streets?" asked Akram.

"I expect they will block the streets, my friend. I am counting on it. We are two streets away, and what we know from others is that there will be high security on the two main streets, the hotel tops, and other measures. We can use either of two exits from the parking area; one down toward 14th Street, and the

From a Vantage Point

other from G Street. We will use G Street so that we can go away from the area quickly."

The men shook their heads, and nodded their approval of the plan.

"Good, now we go to breakfast, and then we will drive through the area in the center of town so it will be known to us tomorrow." Hakim folded up his map, placed it back into his backpack, and rose to leave. The rest followed, including Sira, who had little choice but to follow and hope for an eventual escape.

Department of Homeland Security, Washington DC As everyone filed into the conference room, Alice sat, waiting for an update from the staff on their progress in locating and stopping the terrorists. She had already been briefed by Richard Peabody and his agents on the actions they took at the *Alexander*, gratified to know at least the location of the expected activity, but still concerned that the main players were yet to be identified and found.

"All right, let's get organized here," started Alice, "We have one day left before the Inauguration. Most of you have been doing same hours as me, so you know the around-the clock meetings and calls are rapidly sapping everything out of us. Nonetheless, we must be able to ensure, along with the FBI, that this event goes as planned, and with unexpected hitches."

"Just a short while ago, I heard from NSA that we intercepted the nephew of Amid Fatoullah, and sent him packing back to Cairo. I've asked State to make sure he is on the No-fly list, but this time he came in as a diplomat. Someone in the Egyptian Government gave him UN diplomatic credentials, which have now been revoked."

"Bottom line here, ladies and gentlemen, is the seriousness of our effort. If this guy came to the US, you can be sure it was to make sure things went according to plan. We still have Hakim and his people on the loose. Rick, what about that chase?"

"Well Alice," started Alcorn, "We know he is here in DC. We followed this guy down from Boston, through Philadelphia, and Baltimore and, with the assistance of the FBI and local law enforcement, we closed three cell operations. He left Baltimore headed for DC, we thought, but there was a detour, to West Virginia."

"Let me talk to that, Alice, if I may," interrupted Anderson Cohen. "Two men, probably Hakim's grabbed a young woman, Sira Suleiman, on the streets of Elias, a couple of days ago, then fled East. We later found their car in a parking lot in White Sulphur Springs, but where we believe they met up with Hakim, and moved on into Virginia."

"Yes, they did," continued Alcorn, "We now know they stopped in Covington, rented a van, using Hakim's American Express card, under the name Amoud Said, and later, after a real search in Covington, found their original car in a

From a Vantage Point

Walmart parking lot. They didn't even both to wipe down the car, just left it under a tall light pole."

"Sounds like they wanted us to find it, Rick?" asked Alice.

"Just like they did the other vehicles," added another of the analysts, "Seems like they are waving their exploits under our nose, really." Some of those in the room snickered at the comment.

"Ok," answered Alice, "So they are in a van, all four people, is that right? And they are on their way East again, headed toward DC?"

"Yes," responded Alcorn, "We got them on two cameras on I-66, and another along the GW Parkway coming toward the city at the end of the Interstate. One final camera caught them coming out of the tunnel and turning onto New York Avenue, going out of town. There are no cameras that caught them along New York Avenue, but we have the DC Police looking for the van up in Northeast."

"Just northeast?" asked Alice.

"Well, other districts have the info Alice, but there are many inexpensive hotels in northeast, and a lot of immigrants that stay in them, as they wait for better situations. It's easier to hide up there than in other parts of the city, especially if you intended to go back and forth into the central city."

"Makes sense to me," said Alice. "Any luck on locating them yet?"

"Not so far," answered Alcorn," But we are still looking."

"All right, let's move over to the actual event. What do we know, other than what the FBI has told us? So far, I know they found the boxes at the *Alexander*, reduced the charges in the projectiles, but could not go to duds without tipping off the terrorists. We have Johnson there as well. What's our plan here?"

"I'm working with Roger Doucette on this," answered Anderson Cohen, "We have people on the floor where Johnson is staying, and the room next to his is the comm center. We also have people throughout the hotel to prevent any connection with Hakim or his people, and security around the hotel to prevent escapes."

"How do you know Hakim will even be there?" asked Alice.

"We have now recorded two conversations between Hakim and Johnson, Alice," answered Tom Clements, one of the communications analysts on Sawyer's staff, "Both are pretty consistent. Hakim threatens, Johnson tries to resist, but now Hakim has Sira Suleiman, apparently, his girl-friend, who, by the way is one tough lady. The latest one, just this morning, early, she spoke to Johnson, who seemed visibly upset. As soon as the call ended, Johnson asked the hotel to send up the boxes. From the video in his room, we know he opened them, and read some kind of document in the top of one of the cases."

"The document," Alcorn added, "Is a set of instructions on how to put the pipes together to make a kind of mortar, and the shells are like small pipe bombs. They are all plastic, and designed for one use only, according to the FBI

From a Vantage Point

bomb squad. They can still pack a wallop, but, in this case, as you know Alice, the munitions have been removed, and replaced with black powder. It will still make quite a noise, even break a window perhaps, but there is nothing to hurl forward anymore."

"So, if that is the case, what do you think Hakim's role in all this is, or might be?"

"My guess," responded Alcorn, "Is that there is really a third box, under Hakim's control, which he intends to use, probably in a different location, to add to the carnage the others might have caused. Just a guess, but consistent with the man and the chase thus far. He will do something to be a part of the action. He needs to continue to prove himself."

"So, we still have a big problem gang. Where is Hakim, and what will he do? We only have a day, really less, to answer those questions, and change the rules of the game here." Alice looked around the room, hoping for someone to step up with an answer, although she knew in her heart that would not happen.

"OK, then if nothing else, we need to double the effort to figure out where he is and what he will do. I have a meeting with the Security team for the Inauguration this evening at 5 PM. Get me whatever you can get me by then." Alice rose to leave, as did the staff. She stopped Anderson Cohen and Rick Alcorn by the door.

"I need you two to make something of this mess; make it into a win." Both men looked at her as if the weight of the world had just dropped on their shoulders.

Downtown Washington DC As the van containing Hakim and the others, it looked completely different, driving down New York Avenue during daylight. It became clear to all that this part of town was not like much of the rest of the city, more industrial, a lot of empty space, and many other inexpensive motels, fast-food places, and utilities.

Hakim, sitting in the front passenger seat, told Akram, the driver to stay on New York Avenue; the plan was to go down to 14th Street, and then look around the streets on either side of the hotel, so they could see their escape route on the following day. All three men were amazed at the tall buildings, the myriad of hotels, offices, and restaurants; something not as often seen in other places, like Kabul.

As they reached 9th Street, however, near the Carnegie Library, Hakim changed his mind, and told Akram to go left, down 9th Street to F Street, near the hotel. There, they found a small parking lot where they could park the van, and walk to the hotel, going inside, up the stairs to the bar, and then out again. Finally, they walked down the street a block, found the entrance to the hotel parking lot and, down the small entrance way, they could see the down ramp to

From a Vantage Point

the lower garage. Satisfied, they walked back to the parking lot where they left their van, turned in their ticket, and drove off, back toward 14th Street.

Over the next hour, the van toured the area, driving past the White House, and other monuments, and back toward the I-395 entrance at the Department of Agriculture, which would take them back to New York Avenue, and their motel in Northeast Washington. As he had before, Hakim was making a statement; he wanted the Government people who he was sure were following their moves, to see their van, see them, and so he selected places to walk and drive where there were sure to be cameras to take their photos.

Satisfied they could be seen, Hakim told Akram to drive back to the motel, guiding him through the maze of traffic toward New York Avenue, and relative safety.

The van had been spotted—by Rick Alcorn and his staff, coming up New York Avenue, as they went across the bridge at Brentwood, and into the city. They were followed along in their small tour, and eventually back into the tunnel ending in Northeast. By the time the DC Metropolitan Police were notified of the locations, Hakim and the van were long gone. The police cruisers fanned out again, but by the time they deployed, the van was back at its place to the rear of the motel, not visible from the road.

Inaugural Committee Headquarters, Downtown Members of the Inaugural Committee's team on security began arriving at the Committee Headquarters, just short of 5 PM. The Security Group represented agencies from all over the government, military, civilian, intelligence, city services, the airport authorities, and several others, whose functions were critical for the success of the various events. At the outset, they met weekly, but, as the Inauguration drew closer, they began meeting more frequently; the last ten days, they had daily update briefings, each at 5 PM. The group was chaired by the Committee's Director of Security, a retired Army Colonel whose background was steeped in intelligence and counter insurgency.

"Let's get rolling," said the Director, "We have a long agenda this evening, and I want to move things along, so we are out of here in a couple of hours. You all have critical functions tomorrow, and you all need to be sharp."

"Let's start with the first, and most important outstanding item, shall we?" he asked. "That's this potential terror threat. Alice, what is the latest?"

"Well sir," she started, "We now know there is a definite threat, and that we may have it contained. There was a threat to send mortar rounds against the Mall, and both major avenues, emanating from a hotel on the route. We discovered it, the FBI contained it by removing the munitions from the shells, and replacing it with black powder."

"Why not simply take them out completely, Alice?"

From a Vantage Point

"Well, we know who the players are, and one in particular, who is at the hotel right now. What we need to assure ourselves of is that he is the only active player. We have others around town who have come to DC from overseas, and are directing this effort, but we are not comfortable saying what we have found is everything. My staff, together with the FBI and Secret Service, and DC Metro, have created a perimeter around the hotel, in addition to the usual rooftop and inside security along the route. We want to catch these people, and prevent further injury. We could not do that if we simply arrested the one guy we have now."

"Sounds logical. What other assistance do you need, just in case this all blows up, literally, in our face?"

"We probably need to put more DC Guard troops on the streets. I know we have a lot out right now, but we need them for crowds if something does happen," said Alice, looking at the DC National Guard commander. "You might want to have more ambulances ready as well, perhaps in a staging area along the Mall. Just a suggestion there."

"What happens if there are others, and they blow up their own bombs?"

"We're ready for that as well, Sir," Alice answered. "I have every agent east of the Mississippi available, other than those on critical investigations, more Coast Guard personnel, and a large contingent of ICE and Border Patrol coming in as we speak. We are going to use them to saturate the area even further, with most of them in civilian clothes to mask their purpose. We'll get them. I don't want to say, 'will die trying' but we'll get them all."

"Thanks Alice. You know we appreciate your efforts here."

"OK, FBI, do you have any major outstanding issues?" the Director asked.

"Sir," responded Richard Peabody, "We are working remaining issues. You should know that we did turn around one terrorist in New York, two days ago. Sent him back to Cairo.'

"Why not arrest him?" asked the Director.

"Because he had diplomatic Immunity, Sir. We had no choice, but he is now on virtually every no-fly list, throughout the world. That was the best we could do, with State's help."

"Any others?"

"Nothing major. We have several hundred extra agents coming, or already here, along with nearly 300 US marshals. Adding those to what DHS is providing, and we, have, I think, a potent force."

"General, what about the DC Guard?" asked the Director.

"We have all our Army Guard troops on alert, Sir. The military police units have all been sworn by Metro, and they will be on the streets in and around the area between the Capitol and the White House. We are co-located with the DC Emergency Preparedness Center on the Ellipse, near the Washington Monument,

From a Vantage Point

as we can respond quickly where needed. In like with your request, we have two of our medical units on alert, the Air Ambulance Company, and the Medical Command, both located here at the Ellipse. We are ready for whatever you need."

"Thanks General," responded the Director, "The DC Guard has been a part of the Inauguration program for years. We appreciate your unique service. FEMA, anything to add?"

"We are on target, Sir. The Command Center is open and operating at FEMA HQ. We have a coordinator at the Preparedness Center, and another at the Headquarters."

"Anyone else? OK, let's discuss the overall plans for tomorrow." The director pointed toward a map on the wall, and began to go through the steps involved in the Inauguration with the attendees. He covered over the next hour every step the President and Vice President would take, the motorcades before the ceremony, the parade motorcade after the ceremony, and emergency precautions and alternatives in the event of problems or disaster.

Finishing up, he turned back to the group, saying, "All right. That's all I have, so let's hope that every piece of the puzzle works tomorrow, and we will have a great day. See you all tomorrow. I will be at the Emergency Center, with many of you, but will also be traveling around, so you can get me on a walkie-talkie if you need me for anything. See you all tomorrow. Alice, I want to spend a couple of minutes with you after the meeting." Alice nodded her understanding.

As most of the group left, the Director came over and sat next to Alice.

"Alice, I need it straight here. Do we have a major problem tomorrow, one that has to go up the chain to the President and Prez-elect?"

"I don't think so, sir," she responded, "We have everything we can control, under control. We are looking to be sure that the guys we do not have under surveillance, or under arrest, can't do major damage tomorrow. We will likely have an incident at the *Alexander*, but even that is under control. We are working with the manager, and his Chief of Security is one of my retired senior agents. He knows his job, and what we do. I'm comfortable with that, and not ready to say we need, or should scrap America's Parade. I'll stake my reputation on that. I wish I could guarantee you on that, but I can't—at least not right now."

"Hope you are right, Alice. A lot of us have our reputations on this. Just keep me up as we move into tomorrow. I don't care what time you call; I want to know something first."

"Will do, Sir," she responded. "I just hope I don't have to call."

"Me too," he answered, "Me too. Have as good an evening as you can Alice," he added, as he rose to leave. "See you tomorrow morning."

From a Vantage Point

Alexander Hotel, Washington DC The lobby of the *Alexander* was mobbed. It was Inauguration Day, the hotel was full, and they were running a special buffet for guests, so they could eat and then walk over to the bleachers on Pennsylvania Avenue to see the parade.

Hakim and his men took advantage of the huge crowd, as they wended their way downtown, using much the same route they had the previous day, and pulled into the side entryway for the hotel parking area, drove down the ramp to the next level, and looked for a parking space away from the entrance. They found nothing on the first level, but, on the second, they found an ideal spot, and it was close to the doorway to the elevators.

Looking at his watch, Hakim tried to discern how much time it might take to take the box from the back of the van, go through the doors, and up the stairway from this lower level, eventually reaching the roof, as they planned. He estimated about 14-15 minutes. That meant they had to stay in the garage, and remain out of view for nearly 30 minutes. With Akram, and Sira, who stayed in the van with the other man in his group, that might be a problem. Keeping them in the van was really the only way to prevent disclosure. Hakim looked around, saw no cameras along the walls or the ceiling, and decided to do what his instinct told him—remain in the van until it was time to move.

Meanwhile, there was a knock on the door outside Will Johnson's room. He looked through the keyhole and saw a bellman standing next to a porter car containing two wooden boxes. Opening the door, he invited him in, and quickly had the boxes on the floor in the living room area. He gave the bellman a tip, thanking him for his service, and opened the door for him to leave with his cart.

Once the bellman was gone, Will Johnson eyed the boxes. He knew from his discussions with Hakim that they contained the things he needed to do the job Hakim wanted. Carefully opening each of the boxes, Will found a set of instructions inside the larger one, giving him directions on how to put the plastic pipes inside the boxes together, then use them to send projectiles out of the hotel room. From the drawings, it was clear he was expected to set them up in a way they would blow out the large, wide windows of his hotel room living space, as they then sped on their way toward their destination. As Johnson looked out the window, he assumed that meant either the Mall, or at least Pennsylvania or Constitution Avenue.

In the basement, Hakim knew it was time to leave.

"You,' shouted Hakim, as he turned in the van to face one of the men with him, "You will stay here with the woman. Akram, you will come with me to the roof." Akram quickly left the van and went to the rear door, taking out two backpacks and a large wooden box.

"I have what we need, Hakim," Akram said, loud enough for Hakim, not leaving the van, could hear.

From a Vantage Point

"Keep the woman in the van," ordered Hakim, "And you keep ready to drive out of this place as soon as we return. There is no room for delay."

Akram gave Hakim his backpack, and the two grabbed the handles of the wooden box, carrying it over toward the doorway taking them up the stairs to the roof, as they planned. As soon as they entered the doorway, the security cameras in the corners of the stairwells picked them up. In the hotel security office, one of the guards looking at the various screens started scanning to review the stairwells, but was interrupted by the arrival of his boss, Joe Xanaria.

"Everything all right here, guys?" he asked the two men sitting at consoles. "Watch for anything out-of-the-ordinary."

"Sure will, Joe," responded the guard, turning from his position to face Xanaria, missing the entry of Hakim and Akram. "We got this, Joe," answered the other.

By the time the guard turned back to his console, the two terrorists had moved up the stairway, and momentarily out of sight from the cameras. Seeing nothing, the guard asked the other, "Want some coffee, or something else?"

"Sure, where are you going to get it?" came the response, then he added, "Get me a large black coffee. This is going to be a big day, and we have to stay alert here."

"No problem," answered the other guard, "Be back in a jiffy. Just going to the lobby. Anything else?"

"Sure, if you are going to the small coffee shop, how about plain donut, make it two. Here's some cash." The guard pulled some money out of his pocket to hand to his associate.

"On me, this time," he responded, "You paid the last time we had duty."

"Great, thanks," he said, looking back at the screens. He saw nothing since the two terrorists were now up two floors, and the cameras above the lobby floor were only every three landings. That gave Hakim and Akram a giant head start going up the stairs toward the roof. Without realizing it, the guards had given the two terrorists a free trip to the roof.

Will Johnson, in his room, tried to follow the instructions in the wooden box, taking out the parts, laying them on the floor, and beginning to organize them into weapons, all under the watchful eye of the Federal agents in the next room.

"This guy knows nothing about these weapons," said one of the agents, a counter-terrorism specialist. "This is almost comical, if not for being deadly serious."

"I agree," added Roger Doucette. "What was he in the military years ago?"

"Don't know, but I'll bet he was a medic, and not an artilleryman," came a response from elsewhere in the room. "He has no idea what he is doing," came a third reply, followed by small smirks and laughs from the rest of the people in the room.

From a Vantage Point

"Ok," said Will to himself, "Three large sections, and a small section. A box on the bottom. Put them together," he said several times, as he assembled the pieces. "Does this thing really work?" he shouted out to himself."

Finally, he assembled the three weapons, weird-looking weapons, sitting on bases that tilted about 20 degrees. The final parts he needed to add were smaller sticks, extending from a blob of plastic near the top of one pipe section to the floor. Then, placing the three in place near the windows, he stepped back to see what he had done.

"This doesn't make sense here," said the agent who was the weapons expert. "These things will not fire. All they would do is blow up when he dropped the first charge. They are too light, and too unstable to fire anything successfully. Not even a good design."

That comment perked up Doucette's ears. "OK, so if these things don't work, what are we here for?"

"Roger, it looks like these things are more of a diversion than anything else—designed to make a bang, and kill somebody, but that somebody today would be Johnson. He's being used, I think."

"If that is so," responded Doucette, "Then where is the main game?"

"Connect us to the main security cams, will you?" he asked the agent at the console. In seconds, the cameras came up. "Roll me the footage here," asked Doucette, pointing to the garage entrance.

"Look, right here," yelled Doucette. "It's the van, down in the garage, over in a corner. Get people down to the garage, right now." Two agents spoke into their communicators, and the screen, as it changed, showed four agents in security gear approach the van, take out the side door, and pull two people out.

"Neither of those is al-Azahir," shouted Doucette. "The woman is the one from Elias, Sira, I think is her name. Where did al-Azahir go?"

"The roof," shouted three agents at once."

"Bingo," said the agent at the console, running tape from the entranceway, and then up the stairs, losing contact periodically, but finding the two men again as they approached the landing just short of the roof.

"We got problems, Roger," yelled the agent at the console. "Johnson just looked at his watch. It's five to noon. I think we have showtime."

"My God," shouted Doucette, picking up his communicator, and yelling into it, "Active shooter on the roof. Get the chopper in the air over *Alexander* location. Do not, I repeat, do not allow them to fire their weapons. Use any force necessary."

Just as he finished, and looked toward the console, Johnson put the first of the charges into one of the tubes and dropped it. The explosion noise rocked the air, and they could see only black smoke in the room. Breaking through the door, two agents grabbed Johnson and pulled him from the room.

From a Vantage Point

On the roof, Hakim was also ready, and at the same time as Johnson dropped his charge, Hakim did as well. The difference here was that Hakim had the weapon leaning on the cement façade. In all, he fired two charges, and they soared through the air, headed for the Mall. The helicopter, arriving at the scene, could only look on in horror as the event happened.

"This is Air one. Two charges fired, headed for the Mall. Repeat, two charges fired, headed for the Mall. Just as the pilot said the last words, explosions rocked the air, and he added, "Contact at Constitution Avenue. I see smoke and fire, repeat, I see smoke and fire."

"What about the shooters?" asked Doucette.

"Shooters no longer on the roof. Assume they are on the stairs going down. That's all I can see."

Hakim and Akram were going down from the roof, but only two floors. There, they went through the passageway doors, and mingled with the crowd of guests who had come from their rooms during the explosion. Walking down the corridor to the other set of stairs, the two descended to the lobby, and, still mingling with the hotel guests, they moved out onto F Street, And simply walked away.

Will Johnson staggered from the room, into the next one, where the FBI assisted him.

"Mister Johnson, I am Agent Doucette of the FBI. Please come with us right now." Two agents took Johnson out of the room, toward an elevator, where agents guarded access, and then down to the lobby and the security room, where he was met by Joe Xanaria, the security chief.

"Have a seat, Mister Johnson," said Xanaria, "There is a bathroom over there, if you would like to clean up a bit. Please leave the door open, though." The other agents started to leave, and Will became confused.

"Am I under arrest?" asked Johnson.

"That's up to the Feds, Mister Johnson," responded Xanaria. "They will be down in a minute or two. Go get cleaned up if you wish." Will did as Xanaria suggested, still confused. He took off his coat, and tried to get what he could of the smoke off his face and hands, then returned to the room where Xanaria waited.

Several minutes went by before there was a knock at the door, which Xanaria opened, and a phalanx of men entered, looked around, they brought in Sira and another man from the van. Sira ran over to Will Johnson.

"Will, are you all right?" she asked as she looked him over, trying to see if he was injured.

"I'm fine, Sira," answered Will, "Once I get all the soot off, it will be the same old me," he laughed.

Sira broke down into tears. "I was so worried for you, Will. I did not know what they might do to you," she mumbled through her tears.

From a Vantage Point

"Everything is fine, Sira," Will responded, "Other than a broken window or two, things are a lot better than I thought just a few minutes ago."

"You are a lucky man," Will heard, turning to see yet another person entering the room. "I'm Special Agent Roger Doucette, and I think you know these other two," he added, turning and pointing toward the door, as Anderson Cohen and Tom O'Neal joined the group." Will was astonished.

"You gave us a hell of a ride, Will Johnson, "Announced Cohen. "I wish we could say we enjoyed it. What about you Tom?"

"Right now, I think Will is in shock, Anderson. He just found out that the guy working on his cooperative project is a Federal agent. I wouldn't want that happening to me. By the way, Will, your project is still a go. There is no problem there." O'Neal walked over and shook Will's hand, then added, "It's a great project. I just might come and help occasionally myself. Always wanted to get a farm out in the country."

"So, what happens now?" asked Johnson.

"Right now, the most important thing is your safety, and that of Ms. Suleiman. We're going to protect you both and, at the same time, make sure that al-Azahir cannot bother either of you again," responded Doucette. "A bit later, we will need you and Ms. Suleiman for a de-briefing, but right now, both of you just rest, and let us deal with the issues. Joe, don't you have a room for these two?"

"Sure do," answered Joe Xanaria, "Whenever you all are ready. Our house staff is also working on some clothes for you both. Luckily, there is both a men's shop and one for the ladies right next door. We'll take care of it shortly. For now, just sit and try to breathe normally."

"By the way, Sira," Xanaria continued, "The staff here thinks a lot of this guy. He's been a good customer, and we hope you will all come back occasionally to see us. Try to enjoy the day. Anything either of you want, just call room service. The bill is on us." Xanaria smiled, and added, "OK, so I have to go look at some broken windows that need fixing. That's easy, though. It's Roger who must explain the bombs along Constitution Avenue. See you later, ex-terrorists." Xanaria shook Will's hand and hugged Sira, wishing them well, then walked to the door to leave.

Thanks to you all for what you have done today. I know everything didn't exactly go according to plan, but you saved the day, and the President. We appreciate that," said Xanaria, looking at the assembled group. The agents in the room clapped for nearly two minutes, as Joe Xanaria left the room to survey the damage.

From a Vantage Point

Chapter 44 One Final Chase

Hakim and Akram had been spotted by the helicopter, which blared out, "This is the FBI. Stop where you are or we will shoot." Hakim waved his fist in the air, and the two men rushed toward the door, taking them back into the hotel.

"Shooters no longer on the roof. Assume they are on the stairs going down to lower floors," reported the helicopter pilot. "That's all I can see. Repeat, no shooters on the roof. They have moved back into the building."

The two terrorists raced down the stairs, to the second landing below the roof, going through a passageway door into a hotel corridor. Several of the rooms had open doors, as people were looking out toward the mall at the end of the corridor, and others were doing the same from their rooms. More and more were coming out, as the fire alarm started to sound, wondering what they were supposed to do.

"Come this way," announced Hakim, and he pointed to the stairway at the opposite end of the corridor. "This way to the lobby," he added, then he and Akram mingled in with them, as if they were hotel employees, prodding them along toward the doorway.

Slowly, the group made their way down the stairs, with others from the lower floors joining them as they descended toward the lobby. Finally, they reached a door marked "LOBBY", and the crowd poured out into the concierge area of the hotel.

As they did so, Hakim and Akram moved to the side, eventually slipping out through a doorway to F Street. Once outside, they simply walked up the street, again mingling with the crowd, and disappeared.

At the US Capitol, Washington DC The first indication the day was not going to go as planned came into the ear buds of the Secret Service about five minutes before the Swearing-in of the new President.

"We have shooter situation along Pennsylvania, at National Place. Lock down POTUS, and the rest of the official party," said the message, with urgency. "Lock him down, NOW," the voice continued. "Confirm."

When those messages blared, other dignitaries, some already on the podium where the ceremony was to take place, were also moved, including the Speaker of the House, third in line of succession. The Capitol police moved them inside, and quickly formed a cordon around the podium to prevent any possible intruders.

Just as quickly, observers could see sharpshooters emerge on the roof of the Capitol, the Supreme Court, and several of the congressional buildings. Metropolitan Police, and vest-protected Federal agents also moved into protective mode for the President. No one knew when, where, or if there could be an attack, as was apparently happening down near the Mall.

The outgoing President was still inside the Capitol with the First Lady. The President-elect, and his wife, along with the Chief Justice, who had arrived moments earlier, were in the President's Room, off the Rotunda, waiting to move toward the Inaugural stand. Several dozen Secret Service agents created a human wall around the area.

The Capitol Police also created a zone around the Signing Room, the room the President uses on occasion when he is at the Capitol for ceremonies, and now the location of the outgoing President and his First lady, both of whom were informed of the situation by the Chief of the Presidential Protection detail.

Reports quickly began to come in over the media, and the Emergency Response Center at the Washington Monument went into full security mode. Washington was waiting to see what would happen next. The media was equally quick in its announcements.

> "We are breaking into our normal broadcasts covering the Inauguration today, to bring you an emergency news flash," said an announcer on Channel Five, Eyewitness New, one of the major outlets in the city."
>
> "There were several explosions along both Pennsylvania and Constitution Avenues, just before noon. One location, the Alexander Hotel, appeared to have at least one window on an upper floor blown out, while over near the Smithsonian, at least one section of a museum is in flames, with the DC Fire Department already calling this a three-alarm fire. Trucks and ladders have raced to the scene."
>
> "We have a reporting team on the scene. Jim Snead, what's happening downtown?"
>
> "This is Jim Snead, Eyewitness News, reporting to you from a vantage point along the Mall near 14th Street. Just a short time ago, several small explosions were heard and felt along the mall from 12th to 15th Streets, with one of the explosions know to have damaged a building at the Smithsonian. That building is presently on fire, and ladder companies from throughout the District have responded. Traffic is totally snarled, and plans for the Inaugural Parade are on hold, and may be cancelled."
>
> "So far, the White House has had no comment; the only response to inquiries has been from the Emergency Operations Center trailer, set up at The Washington Monument grounds, and their spokesperson has asked that people stay away from the Mall

From a Vantage Point

and downtown until the 'all clear' has been sounded." We have no word when that might occur. We also understand the Capitol is on lockdown, but there is no report of any activity there."

"Joe Snyder, with us now, was a witness to the explosions. Mister Snyder, what did you see?"

"Well, I was walking along the Mall, just about here at 14th Street, when I heard an explosion behind me, and turned to see what it was. Then, I saw a streak in the air, coming toward where I was, and ran across toward the building, and fell flat on my face. I felt the second explosion, while I was down on the ground. I waited a couple of minutes, and then got up, turned around, and saw the museum in flames."

"What do you think it was, Mister Snyder?" asked the reporter.

"Hey, I was in the Army a long time, and I know a mortar coming in when I hear it. I do not know about the first blast, but the other two were mortar's coming and dropping on the Mall. Must have been from somewhere close."

"Right now, there is chaos down here, although people are beginning to hope that no more explosions will be coming. We will have more in a short while. There is supposed to be a press conference down at the Emergency Ops Center later this afternoon.'

Thanks Jim," said the announcer, "We will interrupt as more news on this disaster becomes available. Right now, we understand there are no serious casualties at the Hotel, other than some glass shard injuries. We have no reports yet on the Smithsonian area."

"In other news,..." the announcer continued.

At the US Capitol "Mister President, I highly recommend the swearing-in be done indoors," said the Chairman of the Inaugural Committee "It would not be the first time something like this has happened. We have had several instances where weather had changed the venue. We need to do it this time as well."

"Five minutes ago, I was the President-elect; now I am the President of the United States," he responded. "We did have a private oath-taking here a few minutes ago, but we will go outside, Mister director, and do it the right way," said the new President, adding, "The American people must know that we have no fear here. They look for strength. We have to give it to them."

"Mister President, I understand all that," the Director of the Secret Service, chimed in, "The place is simply not safe. We have no idea where two of the terrorists are, at the moment. You should not go outside at this juncture."

From a Vantage Point

"We can, and we will, Mister Director," the President responded, "Now get the wheels in motion to do what you must for security—bring in the Army if you need to, but we will go outside, and let the people see the swearing-in. Those are my instructions."

The Director knew he would go nowhere continuing the argument. "Get ready to bring out the Official Party. Everyone is on the alert. We have ten minutes before POTUS goes out there. I want the place as secure as you can make it."

The ear buds buzzed, from multiple agencies. Every available Federal agent, US Marshal, Capitol Police officer, and multiple other jurisdiction officers flooded the area around the podium in preparation for the public ceremony.

Fifteen minutes later, the swearing-in ceremony took place, as it was supposed to happen. The guests re-emerged from the Capitol, taking their places on either side of the area where the President would be sworn in. The Chief Justice administered the oath to both the President and Vice President, followed by the usual inaugural address, although shortened, with mention made of the disaster down town. During the ceremonies, additional military personnel were brought in from Ft. Myer, and Bolling Air Base, to line Pennsylvania Avenue, two-feet apart, between the Capitol and the White House. Roving groups of federal agents in civilian clothes, but wearing flak vests, walked up and down the sidewalks.

By the time the parade started nearly an hour later, the fires were out at the Smithsonian, but the damage was clear. The Emergency Operations Center communications coordinator asked the media, especially cameramen, to limit the shots highlighting the damage to the buildings as the motorcade went by that location. For the most part, the request was honored.

F Street, Washington DC Hakim and Akram fled as quickly as possible toward the northeast of Washington. Trying to stay where crowds gathered, they made their way along F Street, then up 9th Street, until they reached the Martin Luther King Library. Outside the library, they found a car idling across the street, and saw the owner walking over to the library, with some books in his hand. They quickly crossed the street, found the car unlocked, and drove it away, turning Quickly onto G Street, then down to 7th Street and again north to H Street. They were looking for a bus, and found one about to stop at 7th and H streets. Pulling the car over, they raced for the bus, getting on just in time, as the driver pulled out into traffic.

"That will be $2.20 each, gents," said the driver, looking at them.

"Hakim reached into his pocket, pulling out his money, and responded, "I have only a five dollars bill. Take it."

The driver took it, responding, "No change on the bus. You get two seats." He pointed them toward the back, as he drove along H Street toward his next

From a Vantage Point

stop. Sitting about half-way down into the bus, both men relaxed a bit, and sat back, enjoying the ride.

"What do we do now?" asked Akram. "The police will be after us eventually."

"Stay quiet," Hakim admonished, "I will look at my map. We will figure out what to do next." He pulled out his map, turned it over to show the larger map of the city, and plotted where they had been and where they were going.

"We get off here," stated Hakim. "This is near the Capitol, and we can get a new bus at a place called Union Station."

Alexander **Hotel, Washington DC** Will heard a knock on the door of the room in which he and Sira were staying. Originally, Xanaria had arranged for two rooms, but Will insisted she stay with him. Sira readily agreed, the fright still in her eyes told Xanaria it was useless to argue.

"Mister Johnson, it's Agent Cohen," said the voice through the door. Will looked out, and saw the agent standing there waiting.

"Oh, Agent Cohen," he responded, starting to unlock the door, "Welcome. Come in," he added, as he opened the door to admit him.

"Mister Johnson, I wonder if you would feel up to coming over to Homeland Security for short visit. We really need to discuss this whole affair with you—do a de-brief, if you will, and try to put some pieces together. Is this a good time?"

"Well," responded Will, thinking about Sira.

"No, it is a good time, Agent Cohen," responded Sira, coming into the room from the bedroom, obviously just awakened. "It is a good time. I will get ready."

Sira walked back into the bedroom, closing the door.

"She'll be out in a minute or so, Agent Cohen. This really is a good time. We have a lot to say, and want all this behind us. That's why I called you a couple of weeks ago. I was afraid for Sira, and this had to stop. Hakim is an animal. He would use or kill anyone. I know that now. He and Josh used to be my friends. Boy, can I pick friends sometimes."

"Mister Johnson, you did exactly what you should have done. You will meet a lady, a great lady, at Homeland. Her name is Alice Sawyer. I can tell you that she has been following you since Giddons first showed up on your doorstep. She had her people follow you literally all around the world. We had someone in the Middle East, someone in every place you did anything—like Tom O'Neal, who hoped you would do exactly what you did—call us."

"Why did she do that?" asked Will.

"Because Alice is a very interesting and experienced professional. She believed in you from day one, and she kept believing. When you called me, I called her. We told no one else about your call; not the FBI or any other agency.

In some ways, we took a chance and used you as bait to bring out the rats. We knew about Hassan and Sammi; We knew about Sira, but mostly we felt you

From a Vantage Point

would continue to be a loyal American. Like I said, she is an amazing person; one who put her neck on the line for you."

By the way, before we go," continued Cohen, "Officially, you and Sira helped us crack the case. There are no charges against any of you, including Sammi, and there will not be. You might have to testify eventually, but I somehow expect it will not come to that. More likely, Hakim and his friends are headed to Guantanamo, if we get them alive, and for a long time. That story will come out in the briefings, so be prepared for interviews back in Elias. We'll keep the story low while you are here, so you two can take a day or two, see the city, and enjoy the sites. I think Tom O'Neal, and his associate Jim Davis might want to do that with you."

"Jim Davis?" exclaimed Johnson.

"Oh, did I forget to mention Jim? He is a sky marshal working for our counter-terrorism unit. Like I said, we were watching the whole time—mostly to make sure no harm came to you. I'll be down in the bar, so, when you and Sira are ready, come on down, and let's go out to Homeland."

"Thanks again, Agent Cohen. I can't tell you how much we appreciate what you have done."

"Please, call me Anderson. Most of my friends do, and I would be honored if you would as well. I might come and help occasionally too-just to get out of the office, and show Tom O'Neal that he is not the only one who loves farms and produce."

"Thanks Anderson, and call me Will, please." The two men shook hands, Cohen turned to leave. "See you down in the bar, Will."

Will waved, and closed the door, now a happy man.

Department of Homeland Security Alice Sawyer waited patiently in her office for the arrival of Will and Sira. Anderson Cohen called earlier, telling Alice they were on their way. She looked forward to the visit, especially since she had just been in a testy session with her boss on Hakim and his actions, the damage, and the delay in Inaugural activities.

She heard a commotion outside her office, and walked to the door, opening it to find Anderson Cohen and several others about to enter.

As he did so, Cohen turned to Will Johnson and Sira, Saying, "Alice Sawyer, this is Will Johnson and Sira Suleiman." They all entered the outer office from the corridor, and Alice escorted them further into her office, asking them to sit at her small conference table.

"Please, come. I have been waiting to meet you both," she responded, "Are you both well? And you, Ms. Suleiman, do you have everything you need?" She sat with them, and quickly brought the conversation to a very informal tone.

From a Vantage Point

"Well, Mister Johnson, it seems you blew up a window, I have to pay for," she announced, laughing a bit, then adding, "But I would rather pay for a hotel window than have something much more serious happen."

"In all honesty, Ms. Sawyer, when I dropped that charge into that plastic pipe I wondered what would happen. I expected it to blow me up."

"So did we, sir," she responded, "So did we. There was a second or two where some of the agents thought about stopping the whole thing, Fortunately, I knew the charges had been changed. All you blew up was black powder. It made a mess, and did blow out a window, but nothing like Hakim did up on the roof."

"Hakim was on the roof?" shouted Sira, "We did not know that. He took this box from the van, and went upstairs with his man Akram, but I did not know he was going to do more. I thought he was going to meet Will."

"My guess, my dear," answered Alice, placing her hand over Sira's on the table, "Was that the intent was always to get rid of Will Johnson. None of the piping in the boxes brought to his room were strong enough to withstand a real explosive charge. It would have blown him and the hotel up in a cloud of fire and shrapnel."

"I just have one question for you, Will Johnson," offered Alice, "It is clear you would have gone ahead with this. Why? What would make you do that?"

"Because it involved someone I love dearly," responded Will. "She is worth everything to me. When Hakim took her, and threatened me, I felt like I had no choice. I called Anderson because I wanted someone to know that what I might do was not because I was a terrorist, but because I was someone in love. I think he understood."

"Well, eventually Anderson will be coming to see you to get formal statements, but, for now, I think we can have some tea, and simply give thanks you both are alive and well." She buzzed and her assistant came in. Alice asked for a pot of tea and some cups.

"Let's have the tea, and then I have to go do a press conference. You might like to come along. Ever see a government press conference up close?" she asked, looking at Sira.

Sira looked at Will, and responded, "We would love to." As she did, the assistant came in with tea, cups, and the condiments. Alice poured, asking who wanted what. They sat and relaxed until he returned, and told her they needed her in the press room.

"Come on along, let's go do a press conference together."

They walked down the corridor, Will and Sira holding hands, Anderson Cohen, Alice, and her assistant. As they walked into the room, the din of the participants grew quiet, and Alice rose to the Podium to speak.

"Ladies and Gentlemen, this has been an interesting day. Normally, as we celebrate Inauguration Day, everyone looks at TV, some come down to the parade, and everybody recognizes the change in administration," commented Alice, as she started to introduce the press conference. "Some of you were downtown when the blasts occurred, and listened to the meager information available at that time. We have a bit more knowledge of the situation now, and I want to share some things with you now, that might fill in some gaps for you."

"First, let me introduce some of the people here, so that later, as you want to ask questions, you know who to ask. On my right is Richard Peabody, Assistant Director, FBI, and Agent-in-charge of the Washington, DC Field Office. As many of you know, here in DC we also have a unit of the Terrorism Strike Force, which Richard and I chair for the Government. Several of our senior DHS managers are also here, and I will introduce them in turn as we progress."

"Right now, I want to assure you, and the American people, that Washington DC is safe, the Inauguration Parade and evening festivities are moving forward as planned, and the President and his family are in no danger," Sawyer continued.

"For those of you who may not know me, I am Alice Sawyer, Director of the Counter-terrorism Division at Homeland Security. It is my responsibility, within Homeland, to make sure that our cities are safe, people are secure, and we deny entrance, to the best extent we can to terrorists and other law-breakers. I want to assure you that we do that daily, and we do that well."

"In this instance, three people entered the United States, using falsified, but seemingly valid documents, through Boston, Massachusetts. We identified these people shortly after they arrived, with assistance from Interpol, and began the process of following them through several states, until they reached Washington DC, and the events today."

"In your handouts, we have given you pictures of two men still at large in the DC area, the first, Hakim al-Azahir, a known terrorist, deserter from the US Army, and wanted on a RED LETTER from Interpol. This man is considered very dangerous, a known killer, and one who is very dedicated to Jihadism. He was born an American, in Virginia, was drafted during the Vietnam Era, and deserted to Europe rather than serve. Since that time, he has been supporter of al-Qaeda, supplier of arms and equipment to the Taliban in Afghanistan, and a drug dealer working for several interests in Egypt and Libya."

"The second man, Akram Said, is also wanted by Interpol, and the Government of Afghanistan, for multiple deaths involving Afghani soldiers and their families. He too is wanted by Interpol, and considered very dangerous. Both men are at large in the Washington area. We need to have their photos shown as widely as possible. If someone sees either or both, please call the DHS hotline number, noted on your handouts. We want to take these men off the street as quickly as possible, and before they have the opportunity to obtain arms to defend themselves."

From a Vantage Point

"Finally, I want to say how proud I am of both the Federal resources that worked together today to reduce as much as possible the damage along the avenues adjacent to the Mall, and prevent further injury. We will release more information later, but I do want you to know that several citizens assisted us in our efforts to stop this action. We were only partially successful, as you have seen, but so far, there are no deaths, only about ten injuries, but there is extensive damage to a hotel, and to one Smithsonian Museum. Please understand that in this world of terror, we cannot stop everything before disaster happens, but we work unceasingly to prevent what we can."

"I expect another briefing for you in the morning. If you have questions, please see our communications director. I hope you will understand that, at this juncture, we want to give you as much factual information as possible. This is not the time to shoot from the hip on answers."

"Thank you, and good evening." Alice walked off the platform, and returned to where Cohen, Will, and Sira stood on the side of the room. Several reporters came up asking questions, but Alice waved them toward the communications director.

Within the hour, the photos of Hakim and Akram were on every news station throughout the area. It was now a matter of time before they were seen, and captured. For now, Will and Sira felt like most of their pain was gone, and they were free.

Returning to Alice Sawyer's office, the small group was mostly silent. Alice knew she still had a great deal of work to do, but she was certain they would find the two men. And put them away for a very long time. Anderson Cohen was proud of his part, and what he wanted now was to see his two new friends happy, and back at home. He took them back to the hotel, thanked them again, and watched as they walked into the hotel free people.

As far as Will and Sira were concerned, they simply wanted to rest, but, before they did, there was one thing remaining to do. When they returned to their room, Will picked up the phone, dialed a number, and waited for a reply.

"Hello, this is Sammi's Restaurant. Can I help you in some way?"

"We want to order take-out," responded Will.

"Mister Will, it is you. I am so glad. Are you and Sira all right? Is everything all right?" Will motioned to Sira to pick up the other phone.

"Yes, everything is all right," she answered, "But we need two orders of whatever we can get. We are very hungry."

"It is you, Sira. You are free. I am so glad. If I could, I would send you the entire restaurant right away. When will you both come home?" he asked.

"We will be on our way tomorrow, Sammi. The government is calling us all heroes, you too. We will be there for lunch," responded Will.

From a Vantage Point

"I am so glad, Mister Will," responded Sammi. Will knew Sammi was crying from the broken words, but Will knew he had to call to let him know. "I will tell everyone you will be home. We will have a great party. Everything will be on the house. I am so glad, my friend. You two have been through so much. I will welcome you home in a good style, as you say in America. Everyone will be here."

"Whoa, Sammi," said Will, "We are tired, and will come home tomorrow, but do not overdo it. We just want to relax."

"OK, Mister Will, only a few people, then, but we will welcome you because you are part of our family here. See you tomorrow." Sammi got so excited, he hung up the phone. Will and Sira understood, and they did the same. Sira rushed over to Will, grabbed him and kissed him.

"I love you, Will Johnson," she exclaimed.

Will looked her in the eyes, and responded, I love you too, Miss Sira. Will you marry me?"

The rest of the evening was really a blur for Will and Sira. The thought he had come so close to turning into a terrorist was saddening, but having Sira next to him, close to him, and loving him made all that heartache go away. Neither would really remember when they fell asleep, only that they were together.

They awoke the following morning to a bang on the door. Will looked over at the clock, realizing it was after 9 AM, put on his slacks, and went to the door. Outside, was a waiter, a large cart containing food, and a large bottle of champagne. Will opened the door, smiled, and allowed the waiter to enter. Sira, who was also awakened, peered out from the bedroom door, which was slightly ajar.

"Good morning, sir. I hope I have not unduly disturbed you. In the kitchen, we tried to guess what you might like," he said, opening the covers of the several dishes on the tray. "This is all compliments of the hotel, Sir. We all appreciated what you did for us." The waiter smiled, and added, "If there is anything we forgot, or something else you want, please call. We'll bring it right up." Smiling again, he turned to leave.

"Let me get you something," responded Will, fumbling for his wallet."

"Oh, no, Sir. This is from us all. Have a great day, you too ma'am." The waiter walked from the room and started down the corridor, swinging in the air a cover napkin he picked up from the tray.

Will turned toward Sira, still peeking out the door, "How about breakfast?" he asked.

"I am not dressed," she answered.

"Who cares. No one will see you except me. Let's eat," he laughed.

"I will be right back," she answered, going back into the room for a robe, then returning. "Now, let's eat," she added, laughing as well.

From a Vantage Point

Two hours later, Will and Sira were on the road, driving out of Washington, along I-66, headed for Elias.

Sammi's Restaurant, Elias, West Virginia Sammi ran around the restaurant several times, checking and re-checking everything to be sure that the restaurant was perfect. The florist had provided several small baskets of flowers, mostly carnations, Sira's favorite, and the table Will normally sat at was covered with a red, white, and blue tablecloth. All the food was provided by the farmers in the cooperative. Everyone was proud of Will and Sira. Now, all they had to do was wait.

Outside town, off the state road, a police cruiser waited about two miles away. When he saw Will's pickup truck coming along, he called in, and as they arrived, the fire and emergency horns went off, people came out of the stores, and stood along the street, as Will pulled up in front of Sammi's, and parked the truck. There was a sign right in front, saying, THIS PARKING SPACE IS ONLY FOR WILL JOHNSON, HERO, with a big blue star at the bottom.

As he left the truck to walk around to open Sira's door, the crowd broke out in a huge cheer. They were all glad Will and Sira were back.

Elmer Gates stood in front of his hardware store, his wife Ellen next to him and saw them arrive. When he observed Will opening the door for Sira, then take her hand, he said, "What a gentleman. You don't see that much anymore."

"They're in love, you idiot," responded Ellen. "We have to start planning a wedding soon. Haven't had one in a while in Elias." She watched as they continued to hold hands, as they walked toward Sammi, standing at the door to his restaurant.

"Welcome home, Mister Will. All these people came to say hello," Sammi beamed, as he walked over to hug his friend, then Sira. "We are all glad you are safe. We have been worried. Come inside please, my friends."

Sammi and the two walked into the restaurant, where even more people waited, and took them to the table decorated for them.

"Have a seat, both of you. We have many people who wish to speak with you."

For nearly two hours, people came through the restaurant, some just to say hello, or shake his hand; others who wished them well, hoped they were not harmed. Still others simply wanted to be there because Will was one of their home town people.

Will remembered when he first came to Elias with his parents, and the town greeted them with open arms, treated them as friends and neighbors, and, when his parent later passed on, they adopted Will as their own. He never forgot that feeling, and now it was even stronger. As he sat there, still holding hands with Sira across the table, his thoughts were divided; on one side, how much he loved

From a Vantage Point

Sira, and wanted her to be a part of this community, and then how much he loved the community as well. He knew they would be very happy here for years to come.

From a Vantage Point

Epilogue

The End of A Dream

When Hakim and Akram stepped off the bus near Union Station, they had no idea what their next steps might be. They could not know that the report of the stolen car had already become known, and the Metro Police had thrown a virtual ring around the town—every officer looking for two men wanted by the FBI. Their pictures were circulating widely, and teams of officers were in all the major transportation hubs waiting to see if they tried to escape the city.

The bus along H Street stopped at North Capitol Street. From there, it was a one-block walk to Union Station and freedom. In Hakim's mind, looking at his map, they needed to go one block over on H Street, stay off the main road, North Capitol, and wend their way toward the train station. Once there, they could take a train, a bus, or other available routes out of the city to Baltimore, where they still had friends.

Union Station has several police departments monitoring people there. There is, of course, the Metropolitan Police, the District of Columbia police force, but there is also the Amtrak Police Department, managing the station and its trains, and the Metro Police Department, managing the connections with the Washington Metro. It is not unusual to see officers of all those departments patrolling the station together.

That morning, Inauguration Day, is a major travel day for those thousands coming to Washington for the festivities. From Hakim's perspective, it was a great cover for their escape. However, not knowing how these police departments worked, he and Akram had a distinct disadvantage. As soon as the explosions were heard, orders went out to augment security in all Government and historic buildings, including Union Station, and the bus stations surrounding it. The garages were sealed, with inspections for those coming in, and going out, enhanced patrols were initiated, and eventually, early in the afternoon, pictures of Hakim and Akram were provided electronically to every patrol officer, including those on trains, and working in the bus stations.

Hakim realized, as soon as he and Akram approached Union Station, they had a problem. Crowds were rushing toward the station, but several of the doors were closed, and the remainder had checkpoints, looking closely at every person coming into the station. The same was true over at the Metro buses, and the Greyhound station nearby.

Nonetheless, the men decided to attempt to enter and go toward a train. Both men would Enter a different line, to try to enhance their chances of at least one getting through. Hakim stood behind two women, who appeared to be a

From a Vantage Point

mother and daughter, and moved toward the checkpoint. Akram did the same, standing behind a young couple with small children.

As they moved forward, one of the officers monitoring the line looked at Akram, sensing that he had seen him before. The officer quickly realized it was one of the men wanted for the bombings near the Mall, and quietly called on his communicator, giving the code for an alert. Two additional officers came toward the line, coming up behind Akram, and quickly grabbed him from either side, pushing him to the ground, with one officer, his weapon drawn, telling him to stay where he was.

Several other officers looked for Hakim who, sensing he was about to be arrested, grabbed the younger of the women, pulling a small knife from his pocket. He was quickly surrounded as well. Realizing he had no chance, he threw down the weapon, and the officers seized him, handcuffed him, and brought him over to where Akram was still on the ground.

By the time Akram was brought to his feet, the area was swarming with police, who brought the two men out toward the main entrance of the Station. There, they were joined by several black sedans, screaming their sirens up to the entrance. Several Federal agents rushed into the station, went over to where the police had Hakim and Akram, and waited for their boss, Roger Doucette, to arrive.

As Doucette approached, he began the time-honored ritual, "Hakim al-Azahir, you are under arrest for conspiracy to commit a terrorist act. You have the right to remain silent, and the right to have an attorney present before you are questioned, if you so choose. Do you understand these rights?" asked Doucette.

"Who the hell are you, anyway?" asked Hakim.

"My name is Doucette, Roger Doucette, Special Agent with the Federal Bureau of Investigation. Please go with the agents." Watching Hakim taken away, Doucette turned, and said the same thing to Akram, who was then taken to another of the sedans. Once they were secure, the sedans roared off, sirens blazing.

The men were taken directly to the Federal courthouse at Constitution Avenue, and brought before a Federal magistrate. The Magistrate started to read the charges, but was interrupted by the Deputy United States Attorney.

Your honor, we have just received a writ from the FISA Court remanding these two to the facility at Guantanamo Naval Base, pending further action under the Patriot Act. The Government asks that no further proceedings occur here, with your approval, of course."

"I have no problem with allowing the writ," responded the magistrate. "My only function here seems to be ensuring that the prisoners are aware of their right to counsel, and their right to object to the remand of the Department of Defense. Do you object?"

From a Vantage Point

"We have no attorney, judge," responded Hakim. "We do not accept your so-called justice here, so we do not understand the need for an attorney."

"So be it then, gentlemen," answered the magistrate. "You are remanded to the Incarceration Facility at the United States Naval Base at Guantanamo. Take them away." The US Marshals in the court quickly removed the two, turning them over to DoD security personnel who would take them to Cuba. By the late afternoon, the two were on a military plane out of Andrews Air Force Base headed south.

Home of Amid Fatoullah, Cairo, Egypt "Amid, the two, Hakim and his man, were arrested in Washington. They are being moved to Cuba. What is your wish?" asked Ali, his nephew.

"Send word to our people there. They are to be dealt with there, and never return to us. Have it done quietly, but quickly. The other thing, about your return," asked Amid, "Has the problem with the diplomatic mess been dealt with as well?"

"Yes, it has Amid," answered Ali, "The minister in New York has been recalled, and is in disgrace. The United States Minister was called in by the Government to protest their actions, and the Embassy in Washington is continuing to demand that I be removed from the various limitations they imposed. It will be done, but quietly, and over time, since the current US Government is desirous of good relations with the government."

"Good, I do not want your name dragged through the gutter. Do what you need to do to resolve this."

Within two weeks, Hakim was being moved from Camp Alpha, where he arrived and was processed, to Camp Delta to undergo interrogation. On his second day, when he passed by another prisoner, who fell to the ground as they were beside each other, and the guards stopped to aid the prisoner, pulling him to his feet, the prisoner fell forward towards Hakim, then straightened and moved on with his guards.

Hakim went several feet forward before realizing he had blood coming from his side, pouring onto his white robe. When the guards realized what had happened, they stopped, called for assistance, and had him brought to a medical station. A long sliver had punctured his left lung, nicking the lower part of his heart. There was no time to repair the damage. Hakim al-Azahir died within fifteen minutes. The long, thin object with which he was killed was never found.

Akram was left to consider his own fate, and, for nearly six months, he stayed in isolation, reading and praying. One morning, the guards went to his cell to give him breakfast, finding he had choked himself to death by eating pages of the book he was reading at the time.

From a Vantage Point

From a Vantage Point

A Day in Paradise
Elias, West Virginia The Elias Christian Church is small. It contains only enough seats for about eighty people. Sitting in a small glen, with the hills rising on each side, it is an idyllic sight, the white wooden church, with the sloped roof, leading to a spire with a brass bell, and a cross atop it, and flowers all around it, the church is a favorite place for the community to be, both to pray, and to enjoy each other's company.

Today, the church was an even more beautiful sight, decorated with cloth steamers, and the flowers out in full bloom, it was a perfect day, with the sun out high and virtually no clouds; a perfect day for a wedding.

Nearly six months had passed since the Inauguration marred by explosions, something long forgotten, except perhaps for the news media, which ran occasional conspiracy theories about the events. Life had gone back to normal, especially in Elias. A new store in town sold goods from the farms, and had a big sign on its front, ELIAS FARMERS COOPERATIVE, one of three facilities through which the farmers sold their products, stretching as far as Kentucky, and down into Maryland and Virginia. Once each week, out about five miles from town, at a new warehouse building, large trucks came to load produce of all kinds, milk, cheese, and, on occasion, furniture to send to market.

Now, the cars and trucks converged on the Elias Church, parking anywhere they found space, to come together to celebrate another special event—the marriage of Will Johnson and Sira Suleiman. Will drove to the church this time in a car, not new, but new enough that it really looked special. He washed and shined it three times to make sure it looked just right.

Sira came to the Church in an antique Hansom carriage, drawn by two white horses, escorted by Sammi, in his best suit, and a carnation on his lapel. Sira was radiant in her white gown, borrowed from Ellen Gates, and altered by one of the women seamstresses in town, with a long, filmy veil topped by a gold cloth circlet, in deference to her Middle-Eastern heritage. She carried a small bouquet of carnations in several colors, grown by one of the families, and on her arm a small gold bracelet—given to her by her mother, the only thing Sira had to remind her of her family from the old country.

When the carriage stopped in front of the church, the entire community was standing around the edges of the church, waiting to catch a glimpse of her. Inside, Will Johnson waited for his bride with his two groomsmen, Anderson Cohen and Tom O'Neal. Sira too had attendants, her maid of Honor Ellen Gates, and two of the Gates' teenage girls.

As the carriage stopped, Sammi stepped down from it, walked to the other side, and extended his hand for Sira. That was the cue for everyone to clap and cheer. The uproar could be heard for miles. Then, the people filed into the church, many standing along the sides, happy just to be there and share the day with Will and Sira.

Sammi took Sira's hand, and escorted her toward the door of the church where her bridesmaids waited. As they entered the church, Sira saw Will just ahead, near the altar waiting. Looking at him, she mouthed, "I love you, Will Johnson." He looked at her, smiled, making out what she was saying, and answered, "I love you too, Sira Johnson."

From a Vantage Point

PERSONAE

A

Abadi, Hakim al-Azahir's companion in Afghanistan

Ahmad, Fatima, Owner of Ahmad Shipping, and double agent in the payroll of both Hakim al-Azahir and the CIA

Ahmad, Ibrahim, Uncle of Fatima the Owner of Ahmad Shipping

Ahmad, Khalil, Brother of Fatima Ahmad, and owner of the Place of the Dove Restaurant, Khartoum

Al-Asiri, Bomb-maker, and weapons specialist with the al-Qaeda in the Arabian Peninsula

Aldrich, Allie, Reporter, WCHS-TV, Charleston, WV

Al-Azahir, Hakim, Terrorist in Yemen

Al-Zawahiri, Ayman, Deputy to Osama bin Laden, Terrorist

Alcorn, Rich, DHS Team Chief, Security Review for Horizon LLC

Arnold, Thomas, Special Agent-in-Charge (SAC), Atlanta Field office, FBI

Ashkar, Maryiah, woman in Khartoum (Possibly relative of Will Johnson)

Ashkar, Sulieman, Terrorist (Called Willard Johnson)

Ashran, Jamil (AKA Jamil Ahmad), Atlanta Terrorist

Atherton, James, ALIAS of Josh Giddons

B

Basur, Security Officer at Khartoum International Airport

Benazir, Asiri, Cosmetician, Ankara, Turkey

Bin Laden, Osama, Terrorist, and leader of al-Qaeda

Blankenship, Scott, Assistant to the Security Officer, US Embassy, Khartoum

C

Carlson, Samantha, Reporter, Guardian-Mail (UK)

Cartwright, Rick, CIA Desk Officer, Kabul, Afghanistan

Cello, Rose, Eyewitness News, Washington DC

Clement, Tom, Communications Specialist on Alice Sawyer's Staff

Coggins, Tom, CIA, Doha, Qatar

Cohen, Anderson, Special Agent, Department of Homeland Security, Charleston, WV

Corbett, Tom, W. Va. State health Department

D

Davis, Jim, US Air Marshal/CIA

From a Vantage Point

Donohue, William (Bill) Security Director, US Inaugural Committee
Doucette, Roger, Senior Special Agent, FBI Field Office, Washington DC

E
Edwards, Dwayne, Chief of Police, Elias, West Virginia
Ewing, Jack, CNN News

F
Fazeel, Anwar, INTERPOL Officer, Qatar
Flood, Jim, Mayor of Elias, WV
Freitag, Ralph, CEO Horizon LLC, Atlanta GA

G
Gates, Harry, Hardware Store owner, Elias, West Virginia
Giddons, Josh, Terrorist, Mercenary
Greene, Jim, Reporter, WSB-TV, Atlanta, GA
Griffin, Alan, Reporter, WCHS-TV, Charleston, WV
Guerrero, Alfonso, General Manager, Alexander Hotel, Washington DC

H
Hales, Alex, CIA Khartoum Intel Analyst
Harding, Anne, FBI Spokesperson, Atlanta GA Field office

I
Irving, Charles, Security Officer, US Embassy, Khartoum

J
Jackson, Chuck, Doctor, Physicians without Walls, Qatar
Johnson, Willard, Produce Salesman & Terrorist, West Virginia
Jones, Jimmy Ray, News Reporter, WCHS-Radio, Charleston, WV

K
Karim, Akram, Associate of Hakim al_Azahir
Khan, Sammi, Restaurant owner, Elias, West Virginia

L
LeParc, Augustine, Chief, Analysis Division, INTERPOL, Lyon, France
Loomis, Fred, Editor, Elias Newspaper
Lawson, Jim, U. S. Air Marshals Service

M

From a Vantage Point

    Maloof, Ibrahim, Member of the Islamist Training Committee, outside Khartoum, Sudan
    Mansour, Salim, Security Manager, Khartoum International Airport
    Minihan, Bernie, CIA, Deputy Director, Operations
    Minihan, Sarah, CIA

N
Namers, Jeffrey, CIA Station Chief, Doha, Qatar

O
Oakley, Sam, Boxing Promoter, Atlanta, Georgia
O'Neal, Tom, Member of the Terrorism Task Force led by Alice Sawyer.

P
Peabody, Richard, Assistant Director, Federal Bureau of Investigation
Pentopolos, Heraklos, Kabul Businessman
Peshar, Ali, Associate of Amid Fatoullah, Cairo, Egypt.
Pullery, Fred, JTTF Oversight Chair

Q
Quigley, Eric, Chief of Security at Horizon LLC

R
Radan, Jalil, Owner of Near East Imports, Atlanta, Georgia
Reardon, Joe, Signals Chief, US Embassy Khartoum.

S
Said, Kassim, Alias of Hakim al-Azahir in Afghanistan
Saleem, A member of Hakim's group in Afghanistan
Sawyer, Alice, DHS Executive
Scully, Dr. William, Pathologist, Mercy Hospital, Atlanta, GA
Shapiro, Aaron, Staff Lawyer at DHS
Shubo, Jim, WGCL News, Atlanta
Singh, Hassan, Worker in Sammi's Restaurant
Sites, Elmer, Attorney-at-law, Elias, West Virginia
Shadd, James (Jim), Pathology Technician, Mercy Hospital, Atlanta, GA.
Suleiman – Maître' d at the Club Mediterranee, Khartoum
Suleiman, Sira, Terrorist in Elias, West Virginia (Works at Will Johnson's farm)
Smead, Jim, Eyewitness News, Washington DC
Suleiman, Samira, Terrorist in Atlanta, GA.

From a Vantage Point

T
Taggart, Sophie, Analyst, Operations Division, CIA, Langley VA
Torgenson, Olav, Physicians Without Walls, London

U
Usher, Dan, DHS Communications Officer, Tampa-St. Petersburg International Airport

V
Victorino, Dan, CIA Station Chief Cairo, Egypt.

W
Withers, James, President of Diamond Imports, Atlanta, GA. Contact for Hakim Al-Azahir

X
Xanaria, Joseph (Joe), Chief of Security, Alexander Hotel, Washington DC

Y
Yasin, Hassan, Terrorist in Atlanta, GA

Z
Zambino, Eldon, National Security Agency

Made in the USA
Columbia, SC
09 December 2017